Fangs of K'aath
II
Guardians of Light

By
Paul Kidd

Fangs of K'aath Two:
Guardians of Light
Copyright © 2005 Paul Kidd

All rights reserved. No part of this book may be reproduced or transmitted in any form or by any means, electronic or mechanical, including photocopying, recording or by any information storage and retrieval system, without permission in writing from publisher, except for review or promotional purposes.

All characters in this book are fictional. Any resemblance whatsoever to actual persons, living or dead, is purely coincidental.

Cover and Interior art by Monika Livingstone
Copyright © 2004 Monika Livingstone

First Printing January 2006
Printed in USA
By Lulu.com

ISBN: 0-9537847-1-1

Editing: Martin Dudman
Layout: John Tatman

All Inquiries should be addressed to:

United Publications
85 Croydon Road
Keston, Kent
BR2 8HU, UK
up@up1.co.uk

or
Paul Kidd
paul@purehubris.com

Fangs of K'aath II
Guardians of Light

Paul Kidd

Dedication:
For my beloved Sandhri:
Glad you're still there…

Prelude:

In the heartland of an ancient world, in a land of dreaming deserts and shining sapphire seas, an age of heroes came.

It was a time when all the world seemed somehow fresh and new. The reborn kingdom flowered with new ideas. Mariners explored far oceans and discovered strange new realms. Magic and technology took on a bright new lease of life. Religions swirled in the melting pot, blending in strange harmony.

It was a land of hope. A land of colour.
It was a land of scimitars and sages – of ancient magic and astonishing new frontiers.
It was the land of Osra – it was the age of Shah Raschid.

On the banks of the river Amu Daja, beneath the gaze of ancient pyramids, lay Sath, the city of new life. The port thronged with vessels from a dozen lands. Old walls shone new with tiles that shimmered like a million brilliant peacock tails. Minarets soared beside church steeples amidst canopies of cool green palms.

The city gates stood wide and open, thronging with traffic that laughed and chattered as it came. All the races of the world were there within the streets, tails waving, fur a-gleam. Beneath the awnings of the coffee houses and Royal Bazaar, the animal races walked and talked, bought and sold, argued, laughed or sang. Tall, stylish cats walked carefully between the stalls. Foxes, bats, rabbits, mice – towering bears, slim cheetahs, dark jackals and shaggy wolves: They wore the robes of a dozen lands, from desert nomads, to city merchants, visiting westerners and wandering holy men. The people paused at shady fountains. They argued prices in the markets, or sat before a learned man beneath some ancient tree. Light danced with dust motes as it streamed past lattices and rooves, patchworking the streets of Sath with light and shade and mystery.

Caravans bringing trade goods, spices, texts and scholars wound their way into the city walls. Camels padded regally beside fierce horses from the frozen north, passing great painted elephants from the east. There were students, immigrants and refugees, all wide-eyed and anxious as they gazed at the strange, exciting streets of their new home.

There were no beggars in Sath, nor were there slaves.

For this was Osra: The land of new beginnings.

Chapter One:

At the end of wintertime, the hills about the city of Sath grew lush and green with countless growing things. The soil had slaked its thirst, drinking deep from winter rains and sending plant life bursting forth into the skies. As spring came to the land, wildflowers shot into life like fireworks, tipping every tree branch and carpeting the fields with countless stars.

In the orchards, great drifts of flowers made oceans of pink and white. On the roadways, camels strode regally along, tended by their robed and turbaned masters. Fine drifts of petals settled on beast and master alike, making each and every traveler look like a bridegroom strolling happily towards his wedding bower.

Tulips grew beside the roads in their untold thousands. The great flowers stood straight and sturdy upon their stalks, their brilliant colours making the roads into ribbons of life. The ribbons swirled and intertwined – all of them leading onwards into Sath.

Feluccas drifted up and down the river, their sails white triangles perfectly mirrored in the water. Beside the Amu-Daja, small boys ran hooting and laughing as a strange boat thrashed its way along the shallows. The boat had no sails, and jetted alarming clouds of smoke out of a great box mounted in its belly. The boat master stood and waved to his audience, then leapt in alarm as something hissed and jetted steam from deep inside the boat. He raced to frantically tend the machine, and the boat – unsteered – veered off towards the mud flats with a purposefulness that seemed redolent with mechanical malice. The children squealed with laughter as the strange boat ran aground, and soldiers ran to help the boatman, who now was floundering in the mud.

The noise awoke a thin, rather disheveled young man who had spent the night beneath a calabash tree. The grove spread dark green leaves to the morning sun, dappling the dust with sunlight and shielding the traveler from morning dew. The calabash trees had great, strange flowers that were already swelling into infant calabash gourds: the newly opened flowers, however, had drawn an enthusiastic crowd of flying insects all night long. The traveler had spent a night bedeviled by swarms of passing bugs. With red-rimmed eyes and travel stained robes, the youth sat up and stared about himself, gazing soulfully at another strange new day.

He was a youth perhaps eighteen years of age – long and slim, with neat round ears and a nearly invisible stub of a tail. His fur was lush, and pattered in beautiful markings of black and white: Black patches of fur about his eyes made him forever seem to be owlishly wise. The young bear wore a hemp robe and a black-lacquered hat. He carried a drinking gourd, a scholar's sword and the staff of a sage. Most of all, he carried a single bundle that had been carefully shielded from wind and dew. It was a great frame – a backpack made of bamboo that served as shelves for heavy scrolls made out of slatted wood. "Sixteen volume Meng" lacked food, water, shoes and blankets – but through all his travels, he had preserved his books pristine and inviolate.

The youth rose stiffly, his back stabbing with pain. The tall young panda bear beat the dust from his ragged robes, mournfully contemplating the rents and fray marks in his hems. Young, poor and self possessed, he struggled from the grove. He ran anxiously to a little hillock by the riverside, and climbed hurriedly, hoping against hope that finally he would *see*.

She was there!

The young man stood, his eyes enraptured. He stared along the river towards the city of his dreams. Brilliant white walls were topped with gardens of fruit and flowers, and blue-tiled minarets and steeples shone like priceless jewels. The young sage swayed, his head light and his heart alive with joy.

Sath! Today, after a journey of three thousand miles, Sixteen-Volume Meng had finally arrived!

The young sage's fur was dusty. His feet were bare and his legs ached from the countless steps he had taken on his road. Threadbare, worn and rather lost, he stared towards Sath in nervousness and wonder.

A true sage sets no store by wealth, nor does he complain of poverty. He wastes no time regretting what is not, but finds the good in what is 'now'. Unfortunately, at this particular 'now', Meng had neither breakfast nor water. For the last two days he had eaten nothing but a few grains of boiled barley given to him by a farmer's wife. Meng felt his stomach growling like a caged crocodile – made all the more wild by the smell of fish frying on a fire by the riverside. Other travelers were cooking their breakfast, but their stores were already disappearing swiftly down their throats.

Tired – hungry and disheveled, the young man felt pang of self-pity, and immediately dismissed it. Through noble action, he was serving the dictate of Heaven! Heaven would provide! Made thin and rangy by the long, long road, Meng reached down and hoisted up his heavy burden of wooden books, then swung the bookcase onto shoulders long bruised and calloused by the weight. Hungry and teetering, he settled his battered black hat upon his head and looked towards the distant city walls.

Sath! Sath at last!

There were miles yet to go. Meng took a drink from an irrigation bucket, then walked past a field of buffalo and out onto the river road. Tall tulips caressed him as he walked through the fields, and the skies seemed alive with countless giddy little birds. Ibis watched him from the riverbanks, long-nosed and wise. Meng scrabbled up onto the well-paved road, folded his forearms and bowed towards an elder who walked beside a priest. He tugged his rope belt tight about his growling belly, and set out to trudge towards the walls of Sath.

Onward! It was a mandate of Heaven! A sage rests not upon his laurels, nor does he seek honours and offices. The sage seeks to instruct the unfortunate, to uplift the reprehensible, to give skill to the skilless. By example, his very life instructs. Meng had brought the knowledge of the distant East to the realm of Osra, the city of Sath. The land of Scholars would be brought the wisdom of the sages at long last!

Tsau-Yi Meng had traveled three thousand miles, and for the best of all possible reasons. Noble action was its own reward! The prize student of the seminaries of the Yellow Empire – the youngest sage to ever pass the Imperial Exams – had turned his back upon all offices and instead had become a pilgrim of The Way. In a far barbarian land, he would instruct, uplift and set example. His life would be celebrated through the ages!

With his eyes fixed on lofty goals, Sixteen-volume Meng stepped in a camel turd. With a squawk of outrage, he hopped along the road, his library teetering awkwardly on his back. He collapsed against a shade tree and wiped his feet, while all about him ibises spread their wings and cackled their amusement at the skies.

Jerking his robes straight, Tsau-yi Meng, scion of The Way and bearer of sixteen volumes and four commentaries, pulled his robes straight, gave the cackling birds a lofty glance, and marched doggedly on his way.

He walked beside bullock carts laden with dried fish and fruit. He found himself being passed by lofty camels walking end on end in train. The traffic grew ever thicker, and with it came the chaotic babble of voices. A caravan of robe-shrouded travelers threw back their hoods to reveal the tall ears of rabbits. They called out to the local soldiers – foxes, mice, rats and bears. Furry tails waved as women in gossamer pantaloons and veils swayed by with water jugs or baskets balanced regally on their heads. There were stripes and spots, tails and whiskers – pink eyed rodent women with their fur dyed into startling hues. A tide of life swirled about Meng the sage, sweeping him on into the gates of Sath.

The gates were set within a massive archway sheathed in multicoloured tile. The shade of the archway cooled Meng's brow – and then suddenly he was plunged into a mysterious alien world.

Sath's streets were paved with stone and lined with trees. Beside the gates, huge fountains offered rest and drink and shade to every weary traveler. The tall buildings were latticed with covered balconies, shaded by awnings and filled with restless, brilliant life.

The market crowds headed into the great open squares of Sath. Jugglers and balancing acts performed for the crowds. A huge puppet theater entertained an enthralled throng of children, all of whom had fresh-scrubbed faces and a little loaf of bread. The street entertainers seemed to be astonishingly well dressed, well fed, and performed purely for the joy of their art..

A dancing Tora bird fully six feet high at the shoulder gaped its razor-sharp beak and spread its tail plumage like a massive fan, turning to face Meng as he backed away in fright and hastened past. He slid into another street – a place of potted flowers and interesting little shops. Looking owlishly about himself, the young panda wandered onwards, staggering past stalls heaped high with goods from a dozen different lands. He dodged as a fire-breather shot a jet of flame into the air. Meng recoiled into a vast warm wall, looking up in shock at a huge fat feline shopkeeper dressed in turban, robes and sash. With a hurried bow, Meng retreated back out of the markets and found an oasis of peace down an alley lined with palms.

High above, a muezzin sang forth the call to morning prayer, his voice drifting from the heights of an astonishing minaret. In the streets below the mosque, a Christian priest in a tall black hat and black robes played chess with a Buddhist monk dressed in saffron yellow. Both men nodded to a dervish who hurried onwards to make his prayers.

Meng felt a surge of relief. The elders were clearly religious scholars and seekers of The Way. Meng pulled a little book from his sleeve and refreshed his patchy knowledge of Osranii grammar. Approaching the priests, Meng placed his hands inside his sleeves and bowed – careful not to spill his books into the laps of the elders.

"Honoured sirs. This humble one wishes to know how he might see the wise ruler of this land."

The two men looked at him. The Christian priest was a lop-eared rabbit with hair swept back from his brow in a silver stream. The Buddhist was a rangy dog with a face redolent with humour. The Christian knocked out his pipe and spoke to the Buddhist in some strange tongue, then leaned forward to poke Meng in the chest with his pipe stem.

"Boy – are you lost? You're lost, yes?"

"Honoured elder, this one is a traveler of The Way. He has come to bring illumination to the ruler."

"Aaah! Illumination!" The Buddhist arched his brows and scratched his snout, grinning all the while. "You come bearing the one true knowledge - a self evident sacred truth, immutable and unmovable?"

"Yes, honoured one."

The Buddhist coyly sipped tea. "Stay here with us and drink tea, my child. This will be the last peaceful day of your young life."

To face the enemy in battle was the courage of a warrior. To face great odds and adversity was the courage of the sage. Meng bowed seriously, his sincerity and faith etched in every elegant, ragged line of his body.

"Peace will come when The Way is understood by all who are confused." The panda swayed a little – hunger made him a tad light headed. "I must risk the sovereign's displeasure and present him with my gift of knowledge."

The Buddhist looked at the heavy rack of books balanced on the boy's thin shoulders. Meng's ribs showed where the wind pressed his robes against his body.

"Child, you may find your knowledge to be a burden. For all your books, you have apparently learned little."

Meng blinked.

"Honoured sir?"

"It is of no consequence." The monk pointed up the hill towards the center of the city. "The great white building with the open gates – this is the palace. If you seek a man, you should first present your compliments at his home."

Thanking the elders for their help, Meng bowed three times – staggering under the ever growing weight of all sixteen volumes and four commentaries. The Buddhist and the Christian priests were joined by the local Muezzin, and all three watched him go.

The muezzin – absurdly short and with a turban two sizes too large, scratched his ear.

"Taoist?"

"Confucian Moralist. Mencian." The Christian priest poured tea into three cups. "Sticks out like a pimple on a sacred cow's behind."

The Buddhist blew into his cup.

"He could be a Mohist."

"Mencian. He has a scholar's sword." The Christian priest squared the chessboard.

"Heh. Remember the Zen Buddhist?"

"Ah, the Zen Buddhist..." The monk half smiled. *Everyone* remembered the Zen Buddhist. "It's going to be a shock to the boy."

"A shock in the right place does more good than harm." The Muezzin drew up his chair to the games table. "We shall find the boy a chair."

"Whose move?"

"Mine." The Buddhist put butter into his tea. "Now where were we?"

With feet dragging from fatigue, Meng steeled himself and climbed the winding streets towards the palace hill.

It was a long, tiring trudge past houses hung with laundry. Little flightless pet toraki birds lay sunning themselves on doorsteps. Here there was a maze of cool alleyways, open squares and shady trees. Footsteps faltering, Meng slowed to contemplate the long white walls of the palace looming overhead.

How to enter the palace for a direct audience with the Shah? It was vital that Meng not be forestalled and dismissed by mere underlings. But a ruler would be protected by rampart after rampart of petty bureaucrats. Meng had prepared countless moral discourses inside his own head, seeing himself shaming ministers and winning through to the ear of Kings. The sovereign must be instructed as to correct and benevolent conduct.

... Only, when you found yourself sitting beside a blank palace wall, it all seemed rather different... His great rack of books teetering behind him, Meng wearily sat himself down upon a stone and anxiously contemplated the future.

The tail end of a rope hit him in the head from above.

"Hey! Stoopid! Moving the butt!"

The panda looked up in shock to see a taut female backside in white pants poised above him atop the palace wall. A skinny black bat – lean as an eel and with fur as pure as liquid night – straddled the wall and threw a great heavy package down to Meng.

"Ha! Hey – you with the dish rack! *Catch!*"

A hefty basket was carelessly tossed down to Meng, who managed to catch it – although the weight of the thing knocked him staggering. The basket was scorching hot and wafted out mouthwatering odors of roast meat, barbeque and fresh bread. Meng juggled the basket to save his scorched hands. The young scholar managed to find his balance, looking upwards in alarm.

"Madam!"

"Woo-hoo! Good catch!" The bat woman had bare feet, a red fez and robes like a desert raider. She leaned excitedly over into the palace, and began hauling eager little children up atop the wall. "Quick quick quick! Up the v'all and over!" She hefted children one after another and sent them sliding giggling down the rope into Meng's arms. Little girls, little boys – child after child after child. "Go go go go go!"

If she'd had wings, she would have flown. Instead, the bat leapt down from the wall in a sail of robes. She landed on the balls of her feet, grabbed the basket from Meng and snatched him by the arm.

"Come on!"

Hooting with glee, the bat dragged Meng along the alleyway. A dozen children surrounded her, squealing with laughter. Little feet pattered on the road, chickens squawked and fled from their path. Behind the palace wall, a shout of outrage came – a female bellow followed by a great, indignant peal.

"Sandhri! Sandhri – get back here!"

Children swirled all about the bat as she dragged Meng off into a wild maze of palm trees, wells and walls. She had a spicy smell – part dust, part musk, part mystery. A tufted tail like a rabbit's scut jutted from her pants, and sleek muscles slid beneath her jet-black fur. She led her band of reprobates zigzagging through alleyways, and then ducked into a row of stalls inside a little market lane. Hidden badly inside a rack of clothing, Meng pulled dangling pants and robes away from his eyes and struggled to find the bat.

"Madam! This unworthy one begs to ask - why do we run?"

A fez framed by tall black bat ears emerged from a neighbouring rack.

"You v'ant to eat? Sure! Then v'e run!" Her accent was joyous, caroling and downright impossible. Meng's fuzzy black ears twitched in confusion.

"To eat?"

"You know – in the mouth!" The bat slid beside Meng and shoved her head out into the open, scanning the street. Her basket filled the air with its mouthwatering scent of hot food. The bat had a head of hair so long it almost streamed to the ground – pure white, straight and dazzling. She swept a lock aside from eyes bright with greed and joy.

"We lost t'em! Ha! Hey hey! Good running!" The bat's tall ears searched hastily for sound. "Right. Hey, meester dish rack! V'at name iss?"

The scrawny, tall young panda tried to give a lofty reply.

"I am Tsau-Yi Meng, sage of the tenth circle, known as Sixteen Volume Meng." He made to lift a finger and admonish the woman. "Madam, I believe your grasp of propriety…"

"Shh!" The bat watched for pursuit, helped by a swarm of children. "Sixteen, ha? Sandhri hass read lots more than t'at! She can read good now!" The bat dragged Meng along behind the clothing racks. "Keep an eye out for librarians! And iff you see Yariim – *run!*"

Meng blinked, feeling addled. "Yariim?"

"Iss a girlie mouse – blue fur. You can't miss her! Blonde bombshell. Glasses. Tits out to here and a backside t'at just v'on't quit!" The bat gathered children in a gaggle beneath the sweep of her arms. "Right – heads down and across the road. *Go go go!*"

Swept along despite protests, Meng found himself chivvied across the street. Sandhri the bat led her followers into a beautiful little courtyard where a vast old fig tree spread a welcome cool. A terracotta pipe ran water into a little brick-lined pool where blue dragonflies fanned themselves and dozed away the morning heat. With a whoop, the bat jumped up onto the rim of the pool, put down her basket and dragged off her robes, revealing a slim body dressed in harem clothes. Meng could only goggle in alarm.

"You are in a barbarian harem?"

"Pah! Sandhri *iss* the harem!" Sandhri spread her robes as a picnic blanket for the children and plonked the basket into the middle. "Come! Eat, eat!"

The basket was flung open. Inside were earthenware dishes that steamed as they opened, making children gather in a starving mass. There was a bowl stuffed with flat pancakes of fresh-made bread. Saffron rice with duck and peas – chicken legs and fish balls, and a vast plate of roasted lamb so tender it was falling from the bone. The bat dug down and unearthed a greasy cloth filled with her favourite loot.

"Sausages! The good ones!" The bat held a sausage aloft like the treasure of the ages, then jammed it into her mouth. "They neffer get in enough of t'ese!" She jammed the grubby parcel of sausages into Meng's hands. "Hey sixteen volume Ping! To drop the library and sit down!"

"Meng." The panda's shaky Osranii vocabulary was stressed to the breaking point. He remained loftily standing. "Madam. You have food that is not yours. You have escaped from over a harem wall. Am I to understand…?"

Through a mouthful of food, the bat made a gleeful noise of scorn. "Pah! No sure you be understanding much!" The bat waved her hands. "You know v'at problem iss? You talk too much! Iss gabble gabble gabble all the time. How you get so tall v'en you too stoopid to eat?" The bat shoved a sausage into Meng's hand. "Sit, sit! Eat. You looking like a starved mantis up there. To drop the shelving and sit down!"

Somehow, Meng found himself sitting cross-legged beneath the fragrant fig tree. His mind told him to remain chaste and aloof, but his stomach whimpered and craved food. The bat opened pots and sniffed, thrusting one away in disapproval.

"Ick! Chick peas!" The bat made a face. "Who the hell v'ant's chick peas?"

Meng tried to fold his hands regally.

"The sage thinks not of the belly, but upon virtues of the mind."

"V'en it rains, get under shelter. V'en you're starving – eat!" The bat's expressive hands opened wide. "V'y iss it alv'ays Sandhri who hass to teach these people things?" The bat flipped out her great sheets of silken hair and whisked in to inspect Tsau-Yi Meng with a brilliant grey eye. "V'at giffs? Did you fall on your head or somet'ing, or do you alv'ays speak like that?"

Children reached in to snatch food. Sandhri slapped a girl on the hand and raised a finger. Her authority was for some reason absolute. Looking ludicrously pious, she folded her hands in prayer.

"Hey God! *V'e shall forever beauty feel. So thanks a lot for this great meal!*" Apparently this constituted a prayer. "Dig in!"

Starving vultures would have been slower. The children were all well dressed in white robes, red scholar's sashes, and blue caps and trousers, but they ate as though there was no tomorrow. Bread flew out of the basket, and the champ of jaws was everywhere.

The bat spread out a vast piece of bread and sprinkled it with rice. She had a silver Christian cross hanging between her little breasts – and what looked like a silver hilted pistol and a punch dagger at her belt. A bandit! Meng was more appalled than ever. He had half made up his mind to rise and flee, when the bat dragged the massive bread piece over to his side.

"You from real far, yes? Ha! Now v'e show you real food at last." She bit into a sausage that had a skin so crisp that her needle white teeth made an audible crunch. "V'at you want first? Pilaf? You peoples like rice, yes?"

"N-nothing." Meng swayed, weak and starving. "It's – it's not right! And no meat shall pass my lips until I complete my mission."

"Mission, ha?" Sandhri uncorked a jar of yogurt and cucumber dip. "Sure you don't want a sausage in bread?" The bat voluptuously rolled one beneath the Panda's nose. Its skin was crackling brown, and it lay in a bed of onions and cucumber dip. "Pretty crunchy! And with pine nuts in them – juicy sweet!"

They smelled tantalizing! Meng's stomach churned like a caged animal. He swallowed back a gallon of drool.

"It-it is better to conquer a single desire that to accede to ten thousand!"

"Pah! Well here – just hold it for me! I need my hands for talking!" The bat was busily helping a five year old little girl roll herself meat, rice and vegetables inside an envelope of bread. She kept the child upon her skinny knee. "So v'at's this mission?"

"To see the Shah. I have come to instruct him."

The bat turned, immensely amused, and raised one dark, expressive brow.

"So you're – v'at – eighteen? And you've come to instruct the Shah?"

"Yes, Madam."

The bat swelled with delicious enjoyment. "T'at v'ould be Raschid the Great, the Shah of Scholars? T'at's the guy you mean?"

Meng bowed.

"It is this humble one's hope to illuminate the darkness, to uplift the fallen and to open the eyes of the mighty to the true Way of the King."

"Woo-hoo! True v'ay! T'iss I haff to see!" The woman snatched several sheets of bread before it was all gone. It left her with floury fingers. "All those brains must giff you an appetite. Eat! You're too skinny. Eat!"

Meng sniffed.

"You are skinny, too."

Aloof and magnificent, the bat struck a pose.

"Sandhri iss not skinny. I chust haff lines of pure, classical restraint." She haughtily slapped bread down onto the picnic robes. "Eat!"

"I cannot indulge until my mission..."

"I'll get you to the Shah! Now eat before you fall over." She waved a hand airily, utterly unconcerned. "You need meat. How you expect to teachie stuff v'en your ribs are sticking out all over!"

She began making Meng a bread roll. Bread, then rice, duck, yogurt, lamb... It smelled tantalizing. Meng stared at it, salivating, and tried to hold his mind upon matters of importance.

"You can help me see the Shah?"

"Sure! Whateffer – v'y not?"

Meng sniffed. "Truly?"

"Absolutely!"

"But you are a thief!"

The bat grandly raised one finger. "Not a t'ief! Chust a redistribution vector!"

The panda sniffed.

"A mendicant like yourself cannot possibly know the Shah."

"Hey – we're scoffing foods here!" The bat slapped Meng on the back. "Now Shah Smah. You'll get t'ere. Eat!"

The panda peered at the food all about him. The lamb looked exquisite – tender, flaking off the bone and juicy. He picked up a few lean pieces and laid them on his bread.

The bat was having none of it.

"No no no no no! How you get so tall eating that silly v'ay? Like this – yogurt on the bread, then cucumbers, then lamb. Hot lamb!" Sandhri thieved the crunchy end bits of the roast for herself, then heaped Meng's bread high with smoking, juicy meat. "Now bitter orange. Like this!" She squeezed a fruit with a deft, lightning fast flick of her hand, showering juice over the meat. "Then salt, black pepper – and roll it up. Like that! Here!" Sandhri did the whole process herself; an instant later, the bewildered panda held a roll of bread and meat that dripped hot juices onto his legs. The bat bit into her own roll with absolute unfeigned ecstasy – copied by the children all around her, who ate like a pack of starved Tora birds. Sandhri jogged Meng's elbow with her own.

"Eat, eat! If you eat, then maybe t'at hang-doggie look v'ill go away! Eat!"

Meng ate. The meat was delicious. The sharp tang of the bitter orange set off the savour of the meat to absolute perfection. Meng bit – and was transported straight to heaven. He closed his eyes as his senses swam with the simple pleasures of rest, food and chatter. The sage ate steadily, somehow finding a second roll of meat and bread in his hand as he finished the first. Sandhri sat like a frog on the lip of the fountain, watching in sly amusement as he ate.

"Good boy! You mellow and let Sandhri do the t'inking for a v'ile." The bat settled herself against the water pipe, water splashing merrily beside her. She gathered the children in all about her, and they flocked in about her with bright faces and eager eyes. Gardeners, housewives and workmen downed their tools and came over to listen as Sandhri lounged back, settled her fez across one eye and held court.

"Now – V'at shall we hear about?"

The children bounced like eager little balls.

"Animals!"

"Butterflies!"

"Sword fights!"

"A ship that flies!"

The children flew in and gathered all about Sandhri in an eager ring. Taking the smallest girl upon her lap, Sandhri raised one finger to the sky. She rested thoughtful eyes upon Sixteen-volume Meng.

"I t'ink v'e maybe tell mister lofty-volume Wang all about some little t'ings." She clapped her hands. "Now shushing to listen! I clap hands! I clap hands! I bow to God and smile..."

The bat leaned forward to her audience, utterly transformed. Expressive hands swept outwards, and her face became infinitely cool and calm. "A story I haff for you. So shush!"

Surrounded by the fig tree, children and dragonflies, Sandhri leaned back and closed her eyes.

> *"Long ago, after Adamah and Ewah left the garden of Eden, many off the animals also ate from the Tree of Life. The bats persuaded the others, and so t'ey all came to eat the sacred fruit. Everything v'ith fur and paws came scuttling up the tree to take part of the power that had made Adamah and Ewah lords of the Earth.*
>
> *"Still! Some animals missed out on the whole experience! The hooved animals and the fish could not climb the tree, and the birds slept late and missed the whole affair. The insects v'ere perfectly happy as they v'ere, and also refused to eat from the tree. But the other animals changed and grew. T'ey rose up onto two feet, and they knew lust and fear, passion and glory. But t'ey also knew love, and for this, God treasured t'em even though t'ey had disobeyed his command.*
>
> *"God could not release t'ese new Peoples of The Tree onto the Earth, and so he made a new v'orld for them, "Aku Mashad". A gate v'as opened, and all the animals who had eaten of the tree v'ere sent forth from Eden to found new lives.*

Sandhri leaned forwards, miming sadness. The children stared up at her, utterly enthralled.

> *"Left behind in Eden, the ot'er animals v'ere sad. V'ithout the crowds of other species, the garden seemed empty and forlorn. Not'ing changed, and all seemed strained and quiet. Finally, the remaining animals called a conference. Fish spoke to insect, insect spoke to mammal and mammal to bird. The Zebra v'as elected as spokesman, and he trotted forth to haff a*

v'ord to God.

"He found God messing with his petunias, tryink to get the colour just right. The Zebra coughed until he had God's attention, and t'en sv'ept down into a reverent bow.

"God, oh God." The Zebra nodded his stripy mane. "V'e know you are angered at t'ose who disobeyed you and ate fruit from the tree. But t'ese animals have been our friends and companions v'ile v'e have lived in paradise. It iss too cruel to send t'em off into anot'er v'orld alone." The zebra looked around itself, and was encouraged by nods from the other animals. He looked at God and quailed a little, then bowed even more humbly than before. "Great God, we humbly ask t'at v'e be allowed to accompany our old friends. To help t'em and v'atch over them as they try to make new lives."

"God looked down at the animals in thought. These were the creatures that had remained faithful to his commands – the insects, the fish, the scaled animals, the animals with hooves and the ones with feathers. God gestured towards the far v'all of paradise, to where Adamah and Ewah held sway over the other world called Earth.

"My Children – you haff seen across the v'all to the world of Earth. If I send you forth from the garden of Eden, even into the new v'orld I have made for your friends, you v'ill never be at ease as you are here in the garden. For you must know that the gift of the Tree of Life is power over others." God gestured to the new gate that he had made – the gate to our own v'orld of Aku-Mashad. "Children – are you sure that this is v'at you wish? For on Aku-Mashad just as on Earth, the peoples who have eaten of the Tree will rule, and you will foreffer be subject to them."

"The animals looked to v'un another, but they v'ere all agreed. V'at would life be like in the garden without their friends the cunning foxes? The sturdy bears – the brave, bold wolves?" Sandhri arched her brows – skinny as a black eel - and twirled one hand. "What would life be like without the clever twitters of the bats?

One child – a skinny little cat with smoke-brown fur and great blue eyes – began tugging insistently at Sandhri's trousers.

"And the cats?" The little girl looked up at Sandhri. "Did they miss the cats?"

Sandhri sat up, her whole body miming amazed agreement.

"Cats! What v'ould a v'orld be like v'ithout the cats? No style, no grace – and no v'un to shiver their fur v'en you touch their backs v'ith your finger just *there*…" She touched a finger to the little cat's hide, and the child's fur contracted around the point like ripples in a pond. Sandhri laughed, drank water from the fountain pipe, and shared the last piece of bread with the little cat. "Now! V'ere were we? Out off Eden? Good!" The storyteller never noticed that a dragonfly had landed upon her hat, and was slowly fanning its wings. "Ho, you t'ere! Are you alright there, patchv'ork Meng?"

"Quite well, I thank you." Meng had a little Osranii dictionary in hand, and was listening in a panic, as if afraid there might be an exam on the subject later. "Are these the words of some famous sage?"

"Off course! The sexiest in history! Also cleverest, and v'ith prettiest eyes. So pay attention!" Sandhri spread her hands. "Right!"

Meng seemed puzzled.

"I fail to see how this aids us entering the palace."

"Palace, palace! V'y for you in such a hurry? Sausages and shade are here. Not to be sneezed at!" Sandhri raised a finger high in righteousness. "Now, v'ere were we?"

"The animals went through the gate!" A slim, skinny little rat boy – all legs, elbows and knees – adjusted his glasses. "The animals came here to Aku-Mashad."

"And so they did!" Sandhri stuffed the last bread into her mouth, talking with her mouth full..

> "So – the animals v'ere insistent t'at t'ey should travel to join us all here in the new v'orld. And so God opened up the gates and let them through.
>
> "In the new v'orld, everything was vibrant, fresh and new! Each animal made its own compact with the People of the Tree. The sv'ift-running horse became our friend and our ally. The elephant carried burdens – and the cow and lazy sheep exchanged t'eir freedom so that t'ey might live in well-fed herds. The birds and lizards, fish and insects spread out into the v'ilderness, there to make homes for themselves and become the joyous, v'ild things of the world.
>
> "V'un by v'un, the creatures all dispersed. Of all the insects, only the honey bee stayed to help the people – and with her v'as another tiny little insect v'ith gossamer bright wings. She v'as called the mosquito, and she v'as very, very shy.
>
> "The mosquito looked out across the v'ilds, and was afraid. She found the cows in the field, and tried singing them to sleep v'ith her v'ings, but the cows glared at her in annoyance.
>
> "Mosquito, go av'ay! V'e haff big sv'itchy tails, and v'e are going to swat you v'ith them!"
>
> "Terrified, the mosquito tumbled av'ay on the breeze. She ended up in a field full of lambs and ewes. Tired and hungry, she crept up to a sheep, but the sheep glared at her.
>
> "Mosquito, go av'ay! V'e are growing thick v'ool to keep your pointy nose av'ay from our skins. So t'ere iss no food for you here."
>
> "Unwanted, poor mosquito shed a little tear. She flew away along the banks of a stream, until she heard a strange little noise. Creeping through the grass she carefully peeked out into a little shady place, where a hut made out of mud and grass stood beneath a big green tree.
>
> "Sitting outside the hut was a family of dogs – People of The Tree. T'ey wore clothes on t'eir backs and shoes upon t'eir feet. Bread baked in the ovens and fruit sat in bowls. They v'ere sitting and singing v'ith each other as the sun mellowed softly into afternoon.
>
> "T'is seemed so much more friendly than the open fields. Keeping shyly hidden, the mosquito v'ent off to explore around the huts, the trees and lanes. She found a deep, cool v'ell all filled v'ith v'ater – all private and at peace. With a little noise of glee, the mosquito dove down to make her home. Here she could lay her little eggs and make her babies to her heart's content. She learned music from the People, and in return, she danced upon the summers breeze.
>
> "And so the mosquito lived happily. She kept out of sight, creeping out

at night to make her meals on people who v'ere fast asleep. She t'ought it best to stay unnoticed and unseen, in case anyone should object to her being there.

"Meanv'ile, all v'as not so well v'ith the ot'er animals. The horses wanted free feed provided for t'em, but t'ey objected to haffing to carry people on their backs. The oxen t'ought walking in circles pulling ploughs v'ass too boring, and v'anted to be pampered. The v'ild animals had found t'emselves being hunted for food, and v'ere utterly outraged. The animals all made a secret meeting, and decided to bring their complaints before God.

"T'ey raised a mighty cry, and God soon came down to discover v'y the ruckus. He listened to the animals' complaints, but v'as unamused.

"T'is iss v'at I warned you of. The Peoples of The Tree rule here. But still, your species thrive and the natural balance has been kept. V'y do you complain?"

"T'ey make us v'ork for our feed!" Cried the horse and the oxen. "They breed us and eat us!" Bleated the sheep. "Is this not cruel?"

"They hunt us for their dinners" said the deer. "And v'ith the Tora birds so huge, v'e already haff a full job just avoiding being dinner for the birds!"

"T'eir complaints v'ere many, and had some small amount of justice to them. God gave a weary sigh, and sat himself down.

"Very v'ell. I can alv'ays arrange a yearly plague off boils or door-to-door salesmen, if it giffs you any moral satisfaction."

"The animals whooped happily and agreed t'at t'iss might be just the t'ing! God made a mental note not to make himself so available in the future.

"Alright, you unruly beasts. The People of Aku-Mashad shall be punished, but only if you all agree. If no v'un will speak up for them, then I will punish t'em."

"The animals looked from one to another. The vengeful Torah bird clacked its razor beak. The proud horse tossed its mane. No one came forward to plead for mercy for the unfortunate people of the Tree."

Sandhri leaned forward, slyly twinkling her fingers.

"Until shyly – hesitantly – v'ith a v'irr, and a v'ine, and a little buzzy-buzz, v'un tiny little figure came forv'ard. The little mosquito drifted out into the light.

"She v'as very small, and oh-so shy – a dear little thing that quailed when the other animals all looked at her. She saw their eyes scowling at her, but the little mosquito bravely puffed out her chest, and spoke in a voice as quiet as a breeze.

"Please Sir – uh, Mister God? Please, Sir – but I like the People. Please, oh please don't hurt t'em."

"The other animals scoffed, annoyed that the mosquito had even bothered to attend.

"Go av'ay! V'at do you know about t'ings off importance? V'y should v'e listen to a mere mosquito!"

"But the little mosquito bravely stood her ground.

"I am an animal, and I have as much right to talk to God as any of you." The mosquito quailed a little, shivering her wings. God extended a finger for her, and she landed upon it. He looked at her, and leaned in close to hear her speak.

"You are quite right, child. Tell me what you have to say."

"The mosquito sat upon the finger of God, and addressed all the other animals.

"I like the People of The Tree. When no one else would tolerate me, they gave me a home. I think they work very hard growing food for all the other animals they care for. You, horse! I have seen them grooming you night after night. And the runner birds are given kennels that are always swept so clean. They make ponds and pools where other insects can live, and their roof eaves even make a place v'ere swallows can make nice safe nests of mud."

"The animals grumbled. "That is as may be. But v'at haff these People ever done for you?"

"They giff me the means to live." The mosquito hummed. "V'en I need to lay my babies, there is always v'ater v'ere the people are." The mosquito blushed. "V'en they make music in the evening, it greets us as we hatch out from the waters – and it teaches us how to make our own songs as we dance through the sky. And so every mosquito is born into gladness, and knows where its next meal may be found.

"But most of all – they're so very tasty. The birds have feathers that we cannot pierce – the lizards all have scales. The cows tried to swat us, and the sheep grew nasty v'ool. But the People are all just right! Such tasty and delicious blood. We nibble on their ears as they sleep." The mosquito looked at God and pitifully wrung her little hands. "Please – please don't punish the People, or my sisters and I shall starve and die, and our music will not be heard forever more."

The animals were all ashamed and bowed their heads. God lifted the little mosquito in his hand and nodded his wise head.

"Good mosquito, I haff heard your plea. You v'ill live hand in hand with the creatures you haff so ably defended." He released the mosquito up into a warm night sky. As she felt the breeze caress her, the little mosquito began to dance, and her wings made music drift upon the air.

God watched her innocent joy and smiled.

"As long as the mosquitoes dance, the People shall be safe from my wrath. As long as one mosquito sings, I promise that the mosquitoes shall never know hunger."

God faded back away from the open world, leaving the animals to shamefacedly go back to their rather comfortable lives. Above them, the mosquito danced as sunset stained the skies a brilliant hue. She went back to her beloved People, and lived safe and sound forever more."

Sandhri the storyteller lounged idly beside the fountain. Beside her, mosquito larvae wriggled in the waters of the pool, going about their funny little lives.

"And that was that. V'ere t'ere are people, t'ere the mosquitoes ever more shall be. And v'en a mosquito hovers in the bedroom air at night, you can never ever seem to still its song. But be glad – because the mosquito sings your praises to God, and so all of us v'ill be forever safe and sound…"

A horn blew from the palace, and the children all looked up as one. Sandhri gave a great cat-like stretch and stood, showering crumbs from her lap.

"Lessons time! All off you go to school, now!"

The children gave an '*awwwww*' of disappointment, but Sandhri gathered them up, hugged them then chased them off towards the palace gates.

"Off off! Before Yariim has our hides. And shhhh about the food!" She picked up one little girl who had fallen down. "Quick quick! See you later! V'e make puppets before dinner, before you go to bed!"

Wives and workers called out to Sandhri as they went back to work, and Sandhri hooted greetings to them as she shook her robes free of crumbs and put them back on again.

"So hey Meng! You v'ant to get moving?"

The tall young panda blinked in confusion after the departing children.

"Where are they going?"

"To school! Iss a school day. Only Yariim had some stuffy poet comink to read t'em hiss boring odes before school." The bat found a crumb had fallen down her meager cleavage, and she pulled out her top to busily shake it free. "So hey – you like story, yes?"

Puzzled, Meng stood with his hands inside his sleeves.

"Ah. What was the moral purpose of the story."

"Aaaah. Perhaps there v'ass v'un. Perhaps not." Sly and elegant, Sandhri balanced atop a stone. "Perhaps it just says neffer to dismiss little things. Even humble t'ings can be great treasures."

"Truly?"

"I chust tell 'em! For you it iss to decide v'at you learn!" Sandhri pranced. "Ho, mister seventeen volumes. You should think less and learn more. Ha!"

"Ah."

Meng furrowed his brows, and did not see the point at all…

Ever busy, Sandhri helped Meng lift up his heavy rack of books. "Ooof! You must be crazy! You come far v'ith t'ese t'ings?"

"Three thousand, two hundred and eleven miles." Meng swayed a little unsteadily beneath his burden. His meal had stretched his stomach, and the hot food seemed to be spreading a spell of sleep slowly through his body. "Forgive me, but this humble one wonders whether we should rest a while…"

"V'at? I t'ought you v'anted to get into the palace?" Full of eagerness, Sandhri dragged the fellow onwards. "Come on – v'e get you in first, t'en sleepies later. And you need a bath."

"I need no luxuries."

"I vass t'inking off us, not you!" Sandhri gave an expressive sniff. "Hey – haff you been treading in camel turds?"

"I… not on purpose!" Meng tried to stick to the subject. "Madam – I fail to understand how a mere storyteller can get me into the palace."

"Easy peasy!" Sandhri gathered up her empty plates, put her basket on her arm, and headed for the palace wall. "Come on – don't forget the volumes! You gotta look after that kinda stuff! You don't v'ant to be v'alking back to get anot'er load!" The Bat towed Meng by the hand. "Iss pretty important we get you into the palace to get your head screwed on straight!"

The young panda gave Sandhri a lofty glance.

"What can a street corner storyteller know of the way of the sage and the path I must travel?"

"Oh – paths!" Sandhri's beautiful eyes lit with sly little lights.

> *"Long ago, a Monk of Han returned to his mountain monastery after a journey of eleven years. An old friend met him and asked.*
> *"Friend – where did you go?"*
> *He replied. "I traveled to the far ends of Aku-Mashad."*
> *"What, then, did you discover in these far places."*
> *"That I lacked Nothing before I left the monastery."*
> *The friend then said. "V'y, t'en, did you go?"*
> *The monk replied. "Ah! If I had not gone there, how would I have known that I lacked Nothing?"*

Arching back his neck, shocked and amazed, Meng stared.

"Lady – who are you?"

"Pah ha! I am Sandhri al Dinaq – a teller of stories!" The bat swept off her fez and gave a bow, her white hair sweeping elegantly to the ground like sheets of purest silk. Her little tail stuck up into the air. "At your service."

Meng felt a little prod of worry.

"Al Dinaq…?"

"A cool name! V'ateffer!" She clapped her fez onto her head. "Now quick! We're late!" Sandhri the storyteller, consumer of sausages, grabbed the young traveler by the hand. "Hurry up or v'ere in trouble!"

"We?"

"Of course 'we'! Iss part of the plan! I can tell Yariim it v'as your fault! Simple!" She dragged the poor boy up the hill into the streets. "V'y iss you such a sleepy head? Now run! Pick up the feets and run!" Meng was propelled awkwardly up the street. "Alright, big steps! V'e try to sneak in v'ith the school crowds. If anyv'un asks, you're the ambassador from… v'ere are you from again?"

"The Yellow Empire."

"Good name! Yellow Empire. Let's go!"

Sandhri walked them from the alleys and out into the broad, bright streets of Sath. Palm trees sent shade chasing back and forth across a road that swept towards the mighty palace gates. Guards dressed in blue velvet armour and steel helms welcomed a crowd of people who were all hurrying inward through the gates. There were children in droves, young girls with robes over dancing costumes of astonishing beauty – old scholars and serious young men and women locked in their own discourse. Sandhri jumped the entire queue, speeding Meng past a huge armoured tiger who stood happily on guard.

"Hey Saud!"

The tiger beamed and raised a hand vast enough to engulf Meng's skull. Sandhri dragged the confused sage onwards through a towering archway, past marble pools crowded with bustling scholars, then made him hide behind a doorway as she spied out a corridor.

"Madam! Is this legal?"

"Eh – v'at's legal?" Sandhri whisked Meng down a colonnade of astonishing marble pillars, open gardens and coloured glass. "So hey! V'y iss t'iss empire off yours Yellow? V'un too many retreats in battle?"

"What? No!" The panda was incensed. "The emperor wears yellow."

"Hokay! V'ell, v'e can send him some better coloured duds later." Sandhri turned excitedly about,. "Speakink of duds! I got t'iss new number you ought to see. My husband, he comes back tonight after t'ree days upriver! I got this piece that's about two spiderv'ebs of silk and a bit of glitter! Sexy ass it gets!"

"Really." Wracked with nerves, dazed and confused, Meng saw more guards march by. "Look…"

They swept around a corner, and were stopped dead in their tracks.

A woman stood there in the colonnade – a woman as stunning as an angel. A mouse with soft, round ears. Small, straight backed, round and perfect, she had the total grace of a dancer and the poise of a queen. Long blonde hair was caught up in a jeweled head piece. Her robes framed a figure as buxom and as flawless as an adolescent's wettest dream. She had great owlish glasses on her face, and ink stains on her fingertips. Her fur was a pure sky blue, and her eyes as pink as dawn.

The woman folded her arms and glowered at Sandhri, radiating absolute authority.

"That food was for the poet laureate."

"It v'asn't labeled!" Sandhri threw spread fingers against her heart, protesting her innocence. "Hey – T'ere v'ass this guy hanging around the baskets. He must have taken it. Ask the kids!" Sandhri hastily looked for a diversion. She threw an arm about the blue mouse, who tried to remain stiff and seething as Sandhri dragged her towards Meng.

"Hey! Lookie who v'e found! He's from the Yellow Empire. Brought sixteen volumes all the way v'ith him!" Sandhri gave the mouse a loving squeeze and waved a hand from her to Meng. "Hey Meng! This is the lady I told you about! T'iss iss my lovely Yariim!"

"Aaah!" The wandering sage's tired mind made the connection and was glad. "Gentle lady, she has spoken of you! You are the blonde bombshell with the backside that does not quit." Meng delivered the litany as though reciting Yariim's pedigree. He put his hands in his sleeves and solemnly bowed. "I am Sixteen-volume Meng, a wayfarer on the path of enlightenment."

Yariim raised one eyebrow in amusement, and then shot a sidewise glance towards Sandhri.

The black bat clasped her hands in joy.

"He followed me home. Can v'e keep him?"

Sandhri grabbed Meng by the arm and hauled him around the corner. Here in a vast, wide palace square, there were guards in royal blue armour – girls in harem costume performing stretches on the grass. Functionaries and public servants in gorgeous robes stood outside the halls, waiting for the business day to start. The little bat dragged Meng into position and excitedly ran forward.

"Hey Meng! Check this!" She waved towards the crowds. *"Hey efferybody! Good morning!"*

Scholars, soldiers, public servants, harem dancers and their instructors all looked up, smiled gladly, then all bowed low to Sandhri in one gracious flow.

"All joy to the Queen!"

Adjusting her glasses, Yariim turned her glance of the ashen-faced Meng.

"I take it you have met Queen Sandhri, first wife to the Shah of Osra? I am Queen Yariim."

Meng fainted clean away. Yariim settled her glasses and looked down at the poor boy with a sigh.

"Sandhri - you are going to get such a pinch when I get you alone..."

Chapter Two:

In the soft evening light, amidst fields filled with countless blossoming apple trees, a city burned.

It had been a beautiful city – Hadat, an ancient oasis settlement on the long, parched trade route between the Frankish kingdoms and the Yellow Empire. Here, the long rows of two-humped camels had come from the east with their cargoes of silk and gemstones, cinnamon and jade. The one-humped camels had come north from distant Sath, bringing Osra's wealth of magic and perfumes, steel blades, ground lenses and brocades. The Franks came with great cargoes of amber, wines and silver. From far Meepsoor to the south came sandalwood and diamonds, lapis lazuli and hunting birds. Hadat – a city state proud and prosperous, had thrived beside its oasis of sweet water, acting as a melting pot for races and ideas.

Until the coming of the horde.

The coming of The Khan.

They were not nomads, although the nomads were amongst them. They were not mercenaries and adventurers, for now they took no pay in gold. The endless wars that had raged across the steppes had bred vast armies, and now one of those armies had found a *cause*. They no longer fought for land or loot: they had brought the world the death that follows men of holy vision.

For they were the instrument of the Tsu-Khan, the soldiers of a living God.

He had come to them like a vision of pure power. The Tsu-Khan – the Lord of Ghosts. Through him, tiny states had become an empire. Through him, nomad warlords had joined forces with the armies of the steppe cities. Army after army had felt the raw power of his call.

The lord of death. The lord of ice. A creature with a dark, terrifying mission. He had taken the lost, the violent and the dispossessed – all those who had come to revel in the flame of war, whose sole release was blood. They had come beneath his banners made of living, screaming skulls, and felt the dark glory that he gave them. Victory after victory – blood everlasting. Their only pleasure came from serving him. Their only terror was to be unworthy of his glory. The sheer chill of his power swept them onwards like a storm, filling savage, empty souls with deadly purpose.

He was their priest and their messiah – their dream, their living god. No life had purpose unless it served the Khan. No cruelty, no sacrifice could be too foul if it brought terror to his name. Those who valued their miserable lives had run to bow before him: City after city had prostrated themselves before his armies…

… And those who failed to embrace his glory, died…

The city of Hadat burned.

The fires lit the skies, hotter than the stars. Children screamed as they burned alive – women screamed in rape. The light framed a single, small figure that sat upon a blue-eyed horse. A figure clad in jet black armour made from finger bones...

He was lord of the city states and master of three hundred thousand warriors. The Tsu-Khan: The Lord of Ghosts.

He was unsleeping, never resting – focused and unswerving. No pity, no weakness marred his soul. He had come out of the wilderness to bring the steppe warriors his vision: One world serving the Khan. One empire that embraced all of Aku-Mashad.

One dark, immortal Khan…

Osra would be crushed. The Yellow empire would fall, and the lands of the west. Vindahl's rich farmlands and the jungles of the south. All creation would bow before the chosen one.

And now, the last of the City States had fallen. Hadat – the treasure house of the Steppes. The storehouse that would buy more soldiers, more blades, more arrows. All the strength of the ages would be needed to drive the great vision onwards into glory.

Hadat died as a blood sacrifice to the purity of that vision. It had rebelled against him, refusing its tribute – and now it died as a lesson in terror. Half a million inhabitants had dwelled within the city by the wells. By the end of the night, half a million corpses would lie splayed across the grass.

The soldiers were at work. A hundred thousand men could liquidate entire populations in a single night. Each man had a quota of five heads to reap. Each officer made sure his men brought in their trophies for the count.

There was a joy that came with slaughter -a release. To rape a woman across the corpses of her children – to chase fugitives fleeing across the plains, hacking a bright blade into flesh with a sound like chopping wood… these were pleasures mere gold could never buy. The Khan brought his men the gift of slaughter, and in return they pledged their hearts and souls to his dreams.

Hadat died in a frenzied orgy of gore. Screams filled the evening. Blades sliced and hacked into living flesh. A city burned, and the Tsu-Khan stared idly at the flames as though divining messages sent from another world.

Fires threw wild shadows across the hillside. Visions danced insanely in the flames. A carpet of headless corpses spread at the Khan's feet, fanning out to pave the world with fly-blown meat.

He felt them come. Without turning, the slim, slight figure of the Khan lifted up his gaze from the flames.

Dark, half ragged things sped unseen through the air around him. Lord of three hundred thousand blades, the Tsu-Khan looked at his generals through blank, blue eyes. He was a slim, small arctic fox – his fur pure white and his face forever blank and calm. But his soul seemed to seethe around the mere flesh like a dark, half hidden storm. In his armour made of bones, beneath his banner topped by screaming skulls, the Khan turned to watch his men approach.

"General Gurad. General Tsai-Chung."

The Khan's generals were smothered in ashes and blood. Nomad and Osranii, they threw severed heads onto the grass. The trophies rolled to show bright glazed eyes that shone in the light of distant fires.

"Lord, my Lord, My Great Lord." Tsai-Chi, the nomad general, spoke with a voice soft and silken quiet. A snow tiger, his fur glimmered weirdly in the city's fire. "My *tumans* have reaped the trophies of the dead."

"Great One." Gurad, the Osranii general – a scarred leopard with one hand marred by ancient burns, touched his head, mouth and heart in salaam. "Your army has purified the traitors of Hadat."

"Good. Good…" The Khan's voice was quiet – almost absent minded, as though the people all around him were merely puppets in a play. "Have the Guard save the city fathers until last. I wish them to witness the absolute destruction of all that they hold dear." The Khan leaned upon his saddlebow, looking in wrapt fascination at the flames.
"Wait until the last of their citizens is slain before them."
He turned again to look at the interlaced patterns of headless bodies, skulls and blood.

"A fall into madness is made more rich, when total horror is communicated to the heart."

The Tsu-Khan turned to face his generals. Pale blue eyes, clear and childlike in their perfection, looked out through a plain black veil.

"Gurad. You will both take the city fathers, and flay them alive with your own hands. Have their skins used to make my battle drums."

"It shall be done." Gurad's voice shook with love. Blood still dripped from his naked scimitar. "Great Lord – Sacred one. Master of a thousand glories."

General Tsai-Chi bowed. The snow tiger rose in his stirrups and pointed back down the hillside with his rawhide whip.

"Our gift to you, Oh Perfect one! The city's treasures have been found."

Hadat's wealth was in silks and gold, in spices and in grain. But most of all, she had sat at the center of the world's trade routes for a thousand busy years. Magics gleaned from countless ages had rested in her palace chambers. Loot fit to arm the conqueror of a world.

Soldiers brought the treasures on stretchers made of bloody robes threaded upon spears. There were books, scrolls and enchanted blades – bows made from pale blue dragon bone and jars of sacred herbs. A great brass hemisphere as big as a cart sat upon folded metal rods and tubes, carried by bullocks sweating from the load. It would all go to the Khan's capital, Khordesh – there to be sifted for worth in battle.

The brass hemisphere lumbered past. The Khan turned to watch it pass. The shell was hollow, and a round opening was hung with a curtain made of old blue silk. He stared at the cold metal, and let it go.

"Gurad?"

"Yes lord."

"The Great War is almost at hand. You will pick your mouthpiece. We shall move against Osra."

On the plains below, the headless bodies lay. The Khan moved forward, his horse treading heedlessly on rubbery, dead flesh. The warlords cast long shadows across the slaughtered innocents as they rode.

Sitting on his horse, the Khan gazed across the dead with pale blue eyes. He reached out his arms, spreading them wide, and opened his fingers, drawing the stuff of nightmares up out of the dark.

"Arise! Arise and obey!"

A cold wind sprang out of the blood soaked soil. Soldiers gathered, staring in awe as their leader shimmered with a savage, ghostly power. He stood up in his stirrups, caught by a storm that seethed and tore at his robes.

"Creatures of a lesser world, *arise!* By the great seal, obey me. By the lesser seal, you will serve me. By the seals of pain, you will do my bidding and bow before my will.

"Arise! Awake! Arise!"

The headless bodies jerked from the ground, as though still caught in their death throes. Corpses convulsed, then hammered madly at the ground. The severed heads all gave out a moan – a tortured scream of pain that rose and rose like a storm upon the wind. Pale shapes flew up to swirl, caught helplessly in a maelstrom of savage light that spilled out from the Khan's dark robes.

Ghostly shapes wailed and screamed in torment. They screeched in fear, in madness and despair. They were drawn inside the light in their thousands, sucked inwards and shut off from the universe. The light blazed bright – the dead souls screamed - and then suddenly a hidden door slammed shut. The light was gone, the corpses stilled. Only the sounds of a dying city still disturbed the night.

The Tsu-Khan breathed deep, his arms still spread. He opened pale blue eyes and stared into the dark.

"We leave for the capital."

Gurad's horse shivered, sweating white with terror. The general slapped it into calm.

"Great Lord., I shall bring my mouthpiece. But can he do the things you ask?"

"He will do all that we could hope for, Gurad." The Khan breathed deep and calm. All around him, his black-armoured guardsmen gathered – thousands and thousands of them – cold instruments of steel and blood. "He will neutralize Osra. He will allow us to conquer in the east and in the west."

"And then, my Lord?"

"And then you shall have your wish, Gurad, as my gift to my faithful. You shall have Osra placed into your own hands." The Khan reigned in and looked to the South West – towards the distant lands of Osra.

"We shall take the queens of Osra while we crucify their Shah. We will watch their cities burn. We shall slake ourselves upon their childrens' blood, and bring them to know that I am their god, and that serving the Tsu-Khan is their only salvation."

Gurad bowed instantly, ablaze with love.

"Lord…"

"Go, Gurad. There is much work to be done."

The battle lords separated and rode the spattered fields. The Tsu-Khan moved amongst horsemen who abjectly bowed their heads as he passed. Behind the Khan, a new pyramid arose – a monument of severed heads that glistened sickeningly in the light of dying fires.

The Khan rode onwards on his blue-eyed horse, and his horse's hooves left a trail of blood.

*****

In the great palace of the Osranii Shah, there lived a special girl. A girl, all wriggly slim – all whiskers, tail and ears. Green of fur, sly and sleek, with great pink eyes that forever rolled with mischief. Fifteen and three quarter years old, she had long lanky legs for climbing trees, and clever fingers for thieving biscuits from the kitchen baking pans. She had the svelte and skinny build of her beloved Sandhri, and had brand new breasts far more akin to those of her darling Yariim. Her hair was long and golden-bright. She could fly a kite and throw a stone – or dance and play ditties on the Vindahlese sitar. All in all, Itbit was the cleverest of mice.

Whiskers a-twiddle and glasses gleaming, Itbit prowled the gardens of the palace looking out for fun. She peered carefully about the colonnades, her long whiskers hunting for trouble. Her great skinny pink tail twisted like a crafty serpent as she peered through windows, lattices and balconies. It drew attention to her taut little bottom as she hid herself behind curtains and tapestries.

Evil guardians were on the prowl: Somewhere in the palace, a maths tutor was looking for Itbit and simmering in fury. She had taken her favourite horse out for a gallop in the morning, and had jumped a fence only to accidentally trample Lady Fatima's prized flower garden on the other side. Crafty tricks and tricksy ways were safest for Itbit now, otherwise she would find herself in Fatima's deportment class for the entire afternoon. A fate worse than death!

Itbit tip toed happily down a side corridor, sliding stealthily out of sight behind a great brass urn. The royal poet laureate stalked past, his tail a-swirl with indignation, looking for someone who would hear his complaints. Itbit – the cleverest mouse there had ever been – let him go, and then slid into the dead zone that always followed in the poet laureate's wake.

There was a locked door here, behind a forgotten old tapestry.
Sandhri had taught Itbit many things – much to the annoyance of Yariim and Raschid. One of those things was how to keep hold of things that didn't strictly-speaking belong to her. With a merry twirl of her tail, Itbit slid a stolen key out of her cleavage, fitted it to the lock, and slipped through the opened door before anyone could see…

… And Itbit was in the most special, secret garden of them all.

In the back of the palace complex, beside a great, eccentric tower, was the old rear gardens of the college of sorcery. It was overgrown and full of green – a place where gardeners never trod for fear of the sorcerers, and where sorcerers never trod for fear of eerie things living in the grass. Here, great toads with pure red eyes could be found underneath the stones. Little flightless uki birds, small furtive dwellers in the wainscotings of the world, made nests of leaves and fluff beside a beautiful green pool. Here, the experiments of the sorcerers made their homes, fed by Sandhri, Raschid and Yariim, who always came here with Itbit in the cool of the evening.

It was the quiet place – the place where business never pursued them. The back wall of the palace gave easy access in and out for anyone tricky enough to negotiate the creeping vines with their hordes of watchful wasps. Clumps of daffodil-like flowers kept watch from every hollow, hooting like maniacs if they saw anyone or anything they did not recognize.

Itbit slipped through the flowers and found her friends the wasps. The little creatures were busy again with yet another of their endless schemes. They had long abdomens patterned in yellow, white and mahogany brown. The wasps trundled apricot stones over to a garden plot that they had dug all by themselves, keen to grow their favourite fruits in an orchard of their own. The little creatures were an experiment forgotten by the mages, but much treasured by Itbit and Raschid. Itbit bustled over to the wasps and gave them an over ripe nectarine, plus three sewing needles thieved from her old mistress in the dressmaker's shop. They waved to her in thanks, and went back to the heavy work of planting their very own orchard trees.

At this time of day, the college of magicians was busy with its work. The Royal Sorcerer, old Hassan, now found himself presiding over vast new facilities. The old school now had twenty researchers and two dozen students, all devoted to the cause of discovering a proper scientific basis for magic.

Thus far, the results were less than instructive. An explosion came from the third floor of the sorcerers' tower, followed by the wails of a student. A door burst open, and a young man came speeding out with the tails of his robes on fire. He ran for the garden pond, astonishing the red-eyed toads with a leap that carried him a dozen feet out into the center of the pool.

Hassan the sorcerer was an old, grizzled cat, black of fur and thick of whisker. He stumped out of the tower door, looked towards the pond – then took a second look as he saw Itbit eating biscuits beside the daffodils. He unshipped a great brass hearing trumpet and stumped forward through the trees.

"I've told you! We don't take students until they're eighteen!"

Itbit walked over, sticking out her bare pink feet as she came, her hands clasped innocently behind her back.

"Itbit is eighteen – see?" She jutted her chest forward: "Itbit's tits be real fine bits!"

Hassan adjusted his glasses, looking at the proffered breasts. He seemed unimpressed.

"Yes – class mammalia. Very nice." He put his glasses away. "You're fourteen."

"Eighteen!"

"Fourteen!" The old magician began counting off the years on his fingers. "Raschid is crowned. Then there was the year you and that bat girl tried raising bees in the harem garden. Then there was the year you kept that Tora bird hidden in the broom cupboard. Then there was the year you showed those boys how to use that tunnel to peer into the harem baths… Then that year with the boy's gym changing rooms, and the Zen Buddhist…"

Haughty as a queen, Itbit put her nose in the air, making her great spray of fine white mouse whiskers quiver with dignity.

"Itbit was not responsible for silly monk!"

"That's as maybe. But that makes you a little girl of fourteen!"

"Fifteen!" Itbit stamped her foot. "Itbit is a Lady! She is fifteen and three quarters!"

"Which is still not eighteen." Hassan prodded Itbit's ample bosom with his walking stick. "And big isn't wise. You need a good educational foundation if you're going to learn magic. Maths, science, languages!"

The green mouse simpered. "Itbit has education! She is clever. Blue pretty Yariim has taught her dances and songs and histories. Sharpie-clever Sandhri teaches her legends and tales and lots of hidden things. Raschid has taught Itbit numbers and letters and how to make very nice bombs!" Itbit stuck out her chest in pride. "She speakies lots of languages very goodly! Clever words and tricky tongue!" The mouse tried to look superior. "Itbit knows what an Itbit knows."

Hassan threw up his arms. This was a game played out for mutual pleasure a dozen times a week. He turned and stamped back the way that he had come.

"One book, then. And one only! And this time don't draw pictures in the margins!"

Itbit made a gleeful noise and followed after the old sorcerer. They walked past a huge birdhouse filled with happy flocks of flying squid. The squid cart wheeled happily as they saw Itbit, and she ducked a jet of ink that flew carelessly off across the path.

"Hey squiddly diddlies!"

Hassan pushed past a door that hung half off its hinges and led the way into the tower. There were tables strewn with papyri and parchments, and researchers carefully comparing different volumes of text. Three men were hitting tuning forks and watching the effects of the sound upon a dish full of krill. It was the usual goings-on that filled the sorcerers' day. With her hands behind her back, tummy in and breasts stuck out, Itbit rocked on her heels and waited happily as Hassan grumbled his way through a tower of books.

"Here! A book on sprites and spirits – how to address them and how to appease them. Useful defensive stuff." The old man blew dust from the covers. "Here you go."

The curvaceous green mouse girl happily seized the book.

"Itbit will read him good!"

"Read it carefully. I'll question you on it next week – so mind you learn it well!" The old man knocked out his hearing trumpet, and a bemused moth fell out. "Never quite know what you young idiots expect from magic, in any case."

"Itbit will be a sorceress!" The mouse twirled her tail with guile. "She will make mighty spells that will make everybody want to please her!"

"Hmmph. Get your education, and get your mental tools sharp and straight. Any other advantages you'll need in life are already well in place." Old Hassan used a stick to poke at Itbit's breasts. "Now then – go do your lessons. And don't forget the maths!"

The mouse hovered, looking about to see in anything interesting was being made on any of the benches.

"You want to play backie-gammon with Itbit?

"Tonight, after your classes." Somewhat pleased, Hassan blew through his whiskers. "With *my* dice!"

"Itbit is outraged! What do you imply about an Itbit's dice?"

"You've known that skinny one too long. You know the one I mean – with the hair!" The sorcerer waved his walking stick. *"My* dice! And I'll keep you some biscuits!"

Pleased with her day, Itbit hugged the book to herself and skipped off into the secret garden. Sandhri had told her that there were some old ghosts in the north tower, and she was fairly certain spirits must live by the river in the pretty rocks. She would read her book and then go to try and try to find some. Surely they would all be pleased to tell a tale or two to Itbit!

Out in the gardens, the wasps were carrying nutshells of water from the pond to irrigate their seedlings. Itbit wandered past, only to hear a sudden commotion in the vines that covered up the palace wall. Guards heard the noise as well, and came running over to investigate, guns in hand.

The disturbance was caused by a bundle of blackened, filthy robes that hung upside down and trapped in the vines. A male voice squawked in panic as wasps gathered all about the vines in threatening clouds.

"No! no – it's me!" The figure thrashed, totally tangled in black, smelly robes. *"I've got an apple for you somewhere. Really – wait! Help!"*

With a grin, Itbit hitched up her halter and paced over to the wall. An infantry officer with a long pistol in one hand and a gleaming scimitar in the other came to the edge of the wall and looked down at the intruder. An elegant, slim-waisted rat, he magically parted the wasps aside.

"Thank you, ladies! Thank you!" Armed with poisoned needles and lances, the palace's wasps were nothing to be sneezed at. The soldier pushed back his helmet and leaned over the wall. "Sire – are you in need of help?"

From inside the filthy robes, a voice tried to be calm.

"Colonel Abwan is tangled upon the other side of the wall. I wonder if you might help him?"

"A pleasure, Sire."

The soldier sheathed his weapons. Itbit waved to him happily from below.

"Hey hey Spike man!"

"Hello little mistress." The soldier waved happily, then went off to look over the far side of the wall. "Ah, Colonel! And to what do I owe the pleasure?"

"Fer Allah's sake, stop bein' funny and help me up!"

Itbit waited at the foot of the vines. The man in his bundle of robes fought and cursed, trying to get right side up. He was hindered by a jute bag filled with papers, pens, ink and tape measures. Filthy, half drowned and reeking of river mud, he managed to free his head and look frantically about the garden.

Itbit was waiting for him, wreathed in happiness.

"Hey hey Raschid! Clever Itbit is here to get you down."

"Oh, it's you!" The man looked glad. "How did you know to be here?"

"Itbit knows what an Itbit knows!" The mouse climbed the vines and disentangled her friend. "Liftie foots! Now watchie bumps!"

"Wail!"

The man fell with a bump into a pile of weeds. The daffodils all craned to gaze at him, eyes wide and lips pursed. Some crept over on their roots to take a closer look. Itbit helped him stand, pulling at his sodden, filthy robes.

"Itbit say, iss silly Jackal chap! Is all stinky wet with mud!" Itbit was thoroughly muddied herself by the time she got him all untangled. "What you do?"

Long hands wearing archer's thumb rings, left and right, pulled back a mud stained hood. A long jackal's nose appeared – smoke grey, wise and elegant. The Jackal's smooth head had tall, high pricked ears, and great brown eyes lit with quiet, wise humour. Matted by mud, tar, and what looked like soot, he was a little bit the worse for wear. Grateful for Itbit's help, he struggled to his feet, his eyes full of love for his friend.

"Hello Itbit."

"Hello silly Jackal Shah!" Itbit threw her arms about Raschid, heedless of the mess, and lovingly hugged him tight. "How did the boat go?"

"Um – well, I sort of ran it onto a mud bank and fell off." Raschid kept an arm about his beautiful Itbit and squeezed as they walked. "Actually, I knocked myself silly."

Itbit rolled expressive eyes.

"Jackal-fellow keep it quiet! Otherwise Yariim and Sandhri will say they told you so!" Itbit dragged her key out of her ample cleavage. "Here! We go get you in bathies double quick! Itbit make all clean, and then we say 'Jackal, he be doing busy things all morning – not making his puff puff boat crash on river. No way!'"

Raschid al Dinaq, Shah of Osra, sage of sages and husband to two loving wives, hitched up his muddy scholars' robes. "The engine theory is sound. But the engineering is lacking. I've been using brass and copper, but it might have to be iron and steel. And that leads to corrosion problems in itself." The Shah of Osra gave a sigh, letting himself be led past the tiny wasp queen, who bowed to him in return to his *salaam* of recognition.

He came back to reality and raised one brow as Itbit led him through the locked door into the palace corridors.

"Itbit?"

"Yes Raschid?"

"Is that Lady Fatima's key?"

"Iss borrowed! Itbit keep it nice and warm with titties!"

"So I see…"

Ask not the ways of bats and sneaky mice. Raschid rolled his eyes and followed his oldest friend into the quiet places of the palace halls.

Moving furtively, the Shah of all Osra followed the mouse on stealthy paths through corridors and rooms. They flitted past the old Harem, where girls from across the Empire were now taught dance, music and the arts. For those who were curious, it was well known that Fatima still tutored a side course on the erotic arts, with a library well-plundered by Itbit. The Shah crept through a jungle of flowering plants behind a calisthenics class – somewhat distracted by the number of tails and bottoms waving in the air. Itbit tugged him behind a tapestry and the two of them made their way carefully towards the baths.

They went under some windows, and along a hall behind a row of soldiers, and out across an empty colonnade. Puffed with her own cleverness, Itbit pranced on her dainty feet.

"Ha ha! Itbit knows clever twisty ways!" The girl opened yet another door with one of Fatima's keys. "She came this way when she led the boys to watch the senior dance class in the bath!"

Raschid was shocked.

"Itbit! You never!"

"But they sneaked Itbit into the horse races as thank you! Itbit won fifteen gold pieces on a stripey pony!"

The Shah was half certain he would get into trouble over Itbit's excesses.

"Look, Itbit – I'm just not sure you should be…"

"Was fine! The boys liked it very much."

"I'm sure." Taking a sharp look at the mouse, Raschid raised his brow. "Just how often do you sneak into the baths?"

"Now and then. Itbit has things to learn." The mouse looked sly and twirled her tail. "Someday special, Itbit will need to know lots of things."

"IImm." Raschid wrinkled his nose in thought. "Itbit   I think we need a little talk…"

The door opened, echoes from the baths danced in the air – and Shah Raschid found himself face to face with a woman's scowl.

Fatima, mistress of the palace and teacher of arts stood in the doorway. She was forty years old, educated, sensual and beautiful. A pink-furred rabbit, elegant, buxom and intensely intelligent. She lowered glasses down to the end of her nose and regarded Itbit with glacial displeasure.

"Itbit – three of my keys are missing." The rabbit looked to Raschid and bowed in real love – the set of her ears indicating an awareness of his reeking, muddy state and the probable damage to the palace carpets. "My Shah…"

"Lady Fatima. How lovely to see you…" Raschid swallowed. "Um…"

"A tray of biscuits is missing from the kitchens." Fatima eyed Itbit, who took a quick sidestep to innocently hide behind Raschid. "And the new tiger girl that your friends the grooms so admire is missing two sets of underwear from the dirty laundry basket again…"

Itbit looked totally shocked – a skill learned at Sandhri's knee.

"Itbit is alarmed! Nasty grooms must be stealing underwear and looking at it while eating cookies!"

"Quite." Fatima seethed. "And another thing…"

At this point, the poet laureate spied Raschid. The lean, gangrelly Genet cat swiped back his hair and flowed over to bow before the Shah.

"Great Shah! My Lord!" The poet was in paroxysms of over-played distress. "My Lord! My entire performance this morning was cancelled! When am I to deliver my odes?"

"Ah…" Raschid wanted to hear odes the way he wanted fishhooks driven through his skull. "Well…"

"Raschid!"

Blue and beautiful, Yariim came racing over from a corridor, her pink eyes full of concern. "Raschid! Someone says that there was some kind of explosion on the river! Are you unharmed?"

Raschid gathered up his wife in his arms.

"Unharmed! Quite unharmed." The Shah went into a bit of a sulk. "And it wasn't an explosion. We just blew a steam line."

A great peal of laughter, pure, unsullied, raucous joy, hooted out across the hall.

"Bwa-ha ha ha ha! Silly Jackal! V'at iss happening to you?"

Sandhri leaned through a window, her hair spilling to the ground. With a glad whoop of joy, she vaulted across the windowsill into the corridor and hugged Raschid, instantly marring her robes with mud. The bat arched back and looked up at her husband's face. "Iss a mud-fish jackal! Stinky-fresh!"

"I – ah – fell."

Itbit's shapely little figure emerged happily from behind Raschid – just outside the reach of Fatima.

"Is so! Itbit finds him. Itbit say – 'we wash him clean and shiny as new pin!'. Itbit does good things to please everybody!" The mouse began to propel Raschid into the baths. "Family only. Must get stinky Jackal fellow into bath, quick quick!"

She bull-rushed one and all into the great, echoing beauty that was the palace baths. Rocks planted with ferns glistened beside a waterfall that filled the bath house with a soothing rush of sound. The hot pool steamed the cold pool glimmered, all overhung with fuchsia flowers and camellia blooms. A great stone eagle's head lay half out of the water, forming an island on which two mouse girls and a long, skinny Lemur girl from the dance class were reclining nude and lazy in the filtered light. The girls saw the gaggle of intruders – saw the Shah – and plunged into the cold pool with a squeak of surprise. Itbit bustled Raschid inwards, tossing muddy clothing to the floor.

"Sorry sorry! Emergency is! Just stay on other side of rock!" Itbit piled her books to one side and helped Raschid. "Bath time now! Fatima and poet fellow should come back in an hour. Maybe more – much more!"

Fatima reached over one elegant hand and fished a brace of keys out of Itbit's cleavage. She fixed the mouse with an unwinking eye.

"We shall speak of this later."

Harassed, disheveled and forever trying to keep the peace, Raschid bowed to Fatima.

"I shall deal with it. Thank you, Lady Fatima."

"I thank you, My Lord." Fatima twirled the keys nimbly, and let them slide into her own cleavage. As she left, she called carelessly out across the baths to where the skinny Lemur girl was hiding. "Saa'lu! Your skinny ring-tailed bottom would be better employed learning those dance movements you were so conspicuously bad at this morning. Find a towel, and go to practice." Fatima bowed reverently to the Shah, her pink eyes sparking with a private humour. "My Shah…"

The tall Jackal took Fatima's hand, looking at her smile.

"How is Saud?"

"We are both very happy, my Lord. I believe he wants to ask your permission to wed."

"Excellent." Itbit was keen to close the bath house doors. Raschid shouted through the closing doorway. "Send him to me later! At dinner!"

The doors slammed, barring the poet laureate and sundry other well wishers from the royal presence. Itbit raced about the bath house finding towels, leaving Sandhri and Yariim holding Raschid. The trio watched her in bemusement, and then the two women peeled themselves away from Raschid and looked down at the mud all over their clothes

Yariim wrinkled her delicate pink nose, long whiskers twiddling and her brows arching in good humour.

"I thought I had asked you to test that boat on land before you took it into the water?"

"Um – well, we were on the land, and it seemed to be going so well. And the river was just a little step away…" Raschid winced as Sandhri peeled away his robes. "I didn't make it go fast! Just a dawdle!"

He winced as Sandhri jerked his tunic off. Sandhri looked thoughtful, then bent down and inspected the back of Raschid's pants.

"Hey nitwit! You bruised your arse!" Sandhri was much concerned about Raschid's backside – an area she had cherished for quite some time. "Chust how fast v'ass t'iss 'dawdle'?"

"Ah." Raschid tried to look innocently at the high, shadowed ceiling. "Just a stroll. Twelve leagues an hour or so?"

That was a good pace for a cantering horse. For a tin engine made with the shah's own hands, it was phenomenal. Yariim, queen of Osra, state historian and mistress of the royal libraries adjusted her glasses.

"Twelve?"

"Twelve!" Raschid was thrilled. "Easily twelve!"

"Well – that is a triumph, then. Well done." Yariim began peeling off her own mud stained clothes, her eyes on empty air. "With engines like that in our ships, they would never be becalmed. We could explore the far side of the world – past the Yellow Empire and beyond! Who knows what marvels we might find?"

"Marvels!" Sandhri tore off her halter top, revealing skinny ribs, a white streak of ventral fur as soft and inviting as silk, and flat little breasts that bobbed prettily as they came free. "Hey Raschid! We haff a Yellow Empire guy. I just put him to bed. Silly idiot walked here v'ith' half a library on his back. Almost killed himself."

"Poor fellow." Raschid divested himself of coil after coil of waist sash. His curved *yatagan* short sword was placed in the hands of a statue by the water side. Raschid looked suddenly pained. "Please tell me he's not a Zen Buddhist?"

"I wish you peoples v'ould leave that alone!" Sandhri planted fists on her skinny hips and scolded. "Iss it my fault if he takes a vow of silence?"

Yariim leaned forward, unhooked her halter, and swung herself free. Her wise eyes remained on Sandhri.

"You put on a yellow hat, held a lotus flower, then walked around him three times, and told him you would only remove your hat if the first word he spoke was the quintessence of the Tao." Yariim unpinned her hair, and it cascaded down about her in sheets of pure gold. "By the time he finished worrying over why you chose yellow, why you chose a hat, or what the lotus flower meant, he was half way to the nut house!"

Raschid cocked an eye to Yariim. "Has he spoken yet?"

"No. He still hasn't spoken. He's living up in the bell tower, needs help to wash himself and can only eat buns!"

Sandhri bent over and slithered her way out of her pants, freeing her fluffy scut of a tail, and a taut, gleaming little rear. A perfect "V" sculpted above her tail served to plunge the eye down into her curves – a view well worth the trip.

"Iss cool! He'll snap out off it some day. I still have the hat!"

Sandhri grinned. Brat naked and deliciously supple, she vaulted backwards and slid into the vast, hot pool. Yariim sighed, let her harem pants fall, and joined her, splashing the bat in the face.

Itbit gathered up muddy clothes and dumped them in a hamper. She stood on tip toes to kiss Raschid on the nose.

"Time for bath."

The Shah went snout to snout with his green-furred friend.

"Itbit – you *are* going to do your mathematics now, aren't you."

Fairly caught, Itbit gave a sigh. The mouse rested her forehead against Raschid's.

"Itbit will do it. Bat and Jackal and blue mouse want Itbit to learn, so Itbit be good and learn all there is."

"Good girl."

Itbit rose.

"Long bath now. Long, long bath. No worry about palace – Itbit take care of things for a while." The green mouse swayed her bottom as she walked. Yariim and Sandhri both tilted their heads and watched in new amazement. When had Itbit grown so?

Itbit turned to go.

"Sandhri and Yariim should both get out and wash Raschid. Not to let him muddy nice bath. Wash him on a stone." Itbit picked up her course books. "You wash him good! No one takes care of Jackal Raschid Shah as good as Itbit does."

Raschid laughed.

"Stay!"

Itbit poised, looking at Raschid with total fondness. Her long eyelashes made her face look suddenly terribly wise and mature.

"You bath with your ladies now, who love you. Relax now, and many happywriggles." The mouse hoisted her books. "Itbit has study to do. She is fifteen and three quarters, and soon she shall be sixteen. Then she will be a real lady at long last." The mouse bowed. "Baths iss for wriggle friends and happy families."

Raschid looked at her a little sadly.

"We *are* a family."

"No. But in the heart, yes." Itbit kissed Raschid again – then Sandhri and Yariim.

She left them in the bath, closing the doors behind her. One jerk of her thumb brought a guard running to protect the royal privacy. There were generals and warlords with less authority than Itbit.

The green mouse squared her shoulders, puffed out her chest, and lifted up her chin. It was time to do her wretched maths – then her study, then read and plan. Itbit would be sixteen years old in a few weeks time. Then everything would change. She would be forever with her friends and loved ones, Sandhri, Raschid and Yariim. No more barriers. Total happiness.

"Itbit is going to be family very soon now. Very, very soon."

She would be family.

She would be third wife to the Shah.

With a happy lift to her steps, Itbit paced off into the palace, setting off about a busy day.

Chapter Three:

In the evening, with sunset streaming scarlet banners all across the sky, the palace of Sath sparkled like a mountain of stars. The waters of the river delta glistened eggplant blue, while high above the moon swam through wisps of cloud. A last few boats glided up the river above their own perfect reflections, and the city swam with the countless sounds and smells of night.

Families gathered in the broad courts between the houses, sitting in the evening cool as music was played. Night beetles, purple-black with huge orange wings whirred between the palm trees, and children ran shrieking with laughter as they chased the insects through the streets. Lanterns softened streets into places of warm light and velvet shadow, and windows glowed bright with candle light.

At the heart of all the lights, the music and the laughter, the palace was the brightest jewel of all. Her gates stood open, and the soft grass of the outer gardens was host to a hundred families. The moon fuchsias opened up their flower buds to glow like countless paper lanterns beside the garden paths. Beautiful insects bred by the sorcerers flew merrily through the trees, each tiny animal glowing like a star.

Awakening at the setting sun, Meng could only stare and wonder. He had been lain down in a colonnade with a dozen other quiet pilgrims. A jug of water was at his feet, and plain white robes lay at his side. His books were neatly stacked in their rack beside him. Figures strolled the courtyard or sat in their niches, discussing science and philosophy as they walked.

A delicious scent of frying meat, of sizzling garlic and hot bread had aroused Meng from total slumber. He felt dazed, his body stunned by months of effort and sudden, total relaxation. The boy sat up, blinking, eyes wide as an owls and images dancing in his mind.

On a pallet beside him, there sat a thin, wiry, tuft-tailed mouse. He was swathed in desert robes, with a *keffiya* headdress that covered up his face. A curved dagger, sword and a brace of pistols glittered in his belt. Beside him a jet black fox, so skinny as to seem almost skeletal – a creature with hair that stood out in a bizarre cloud about his head. The fox wore almost nothing except a loin cloth, and countless deadly weapons slung about himself on leather belts.

Both men sipped from steaming cups. With a deep, melodic voice, the desert mouse spoke to Meng.

"The holy fool has arisen." The mouse pulled down the face veil of his headdress, revealing long mouse whiskers and eyes as dark and sardonic as a demon's. "Greetings, fool."

"Fool?" Meng's brain was half asleep, and half of him was still plodding along the endless roads that had led to Osra. "Forgive me. Your language is difficult. Did you say fool?"

"A fool." The mouse poured tea from a little iron kettle. "You knew enough to fear the city states of the steppes. Those lands are given to death. But you were a fool to risk wandering the southern desert. The desert eats the flesh of all who would defy her."

He pointed a riding crop towards the other man, who sat there stonily drinking tea.

"Here, fool, is a man who opened the wells that lay in your path. Three times his men slew Torah birds that would have eaten of your flesh as you slept. To him, you owe remembrance in your prayers."

The young panda blinked. The black circles about his eyes made his astonishment seem huge. He placed his hands inside his ragged sleeves, and gave the black-furred fox a reverent bow.

"This humble person thanks you for your guidance. This was benevolent action, and it shall be a beacon to me." Meng then bowed to the desert mouse. "I thank you for pointing out my errors."

The mouse merely inclined his head. Meng sat up, still dazed, and looked at the two warriors.

"This person begs to ask - why did you help me?"

"To walk alone through the deserts, shoeless and with no water? To carry books so far? Clearly you were mad." The mouse lifted the teapot's lid and gazed inside. "We cherished you. Madness is sacred to God. For only the mad speak the truth."

The fox with the shock of fuzzy hair gave a grunt of agreement, but said no more. In response, the desert nomad turned and pointed with his cup towards the palace halls beyond.

"This is a house of madness. They are all mad here, sacred to God, and God cherishes them."

Somewhat shocked to hear royalty spoken of so, Meng started at the palace in amazement.

"Mad?"

"Quite mad." The nomad swirled his tea. "The Shah is a fool because he believes in the essential goodness of man. The little knife girl is mad because she believes love is greater than hate. The dream dancer is mad because she believes that hope is in everything, and that all things are lights." He swigged back his tea. "And we are mad who follow them, and help to make the madness real."

The fox moved. He was pure muscle – lean as a snake, with eyes like jet. He looked Meng quietly over with one flick of his eyes.

"I shall not drink tea with him."

"It is improper." The mouse nodded, then eyed Meng. "You have missed the evening prayers"

"Ah." Meng had passed through Islamic towns on his journey – through Christian villages, and even Pagan places in the Jungles of Meepsoor. "You are Islamic? Christian?"

"We are all of The Book. Christian and Islam are but sects of the same. The Shah – blessings and peace ever be upon him - shows us that even the Hindu idolaters of Meepsoor worship the principal of God, giving him many faces." The man breathed in the fumes of his tea. "God is inarguable. How we worship him is the business of each man, and not a thing for wars and bloodshed."

Meng sat back, feeling a tingle of awe.

"Yes. Madness."

"Priceless madness." The desert mouse shifted position to look at Meng. "You cherish God?"

"I serve the great principal. The Tao – the power that is within and without us all."

"Hmmph." The mouse nodded. "Then when you pray, remember to give thanks. God has smiled upon you, for you have come to a land of heroes, fools and dreams." He stretched. "Pray. And when you return, you will drink tea with us."

Meng struggled to his feet, breathing in the crisp night air. He looked at his books beside the bed made for him in the colonnade, then decided the volumes would be safe. He looked about himself, and through an archway he saw the gardens dancing with fairy lights, and people gathered beneath the palms.

The mouse pointed with his riding crop.

"Through there. The little knife girl will cherish you. You are in Osra, where no man hungers and all men are free."

The panda slid his arms inside his sleeves and bowed.

"I shall seek as you say." He closed his eyes and bowed more deeply. "I am Sixteen-Volume Meng, of the family Tsau-yi. May this humble one know the names of his benefactors?"

The mouse flicked his riding crop to indicate his fuzz-haired companion.

"This is Kors Jakoob, Chieftain of the Beni Haasi. I am Raas Yomah of the Beni Mus." His tufted tail could be seen curling neatly about his feet. "We shall care for your sixteen volumes. Now hurry, before the best food is gone and you will be a fool indeed..."

Osra was a land that had no orphans. Children with no parents, who had no family to care for them, were taken under the wing of the Shah. They carried the surname "al Osra", and lived either in the royal palace, or in the palace of the governor of their home cities. They were raised, clothed and fed from the Royal exchequer, and were given an education second to none. Raschid, Sandhri and Yariim had taken the waifs of the street, and were raising a generation of citizens.

The first years of the Shah's reign had been difficult. The economy had been in uproar, and rebellions had been crushed. Slavery had been ended – often at gunpoint - as the rich were made to give up their trade in sentient lives. The great estates had been broken up. The private armies of the great nobility had gone. Instead there were royal regiments, with young nobles sitting exams at officers schools and at the administrative academies. Universal religious tolerance had led to savage reaction from the most fanatical sects:

The people – the poor, the freed slaves and the just at heart, all had flocked to Shah Raschid. The Shah had made his changes all in one sweep, in the aftermath of civil war.

They had swept the country almost overnight, and then were locked in place. Old reactionaries might grumble – but the kingdom had an energy and a purity about it that could not be ignored. The zealots and the plotters had been offered peace, and then escorted to new lands once coexistence proved impossible.

Both day and night, the palace doors were open. They came here to be with their Shah – the citizens and the travelers. The outer lawns and colonnades were open to the people. The royal orphans were fed here. The elderly who had no children to support them, the lost, the destitute… all came here to be fed by the Shah. In Osra, no person went in want when another had excess.

The evening spread magnificently across the sky. Children ran in unruly mobs through the trees, while adults sat around picnic cloths spread beside the paths. At the heart of it all, there was a great sprawl of ovens and open fires. Meat barbequed beside simmering vats of beans, while girls patted dough into discs of bread and baked them on the fires.

Meng found Queen Sandhri, first wife to the Shah of Osra, adopted scion of the Beni-Mus and Mistress of ten thousand tales, dressed in a white smock and dusted from head to foot with flour. A head scarf contained her great cascade of pure white hair, and a kitchen knife big enough to disembowel an elephant swung from her belt. Barefoot and happy, she mixed bread dough in a huge pottery bowl, working hard and fast to keep the hungry masses fed.

"Meng!"

She saw the wandering sage and gave a floury wave. Shocked, Meng approached. At the proscribed distance, he bowed three times, each bow lower than the last.

"This humble one greets Osra's Queen, her Queen, her Great Queen." The panda could not help but open anxious eyes and peek at the sight of royalty cooking bread like a kitchen maid. "You…. Are making bread?"

"Bestest kind! Hill bread!" Sandhri turfed a great lump of dough out onto a floured board. She rolled it into a vast sausage, then used her knife to slice off precise-sized chunks which flew along the table into the hands of the bakers. She never even looked at her work as she spoke. "Aaaah! You're new. T'iss is v'at I do! Two days, maybe t'ree days a v'eek, I cook for the people here."

The scholar was totally bewildered.

"Forgive this one for his curiosity –but why?"

"V'en I had no bread, someone who had two pieces gave me v'un." Sandhri tipped more ingredients into her bowl – oil, salt, yogurt, flour and sesame. "Now I haff much bread – and efferyone can eat." She kneaded dough with powerful hands, her black fur showing hard muscle beneath. "T'iss iss how we live. T'iss is our rule. Efferyv'un works, so efferyv'un shares." She punched at the dough, her face intensely satisfied. "Raschid's rule."

"The – the Shah cooks?"

"Pah! That silly Jackal? T'at man could burn v'ater!" Sandhri pulled at dough, folded and shoved the mass into order. "No – he grows things. There – the vegetables are his. Try the tabouli! Hiss parsley really came on this year!" Sandhri began slicing dough again. "Hill food tonight! That puts me in charge."

The panda arced brows in surprise.

"Does the other… Queen… cook too?"

"No no. She hass to limber up – she'll be busy at the banquet tonight." Sandhri paused, tired but elated. "She makes v'ine, though. Iss her hobby. I help!" She looked left and right, then drew in closer.

"Actually, I just like v'atching her stamp on grapes and get all gooey. V'en v'e both do a special vintage, iss a special vintage!" The bat whisked in close, whispering behind a floury hand. "Simmered in our own juices!"

Agog, Meng froze in a polite half smile. Sandhri was stepping back from the table. She threw her cooking knife at an old tree stump with force enough to *thunk* hard into the wood. "All the kids are fed? Yes? Hokay – no v'un gets dessert until you eat two vegetables. I mean it!"

She abandoned the cooking tables and accompanied Meng.

"Hokay! Hungry? I am! Ve've been smelling t'iss stuff for hours now! Come on!" She grabbed Meng with a flour smothered hand and dragged him into a colonnade. "Here. T'iss v'ay!"

She washed her arms and hands in a big earthenware bowl held by the titanic tiger soldier Meng had seen before. The bat used a brush to dust herself clean, then dodged into an alcove and dragged a curtain shut across the door. Meng was left standing uncomfortably outside, wondering what in the name of the Tao was going on.

Sandhri's apron sailed over the curtain and hit him in the face.

"Hey Meng! Hold this!"

"As you command, Great Majesty." Meng bowed. A vest smelling fragrantly of bat hit the back of his neck.

Rising, Sixteen-Volume Meng delicately cleared his throat.

"Majesty?"

"Ya?" Sandhri sounded as though she were busy. Her hair scarf was tossed over the curtain rail. "V'at giffs?"

"You feed all of the destitute? Every evening?" Meng looked back over the lawns in thought. "Are there not those who take advantage of the royal bounty?"

"Pah! You are talking to Sandhri, here!" The bat extended an arm above the curtain, twirling it in easy superiority. "I haff my eyes and ears. Every governor in every city hass the same."

"Forgive this one's curiosity, Majesty." Meng bowed reverently, even though the bat was out of sight behind the curtain. "You have people watch to see who comes to these meals?"

Sandhri's head appeared over the curtain. She was tugging down the string on which the curtain was hung, and it seemed that she was quite naked.

"Hey you! T'ese people don't *take* food! V'e giff them ingredients. They cook, they serve, they clean the mess. If you're destitute, and v'e see you here frequently, t'en v'e reach out a hand. Jobs can be found, help given. T'ese food crops are all grown by people who had not'ink a few years ago." The bat let go of the curtain, and it jerked up, hiding her face. It now bared her shins, and Meng saw her pants and underwear go sliding to the ground. "Believe me – I know v'at the poor need. And t'ese days, they get it!" Her face appeared again. Her hair was part way through being brushed to a dazzling white glow. "T'iss iss Raschid's Osra! Here, no v'un gets forgotten. Here' everyv'un hass a chance to excel!"

The curtain whipped away. Queen Sandhri stood posed saucily in magnificent harem clothes. Transparent pants of gauze lovingly displayed the shapeliest legs Meng had ever seen. Modesty was covered by sheer red velvet strips that shimmered with countless tiny jewels. Mica dust had been brushed into her fur, giving Sandhri's fur a secret golden sheen. A tiara shimmering with rubies framed the Queen's face, and a rope of gems ran about her narrow waist and pure white belly fur. The line of the gems drew the eye plunging downwards.

A tiny flick of gossamer-soft pubic fur just peeked into view above the velvet covering Queen Sandhri's groin.

She was as lean and perfect as an adolescent dream. Framed by the pure cascade of her hair, she twirled a pirouette for Meng. Her eyes were wise and sly.

"You like?"

Osranii women were famous across the entire world. Meng stared, somewhat ashen. Sandhri lifted out her hair and jutted out her chest. "I alv'ays v'anted pomegranates, and instead I got some grapes. Still! Comes out alright, ha?" She stretched joyfully; Sandhri had the backside of a goddess. "V'en the hawk iss sleek, don't v'eigh it down v'ith harness!"

Meng understood.

"There is a banquet, oh Queen?"

"V'unce a v'eek! All the admin guys, Generals, lords and ladies komm! You're invited." The Queen struck a pose to display her costume. 'Not too much for a mere ex-beggar girl?"

The young sage looked at the Queen's magnificent costume, placed his hands in his sleeves and reverently bowed.

"When the Sage-King Shun was poor, he ate simple food with pleasure, wore simple rags, and enjoyed the river flowing past the fields. When he was lord of empires, he ate royal food, wore silk and was served by the daughters of Lord Shi of Wu." Meng bowed once more. "The superior person adopts all things appropriate to their times and station."

Sandhri looked at him, extremely pleased.

"I knew t'ere v'ass a reason I v'ass keeping you around!"

A gong chimed somewhere in the palace. Sandhri instantly shot forward and grabbed Meng by the hand.

"Hey, come on! You haff to meet Raschid. Sit near us. I'll move a General or somet'ing. Make sure you get a spot near the cakes!" She propelled Meng from behind, steering him towards a great hall that stood beneath a pure blue dome. "Hey – t'at's really hard back here. V'ere you get such a cute backside?"

"I have just walked three thousand miles, lady."

"Ha! Maybe I recommend t'at to Yariim's calisthenics class!" The bat bustled. "Now hurry up quick, or all the nibblies v'ill be gone!"

"Bow ye, bow ye for Raschid of the House Dinaq, Shah of Osra, guardian of the tombs and shrines, keeper of the sacred places. Beloved of God and all the Prophets. Shield to his people, protector of the weak. Well of wisdom to the weary." The chamberlain was tall – a cheetah with fur sheened a steely grey. He had a moustache so huge it seemed to have a life all of its own. He knocked his staff imperiously against a floor fantastically inlaid with marble flowers. *"Bow ye to the favoured one of the Angel of Peace. Lord of scholars, friend to women. Bow ye, bow ye to thy Shah!"*

The great palace of Sath boasted one titanic room which outshone any other palace in the world. Beneath a vast dome of blue and golden tile, a marble floor had been worked into an image of the tree of life. Every animal, every race, every plant known to science had its place upon the tree – intricate little figures that intertwined and shimmered in an endless dance. Balconies ringed the inner dome, and from these there cascaded brilliant trellises of flowers. Butterflies fanned themselves upon the blooms, and tiny glow beetles danced high in the air.

It was a room that lived. Tall pillars had been sculpted into reliefs that teemed with insects, animals and herbs. From each pillar flowed a fountain of bright water, splashing through rocks and little gardens to meet in a ring of streams that encircled the marble floor. Ringing the great central floor, with the stream at their backs and the ferns bright and green all around them, the Shah's guests bowed their heads to the ground in a single graceful wave. Their robes crossed all the colours of the rainbow: Nobles, adventurers and harem girls dressed in silks and satin cloth. The stark black and beige of imams and priests mixed with the pure white of scholars. Merchants, sailors, doctors sat beside soldiers in brilliant uniforms. There were shaman women from the western marshes sitting next to nomad lords. Sewn in and around it all, like gems in a gorgeous setting, the palace women moved in glittering display. All bowed reverently towards the presence of the Shah.

In public amongst his people and his foreign visitors, Shah Raschid made an imposing sight. He was a Jackal – towering, long necked and elegant, with tall ears and a long, grave nose. His fur gleamed a gunmetal blue, and his bulk hinted at wolf-blood somewhere in his ancestry. Young for his office, he moved quietly and easily. Seated in the front row of the guests, Meng felt a light of surprise inside him as he saw the Shah's warm, intelligent brown eyes.

The Shah of all Osra chose to appear in the simple robes of a desert scholar. There was armour beneath the robes; a pen and writing tablet hung from his belt. An old *yatagan* short sword with worn, plain grips jutted through his sash.

Erect and graceful at his side, were Shah Raschid's two wives. Sandhri – slim, elegant and black as night, covered her exquisite harem clothing with a golden robe embroidered with the words of countless fairy tales. On Raschid's other arm, Yariim came, serene and beautiful. She wore a sage's robes in gold and sapphire blue. Her sky-coloured fur gleamed in the lamp light, highlights rippling over her sleek curves as she paced by her husband's side. The royal family of Osra walked graciously to their place, and then quietly sat down.

The people bowed profoundly low. Old battle comrades, scholars and administrators. Young nobles full of Raschid's fire, and even old noblemen. The Shah returned the bow to his guests, acting as host instead of sovereign. His voice rang genially out across the massive hall.

"Welcome. Welcome to our home."

In a great rush of release, people rose from their homage. People began to talk, and greetings called across the room from a hundred tongues. Raschid looked over the heads of guests and signed to Lady Fatima, who sat at the strategic location near the kitchen doors. Fatima inclined her head, clapped her hands, and music began. A stream of dancers and musicians – the palace's famous students – flooded out from the ferns and pillars and brought the celebration instantly to life.

Yet more women came running from the kitchens bearing finger bowls and towels. The girls quipped with favourite guests, or spoke politely to foreign dignitaries who seemed at a loss with local ceremonies. Yariim had positioned her brightest girls to be hostesses to the foreigners, and all seemed well. She cast a searching glance over the hall to make sure that all was proceeding happily, and then relaxed to lean back against Raschid.

The blue mouse gave a sigh, ready to enjoy the evening.

"Is it my imagination, or is the Chamberlain making your introduction longer every time?"

"I believe he rather likes it." Raschid put his arms about his wives and squeezed. "I tried to talk to him about it, but he gave me such a hurt little look…"

Eagerly sighting a serving girl, Sandhri beckoned her over to inspect her tray.

"V'e should get him to chuck in a few loony v'uns, just to see if anybody's listening!" She found the tray had her favourite prawn dumplings, and immediately took possession.

"Hey, v'e gots t'ese things again? Anybody v'ant v'un?"

Yariim cocked one eyebrow.

"Don't prawns make you frisky?"

By way of an answer, Sandhri looked at Yariim and immediately ate two. Yariim thieved one for herself before the entire plate was gone.

Raschid raised a hand in greeting to specific friends in the hall. Kors Jakoob and Raas Yomah he greeted with great joy. Yariim bowed to Raas Yomah gracefully, pinking slightly about the ears.

Every week, a royal dinner was held. The royal family invited the heads of noble families and merchant clans. They invited their military officers, the captains of their exploring ships – priests, shamans and scholars. They brought the heads of royal enterprises such as the academies and hospitals, research institutes and laboratories. The elected heads of each district of the province would attend; nomad chieftains and foreign emissaries were always welcomed. The meals were a time when the Shah could ask each person about their progress or their needs – when new discoveries could be aired and programs suggested. The government could be seen at work, and all grievances could be aired in good company.

People would approach the Shah after the main course was eaten and cleared away. This was Sandhri's idea: a good meal made petty grievances fade, and sent some of the more pompous guests off to sleep. Until that time, the hall seethed with chatter. The Osranii were a voluble people, and dinner made the talk flow as fast and gay as wine.

Intercepting food for Raschid and taking a bite from each plate, Sandhri cast an eye over the crowds.

"Aaah - V'e haff four Franks over t'ere. Two off t'em look like t'ey haff bad smells beneath t'eir noses."

"Ambassadors. Two D'Orrians, and two Westerners?" Yariim looked carefully at the visitors. "The D'Orrians look as though they expect a fight."

"Trade troubles again. V'e sunk some D'Orrian slave traders who v'ere raiding the southern coast."

Sandhri raised a finger, and a serving girl leaned in close. The cat girl's long tail switched as Sandhri murmured softly in her ear.

"I v'ant two teams on the Franks. Follow t'em after the feast. Keep our people on t'em. Report to me tomorrow."

The cat girl nodded, then went off with an empty tray. A silent glance from her made soldiers and servants unobtrusively leave the feast to follow her. Sandhri went back to thieving prawns, and Yariim poured the three of them their wine.

Sandhri's eyes and ears were everywhere. The bat made no comment, but went about her meal.

Serving girls, dancers, musicians and hostesses made a flow of brilliant costumes all throughout the hall. Women were everywhere. The Shah cherished them, and they came to his house to study in his academies and take their place in schools and government. While one woman stood, the Shah's power was safe. Sitting close to the royal dais, Meng could only stare at the ladies of Osra in shocked bewilderment.

In the Yellow Empire, a young lady would dress in layer after layer of carefully selected robes. Here in Osra, they bared far more than they concealed! Harem pants of transparent silk made legs gleam beneath enticing mists. Garments of sheer satin, velvet or thin silk inflamed the imagination with the glories hinted at and half concealed. Each girl decked herself with belts of bells or jingling coins – anklets, necklets headdresses and caps. They had turned themselves into vibrant, walking works of art.

A lemur girl – white furred with black markings like a mask across her face, and with a long, waving tail striped in fuzzy black and white, bent over to pour wine for the guests. Meng stared at her backside – it was beautifully shaped, and cunningly clad to make the most of the girl's rangy build. Meng was just coming to terms with it artistically, when a huge elbow eagerly jabbed into his ribs.

"Ha, boy! That one! Do you see the striped one, boy?" A hand with fingers the size of sausages pointed out salient points of the girls taut rear. "Perfect! Damned perfect! I'll bet you never saw an arse like that in the Yellow Empire!"

The speaker was a huge black bear with flashing teeth. A monument of muscle, he was wearing an intricate armour of engraved plates and iron mail beneath gorgeous brocade robes. He hugged Meng against his huge bulk, almost crushing the boy's bones, and made him gaze upon the girl.

"Fantastic! Simply fantastic! If she wishes to be my mistress, she need only apply!"

He kissed his fingertips in loud appreciation. The lemur girl looked back at the huge warrior, gave a wry glance, and hiked her tail a little higher in challenge.

The bear splashed wine into two goblets, and thrust one into Meng's hands.

"General Ataman! Ataman! That's a northern name. We were nomad lords who liked Osra so much we let them invite us all to stay!" He crashed his goblet against Meng's, almost drowning the boy. "You're Han, from the East? I know of the Yellow Empire! My brother owned a Han girl slave – a pretty little thing, dainty as a doll! That was before the Shah arose, may blessings shower upon him. Slavery abolished, so my brother had to let her go!" The huge general waved his wine. "My brother liked her so much he had to marry her to keep her! That makes us almost related, you and I. Call me cousin! Cousin Ataman!"

The huge man roared with laughter at the thought. Out on the floor, the Lemur girl turned to go. Ataman immediately threw open his arms.

"Wait, girl! No luck could be greater than your luck tonight! The great Ataman wants you to share wine with him and both be merry!"

The girl gave a toss of her head and went away. Ataman seemed unblunted. He eagerly crushed Meng beneath his arm.

"Ha! She likes me, I can tell! Take my advice, boy. When you take a bride, look for brains, attitude and tail!"

Sandhri noticed Meng being slowly crushed to death by Ataman. She quaffed down her wine and shot to her feet, abandoning her golden robes. Speeding like a black arrow, she flitted to Meng's side.

"Meng! How v'onderful off you to come! And after so long a journey." She managed to extract Meng from the General's grasp. "General Ataman! I chust haff to borrow Meng here. The Shah *so* v'ants to meet him."

She rescued Meng with a deft jerk of her arms, hoisting the scholar to his feet. Shaken, the young Panda was led tottering away from General Ataman, who was roaring a merry greeting to scholars from the science institute. Sandhri patted Meng upon the hand as she led him away.

"You know, t'at man v'unce head butted a v'ater buffalo, and the buffalo died."

"Truly?"

"Hey, t'iss iss Sandhri talking! The very heart and soul of truth!" The bat laid a protesting hand upon her meager breast. "Hey, v'ould Sandhri lie to you?" She pulled Meng's tattered clothes into place like a mother fussing with her young. "Now big breath, and come and say hello to my Raschid."

And thus, Meng found himself face to face with the Shah.

The panda dropped to his knees and bowed, knocking his head against the floor three times. With a lackadaisical flip of her hand, Sandhri made the introductions.

"Tsau-yi Meng, t'iss iss Shah Raschid the great, beloved of tiddly pom and guardian of fiddle dee dee! Raschid, t'iss iss 'Sixteen-Volume Meng' – a lovable nitwit who walked three thousand miles to see you."

She coaxed Meng up out of his abject bow, and the young man met the eyes of the Shah.

Shah Raschid was warm as summer, as boundless as oceans. Calm and powerful – flowing with the essence of the Tao. He bowed in the precise manner of a courtier of the Yellow Empire, and spoke to Meng is his own native tongue.

<<You honour this house, scholar. These humble ones are overjoyed that you have chosen to rest with us.>>

Face to face with the Shah at last, Meng could only stare in wonder.

<<Majesty.>>

<<I trust you do not find us too eclectic.>> The Shah bowed slightly as he quoted <<*There must be a path, and it should be a crooked path. It will reach a tree, and it should be a knotted tree. There will be a gate, and the paint shall not be too newly laid. There will be a porch, and the porch should lie cool in summer afternoons.*>>

His accent was eccentric, but the words were precise and calm. Meng blinked, and Sandhri nudged him happily in the ribs.

"Told you he v'ass smart, my Jackal! Speaks Han good, ha?"

The Shah was apologetic.

"I do not read it well. Only a few symbols." Raschid shrugged ruefully. "Perhaps we can correct this fault, now that you are here."

"Majesty, you do me honour."

"Pray, call me Comrade! We are scholars." The Shah poured wine for his guest. "You have come to us and I believe we can help you find your way."

They ate, they drank. Engineers came to show papers to the joyous Shah. Yariim spoke earnestly with school administrators.

Meng watched and learned.

Here was an dedicated ruler, with able ministers. In return, his people cared for him. The Osranii were careful with their Shah. Meng saw that blue-armoured sharp shooters were in the shadows of the balcony up above. His fiercest supporters – Kors Jakoob and Raas Yomah, General Ataman and the scholars – had deliberately been seated closest to him. The Shah seemed hardly aware of it, but he was guarded loyally and well.

… *Extremely* well. Meng slowly realized that Queen Sandhri was armed. It took a while to realize it, but a black-hilted punch dagger hung behind her belt, and a throwing knife was up her sleeve. She would take a bullet or an arrow for her husband – of that there was no doubt.

Yariim looked up from gazing at a proud young artist's work. She adjusted her spectacles and looked into the crowds.

"General Ataman!"

"Yes, Majesty!"

"Are you ready to dazzle us?" The blue mouse smiled. Ataman met her gaze with huge teeth bared in a grin.

"I am ready to astound you, Majesty! Tales of battle that will make you all weak-kneed with awe! Tales of exploration and adventure!" The huge bear waved a finger at the lemur girl who was still serving wine. "Listen, girl! This you will love!"

He strode over to the Shah, and Raschid rose to meet him. They clasped forearms hard, and then sat, facing each other. Raschid joyfully signed for coffee. Ataman drank off the absurd little cup with a single flick, making a huge noise of satisfaction.

"Aaah! And now, my Shah – and now, a tale of adventure on the seas. The seas!" Ataman seemed genuinely amazed. "Does it not astound you? Sinbad himself never sailed so far or fought so well!"

General Ataman was a land soldier through and through. To him, the ocean was merely a place where other people went to fish on their days off. He rose to his feet to bellow his achievements to the crowd.

"The orders said – 'pursue the raiders'! And the raiders took to sea! So we followed. Right out of the middle sea, and then sixty days, we sailed! All down the coast, with that fellow BaBarad at the helm. Two ships, heading down a coast that was as dead as hell. Rocks and sand – lizards the size of camels! Then finally jungles – endless jungles! BaBarad, he simply steered onwards. He claims he took his woman there on honeymoon, to show her a land where the fish walk from the rivers and where there are birds with tails a yard long up in the trees!" Ataman leaned conspiratorially towards the Queens. "So you see – we were in the hands of an idiot. Important that a sure head take command!"

Yariim cut the General a haunch of meat, thoroughly enjoying him.

"Did you find one, oh General?"

"On the high seas? Never!" The general snatched up the proffered meat in one hand and ate. "So by default, I was forced into the role. It is hard for a cavalryman, when his horse is not there to do his thinking for him!"

The audience laughed. Ataman reached for wine and drank like a dry sponge.

"But imagine our surprise. There is a kingdom there, in amongst the jungle trees. BaBarad will show you the maps – but we found burning villages. Dead were rotting on the ground. Someone had killed the old and the very young – the sick in their beds and the infants on the breast."

Raschid's hand was on his yatagan.

"Slavers."

"Slavers!" Ataman said the word with huge satisfaction. "They were gone, but their muck-filth was left behind them."

Fascinated by the tale, Sandhri leaned in close.

"So v'at you do?"

"Do? We went ashore!" Ataman opened his hands wide. "Why not? We are Osranii – and we have a special place in our hearts for slavers! We found what was left of the local's capital – a city all made of mud. Good people – damned scared! The slavers brought a sickness they did not know how to cure. And the Slavers had another tribe catching these folk as they went to till their fields. Penned them up and sold them onto slave ships bound to the north!"

Ataman walked the circle of the central hall like a barbarian hero chanting out his deeds.

"They gave us meat and sang us songs. So we did as men do! We told them we'd kill the bugger slavers for them! So we stormed their slave stockade at night and freed the prisoners. Then we landed guns and dug in deep. Made furnaces out of mud, and watched like hawks.

"And they came! In the dark of the moon, three slave ships came. Right into our arms!"

Sandhri could see it in her head.

"You ambushed t'em!"

"We led a boat attack at night – cut out one ship neat as you please. The others slipped cables and made a run. The shore guns fired shot heated in the furnaces. We burned one ship, and BaBarad chased the other and ran it hard aground on a sunken bar of sand." Ataman laughed, his belly shaking like a pudding. "They tried to swim for shore! Don't eat shark from that bay! You may get more than you bargained for!"

He laughed raucously. Raschid nodded slowly, weighing a hundred factors in his mind.

"What did you do to the prisoners?"

"My Shah – I gave them to the local king. Their offense was against his people! I believe they fed the buggers to the crocodiles."

The Shah stroked his chin.

"And the local tribe? The slavers' allies?"

Ataman grinned. "We gave all the guns we captured off the slavers to our friends. Taught e'm how to shoot, and left 'em five good sergeants. Next time the slavers come, they'll find themselves up against cannon and muskets! Ventilate a few of the buggers, and they'll think twice about selling folk like cattle!" Ataman knelt before the Shah – a huge, massive monument of muscle, steel and fur. "We left the captured ships with the local king, with some of our sailor-buggers to teach them how to sail. They can learn how it's done, and chase slavers for themselves next time!"

Queen Yariim lowered her glasses in awe.

"And so you all returned?"

"I came back here, beautiful Majesty! BaBarad, he took one ship onwards. He believes there is a passage to the south that leads to the Golden Ocean. The Yellow Empire!" The huge General thumped Meng on one shoulder. "A sea route! So next time, you don't have to walk. You can spend half a year puking up into a bucket instead, ja?" Ataman turned to the Shah. "I bringed some of the mud fellows with me! A prince, a sort of minister, a princess, and a sort of fellow who remembers history in his head. No writing! They speak a little Osranii – not good like Queen Sandhri and me, but speak. Yes!"

He looked about the room, nodding hard. The big man leaned forward towards the Shah.

"I know I am a cavalryman who should let his horse do the talking. But chase raiders, you said. I took two companies and chased! We found new folk – what could we do? I do as I think maybe Shah Raschid would do. Slavers no good! Mud fellows – they're jolly good people. Call themselves *Ha'kuto Hanin!*"

The big man half rose and waved. There was a stir at the door, and the crowd of diners turned to see. Men and women gasped in awe, and people sat tall, straining to see over the heads of their neighbours.

Four tall, slim strangers walked hesitantly into the palatial hall. They were alien, barbaric and utterly entrancing.

They were led by two cat-people; leopards with a rangy, limber build. The male was a young man with jet black fur, faintly marked with darker spots. The female was young, perhaps only sixteen, with fur a rich, deep orange patterned with great black spots.

The young woman wore head ornaments of hammered gold. She was bare breasted, and wore nothing but a little curtain of shell beads. Her arms were ringed by countless copper bracelets. The young man bore a shield of striped hide, and a spear with a wooden head fancifully carved into a swirl of animals. Behind them came two older men – one in robes of red-brown cloth, and the other naked but for a loin pouch and bandoliers of little gourds. Osranii sailors came behind them – piratical figures in turbans and pantaloons, happily carrying six whole elephant tusks, and two hefty palanquin loads of treasure.

The four emissaries stooped, blowing outwards through fanned fingers. The black leopard took a pace further forward, remaining stooped. He kissed his folded hands and pressed them to his head, staying in this pose before the Shah.

Raschid stood, spreading wide his robes in welcome. He spoke quietly to the black leopard – soothing, calming – then lifted up his head to address the room.

"Deeds were done, and now these people have come to us as emissaries." The tall Shah stood with one hand on his yatagan. "Does any person here disapprove of Ataman's acts? Let us hear it now, where we may discuss repercussions in full."

There was a murmur in the room – merchants talking over events with sailors and soldiers. Suddenly a loud voice called across the hall.

"We protest these acts! We claim right to address the Shah!"

The Chamberlain indicated the speaker with a tilt of his staff. Raschid lifted up his hand.

"Stand, then, and be heard."

Three men stood. Two 'Franks" – tall westerners in outlandish garb, and a dark robed priest who translated for them. The two other westerners – dressed in white and gold, remained seated and uninterested.

The priest and his two masters came forward.

"Oh Shah – this is an act of war!" The priest walked slowly, turning to send his message throughout the hall. His two masters stood dark and dour – one of them an otter with grey streaks in his fur, and the other a sharp faced fox. "Those vessels were owned by subjects of the King of D'Orran, guardian of the Holy Word and Sword of Christ! The men your servants slaughtered were my master's servants! The blood you spilled was D'Orran blood. To prey on our trade is piracy, and pirates will be blown from the seas!"

Osranii murmured – soldiers started forward, and merchants muttered behind their sleeves. All of a sudden, Queen Yariim stood, and Raschid bowed to her, granting her a turn to speak.

She pulled her robes tight across herself in sheer dislike as she stared at the Franks.

"A slaver is an enemy of freedom. All sentient creatures owe a duty of conscience to guard freedom and defend the weak!"

A merchant stood, and was recognized by a wave to the Shah's hands. The man gathered up his robes.

"Ataman may have overstepped his bounds. Without recourse to diplomatic protest or possible lesser action, he has opened fire upon ships of another kingdom!"

There was a back-murmur of agreement, countered by a sharp snarl of protest all about the hall. Ex-slaves were a good percentage of Osra's citizens, and she had drawn praise from priests and scholars all across the world for her stand.

An argument arose. In the middle of it, a slight, outlandish figure rose gently to its feet. Ragged and alien, Sixteen-volume Meng bowed to the Shah. All voices were forcibly stilled, and Meng stepped forward.

His quiet voice echoed beneath the mighty dome.

"Allow this one to clarify, unless all fall into error." He placed his hands into his sleeves. "The man Ataman seems to have acted with a pure heart, without malice. He acted instantly, according to principals of his heart. He has done good, as he sees it." He looked quietly about the room. "You must decide whether his principals are the ones you yourselves claim to uphold. If so, then you must support him, or confess yourselves to be hypocrites."

"Right principals – right action."

Meng bowed again, then quietly sat down.

The Franks from D'Orran listened to their translator. They hissed in the man's ear, and he lifted up his head.

"Principals? This is a matter of honour! Blood has been spilled! Restitution must be made!" The priest leaned closer. "We have ships – bases! Osranii trade will be attacked upon the seas!"

Shah Raschid lifted up his hand. He turned his back upon the debate. Queen Sandhri and Queen Yariim both stood, but he held them back.

The Shah paced slowly. He turned, and reached out a hand to lift the kneeling *Ha'kuto Hanin* prince to his feet.

"This, then, is our decision. The Ha'kuto Hanin are most welcome as partners in the community of nations. In friendship, then, we shall send them sorcerers to cure their plague, scholars to learn their lore, scientists to explore their lands and learn about their people. We shall send them teachers to show them how to dig and smelt their own steel, and to make ocean-going vessels of their own. We shall do as a brother must, and give them the tools to defend themselves." He opened up his arms. "We welcome their people as equals, and look upon them as a Light of God.

"To the King of D'Orran, I say this: We find slavery to be a blasphemy against the laws of God. Greed has clouded the judgment of your councils. Do not defend a cause that is morally bankrupt, or you shall find yourselves abandoned by your people and by God." He pointed a hand solemnly at the Franks. "The deaths caused by our navy are regrettable. But your ships were pursued because they were raiding our coasts. They were murderers, thieves and pirates – and were hunted down to the ends of Aku-Mashad. *This* is how we deal with attack.

"If your King sends emissaries to *Ha'kuto Hanin,* we shall help them establish a relationship of trade and mutual benefit. We shall treat with you as servants of an honourable nation. But if your King officially supports murderers and pirates, then we shall treat with you as murderers and pirates.

"We urge you instead to come to us in friendship."

The Franks blustered, but the Lord Chamberlain came forth and banged his staff against the ground.

"It is now written. So it shall be!"

The D'Orrians swept out of the chamber in a fury, watched nervously by the Ha'kuto Hanin. Sandhri narrowed her eyes and watched them go.

"Franks. T'eir Knights can charge clean t'rough the v'alls of hell itself. They fear not'ing except to die in bed."

"Bravery does not equate with virtue." Yariim was bitter. The issue of slavery touched her to the soul. Despite all the skill of the royal sorcerers, her throat still bore the faintest of white scars – a reminder of her own life in chains. The beautiful blue mouse lifted up her chin, proud and regal, and called out to the other Franks present in the hall.

"And you! You other Franks. Where do you stand?"

The two remaining westerners had remained quiet and distant at the far edges of the hall. They were big men – a lion and a badger, hefty and scarred. Each one wore a fantastical suit of steel plate armour beneath white robes marked with an image of a golden sun.

The lion moved softly into the light. Grey streaks glinted all throughout his mane.

"We are Brothers of the Order of the Sacred Light, and we have no King but God." The lion bowed slowly. "We have come to see the mettle of Osra. We have now seen."

Both men bowed slowly to the Shah, took three paces backwards, and faded back into the shadows. Their heavy armour rattled as they walked, and they were gone.

A heavy silence reigned. The dinner guests sat back in their places, contemplating. Others murmured to one another in soft voices. In the middle of it all, Queen Sandhri rose happily to her feet. She alone seemed eager and full of joy.

"Hokay! Heavy business done. D'Orrans sent packing." She pointed a finger. "Ataman! Tomorrow night, v'e party. Looks like the lemur gal is keen to be pals after all. And you folks!" The bat bustled over to peer into the faces of the bowing Ha'kuto Hanin. "V'un of you iss a history remeberer? So you know stories and stuff? Here – over here. Sit! Eat, eat!" She had the leopard princess on one arm and the naked shaman on the other, looking in fascination at the gifts the delegation had brought. "So v'at's in here? Chilies! Pepper! Iss it you that grows t'ese t'ings…?"

Overjoyed, the bat took the foreigners in hand. The party mood slowly reemerged. As musicians played and dessert came trooping out from the kitchens, Raschid sat down and put his arm about Yariim's shoulders.

The mouse looked up at him lovingly. He tried to brush the memories back away from her mind.

"It will be alright."

"I know." Yariim sighed and lowered her head. "I hate it. I hate knowing that it goes on."

Raschid held her tightly. "We do what we can. Enough little actions can make a mighty change."

The blue mouse looked at the Ha'kuto Hanin Prince and Princess in unfeigned admiration. They were slender and absurdly tall – exotic in their outfits of beads and hammered gold.

"They're magnificent, aren't they."

"Spectacular. I'm so glad that Ataman and BaBadur found them." Raschid watched Sandhri as she pantomimed a story to the enraptured visitors. "Their storyteller is going to be popular."

"A hill woman always makes her guests feel comfortable." Yariim gave a wry smile. "Sandhri is going to wear one of that girl's outfits tomorrow – I just know it."

"We may have to keep that out of public view. Osra might not be quite ready for a topless queen."

Yariim shook off her pensive mood. She faced her husband, then bowed gracefully down to the floor, her blonde hair gleaming in the light.

Yariim gave a little smile.

"My Lord? If you are ready, then someone very special has been waiting nervously in the wings to bring you something."

"Ah." Raschid sat back, wreathed in joy. "By all means, please do begin."

Queen Yariim leapt up, signed to three or four of the serving girls, and swept off into the outer palace. Sandhri drew her guests out of the central hall and cleared the floor. The entire gathering shifted to make space, gathering drinks in a flurry, clearly anticipating something special. A tad lost, Meng could only look about himself and blink.

The Shah held out a hand and beckoned Meng to sit out of the way at his side.

"Sixteen-volume Meng." Raschid cocked an eye. "Why 'sixteen volume'?"

"Oh Shah, I was so called this because I had mastered the sixteen great philosophical volumes before my coming of age. I then wrote four commentaries upon the works of Mengzi, Kunfuzi and the analects."

"Why, then, did you not enter service as an administrator or a minister in your own land?"

Meng actually felt his ears blush. "Great Shah – this one wishes to model himself upon Confucius. The Great Sage forewent all honours, that he might instruct the great ones of his age."

The words seemed pompous. In the face of the Shah's wise and smiling eyes, he felt a little ridiculous, and so he bowed. The Shah put a hand upon Meng's shoulders and gave a happy nod.

"Meng, you are unique. Please stay with us. I shall be pleased to read your sixteen volumes and four commentaries, and to talk with you about them through and through." The handsome jackal tapped his long grey nose. "Yes. You have patience, and a great deal of fortitude." He bit his lip. "Do you know mathematics at all?"

Meng bowed. "This humble one has taken instruction in three levels of abstract mathematics, as well as in astronomy."

"Ah!" Raschid felt enormously pleased. "Then Meng, I may ask you to stay with us as a teacher! I have a… a most difficult student that may benefit from your skills."

"Great Shah, I would be honoured."

With a wild ringing of bells, a stream of women sped out into the hall. They were the royal musicians, full of life, and they flitted into position with an easy, practiced grace. Long necked lutes were tuned and flutes were blown. The senior musician chased quickly up and down the orchestra, checking all was well.

Hill men came behind them, dragging drums and great long drone-pipes, bells and round clay flutes. They gave one look to the senior musician, and then the entire orchestra came alive with sound.

Dancers span out into the hall – women swirling in silks and gems. Bare feet hit the floor with perfect skill, and the audience gave a wild cheer of joy. The dancers fanned out in the pattern of the tree of life, and with impossible grace, they danced before their husbands, their lovers, their parents and their friends.

At their head, there swirled Osra's most cherished dancer, Queen Yariim. Utterly given to the dance, she was a thing of pure and elemental beauty. Meng felt the Shah rise in his seat, utterly enraptured. Yariim looked to him and smiled – locked eyes with Sandhri in a gaze of total love, and then swept back to dance across the palace floor.

In the middle of the tree of life, there was a little seed. Silks were piled across it, and the dancers pulled them free. Whisked away, the cloths swirled and shimmered like spring leaves. A single little figure was uncovered on the floor.

A girl lay on the floor – slim, delicate and stretching upwards in new birth. She blinked about herself, and froze in stage fright. Yariim enfolded her, then gently drew her up into the dance.

Meng stared, and the world about him faded clean away. He forgot the wondrous dancing Queen, forgot orchestras and Kings. A journey of three thousand weary miles simply fell away…

Before him, there shone a treasure that spoke straight into his soul.

The girl…

She was willow thin and graceful, with a face alive with an innocent and timeless joy. Her perfect figure swayed with the sheer grace of a born dancer. Perfect breasts, a smooth, slim waist and a backside fit to die for. Great pink ears framed her face, and whiskers quivered long and delicate out from a muzzle tipped with a wonderful pink nose. Her pink-hued eyes sparkled with a tireless, wonderful vivacity and life.

A mouse girl – a girl of Osra. Her eyes spoke of a thousand jests, of vivid dreams – of adventures, plot and plans. She was yang to Meng's own yin; life to his shyness, laughter to his wonder, love to his loneliness. Shy at first, she soon lost herself inside her dance. She swept past Meng, confident and free. He stared enraptured at the highlights shimmering in her perfect, leaf-green fur.

Meng's universe stood still. It held nothing but the girl.

At his side, unheard and all but forgotten, the Shah watched the dance, smiling at the girl with bright green fur.

"Itbit. My dear, dear Itbit. Your new student."

Beaming gladly, Raschid patted Meng upon the shoulder.

"I do so hope you will both be friends…"

Chapter Four:

They made love together as they always had, simply adoring one another. No jealousy, no hurry, simply reveling in one another. When it came to making love, three matched souls could share an intensity never known by two.

Yariim – always excited and full of life after a dance. Raschid – powerful and gentle.

...And Sandhri: passion without end.

When it all melted to a close, they lay together, gazing out across a world of tree shadows, roofs and stars. Sandhri lay with Yariim in her arms. Raschid held Sandhri from behind, around her and inside her the way she loved. Yariim and Raschid dozed in an ocean of afterglow, but Sandhri lay awake and thinking, holding her lovers tight and staring at the stars.

She wept a little – strangely happy – without quite knowing why.

The city slept. Minarets made tall shapes against the deep, dark sky, and the universe felt utterly at peace. A little rain shower came, bringing with it the wonderful, sharp scent of rain on hot tile roofs, on cobblestones and parched, dry dust.

It was a breath of life – absolute and bewitching. Sandhri carefully slid out from between her lovers, her black fur gleaming over slim muscles in the moonlight. Pure white hair cascaded down across her back, cloaking her almost to the floor. On soft feet, dazed and in a dream, the slender bat wandered quietly across the room.

Tingling and strange, she made her way to the balcony and quietly sat down. A sharp breath of air lifted through her hair. Her fur seemed impossibly alive – her skin shivered happily to the chill. With eyes closed, she lifted her pink nose and let her mind drift with the wind.

There was a scent – a warmth, a presence. Naked and quiet, Yariim came to the bench beside her and sat down. With her eyes still closed, Sandhri could see her hair, her form –

the wise, quiet lines of her face. Sandhri reached out for one of Yariim's hands, kissed it quietly, and held it gently against her heart.

They sat for a while in the peace and quiet, smelling the aftermath of the rain. Frogs crept up out of the palace ponds, moving with stealthy little feet. Sandhri breathed it all inside herself, feeling the life that stirred so softly in the night.

When she spoke, it was as quiet as the breeze.

"Am I different?" She remembered a time of raggedness – of hunger and proud pain. "V'e married six years ago. Do you t'ink perhaps I've changed?"

The blue mouse quietly slid an arm about her, warm and thoughtful. They sat together for a while, as Yariim stroked gently at Sandhri's hair.

"You changed. More secure. Deeper? I don't know." The mouse rested Sandhri's head against her shoulder as they watched the stars. "We changed together."

"Yes." The bat was quiet. "But do you like it, you and our Raschid? V'ould you prefer it all to be exactly as it v'ass?"

The mouse's hands were strong and comforting.

"No man may step into the same river twice. We all grew into a new life, and love guided how we grew." Yariim stroked loving fingers on the back of Sandhri's neck. "But the core – the love – has stayed the same. Some things in the universe are eternal. God, time, the stars, and Sandhri."

Her heart pounding hard, Sandhri lifted up her head. She stood softly, tall and slim beside the seated Yariim. The starlight seemed to tingle in her fur.

"I love you, my sister. Forever and alv'ays."

Yariim looked up at her, bewildered and concerned.

"Forever and always."

Sandhri felt her pulse at her own throat with her hand.

"T'rough efferything, t'ere v'ass alv'ays something I thought I might neffer be able to giff to both of you. Ever…"

She bowed her head. Her hand crept down her pure white belly fur to rest below her navel. She felt herself tingling, and she *knew*…

She looked to Yariim with a watery, hesitant, joyous little smile.

"I'm pregnant."

The mouse stared at her in shock, in joy. Silently, worshipfully, she drew Sandhri against herself. Their hands clenched tight – the grip had a silent, perfect joy. Yariim kissed Sandhri's belly and laid her face against her silky-soft fur. Her fingers clenched into Sandhri's backside.

She held Sandhri tight, sure she could *feel* the life inside her. Caressing her, the mouse lifted up her face, her eyes bright with tears.

Hybrid children were rare – so rare that they were spawned only by true love. Rare enough that it had been impossible to hope.

"You're sure?"

Sandhri was dazed to tears by joy. She was so excited that her head swam – so happy she felt herself cry.

"I'm sure. Hassan the Sorcerer spun the ring today. I'm sure!"

The mouse stroked Sandhri's little tummy in amazement. "A child. Our child. *Our child!*" Yariim surged to her feet, unable to let go of Sandhri. She held tight onto her friend, feeling utterly reborn with joy. "You're sure? How far? When did it happen?"

"I've missed tv'ice." They caressed Sandhri's belly together, half wanting to laugh. "Tv'ice! Eleven v'eeks."

"Raschid's birthday night." Yariim laughed, wiping tears back from her face. "You gave him more than we knew."

The two women cried together, with no idea of why. Standing naked on the balcony together, foreheads leaning against each other, they wept together and wiped each other's tears. Sandhri brushed Yariim's hair back from her face, and looked into her eyes.

"You don't mind? That it's me first, I mean…?"

"It's right. It's how it *should* be." Yariim proudly wiped back Sandhri's tears, and then her own. "A son! Raschid's son!"

She pulled back Sandhri's hair, pointed her towards the bed where Raschid slept in peace, then slapped her on her naked rear

"Wake him. You tell him."

"V'e both tell him." Sandhri reached out and took the mouse's hand. "Toget'er."

Sandhri felt life flooding through her, proud and full of hope. Her whole body seemed to flow with a sudden rush of fire.

"A child! I'm going to haff our child!"

She took Yariim by the hand and they ran to the bed, kicking Raschid awake where he lay. She sprang atop him and told him all, with Yariim laughing at her side.

It was springtime in Osra, in the age of Shah Raschid, and all was pure and wonderful with the world.

***

In the Yellow Empire, a new day had already dawned. The Palace of Eternal Serenity glittered under the bright sun of the morning, its pagoda roofs soaring high into the sky. Gardens of chrysanthemums and cherry blooms shone more beautiful than silk brocade. The sculpted gardens echoed to the sound of waterfalls, of caged nightingales and wandering streams.

Beneath the flowers, splashes of still more brilliant colours lay. There were flowing patches of apricot, azure and spring green; sapphire blue chased with patterns of swirling phoenixes and blooms. Delicate women, fat courtiers, princes, queens and little girls – all lay sprawled or huddled all across the palace lawns.

Bright blood made fantastic patterns across the cobblestones, dripping red curls into the gently flowing streams. The curls mingled prettily with one another, one after another, more and more, until a river of crimson drifted through the gardens and out through the palace walls. The cage birds twittered, and all was calm as day came to the hub of Empire.

A slight, quiet figure walked amongst the corpses, stopping to contemplate the most interesting amongst the dead. He was a pure white fox with eyes of empty, arctic blue. Beneath long black robes, he wore armour made of severed finger bones. The Tsu-Khan gazed upon a garden of death, and breathed in the scents of slaughter. Satisfied, he placed his fists upon his hips and stood in the morning sun.

"Exquisite…"

The Tsu-Khan had only a limited manpower. He could not conquer all of his enemies at once – and yet he must act now, while his victims were unaware of how close their danger loomed.

Troops from the Yellow Empire had overrun the palace before dawn. It was Imperial troops who had made the slaughter. Imperial troops that had died fighting their own emperor's guard. They were hungry for rewards, and they were led by their own generals. The empire had fallen in an internal coup – a coup generated by the Khan. For his control spread beyond the sight of mortal men, and crept into the heart of darkness.

One of his own men – a Steppe Warrior in looted robes, came towards him, reversed his sword and knelt upon the ground.

"Great Holy One – we have found the Yellow Emperor, and his head has been severed from his body." The man put his forehead to the grass. "Shall we punish the man responsible?"

"No." The Khan's voice was quiet and husky. He looked sidewise with eyes as pure as winter sky. "We shall work with what we have.."

"Bring the turncoat General here."

Beyond the palace walls, the city lay silent. The City's governor had ordered the city guard to stay in place – for he had already seen the Tsu-Khan a few short days before. He had conducted General Hzi Chi Zhao into an audience with the Yellow Emperor. He had stood back and watched as the General's troops slaughtered his own overlord and all his household. When a princess had fled into the governor's arms, he had cut her throat with a single, ice-cold stroke.

- The Yellow Empire had fallen.

With a clash and rustle of red silk armour, the General came. He was a Raccoon-Dog with a mask of fur across his eyes, a dense pelt of fur and a tail that swept bloodstains across the grass. His huge broadsword had nine brass rings threaded along its spine, and he held the head of a nobleman in his hand. With his sandal bearer and his banner man behind him, General Hzi Chi Zhao strode before the Khan.

The Governor of the capital and the Khan's own troops had gathered in the garden. The Imperial General tossed the severed head at the Tsu-Khan's feet.

"Dead! The crown prince was visiting his father. Now we have no need to clean up his fortress of Zhaoli!"

The Governor of the capital city was dressed in robes and a hat with many dangling beads. Hands in his sleeves, he bowed to the Khan.

"It is complete, oh Khan. The populace have remained indoors, as I instructed."

The Khan nodded. The arrangement of the dead girls strewn across the garden was an ephemeral moment of beauty. He gazed upon it critically, as though assessing an art piece that would soon be lost and gone.

The Imperial General looked about the gardens and gave an oily smile.

"I am ready to rule the Empire - taking all guidance from your every wish, of course!" The man opened his arms to encompass the strange, alien beauty of the palace.
"You are wise, Khan! An invader never rules in safety. He is alien! A people are only ever pacified when ruled by their own."

"Yes."

The Khan was far more interested in a dead girl lying at his feet.

"Yes." The Khan turned his blue eyes upon the Governor.

"Kill him."

The General jerked, but it was to no avail. The city governor whipped his arms up and caught the General in a grip of terrifying power. Hzi Chi Zhao desperately tried to wrench free. He screamed – but screams were pointless in this place of slaughter. He disturbed nothing but the nightingales.

One of the Khan's soldiers slit the General's throat – just a single small cut beneath the collar of his robe. Blood jetted high, and the General babbled in fear. His struggles grew weaker and weaker as his life blood drained. The Governor held him in place as the Khan approached, held back the General's head and quietly watched the man die.

The wound was small, and it was beneath the line of his clothing. The Tsu-Khan nodded idly. He tilted his head slightly to one side as the light faded from his victim's eyes.

Hzi Chi Zhao gave a rattle. Drained like an animal in a slaughter house, his corpse was dropped onto the grass.

Walking slowly about the corpse, the Khan signed to his men. A jade jar was brought forward and put in place beside the dead General's head.

The Tsu-Khan looked quietly down at the jar.

"How did he die?"

"He was crippled in battle, Beloved One. During the siege of Murek-ghan." The soldier who had carried the jar bowed low. "When he was offered the chance to serve, he slew himself at once."

"Good. Good…"

The Khan threw back his robes. His white fur seemed to shine blue with power, and a shimmering light suffused the air about his flesh. The beloved one of the steppes, warlord of life and death, took an idle breath. As the jade jar was opened up beneath him, he extended his hand.

"Join…"

A ghostly shape swirled upwards from the jar. It flew above the General's corpse, and then settled like a blanket all across the dead, warm flesh.

The Khan lifted up one hand.

"Arise. Serve."

The General sat. His eyes opened. Like a sleepwalker, he arose. Swaying on his feet, he looked down at his fingers, opening and closing up his fists.

The Tsu-Khan quietly closed his robes.

"You are Hzi Chi Zhao, once General of the Yellow Empire. Now you are Emperor by right of arms. The armies of the West are yours. The army of the North is run by one of my own Chosen, who you will now know as Yueh Qui. This is Hu Hao, Governor of the Capital; He is also of the Chosen." The Khan walked slowly around the newly animated corpse. "There is a southern army that will oppose you. Crush it. They are monks and scholars, not warriors. Make war, and rule in my name."

White and slim, death-quiet and slender, the Tsu-Khan faced the General.

"Pray in *my* name, and this new body shall not putrefy. You are immune to poison, to pain and fatigue. You have the brain of Hzi Chi Zhao to rifle for memories; keep your nature a secret from all but our own…"

Another soldier bore a shrouded shape – a small box beneath a scarf of dark green silk. The Tsu-Khan looked towards him, and the man came to kneel and proffer up the box.

The Khan opened the box. Inside, there was a small glass mirror. He waved his hand above it, and spoke.

"Gurad."

The mirror remained dark for one long minute, and then finally cleared. General Gurad's face appeared within the glass. He was armoured and riding under a cold dawn sky. He was gazing into a mirror of his own.

"Holy One! I am here."

"The Yellow Empire has fallen. We will take treasure, siege engineers and eighty thousand of their men, and we will travel West to join you."

"Yes my Khan."

The Khan looked up at a springtime sky.

"We will reach you in three months time. And then it shall be time to march." He dropped his gaze from the clear, bright clouds to the figure deep inside the magic glass.

"Winter, Gurad. We shall invade the West in deep winter, using the Northern steppes, when the rivers are frozen and we may pass them with ease. We will take the power of the East, and crush the West, and make all Aku Mashad into one domain."

"So it must be, Holy Person." Gurad bowed. "I will prepare supplies for the campaign."

"Good, Gurad. All has come to pass as I have foreseen."

The Tsu-Khan closed the mirror box, and turned away. The undead General, the undead Governor and the Tsu-Khan's soldiers followed him in silence as he walked through a garden made beautiful by the bodies of dead girls.

Served by the living and the dead, lord of armies and master of ghosts, the Tsu-Khan walked from the palace, and on into a city that lay quiet as a grave.

**

Sath's dawn came with that most annoying Islamic habit, the call to prayer. Musical and colourful as it was, Meng truly resented it. He resented being pulled out of a perfectly good sleep – the first total relaxation he'd had in a year of travel.

To walk three thousand miles is a simple enough thing: walk ten miles a day, and in a year, you will have reached your goal. But this was ten miles a day come rain, hail, snow or shine. It was plodding onwards, wondering if there would ever be a stream from which to drink. It was begging food as a mendicant from caravans and homes. It was looking forward, and seeing no goal – looking backwards and seeing no home. It was the incredible tedium of walking, walking, walking without end…

To sleep on a mattress in a marble colonnade. To smell the scent of women all around him. To know that today of all days, there was no march to make, no trudging to be done….

Ecstasy!

A scent wafted into Meng's nose – sharp and intensely delicious. It was part frankincense, part sandalwood, and partly sun-warmed fur. It had a sharp, wonderfully exciting undertone of feminine musk. Here and there were hints of grass stains, stolen peaches and baked goods. Meng rolled onto his back, drew the wonderful smell deep into his lungs, and opened up his eyes.

Her!

He found himself looking straight into her face: Itbit, green fur gleaming and huge fine whiskers a-twiddle, sat cross legged beside him as he slept. She had peaches and hot cookies spread out on an old blue towel, and she wore a vest and harem pants made out of much-loved muslin cloth. She saw Meng awaken with a start, and spread her arms out wide.

"Morning time! Itbit say hello hello to Sandhri's good friend Meng!"

The great sage, bearer of truths, simply stared in shock. To a confused morning mind – after a night of dreaming of her – Itbit was startling. Slender, with a bottom as smooth and invitingly round as the peaches she was happily eating, she looked like a goddess of the spring. Blonde hair bound in a high pony tail caught the sunbeams slanting through the hall and lit up like the dawn. The girl saw him staring, gave a sly simper, and tossed Meng a peach.

"Good dreams, yes? Itbit think so. Meng, he smile, but restless. Always means happy-wriggle dreams!" Itbit bit into a peach and relaxed back against a marble column, happily at ease. Her pink eyes gleamed. "You come long long ways! Yellow Empire, yes? Aaah – Itbit, one day she travel far. See everything there is to see. Make a flying carpet and take all her family, all her friends. We find wonders." The girl shook her half-eaten peach at Meng. "So Itbit say – you tell her all about your travels. Every little bit!"

Sixteen-Volume Meng sat carefully upright. Osranii nights were warm, and he had slept naked out of doors, covered only in a sheet. He was acutely aware of this, and he sat with the sheet gathered about his loins.

The pink eyes were on his as he stretched. As Meng moved, his black and white fur gleamed in the morning light.

"Itbit has never seen suchie person before." Itbit leaned eagerly forward, peering this way and that at Meng's fur. "Very fine! Very plush! Is nice to have colours done just so! Is dyed?"

"No no. This is natural." Meng sat up, straight and dignified – somewhat spoiled by the early morning ruffles in his fur. "I am a Panda. We are a type of bear. We are all marked this way."

"Hoo hoo! Itbit is fine colour too!" Itbit eagerly held out an arm. "Is dyed when she was very little. Stays forever! Slave thing they do to white mouse, white rabbit, white rat. Now is fashion! Itbit is very beautiful!"

The mouse jumped eagerly up.

"Raschid say, you teach Itbit now. Yes?"

"Yes… Yes, he wants me to be your tutor." Meng caught his breath and solemnly bowed. "It is a great honour to serve you so, my lady. It is this humble one's pleasure and his duty to help you place your feet upon the path of the Tao."

Bowing forward had made Meng's bare bottom rise up out of the nest of sheets. He felt the breeze, goggled, and sat hurriedly back down.

For her part, Itbit stood – coltish, long legged and full of life, and clasped her hands.

"New teacher! And a funny fuzzy one! Good!" She reached down and grabbed Meng by the hand. "Come quick, yes? Itbit think be busy day. Time to do all things that an Itbit docs!"

In a sudden shocking rush, Meng found himself standing. Itbit dragged him off along the corridor. He squawked and clumsily wrapped a sheet about himself, clasping his clothes frantically against his skinny body.

"Lady! What – where…?"

"Hurry! Or we miss all goodie good stuff!"

The girl dragged Meng into a clumsy run. He followed willy nilly as she went through doors and scrabbled up rocks in the gardens. Triumphant, she stood above him, legs splayed wide like a mighty conqueror, and flourished her hand.

"Iss bathie time! See – before silly girls get here and mess it up with blah-blah-blah. Meng bath now, and Itbit fix all raggedy-tatter clothes. Is good!"

In a nest of rocks in an open garden, there was an open air bath that steamed in the sun. Itbit scampered over to a great big boiler hidden behind the boulders, and opened up an iron door.

Heat billowed forth. Itbit chattered away to something inside the ovens, and rooted about in a box to find a choice lump of coal. She fed it to something in the flames, and happily beckoned Meng over to her side.

"Come and see! Is a little salamander there. Little fire fellow! Sandhri found him in a burning house, and told him stories until he follow her home. Now he sits here and helps keep water hot, and we feeds him and tell him all our tales!" Itbit eagerly beckoned Meng over. "Say – 'hello salamander. I am Meng bookie fellow'. Iss nice salamander! Nearly never bites!"

Meng edged over, trying to keep his sheet in place. Inside the red hot fireplace, he saw a great skinny thing that looked like a dappled orange skink. The creature stared at him with eyes like molten gold, and stuck out a tongue that danced with licking flames.

The sage bowed. The salamander made a 'huff' of dismissal. Itbit shut the oven doors.

"He not like the chill when we open doors. But later – you tell him things when you teach Itbit. This be fine place for lessons." She mounted the rocks, her backside and her thighs taut and perfect as she climbed. "But quick now! Take off silly sheet, and you bath well! No ticks and fleas will you put on poor pretty Itbit!"

She fussed and ordered until Meng nervously slid into the bath – sheet still held firm. Itbit made a great noise of dissatisfaction, and sat down on a rock above.

"Itbit will not peek! Take off silly sheet."

"Madam – it would be improprietal?"

The girl looked up from arranging Meng's tattered clothes upon the rocks above. Washed and clean, they were sadly frayed.

"What iss 'improprietal'?"

"It means 'unseemly' – outside the proper order of politeness and social dictate. It is not allowed under the rules."

"Ah – rules!" Itbit pulled needle and thread happily out of her bag, flattening Meng's threadbare tunic on a stone. "Itbit has no rules. Itbit does what an Itbit does. Is good for everybody!"

"Everyone has rules." Clutching his sheet, Meng stood in the pool, bedraggled fur trailing from his wet cheeks, trying to look and sound lofty. "Whether you realize it or not, you are bound by an unspoken social contract that dictates your behaviour."

"Nope!"

"Yes!"

"Nopie nope!" Itbit cut thread with her chisel teeth. "Remember to wash behind fuzzy ears. Fleas hide there!"

Meng resentfully did as he was told. "This is the sort of thing I am here to teach both you and the Shah! You have a free and easy attitude here, and have replaced an old social system with a new. But too much freedom creates dangers. When people do not know their place, then they are misled by dreams of ambition or by nightmares of instability. A stable society must lock itself down into rules, orders and rituals."

Itbit was carelessly sewing a patch on the seat of Meng's trousers.

"Nope!"

"Stop saying that!" Meng stood, indignant, utterly unaware that he had dropped his sheet at last. "Rules are essential! Without rules, there is no guidance. Without guidance, human nature leads us into error! Rules prevent error."

Itbit sewed happily onwards, scarcely paying him attention.

"Itbit say – rules are for people with no trusts in brains. You follow rules because person who makes rules says he brainier than you be. So you believe him! Maybe he is, maybe he not." Itbit stitched with remarkable speed and precision. "But Itbit is smart! Itbit knows as much as anybody. So she look at rules and say – 'hey, Itbit knows why you say that. But Itbit knows a little bit more – so she take care in her own way!" The mouse tugged at her repairs critically, then decided to double stitch. "So in the end, rules and orders is for stupid peoples. But when all peoples are smart, and all take care of everyone around them, then there is no need for rules. Much happier! Less rules means more happy!"

Meng stood, feeling strangely sulky.

"I do not concede the point."

Itbit now wore glasses to help her with her sewing. She lowered them down her nose and peered at Meng.

"Is as you choose." The mouse wriggled her pink nose. "Willie is showing."

Mend sat down at once. Above him, Itbit spread out his clothes in sun to look for wear and tear.

"You got skinny! Skinny as silly bat. Look at these clothes. You were much bigger when you bought these things!"

"They were made for me by my mother." Meng was scrubbing at his feet – now rather horny objects: he had worn through his shoes somewhere in eastern Meepsoor. "She wanted to give me room to grow."

"You have a mother?" Itbit shot her head over the lip of the rocks above. "You left your mother all alone? To go walking all this way?"

"I did, and she understood my drive to follow my duty." Meng was proud. "Mothers must support their sons when duty calls them."

"Itbit does not have mother."

"Ah." Meng looked up at her, a little saddened. "I am sorry."

"Iss not sad. Is good! Itbit has jackal, bat and blue mouse now." The mouse was lying on her belly, head over the rim of the rocks, her elegant pink tail waving sinuously above her. "Hey – was it a long long way? How do you get from Yellow place to Osra place in one piece? Itbit has to know these things for when she does her travels."

"In theory it is simple enough." Meng sat in the shallows. "You take the west road out of the capital. It takes you through the provinces of 'river willows', 'evergreen', 'yellow heng' and 'fulsome emptiness'. Then there are two caravan routes. North across the great steppe, through the steppe cities and to Osra. Or the long way, south west, across the great ice mountains and into Meepsoor."

The mouse tossed down a cookie.

"Which way you take?"

"I went across the mountains and south west." Meng tried the cookie, and found it sinfully good. "The steppe cities are always at war. No one goes that way any more."

"Ah." Itbit lounged, her feet a-wiggle. "Did you see beautiful things?"

"Beautiful?" Meng settled in the water. He closed his eyes and rested back his head, bringing back to mind all the strange, undying wonders he had seen.

"Beautiful beyond imagining. The southern mountains are stark and ancient. Huge waves of rock thrown high into the skies! The valleys are great forests of rhododendron flowers, with bees as big as uki birds whirring through the blooms. There are cows there, and green fields with little houses made from stones. Everything there smells of ice water running fresh in all the streams.

"The mountains are high! So high that they are always covered in snow, and the air is so thin you grow dizzy. But monks will help a traveler. They drink tea with butter in it, and have great monasteries built upon the mountain passes. In the evenings, you could sit there with your feet above the world, looking out and down across all the lands spread out below. Stony paths hung with spears of ice. Shrines with statues of red painted monsters, planted about with little flowers. Sometimes, you heard great horns echoing about the mountains, and the chanting of monks let you know there was somewhere safe and warm to sleep the night."

The furnace doors squeaked open. The salamander peeked forth, listening to the tale. Itbit listened in utter fascination.

Meng lounged in the water, his hands behind his head as he stared at vistas in his memory. "On the far side of the mountains is Meepsoor. Rich, green jungles overrun with living things. Flying lizards leaping from tree to tree! Crocodiles as long as your forearm chasing little fishes in the streams. Tora birds with brilliant green feathers make huge mounds out of shiny objects they scratch out of old ruins. They dance and sing wild songs to attract their mates in places where old temples molder and huge statues lie covered in veils of living flowers.

"It grows hot as you go south and west. The roads are trod by elephants with great soft feet – painted all the colours of the rainbow! Ladies dressed in nothing but a belt of gold wave at you from above. In the towns, holy men will speak with you as they sit naked in the dust. Warriors on horses painted bright red with henna dye ride past, swapping tales of the hero Shah of Osra. The temples tower high on high, every inch of them carved into gods and mortals, elephants and demons. In the evenings, the holy travelers sleep in the warm grass about the temples. Women from great houses come and bring saffron rice to all the pilgrims and the holy men. Children wearing thin copper bangles on their wrists dance for the pilgrims as the evening comes, and all the land twinkles soft with fires."

Above Meng, Itbit lay her face upon her folded arms, hushed and entranced - her pink eyes never leaving him.

"Where then? Where did you go?"

"A long, long way through Meepsoor and west into the plains. They call it Vindahl, and it is so hot in the day that the red soil shimmers in the heat. There are ruins there – old fortresses and temples. Islamic warriors fought the Meepsoori there long long ago, and all the irrigation tunnels were destroyed. So now there are just city states at the river banks, and all the rest is empty space, old ruins and quiet dust. Huge vultures soar the skies, and herds of great flightless birds run fast across the far horizons.

"After two months on the plains, you come at last to something I had never seen before. Past Vindahl, you reach the ocean!"

The little green mouse lay quietly, her eyes dazed with sights from Meng's tales.

"Itbit knows the ocean. Itbit has a boat with yellow sails. Sandhri's friend Zhu taught all of us how to sail the boats, and we race her across the river mouth."

"Well I had never seen it in my life." Meng lay on his side, head propped on one hand. "It went forever, clean and bright! And there were seal women lounging on the beach!"

"What is a seal?"

"People with sleek fur, built like dogs but with no ears, who swim as easily as other people walk. These ones were from the far West, with a language no one spoke. They swam to keep cool. They had come to trade for incense down in south Meepsoor." The young sage swirled the bath waters with his feet. "They gave me a ride in their strange, high boat to the western shore of the gulf. Here they left me in the town of Malakh, at the edge of the great sand desert.

"There were nomads in robes. And camels! Huge camels! And men rode pure white horses on the beach. But I turned and walked out into the desert. Into a land of huge white dunes."

"Itbit knows the dunes." The green mouse waved her tail. "The sun is so bright, you get headaches behind your eyes, and everything shimmers. The sand makes a noise like hissing coals as it slides away from your feet."

"And there are ruins! Huge old ruins." Meng stared at the sky. "But from somewhere, I would always find a trail leading to a well. The nomads – they were helping me, even though I didn't know." The sage flexed his fingers in the water. "Soon, I found lines of trees, all planted beside a huge pipe made out of poured stone that ran right through the desert. There were people there who said the Shah had made water come to the desert. That there was life where nothing had lived before."

"That is my Raschid's pipe." Itbit said with satisfaction. "Itbit planted fifty trees all by herself!"

"Beautiful. At night, the tent towns bloomed, and fires glimmered on the sands. Women in black gauze danced, and men made songs with the strangest sounding instruments. They fed me dates and millet bread, and pointed me west – always west."

" – To Osra."

Itbit watched him carefully.

"How long is it take you, to walk so many ways?"

"Three hundred and sixty one days." Meng was proud of his record. Even in the freezing cold mountain passes, he had still managed to make ten miles or so a day. "A year of walking without pause."

Itbit was impressed.

"Strong! Must be why Meng has such tight tushie!"

She gave a sigh and levered herself up. The salamander had crept right out into the rocks, and it gave an appraising, tolerant look to Meng before scuttling back into his flames. Itbit tossed clothes down towards Meng.

"There, Itbit fix! Meng has strong trousers now to hide cute tush." The girl stood, stretching. "Out of bath now. We go find everybody. Is an important day. Big secret be out!"

"Oh?" Meng used the wet sheet as cover to slide behind a rock. He awkwardly put on his pants. "What secret?"

"Aaaaah!" Long and limber, Itbit walked from rock to rock with pretty, pointed feet. "Itbit knows what an Itbit knows! Black bat, she sneakie in to sorcerer! She throw up breakfast two whole times! She lie in garden when no one lookie and spins wedding ring on thread above her tummy!" The mouse looked slyly over her shoulder. "Good thing they have Itbit. She be sixteen soon. Be family then. They need her to help. Good timings! Itbit make everything good for everybody, and we all be happy forever and ever, with green mouse, blue mouse, bat and jackal. Ever and always!" The mouse paused with her back to Meng – her backside perfect. She looked back at him with a smoldering little smile.

"Itbit will learn the happywriggles at long long last. It will be good – yes?"

"I…" Meng had no idea in the world what she was talking about. "I imagine so, yes."

The mouse looked out over the palace, her face proud and full of joy.

"Itbit will be the best ever."

A great noise sounded from somewhere over the south wall of the palace – a crackling explosion that went on and on. Itbit craned onto her tip toes, made a happy noise, then leapt down to collect Meng.

"See – is beginning! Happy times for all. You come now! Come with an Itbit, and you see something really good! Everyone happy today. Big holiday!" She dragged her hapless tutor away from the bath. "Run! We be quick. Say bye bye to Salamander, and we go!"

With a wave at the salamander, Meng was dragged off into the palace. Through the kitchens, past guards and officers and out a postern door, then down a shady street. Itbit ran out through a gate in the city wall, to enter a huge flat field spangled with grass and poppy flowers.

It was a field alive with hundreds of soldiers. There were Royal guards in blue brocade. There were men in the white robes, red caps and white turbans of the royal *tefekchi* – the musketeers, armed with scimitars and long Osranii guns. Most spectacularly of all, there was the cavalry, resplendent in silvered mail, velvet brigantines and silken robes. Their horses were sheathed in brocade and glittering with steel. The field was alive with joy.

Mounted on a great, scarred, disreputable camel, the Shah of Osra was amongst his men, clasping hands that reached eagerly up to him. Another camel sat daintily upon the ground, and here Sandhri and Yariim were mobbed by laughing soldiers and their wives. Men fired muskets into the air in celebration, over and over again.

A huge tiger soldier in the blue armour of the Royal House lifted Sandhri up on high in triumph. She laughed and shook the soldier by his ears until finally he put her down.

With Meng in tow, Itbit padded guilessly through the jubilant crowds of soldiers. She presented herself beside Sandhri, Yariim and Raschid.

"Itbit! There you are!" Raschid was bright with joy – dazed and starry eyed. His camel made a skillful turn, and Raschid swept Itbit up into his arms. "There you are! We've been looking everywhere!"

"Aaah?" Warm and seductively comfortable in Raschid's arms, Itbit leaned back and innocently rolled her eyes. "Itbit says – bestest friends have news?"

"News – wonderful news!" He squeezed Itbit tight, then held her away from himself, looking a little anxious. "Well – we hope you will think it is good news."

The camel knelt awkwardly beside Sandhri and Yariim's mount. The endlessly firing muskets sounded like a battle. Itbit shouted to be heard above the deafening row.

"Itbit knows no news. But Itbit has a present. Itbit say – she made a little thing. Here it is. Be present. First present!"

She delved into the jute bag and came out with a little parcel that she managed to get into Sandhri's hands. She shouted over the never ending *bangs*. "Is present!"

Sandhri blinked, unfolded the cotton wrappings, and found a soft little thing made from silk. She held it out to find a hand-embroidered baby's swaddling robe. Overjoyed, Sandhri held it out into the light. The robe must have taken days to make.

"Itbit!"

She looked at Itbit in astonishment. The green mouse gave a sly, innocent smile.

"Itbit knows what an Itbit knows!" The mouse came into Sandhri's arms, and in all seriousness patted Sandhri's flat belly.

"It will be alright now. Itbit is here to look after things. That be lucky! You need someone smart in family!"

She held Yariim, Raschid and Sandhri tight.

"Itbit will be close to look after all of friends. Never be worried. Itbit is here."

Meng stood amongst the soldiers who jubilantly congratulated their Shah. One of the galloper batteries of cannon had swung swiftly into place, and it added its apocalyptic noise to the tumult. Shah Raschid ducked as the cannon roared, and saw Meng standing nearby. He reached joyously out to seize the sage and tell him the wondrous news.

"Meng – I'm to be a father! A father!"

The panda took on a look of joy, and bowed reverently five times.

"A thousand years is insufficient to express this humble one's joy!" He bowed to Sandhri, who was isolated from him by the storm of noise. "May the wellspring of peace flow forever in your family's heart."

"Ha ha! Well said!" Raschid beamed, made huge with the sheer joy of his discovery. A father! He would have a son! The thought of it still dazed him. He felt so full of happiness he half thought that he might burst! "So, Meng – you found Itbit?" He pulled Itbit onto his lap. "And what did you do with yourselves this morning?"

Itbit's halter top was made from thin muslin pulled almost to its bursting point. She seemed unaware of its effect, even as it froze Meng in hypnosis. She threw open her arms and looked happily upwards at Raschid.

"Busy morning. Busy, busy! Itbit and Meng have been in lessons. We do political philosophy, and lots and lots of geography!"

"Excellent!" Raschid was truly pleased. "That's excellent! Well done, Meng. Good man!" Full of life, Raschid felt himself warming enormously to the young scholar. "Come then. It's a holiday! Work tomorrow. We'll ride, and the army is going to shoot! We'll make it a festival, and go down by the river!" The Shah of all Osra had no camel at hand to offer Meng, and so he walked beside him, throwing an arm about the boy. "Did I tell you it will be boy?"

"Yes, my Shah…"

"A boy, Meng! A boy!" They walked off, surrounded by hordes of troops. "We're going to have a boy."

"Yes, my Shah."

All about them, muskets fired. Meng decided he was in for a strange day.

"There. Do you see that? There is the last one." A quiet voice, hissing with urgency, whispered in the watcher's furry ear. "You will see a small mouse girl with fur of green. That is she – the last of the Shah's women."

They lay behind the balcony railings of a tall, thin minaret. The priest – a skeletal black cat with one ragged ear, crowded his companion, who lay watching the field through a long brass telescope.

The man with the telescope was sleek and elegant – slim, muscular, and immaculately clean. He wore robes in the style of a Yellow Empire nobleman, but with the turban of Islam. An Osranii scimitar hung at his belt – Osranii steel was the finest in the world. He was a mouse – his fur a soft creamy white, and his nose, lower limbs and ears a dark smoky brown. He kept his telescope focused on the far away field where Raschid and his family were surrounded by their celebrating men.

Behind them crouched a long, limber nobleman – a cheetah with a scar across his cheek. The man wore the robes of an Osranii nobleman.

"Do you see them? The Shah is there?"

"The Shah is there." The mouse with the telescope had a rich, droll voice full of amusement and self satisfaction. "My eyes work well enough, Haduh Had'idh."

"Three women! One green, one blue, one black! They are never away from him." The priest kept hidden behind the minaret rails. "Even in battle, they are at his side!"

"Loyalty in a bride is a commendable thing." The mouse lowered his telescope. He had a slim, sardonic face, with exotic, tilted eyes. "A worthy man would choose a worthy wife, do you not think?"

"Worthy!" The Osranii nobleman spat to avert evil. "Slave women and commoners. He defiles the royal bloodline with the wombs of mendicants, beggar girls and slaves!"

"An infidel!" The priest hissed, his fangs barred. "He intermingles faiths until he claims that all are one! He spits on the prophets in the name of reason!"

"Ah." The mouse sat up, languidly dusting off his immaculate yellow satin robes. "Is he, then, reasonable?"

"Reason is the enemy of faith!" The priest looked to the Osranii noble. "His reason turns our nation into a mockery before God!"

"The rabble follow him like a messiah!" The Priest hissed, as though people on the streets a hundred feet below might somehow hear. "It is the age of the mob!"

The white-brown mouse stood, stretching elegantly up on felt boots. He wore the rawhide riding whip of a steppe nomad about one wrist.

"It would seem the army is drawn from that rabble. He is inordinately popular."

"They are fearsome." The Osranii nobleman joined the mouse at the railings. "Powerful street fighters – but worthless in an open field battle."

The mouse raised one brow. "You have faced them in an open field battle, Had'idh?"

In reply, the nobleman jerked his chin contemptuously at the smoke hanging over the cheering battalions of infantry. There were now at least three thousand men out on the field.

"You can see it for yourself. Muskets. The entire infantry arm is equipped with muskets. Accurate only to a few dozen paces – and a bow fires twelve shots to their one." The noble let contempt and hate mar his face. "But effective in the streets. They slaughtered cavalry and bowmen in the Shah's revolution. At street ranges, they are devastating."

"Then we must avoid brawling with them in the streets." The mouse raised his telescope again. He saw a huge tiger soldier in blue armour walking with an exotic harem girl on one arm, and his other hand resting on the shoulders of the blue queen. The man looked big enough to crush a boulder with one hand. "Yes – we shall certainly be very good boys."

He closed up the telescope and held it up before him, looking at it in puzzled admiration. "This device is really quite miraculous. Locally made?"

The priest bowed.

"Local, my lord. Designed by the Shah himself, it is said."

"Interesting…"

The mouse lowered his chin to his chest in thought. Only Osra had the ability to make such baubles. Only Osra could make glass so pure it could be used for spectacles, lenses – and now apparently these viewing tubes. Osranii steel was the wonder of the world. Rebellious local voices treated technology with contempt, but the mouse came from a world where any unknown quantity could mean death. The steppe cities were no place for fools – nor did the Tsu-Khan place his trust in any but the most competent of men.

The mouse looked out over the distant field once more. A true celebration seemed underway. He pulled kid-leather gloves onto his hands and prepared to start his work.

"Very well – you have given me dossiers on the Royal Household. We have seen them from a distance. It is time to see them face to face, I think!" He paused, one gloved hand half raised, and gave a smile full of languid charm. "Time to show the Shah the friendship of the mighty Khan."

The Priest crouched expectantly.

"Time to show them the red blade of war?"

The mouse smoothed his whiskers with an arch little smile. "No, my dear! Time to show them that Osra is not alone in having civilized charm."

The mouse looked for the priest's telescope and appropriated it, shoving it through his own belt.

"You shall have your faith purified, priest. You shall have your noble houses restored, Haduh. There will be an Osra of which you may approve – never fear." He took a swift look about the balcony. "All packed up, are we? Then let's be off."

Yet another spatter of musket fire erupted from the field, as a new regiment came running onto the field to greet the Shah. Turning, the steppe mouse frowned as the musketry surged in volume. The field was completely covered up in smoke.

"How many infantrymen is that, Haduh?"

"The guard, plus two battalions." The nobleman sniffed. "Three thousand men."

The mouse raised his telescope once again, but now saw nothing but a fog shot through with countless stabs of flame.

"That is a very great volume of fire to be coming from a mere three thousand men."

"They have pistols in their belts .They must be firing them as well."

"Ah. I see." The mouse closed the telescope again. "Well, lead on! I believe there is a wonderful Meepsoori restaurant beside the market place. You shall have the honour of purchasing me an early lunch."

On the field far away, Sandhri laughed, sheltered under Raschid's arm. Beside them, the army celebrated, firing muskets and laughing aloud

With a bellow of joy, his fiancé Fatima beneath one arm, Saud fired his musket up into the air. The big bullet hammered skyward, the musket kicking back in Saud's powerful hand.

Saud worked the lever underneath the rifle butt. The rear of the barrel unlocked and swung to point upwards. Saud fished a paper-wrapped cartridge of bullet and powder from his belt, stuffed it nose first into the open breech. He worked the lever and closed the breech, the action sheering off the tail end of the cartridge to expose the powder and simultaneously prime the firing pan.

He cocked back the hammer and fired again, whooping for joy! All around him, other men did the same.

One shot in four seconds. As fast as a bow.

The army celebrated, while in the town, traitors took an emissary out to a very long and expensive restaurant lunch.

Chapter Five:

Luxuriating under the stroke of a body brush, Sandhri the Storyteller lounged in supreme comfort. She lay on a balcony overlooking the gardens, buck naked and drowsy with satisfaction. The entire balcony was hip deep in cushions – impossible to walk through, and absurdly delightful to lounge about in. Yariim sat cross-legged beside Sandhri's naked back, patiently brushing her friend's black fur to a lustrous shine. A sheet of scrap paper lay on the broad stone windowsill, and Yariim scribbled notes with her other hand.

Sandhri made delicious noises under the brush. Her pleasure was best seen by the clench and wriggle of her long bare toes.

"Oooooh…."

Yariim kept brushing. "Is that getting the right spots?"

"Oooh – my fur feels great." Sandhri purred. "You haff to put a lot off time into keeping your fur in condition v'en you are pregnant. All the books say so!"

"Uh-hum." Yariim was amused. "You really must show me these books sometime."

"Oh – hokay!" The bat lifted one leg. "Right after you massage my little feets."

"Quite."

There was a clatter at the window. Raschid made a classical entrance via the climbing vines. He wore a musketeer's robes and had powder marks up the side of his face from flashes in the musket pan. He was a thoughtful Shah, and carried a pair of long red roses in his teeth.

He became stuck at the windowsill. Yariim heaved and handed him in, and Raschid almost drowned in the ocean of cushions. He floundered, yet still somehow managed to pass out the roses to his lady loves.

"For my darlings."

"My love!" Yariim was delighted by the rose, and she kissed him warmly. "Oh, it's beautiful!"

"Hey Jackal fellow!" Sandhri made a vague wave of her foot, too boneless to move. "Hey – v'ith all the hybrid-thing? I finally figured out v'at v'e are having. He'll be a bouncing baby Battle-Jack!"

The blue mouse rolled her eyes, putting away the brush. Sandhri made a whimper.

"You missed a bit – t'ere, right above my tail."

Yariim stripped fluff out of the brush and eyed the boneless bat.

"You wouldn't be exploiting this situation at all, do you think?"

"Me? Neffer!" Sandhri idly raised one finger. "I haff to relax for *two*, now!"

She sank into the cushions. Clambering over from the windowsill, Raschid held up a list.

"Alright – I have more names here on the list." Raschid smelled of powder smoke. Osranii regiments rotated through the capital month by month, and Raschid always drilled and ate with the men. "Abwan's regiment took a vote, and they all suggested we call the baby 'Abwan'."

"Ahh – Abwan." Yariim gave an indulgent smile. "We shall thank the Colonel for that suggestion. Any others?"

Raschid nodded in all due seriousness.

"Saud said we can borrow his name, because Fatima calls him 'darling' these days, so he isn't using his name as often as he used to."

"Ha." The blue mouse leaned back against the pillows in thought. "Well, there's all the traditional throne names. Salah, Akhbar, Abbas…"

Sandhri made a snort. "Hardly!"

"Marwan, Maradh, Shaviik…"

"Too much of a mouthful!" Sandhri lolled. "T'ey don't grab me."

"Hmm." Raschid peered at his ever-growing list. "Um – Raas Jakoob suggests 'Dhavid' or "Suliman' – something strong and biblical."

"Biblical?" Sandhri lifted a foot straight up out of the sea of cushions. It was the only way to mark her location. "Hey, ve' could call him 'God'! God Dinaq! T'en v'en anyone says 'God damn it', he'll alv'ays haff employment!"

Yariim lowered her glasses down her nose. "Really…"

"No – v'ait! V'ait! I've got it! I haff a name!" Sandhri shot up out of the cushions in sudden enthusiasm. *"Sinbad!* Prince Sinbad!"

Raschid and Yariim both swapped a patient gaze, then eyed Sandhri.

"Sandhri - We are not calling the heir to the Osranii throne 'Sinbad'."

Sandhri was hurt. "V'y not! It hass echoes of adventure! Travel! Cunning! And really good sword fightie stuff! I love that!" Wallowing in cushions, Sandhri made mock swordplay with her hand. "Wow! Girls v'ould love it! V'e've got his romantic life *made!*"

"Um – let's just pencil it in as a 'maybe' and move on." Yariim made a careful note on a page. "Well – we have 'Nashwat' suggested by the Udh valley member of parliament…" Yariim shrugged. "In the local dialect it means 'Hope star'. Unfortunately in the neighbouring highlands it means 'fallen meteorite', which might be a bit of a public relations embarrassment."

Raschid lay on his back looking up at a list. "Why does it have to be so difficult? Somehow we have to keep everyone happy!"

"Siiiin-baaaad…." Sandhri slyly emerged amongst the cushions like a shark surfacing from the deep. "I tell you, iss the only v'ay!"

Enthused, Sandhri sat up, one finger in the air and her eyes full of inspiration.

"It v'ill be fantastic! Sinbad! We teach him sword fighting, and how to ride, and how to shoot…"

Yariim reclined, smiling.

"You seem bloodthirsty all of a sudden. Is this a pregnancy thing?"

Sandhri planted a hand against her chest in magnificent protest.

"No! New life inside me hass giffen me a new respect for creation. For instance, I am now a vegetarian!"

Yariim shot a dry glance at the sausage-happy bat.

"You?"

"Yes, me!" Sandhri held up a finger. "I haff sworn an oath neffer to harm another living creature, unless it is either tasty or annoying."

She gave a great, wide yawn all filled with sharp white teeth, then stretched her pretty feet.

"I haff a story. Someone do my feet v'ile I tell it to you. Pregnancy iss very bhad on the feet."

Yariim gave a profound bow. "Shall each of us do one foot, your Fecundity? Or shall we split our efforts between your feet and your poor fevered brow?"

"Yah – that sounds good! Now – v'ere shall I begin…?" The bat lounged back between her partners. *"V'unce upon a time, there v'ass a beautiful storyteller girl. She vass lean and svelte, v'ith curves in all the right places as long ass you liked them racy and not plush…"*

Yariim began massaging one of the bat's feet.

"I believe we may have heard this one."

"Impossible!" The bat held up one finger. "I just made it up just t'en." She opened one eye. "Did I mention this bat had a really sexy rear?"

Raschid nodded. "It may have come up in a previous version."

"Ah well." Sandhri flipped out her great sheets of pure white hair. "But it iss an important story. I will write it down – so I v'ill!"

The blue mouse gave a sudden smile.

"What's this I hear about mosquitoes? What story was that?"

"Ah! Iss a new one! Listen!"

Sandhri sat up and recounted her mosquito story once again. She acted it out with a great deal of buzzing and creepy-crawling with her hands. At the end, Raschid laughed in delight.

"Well that's wonderful! Did you make it up last week?"

"Hell no!" The bat was indignant. "That Meng person v'anted a story, so I made the whole t'ing up for him on the spot, right t'ere and t'en!"

Raschid was quite overjoyed. "You never!"

"Of course I did. And t'iss evening, I write it down into my big book, so t'ere!"

Yariim ceased massaging Sandhri's feet. "Aaah." The book grew bigger and bigger every day. It was already huge enough to stun an ox. "When exactly will you let us put this book into print?"

"Soon! Just a little longer." In all due seriousness, Sandhri put her hands behind her head and looked up at the roof. "You haff to be careful v'ith stories. A storybook iss a door into the v'orld of dreams and tales. Not'ing ever ages t'ere, nor can it effer die as long as love and v'onder still live in the v'orld. Every hero you ever heard of – every love you ever dreamed. Every adventure, every fight and every joy live there alv'ays and forever. Alv'ays evolving, alv'ays new."

Sandhri lay back and nodded.

"You must be careful v'en you make a door. T'iss iss v'ere you v'ill live. And after all, you are inviting ot'ers to visit you." She yawned. "A few more stories in the book. It needs v'un last, Great story. V'un that shows some mettle."

Yariim nodded.

"You are working on a story like that?"

"Right now, I am struggling v'ith the fact I haff to pee." The bat lazed in the cushions. "Pregnancy iss not all cheese and bananas you know!"

A gong sounded – it was a mere ten minutes until the Royal Council convened, with parliamentary delegates and representatives from half a dozen tribes. Raschid stretched in the cushions – regretted not being able to take a morning snooze – and levered himself wearily up in his seat.

Yariim had already found him his turban.

"Council?"

"Council." Raschid battered his red cap and turban into shape. "Today we try to balance small business tax incentives. I've asked our Ha'kuto Hanin friends to attend. We can start working out a trade agreement, and I want to see about using their ports to pioneer new sea routes to the south." The Shah paused in thought. "I think we really might be able to open out the whole wide world. Aku Mashad could be a community of brothers instead of rivals at arms."

He was pure and unbowed: At that moment, Yariim knew why she loved him so. She kissed him softly, took up the flower he had given her, and stood.

"Time to go."

A polite, firm knock came at the door. Raschid spoke, and the balcony door slid open. Fatima, the Major Domo and mistress of the household knelt on the floor. Beside her were the Shah's day guard of blue-armoured riflemen.

"My Shah. My Queens." The long, buxom pink rabbit gave a perfect bow. "It is time for Council, my Shah. The delegates have gathered in the hall of whispers'."

"Good. I'm coming!" Raschid took Fatima's hands and kissed her as she stood. "Yariim? Sandhri? Are you coming today?"

The blue mouse shook her head.

"I have the library to attend. The palace press is printing three books on science over the coming month, and if I don't make the final proof reads, they'll get the whole thing wrong again."

"Ha!" Sandhri was pulling on her much beloved pants and robe. "Now I haff a perfect day! I make stories this morning, inspect markets at lunchtime, and I still get you two to giff me foot rubs this evening!"

"Except for the new activities we have scheduled." Fatima slipped on a pair of glasses and inspected a tablet. "Yes. I have laid you out an exercise program to strengthen you for birth. An hour each day, starting today. Starting *now.*"

"Exercise!" Looking aghast, Sandhri shrank away in alarm. "Look – I haff things to do…!"

"It is all perfectly fitted in with your schedule." Fatima arose and held out a hand for the bat. "We are waiting for you in the courtyard below."

"I don't exercise – I *v'ork!*" Sandhri went into a panic. "Not v'ith weights? Not v'ith anybody v'atching!"

Fatima adjusted her glasses evilly.

"Only those people you usually laugh at when it's calisthenics time."

Disbelieving, Sandhri found herself on her feet being led outside. Yariim wore a devilish smirk as she helped Sandhri through the door.

"I believe I shall watch this first session. I think it should be *very* lively!"

"You can't do this to me! T'iss iss cutting into my nap time!" The bat wailed as she was led out to where Fatima's exercise class awaited. "Raschid – this iss kidnap! Raschid, save me!" She gave another wail. "Ack! Now I really, *really* haff to pee!"

Raschid laughed. He was sorely tempted to watch a grumbling, sour-faced bat being put through her exercises – then decided that there would be too much hell to pay.

One of the guards waited until the women were out of sight, and then leaned in to murmur quietly in his Shah's ear.

"My Shah – there is a Chieftain from Kakuzan who you may wish to see before the council begins."

"Kakuzan?" Raschid scrubbed unsuccessfully at the gunpowder smudges on his cheek. "Yes. Take me to him."

Something was in the air – something strange and discomforting. With a disturbed glance into the empty air, Raschid followed after the guard.

As he left, he took up his battle sword from its hooks and thrust the weapon down into his sash.

Dark with thought, Raschid arrived late for the meeting. He approached the hall, accompanied by two of his ever-watchful royal guards, and there he found Raas Yomah. The nomad chieftain stood scarcely chest high to the Jackal Shah, and yet seemed to fill the room with a suave and ominous presence. The mouse chieftain of the Beni Mus opened up his arms, spreading his robes in welcome as he embraced the Shah.

"My Lord of Lords!"

"Master of the Noble Vagabonds!" Raschid gripped Raas Yomah, so damned glad to see him. "How is Hanna?"

"Hanna has made me a happy man, my Shah. A civilising influence – although she still refuses to drink tea."

Raschid nodded, his mind far away – his eyes sharp and his thoughts racing. Raas Yomah tilted his head to one side, chewing thoughtfully upon a piece of grass.

"You are worried about news. It is the mountain men – the Kakuzaks?"

"They bring news." Wiping his face, Raschid looked about the palace guards, trying to remember days when these buildings had been awash with blood – when swords and gunfire had ripped a summer's night apart.

The desert mouse watched him carefully, his head still tilted.

"You should drink tea, Rashid-dah. Before battle, a nomad drinks tea. It focuses the mind."

"Then we shall drink tea, my friend." Raschid led the way towards the council. "Sit beside me, and we shall see…"

With one arm about Raas Yomah, Raschid marched beneath a vast archway and into the Hall of Whispers.

The room had been turned into a chamber for the great council of Osra. Every city, every district and every nomad tribe sent their elected representatives here to govern the land hand in hand with their Shah. One hundred men, and eleven women: Raschid had worked hard to bring Osra's women to the heart of political power.

They sat in ranks about a central floor. All bowed to the Shah. Raschid touched his hand to his heart, his mouth and forehead in salaam, bowing equally to the delegates.

"My honoured council…"

He got no further. Shooting out of the woodwork came the royal chamberlain, moustache and all, who grandly slammed his staff against the floor.

"Hear ye, hear ye! Hear now the words of the Great Shah! Descendant of Offam Dinaq, the slayer of demons! Great great great grandson of Uffaq al Dinaq, builder of kingdoms! Great great grandson of Burad al Dinaq, the terror of the Franks…"

Raschid nervously raised a hand and managed to interrupt the Chamberlain's flow.

"Hi! Yes – thank you, Chamberlain. Thank you." The Chamberlain gave Raschid a hurt look, and the Shah hastened to ease the blow. "Pray – Queen Sandhri has asked if you might turn your knowledge to thoughts of a suitable name for our Son. We should so value your assistance." The Chamberlain brightened and sped off. Raschid called after him. "She is in the summer garden!"

The tall, steel-blue jackal shared a relieved glance with his counsellors. Raschid took his place at the head of the room, and the palace guards bowed and sealed the room.

The army had a representative, who was accompanied by the hulking General Ataman. Raschid went through the meeting preliminaries, accepted a proposal for a dredging project to open up the old harbour of Huddan, and then waved to catch Ataman's attention.

"May it please the council, but we had best hear the report of the military attaché before we proceed to further budget talks." Raschid motioned Ataman and the slim military attaché to take the floor. "May we have your report, General Ataman?"

The attaché made to speak, but Ataman flexed open his muscles gladly with an audible 'crack', and happily addressed the crowd.

"We have the regular army complete at last! In my absence, the buggers successfully completed an army-scale manoeuver – meaning the buggers apparently don't need me on the pay books at all!" Men laughed, and Ataman barked in laughter with them. "But here! My Shah! Honoured delegates! We now have two guard cavalry regiments and nine heavy regiments at full readiness. We have another two in training – southerners. We have six light cavalry regiments – two of them Hill-people riflemen mounted on Tora birds. There are two guard infantry regiments, twenty Royal infantry regiments, four light infantry regiments…The nomads in addition have three camel regiments. Oh – and there are those damned gunners! Four galloper battalions, four heavy battalions, and the siege train." The General gave a proud roar. "Sixty thousand men! We are clothed, armed, equipped and paid by the state! Never has the world seen such an army!"

A sharp-eyed woman from the Southern city of Jaliq sipped at coffee from a tiny cup.

"What of the new weapons?"

Ataman turned to the military adjutant. The slim little officer pulled spectacles out of the pocket of his long robes.

"Council – most revered Shah. The new rifles designed by the Shah are truly a miracle. But in all the world, only in Sath can we make the steel for these new guns. Manufacture has been slow" The little man produced a list. "The core field army has almost received its full compliment of breech loading rifles, as have the nomads. We have not yet supplied the border battalions with new firearms." The adjutant held his spectacles like a magnifying glass over the lists. "One of the heavy artillery batteries now has rifled cannon. The navy has taken precedence for artillery equipment – although we now beg the council to reconsider."

A sleek grey seal – one of the islanders from the inland sea – stood and raised a hand.

Raschid nodded to him to speak.

"My Shah. Council. It must be asked. Surely this army is a constant drain on the exchequer!" The seal-man paced the floor. "Why does a peaceful nation require an army?"

A delegate from the coal miners gave a hoot from the back of the hall.

"Because we wish to remain a peaceful nation!"

Delegates laughed. The seal shrank with embarrassment, but Raschid spread his hands and waved the laughter down. He answered the seal in all due seriousness.

"We have abandoned a feudal military system because we are a community of citizens, and not a collection of noble estates." Raschid folded his arms inside his robes. "As to why we need an army – We have been asked to give an audience to Hettman Koba of the Kakuzaks." The Shah bowed. "With your permission…?"

Two blue-armoured guards bowed and opened up the chamber doors. Three tall, limber men stood waiting – hares clad in long, dark coats, cylindrical fleece hats, and with sashes festooned with weapons. Cartridges were stored in rows across their breast pockets, and yet more cartridges were kept in waist belts and bandoleers. The wild riders looked as though they came ready for a hundred years of war.

The Kakuzaks were from the mountain country which bordered the desert and the northern steppes, and they were a people constantly at war. Their felt boots made little noise as they came forward, knelt and nodded their heads to the Shah. Raschid stood and came forward to greet their leader – a pure grey hare with eerie mismatched eyes.

"Salaam alaq, my friends."

"My Shah – Salaam alaq." The Kukuzaks were ferociously Christian. They still found it strange to be greeted as brothers by the Shah. "As you have bidden, we have come."

"I thank you, my friends." Raschid motioned for the men to stand and speak. "Tell us of the north."

The grey hare wore a long *shashka* – a sabre without a hand guard. He leaned upon it like a teacher leaning on a staff.

"To you of Osra, we give greetings." The hare's voice was rich and deep. "We are not of this council, although your Shah has asked us if we will join. We are not a part of Osra, nor of the steppes, nor of the desert lands. We are the mountain clans, and we call no man Lord." He held up a hand as if to still protest. "We say this with advisement. The Osranii Shah we call Comrade. Osra has long been our protector, and a haven for our men of war. The Osranii pay our young men to be soldiers, and give our old men comfort in honourable old age." The grey hare bowed solemnly to the Shah. "We guard the mountains that lead to the great rivers and the steppes. We guard the gateway to the West."

The man walked across the floor of the whispering hall. The floor had been inlaid with a map of the known world. At its center lay Osra, with all the other lands radiating outwards and beyond. The Kakuzak chieftain tapped the golden circle that was Sath, traced a path along the sea coast to the north, and thence tapped the mountains that were his home.

"Beyond here is the steppe, and here the great city states lie. To the far east – the Yellow Empire. To the West, the lands of Franks." He looked about the room. "They are a hostile people you may not know. They ride horses as big as houses, and dress themselves in steel."

Raschid nodded.

'We know them, Hetman.'

"Ah – good." The hare poked his sword at the dots that marked the great city states of the steppes.

"Kakuzaks make good money from the caravan trade between Osra and the East. We escort the caravans, and we have markets where the Franks and the Pulski come to trade. Our great churches have domes covered with leaves of gold, and the monastery at Kobekh has a thousand books! We are not an ignorant people." The Kakuzak looked about the room in challenge. "So it is not from ignorance that we tell you that a great storm is coming. Soon there will be a time of blood. Osra should summon its soldiers and join with the horde of Kakuzak. We must prepare for war."

Councilors started up. Men spoke in shock and anger, women buzzed with talk. Raschid rose and held up his hands for silence, suddenly regretting the missing Chamberlain.

"Silence! Silence – not all of us may speak!" He pointed a hand at the delegate from the mercantile district of Sath. "Delegate Haida?"

The merchant nodded to Raschid and addressed the Kakuzak in puzzlement.

"We do not understand! With whom will we war?"

The silver sheath of the shashka sword pointed at the great cities of the steppes.

"With the Tsu-Khan. The Lord of Ghosts."

The Kakuzak chieftain stood with one hand on his hip, posed magnificently in his coat and furs.

"You are men of the south, and you do not know the lands beyond our mountains well enough. The city states of the great steppes are mighty! Great plains of grass feed their herds, and deep springs water their people." He tapped at the symbols for the city states, one by one. "They are mighty, but one after another, all have fallen. All are now crushed by the Tsu-Khan."

One of the other Kakuzaks – this one in a wolf grey coat – joined his chief.

"The cities bow before him, or are destroyed. He has massacred all who stood before him. We are told that in cities he has severed the heads from every living being - men, women, children, horses, tora birds, sheep… He has made pyramids of their skulls to mark his butchery."

A tall Osranii nobleman – delegate for Hadul city and Minister for agriculture – opened his hands in total disbelief.

"Absurd! Why would a man conquer a city only to raze it? Dead men pay no taxes!"

The Kakuzak chieftain addressed himself regally to the Shah.

"He does this to spread terror in his name. When a man knows the penalty for resistance, he will hasten to surrender his freedom and his honour to the Khan."

"He claims to be holy. They treat him like a living god!" The grey-clad Kakuzak leaned forward.. "He was once nothing but a minor nobleman. Then he went into exile in the ice mountains. He returned with powers such as no man has ever seen!"

The third Kakuzak – a hare of a different tribe, his shoulders covered with a great square cornered cloak, hissed and made a sign with his right hand.

"He has no need for God or Satan. The Tsu-Khan is a god unto his people, and damnation to the world."

The council absorbed this news with the reserve due to reasonable men. Looking about the hall, the grey hare leaned upon his sword.

"Lord Shah, you wish to hear only facts. This, then, we know for certain. The Tsu-Khan's horde numbers perhaps three hundred thousand men. No caravans have come from the Yellow Empire for a year. This implies a war along the trade routes. But now the Tsu-Khan's men have disappeared from our borders. A man pulls back his outposts only to gather his strength for attack."

A Christian priest – delegate for Western Sath – spread his hands in wonder.

"But an attack where? On Osra?"

Raschid had already spoken to the men of Kakuzan. He had already spoken to Ataman and his generals. He walked forward slowly, throwing back his robes. Mail gleamed beneath his tunic. Raschid drew his yatagan and pointed down at the map.

"The steppes cross the north of the continent, bridging the vast gap between the Yellow Empire and the West." The sinuously curved blade of the old, battle-tested yatagan traced the barriers that lay between the steppes and the south.

"To attack Osra, he would have only two choices – to go through the great sand desert and die of thirst, or force through the Kakuzak mountains, with a musket behind every rock and an ambush in every pass. The Kakuzaks would slow any invader down to a halt, and the Osranii army would be able to advance and block the invasion routes."

Other delegates – noblemen long skilled in war leaned forward. One man pulled at his chin.

"Then it is not Osra he wants?"

Shah Raschid walked slowly across the map floor, west and north of the painted Kakuzak mountains. As he headed west, he tapped the shapes of the kingdoms of the Franks.

"Across the great northern river, we have Pulak – a land half Frank, half steppe nomad. Then the many kingdoms of the Franks. They are always at war with one another, and are wealthy." Raschid stood amongst the scattered kingdoms like a giant, his hands on his hips as he looked down at the world. "They are divided. They would be rich pickings, falling one by one."

A delegate looked uncomfortable, but shrugged.

"It is the Franks, then. What is that to us?"

Raschid walked across the sea that separated Osra from the Franks.

"With the west under this Khan's domination, he could turn south. He would have all the navies of the Franks at his command. Could we hold Kakuzan and our western coast at the same time? Or perhaps, God forbid, he turns and conquers the Yellow Empire? He could turn down into Meepsoor, and attack us from the south east." Raschid looked at the invasion routes in thought. "No – if this Khan is as terrible as we have heard, then all these thoughts shall already be inside his mind. If he is bent upon conquest, then he has marked Osra as an enemy."

A throat cleared itself loudly amongst the delegates. Raschid looked up, his tall figure framed against the shutters. He saw that one delegate had stood forth from the crowds.

The man was a tall, harshly muscled Cheetah, with a scarred face and opulent robes. He came from the estates north of Sath. He spoke loudly, in a gravelly voice that carried clear across the hall.

"The tales of this Khan's butchery have come to us third hand, oh Shah!"

The Kakuzaks growled and kept their hands near their weapons, but were deterred by the sight of the ever-watchful royal guard. The cheetah strode out into the middle of the hall.

"I must ask you a question, my Shah. Is it reasonable and just to condemn a man or a movement with their case unheard?"

Raschid motioned the Kakuzaks and guards to be calm.

"You are?"

"Emir Had'idh, my Lord."

"Then Emir Had'idh, know that a man of reason should condemn nothing out of hand. He approaches all problems through knowledge and insight."

The Cheetah bowed.

"My Shah, with your permission, I would like to bring a guest before the council."

Raschid weighed his thoughts, and then nodded to the guards. Once again the doors were opened – and this time, a slight, dapper little figure stood silhouetted in the sun.

"Ah! Thank you, my dear fellows – thank you." The newcomer made suave, snappy little bows to the guards, hugely amused by their watchful hostility. "Thank you indeed!"

The mouse had fur the colour of coffee-cream – subtle, plush and gleaming sleek as satin. His muzzle and his ears were darkened to a deeper hue, as rich and mellow as warm teak. He wore the felt boots of a steppe dweller, and a long coat of magnificently embroidered satin. The coat came from the Yellow Empire, and was smothered in images of dragons, carp and birds. He had kid gloves on his hands, a riding whip swinging from his wrist, and a slim, plain sabre that he handed to a guard. His face was slim and brim full of good will – lazily handsome, and filled with a sense that he had a hundred jokes bubbling away inside him still untold. The mouse undid his sword belt and draped it across one shoulder, then strode a few paces into the room. He bowed left and right to the royal council, and then knelt ritually before the Shah.

"Lord, my lord, my great lord! I am Prince Tulu Begh, commander of ten thousand and son of the Sultan of Tugukh! I bring you greetings from your royal cousin, the great Tsu-Khan of the steppes, leader of the peoples of the ocean of grass."

"Rise, Tulu Begh." Raschid stood before the mouse, his thumbs through his sash, looking down at the creature in calm reserve. "We are interested. What brings a Prince of the Steppes to Osra at such a time?"

"Politeness, and the joy of new birth, oh Shah!" The mouse sprang upright, spreading his arms wide. "We have been remiss!" The young man was open, friendly and beamed good cheer across the hall. "Our wars are over, and it is time to make all the proper overtures at last! The Steppes are a united kingdom at last, and as a kingdom, we extend greetings to our neighbours, who we hope will look kindly on us and extend a helping hand."

Raschid walked across the map of Aku Mashad.

"We have been discussing your Khan's hand." The Shah was a swordsman. It showed in the way he moved. "You have come far, Prince Tulu Begh. Was it merely to give us your king's greetings?"

Tulu Begh gave a smile as though he quite understood the diplomatic language of Shahs and Kings. "I cannot deceive you, Great Shah. My Khan is a very practical man, and he asked me to consult with you on practical arrangements. The steppe wars are over! Now there are trade routes to re establish, and bonds to rekindle. And, if you will forgive me, we have so much to lean about your world!" Prince Tulu genially interlaced his fingers. "But I am a simple man of the steppes. Perhaps I have broken etiquette? I have perhaps come at a bad time?"

Councilors stirred. Raschid felt a sly glow almost worthy of Sandhri.

"Your timing is quite perfect." He stood and pointed at the maps. "We were discussing the possible routes your Khan will use to invade Osra."

"An *invasion*, Great Shah?" The mouse prince looked wonderfully aghast. "Oh Shah, you must understand that we are a war weary people! Now that we have unity, we have nothing but a desire to live in peace."

"Logic rarely plays a founding role in war." Raschid looked down at the maps. "It is because only fools would risk death for so useless a thing as temporal power."

"Ah – there you find me in complete agreement, oh Shah." Tulu Begh gave a bow that brimmed full of peace, humour and satisfaction. "Our Khan is a holy man. A sacred saint! He, too, upholds the spiritual above the temporal. In this, perhaps, you would find yourselves to be kindred spirits."

"You have no idea how much it would please me, were it so." Raschid had a flat, metallic taste in his mouth. He believed in the inherent good of decent people – people given education, hope, respect and freedom. Reminders that the world contained far darker things left him with a bitter aftertaste.

He paced with his yatagan held behind his back like a walking stick. With a jerk of his chin, Raschid directed Prince Tulu's attention to the Kakuzak warriors.

"You are familiar, of course, with our old allies, the Kakuzaks. The 'guardians of the gate'?"

Tulu seemed delighted.

"We know them well, great Shah! The Kakuzaks are bandits! Heaven help any man who does not pay their protection money." He spoke utterly without rancor, as though pleased to find Kakuzak warriors at hand. "But bandits have the virtues of bravery, of cunning and great strength in adversity! We honour the Kakuzaks greatly as foes – and as inventors of fairy tales."

His last words were said with a warm, amused look – a challenging raise of one brow. The Kakuzaks crouched, battle ready, but refrained from attack. Raschid looked to his council, found Raas Yomah, and nodded to him slowly.

"We are connoisseurs of fairy tales. Indeed, we shall send you to where you can hear the very best." Raschid turned and signaled for his old companion, Colonel Abwan of the Guard. "Abwan, my friend – please convey Prince Tulu Begh to an apartment in the palace. Have Fatima see to his needs. Let him never, *ever* lack for companionship."

"Yes, My Shah." Abwan gave a satisfied smile. Tulu would be watched like a hawk! "I shall see to it myself."

"Good."

Prince Tulu bowed, threw his sword belt about his waist once more and left. He had a spring in his step, and a delighted air like a tourist. He bowed cheerfully here and there to members of the council, and happily departed the hall. Raschid came forward and had a quiet word to the Kakuzak warriors, who bowed to him and left to accept the palace's hospitality. He would give the men fine horses and fine guns in personal thanks.

After they had gone, the council hall remained strangely quiet, until a merchant delegate looked up at Raschid in evident relief.

"My Shah – there may be an opportunity here for a new friendship."

Some faces nodded. Others looked unsure. They looked to the Shah.

The tall, grave jackal stood gazing down at the map.

"General Ataman – send scout riders to investigate the Steppe cities. Look for evidence of massacres. Have your men speak to the local population and find out about this Khan. " He looked up and singled out the merchant delegates. "Gentlemen – find me traders who once did business with the East. Have they heard reports from the Steppes? What information can they provide ?"

A merchant bowed.

"It shall be done, Lord."

"Excellent. Let it be swift."

Men left to do the council's bidding. Raschid paced as the council members began to loudly debate the shocking news of the day. The jackal bowed his head in thought, oblivious to the noise.

He would set Sandhri to it: she would find traders, travelers, vagabonds and monks who would know whispers from the East. He would speak to young Meng once more, and see if the boy had heard of this Tsu-Khan.

…And he would ask the sorcerers why this Khan was called 'the Lord of Ghosts'…

The council adjourned until the morrow. Quiet and thoughtful, Raschid walked past Raas Yomah.

"My friend - find the old comrades. Ask everyone to meet me in my study after fourth prayer. General Ataman, too." Raschid looked up at the outside world as the shutters were unsealed.

"We have work to do."

Chapter Six:

Itbit knew what an Itbit knew. She sat upon a cannon that stood upon the palace's south wall, carving an apple with a little knife. She ate the crisp, fresh pieces with a great deal of gusto. Sitting on the walkway at her feet, Meng looked up at her, marveling at Itbit's wonderful, unstudied grace. Every line and curve was like a song – something gentle, lilting and wonderfully alive. With his heart in his mouth, the young panda spoke a gentle poem to the breeze.

> *"A lute plays softly*
> *The cadence perfect and precise.*
> *But she – she moves with artless grace.*
> *Peach blossoms drifting in the breeze ..."*

Itbit looked up gladly, a piece of apple speared on her knife.
"Is pretty poem, but it does not rhyme!"
"Not all poems rhyme." Meng sat straight backed, but his face was forlorn. Itbit was a girl of a far country, and a sage should never dwell on worldly things. But she moved with such wild, unconscious life that it almost made his soul sing. "A poem is a sequence of imagery designed to evoke an emotional response."
Itbit fed herself a piece of fruit, lounging back against the battlements. Her long hair spilled unconsciously downwards in a cascade of gold.
"It still does not rhyme." The mouse lifted a finger in an oratorical pose.

> *"Bright white whiskers, all a-twiddle.*
> *Cookies filling up her middle.*

Crafty eyes and tricksy ways
Hair like golden summer days."

Itbit eyed Meng. "Now that's a poem! See – it rhymes. Itbit's Raschid made up that one as we both rode on a camel. Marwan liked it, and he knowsies good poems!"

Meng frowned.

"Marwan – the previous Shah?"

"No no – Marwan the camel! He is very big, and a very wise camel. He walks through snow as easily as he walks through sand."

Itbit's tutor looked up at her, wide eyed. "You took a dromedary camel in the snow?"

"Ha! Silly bear man thinks Osra is all sandy-hot! But in hills and mountains is snow in winter time. Itbit made a snowman taller than a horse, and Sandhri made a wife for him that had three heads." Itbit hurtled an apple core towards the palace stables. "Sandhri, she made Itbit a story about it right then and there. Stories are what we do together."

Itbit knew what an Itbit knew – and she caught a strange, yearning flash in Meng's eye as he looked at her. Itbit sat a little straighter, obscurely pleased, and reached for another apple.

"Itbit has given you a poem that rhymes. Now Meng man should givsies her a poem that does not rhyme, and we see if rhyming is better." She cast a sly pink eye at the panda bear beside her. "Iss nothing you can think of as a poem?"

Feeling torn and unhappy, Meng looked away – out over the palace battlements. The river shone pure and clear, dotted with white sails. A pile of ruins in the shape of a huge beast stood beside the river mouth, and was overgrown with little flowers.

Meng closed his eyes.

"I heard love's voice ring out beside the stream.
Laughing, she stood with locks streaming in the breeze,
Far brighter than the ribbons trailing in her grasp.
Hand raised, I want nothing more than to speak.
- But she turns, laughing at another's words."

He spoke quietly, his voice the barest whisper on the wind. Meng bowed his shoulders and sighed, feeling torn and miserable.

Itbit quietly sat up and blinked. She looked at him and bit her lip, not quite able to understand…

"Itbit thinks maybe… Maybe your one was better."

The uncomfortable silence was broken by the soft sound of footsteps on the stairs. Arriving happily up upon the battlements came a slim, upright young man in yellow satin robes, wearing a steppe nomad's hat and carrying a sabre on his belt. Behind him strode two of Abwan's best men – officers of the Guard armed with pistols and well renowned for their diplomacy and accuracy.

Lazing away atop the cannon, Itbit waved a hand.

"Hello man."

The newcomer took on a look of reassured delight. He swept down in an elaborate, courtly bow.

"Each turn, each new vista in Osra brings a greater wonder than the last!" He bowed yet again. "A mere fancy, of course. Not all the jewels of Sultans could ever surpass this."

Surprised and pleased, Itbit stood. The stranger took her hand and kissed it in the manner of a Western courtier.

"I am Prince Tulu Begh – a rider of the Steppes here to raid Osra for its finest jewels." He smiled. "I had though rubies to be fine – but I never before beheld an emerald…"

Emerging from amongst the books and scrolls, Meng arose. He gave the newcomer a cautious bow.

"Great Prince, I am the Sage Tsau-yi Meng." He tucked the slim sword that jutted through his sash to a better angle. "I am this Lady's tutor."

"And what can be a greater gift from heaven, than to be commanded to keep such company!" Tulu reached quietly into his sleeve and produced a small sealed box of sandalwood. "My dear Lady Itbit – please accept this – a tiny treasure from my own domains."

Moving quickly, Meng intercepted the box.

"Lady Itbit thanks you." Meng stepped to keep himself between Itbit and the intruder. "Your gift is most appreciated."

"Ah – is it, indeed?" Tulu watched in languid amusement as Meng opened up the box. It contained a grease that shimmered a warm amber colour in the light. Tulu leaned in a little closer, like a conspirator, and whispered into Meng's furry ear. "It is a woman's perfume, dear boy. You might try it on, but I am afraid people in the palace might talk…"

Meng gave the man a glare.

"It is improprietal to touch hands with a lady not of one's own family, unless an understanding has been made." Meng passed the box to Itbit. He had never been so instructed, but he presumed that he was Itbit's body guard as much as he was her teacher. "I am here to teach my Lady Itbit the proprieties."

"Of course."

Itbit had opened the box, and she breathed in the subtle perfume, glorying in its smell. The scent was quiet, alluring and unutterably sensual. Her long whiskers quivered as she drank the odor in. Tulu gave a smile, bowed once more, and leaned back against the battlements.

The mouse's handsome face with its smoke-brown snout tilted towards Itbit. He gazed at Itbit with dark, delicious eyes.

"I may achieve no diplomatic triumphs upon this journey, but at least the trip has been worthwhile." He watched as Itbit cut fruit with her little knife. "Perhaps you might offer some fruit to the guards, my dear. It is a rather hot and sweltering day."

Tulu had handsome features, a languidly athletic build and a self-assured air that made Meng bristle. He tried to loom above the mice like a great scholar should, gazing down at lesser creatures from heavenly heights.

"Sir. I notice that you wear clothing of the Yellow Empire." Meng speared a glare at the intruder's yellow robes. "You are a man of the Bandit kingdoms?"

"The steppe cities." Tulu accepted fruit from Itbit thankfully. He held the piece of apple up in thought. "A prince and a jongleur, a singer and a poet! In effect, I am a citizen of the world."

"And a rider." Itbit cut apple with a deft twist of her knife, her eyes sly. "Itbit sees that reins have creased Tulu man's gloves. Boots be worn from stirrups. Itbit thinks you have ridden muchly far and muchly often, yes?" She pointed her knife at Tulu's plain, unadorned sword. "Itbit say – this be fighting blade, not blade for show. Tulu man rides with armies."

Prince Tulu made an arch of his brows, and then gave a theatrical bow. "I am revealed as an adventurer." He smiled. "But an adventurer at your service…"

Meng sniffed.

"Your robe is yellow, Sir. Perhaps you do not comprehend its significance." The Panda stood proudly erect. "Yellow is allowed only to the emperor."

"And it is the Emperor's own robe!" Tulu held it out for a pleased Itbit to inspect. "I snatched it from a caravan with my own two hands. They were bearing the emperor's concubines, his furniture and his wardrobe to the North so that he might spend a nice, cool summer." Tulu leaned on one elbow beside Itbit, who was extremely pleased. "I made off with his clothes, but alas, the concubines were far too nimble to be caught."

"Aaaaah." Itbit wriggled her long, fine toes. "Concubines can be that way."

"So I saw…"

Flushing beneath his fur, Meng squeezed his fists shut tight.

"Lady Itbit, perhaps we should continue with our lesson." He shot a dire look in the direction of Tulu Begh. "I am unsure that you should be in such proximity with foreign persons who are armed."

He ushered Itbit away. Tulu Begh gave an airy twirl of his hand.

"Never fear, dear sage – I have my tall blue shadows." Tulu gestured happily to the guards behind him. "The lady is quite safe."

Turning a glance over her shoulder, Itbit gave a sniff which set her whiskers all a quiver.

"Itbit can takie care of self."

Itbit threw her fruit knife. The blade flew and *thunked* into the gun carriage beside Tulu Begh. He turned a pleased eye towards the girl, never even sparing the knife a glance.

"But now you have no knife."

"Itbit was taught by Sandhri the storyteller." Itbit let a new knife slide from her sleeve. "Always keepsies one cheap shot hidden up your sleeve…"

She allowed herself to be led away, down the stairs towards the gardens. As she walked away, Itbit gave her tail a swish and her backside a saucy wiggle. She risked a glance behind herself to see if Tulu Begh had seen.

The handsome, honey-cream mouse was still lounging against the big brass cannon, with his eyes resting upon Itbit's every curve. She felt the admiration in those eyes, and Itbit felt herself flush bright red all out along her snout.

From the gardens down below there came an incessant grumbling. Walking painfully along the path, Sandhri let heaven and earth know all about her complaints. Long suffering and with their eyes rolled to plead to the powers above, Yariim and Fatima tried to help Sandhri make her way along the path. They received swatted hands and insults for their pains.

Exaggerating her limp, Sandhri irritably battled her way up slope towards the battlements. She felt smothered, pressured and much put upon. In a magnificent sulk, she tromped her way uphill, scattering the peaceful insects that were living in her path.

"Flex! Flex! All dancers ever think about is flex!" The bat held up one finger, proud as a goddess. "If you peoples iss all so keen to do the splits, t'en you do them! Let your betters spend their time in peace!"

Yariim rolled her eyes.

"Darling, we don't want you to do the splits. We're simply saying that some pelvic exercises…"

"My pelvis gets a pretty damned good workout effery evening, thank you much! And some lunchtimes – and some mornings, too!" Sandhri raised her brows and leaned closer to Yariim. "You off all people know that ass much as anybody."

"Quite." Yariim was not giving up. "I'm not joking, Sandhri. We're doing this pregnancy right. That means one hour of properly monitored exercise every day."

"My tits hurt, my dreams are ga ga, and now the smell of bacon makes me puke!" Sandhri jammed her hands in her pockets and grumbled. "I can't v'ait until v'e get your butt pregnant, too. T'en ve see how much you feel like exercise...!"

Quite agile, perfectly flexible, and not the least bit hurt, Sandhri took the steps up to the battlements like a champion. She was skinny as a snake, and up until this morning had been perfectly capable of climbing trees. Mounting the battlements, she saw Itbit and Meng standing together. Tulu Begh she managed to ignore.

"Hey you two! You study hard, ha?" The bat threw back her hair and worked her chops, looking about the battlements. "Does anyv'un haff anyth'ing salty?"

Everyone looked around. Straightening up, Tulu Begh opened the pouch that swung beside his sabre and retrieved a hard, salt dusted soldier's biscuit. He proffered it between two fingers. Sandhri took the biscuit, leaped up to sit upon the battlements, and perched with her backside high above the rooves of Sath.

She crunched the biscuit, heaving a sigh of relief. Her saliva glands had been running, and she had been just short of puking right over the palace walls.

"T'anks. The dry salt makes it better." The bat cast an all-knowing eye casually over Tulu Begh. "Steppe bandit?"

The diplomat gave one of his wonderful, sunny bows.

"To my mother's disappointment, Lady, I regret it is so."

"Pah!" Sandhri made a noise of friendly derision. She gestured with the biscuit to Tulu Begh, showering him with crumbs. "He's smooth!" She shot Tulu an arching glance. "Ambassador?"

"An Emissary, lady. An emissary for peace." Tulu gave a simple smile. "Why else should I be here?"

"V'y else?" Sandhri sat cross legged on the battlements. Yariim and Fatima sped to her side to take surreptitious grips upon her sash, lest she should fall. Sandhri gave a great yawn and ignored them.

"A long time ago, t'ere v'ass a great green slithery snail. That snail v'anted to be the biggest snail in all the v'orld. He knew that the only v'ay to grow so big v'ass to steal from people's gardens and eat t'em out off house and home." Sandhri tapped her biscuit with one finger, delicately dislodging crumbs. "But – the garden paths v'ere littered v'ith the shells of ot'er snails who had tried and been thoroughly trodden on. How to know v'ich gardens v'ere safe to enter?"

Sandhri leaned against a crenellation and looked at Tulu Begh.

"Aaah. But this snail v'ass clever! He crept to the very edge of the garden, and he pressed his head against the fence. And he strained, and he pushed, and he stared real hard – and slowly his eyes grew out on stalks!

"T'iss made things easier. So greedy sneaky slippery snail learned to always poke his eyes into a place to look for unguarded loot before he exposed himself to danger." Sandhri clicked her fingers. "Quite a clever snail!"

Tulu Begh looked at Sandhri in amusement. "But dear lady – whatever happened to the snail?"

"Oh, that!" Sandhri tossed back the half uneaten biscuit. "He forgot - Salt does not go v'ell with snails."

She leapt up and stretched – the very picture of lean health. The bat gave a great yawn, then reached out for Yariim.

"Hey blue butt! You v'ant exercise, then you two come on a camel ride. The beasts need a run."

Yariim rolled her eyes. "I have told you, I am learning Frankish."

"Frankish iss easy! Just keep your *ibids* before your *ipsums*, and you'll do fine!" The blue mouse took Sandhri's arm. "Since when did you speak Frankish?"

"I'm a storyteller! V'e know everyt'ing!"

They turned to leave. As they want, Yariim bent her head and beckoned Meng to lean down to speak with her. Yariim's glasses hid the sharp concern deep in her eyes.

"Sir Meng? A word. Itbit – pray let us speak."

They moved down the stairs, away from Tulu and his guards – away from listening soldiers and passing serving girls. Walking to the edge of the sorcerers' gardens, Yariim took Meng and Itbit, Sandhri and Fatima into the shade of an old green tree.

She took Itbit by the hands. It half surprised her that she no longer needed to bend down to murmur into Itbit's ear.

"My darling, we have a very important meeting to attend to." The beautiful blue mouse kept her eyes scanning for eavesdroppers. "Did you see that man – Tulu Begh?"

"Itbit saw." The young girl simpered. "He thinkie he be clever."

"Well then you be more clever. You be smart as only an Itbit can." Yariim kept a wary eye upon the battlements. "You keep a quiet eye on that man, Itbit. You do it so he never knows – and watch for all his tricks."

She straightened, saw Itbit's face so confident and sly, and stroked the back of her hand softly down Itbit's silken cheek. Yariim gave a quiet smile.

"When did you become so beautiful?"

"Itbit has always been beautiful. Now she is just big enough for jiggle-mouse to see!" Itbit swirled her tail and looked archly at the battlements. "Itbit watch Tulu-man. Never fraidie be!"

"Well, be my eyes, beautiful one, and be clever. Clever as only you can."

Sandhri was conferring in quiet with Fatima. She looked up, her thin face alarmingly innocent.

"But Itbit! You spend some time with Meng alone." Sandhri tilted her head to one side, weighing intuitions. "Do your lessons alone v'ith him, and make sure you get time alone just to v'alk and talk." She assumed a pious look. "It clears the mind."

Itbit blinked.

"No needies! Itbit's mind be clear!"

"Then clear it again." Sandhri shot one sharp, evaluating glare up onto the battlements towards Tulu Begh. "Iss afternoon prayer time now. V'e all meet up before dinner, and I v'ill do your hair."

Saud – vast, ever dependable Saud – loomed in the shadows, waiting to collect them. Sandhri kissed Itbit, handed a peach to Meng and put her arm through Yariim's. With Fatima beside them and Saud behind, the two queens moved on into the palace.

Yariim turned a glance back towards Itbit and Meng.

"What was that all about? Why do you want her spending time alone with that fellow Meng?"

"Because Sandhri knows v'at a Sandhri knows." The bat lifted a finger wisely. "I am hoping many lessons v'ill be learned."

They walked on. Above them on the battlements, Prince Tulu Begh, commander of ten thousand and emissary of the great Tsu-Khan, leaned on the wall and watched them go. His gaze lingered narrowly upon Sandhri and Yariim – then switched to watch Itbit walking gaily down a row of rose bushes side by side with Meng. The Prince stroked his whiskers thoughtfully, then drew back from the wall. He collected his two guards and went on about his guided tour of Osra's royal palace.

The Shah of Osra was a father to his people. The Shah of Osra believed that good blossomed only when freedom of conscience reigned. He had worshipped in the high Mosques of every Muslim sect within his kingdom. He had stood in synagogues as an honoured Gentile, and had attended the services of the Christians. But here in private, his beliefs were his own. He did what he so very rarely had done, and returned to his roots. Raschid al Dinaq, Shah of Osra, knelt on a plain white mat upon his own balcony. With Raas Yomah and Kors Jakoob beside him, he heard the Muezzin call from the minaret, and bowed his head in prayer.

Raschid knelt, then bowed to touch his muzzle to the floor. He sat up to look into his own open hands, and recited the old, old words. Words that seemed to come from another world, another time. High above the palace, the priest sang his words that drifted out across the rooftops of a quiet afternoon.

"*In the name of Allah, the just, the merciful.*

Blessed is he who takes comfort in Allah. Blessed is he who lives within the house of seven pillars. I have turned my face to Allah and I have been shown the way of righteousness..."

The Shah in his scholars robes – Raas Yomah in his nomad dress, and Kors Jakoob in his loincloth and vast shock of fuzzy hair: They prayed quietly together, and beside them lay their tea cups, pens and swords.

Sandhri entered the room quietly, for once treading carefully and keeping her silence. The Crucifix about her neck was silver, and the back was inscribed with the name of Saint Christobel - the patron saint of liars. Yariim came with her, and behind them were Fatima the house mistress and the huge, looming figure of her husband Saud. They stole softly across the room behind the praying men and filtered into the sitting room. Raas Yomah had been brewing tea, and Fatima fetched the iron teapot and filled it up with water from an urn.

The door whispered open again. Passing through the royal guards on duty just outside came old Abwan, followed by two infantrymen: Marsuk – a grey whiskered mouse with a patch across one eye, and Spike – a long, lean and dapper rat who carried an immaculate, curved sword. They were old companions and old, old friends. Sandhri flitted quietly over to hug them, and Spike rested his hand gladly upon her belly as they whispered of the child inside.

The hush was unnatural and strained. Everyone mouthed words of exaggerated thanks as the tea was poured. The clank of the teapot lid seemed hideously loud.

The final arrival whispered through the door – a fox woman with a long pointed nose, a great fluffy tail and luminously beautiful eyes. Her bracelets made a musical little noise as she sped tip-toe across the carpets and into Sandhri's arms. They made hushed noises of delight, the fox touching Sandhri's belly and then squeezing her tight. Sandhri held onto the fox for all that she was worth.

"Zhu! My Zhu!" Sandhri's whisper rang with life. "Zhu!"

They kissed. Zhu kept a marveling hand upon Sandhri's belly, excited beyond belief.

"I heard, I heard. When is he due?"

"Winter!" Sandhri was excited. Her eyes lit with fantasy. "Maybe on a storm-lit night v'ith snow flying in the sky!" She poked Zhu the fox in the rear. "How are your boys?"

"In school today. Their Father's on a voyage down south." Zhu's husband, BaBarad, was one of the most celebrated mariners in all of Osra. Zhu gave a sigh. "Who knows when he'll be back."

"He spends the time he's on ship longing for home, and the time he's home 'vondering about his next ship. Good t'ing his homecomings are v'orth looking forv'ard to!" Sandhri led Zhu down amongst her friends. "How's the theater?"

"Fantastic! I have two plays in performance. Fallahim's working on a musical with a bunch of Franks. Defrocked monks or something." Zhu's whisper was absurdly loud. "Fallahim said you should come down to the theater soon. He want to talk to you – something about Ibises!"

Raschid appeared, tall and quiet and solid in his pure white scholars' robes. He opened out his arms, and Sandhri and Yariim came to him. Sandhri's eyes were grey – as grey as a storm-lit sea. Yariim looked up at her husband, her face sharp and intelligent.

Raas Yomah and Kors Jakoob came from their prayers. The group of old companions sat together in a ring about the tea kettle and the stove. Old difficulties were long, long past. These were folk who had shared danger, battle, plot and adventure. The soldiers had faced war and sorcery. Fatima had lived through palace plots and revolution. The women had wits sharpened in the streets and alleyways of Sath.

They were all minds who could be relied upon.

The men carried swords. Sandhri wore her knife and had a pistol through her sash. Yariim carried an intricately painted silken fan. Fatima bore the palace keys. They were all the symbols of official business. Old friends met to debate the fate of a world.

Sandhri looked to her husband.

"You do not often pray."

"I never like to bother someone who must honestly be busy." Raschid sat with his friends without ceremony. "But we have prayed – and we have tea."

Raas Yomah's beautiful rich voice drifted through the room.

"We have prayed, because God may be willing us to war. If we are to be his instrument, then we shall obey with gratitude."

Raschid looked out over the steam rising from the old iron kettle.

"He breaketh the bow and cutteth the spear in sunder; he burneth the chariot in the fire.

...I shall be exalted amongst the heathen. I shall be exalted upon the earth. For the Lord of Hosts is with us."

It was from the psalms – quoted for Sandhri. Raschid looked to her, his eyes concerned – already seeing deeds his heart could not dwell upon.

He sought out Sandhri's wise grey eyes.

"Tell me, my Storyteller. Tell me of the Steppes."

Sandhri took tea from Fatima, and breathed in the steam.

"The steppes are *old*. Older even that Osra. Older than the Yellow Empire or the Franks." Sandhri's great pointed ears stood tall, and her gaze was far away. "Magic comes from there. The old magic – blood and spirits, howling storms."

Yariim listened carefully, as did all her companions. These were all people who had seen the evil of K'aath, and they did not take sorcery lightly.

Yariim leaned closer to Sandhri.

"There is black magic on the Steppes?"

"Oh yes." The bat still stared into blank air. "The best storyteller I ever met came from the steppes." Sandhri shook her head. "V'onderful tales! Of an mad v'itch who roamed about in a house that stood on chicken legs. Of a king whose head v'ass on backwards, and who rode backwards into war…"

"Suddenly the bat quietened.

"And other things. Things of v'ich even storytellers do not tell to any but t'ere own…" Raschid rubbed at his eyes.

"These tales of massacre. Are they merely more fairy tales?"

"No. Oh no." Sandhri slowly shook her head. "My love, I t'ink they are real because it iss not a tale any man v'ould bother to invent." She sipped absently at her tea. "To shock a man, you give him somet'ing he can grasp. A hundred people being massacred iss utterly believable. We can hold it in our minds. A t'ousand – perhaps so."

She sounded lost and hollow.

"…But hundred s of t'ousands? Pyramids of skulls reaching high into the sky? My agents haff met refugees who tell of oceans of the dead – children impaled on poles to line this Khan's processions." Sandhri shook her head. "It iss literally unbelievable. We reject it out of hand – V'ich iss v'y I think the tales are real. These are not things a storyteller invents to make a tale ring true."

Raschid gave a sigh, and reached for a vast roll of paper. He spread it out across the central carpet, revealing a giant map of all the world. Yariim brought forth a box of letters and documents, and placed it on the floor near to hand.

The group gathered, looking down at the map. Raschid knelt over the map, reaching awkwardly across the huge surface. Yariim perched glasses on her nose and read from her notes, helping Raschid place coloured pebbles all across the map. They consulted for a moment – shifted pebbles here and there, and then sat back to survey the results.

Osra sat at the world's hub. Above her lay the route from eastern world to west, across the massive steppes. Below her lay Meepsoor, and then the half-known jungles of the south. Shorelines of lands across the seas were penned in here and there – Zhu's husband and his men had just begun to touch upon a greater world.

In Osra, blue pebbles were gathered. More blue pebbles dotted the desert, Kakuzan and the allied state of Meepsoor. Red pebbles smothered the steppes. Yellow pebbles filled the Yellow empire. But to the west, where a dozen kingdoms fought their eternal wars, the pebbles marking out the Franks were a mad clutter of discordant colour. Black and white, orange, green and grey…

Raschid sat before the map. He reached out to point to the blue pebbles with his enchanted scimitar.

"Here is Osra. We have a regular army of sixty thousand. Nomads – five thousand. Kakuzaks, five thousand. Below us and to the south east, our brothers from Meepsoor. A hundred thousand troops, but mostly infantry levies. Good cavalry. Elephants. Some good heavy guns."

The scimitar moved away from the solid area of blue pebbles, and pointed to the west.

"Here are the Franks. We have good estimates from our intelligence. Overall, there must be a hundred thousand troops. But they are divided into twelve different kingdoms, perpetually at war. The black pebbles mark the Pulski – half Frankish, half nomad. D'Orran trading colonies with garrisons are dotted *here*, *here* and *here* in the inner sea."

The Shah gestured vaguely to the Yellow Empire. "Here we have the far east. These are estimates provided by traders, and by our good friend Sixteen-Volume Meng. Total military strength of the Yellow Empire is half a million – but only a hundred thousand troops are anything better than mere rabble. They are scattered into a vast geographical area. I have only marked those hundred thousand battle troops."

The yellow pebbles and the blue made solid power blocks. Raschid moved his sword to outline the red stones piled high upon the northern steppes.

"And here - the red. This is the army of the Tsu-Khan."

The red pebbles hung at the apex of the world. They far exceeded Osra and her allies in sheer number. They outnumbered all of the Franks together, or the Yellow Empire's troops. From their position straddling the three neighbouring zones of the world, the red pebbles were well placed to strike against whomever they pleased.

Raschid spoke to friends who leaned in carefully to look at the maps for themselves.

"For hundreds of years, the steppes have always been a jumble of little states and nomad hordes – a bramble patch most other nations have avoided. But a force has been at work here. Almost unnoticed, one commander has taken the steppe cities one by one. He now controls both the city states and the great Steppe hordes. Ten little nations have become one super state – a state devoted utterly to war." Raschid sat and mused upon the red pebbles piled on the map. "We estimate his army at a quarter of a million first class fighting men. Armoured cavalry trained in steppe warfare."

Kors Jakoob gripped his tea cup and leaned in towards the maps. He flipped his hand towards the pebbles.

"Nu! Are such numbers possible?" He looked up at Raschid. "Are they correct, my Shah?"

The jackal looked quietly at the map. "We may be under estimating. He may have as many as four hundred thousand men."

Raschid let his sword slide down to rest on the carpet beside him. Feeling tired and concerned, he pulled back the sleeves of his robe.

"The Tsu-Khan has just consolidated an empire. He clearly has a thirst for war – and a predilection for atrocity. He seems to see himself as a messiah." Raschid had laid aside his sword for a pen and parchment. "What will he do? What must we prepare for?"

The group of friends sat in silence.

Zhu leaned back in her sea, pondering. Yariim had steepled her fingers. The soldiers all leaned carefully forwards to inspect the map and all its pebbles. Cloaked beneath the pure white cascade of her hair, Sandhri sat like a frog, her sharp eyes flicking fast from city to city, pebble to pebble, running a hundred scenarios swiftly through her mind.

Marsuk – one eyed and grizzled, pulled at his whiskers with one hand.

"Mmmmph! Alright, then. Three possibilities! He takes on the Yellow Empire, and gets bogged down in a huge war in the East. Or, he turns south to hit Osra via Kakuzan. Or he invades the west and tries to conquer the Franks." The ex sergeant sniffed. "If it were me, I'd sit on what I had. The Yellow Empire won't conquer you, Osra can't hold terrain north of Kakuzan, and the Franks are too busy piking each other in the arse to bother with a new crusade into the east."

The two desert nomads had long, harsh experience of war. They conferred, their slim hands pointing at the pebbles.

Kors Jakoob chewed on a straw, his head tilted to one side, his hair standing like a vast pom pom all around his skull. He pointed to the pebbles with his straw.

"Yes, yes… This Khan will not attack Osra. The Franks are on his border, and they would snap up his outlying cities. They like loot, the Franks. Yes, yes…"

Captain Abwan scratched one of his lolling canine ears. "He might not care. If he likes massacre, losing a civilian population may not fuss him."

Yariim carefully stroked her chin. "But it is inefficient. It makes him look weak. This Khan vanquishes his enemies through fear." The blue mouse nodded. "Yes – that is why he uses massacres. Terror is his tool."

"Quite." Raschid creased his brows in thought. "If he attacks east into the Yellow empire, he risks a long war. Again, he leaves his south and western provinces open to attack by us or the Franks."

Fatima – pink and elegant, and with hard, calculating eyes, sat beside Saud, her husband.

"That means the west, then. If he was going to attack, he would head west. The Yellow empire does not expand out into the empty steppes, so his eastern border is safe. He can snap up those little Frankish kingdoms one by one."

"But would he?" Raschid tried to live in his opponent's mind. Impossible when one knew nothing about the man! "It would be a needless war! He might just sit there and enjoy making the steppes into a real kingdom at last."

Sandhri looked at him.

"You are too good a man sometimes."

The bat had no problem projecting herself into another mind. She saw herself as a warrior of the steppes, measuring wealth in horses, slave women and gold. All these things could be torn from other lands. Looking like a witch leaning over a potion, Sandhri cradled her tea.

"T'iss Khan has come from nothing to rule a vast empire. Hiss men follow him because he giffs them victory after victory – blood and yet more blood! He will keep on conquering, because he has never yet failed. In hiss mind, the v'orld iss already his for the taking!" The bat leaned forwards through the steam from her tea cup. "T'iss man iss a vampire that feeds on blood."

Sandhri thrived upon theatrics. Raschid scowled. In reply, the little storyteller jerked her chin towards the map.

"I'm telling you! Iss going to happen!" She looked across the room. "Saud! Hey, back me up. Think like a nomad king. You've just conquered a kingdom by right of sword. You haff warriors flushed with victory! You haff a few screws loose, and the cups in the cupboard don't quite add up!" The bat waved a hand over the map. "The whole v'orld's here at your feet. So v'at do?"

Rising to his feet, Saud lumbered up and down the edges of the map, staring down at all the pebbles. The vast tiger swept the carpets with his tail. Finally, he nodded his head, each thought coming with careful weight.

"Saud thinks this man is strong, and he feels powerful. He will fight something soon, so everyone remembers to know that he is strong." The tiger peered awkwardly down at the maps. "Bullies don't like even fights. Saud thinks this fellow, he might take little enemies first. Here." He prodded at the lands of the Franks with the tip of a sword that was big enough to split open an elephant. Pebbles cascaded from their piles. "Saud would attack here." He frowned. "What are these?"

Everyone leaned in to regard the map again. Raas Yomah smoothed the whiskers back from his face.

"The Queen and the Tiger speak sense."

"Sense? Off course v'ere talking sense! Saud and I, v'e're the brains of the outfit." Sandhri spoke with automatic patter, but her eyes were hard as she looked at the maps. "V'est. The hordes will go v'est."

Abwan looked at the huge rivers which crossed the steppes north to south, barring all route to the West.

"What of the great rivers? Some of these things are half a mile wide."

"They are steppe nomads. They do not fear the snow." Yariim looked over her sheaf of notes. "When the Khan invaded the city of Bulu, he waited until winter and rode cavalry across a frozen river and into the city docks."

Raschid sighed and leaned back against a wall, closing his eyes. He could see the snow covered wastelands in his minds eye.

"Winter. The big rivers protecting the west will freeze solid during the winter."

The Shah sat for a while. What to do? What was the moral thing to do? What guarded his people – but more so, what guarded the *right*? In the long term, was there a choice that somehow made the world a better place?

Yariim rested a hand upon Raschid's thigh.

"If the Khan attacks the west, then our own army can enter his lands behind him once he is past. We could destroy the Khan between the anvil of the Franks and the hammer of Osra."

"Yes." Raschid nodded. That was how it must be. "But will the Franks ally with Osra? Will they stand against the Khan?"

The blue mouse sat proud and strong at her husband's side. "We must lay the ground work. We must make it happen."

There was a quiet clearing of a throat. All eyes looked to Zhu, who nervously fluttered forwards.

"My... Raschid." She waved a vague hand at the map. "Why are we... well, why should we be concerned about a war between the Steppe dwellers, and the Franks? The Franks have been our foes for centuries?" She looked levelly at her Shah. "Why should Osranii blood be spilled to stop an invasion of the Franks?"

Raschid heaved a sigh. He had seen too much war.

"Because it is right."

He rose slowly to his feet, and walked to the lattice that shaded the balcony. He looked out into the palace, where young men sat beneath a tree taking their lessons from a muezzin and a Christian priest.

"Perhaps Osra will be in danger if this Khan conquers the West. Perhaps. But the reports we are receiving tell us that the Tsu-Khan has massacred hundreds of thousands. A people left to him means a people consigned to death and terror." Raschid looked out of the lattice work with a quiet intensity.

Raas Yomah drank tea.

"The steppe men might never conquer Osra. For we are men of The Book, and we are men of the pen, and Allah had shown us sciences to make us mighty." The nomad's slim face looked up at Raschid. "But I say to you, my companion – you have made a new Osra. It is as though the songs of old were true at last, and a promised age had come. Other lands may come to such an age as well – but not if they lie dead upon their hearths, or scream out their lives upon the Khan's impaling poles."

Raschid lifted his face towards the sun, the lattice making dappled shadows all across his fur. He remembered a time, long, long past, when he had spoken a holy sura to a dusty, tired beggar girl sitting in the street.

> *"By the noon day brightness, and by the nights when it darkens. Thy Lord has not forsaken thee, nor does he hate thee.*
>
> *The future shall be better than the past, and in the end the Lord shall be bounteous to thee.*
>
> *Did he not find thee as an orphan, and give thee a home?*
> *And find thee erring, and guided thee?*
> *And found thee weary, and enriched thee?*

So then- as to the orphan, wrong him not.
As to those that asketh of thee, send them not away.
And as for the great favours of thy Lord, share them forth to all in need. For thus is His work to be done."

Zhu looked at the map, lost and forlorn.

"But we have only sixty thousand men…"

"Sixty thousand *rifle* men." Marsuk swelled, half anticipating the fight to come. "We have a new way to wage war."

Sitting amidst the steam from his tea cup, Raas Yomah looked quietly at his friends.

"It is not for man to truly know the intent of God. But we may have been granted the right to be in this place, and at this time, to serve a greater world."

Raschid looked to Yariim. The blue mouse looked at the map, and nodded carefully.

"Mobilised, we become a player. Our mere presence may be enough to circumvent the war."

They all looked up to the Shah one by one. Raschid crossed to the door and opened it. Guards bowed. Waiting for him in the corridor was the huge, scarred, mail clad shape of General Ataman. Raschid nodded softly to the General and brought him to the map.

"General Ataman. You will issue a mobilisation order to the army." Raschid picked up his sword, held it balanced in his hand, then quietly fixed it through his belt. "Commence concentrating our field army. We will march to the mountains of Kakuzan."

The General bowed slowly and deeply. He rose, whirled about, and marched swiftly from the room. Vast as a storm front, the General swept into the palace corridors. His huge voice boomed through the halls.

"Guard! Turn out, you buggers! I want couriers, now! On horses with all four legs intact!" The General bellowed. *"Move, you buggers! We have a world at war!"*

Yariim held Raschid. Sandhri stood and came to them, and Raschid folded his women inside his robes.

"Our Children shall not know war."

Old friends stood and joined them as they turned to look out through the lattices. In the courtyard, the palace guard gathered about General Ataman. Other officers came, conferred, and aides marched swiftly to write orders and start the machinery of war.

Holding her husband and Yariim, Sandhri leaned her head against them both. She rested a hand upon her belly, and quietly closed her eyes in prayer.

Chapter Seven:

Evening spread moth-grey wings across the springtime sky. For four days, couriers had been swarming through the palace, taking orders to the scattered regiments of the army. Four days of generals, officers and quartermasters. Yariim was ink stained from correspondence, and Sandhri tired from talking to scouts and travelers. She did what she could – sent out her spies. All that could be done to help the kingdom was put into hand.

Sandhri lay bonelessly nude upon an old quilt. The quilt had been spread upon the flat roof of the western palace. Raschid was there beside her – Yariim lay with her head in Raschid's lap, looking at the stars.

A tired time. A quiet time, dazed with vague, unbidden thoughts. Sandhri lay on her side, protective of her belly, and stared out across the roof-gardens of Sath.

She spoke quietly, her voice weaving into the evening like a magic spell.

"In a far, far land, in a tower by the sea, t'ere lived a young sorcerer named Benjamin Ben-Zalu. His tower was white, with seven balconies, and it vass as old as old as hills. It stood on a limestone cliff beside a little village v'ere fishermen hung their nets out in the evenings to dry. The fisher girls were long and slim, with dark eyes and dazzling smiles. T'ey danced beside the fires on the beach at night, sending shadows chasing merrily all along the sands.

"Benjamin lived all alone. He vass a fine red fox v'ith a long, long tail. Tall and slim, he v'ass quiet and shy. He v'ass handsome, but he never spoke to the girls upon the beach. They thought him very different to t'emselves, and remained polite, but alv'ays distant from him.

"Benjamin studied magic. He tried and tried, but he found he could only do quite little things. But he persevered, because he believed that v'un day, if he neffer wavered, he

v'ould somehow become a great sorcerer and be a hero. He v'ould right many wrongs and make food for the needy. Then the people v'ould not find him so strange, and t'ey v'ould love him simply as he v'ass."

Sandhri lay with her head propped upon one hand, staring out into the quiet sky. It was as though she saw the story happening before her, and quietly passed on the tale.

"Behind Benjamin's tower, stretching off into a quiet land of wind and sands, t'ere v'ere ruins from an ancient time. Here, Benjamin liked to v'ander and explore. He v'ould uncover sculptures t'at lay quietly in the dust, or find walls covered with pictures that seemed so vividly alive. Sometimes he v'ould study his magic out t'ere in the ruins, v'ere all v'ass quiet, and the whole world seemed at peace.

"T'ere v'ere bones t'ere in the dust as well. The bones of all the people who v'unce had been inside the city. T'ey lay in tombs that seemed so peaceful and calm. V'en he v'ass troubled, Benjamin liked to sit down in the shade of the nice cool tombs, down amongst the grasses and wild flowers. He v'ould lie back in the cool and v'atch the sky – he v'ould sleep, and he v'ould dream."

It was quiet in the palace today. Guards paced the wall watchfully, and the people had not yet come to the palace lawns for the evening meal. The loudest noise was a pair of turtledoves nestling together in the trees.

Sandhri closed her eyes.

"He dreamed... He dreamed t'at he v'alked along beside a cool old sandstone wall somev'ere near the sea. He could feel the sand beneath his feet – could smell the tang of sea salt and sage upon the air. All seemed empty, and yet t'ere v'ass a hidden life always just out of sight around the corner. T'ere were no sounds but the v'ind, and yet unheard voices seemed to hover in the breeze.

"Benjamin came here time and time again, and each time the lands beside the dream wall seemed more vivid. In time, he walked further and further. Now at last there v'ere small shapes like birds flitting half unseen in the scrub. The sound of the ocean grew stronger. Benjamin came to a place where the wall sloped down towards a great, quiet sea shore – and here he looked around himself in v'onder.

"The wall grew lower here, and it headed out and dipped down into the sea. Clean white sand stretched off along the shore. T'ere v'ere distant things off to one side – perhaps a forest, and a hint of wood smoke in the air. But Benjamin v'ass most interested in the great stone wall. He could wade out into the ocean and swim over it, and see the far side of the v'all at last.

"As he walked into the water, a quiet voice came from behind.

"Traveler - You must not go that v'ay."

"Benjamin turned. There, on the sand dunes and facing out to sea, there sat a thin, quiet girl. She had glasses and long, fair hair, and her face was a fox's face, pointed and wise. She sat on the sand with her knees hugged against her chest, looking quiet, and perhaps a little sad.

"Benjamin looked at her.

"V'y? V'y should I not pass the v'all?"

"The girl never looked at him. She had eyes only for the sea.

"Because it iss the land of the dead."

"She stood, and seemed to somehow turn sideways. The girl disappeared like a piece of paper turned on edge. Benjamin awoke and found himself back in the v'aking v'orld. The sun had set, and the fisher girls v'ere dancing by their fires.

"All the next day, the image of the girl upon the beach haunted Benjamin. He paced, agitated, and could neither read nor eat. He ran into the tombs just after mid day, and lay restlessly on his back amongst the wildflowers, wishing for sleep. He lay awake for long, long hours, and finally he found himself wandering in his dreams. He walked beside the sandstone wall again, heading towards the distant sea.

"Benjamin hastened his footsteps. When he reached the ocean, it lay as before – empty and grey, yet somehow infinite. On the horizon it seemed as though there were islands. Even the clouds seemed to have a solidity all of their own. He looked carefully up and down the sand, but the girl with glasses was not there.

"Musing sadly, Benjamin walked along the water's edge. He saw shapes within the silk-grey waters – sinuous and lazy, curious and gentle. He heard a quiet whisper, and looked down at the sand between his feet.

"A silver shell lay there. Benjamin picked it up, and heard his own voice whispering from the shell. It was his own voice as a child, recounting a day spent playing in a tree with an old, old friend. Benjamin blinked and quietly held the shell in his hands.

"A soft female voice spoke beside him.

"It is the day you found the great almond tree. A tree filled with flowers." It was the girl with glasses, and she walked softly at Benjamin's side, her feet leaving footprints in the cool, wet sand. "The shell is memory. Here you find all sorts of things you have almost forgotten, and never knew quite where to find."

"She was slim and quiet. She looked a little like a girl Benjamin had pined for once when he was twelve. She looked a little like the big sister of an old, dear friend – a sister who had once bandaged his torn knee. But she had a strange life of her own – a haunted light in her green eyes. Her smell was sharp and feminine, rich with sandalwood and herbs.

"Benjamin looked at her.

"Who are you, lady? Why are you here?"

"I am here because this place needed me. I am here because I am…"

"V'ith that, she faded, and was gone.

"Another restless day passed for Benjamin in his tower. He watched the fishing boats without caring for their beauty. He ate food as though it were nothing more than wood and paper. This time he worked, and worked hard, tiring himself so that he v'ould sleep. He ran into the ruins, found his place beside the tombs, and settled down to sleep.

"Again he walked the wall. Again he found the beach. This time, she was standing there v'aiting for him to come. With the scent of her hair all around him and her skirt whipping in the breeze, she walked with him towards the forest far along the beach.

"He gazed about the sea and stood, watching the grey silk waves.

"What is this place?"

"This is the land of dreams." The girl's voice was quiet. "It borders on all lands – even the lands of the dead. It is the one place where all are free to come, and free to stay – though few people are ever strong enough to reach here. This is the ocean of stories at the shore of dreams. Out there lies everyplace that has ever been believed in – every image that has been given soul through love."

"They reached the end of the beach. A promontory stood above, and here there was a town of wooden houses swept by quiet winds. Flowers in flower boxes whipped in the breeze, and suddenly Benjamin seemed to be standing in a field of grass.

"Who are you, lady?"

"Waves rippled through the grass as the winds ebbed and flowed. The girl closed her eyes and put her nose into the breeze.

"Thiss iss the land of tales and dreams. Because you haff invented me, I am here.

Because you believe in me, I have being." The girl stood and looked back over one shoulder at Benjamin. The v'ind tossed t'rough her skirts and hair, making her look so thin and beautiful against the light. "You need neffer be afraid of being lonely. I am here, and pure dreams never fade."

"V'en Benjamin awoke, he had tears dried upon his face. He sat up amongst the tombs and stared into the predawn light for a long, long while..."

Yariim and Raschid sat quietly, listening. Each of them stroked a hand softly down Sandhri's spine. The bat hardly even moved.

"Benjamin spent each day studying as hard as he could. In the evenings, he lay down with the tombs and bones and dust, and slipped away into the land of dreams. The girl met him there, always with him but never touching him. She was a dream, and dream could never touch flesh. But she went with Benjamin as he entered the old wooden town and found a strange new world.

"The buildings were old but well loved. A spring grew beside the stream, and beside it were pure white berries. A stone beside the stream slowly stirred, and looked up at him with the face of a frog. It spoke quietly to Benjamin, telling him how to use the berries to cure the sick. Benjamin thanked the stone, and in another dream brought the stone new flowers for its stream.

"He found a great coral dragon skull in a cove beside the sea, and it told him how to cast spells of fire. In another place, he found a lizard made from living water that taught him how to conjure food and drink when he was hungry. All these spells he mastered, and took with him into the living world. To his astonishment, he found that he could make magic at long last.

"In the evenings, the girl was there waiting for him. The scent of her hair was pure and wonderful, and she now looked at him as he spoke to her. Her eyes were pools of perfect forest green, and the whole world seemed to catch its breath when she finally smiled.

"One evening, they sat side by side upon the shore. There was life here now; Benjamin could see it at last. The creatures in the water softly sang, and delicate little winged frogs flew in the dark.

"His heart aching, Benjamin turned to the girl.

"If you were alive, would you love me?"

"I am here, and I love you." She said. "You know I do."

"Benjamin sighed. "You love me because you are my dream, and in my dream I want to be loved. If you were real, you would have to decide whether you love me for myself."

"The girl looked at him sadly.

"Do you not believe you are worthy of love?"

"Benjamin could only gaze across the soft grey sea.

"I do not know..."

"The girl reached out for him gently, yearningly – unable to touch him.

"I am not a soul who has wandered over the wall, Benjamin. I have nothing of my own to give you – I can only give you what is yours."

"Benjamin awoke weeping again – but this time he awoke with a great resolve.

"He had brought many spells with him from his dreams. Benjamin put on the black robes of a sorcerer, and fashioned himself a staff of ebony. With a sword at his side, he followed the paths into the tombs, and there he moved quietly amongst the bones. He finally found what he knew would be there; the delicate skeleton of a female fox, so fine and perfect that it shone like silver in the sand. He carefully dug up the skeleton and carried it piece by piece into the tower by the sea.

"That night, Benjamin did not sleep. He made a bed of flowers, and wove spells taught to him by the rocks, the coral dragon, the water lizard and the forest of dream trees. He poured all his love into the skeleton, and he slowly gave it flesh. He made his dream girl a body, and it was as perfect as his dreams. Finally, exhausted, he carried her lifeless body out into the tombs. He lay her down amongst the weeds and flowers, and fell asleep with her cold flesh cradled in his arms.

"In the land of dreams, he found her. She looked at him with trepidation as he pulled forth a glowing ball of light. She drew back, but he placed the light inside her hands.

"This is yours now, and wholly yours. None may ever take it away." Benjamin looked at her in absolute, devoted love. "I give you half of my life. You have a life of your very own now. I beg you – come with me to the land of sun and stars. Awaken with me, and be my love forevermore…"

"The dream world faded. Benjamin awoke amongst the tombs and the flowers. The girl's body lay in his arms, cold and unmoving. He wept quietly and hopelessly, knowing he had failed.

"…V'en suddenly, subtly – the girl grew warm.

"She heaved in a great, shuddering breath! The girl's body arched upwards, clawing at the air. With eyes wide in wonder, she became alive in his grasp, panting with the wonder of being born.

"She looked up at Benjamin, weeping for joy. She took him and she kissed him with pure and yearning love. She called out his name, laughing and crying in ecstasy.

"They made love beneath the stars, then sat together, simply touching. She never tired of holding him, and he never tired of burying his face within her hair. They went up together into his tower with seven balconies. There they ate and danced, made love and sang. They dressed and walked hand in hand along the living beach while seagulls wheeled high in the summers air.

"Benjamin named her J'alae. He had divided his life in two to give her his gift, and so they had to move carefully. They tired when they walked too far, and yet it was so perfect to swim together in the ocean. They slept together, and found themselves walking together in the land of dreams.

"Happy and confident, Benjamin took J'alae down into the fishing village by his tower. Here they ate fish cooked fresh by the sea. In the evenings, J'alae joined the fisher girls in their dancing. Benjamin cast a spell to protect the boats when they went out to sea, and soon the fisher folk came to his tower with gifts of food."

Sandhri. lay on her side – naked, sleek and black as an eel. She gently held her Raschid's hand.

"But then, bad times came to the village. A war swept the land, and it brought with it many curses. The fields were burned- but Benjamin had learned in the land of dreams to cast a spell that summoned food, and so no one starved. A pestilence came, but the frog-stone had shown him how to cure disease. Throughout the war torn lands, word of the peaceful sorcerer began to spread. Refugees and the desolate, the victims and the needy came to live there beside the sea, and he did his best to care for them. He healed their sick and fed the hungry, and J'alae was always at his side.

"They grew tired so easily, but their joy knew no bounds. Although the times were hard, Benjamin and J'alae were happy. She loved him with a quiet passion that never slept. He adored her totally. The people of the sea village and all the refugees called them their lord and lady, and they remembered them always in their prayers.

"Then v'un day, word of the sorcerer spread too far.

"A bandit king – a great, ragged wolf – brought his men to the settlement by the sea. He had an army behind him, and blood was caked thick upon their horses hooves. With armour of steel and battered blades, they had come from the wars, now fighting purely for v'at they could take and steal. The settlement of refugees was a great, fat prize: the prettiest girls had flocked here for protection. The old and infirm would put up no fight. There v'ere hundreds of people that the wolf chief could enslave and sell. V'ith a hundred of his men behind him, the wolf chief spurred into the town.

"Benjamin saw them coming from one of his seven balconies. Tired after a day of making spells to heal the sick, he took up his black robe and his staff of ebony. He took his sword down from the wall and buckled it about his waist. He bid J'alae to hide in the ruins with the pretty girls, but she refused to go. She walked beside him as he marched off to confront the bandit chief.

"The Bandit chief was full of fleas. Pistols jutted from his belt. On his blood-stinking, mangy horse there hung silks looted from the bodies of butchered girls. He spurred through the village, scattering the refugees. His hundred men were more than a match for poor peasants who had lost their homes.

"When the Bandit chief saw Benjamin, he threw back his head and roared!

"So here is the gentle sorcerer! Here is the man who heals the sick!" The huge wolf brandished his blade. "I shall make my fortune once I have you in chains! I shall sell your services to kings!"

"Benjamin stood quietly in the center of the street, leaning on his staff.

"I am Benjamin Ben-Zalu, and I am privileged to care for all these people. Here, they are safe from your wars and all their curses – safe with the gifts I bring them from the land of dreams. Put aside your guns and swords, and enter here in peace, and you are welcome to share in all we have. Dreams have no wish to be the enemy of any man."

"When the bandit chief heard this, he gave a raucous laugh of scorn. He waved his sword and signaled his men to attack.

"Rape the women! Bind the men! And bring me the sorcerer so that he may be our slave!"

"Benjamin sighed and lowered his head. He did as the coral dragon had showed him, and brought forth flames. The fires burst upon the bandits, scattering them like chaff.

"As the horses reeled, the fishermen of the village raced forward with nets to capture the bandits. Other men brought brickbats and oars as clubs, while girls lined the rooftops throwing stones. The bandits were burned and blasted, snared and battered. They fled in terror, leaving half their number dead upon the sands.

"Exhausted, Benjamin ceased making his fire magics. He looked wearily at J'alae, giving her a watery smile.

"Behind him, the bandit wolf lay dying. With a curse, he dragged forth his pistol, and he fired.

"Benjamin fell, shot through the back. J'alae flung herself forward with a scream, catching him as he fell. Mortally v'ounded, the sorcerer could only lie in her arms and take her by the hands.

"My J'alae." He sighed. "I love you, J'alae. I thank you, for showing me how to bring the people dreams…"

"He closed his eyes and lay dying. J'alae looked about herself at the people of the village – young girls, appalled and weeping. Horror stricken old people, and the grieving young. She looked at them, and then turned to Benjamin, softly stroking his cheek.

"My Benjamin. You once gave me something of my very own. Something no one could *ever take from me. A chance to make a soul all of my own."*

"She let a tear run softly down her cheek.

"*You cannot leave yet, my love. To these people, you are strength and hope. To these people, you are life. With you to watch over them, they have a future – a chance to find dreams of their own."*

"J'alae closed her eyes, and softly kissed her love.

"*Benjamin. I give you back the life you gave."* She clenched her hands inside his fur. "*I give it to you in love…"*

"*Benjamin ached. His chest heaved, and a fire seemed to blaze in his breast. A pure blue ball of light seemed to glow inside him. He awakened, his wounds gone and his body healed.*

- *And all that lay now in his arms was a pile of dead, dry bones…"*

Yariim sat, ashen, a tear in her eye. Sandhri quietly took her by the hand.

"*Benjamin Ben-Zalu arose, and went about his work. He cared for his people, and he was their hope, their life, their strength. In time, he showed them how to bring to life dreams of their own.*

"*But in the evenings, when all was still, he would walk quietly to the old tombs and the gentle dust. He would lie amongst the flowers and watch the sky. Time after time he lay there, but dreams never came to his broken heart.*

"*… Until, one evening, he found himself walking in sand as fine as powder snow. The air carried a hint of sage and salt. Beside him ran a worn stone wall that seemed felt cool and rough against his passing hand.*

"*He walked along the length of the wall, towards the sound of sighing surf. There, beneath the endless skies, where the sea of dreams led out to countless distant isles, J'alae sat waiting for him. He had given her freedom, and she had dreamed a soul of her own. She sat upon the old stone wall that ran beside the land of death, watching for him, pulling the hair back from her eyes.*

"*Here, all things cherished lived forever. All things pure found their home.*

"*J'alae came to him. They could not touch, for he was not yet ready to leave the land of life and live across the wall. But she was there – and he was there – and both of them went together into the land of stories, tales and dreams, which borders every land.*

"*Talking quietly, they v'alked off along the beach to where old friends waited, and where the ocean rang forever with a thousand sighs…"*

The bat's tale came to an end. Raschid sat quietly. Yariim wept, turning her face away. Sandhri lifted up her head, saw her friends, and gave a watery smile.

"Hey. Iss supposed to be a happy tale. After all – t'ey are toget'er."

Yariim wiped her face, looking desolate.

"I love you."

"And I love you, my darlings." Sandhri heaved herself up, putting an arm around Raschid and Yariim. "Hey now. Hokay – was not a good choice of story for right now."

"No." Raschid put his arms about Sandhri and held her tight. "It was a good story. It was one of the best."

They sat together on a rooftop beneath an evening sky. Below them, outriders from new regiments arrived in the capital. Sandhri held her friends within her arms, covering them beneath the white cloak of her hair.

On a far roof, Meng lay with Itbit, staring up at the sky. The clouds hung in stutters up above, streaked like paint spread with a worn old pallet knife. With the day fading, the night was starting to emerge blue and clear in the sky. The first stars began to gleam past the fading light of day.

"There!"

Meng pointed a finger, directing Itbit's eyes to the highest part of the sky. A big blue star gleamed like a friendly, watching eye. "There, lady! That one is the planet Beru. See – it is blue, the colour of peace. And… just there, behind the cloud that looks like a rabbit? Those are Beru's sisters, Skurdu, and Urdu."

Quiet and thoughtful, Itbit lounged on the tiled roof of the library and looked up at the stars.

"Itbit has never heard these names before."

"Ah – in your language, the names are different. But I cannot find a book that tells me about stars."

Itbit felt… peaceful. It was a strange time for her. Part of her knew that something was ending, never to return. She savoured all those moments of peace and simplicity that she could find. The simplest times – the nicest times – were lounging about quietly with Meng.

She teased him, and she frustrated him: but part of Itbit realized that Meng always listened to whatever she had to say. Itbit bobbed her feet, wriggling her long toes. With her hands behind her head, she gazed up past the clouds.

"Most books on stars are not here at the library. They took them up to the observatory." Itbit waved a hand. "In mountains, up high over there. They be writing new books all about the stars now."

Meng's panda ears rose. Osra never ceased to enthrall him.

"They are re writing all the books?"

"Because of all the new starsies they find. And Raschid says everything goes around and around the sun now. The star watchers told him." The green mouse watched the planet Beru gleaming clean and sweet high up above. "We should go and see. The observatory has the biggest big telescope in the whole wide world! It is in the mountains, and Itbit helped make the lens. The glass was bigger than a horse is long, and round as a plate!"

Rising up onto one elbow, Meng looked at the girl in admiration.

"You all made this?"

"Raschid was visited by sailors and a scholar man. They told him they could see stars better with a big big telescope." Itbit lay on her side, smiling at Meng, her curves round and soft in the twilight. "Raschid, he listen carefully, and then he said he would take all the money he made from his own farm in the hills, and use it for the star watchers. So they bought bricks and tiles to makie buildings, and we bought lots and lots of glass! We went to watch when they poured it into the moulds. They got it wrong the first time, and we had to do it all over again!" The girl rolled and splayed on her back, arms flung wide. "To polish the lens, we usied river mud! All oozy-stinky mud! Itbit worked in the nude!"

Meng felt a most unscholarly pang of interest. He forced down the images that danced free and happy in his skull.

"Ah – the – ah – the nude." He nodded thoughtfully. "That was the most efficient way to do it, of course." He folded his hands as a quick means of keeping the damned things still. "So was it… just you doing the – the mud polishing?"

"No no! Lots of good friends. Jiggle friends! But was for girls only!" The mouse ticked people off on her fingers. "Sandhri and Yariim and Hanna, and Zhu and seven girls from dancies class. We polished all day long, for hours and hours." The girl's brow creased in a thoughtful scowl. "Very hard on Itbit's arms – and her bare bot bot became quite cold. But the mud made it very funny!"

Meng gave a cough. 'Yes! I can imagine."

"Aaaaaah…" Itbit made a knowing little noise. She looked left and right, then motioned Meng closer. She whispered into one of Meng's furry black ears.

"Is a magic mirror, because it had a special polish late at night. Sandhri, Yariim and Raschid, they sneak in and have happywriggles in mud on the lens."

The young sage raised his brows imperiously high.

"How would you know that?"

"Aaah, Itbit knows what an Itbit knows!" The girl slid a sly, knowing glance at Meng. "Nudie muds make lots of folk think all about happy wriggles…"

She sat up and stretched – her silhouette an alarming collection of boobs, back and bottom. Itbit flicked back her great, streaming ponytail, and looked up past the palace rooves, up towards the sky.

"And then we founded all the stars." The girl's voice was lost in the wonder of it all – quiet and alive with remembered joy. "Itbit saw the moon, with hills and valleys and great seas. There were starsies red and blue and gold… a planet as orange as a ball. All silent and so beautiful…"

The girl looked up into the night.

"We made it together, and we all touched the stars…"

Meng watched her, touched by her sense of awe. They sat together side by side, and the wind caressed their fur.

It was almost time for dinner on the lawns. Tonight, however, the usual festival atmosphere had faded. A regiment of infantry had left at dawn, marching onwards towards the north, and it had left an anxious cloud of sweethearts, wives and children behind. Itbit saw Sandhri far away across the lawns, tying her hair back and fumbling on an apron as she headed for the bread ovens. Itbit sighed and decided it was high time to help. She slapped Meng on the thigh and rose, hunting for the stairway back down to the lawns.

"Hey de ho. Itbit go help silly bat and mouse make dinner now. They be sad." She poised astride the tiles. "Coming now with Itbit?"

Sitting up to look at her, Meng felt an unhappy pang. He wanted to start up and follow the girl, but instead, he settled on the roof and clasped his hands together tight.

"I shall follow soon, Lady Itbit." The young scholar made himself pledge not to look at her standing there so achingly beautiful in the dark. Itbit's scent of mischief, grass stains and spice jabbed into his soul. "I… I will make a few star observations first."

"*Lady* Itbit!" The mouse stood a little taller, her teeth flashing. "Only you be saying that."

"You *are* a Lady, my Lady."

Itbit looked out towards the setting sun, her silhouette alive with yearning and joy.

"And Itbit will be royal, soon. Very soon now…"

She flitted off across the roof, her bare feet padding softly on the warm blue tiles. Itbit peered over the edge of the roof into the palace's parade ground. Out on the grounds, a dozen pieces of field artillery were ranged beside their ammunition cases and supplies. Gunners in dark robes were testing chains and straps, ready to limber up the guns and take them away to the north in the morning. Spying a darker shape lounging bonelessly beside a nearby fountain, clever Itbit sprang from the roof and sailed over to a tall poplar tree. She slithered down the tree trunk, quick and silent as a snake, and ended up behind the figure lazing at the fountain.

With two guards and a watchful servant girl beside him, Tulu Begh sat with his back against the fountain eating rosewater cookies. He was looking at the artillery pieces in idle interest, watching the gun crews at their work.

Itbit made her presence known.

"They be called cannons." Itbit posed with one hand on her hip, her silhouette an impudent shape against the stars. "Medium caliber rifled field cannon. Osra army men have lots of cannons."

Utterly unsurprised at Itbit's sudden arrival, Tulu Begh proffered her a cookie.

"They seem ridiculously small." Tulu Begh airily twittered his fingers. "The Khan has bombards that could fire those little pop guns as ammunition."

The mouse girl shrugged as if it were irrelevant. She sprang up and sat upon the side of the fountain, looking at Tulu Begh.

"Lots of regiments marching. Lots of things happening."

"Ah, the military." Prince Tulu Begh gave a despairing shake of his head. "I am a poet and a gentleman. I confess a great aversion to war."

Itbit shrugged, dismissing it all quite happily.

"No war! Khan will not attack west if Osra army men be just below. Like in Chess game – check!" Itbit seemed happy with the state of affairs. "No war, so all will have to be friends instead."

"Ah." Tulu Begh sat up, frankly admiring Itbit. He had a way of focusing his entire attention upon his guests. "All this grim fixation upon war." He gave a deep, unhappy sigh. "I do feel like such a failure. It appears I make an extremely poor diplomat."

"No! No no!" Itbit hastened to be a comfort. "You be very good! Not to be sad! Is other things. Lots of things happened. No fault to Tulu Begh!" The girl faltered, risking a look at the handsome diplomat.

"Itbit think you be a very splendid diplomat…"

Tulu Begh made a look of relieved gratitude which made Itbit's spirits soar.

"I thank you, my Lady. If I have made only one friend here in Osra, then my troubles have been worthwhile."

He moved, and his hand rested beside Itbit's own; she could feel the heat of him, making her fur stand on end. Itbit felt her heart give a strange little flutter. She stayed perfectly still, not wanting to scare Tulu Begh into moving away.

The diplomat's honey-crème fur gleamed in the evening light. His eyes were dark and sparked with life. He tilted his head and gazed at Itbit with a quiet smile.

"And so the days march onwards. You will be royal soon?"

Itbit blinked nervously. She looked down, trying not to blush.

"Soon. Itbit will be of age very very soon."

"Yes."

Tulu looked at Itbit, leaning closer so that he could drink in the soft scent of her fur. He gently reached up and traced the back of his fingers oh-so slowly down a strand of her golden hair.

"My sweet, wonderful Itbit." He let his hand stroke ever so gently at the edge of Itbit's cheek. "So much ahead of you. So much to learn…

Hypnotised, Itbit arched helplessly into the touch. Suddenly she stood up, jerked back two steps and stood staring at Tulu Begh, her hands clutching her breast and her breath ragged in her throat. She stared at him for a moment, then turned and fled away into the dark.

Pleased, Tulu Begh ate a last cookie. He stood, smiled for the savage looks shot at him by his two armed guards, and then headed off towards the palace lawns.

The Osranii commoners seemed quiet tonight. The usual barbeque beneath the colonnades was already underway. Noblemen stood in groups, talking with military officers, and a large number of uniforms were to be seen. Prince Tulu wandered happily about the tables, returning suspicious looks with bows and smiles. Fresh bread, barbequed lamb, sour orange and a green salad were the perfect compliment to a warm, fresh evening. Tulu Begh took his bread from an absurdly pretty, limber young Lemur girl, whose tail flourished behind her, threatening to spill frying sausages all over the ground. Her breasts had floury hand prints upon them. Tulu took his food with airy gratitude, and ambled off across the lawn.

His guards refused to eat or drink, keeping their hands near their weapons. Just to be annoying, Tulu sat so that the guards were downwind of the griddles heaped with frying meat.

He ate, nodding genially to Queen Sandhri, who for reasons best known to herself was making bread for the peasants. She nodded back to him, but not without flicking her sharp eyes to Tulu's armed guards – as well as to the rooftops. Tulu Begh had long suspected the Queen had arranged for a sniper to keep watch on him. She was good, but little signals gave her away. Tulu Begh bowed to her with a knowing, genial smile, and went back to his food.

The Osranii marched out their regiments before first light, addling Tulu's spies' attempts to count them accurately. Accurate numbers were unimportant. What mattered was the scale of effort: the main Osranii field army was on the move. Deciding that he really ought to end the day by having done some work, Tulu Begh washed his hands in a bowl, dried them with a towel, and then ambled forth to find a public privy.

He found one deeper in the palace, discretely hidden behind a string of fountains. He wandered into the privies and found a magnificent four-seater, complete with hand basins and perfumed towels.

The guards entered with him. Tulu Begh turned the men an apologetic eye.

"Would you mind awfully? I suffer from stage fright."

The huge soldiers cast an eye over the room, checking outside the windows and behind the doors. With a nod to one another, the guards departed, leaving Tulu Begh to his privacy.

With a happy sigh, the Prince took off his hat and sailed it over to a hook. He dragged his sword belt into position, took a seat, and then slid a hand mirror out of its sheath upon his belt.

He held the mirror up, pressed studs about its rim, and then gave a happy whistle. He tapped the surface of the mirror with one fingertip, peering into the mirror with a curious eye.

"My Lord Gurad? Have I caught you at a bad time?"

Mists swirled in the mirror. The view cleared, and finally revealed a view of open ground. Armoured, kneeling and in the dark, General Gurad's scarred feline face glowered forth.

"Tulu Begh."

"My dear General." Tulu Begh lounged back against the marble wall behind him. "I have caught you at a bad time?"

"It is time for the evening meal." Gurad's voice rumbled with scorn. "You do not eat at sunset, Prince Tulu?"

"Ah - I have been tied up with… affairs." Tulu Begh gave a smile. "In any case, the Osranii sunset was about thirty minutes ago. I'm sure the Shah here would welcome this as yet more evidence of the world being a sphere."

General Gurad was unamused. "They should take their scientists and poets and train them to be soldiers!" He sniffed in derision. "I told you about their ridiculous obsession with learning."

"Indeed, General. But you did manage to forget to tell me about the girls." Tulu kissed his fingers happily. "Magnificent! Here is sheer perfection! I believe they fit more curves under less clothing than anywhere else on Aku Mashad."

Tulu kept a weather eye upon the privy door, keeping his voice low enough to be masked by the sound of the fountains outside. He leaned closer to the mirror, his slim face suddenly hard and sly.

"I have explored the palace. The Osranii are a difficult proposition."

"We sent you to find answers!"

"Indeed you did." Tulu Begh gave a sigh. "You are itching to assassinate."

The Prince held the mirror out and looked the General in the eye.

"Very well. This, then, is my professional opinion. The Shah is beyond our ability to assassinate. The man is loved. No dagger strike or sword blow could land before an assassin was seized by the Shah's companions. Poison is useless – their sorcerers could neutralize any dose we might concoct. A sniper would be too unsure. He is never alone, and his wives are careful to ensure he is guarded at all times."

The General hissed in hatred, unhappy with the report.

"Look for councilors, then! If we can assassinate them and replace their souls with those of our own men, we will control the Osranii Shah."

"Osra's council is a parliament. It has about two hundred members." Tulu Begh made no pains to conceal his amusement. "Assassination on that kind of scale is sure to raise a smidgeon of pubic interest, don't you think?"

"The Queens, then!" Gurad leaned forward in anger. "We can slay the queens!"

"No being alive or dead could replace the senior queen." Tulu shook his head in amazement. "She never stops talking! When she isn't talking, she's eating, organizing other people's business or making mad passionate love." Tulu fanned himself with the mirror. "Makes me exhausted just to think about it!"

General Gurad gave a growl.

"What of the other one, then? The second wife?"

"She is fluent in five languages, organizes the royal library, and is an accomplished belly dancer. Not the easiest skill set to find amongst our faithful." Tulu Begh examined his perfectly manicured nails. "And since our replacement would also have to be a passionate bisexual skilled in ménage-a-trois, I think that narrows the field just a tad too far…"

The General gave a dangerous growl.

"You are telling me there is no solution, then?"

"My dear Gurad, of course there is a solution! After all, I am Tulu Begh!" The prince lounged happily against the wall. "No no – I believe I see a way to totally neutralize our dear Osra. This country has one crippling weakness – and they are too full of the milk of human kindness to see the danger."

"Shall I send you assassins?"

"No no, my dear general. This is a task better left to my own, long perfected talents." Tulu sat up. "We shall neutralize Osra by the time the Khan begins his campaign. You need fear no Osranii army to your south."

"Good." General Gurad breathed a long, slow breath of calculation. "Do your work, and you shall be rewarded, Tulu Begh."

"In this case, my dear general, the reward is all part of the work."

The Prince closed off the mirror and put it away. By the time his suspicious guards entered the room to check upon him, Tulu Begh was already at the hand basin, drying his fingertips.

One guard searched the room again, while the other grudgingly bowed to Tulu Begh.

"You are invited to take coffee in the Whispering Hall. Queen Yariim is going to dance."

"Is she indeed?" Tulu Begh moved with sudden enthusiasm. "Then come along. Let us not miss one peek, hint, swell or curve! And let us sit where we can see her special apprentices."

The steppe Prince swept happily out of the room. A last guard lingered, hunting suspiciously for signs of wrong doing, then shrugged and hurried on after Tulu Begh's elegant pink tail.

Chapter Eight:

Springtime yellowed into summer as time crept slowly past. In Osra, it was a time for crops to grow and grain to be harvested beneath a blazing sun. Troops in white uniforms and red turbans marched along dusty roads heading to the north. Artillery jounced along the roads, horses sweating and harnesses jingling. The great wheels of the gun carriages sent dust plumes drifting off across the fields. At the end of a morning's march, the troops would fling themselves down beside streams to drink and rest. Cavalrymen sweltered in mail armour as they stood watch on hillsides all around the marching regiments.

All in all, summertime was a vile season in which to go to war.

On the steppes, a vast army marched in one huge, churning mass. Imperial soldiers in the service of the Tsu-Khan walked the grasslands mile by mile, terrorized by the ghosts who hung keening and shrieking at the edges of their dreams. Disease and the savage discipline meted out by the Khan took their toll, and corpses littered the steppes in their wake – but sixty thousand men reached the steppe cities by high summer. There were pikemen and crossbowmen, swordsmen and artillery crews. They brought rockets, siege engines and great brass mortars designed to bring the cities of the Franks to heel. The Yellow Empire soldiers were terrorized by the Khan's officers – then broken, remolded and made complete. The dead walked among them, and every man amongst them had seen the Tsu-Khan's power.

In the lands of the Franks, Osranii ambassadors appeared. They came in quiet dignity, always with a Christian priest and a scholarly Imam. They spoke at great length to Burghers and to Regents, to Emperors and Kings, and then went on their weary way in disappointment.

In Sath, at the heart of Osra, old allies gathered – and a very special time drew slowly near.

****

Six months into her pregnancy, Sandhri looked like a stick insect that had swallowed a drum. Lean and sleek, she had stayed skinny – all except for her pregnant belly, which swelled as taut as a gourd. She spent a great deal of time in two-way conversations with her unborn child, telling him stories and sharing off coloured jokes. The Queen ate everything that was not nailed down – and pity help anyone who left food in an accessible place. Of an evening, she wallowed in the baths like a leviathan, hooting with laughter as Itbit decorated her belly as a floating island or a whale.

There was a gentle conspiracy afoot. Itbit was aware of it, but artfully pretended to know nothing. Sandhri and Yariim were at the heart of it, and were full of secret smiles. Raschid – always tired, and often touring the army encampments far in the North – would arrive on Marwan the camel, sweaty and smothered with dust. Itbit would streak out of the palace and fling herself into his arms, and he would hold her high and laugh with her.

In the evenings, when Yariim came in from organizing the army's administration, and when Raschid came back from the troops, they would all sit together. Sandhri, Raschid and Yariim would whisper smilingly together, watching Itbit covertly as the green mouse painted, wrote or sewed. They would see that she had noticed them, and beckon her to come. Itbit would nestle in amongst them lovingly, and all was well in the world.

For a few brief hours, there was simply the feel of *family*, and no worries about war.

In the Whispering Hall, working committees of the Royal Council were constantly in session. Parties orgaised new stocks of cloth and feather-down to make winter uniforms for the field army. Two new musket manufactories were slowly coming into being, but the special minerals that made gun-steel were still hard to come bye. Raschid felt a weary resentment at seeing talented people waste their time on the minutiae of war – but he was proud of the energy and dogged attention to detail which his elected council brought to bear.

Sandhri sat beside Raschid upon a cushion. She had a plate of chicken legs in black sauce, some sesame bread... and a few lamb cutlets just in case she became hungry later. Sitting with her pregnant belly jutting in her lap, she awkwardly read through some reports. Reading and writing now came naturally to her, but she far preferred the cut and thrust of the spoken word.

The girl took a hefty bite of chicken, and read through a letter that had been encoded in invisible ink. She read the lettering through a magic lens.

"Pah! Bugger!"

Sandhri set down the letter and gave a frown.

"We got two of theirs, but t'ey got v'un off ours. I've lost my spy in the Tsu-Khan's base camp." The Bat seethed with frustrated plans. "He v'ass just about to assemble a report on this guy's so called magic powers. How the hell did t'ey find him?"

Raschid looked down at his wife.

"How do you find *his* agents?"

"Because I'm a genius, and I set bitchy little traps." Sandhri waved the encoded letter. "I had t'eir pipeline all v'orked out. Passed messages to their spies and tagged their couriers

"– t'en replaced them v'ith our own." Sandhri made a frustrated noise, and decided to eat the cutlets. "Now v'e haff to start the whole damned thing over again!"

"Ah." Raschid was uncomfortably aware that his wife fought an unseen and particularly nasty little war all of her own. "So – we're doing well?"

"Iss stalemate." Sandhri passed her man a cutlet. "T'ey can't get messages out of Osra. But on ot'er hand, v'e get no information from the Steppes." She leafed through a pile of reports with one greasy hand. "Here v'e go, though. I have three families of refugees who claim that Yellow Empire soldiers are camped at the ruins of Hera. Here's another report that the Tsu-Khan can make the dead walk."

"Yellow Empire troops!" Raschid looked up from his own paperwork. "Are they sure? They mean troops dressed in Eastern style armour, yes? Many of the eastern steppe people wear that sort of clothing."

"I'm chust telling you v'at the report says! Yellow Empire soldiers." Sandhri held up the letter and grumbled. "And t'iss dickhead sends no estimate of numbers. I haff anot'er report saying sixty t'ousand pairs of shoes v'ere delivered north from the Surat depot a month ago. Maybe iss for these Yellow troops?"

"Sixty thousand…?" Raschid shook his head, weighing the numbers. "They *can't* be Imperial troops." He looked to his guards nearby. "Saud! Any sign of couriers from the Yellow Empire mission?"

"No, my Shah." Saud helpfully lashed his great hefty tiger-tail. "That Meng fellow now, he did say it was a very very long way."

"Yes." Raschid had no information from the east at all. He rose and looked up at his situation map. "Are there other couriers?"

"Three, sire. From the west."

"Show them in when they have eaten and drunk, please Saud. I shall be here for at least another hour."

A guard brought in more letters. Sighing, his back and shoulders sore, Raschid stood and read the message. He moved his lips, scowled, and then went wide eyed with joy.

"Ah! It's from the Ha'kuto Hanin king! They've sent us a ship load of *shuradh* ore." He let the letter fall in his hand, relieved. "God bless the Ha'kuto Hanin. Now we can make gun steel again!" He looked again at the letter. "He is sending two hundred of his royal guard to join our army."

"V'at they'll make of the Kakuzan mountains iss anybody's guess." Sandhri peered with interest at the letter. "Did they send me any more chilies?"

They had, but Raschid kept the news to himself. "Last time you ate chilies, you had gastric reflux for two days."

"That v'ass a minor accident." A flying squid cruised merrily in through a window. Sandhri caught the creature and fed it a morsel of food, to be rewarded by a great affectionate rub of the creature's head against her neck. "Hey squiddly did!"

The squid had a message in a capsule carried in its crop. The creatures were smart enough to make phenomenal homing pigeons – if a tad disturbing. Sandhri unrolled the message and read, then made a face.

"Crap. D'Orrians are trying to infiltrate the market v'ith spies again. Time to make a whole new coup back home to occupy t'eir time." The woman suddenly looked incredibly annoyed. "Damnit! I haff to pee again! T'iss iss ridiculous!"

Sandhri dealt with her secret correspondence by clapping it between two cutlets and eating it. She rose and collected the squid. "Here squiddly! You come v'ith me! And don't get ink on the tiles."

The first Queen of Osra kissed her husband and then waddled away. Raschid watched her go, then turned away as guards opened the doors to the hall. A weary Christian priest was ushered in through the door – a tall, lean bear with tar marks on his fur. Raschid collected his senior council men and swept towards the newcomer. Saud ambled helpfully over with ice water and the coffee pot.

The Priest sat and gratefully drank. He bore no good news – happy men did not hesitate to speak. Raschid raised a finger and summoned over an aide.

"Please see to Father Kuruban's traveling companions and his ship's crew. Please house them in the guest house and see to their comfort."

A councilman poured coffee carefully into little cups the size of thimbles.

"You seem weary, Father."

"I am weary, Councilor Emir Zocci." The priest took iced water first, drained the glass carefully, and then quietly took up his coffee. "Weary…"

"You bear news?"

"Of a sort." The priest sighed. He reached into his robes and withdrew three folded letters, each one sealed with wax. "The official words are here, my Shah, my Council. They are dressed however the Frankish kings saw fit. But Angevan, the Free Cantons and D'Orran have all refused to send troops into the East. They claim that the territory in question is nominally subject to the Pulski King, and that it is his privilege alone to defend it." The Priest gave a sour heft of his tiny cup. "However they phrase it, it boils down to this: The Great Frankish Kingdoms will not aid peoples that they perceive as being heretic foreigners."

The idea of a grand Frankish alliance, protecting the Frankish kingdoms from the Khan had died stillborn. There was no anvil to Osra's hammer. The tiny Pulski army, ferocious and flamboyant as it might be, would barely slow the horde and its quarter of a million men.

"It was not all bad news, my Shah. While on the north coast of the Frankish lands, we received a visit from a representative of a man called "The McCallum." He asked if it would be a good fight, and then asked for precise direction by sea to Sath." The Priest shrugged. "What it means is anybody's guess. When we asked other Franks about these people, they derided them as being homicidally insane, tone deaf and purveyors of strong drink."

Raschid carefully poured coffee, careful to keep his face controlled and calm. "Then they will apparently be a good match for the Pulski. We hear that their cavalry wear wings made of vulture feathers, and fear nothing but the falling of the sky."

"Colourful." The priest reached out for a hard cone of sugar, and rapped it with a little hammer to free more sugar chips for his coffee. "It would seem we are effectively alone."

A female councilor peered into a container of cookies – found it mysteriously empty, and pushed the container away. "Our army still acts as a deterrent. Unless this 'Tsu-Khan' is mad, he will accept the stalemate we have imposed." She took a double helping of sugar for her coffee. "Our new army is not dependent on feudal service. We can maintain it indefinitely in the field."

"Expensively in the field." A second councilor grumbled. "Raising new regiments is cutting deep into the public purse."

The Shah quietly set his coffee cup aside.

"We have enjoyed a golden childhood, councilor. But now there is work to do." He looked across the hall to where royal orphans could be seen playing just outside of the windows. "Think for a moment on just how many of *them* would survive the Tsu-Khan's reign, and you will cease worrying about mere coins."

With a heave and crack of joints, Raschid stood. He swept his robes into some sort of order, and found his sword.

"Thank you, Father, for all your long months of effort. It has not been a waste. Perhaps wheels are turning that we cannot see." A rumble of cannon fire came from somewhere in the distance – a common sound these days, with units training hard at their weapons. "I thank you all for your efforts, and your talent. Please join us here tonight for the evening meal."

Raschid coldly marched the palace corridors, accompanied by Saud and shadowed by four of Sandhri's sharp shooters. Saud the Tiger's huge presence was always strangely comforting. Raschid waited until he reached a private garden before he let his fury fly. He slammed a fist against a cherry tree, startling the squids perching in the branches.

"Damn!"

Bastards! Not one Frankish kingdom was willing to put aside its hate and make a stand! Not one!

"Idiots! Fools!"

"You're no good at swearing. Let me do it!" Sandhri was kneeling beneath another tree, happily seeing carrier-squids into a cage. "Goddamned soft cock Franks! May they be buggered by passing circus freaks until their hemorrhoids flail out off t'eir arses like a pair of hellish tentacles!"

The Shah gave a tired smile.

"You're really very good at that."

"Eh. Iss a talent!" She would have bowed, but pregnancy prevented it. Instead, Sandhri blew out a breath and looked up at her husband. "The final ambassador to the Franks came back?"

"He's back." Raschid sat wearily on the rim of an old stone seat. "And none of them will help."

"I told you so!"

"How did you know?"

"Hey – I haff ears in every port. Big ears, too!" The bat twitched her huge, tall ears. "Don't despair. T'iss v'ill not be a thing of nations. T'iss iss for people and belief."

The Shah leaned forward onto his elbows. He felt tired and worn.

"Belief." Raschid sighed. "Our belief has made a whole new age of technology and tools. I trust the tools, and I trust the hearts behind them – but I would have liked some show of faith from the people we intend to help!" The Jackal wiped his hands over his face. "Bastards! They wouldn't send us even a single man! I don't know why I bother to agonise over their fate!"

"And t'ere v'e haff the differences between us, my darling. Sometimes I t'ink I am not a very good person deep down. There iss a big part of me that says 'v'y not let the bastards burn!' But I know *you* v'ill neffer let them down." Sandhri quietly took her husband's face between her hands. For once in her life, she was serious. "Right now, the v'orld needs you. V'e need your faith, and your purity."

Taking Sandhri's hand, Raschid looked up at her, tired and embarrassed.

"Purity?"

"You believe in better possibilities." Sandhri held his hand against her face and looked up at him with her fathomless grey eyes. The little market place storyteller was still there to see. "It iss v'y I love you."

They rested their heads together, forehead to forehead, muzzle to muzzle, and sat for a while in silence. The leaves of the cherry tree whispered in the breeze, while flying squid crept through the branches to peer curiously down from up on high.

Sandhri gave a sudden smile. She grabbed Raschid's hand and put it quickly down upon her middle.

"T'ere! Did you feel that? Raschid concentrated, his hand pressed against the taut swell of Sandhri's belly. Suddenly he felt a shift and heave inside her – a press of something small pushing back against his hand. He concentrated on the moment with all his heart, thrilling to every little quiver he could feel.

"He's rolling!"

"He does that. He still hasn't settled down." Sandhri gave an indulgent, annoyed sigh. "I bet he's going to be breech."

"Breech?" Raschid was alarmed. "Isn't that dangerous?"

"All cantankerous types are breech. I sure v'ass!" Sandhri sat back and gave her belly a poke. "No need to v'orry! A good sorcerer-midv'ife can take care of it. Iss not like t'ere v'on't be any help at hand." She rapped Raschid's skull. "Touch wood."

They smiled together, both of them keeping hidden the one unspoken thought. It would be three months until the child was born – right in the heart of winter.

- When the Tsu-Khan's men would begin their attack.

Raschid looked to the north. Sandhri quietly held his hand.

"You must go to the north soon. To the army. You v'ill haff to be t'ere by v'inter." She nodded slowly. "Yariim and I v'ill stay here. V'e can keep things running v'ile you do your v'ork."

He did not want to leave her pregnant and alone. He did not want to drag her into the cold mountains in the winter when she was in danger of labour. Sandhri saw it all inside him. She gripped Raschid's wrist and kept his hand held against her face.

"T'ere iss no distance between us. T'ere iss no parting, and no emptiness." Sandhri held her husband tightly "Remember. Beside the wall, upon the beach – I am alv'ays there…

"V'e need you. And I am mature enough to let you do your v'ork – and get on v'ith mine."

She stood awkwardly up, and took Raschid by the hand. One of the new palace clocks boomed out its bell, and it told of new appointments and new jobs to do. The guards cavalry brigade had maneuvers scheduled in the afternoon, and Raschid had to be in armour, mounted and in command.

Husband and wife, Sandhri and Raschid: They walked along into the palace, surrounded by Raschid's ever-watchful guards. Sandhri gave a sigh and yanked her Jackal by the tail.

"Never to v'orry, silly jackal. Hey – v'e haff Itbit's birthday in a week. Her special surprise."

Raschid's tall ears rose comfortably as he smiled.

"It's all arranged. You don't mind?"

"I t'ink it's *v'onderful*." Sandhri hugged her husband's arm. "I'm the last v'un to v'orry any more about precedence."

"Well, finally we can give her something that will be hers forever."

"Yes." Sandhri drew in a breath, happily straightening her back. "Family."

They walked on together into the palace halls, while somewhere in the distance, cannon rumbled in the autumn heat.

Osranii armour blended plates and mail in a symphony of art. Mounted on a dust-coloured horse, a figure in sleek armour that shone royal blue cantered along behind a battery of artillery. The whole world rumbled to the sound of cart wheels and harness chains as the cannon jounced and clattered across the dusty fields.

"Halt! Action left! Deploy!"

The formation wheeled to the left in one perfect arc. Cannon slewed around as the heavy horse teams brought their weapons to bear. Gunners leapt from their horses, uncoupled cannon from their limbers and raced to unship buckets, rammers and ammunition. The carriage teams of horses were raced back behind the guns, kicking up vast clouds of dust that swirled chokingly in the humid air.

'Target – five hundred yards!"

The armoured figure sat on its horse behind the battery, beating time with a painted silk fan. Artillery officers sat on their horses behind the guns, calling orders to the troops.

"Three rounds, rapid fire!"

The fastest crews were already on line. Long solid shells were already rammed home into the muzzle-loading guns. Men skipped aside, the gun layers gave a last squint over the gun sights, and lanyards were smartly pulled. The first gun bucked madly backwards, belching smoke. Its missile could be seen streaking hard and fast down across the plains.

Eight guns fired in rapid succession, each one slamming backwards with recoil. Solid shot kicked up lines of dust across the plains. The target – a square of old sacking stretched over a wooden frame – rocked from near misses, and then finally took a hole punched through its middle. Seconds later, another shot hit the frame, and wood flew into the air. An officer turned in excitement to the armoured rider at his side.

"Two minutes! We must have scored a hit in under two minutes!"

"Two minutes and ten seconds." Yariim's armour clanked as she moved. She counted the cadence with precise little beats of her fan. "We are still trying to beat five minutes for three rounds."

It was virtually impossible: Only the guard artillery ever reached such prodigious speed. But the second Queen of Osra – Queen Yariim herself! - had been with the battery every day as it trained. They felt themselves special, and worked with dogged speed. The last string of shots stuttered out. Yariim deliberately miscounted, tapped her fan an instant after the last gun fired, and threw up her hands in glee.

"Five! Five minutes exactly!"

Dusty, powder burned and sweating, the crews leapt about and cheered. The cannon muzzles leaked smoke like scheming dragons as the men slapped their weapons on the breech. Officers came spurring over to Yariim, keen to be praised. Yariim pulled the silk veil from her face and took her helmet off, shaking her sweat-stained hair free.

"Well done! Well done everyone. We made it at last!"

They were militia – part time enthusiasts who were keen to help by going full time into the army. The artillery regiment was made up of fishermen, shopkeepers, market boys and office workers from the streets of Sath, and officered by merchants and old soldiers. Their Lieutenant Colonel was a great, hefty badger with a muzzle streaked entirely grey, his mouth hidden beneath a fantastically elaborate moustache. He preened openly, puffing like a peacock as his Queen spurred her horse over to his side.

"Colonel!"

"They did it! All those years serving the fortress guns, y' see? They don't fear the bang. Not like all these young fellas today. Too many people fear a healthy bang!" He caught himself and blustered. "Savin' your august presence, Majesty."

"I can be quite fond of a bang." Yariim gave a slight smile. She looked about the clouds of dust and smoke to where the men all looked towards her. "Beautifully done! I want you all to dinner in the palace grounds tonight. We'll take you up to see the Shah!"

Men cheered and slapped each other on the back. One gunner surged towards Yariim, nervously stopped, and was urged forward by a dozen of his friends. The man bobbed in a bow, then bobbed again and made his best salaam.

"Majesty! We wanted to ask! I mean – now that we broke the five minute record and all…" The man looked about for support, then looked up at Yariim and blurted out his message all in one stumbling gasp. "Majesty! We ask permission to take the title of 'Queen Yariim's Own Artillery.'" He bobbed again, and then blanched. "Please!"

Yariim laughed aloud. An ex-slavegirl and a professional dancer knew damned little about cannon. She had joined the boys mostly as a morale exercise for the enthusiastic militia. She waved her fan at the men as they laughed with her, and she stood in her stirrups – her breasts making an impressive swell beneath her mail armour.

"I'm told I make a good figurehead!" Yariim laughed with the men. "I'll ask! The Shah will say yes. Does that make me an honourary Colonel?"

"Yes, oh Queen." The Lieutenant Colonel puffed out his chest. "If the Shah agrees."

"He'll agree." It would be a good exercise in morale building. "And I'll send you sashes. Blue sashes! You're a royal regiment now!"

They cheered her as she caracoled her horse. Waving happily, Yariim trotted along the ranks of gunners, then spurred into a faster canter. Leaving the men behind. She cantered over to the trees shading the eastern edge of the field, where a single lonely figure waited for her, books in hand. Tail high, her horse whickered as it recognized a stable mate. Yariim reignedin and wiped the dust out of her eyes. She gave a pleased wave to the ever-anxious Meng.

"Five minutes! Did you see that? From full gallop to three rounds in five minutes!"

"Prodigious, my lady." Meng had no idea how swiftly cannon were supposed to fire. The ones he had seen at home were as big as a house, took sixty oxen to move them, and fired stone balls the size of cattle. He had a vague impression that he was seeing something entirely new here, and was missing the point. "I am sure they are very fine, Majesty."

Yariim hung her helmet from her saddle bow. The damned helmet weighed a ton, and gave her a headache if she wore it for too long, but the men seemed to like it. Part of the job of being royalty was being seen, and men going into battle liked the idea of a warrior Queen. Once upon a time, Sandhri would have done the job, but she was forbidden to ride now. Yariim had taken on the task with a certain amount of trepidation, and now suddenly found that she enjoyed it.

She rode well. The discovery pleased her. Raschid had taught her patiently, and now the results finally showed. Absurdly pleased with the afternoon, Yariim rode side by side with Meng and looked him up and down.

"Meng! You ride very well."

"I was raised in a noble family, Majesty." He tapped the slim sword that hung always at his belt. "It had its obligations and its burdens." Meng looked about at the soldiers far behind them. "Do you ride frequently with Queen Sandhri?"

"Sandhri doesn't ride horses. No one rides horses near Sandhri."

"Ah." Meng nodded, not understanding. "I see."

"She's a camel girl. – with occasional outbreaks of elephant." The blue mouse gave a laugh as pure as morning dew, her golden hair flashing in the breeze. "You should see her steer an elephant! God help you if you don't get out of the way!"

The lanky panda looked once again at the artillerymen, then cleared his throat – a sure sign he was about to chastise his betters. Yariim gave a smile and flicked her pink gaze sideways.

"Yes, my friend Meng?"

"About granting this group of soldiers this title they desire, Majesty." Meng looked at the mouse. "Is it a benevolent act, Majesty, to sway the hearts of men with the lure of Pride?"

The queen kept her eyes on the road, riding straight backed beneath the autumn trees.

"It is benevolent, Meng, if it creates good and causes no evil. If pride makes them get in one vital extra shot when it counts, then it has all been effort well spent."

"Ah." Meng sounded disappointed. "That point of view is… utilitarian."

"Do not dismiss the useful just because it seems obvious, my friend. A reality turned to good use is surely a boon?"

Not conceding the point, but willing to let it lie, Meng gave a sigh. Yariim looked at him and nodded quietly.

"You are correct to bring forth your point of view, friend Meng. Never fear."

"This unworthy one thanks you, your Majesty."

They rode a while beneath the dappled shadows of the trees. The city of Sath spread out before them like a magnificent dream, her blue tiled walls gleaming in the sun. Great ships were cruising up the river delta, their sails billowing tight in the afternoon sea breeze. Yariim drew her horse to a halt beneath a sycamore tree and gazed out across the view, looking at the tranquility and the beauty of her home.

The city shone white and wonderful beneath the summer sun. Palm trees threw shadow down into the streets, and the river shimmered with glints and ripples as far as the eye could see. The pyramids hovered, half lost in the haze. Summer was dwindling; autumn brought its promise of rain and brand new life….

Beautiful.

Yariim gazed quietly at the city for a long, long time. When she spoke, her voice was low and quiet.

"It is beautiful, isn't it, Meng. We have been building such a dream here. I so wanted you to see and feel the things that we have done…"

The young scholar looked at the city, and indeed it was beautiful. It was like a place out of a waking dream – beautiful and full of joy. Meng thought of all his long, weary journey to this oasis, and gave a rueful sigh.

"You have laboured well, your Majesty." He shook his head in self-depreciation. " For my part, this humble one has achieved so very little. I have yet to teach the Shah anything of Benevolence or Propriety."

"You must read your Lao-Zu, my friend." Yariim stopped to brush a rogue strand of hair from Meng's eyes. Her smile was warm and infinitely wonderful.

"When hearts are pure, all responses are spontaneous. When hearts lose their way, responses are dictated by guidelines of imposed morality and propriety." She held the back of Meng's hand and squeezed. "You should be easy in your heart, Meng. As Sandhri would say – 'Put the feets up, haff a sausage and relax."

The scholar fretted unhappily.

"Then why? Why am I here?"

"You are here because you needed to be here. There were things you could find only amongst us." Yariim twitched her heels and rode on. "We are happy to be of use. You are a *light*, Meng. We must give you a chance to shine."

The young man rode beside Yariim, fretting uncomfortably with his reins.

"I am useless to you. Today, only skill at war has any real utility."

The Queen gave a snort. "I shall tell you a secret about war, Meng. God favours the smart. And here in Osra, we are very quick with our wits indeed." She took on a hard look – half predatory, half proud. "The world has never seen how heart and science fight as one. The Khan will regret the day he cast covetous eyes at Osra." A carbine hung from her saddle alongside her unaccustomed sword. "Twelve aimed rounds a minute, Meng. *That* is insurance worth banking dreams upon."

Sitting on a green-dyed pony far away down the road, Itbit stood in her stirrups and called out something happily as she saw Meng and Yariim. The blue mouse waved, and Itbit turned her pony and raced towards them at breakneck speed. With her hair flying and her body poised against the horse, the green mouse looked utterly breathtaking. She screeched her horse to a halt in a shower of stones, flinging herself into Yariim's arms.

The green mouse was utterly alive – vibrantly feminine, full of energy. She kept her hands caught avidly in Yariim's fur.

"One day to go! One day – then Itbit will be a woman!" Itbit puffed out breasts that went far beyond being merely impressive. "No more little Itbit! Hello It-mouse titmouse! Big girl Itbit at long last!"

She was so excited she was almost bursting from her skin. Yariim laughed and kissed her, surprised at the avid response. Itbit spun her pony and punched Meng on the shoulder.

"Hey Meng! Itbit be birthday girl tomorrow!"

"I have been preparing you a gift." Meng bowed – and his painful, hidden infatuation made Yariim's heart ache to see. "I do so want you to be happy, my Lady."

"Happy Itbit will be!" She rode around and around Yariim. "Itbit will make you proud! She will be the bestest partner ever there was! We be four together!"

There were yet more riders on the road. Armoured horsemen with bows and sabers at their belts. The leader clattered to a halt, his horse's chain mail armour tinkling like a thousand tiny bells. The man made a grave *salaam* to Yariim.

"Majesty. We thought perhaps to escort you on the road back to the palace?"

Haduh Had'idh, Emir of the second order, bowed toward Yariim. The long, lean, feral Cheetah made his ritual obeisance and kept his eyes low. "It is not fitting that a Queen of Osra ride without full escort. With your permission, we shall ride with you on your way."

It was a well-meant request, but Yariim sighed. One of the irksome things about life these days was that times in hand-picked company were limited. Yariim kicked her heels into her horse and brought herself level with the nobleman.

"Thank you, Emir. You are kind to think of me."

"My Queen, you are on our thoughts both night and day." Emir Had'idh waved his hand, and his men fell in behind the Queen. "We are always happy to be of service to the crown."

The group rode onwards happily. On a tower of the palace, happy as can be, Tulu Begh watched them through his telescope, and broke into a smile. He was still smiling as he turned to his two guards, indicating that he was done with walking on the battlements. With a peach in one hand and whistling happily, the Prince descended down into the palace.

…There to wait for the adventures that tomorrow was about to bring…

Chapter Nine:

"Ten thousand years! Ten thousand years! Blood and steel, ten thousand years!"

Heavy male voices thundered in unison a hundred thousand strong. The sound struck city walls like a thunder blast, making birds start up in their thousands from the trees. Drawn up in ranks across a muddy plain, division after division of the steppe-lord's army bellowed homage to the great Tsu-Khan. Big armoured men on armoured horses pumped their lances up towards the heavens, their voices booming in a rhythm that numbed the mind and soul.

"Ten thousand, ten thousand, ten thousand years! Ten thousand years reign to the Khan!"

He rode before them on a pale horse – a small arctic fox, slight and straight-backed. His dead blue eyes looked upon the troops, each man feeling singled out for divine scrutiny. Ghosts flew beside him, and bones rattled from his horse's harness. The Khan's own battle armour was sheathed in fine finger bones ripped from the living hands of princes, generals and kings.

One hundred thousand men. One hundred thousand horses. An ocean of flesh, leather, iron and steel. A tidal wave with which to smash a world. The ranks of soldiers went on and on, stretching across the plains. Their banners were tall poles hung with the flayed skins of the wives and daughters of their enemies.

Total silence fell. The men fell silent, and only the steppe winds still sang and moaned above the plains. The Tsu-Khan drew his horse to a halt, turning to face the army. A moaning, skeletal ghost swirled past him, sniffing avidly for the scent of fresh-spilled blood.

He faced the army and gazed upon it. Rank after rank of men, all of them given to the way of blood and steel. All of them murderers, executioners and soldiers – all of them caught up in the great, all-powerful vision of their Khan. They had no conscience except that which he allowed them – no mercy, no weakness, no idleness, no fear. He would take these men, and he would stab them into the shrieking heart of the world, bursting forth an ocean of blood. The blood would drown a world in terror, leaving nothing behind it except obedience to the great Khan's will. The Tsu-Khan closed his eyes, feeling the spirits of a hundred thousand men pulse like water flowing through his soul.

There were other souls trapped within the Tsu-Khan's power. He had imprisoned ghosts in their tens of thousands, holding them adrift inside an ocean of pure pain. Torture, suffering and madness ripped at them, tearing minds to ribbons and leaving nothing but a ravening intensity of hate and pain. It was a tool that could be used to shatter empires.

Aku-Mashad: the sub world. The lesser shadow of creation. The Tsu-Khan would complete the task he had been held from long, long ago. He would crush this world beneath his heel, draining it of power. The under beings would become slaves to his undying might. With real power in his hands, he would turn to conquer the lost world of Earth. All of creation would be enslaved to him; all of creation would kneel in abject worship before the Khan…

He gazed upon his followers, and saw the total obedience in their eyes. He let power from the stolen ghosts trickle forth into his men, and they swayed as pure pleasure, pure fulfillment suddenly flooded through their souls.

"It is good…"

General Gurad was beside him, as was his duty. The officers of the divisions – each one a commander of ten thousand, were ranked kneeling on the ground, their sword belts thrown across their shoulders in homage. The men each held their war horses by the reins, and the animals stamped and tore the muddy ground with their hooves.

Mud. Storm clouds gathered overhead, and soon it would rain. The steppes would be swept with cold and water, and the freezing time would come. In two short months, the great ice would come to the lands of the north. Rivers would freeze, and the way into the heartlands of the west would lie open and exposed like a sleeping virgin beneath the Tsu-Khan's blade.

It was good. The Tsu-Khan's soft voice drifted out into the breeze.

"General Gurad – your warriors are worthy."

The General bowed. His officers bowed. They made the motions with absolute reverence – with total dedication. The very presence of the Khan was like water to a thirsting man – like air to the drowning, like life to the dying. All around him, men felt their strength increased a hundred fold as the great holy one drew near.

General Gurad kept his eyes upon the ground as he made his report.

"Our second army is concentrated on the Osranii border. One hundred and fifty thousand men. The Yellow Empire troops are encamped in the ruins of Hadat." The old wolf flexed his fingers, craving Osranii blood. "We have made great hunts. All animal flesh from the western steppes has been harvested, dried and stored. The army has iron rations to last ninety days of campaign."

"And beast fodder?"

Gurad gave a nod.

"The granaries of the city states have all been seized, Holy One. The farms have been ransacked for hay. We have stored all the fodder at the city of Urut, and we shall be supplied by caravan."

"Excellent." The Khan left mere details in the hands of worthy subordinates; a living god had other things to occupy their minds. Your men are properly prepared, General."

The Khan looked the warriors over, scanning slowly along the lines like a man taking in an elemental vision of the mountains. "We are pleased."

The Khan made a sign, and men brought forward the horses of the ten commanders. The animals grew nervous, rolling white eyes and edging back as the Tsu-Khan slid onto the ground.

He reached into the unseen gate, and *pulled*…

They fought him, but the Tsu-Khan was mighty. He found the spirits he desired, red raw with hate and rage. He tore them from the unseen world, and brought them raging and howling into Aku-Mashad.

Ten chosen spirits – elemental beings that had transcended the weakness of mere mortal souls. The Khan hurtled the spirits into the ten war horses, and the spirits screamed in lust as they plunged into the animal's hot, sweet flesh.

There was a jerk of pain. The horses stood stock still, paralyzed, and then suddenly their torment began.

The horses reared and screamed in agony, blood flying from their mouths. Red foam jetted from their nostrils. The animals fell, kicking and tearing at the ground, their hooves flailing wildly in the air. Men leapt clear of the maelstrom, watching cautiously as horses and spirits warred for possession of the flesh.

A horse jerked upright. It stared across the mud fields, then surged up onto its feet. The black hide shivered, running white with sweat. Dragging air into its lungs, the beast looked about itself, then reared and gave a cry of raw animal rage. With eyes now glowing a stark, blank blue, the horse stood, huge and cunning, its lips still drooling ropes of blood.

The other horses joined it one by one. The Tsu-Khan waved a hand, and each horse moved to find its master.

"To my officers, I grant tireless hooves." The Khan turned his ice-blue eyes upon his commanders. "I grant mounts with lust for war and lust for blood. I grant you power of horse."

The men bowed to the Khan, fangs gleaming in their snouts. The demon horses were a priceless gift. The officers sprang into their saddles and raced off to parade before their men, and the soldiers bellowed in approval as the demon horses reared and screamed.

As the accolade swelled and surged, the Tsu-Khan remounted. He stirred his horse forward and turned to General Gurad.

"What is the status of General Tsai-Chi's southern army?"

General Gurad swiveled his head to the south. His lamellar armour rattled as it moved.

"Tsai-Chi has one hundred and fifty thousand men placed ready to block the Osranii invasion route through the passes. We could strip that force to only thirty thousand, if we accept their role to be delaying tactics in case of invasion."

The Khan joined his General in looking to the south. "Thirty thousand men would not halt the Osranii. They are our most dangerous foe."

"Yes, Sacred Person."

"Dangerous…" The Khan's voice trailed softly into the rain-swept breeze. "The Osranii embody something that must be crushed, Gurad. They must be… purified."

"Yes, Holy One!" Gurad thirsted for the moment. "Will it be soon?"

"Patience, Gurad. Build upon the rock, not upon the sand."

"My Lord?"

"A Christian parable first told in another world..." The Tsu-Khan brushed the tips of his fingers as if scattering an influence that was unclean. "It means that the great endeavors should only be launched when a solid foundation is at hand."

The empty blue gaze turned upon Gurad.

"Is our man ready, Gurad?"

"He is, Holy Person." The General looked to the south. "The third day of the third month of the third season."

"It is good, Gurad." The Tsu-Khan's armor rattled softly as wind passed through the layer of dead, dry finger bones. "Your man's plan is excellent. We need only a single season's grace. Three months of inability and hesitation."

"He is clever, Holy One."

The Khan was surrounded by the faint wisps of moaning ghosts. "We embrace cleverness, Gurad. We embrace it as long as it bears us results."

"His assessment was absolutely precise, Holy Person."

A cold wind blew. Rain could be seen slanting downwards through the skies somewhere off across the steppes. The Khan looked to the storm clouds, and tilted his head quietly to one side.

"The rains come. Soon the steppes will be cold. In the north, the great snow will soon begin."

The Khan twitched his reins. His horse – blue eyed and moving with a serpentine grace – turned towards the city. With a vast army fanned out behind him and storm clouds in the sky, the Khan looked to the north – to the west, and felt dead spirits fly.

"Just one season, Gurad. One season, and we shall own it all."

He rode towards the city, and his horse's hoof-falls echoed in the wind. With a deep indraw of breath, General Gurad straightened. He looked West towards the rich lands of the Franks – then south towards the promised blood bath of Osra. With a glad shout of lust, he stabbed his heels into his mount and rode to join his officers and men.

***

The third day of the third month of the third season! As dawn came, Itbit scrunched up inside her blankets, a vast ball of gladness swelling up inside her heart. Her fuzzy fur seemed to tingle, and the whole world seemed wonderful, warm and new. Waking slowly in the dawn, Itbit clung to sleep, reaching out with her ears to hear the birth of a whole new life.

It was dawn in the palace. Little birds flocked twittering beneath the palace eaves, and a fine rain fell across the rooves of Sath. The rain made a gentle wash of sound, and brought with it a sharp, clean smell. The dust of summer had long faded, and green grass grew in all the fields. The Great River Amu Daja swelled as countless streams ran sparkling from the hills. In the skies above, birds wheeled in great shimmering flocks, migrating southwards from the icy lands of the Franks to winter in the gentle fields of Osra. Farmers had their second planting of crops well underway. The barns were full, the temperatures were down. Autumn was Itbit's favourite time of the year.

But best of all was the third day of the third month. Itbit's birthday.

Her Birthday! The thought brought Itbit beaming out of bed. She sat up, naked and warm, the sheets smelling beautifully of warm, round girl. With green fur fluffed out and her tail stretching out its kinks, Itbit looked around her room in simple utter joy.

Today was the day!

Naked and happy, Itbit leapt up out of bed. Her room was a dear, sweet place, scattered with the countless little treasures that made it home. There were dice and cards, pet uki birds and cuddly stuffed sea serpents – silks and patterns, needles and thread, half made dresses and comfortable clothes. Itbit had thieved her favourite books out of the library – including a picture book from Meepsoor she had gone to great length to study page by page – because tonight was the night – and Itbit had to know what an Itbit had to know.

Her room! This had been her last night alone inside her own room. From now on, it would be the marriage suite of the Shah himself. Itbit would keep this room as her private hideaway; the tree outside the window gave rapid access to every important point in the whole world – the stables, the kitchens, the library and the baths. It was too good a room to give away.

But tonight – she would be in a very big bed, in a very big room. Itbit shivered with delight, and felt a now familiar squeeze and tingle of anticipation underneath her tail. Tonight she would be a woman at long, long last.

Tonight, Itbit would be a lover.

She thought about pages seventeen and eighteen of her picture book. Then about pages twenty and twenty eight. An unbidden image of page fifty two came into mind...

Sugar. Mistress Fatima had confided some secrets once late at night. You needed lots of energy, a dash of sweet oil – and pace yourself.

Pace yourself. So – Itbit would be calm, be passionate, and pace herself. And in case that didn't work, she had laid in a jumbo sized bottle of *chezbah* and three straws...

Itbit felt like she was going to burst out of her skin. Full of jitters, she flitted abut her room, jiggling, naked and absurdly happy. What she needed was cold, clean air! She ran across the room and flung open her windows, flinging them wide-open to the dawn.

A figure in the tree right outside her window stared at her in shock. Only two feet away from Itbit's naked breasts, Meng goggled at the girl. Itbit stared in shock, then gave a squeal of fright.

"Eeeeeeeee!"

Meng half fell out of the tree, catching himself upside down by his knees. He flailed madly about, a book flapping in his hand. Guards came racing across the garden, rifles flicking up to take sight on the scholar hanging helpless in the tree. Meng gave a hasty squawk of panic.

"It's alright! It's only me! It's only me!"

"It's only him! Iss fine!" Waving to the guards, Itbit grabbed the boy's flailing hand and hauled him up towards the window. "You silly Pandie-bear! You could have been shot by guards! Itbit be an important lady!"

She was cross, her chest was puffed out in excited disapproval – and she was still naked. Dragged awkwardly across the windowsill into the room, Meng ended up with his face crammed into Itbit's breasts. He froze, lost in a wealth of softness, then swallowed and looked up at Itbit's disbelieving face. The girl scowled magnificently down at him, then hit him right between the eyes.

"Itbit's tits be not your bits!"

Meng saw stars and crawled about upon the floor. He ended up lost in a pile of Itbit's underwear. He unconsciously used a pair of panties as a pad to soothe his poor aching head.

"I am innocent! My lady – I was merely.... Merely climbing a tree!"

Shrouded in a length of curtain, Itbit expressively raised one brow.

"You have been climbing trees to perve at Itbit's bits!"

"No no! I swear!" Meng waved the panties in his hand as he protested his pure innocence. "My lady – such a thing would never cross my mind!"

Stiffening - and incidentally jutting out her breasts – Itbit gave a displeased little sniff.

"Why not? Does Itbit not have beautiful bits?"

"Exquisite!" Meng's voice dripped misery and yearning. "I mean – to those who… who would be so improprietal as to think upon it." Meng mopped at his face with the panties, then suddenly recognized the silky little garment and threw it away. *"Wah!"*

"Leave Itbit's undie-pants alone!" The girl jerked the curtain tight about herself, making the most toothsome bits of her bulge out from the restraint. "You looked! You camie up tree to peekies through windows!"

"No no – I swear." Kneeling, Meng planted his hands on the ground and pressed his face to the carpet in abject apology. "I never looked. I swear." He discovered his nose was now pressed into the fallen panties once again. *"Waaaah!"*

Meng did a mad dance, trying to free himself of Itbit's undergarments. Her face indulgent, Itbit watched him for a while, then deftly took her panties from his hand.

"Hand Itbit the robe! The yellow robe!" She swatted the panda on the rear. "And be still! Stop babbling!"

Meng found something sheer and satin hanging carelessly from a cupboard door. He gingerly held it out to Itbit, and the girl seized it happily with both hands. The curtain fell, and Meng did a swift about face to stare at the opposite wall.

A full length mirror met his eyes: A mirror filled with an image of Itbit naked behind him. Meng quailed and swiveled to face another wall, thankfully finding nothing there but blank paint and shadows.

Behind him, Itbit threw the robe over an open window shutter. Standing naked and magnificent, she began to brush her gleaming golden hair. She smiled fondly, watching the Panda's back.

"You silly panda.. What you do outside of Itbit's window in the rain?"

Her shadow looked magnificent. Meng folded his hands up inside his sleeves and tried to keep his mind focused upon benevolence and propriety. It was difficult when the bed beside him smelled warmly of Itbit's tantalizing scent.

"I… I wanted to bring you a gift, my lady. I wanted my gift to be the very first one that you found."

"Oh!" Itbit froze, truly touched. She hugged her hairbrush to her heart. "So you climbie that hard tree for me?"

"Yes!" Meng swallowed. "That was all it was. Truly, I do swear…"

"Itbit does believies you!"

Itbit bent over, bottom high, and pulled on fresh underwear. The shadow on the wall was educational, curvaceous and explicit. Meng gave a yip, tried to force away unbidden thoughts, and tried to pretend that the mirror did not stand so horribly horribly close to hand. He risked a single glance sideways – was well rewarded, and was instantly consumed by guilt. He clapped his hands hastily together and frenziedly began to pray.

"Oh great Buddha! Merciful patron of the mind! Help me now keep focus upon the true demeanor of the sage. Help me focus on the demeanor of a sage! Help me…" Itbit limbered up by touching her toes. *"Help me!"*

With a happy sigh, Itbit bounced across the floor and threw herself into the yellow silk robe. "What you say?"

"Nothing…" Meng stared at the wall. Seen as a shadow with the sun streaming through her robes, the cheeks of Itbit's backside just peeked into view from behind as she stood with legs akimbo. Meng swallowed carefully and reached into his sleeve. "I merely meant to say – here is a gift I have brought you for your birthday…"

Dressed in her robe, Itbit gave a squeal of joy and jounced over to Meng's side.

The silk robe did little to hold back the girl's bouncing exuberance. She hugged him tightly, squeezing hard, jiggling excitedly up and down.

"Meng! Itbit's lovely, thoughtful Meng!"

He passed her a small book – beautifully hand made and hand lettered in Meng's own patient hand. The covers were the same green sheen as Itbit's fur, and the whole book had been hand bound by cords wound into a starkly beautiful string of knots. The whole gift seemed to breathe with reverence and love. Itbit took it carefully, holding it like a priceless treasure. She carefully opened the book upon an inside page, and there saw a map of constellations seen against a pure black sky.

Awed, Itbit stared at the page.

"Meng! What is it?"

The sage swallowed in embarrassment. He looked down at his hands.

"I have been to the observatory. To the great telescope. Now that the autumn has come, new stars are in the sky, and... and while I was there, I discovered a whole new star in the heavens. It is a beautiful, flawless white, at the heart of the constellation of the mouse. And so..." The scholar's ears blazed with the heat of embarrassment. "and so I was allowed to name it after you."

Itbit looked up, her eyes huge with amazement.

"Meng!"

The young scholar coughed, and fumbled with the book.

"So... so this is all the data on the star. Here is the constellation. Here is a horoscope. And....and the rest of the book is all simply poems."

Itbit's pink ears rose.

"Poems?"

"Poems all inspired by..." The sage faltered. He could not bear to look up from his hands. "Well, I... I have thought of them when we have been together."

Absurdly pleased, Itbit took her reading glasses from the stand beside the bed. Meng almost leapt out of his fur with shock.

"No no! Don't read them now!" He looked for some way to escape. "I mean – surely alone would be the best..."

With a sigh for Meng's silly ways, Itbit took him by the hands.

"You are a silly creature, and Itbit thanks you." She drew him fondly close, took his face in her hands and kissed the panda smack upon the nose. Meng almost expired. Itbit put her face against his cheek. "You are Itbit's good good friend, forever and always. And she will try to be a better student."

She sat holding both of Meng's hands in her own. Meng gave a timid smile, then looked up at her and tilted his face in fascination.

"They look bigger..."

"Oh?" Itbit pulled her glasses slightly down her nose, her cleavage jutting. "Whichies do you mean?"

"Your eyes! With the glasses, I mean!" Meng had fallen over his own tongue again. It was a strange effect only Itbit seemed to have upon him. The green mouse gave a little sly smile.

"Aaaah." She kept her glasses perched at the very end of her nose.

"Men likes to make passes at mouses with glasses.
Especially the ones who have fabulous... eyes."

She made a pose. "See. Iss a poem, and it does not rhyme – just like you taught." She squeezed Meng's hand fondly. "You see? Sometimes even Itbit can listen and learn."

Trumpets sounded outside the window. Shocked at so much noise so early in the morning, Itbit and Meng both turned to the window. Itbit leapt up and looked outside, leaning far over the windowsill. Her ample bosom almost spilled out of her robe.

"My Lady Itbit!"

Prince Tulu Begh stood in the yard, magnificently attired in satin robes, felt riding boots and cap. The mouse's dark muzzle and ears lifted, his face lighting with a sly, knowing smile.

The steppe mouse gave an elegant bow, sweeping out his hands.

"My Lady! Greetings to you on your birthday! Greetings upon your coming of age!"

The prince had two men with him, each one carrying a herald's trumpet. Itbit laughed down gladly at the handsome prince beneath her windowsill.

"You silly person. Itbit thinks you will wake the whole palace up!"

"Hopefully yes! For this is no day for sleep!" Tulu Begh climbed half up onto the roots on the tree beneath the window. "Now hurry my lady, and do come down. I have something special for you. Something you might rather like!"

Trotting out from behind the trees all of its own accord, there came a muscular, magnificent horse. It had a hide of pure buff yellow, and a mane stiff as a donkey's brush. It had a saddle fabulously chased with gold and smothered in silk tassels. Exotic, high stepping and spirited, it came prancing to Tulu Begh's side and stood pawing at the turf.

"Do come down!"

Itbit started at the horse in shock. The creature was utterly magnificent. With a squeal of delight, she overleapt Meng and grabbed for her riding pants, making sure she tucked Meng's book into her robes.

"So you only want Itbit to read this later?" The girl double checked with the scholar as she raced past. "Okie day! Itbit readies when she is all by herself."

She leapt straight out of the window and slid down the tree, athletic and beautiful. Breathless, Itbit arrived beside Tulu Begh, who held her by the waist and helped her down.

His hands were warm and firm – and he had no trouble holding Itbit's weight at arms length. The prince held Itbit above his head, looking at her with a sly, smoldering expression that always made Itbit think funny thoughts. She curled into his arms, landing on the ground, and then spun free with a dancer's effortless grace.

Itbit stood before the foreign horse. Its harness was alien and entrancing – rich beyond Itbit's wildest dreams. But it was the horse itself that was utterly bewitching. Muscled like a hero – perfectly proportioned for Itbit's size and with a sculpted majesty that made the girl gasp for joy, the horse was a study in absolute perfection. It came forward of its own accord and tossed its head, proffering Itbit its reins.

The girl blinked, adjusting her glasses, her whole body craning towards the horse.

"Is it…?"

"Yours?" Tulu Begh made a sly smile. "Of course – with compliments to the most beautiful *woman* I have ever known." He handed the girl the reins, coming close enough for her to smell the warm, exciting scent of his fur. "I wanted to give you a horse. A horse like no other on Aku-Mashad. Something big, powerful and spirited that can be… ridden into submission."

Itbit began running her fingertips avidly over the horse's face.

"He has blue eyeses!"

"And he never tires. He is a steppe horse – the demon breed." Prince Tulu linked his hands to offer Itbit a leg up onto the horse. "A gift suitable for a woman of spirit."

Ignoring the proffered help, Itbit took a fistful of the horse's mane and made a fluid leap straight up into the saddle. Her feet unerringly found the stirrups, she dug in her bare heels, and the horse instantly sped off across the grass. It gathered to leap over a low hedge, and Itbit sat perfectly poised as the horse sailed through the air. She reached the open path and gave a wild sound of delight, sending the horse shooting like an arrow down the path.

Tulu Begh had his usual two guards – plus another one unseen lurking in the palace windows with a gun. They all turned to watch Itbit riding like a creature born of wind and storm. Tulu pushed back his hat and laughed in delight as he saw Itbit's slim, perfect figure gripping perfectly against the horse.

Meng sat in Itbit's window and sadly watched her go. It was for the best, perhaps. She was to be the wife of a great Shah – an insightful, honest man that Meng totally admired. It was best to abandon fantasies and dreams. A sage had no reason to become lost in yearning for the unreachable.

- Let it all be just poems spoken to the wind...

A quiet tread sounded on the carpets behind him. Meng recognised the presence of the Shah, but for once, he could not find the energy to stand, turn about and make his obeisance. Shah Raschid al Dinaq came quietly to the window and sat himself beside Meng, joining the scholar in looking out across the palace lawns.

The big, muscular grey jackal sat with his booted feet dangling in mid air. Raschid's elegant nose tilted to look warmly at Meng.

"Good morning, my friend."

"Good morning, great Majesty." Meng bowed forwards, feeling a pain inside his heart. He half wondered why he did not simply let himself fall out of the window. "Best fortune for the day."

"I hope so, friend Meng. I hope so. Big changes – and hopefully for the best." Raschid put a hand on the panda's shoulder – a familiarity which would have utterly shocked Meng a few scant months ago. "I take it Itbit has already raced off on her affairs?"

A piercing whistle sounded from outside. Sandhri stood outside – sleek, black and well robed against the cold. Her pregnant belly looked taut, healthy and resplendent. With a basket on her arm and a dancing girl at her side, the bat was looking about the garden. *"Itbit? Hey! Get your green birthday backside over here!"* There was no sign of Itbit, and Sandhri gave a frustrated sigh. She looked up at the window above, and was instantly all smiles.

"Hey Meng!"

"Good morning, My Queen." Meng bowed – and this time almost lost his balance were it not for Raschid helpfully securing him by the sash. "How is the prince?"

"Still breech, still unnamed, big as a sheep and tap dancink on my bladder!" Sandhri waved happily, then made her way to the tree and began to climb. "Ach! Iss a good view from t'ere? I brought breakfast and I..." Annoyed, Sandhri swatted at the dancing girl who was pulling at her with her hands. "V'at iss it?"

"My Queen!" The lemur girl's long tail looped in an agony of distress. "Not the tree! The stairs, madam. Pray – use the stairs!"

"Will you... get off! Quit touchink me!" Sandhri tried to kick the girl away, keen to go tree climbing despite being seven months pregnant. "Get – look! Stop it!"

"But my lady...!"

"Yariim put you up to t'iss! T'at jiggle-titted bluebell!" Sandhri had found herself incapable of climbing the tree anyway, but was unwilling to let go of the argument. "I v'ish you'd all stop tryink to molly coddle me! In the hills, ve used to..."

The hills again. Raschid rolled his eyes. He spied Yariim at the far end of the courtyard draped in a golden shawl, and waved her over hastily. Yariim took one look at Sandhri in the tree, and marched over with narrowed eyes.

"What are you doing? Get down! The very idea of it!" The mouse held out a hand to Sandhri, offering her aid in a manner which brooked no argument. "Down! Right now!"

"Chust because I let you go on top…" The bat grumbled as she was handed down from her dizzy perch a full three feet above the ground. "You people are drivink me nuts!"

"You are in a delicate condition!" Yariim and the lemur girl both steadied Sandhri on her feet. "Please do be careful."

"I'm not made of bloody glass!" Sandhri lifted one finger on high, about to deliver another lecture. "You know, in the hills…"

"Your people ate broken glass on plywood for breakfast, had sex with mad tora birds three times before lunch, and still had time to be pregnant nine months out of ten." Yariim kissed Sandhri on the head. "We know, dear. You are a paragon of pregnancy." She took Sandhri on her arm. "Now upstairs the proper way. Easy does it on the stairs."

Sandhri fixed her best friend with a wicked eye.

"Who made you into such a v'icked bossy britches!"

"You let me go on top." The mouse hustled Sandhri upstairs. "Remember the agreement – it lasts all day."

"Tyrant."

Saud and three other guardsmen came ambling over to change Raschid's personal bodyguard. Lady Fatima came flitting over, tippie-toe and tousled, wrapped in a silk robe that didn't quite meet up. She came racing after Saud holding his breakfast and a gourd of cold iced milk.

The rabbit gave her husband a doting kiss, and he held her up like a toy and rubbed noses with her. Fatima had been a harem slave, a harem mistress, a courtesan and concubine who taught the love arts to hundreds of eager students – and she had never been so happy as she was right now. Saud put her down carefully, towering above her, then slung his massive sword over his back and walked towards the Shah. The stairs creaked underneath his weight.

"Hello Shah Raschid. Hello Queen and Queen." The huge man held his breech-loading rifle in one massive hand as though it were a toy. "Hello Sage. Fatima says to tell you she has found green tea. She has it in the big red jar in the kitchen."

"I thank you." Meng bowed. "Lady Fatima is too kind."

"Fatima iss much changed. S'veeter in disposition – unlike some." Sandhri shot a covert glance at Yariim that the mouse was not supposed to miss. "Hey Saud! How's my favourite tiger?"

"Saud is good! He has a present for Itbit in his bag – and also from Spike, and from Abwan. Colonel Abwan!" The tiger seemed immensely pleased with his old friend's rank. "And Marsuk, he will bring a present when he comes to the ceremony tonight." Saud looked around once more. "Where is Itbit?"

"I t'ink she's gone." Sandhri settled herself awkwardly on the bed, finding a pair of panties on the mattress and tossing them to Meng. "Unless I just sat on her."

"Yes, where is Itbit?" Yariim scowled, looking at the extravagant mess of clothes, used underwear and books strewn about the room. A pornographic picture book thieved from the library jutted out from hiding underneath the mouse-girl's bed. "Meng – have you seen her today?"

Raschid gave Meng an understanding squeeze on the shoulder. Meng hung his head.

"She went off riding, Majesty. The prince from the steppe kingdoms gave her a horse for her birthday." Meng knew that he sounded miserable. "A beautiful great spirited horse."

Sandhri and Yariim had both seen Meng working upon his book of poems. They exchanged a silent look across the boy's bowed back that spoke volumes. Sandhri scratched Meng comfortingly between his fuzzy ears.

"Hey hey. Don't v'orry about it. A steppe barbarian knows not'ing but horses, swords and booze. So v'at else v'ould he give her?" Sandhri ruffled Meng's deep, scruffy fur. "But poetry? T'at comes from the heart."

Raschid looked out of the window to where Prince Tulu Begh stood idly sipping tea. The exotic, handsome mouse saw the royal family gazing down upon him, and put on a confident, extravagant bow, almost mocking them with its carefree sincerity. Sandhri gave a great big smile and waved at their guest from up on high.

"Hi t'ere! Good morning!" Sandhri leaned over to Yariim. "Damnit! I t'ought I ordered him poisoned!" The bat suddenly chewed a finger. "Oh, t'at's right. He v'ouldn't eat his kebabs. Oh v'ell! T'at just means Meng can haff plenty of leftovers for breakfast!" She saw the young sage's drawn, desolate features, and took him underneath her arm. "Hey hey – iss chust a joke! Cheer up."

In all due seriousness, the Shah looked at Meng.

"Never fear. Sandhri would never poison kebabs. She would never adulterate good food."

"Nope. I'd shoot him in the back, the v'ay all good girls do!" Sandhri cast an eye at Saud's gun. "Hey Saud! Iss that t'ing loaded?"

Raschid gave the bat an indulgent look.

"We might need him as a messenger."

"Spoil sport." The bat sighed. "Aaaah v'ell. Hey Meng – did you effer see me shoot?"

The young sage was amazed.

"You shoot, oh Queen?"

"Ha! I'm a diva!" The pregnant bat aimed an imaginary gun at Tulu Begh's crotch. "I haff my own rifle – longer than Saud's! And a muzzle loader from Raas Yomah." She remembered the pistol eternally hidden in her clothing and pulled it free. "Hey – later on today, v'e…"

Yariim and Raschid gave Sandhri *that* look. She guiltily put the pistol away, and gave a sigh.

"Later. V'en I lose about a million pounds…" The bat heaved a sigh and rested one elbow on her belly. "You know, I thought pregnancy v'ould get me cut a lot more slack than it does…"

A faint sound of galloping hooves echoed in the morning hush. A high pitched, girlish squeal of joy came distantly through the dawn.

"There!" Raschid half rose from his seat, his long Jackal neck lifting high. "Look at the speed that horse runs!"

A golden streak sped over the palace parade grounds. Itbit rode insanely fast, laughing happily as the cold autumn breeze whipped through her hair. She reined in, turned the horse, and marveled at the animal, then stabbed home her heels and shot off at a gallop for the west wing of the palace. Raschid clambered heavily to his feet.

"We'll catch her at the stables." He helped Sandhri surge up to her feet. "Let us take a look at this steppe horse. The animal seems remarkable."

Feeling warm with the good things planned for this day, Raschid took his wives out into the sunshine that slanted bright across the palace walls. The winter birds wheeled overhead, come to roost in the warm river deltas of Osra. There were little finches, swift flying swallows, and absurdly regal herons with their necks arching tight. They came to bask in the winter wet and escape the snows of their far homes.

Out in the garden, Sandhri gave a hiss and pressed her hand into the small of her back. Raschid rubbed the spot for her, and the bat gave a grumble.

"I slept wrong."

"Well – it must be hard to find a position."

"Iss bloody impossible." Sandhri moved with the heavy walk of a very pregnant woman. "Iss alright. Pregnancy iss fine. I just get so tired so easily." The bat was utterly unused to confessing to limitations. "Ah well. It iss going to be a busy day. I v'ant chicken."

"Chicken?"

"Chicken, and my family happy, Itbit secure and about a half million dead barbarians littering the steppes." The bat sniffed at the air, hoping for a scent of her second breakfast. "Chicken first, then Itbit." She yawned. "The barbarians can v'ait until after I get a little sleep."

At the stables, Itbit had finally slithered her statuesque new horse to a halt. She was with the grooms – her usual accomplices in mischief – checking the animals' hooves. They marveled at the horse's fetlocks, his deep chest and powerful flanks. The horse stonily ignored them all, stamping and champing as though restrained against its will.

Itbit saw her beloved friends enter the stable yard. With a dance of joy, she posed and waved excitedly at the horse.

"Lookie look! Itbit gets a horse! Itbit rode to the city gates, to the sphinx ruins and back again, and mister horsie does not even show a sweat!"

Marwan the camel – a huge, slavering creature as ugly as a baboon's backside and smelling twice as bad – took one look at the interloping horse and bared savage yellow teeth. The huge camel snarled and suddenly lunged at the walls of his stable. The *boom* of the huge creature crashing against wooden posts sounded like a cannon shot. Grooms started, and Raschid whirled in dismay.

"Marwan!"

Marwan was climbing over the railings in a ravening fury. Itbit's new horse skipped cautiously away, keeping its distance. Marwan subsided as the horse moved away, but paced like a leopard in its cage, his bloodthirsty eyes never leaving their lock upon the horse.

Itbit sheltered her horse in annoyance.

"Marwan, you leave him be! Is no time for jealousy!"

Marwan was now the patriarch of a family of camels – most of them sired upon Sandhri's own brace of dainty white dromedaries. Her personal camel was pregnant even now, her belly swaying, agitated by Marwan's violent display. Sandhri shushed her camel and scratched her hard behind one pretty ear.

"Hey – he's really angry."

"Why? What's the matter, old friend?" Raschid approached the stall. Furious, bristling and champing yellow teeth, Marwan moved to put himself between Raschid and the new horse. "Hey, hey! Shhhhh! What's wrong?"

Raschid reached up and took the camel's neck and dragged its head against his chest. He was the only man on Aku-Mashad who could have survived such an act with his nipples intact. Marwan growled and snarled his troubles into Raschid's robes. The Shah hugged his camel, scratched its ears and made understanding noises in return.

Yariim had long experience and vast respect for Marwan the camel. She looked at

Itbit's horse and tilted her head in a frown.

"Itbit – did that horse try taking a bite out of Marwan?"

"No! He's a good horse! Itbit would not let him bite smelly old Marwan." The mouse girl cosseted her new horse, which stood like a stone gazing at the camel through dead blue eyes. "Itbit will name him 'Fireblade', because he is so golden and so fast."

She left the horse in the care of the grooms, and the group retired away from restless camels and enigmatic animals. Yariim opened up her arms, and Itbit came bounding over. They hugged lovingly, and Yariim gave the girl an adoring kiss.

"Happy birthday Itbit."

Itbit extended the hug with a loving squeeze, then made her way into Sandhri's arms. Finally she ended with Raschid. She stayed cuddled in his arms – all long hair, round breasts and breathless excitement. Itbit was tall enough to reach almost to Raschid's chin.

Raschid kissed the mouse, held her cheek against his face, and spoke warmly into her great pink ear.

"Happy birthday, Itbit. Bless you on your coming of age."

"At last." Itbit held him tightly around the neck. "All will be different now."

"Well, not too different!" Raschid kept Itbit under one arm and led the womenfolk over to the Sorcery gardens. Wasps armed with long lances and little bows whirred around the visitors as an honour guard. "But different enough. You'll see!" The Shah felt smugly ingenious. "We have a special ceremony arranged for you tonight."

"Aaah." Itbit tried to look as though she had suspected nothing. "A ceremony?"

"A ceremony." Raschid would say no more. "But lots of important people will be there as witnesses. The Sultana of Meepsoor will be there, and all the Emirs."

"And Kors Jakoob, and Raas Yomah, and the Ha'kuto Hanin fellow-me-man." Itbit looked as smart as a whip, archly gazing back at Raschid. "What could it be, that makes all these people come here to see Itbit?"

Yariim arched her brows in suspicion and amusement and looked at the birthday girl.

"What do you know about the Ha'kuto Hanin and Raas Jakoob? They only arrived this morning!"

"Aaah, Itbit knows what an Itbit knows!" The girl gave a scheming smile. "Is going to be an interesting birthday."

They sat beside the pond in the old sorcery gardens, surrounded by the strange creatures which called the garden home. Sandhri had chicken wings in her basket – bread, fruit, cream and honey enough to feed the five thousand. For the wasps, she had brought sugar water and tiny cubes of Turkish delight, as well as little silk ribbons as presents for their queens. Flying squid hooted from the aviary, and she tossed the creatures sardines she carried rolled up in a grubby cloth. Surrounded by a guard of wasps, with Saud and his men comfortably eating chicken wings, the four friends made a birthday breakfast and wished Itbit a very happy day.

Yariim had brought wine – a strange concoction from the land of the Franks that bubbled as it flowed. She poured glasses for her friends – albeit a small glass for Sandhri – and held her cup on high.

"To beautiful Itbit. Love and joy."

"Love and joy!" They drank to her while Itbit swelled, so pleased she felt that she could almost burst.

"To Itbit!"

Chapter Ten:

    The evening threatened rain. Dark clouds hid the stars, and the air smelled wet and sharp with the impending downpour. The wide river delta shone a stark gunmetal grey, stretching off to meet a distant ocean. Here and there an ibis flew low across the shore, heading for shelter in the brief peace that came before the storm.
    Sath's glow was subtle, lamp light peeking out through lattices and shuttered windows. The tops of tall palm trees shook and rustled where breezes tossed back and forth high above the city rooves. But at the palace, light bravely shone from all the battlements. Cold soldiers sheltered in doors and niches from the breeze, holding lanterns aloft to light the palace for the ceremonies to come.
    Raschid wore a brocade robe to keep away the chill. He crossed the 'dreaming courtyard' to reach the guest rooms, Saud and three guards coming before and behind. The Shah thrust open the door into the palace corridors, bringing with him a swirl of breeze. He let his guards stream in, then shut the doors and swept back the hood of his robes.
    The common room of the visitor's hall was crowded tonight. Representatives from each of the Nomad tribes of the desert had all come for the ceremonies. Every council member had been invited to attend, and many had traveled an indecent way from home. Emissaries from Vindahl, and some of the Sultana of Meepsoor's courtiers had also spilled over into this wing of the palace. With baggage piled in the halls and pet animals running riot on the windowsills, the place was looking like a halfway home for refugees.
    The wholesome scent of tea wafted from a nook beneath an open portico. Raschid acknowledged the bows of his many visitors, and then thrust through into the portico. Here, sheltered from the wind and enjoying an outlook on the storm, Sixteen Volume Meng sat with Kors Jakoob and Raas Yomah. A grizzled, one-eyed old mouse in military uniform was showing off a magnificent scimitar to Meng, helping the sage to see the patterns in the

watered steel blade. He looked up in joy as Raschid entered, leaving the sword lying in Meng's hand.

"Marsuk!" The Shah embraced the old soldier. "Salaam al adakh!"

"Salaam al adakh, my Shah." The soldier held Raschid at arm's length. "It is good to see you again."

They sat and drank tea. Lightning lit the tops of far distant clouds, and here and there a bird flew slowly against the mounting wind. Raschid adjusted his sword and yatagan, then sat down, chainmail armour tinkling beneath his brocade robes.

"So how are you, Marsuk? How is your new regiment?"

"As good a bunch of boys as there ever was. Spike's got my Light company. We're bumping him to Major – but you knew that." The old mouse poured tea. "We've been training in the Kakuzan highlands. Skirmish drill and battle line." He sipped tea, making a face and regretting that it was not something stronger. "Good lads. Good as the old bunch."

"Ah – the old bunch." Raschid smiled and remembered, hefting his tea. "Abwan will be here tonight." He nodded to the huge, genial, watchful Saud who stood like a juggernaut of blue armour nearby. "And Saud is always here."

"Ah, Saud!" Marsuk pulled a bottle from his robes. "How are you, my friend?"

"Saud is good. Saud is well!" The big tiger beamed. "Fatima is having Saud's baby soon. In summer!"

"Summer?" Raschid was delighted. "Saud! Congratulations!"

"We be fathers together." The huge soldier nodded. "And little Saud can look after little Raschid. That way they will never have troubled times."

"Well good for Fatima. Though God knows why she hasn't announced it." Raschid signed for a guard. "My compliments to mistress Fatima, and may I see her at her convenience after the ceremony?" The Shah felt immensely satisfied. "I shall have to find you bigger quarters!"

Raschid sat with his tea perched on his belly, looking fondly out towards the storm.

"We will ask Zhu's husband to find us a boat for our sons! I would like my boy to sail. I've never been an ocean man."

Marsuk gave a sigh.

"Thankfully, an officer can occasionally get by with riding a horse, so my feet don't hurt. Now, it's my backside that aches." The mouse scratched beneath his eye patch. "And how goes things here?"

"Alliances and diplomacy, most of it coming to naught." Raschid downed his tea. "I have been drilling the cavalry. Regiment, brigade and division. I'll be bringing up the heavy divisions to Kakuzan after the ceremony."

Marsuk made a show of shaking his head. "Cavalry? Well, who knows. We may find some use for them!" The old soldier had facial fur permanently discoloured from powder flashing in musket pans. "Well, here's to us. Saud – here's to offspring!"

He waved a glass bottle, then drank. Quietly feeding sticks into his little stove, Raas Yomah shot a dark, disapproving glance at his comrade the mouse.

"You should not drink spirits."

"Should not – but do." The old mouse uncorked his bottle and hefted it in salute to one and all. "Kakuzak plum brandy. We use it to clean musket barrels." He tossed the bottle to Meng, who sat quiet and miserable to one side. "Meng, lad! Stop looking like your pet toraki died. Get that down you. God knows how long these ceremonies will last. Our royalty do seem to love the sound of their own voices."

Meng nervously looked at the bottle, and passed it back untouched with a polite bow. Raschid put his hands out and relieved the young sage of the scimitar that lay across his lap. The jackal's tall ears rose as he felt the heft.

"Well balanced!" He tilted the blade, looking at the tube running down the spine of the blade. He gave a smile. "That's for Itbit?"

Marsuk coughed as he finished another swig of his bottle.

"Same smith who gave me the blade I gifted to Queen Yariim." The mouse looked to Meng, who seemed puzzled. "A woman can't work a heavy blade, so he makes them slim – but the watered steel makes it strong." He jerked his chin at the sage. "Do you fence?"

"I can fence, Colonel Marsuk." Meng motioned wanly to the slim, plain-hilted straight sword at his side. "But I do not think I would be much use in battle."

"Of course not! Only idiot cavalrymen and dandies like that idiot Spike waste time with swords." The mouse motioned to the musket that swung over Saud's shoulder. "Carry one of those, lad. If you have to go hand-to-hand, hit him in the nuts with that! A good musket stock will crush a steel codpiece like an eggshell."

Appalled by the whole concept, Meng gratefully bowed.

"I shall endeavor to remember your advice, honoured soldier."

"Good lad. Remember the wise words of Queen Sandhri: gills are for fishes, wings are for birds, but to solve an argument, use a swift boot to the happy sacks." Marsuk looked up as a gong rang and trumpets blew. "Whup! Is that us?"

"That's us." Raschid rose to his feet. Regretting the loss of warmth, he took off his brocade robe and changed into the white gown of a scholar. Tonight, he was in full armour beneath his robes, and light gleamed from silver plates and polished mail. He set his yatagan through his sash, his long scimitar in his belt, and his nomad dagger settled into its sheath on his arm. He motioned the others to precede him to the ceremonics, and then moved quietly aside with Meng.

The Shah grimaced a little at his warlike garb. He gave a smile of embarrassment to Meng.

"In times of war, they might feel better if they see a martial Shah." Raschid brushed at a score mark across the breastplate. "It is a 'working suit', however. I never commissioned a suit just for show."

He heaved a sigh.

"Walk with me a while, Meng. Let us go and view the storm."

People were crowding out of the doors and heading for the Hall of Wonders. Raschid opened up a window and awkwardly stepped out, then helped the smaller panda to alight. They stood in a courtyard half sheltered from the building wind. Dead leaves whirled down the colonnades.

As the guards clambered into position, Raschid saw two more of his men hunched over in the wind, escorting a figure that seemed quite at home in the breeze. The figure wore yellow satin robes, bore a slim sword, and had his handsome, raffish head bared to the winds. Shah Raschid could hardly help but admire the man.

"There goes Tulu Begh – always with fresh gloves on, and always in a brand new robe. A man who scores high for persistence and style, if not for integrity."

Meng felt crushed. He spared the steppe prince a gloomy look.

"Itbit seems to like him, my Lord."

"Itbit was told to keep a close eye on him – and so she has." Raschid glowed with pride. "She is a good girl – woman! A good help to us." The Shah smiled. "What would I do without her?"

Meng was terribly quiet. He looked away towards the storm, ashamed of the swooping, sick feeling in his soul.

"From tonight onwards, you shall never have to be without her, My Lord."

"Indeed?" Raschid wondered how the sage had known – but they were both men of education and intelligence. He gave a smile. "Well – here's hoping it's for the best. I was very worried about precedence, but Sandhri seems quite happy with the arrangement."

"It is a problem she has handled well before, my Shah."

"Eh?" Raschid had only half heard. He was watching Tulu Begh walking carefree into the empty guest halls. "I suppose so."

A thought came back to Raschid. He immediately took Meng by the arm.

"Now – Sandhri is what concerns me." The Shah scowled in thought as he walked. "Meng, I will be going to join the army in the field soon. Much as Sandhri wishes to accompany me, I cannot have her living in a tent at this important time…"

Meng nodded.

"Yes, my Shah."

"I was wondering if I could impose upon you to be a companion to Sandhri while I am gone. You are a voice of reason, and you might temper her otherwise…"

"Impulsive urges, oh Shah?"

"Ah." Raschid gave a fond smile. "I was going to say 'damned annoying', but you seem to have the idea." He gave a sigh. "Also – as a man of reason, intellect and medicine, you will clearly be a valuable attendant during the lead-up to birth. At least we scholars know a thing or two about birth and medicine, eh Meng?"

The panda sage blanched: Meng knew nothing of the sort, but he could not admit as much when faced with so much trust. He put his hands inside his sleeves and gave a profoundly grateful bow.

"I shall endeavor it, my Shah."

"Good, Meng, good." He squeezed the panda's thin shoulder. "But if a campaign begins, I will allow you to join us. You might be an invaluable historical witness, and your advice will always be welcome."

"Thank you, my Shah."

"Thank you, Friend Meng." Raschid looked troubled. "Look after her for me. She likes you – and she needs someone to talk to who has no worries on their mind."

Sensible of the enormous trust and honour that was being given to him, Meng bowed low before the Shah. His heart gave a pang of guilt, and Itbit's name called out inside his mind.

The gong sounded again. Raschid's long jackal nose turned to look towards the Hall of Wonders. He straightened his robes, and gave Meng a watery smile.

"Well, Meng, it is time. Let us go make one person very, very happy."

In the deserted guest halls of the palace, Tulu Begh heard the gongs toll. He ignored the call, and headed towards the privies, whistling tunelessly between his rodent teeth. He halted before the privy door, and bowed low to allow his guards the privilege of searching the room for conspirators, carrier pigeons and spies.

The first guard went past. As the second man passed, Tulu Begh straightened from his bow and gave the man a smile.

A dagger whipped out of its sheath inside the forearm of Tulu Begh's robe. In a violent blur, the blade slashed across the guard's throat, spraying blood in brilliant jets across the walls. Tulu Begh swung gracefully aside with practiced ease, allowing the blood to miss his robes.

The first man heard a noise as the bleeding guard fell crashing to the ground. He turned, and saw the dagger flying straight for his eyes. The guard ducked, and the dagger glanced from his helmet bowl. Shouting for help, the guard cocked his rifle and swung the weapon around to fire.

Tulu Begh lunged, his slim, plain sword piercing through the plates of the guardsman's brigantine armour. Run through, the guard staggered back. He fired at Tulu Begh, but the Prince flung himself aside. The guard fell in a welter of blood, reaching clumsily for another cartridge for his gun.

He fired again – but Tulu Begh was already outside the halls. Thunder boomed across the rooves of Sath. Cursing, the Prince put a hand to his ear and discovered a hole nicked into the edge.

A quiet shape moved. Rising from a roof nearby, a priest in white robes waved to Tulu Begh. It was a black cat with one ragged ear – the ally of Emir Haduh Had'idh. The priest sheathed his own knife, and one arm of a murdered sharp shooter lolled down over the edge of the roof.

His guards were eliminated. Tulu Begh took a plain robe that had been hidden beside the stables and swathed himself in a turban. He moved to the stables, where Emir Had'idh's men had a horse awaiting him.

A black horse with stark, blue eyes…

The steppe Prince looked to the Emir's men, and nodded once. They nodded once in reply. Slamming his heels into the flanks of his horse, Tulu Begh sped away. He rode out through the ever-open gates of the great palace of Sath, past the poor and the orphans who ate in the outer colonnades. With a demon horse beneath him, the steppe prince raced off before the winds of storm, his laughter swallowed in the thunder of a great, onrushing gale.

***

"Bow ye! Bow ye down! Bow ye before Shah Raschid the Just! Bow ye before the light of faith and mercy! Bow ye, bow ye, bow ye!"

For once, it was too good an evening to cut the Royal Chamberlain short. Raschid settled happily into his cushions with his wives at his side. Sandhri glowed with health, radiant and sleek, her belly hung with subtle little magic charms. Yariim coiled elegantly at his side, her eyes bright with delight – so beautiful that men cast glances of admiration at her whenever they thought she might not see. The Royal Council all beamed, people gossiped and babbled happily. For once, it was a time to forget all about war.

Tonight, it was all about *family*.

A fourth place lay vacant beside the royal trio – a place of honour decked out with a golden cushion. A priest stood behind the cushion in the shadows, and the Chamberlain's clerks stood ready with paper, pens and a great painted scroll. The audience looked smugly at the vacant place, and whispered in satisfied voices behind their hands. Outside the hall, rain began to fall. Lightning flickered in distant hills, and the boom of thunder rolled across the palace. But the Hall of Wonders was an oasis of light – a place where joy would rule for one golden evening.

A stir came from the doorway. With a smile spreading on her face, Sandhri sat herself up as erect as she could go. Raschid arranged his sleeves and made a formal posture. He raised a pen to signal to the guards upon the door.

"Please bring our guest to the hall before us!"

Two grinning men in blue brigantine armour opened up the great doors to the hall. The outer world shone a weird pearl grey, as light filled the stormclouds up above. Standing on the doorstep, small, nervous and demure, was a sweet little figure all dressed in white and green.

Itbit stood, her heart fluttering madly in her chest. She saw hundreds of people looking at her – smiling for her. With a clench of her hand against her heart, the little mouse strode forward, trying to keep her head lowered and calm. The excitement shone in her eyes, however, letting the whole assembly see her joy. She risked a glance up at the dais, and saw Sandhri, Yariim and Raschid beaming at her in expectant joy.

There was a priest beside the empty cushion at Raschid's side. Itbit's heart gave a leap. Dressed in flowing white robes, she strode forward, the hall echoing to the tinkle of little bells she wore about her waist, her arms and feet.

When an Osranii woman married, she covered her head with a silken scarf during the ceremonies. Ever clever with a needle and thread, Itbit had made herself a magnificent scarf all covered with glorious embroidery. She had it folded up and hidden beneath her robes – her clever trick to pull out once the 'surprise' was sprung upon her at her birthday party. Itbit looked up and saw Raschid's face – ever kind, ever loving, ever wonderful. He smiled a smile that he had always kept only for her, and Itbit felt her fear fly away.

She bowed left and right to the Royal council, then sank gracefully down to kneel upon a golden mat that had been placed before the royal dais. With a dancer's fluid perfection, Itbit bowed her head to the floor, bowing to her own beloved Shah.

Raschid beamed down at her.

"Happy birthday, my darling Itbit."

Raschid stood, throwing back his robes to show the armour, the sword and pen that lay beneath. He spoke proudly, his voice booming out across the hall.

"When I was young, someone even younger showed me cleverness and wisdom. When I was troubled, a companion came to give me friendship. When I was in want, they gave me humour, spirit and their trust."

The Shah turned and contemplated Itbit, who bowed even lower – her ears blazing bright red in embarrassment. She felt giddy, and wondered if her tail could ever stop its quaking. Raschid looked down upon her with a radiant smile.

"We have thought long on what to do – what to give as our most precious gift in return. With her sixteenth birthday, Itbit is a child of the palace no longer. She is a woman – and deserves a woman's place and respect. My wives and I want all of Osra to know the love which we hold for her."

Raschid signed to the priest, who stepped forward. Itbit felt a surge of fear and pride. Raschid held up his pen before the crowd.

"Itbit, you are slave born, and have no family name. Today we give to you a name!" He drew a breath and let the announcement peal out across the sound of rain and thunder.

"Let the priests record! Let it be written and let it be known! The woman known as Itbit, child of the palace, having come of age, is hereby adopted into the Royal family! Flesh of our flesh, blood of our blood. She is our child, of the line of Dinaq. Henceforth, she shall be a Princess of Osra, and inherit all rights, honours, titles and duties that fall upon a child of the crown!"

The crowd surged to their feet, applauding in joy. Men bellowed their approval – women wept for joy. Sandhri and Yariim rose to their feet, bowing to Itbit, their happiness at a surprise well given shining in their faces. Raschid opened up his arms to Itbit, bending down, inviting her up into his waiting embrace.

Itbit knelt on the floor and stared. Every face around her laughed and shouted. Her whole world disappeared, and she seemed to be shrinking to a dot upon the tiles. She stared at Raschid in shock and anguish, utterly betrayed.

"No..."

She looked about herself, tears standing in her eyes. The laughter ripped about her like a maelstrom of swords.

"No. No no no..." Itbit backed away, staring in disbelief. *"No!"*

The little mouse's shout stilled the laughter. Sobbing hoarsely, Itbit clutched her heart lest it rip in two. Aching, she backed away from Raschid.

"Itbit is not a child! Itbit is a woman. A *woman*!" The mouse stared at Sandhri, Yariim and Raschid, totally destroyed.

"Itbit is not a child!"

She whirled and fled, her white robes falling from her as she ran in tears. Thunder boomed and lightning flashed. The girl sped past the astonished guards at the doors and fled weeping out into the night. Rain spattered on the ground outside, hiding the sound of Itbit's tears.

Guests were in turmoil. Raschid ran after Itbit, reaching the doors only to be half drowned by a sudden downblast of rain. He stared into the empty courtyard, trying to see where the mouse had gone.

"Itbit!"

Sandhri dismounted awkwardly down the dais. Yariim helped her, then raced forward to Raschid. Left behind, Sandhri waddled forwards with her belly swaying, and then knelt heavily down beside Itbit's abandoned robes.

The bat leaned forward, questing and intelligent. She saw something gleam, and quietly reached out for it. She held it in her hands, and suddenly felt infinitely sad.

Sandhri hung her head, and held the embroidered scarf against her face.

"Oh Itbit..."

Yariim came running back. She saw the tears standing in Sandhri's eyes, and looked questioningly at her. Sandhri lifted up her face, and held out the marriage scarf.

Yariim sagged, feeling impossibly, incredibly stupid. She ached as though a knife had plunged into her soul.

Raschid approached. He saw the scarf, closed his eyes in pain, and then turned to face the anxious guests.

"Stay! Please stay." The Shah waved his hands to calm the Councilors who came anxiously towards him. "A misunderstanding. All will be well. Pray, please stay calm." Standing at the edges of the crowd, Lady Fatima caught his eye, and Raschid nodded to her. "Food will be served. All make yourselves welcome. Pray please wait for our return!"

Sandhri had already lumbered over to the door. Rain came hissing down across the rooves, hitting so hard that the droplets bounced up off the pavements. The bat sheltered herself behind her arm and tried to pierce the storm.

'Itbit!"

Running, weeping through the rain, Itbit fled into the rainstorm. Water hammered down from the skies so hard that it left a fog of mist in the air low to the ground. The droplets stung like pebbles as they slashed into her fur.

She fled using instinct alone. Itbit had lived inside the palace all of her life, and she found her way by the look and feel of stone walls beneath the storm. She pushed through a gate and found her way into a sheltered corner of the buildings; water poured down from the verandah rooves in a solid, clear cascade. Itbit ran through a waterfall that roared from a broken gutter, throwing her head to clear the water from her eyes. She shoved against a wooden gate, never once slowing from her maddened run.

She could still hear them laughing at her! And their eyes – so understanding – so tolerant! Clutching at her skull, Itbit staggered and fell against a wall. She heard a loud, animal roar, and looked about herself in confusion.

She was in the stables – and there was her horse! Saddled and waiting for her, looking back at her and pawing at the ground. Itbit wanted speed! She wanted to race into the rain, to run and hide forever! To leave everything behind. Sobbing, she threw herself at the horse, sailing into the saddle with one effortless flow.

Marwan the camel roared and raged in his stall. The big camel began to claw over the railings, clambering out of his stable to reach Itbit's side. The girl landed in the saddle, and her horse instantly reared and clattered madly for the doors.

Marwan shattered his stall railings with one savage heave of his bulk. Teeth bared to kill, he lunged for Itbit's horse an instant too late. The horse raced clear with nothing more than a rip across its haunches. It ran with impossible speed, shooting out into the rainstorm and vanishing from view. Tangled in his broken railings, Marwan could only bellow in helpless alarm.

Itbit clung low across her horse, the ache in her heart turning into anger. Weeping bitter tears, she raced through the palace gates, guards sheltering in the cavernous archway looking after her in bemusement. Out into the rain again, Itbit touched the horse's flanks and felt it respond with manic speed. She raced through the streets of Sath, the horse throwing up great sheets of spray with its hooves.

Itbit's mind whirled with grief – her heart ripped itself in two. Pride tore its way up through the ruins, making the young mouse burn.

She would show them! She would show them all! She was not a child anymore!

The horse ran its own way, and Itbit paid no attention to where she went. The mad rush of speed was enough. The horse raced through the city gates and out across the open fields, while behind Itbit, all the world seemed to fly apart in flood and spray.

"Itbit!"

Rain crashed down across the palace, making the air thick with mist. Rain droplets hit the marble pavements so hard that they seemed to blast apart like bombs. Trying to somehow see through the stinging fog, Sandhri crouched beneath the shelter of her own hair, peering into the gardens beside the whispering hall.

"Itbit!"

Yariim came racing up, drawing a shawl over Sandhri's head as protection from the rain. She sheltered the bat underneath her arm.

"Did you see her?"

"She went this way! I'm sure she did!" Sandhri could scarcely see her hand before her face. Rain-spatter stung madly at her legs. She looked down a nearby colonnade and stared. An awful thought suddenly leapt into her mind.

"The stables!"

"The stables!" Yariim started after Sandhri, and the two of them raced off into the rain. Overhead, a blast of thunder shook the palace to its very core.

Raschid came hunching out into the rain, one arm lifted to shield his eyes from the explosive downpour. He peered under the colonnades and saw the tail ends of his wives racing off across the palace yard.

Meng hurried to accompany the Shah. His head swirled – half in panic, half in joy. Itbit was not to wed the Shah! He ran to Raschid's side, bowed, and removed his robe to serve the Shah as an umbrella. Raschid met him underneath the flimsy shelter and shouted in the panda's ear about the roar of rain.

"Meng! Go with Sandhri! Make sure she doesn't hurt herself. I'll go check Itbit's rooms!"

Meng nodded. Two guards came running clumsily from the hall bearing swords and oiled silken umbrellas. They accompanied the Shah as he ran off into the buildings. Meng hunched beneath his uplifted robes and made his way across a courtyard, trying to catch up with Sandhri and Yariim.

The stables were in an uproar. Marwan the camel bucked and roared. A stall was shattered, the doors to the courtyard hung open, and water ran in a muddy river across the earthen floors. Sandhri shouted in the ears of a groom, who nodded and tried to point out into the rain. Yariim ran to the doors and looked out into the yard.

"She's gone!"

Itbit's horse was gone. She could never have saddled the monster in time – which meant that she was racing bareback through slippery roads in the rain. Yariim, Sandhri and Meng stood side by side, appalled and helpless, staring into the rain. Behind them, Marwan the camel fought his grooms and bellowed outrage out into the skies.

Sandhri threw Marwan's reins to a groom.

"Saddle him! Quick!"

Armoured figures came racing through the rain. They saw Yariim and Sandhri, changed course, and came running up to kneel before them in the downpour. At their head, Emir Had'idh sheltered his scarred face and shouted to be heard through the chaos.

"My ladies! Quickly – there has been a fall!"

Yariim gripped Sandhri's hands in fright.

"Itbit!"

"We found her on the road, my ladies! Come quickly!"

Horses and a camel were at hand. Emir Had'idh and his men helped Yariim to mount, racing to take up their own mounts. Sandhri hesitated, but Emir Had'idh reached out to her and made a plea.

"My lady! She needs you!"

Marwan bucked and roared, held down by three panicked grooms. Sandhri gave the animal one glance, then found a camel waiting, saddled and bridled by the door. She climbed awkwardly into the saddle, fighting her pregnant belly and moving with speed. An armoured man took her reins and led the camel out into the rain, the whole group picking up speed to canter through courtyards sheeted white with downpour.

They cantered through the palace gates, confused guards bowing and racing aside for the queens. Soldiers ran after the cavalcade, hoping to assist, but were swiftly left behind.

Back in the stables, Meng watched them go. In a panic, he looked about, seeing no animals at hand until the Shah's huge camel gave a roar and surged towards the door. Meng felt his heart leap in fright, and then he took a run and leapt to clutch precariously to the animal's hump. He dragged himself atop the beast's saddle, and Marwan gave a roar and lumbered out into the rain. Meng frenziedly clung across the camel's back.

"Beast! As a scholar, I am your intellectual superior. I ask your cooperation in the name of rationality!"

Marwan took off into the rain at a great rate of knots, his hump swaying like a boat caught in a storm. Clinging on for dear life and screaming in fright, Meng was carried off into the rain.

In the streets of Sath, Sandhri clung to her camel's saddle and rode past houses and empty yards. Spray thundered up from the hooves of the war horses all around her. Shivering at the noise of hooves, in terror for Itbit, Sandhri spurred her camel on and drew up next to the Emir.

"Emir! V'ere iss Itbit?"

"Close, Majesty! Just outside the gates!"

Sandhri ducked the fronds of a palm tree. The city gates were down the wide broad road, a good few minutes hard ride from the palace. Sandhri felt confused.

"How did you find her?"

"We passed her in the road!"

They were already through the city gate. The infantrymen on guard were sheltering from the rain. Yariim rode fast and hard at the column's front, nothing but Itbit in her mind. Sandhri blinked, passed out of the gates and saw the deserted, empty roads.

"Shit!"

An armoured man rode right beside her. He saw Sandhri's sudden surge, and snatched for her reins.

Sandhri whipped out her punch dagger and hammered it home. The blade pierced beneath the armpit of the warrior, stabbing deep into his flesh. The bat viciously twisted the knife and ripped free the blade. Her victim fell screaming into the road. Yariim and the soldiers up ahead heard the cry. Yariim looked back to see Sandhri wrenching her camel about in the road. She waved Yariim on.

"Yariim*! Go!"*

Armoured horsemen surged towards Sandhri, hemming in the slower camel. There were six armoured men, and there was nothing Yariim could do! The blue mouse hesitated, her horse skittering in place, and then she saw a bridge house a hundred yards away that had soldiers working in the yard. She kicked her heels and raced off down the road.

"Assassins! Assassins!"

Emir Had'idh pushed back his helmet brim and pointed a mailed hand to three of his men.

"Get her!"

Sandhri was at the center of a furious melee. War horses backed and bucked, terrified of the woman's angry camel. The camel showed yellow teeth, rearing up to try and crush the smaller horses with its weight. The warriors reached clumsily for Sandhri, unwilling to risk harming her by striking out with fist or sword.

Pregnant and screaming with hellish fury, the bat fought back. She dragged out a pistol from her sash and leveled it at the Emir, but the flint fell on a sodden pan. A man reached for her, and she broke his teeth with the pistol, then hammered her punch dagger at his ribs. Sparks flew from armour plates, and then a curse came as the bat drew blood. The man reeled backwards, and Sandhri kicked her camel into a lumbering run. The beast shoved horses aside and made its way towards the city gates.

Emir Had'idh whipped a steel javelin from his saddle case and threw. Sandhri's camel staggered, hit in a rear haunch. An instant later, the Emir's men were all around her. The camel slipped and faltered. Sandhri tried to stab a rider in the thigh. Forcing through the melee, Emir Had'idh dragged his scabbarded scimitar from his belt. He waited, poised, then hammered the weapon down onto Sandhri's skull. The bat reeled in the saddle. Had'idh dragged her from the camel and gripped her in his arms.

"She'll live!" He felt a mad surge of triumph. He had the Queen! He had the unborn heir! *"We have the Queen!"*

Yariim rode in a panic for the bridge house. Something hissed past her in the rain, and then suddenly she felt her horse stagger. An instant later, something ripped into Yariim's left leg. A blaze of pain made the mouse reel and scream.

Her horse was turning – spinning, dropping. Yariim tried to kick her feet from the stirrups, but the surge of pain from her left thigh made her leg explode with agony. She felt herself crash into the ground, her horse pinning her . The beast fought, surged to its feet, and battled clear. Yariim tried to crawl after it, but her leg seemed to claw at her like a ravening animal. She dragged herself through the mud, and then hooves thundered all around her.

"Get her! Get the Queen!"

Gunshots sounded. There was a sound like an axe hitting a butcher's block, and an armoured figure crashed to the ground at Yariim's side. A second later, she was hauled up to hang face down over a saddle bow. A big horse surged beneath her, tack jingling and hooves hammering. The animal rode hard into the rain, and Yariim felt her leg turning icy cold.

Meng rode hard in the rain. He somehow clung onto the camel, finally climbing up into his seat. He held on as palm fronds slashed at his face, or as thunder blasted in his ear. He rode to the city gates, where soldiers were running into the archway to stare in shock out into the road.

Armoured horsemen fought a wild melee a few dozen yards down the open road. Soldiers from a bridge house down the road fired at another group of riders further off in the rain. Confused soldiers in the city gate stared, then surged forward as they recognized the thin shape of Sandhri fighting the horsemen with a knife.

"The Queens!"

Men instantly drew scimitars and charged towards the horsemen. Others crouched in the archway, cocking their rifles and trying to shelter their flint locks from the wind and rain. An officer bellowed frantically at the swordsmen charging towards the melee.

"Clear for fire! Clear for fire!"

It was too late. Whatever had happened out in the road, it was over in an instant. There was a camel staggering bloodily into a field. Another horse thrashed in the mud beside an armoured corpse. Horsemen spurred away down the road, carrying the lolling bodies of Osra's two Queens. Tufekchi came running from the bridge house. Officers pelted out into the rain – a messenger turned and ran for a horse. Meng clung to Marwan the camel and watched it all, then kicked the huge camel in the ribs.

Marwan gave a savage roar of vengeance and lumbered forward down the road. Meng found an officer and bellowed down to him through the confusion.

"Sir! Tell the Shah that this humble servant is obeying his commission!"

He kicked the camel into a charge, and Marwan took off at a lumbering run. They passed corpses and soldiers, speeding onwards into the mud and rain. Meng and Marwan left Sath far behind, doggedly following distant figures that dwindled and disappeared into the gloom. Lightning flashed, rain poured –

- And Osra had lost her Queens…

The horse ran and ran far into the night. Itbit was at first dazed by it, then frightened by it. She tried pulling the animal to a stop, but it ran and ran and ran – through shallow rivers and under trees. Itbit thought of leaping free, but then she thought of limping ignominiously into the palace, having lost her horse, and she let the ride go on. The horse seemed to know where it was going, and Itbit was too broken with anger, loss and bitterness to care what it did.

Night fell, and still the tireless horse ran though the rain.

Finally, the horse reached an old hut which stood by an empty road. A second horse stood nearby – a fine black animal with the same eerie, empty blue gaze as Itbit's own. Itbit's horse scarcely slowed. One moment it was racing through a world turning dark with night: The next instant, the horse was standing still beside a hut, motionless and calm. Itbit slid slowly from the saddle, dazed and wondering. Her senses whirled, and the sudden total absence of light and noise hit her like a blow.

There was no more rain. No city, no thunder. In the emptiness, Itbit felt herself weeping again. How could she go back? How could she ever go back? And what was there to go back to? She was nothing but a child…

"Itbit!"

It was a voice she knew – a voice that always sent a forbidden, unacknowledged thrill rippling through her heart. Prince Tulu Begh stood in the hut's door, warm firelight from a well laid hearth outlining his figure. Itbit wept and ran to him, and he took her inside his warm, strong arms.

She felt him hold her tight. She was miserable, wet and afraid. Tulu Begh made soothing noises and rested his face against her hair.

"Sssssh. Shhhh, my lady. No need for tears – you're safe now. You are in my arms."

Itbit was freezing, wet and cold. Tulu Begh took her into the hut, where a wide bed with white sheets and a down comforter lay spread out on the floor. There was meat toasting on the fire, and wine mulling in a copper urn. The Prince pulled an old blanket around Itbit's shoulders and used it to scrub her dry.

"No no – this is a shock. Shhh – no tears now. No tears." He held the girl tight and sat her beside the fire. She felt herself trembling in his arms. "No need to speak. Here – this will warm you."

He gave her spiced wine laced with spirits, and she drank it down. The alcohol burned Itbit's throat, clawing its way into her stomach where it seemed to catch on fire.

Outside the hut, the horses shifted. Itbit could hear them move. Tulu Begh kept an arm about Itbit and softly stirred the fire.

He looked towards the unseen horses and gave a smile.

"Stable mates. Your horse must have known I would be here. This is where we stayed when we first came to your land."

Feeling shrunken and tawdry by her friends' betrayal, Itbit could speak only a few hoarse little words.

"T-Tulu Begh is leaving?"

"The Shah and his wives are determined to treat me as an enemy. I am heading back for home." Sitting quietly on the bed, The Prince gave a sad sigh. "I have been an utter failure. It is time to go home."

"Why? Why did you stay so long?" Itbit rested against him. His chest felt hard and muscular against her breasts. "Why?"

"There were things in Osra I found too… fascinating to leave." Tulu Begh gave the girl a sad glance, and kept her softly held against himself. Itbit found herself sitting in his lap.

The girl swallowed.

"Things?"

"Things." Tulu Begh gave a sigh for lost dreams. "I had to leave without telling you goodbye. It was like cutting my heart in two." He hung his head. "I left you a letter…. Cowardly, I know. But a long, long letter, and thought maybe in days to come…" The Prince subsided unhappily. "But no. A girl like you is destined to be a Queen of Osra. You would never be content with a simple Prince, the steppes, and a castle underneath the moon…"

"A letter…" Dazed and wilting, Itbit felt a pain crippling her heart. "Itbit did not see."

"You were to find it after the ceremony." Tulu Begh looked at Itbit in a slight twinge of confusion.

"My Lady – are you not now a Queen of Osra?"

Itbit stiffened, and then her body came alive. All the laughter, all the voices in her head stirred her into heat. The mouse girl surged upright in Tulu's lap.

"Itbit is not a Queen. They did not want her!" She felt the tears starting afresh, and she let them fall. "They think of Itbit as a child! *A child!*" The girl's anger burned with a wild, white heat, all mixed with shame and love. She wept again, and now she hung her head, ripped by the misery of it all.

"Just a child."

She clung against Tulu Begh. Her young, taut body – infinitely smooth and lush, pressed against him. Tulu Begh slowly caressed her face, the back of his hand brushing away her tears. She felt his hands – so firm and sure. He lifted up her furry chin, and Itbit looked up at him, still weeping. She stopped as she saw the look in his eyes, and felt his fingers twining in her hair.

The steppe lord spoke to her in a low voice that shivered Itbit's very soul.

"I do not think of you as a child."

He touched her, and she let him. He kissed her, and she let him. She was proud as she felt herself respond. She kissed him with a passion born of bitterness, and she felt him sliding her softly from her clothes. She felt his excitement as he touched her, and the knowledge brought pride to her injured soul.

He never asked, nor did he treat her with kid gloves. He took her as a woman, and she took the pleasure a woman was due. When he finally entered her, she made him do it *hard*, wanting it to hurt. She wanted the others to find a bloody wedding sheet and *know* what they had done to her.

When it was over, Itbit lay on the bed, feeling filthy – feeling soiled – but proud and defiant deep inside. Tulu Begh lay on his side so that he could touch and marvel at her, like a conqueror who has seized a priceless new possession. He caressed her, and Itbit made a show of reveling in it, letting him show her how to pleasure him as a steppe lord's woman should.

He paused before entering her again, and Itbit drew a deep breath, looking deep into the fire.

"Take Itbit, Tulu Begh. Take Itbit to your castle of the moon."

They made love again. Itbit took her pleasure and her pain as one, wishing that her old friends could see her now and know that Itbit was all grown up at last…

***

In a room tiled with blue and gold, a quiet figure sat cross-legged on a rug made from flayed hides. With a book open on a stand before him, the figure quietly read. Windows looked out into the night, and cloud tails hid the stars. Candles burned with eerie light, while unseen spirits moaned and stirred in pain.

Golden doors slid quietly open. None dared enter the Tsu-Khan's private shrine. Unseen forces could be felt lurking just beneath the skin of existence – for the Khan held the keys that ruled the gates between the world of the dead, and the world of men.

General Gurad, General Tsai-Chi and three officers knelt with their sword belts over their shoulders in formal obeisance. The Khan finished reading his page, closed the covers, and carefully slid three locks in place, before looking up towards his waiting men.

Gurad lowered his face towards the floor.

"Great Holy Person – it is done." The General's voice held a note of vicious pride. "We have the Osranii Queens."

The Tsu-Khan quietly stood, his robes making no noise in the stark, still hall. He placed the book inside a cabinet, and lifted his muzzle to look coolly from the tower window.

The wind blew from the north, and it brought with it the scent of snow.

"General Gurad – the army of the Khanate will march at first light." The chill air ruffled gently at the Tsu-Khan's fur. "We march west, upon the Franks."

"Yes Holy One!"

The officers departed in savage joy. Left alone, the Tsu-Khan looked into the air above and opened up his arms, breathing deep and tasting of the carnage, the terror and the glory which would be shaped beneath his hands.

Chapter Eleven:

The throne room of the royal palace was seldom ever used. The great dais with its canopied throne was all made from pure blue crystal, and the walls, floor and ceiling were intricately inlaid with calligraphic names of Allah. Sitting at the edge of the dais, his sword lying uselessly at his feet, the Shah sat with his head in his hands. Saud kept his bodyguards well away, and men walked with quiet feet. The light of a rain-swept dawn was only just beginning to creep inwards through the windowsills.

A sleek, solemn pink figure appeared at the door. Tall and soft footed, her glasses making her face owlishly wise, Lady Fatima tiptoed into the throne room and whispered into her husband Saud's ear. They conferred a moment, and then approached together. Saud knelt at Raschid's side, grounding his titanic sword. Fatima knelt softly beside the Shah, and whispered quietly to Raschid.

"My Shah? I have news."

There was total silence. Raschid remained utterly still. Fatima lovingly laid a hand upon his shoulder.

"Raschid? Raschid, it is I, Fatima. Abwan and his men have returned."

The jackal gave a long, slow indraw of breath. He gradually rubbed his eyes and lifted up his head..

"Thank you, Fatima." She kept her hand upon his shoulder, and he kissed it gratefully. "Please bring them in - and ask the others to join us."

The rabbit bowed low, quietly arose, and walked with whispering feet across the hall. She was met by men coming quickly in from the stable yard – men with mud on their boots, filth in their fur and the eyes of tired, disappointed men.

Raschid saw Abwan's face, and saw the news he had expected. He looked down at the yatagan lying in his lap - a long, forward curving blade with a worn handle made of ivory.

The yatagan was old. His father's Grand Vizier had owned it before him, and had given it to Raschid before Raschid had first gone into battle. He held the worn grips and thought of that fine old man as the guards ushered Abwan's mud stained, dripping men across the throne room floor.

Abwan looked worn and drained – a grizzled old dog with the scars of old fights showing stark beneath his bedraggled fur. Six men of the royal guard cavalry had ridden with him, and all of them looked frozen and exhausted. Raschid beckoned a haggard dancing girl – a student of Fatima's with a name he could no longer remember, and the girl came running to his side.

"Yes, my Shah?"

"Warm robes. Hot drinks. Coffee. Warm food." Raschid waved listlessly towards his half-drowned men. "Please make them comfortable. And bring food for yourself." The girl had been quietly attending him all night without food, rest or sleep. "You do not have to stay."

The girl – a skinny lemur with a huge, stripey tail and luminous amber eyes, bowed low before her shah, adoration shining in her face.

"I… may I stay, my lord? I do not want to go."

"You do not have to go, my dear." The Shah reached gently forward to put a straying curl of the girl's hair back into place. "Bring yourself a pillow and a blanket, then, in case you grow tired. You can sleep here by the throne."

The girl gave a profound bow.

"Thank you, my lord."

"Thank you…." Raschid searched for the girl's name. His mind felt grey and blank, like old, flat stone. He thought for a moment, then found the girl's name already in his mouth.

"Saa'lu." He tasted the syllables as if remembering something precious for the first time in a long, long while. "I thank you, Saa'lu."

"My Lord…"

Raschid held the girl's hand and looked into her eyes with his sad, brown gaze. Almost expiring with love, the Lemur girl backed away. She remembered to bow – bowed a few more times for good measure and ran flitting from the hall. Long yards of stripy tail slithered after her backside as she disappeared.

Captain Abwan sat heavily on a camp stool. His clothes dripped water to the tiles, and his body shivered with chill. He took off his helmet and simply let it fall.

"We have not found the Queens, my Lord. Nor is there any sign of Itbit." The man gave a desolate sigh. "In this rain, no one was even out on the roads to see them pass."

Raschid nodded. Logic had dictated that good news would have been quicker in arriving – but the illogical part of him had still held out its hopes. The Shah rubbed his eyes, trying not to be sick. He fought to keep his hands from shaking as he massaged his eyes.

Saa'lu came racing in with a scalding pot of coffee and old tin camp mugs. She chivvied in a procession of Yariim's library students, all carrying hot bread rolls and sausages. The smell of sausage made Raschid jerk aside with a pang. Saa'lu gave the Shah a guilty look, but he waved thanks to her and then leaned forward to talk to his men.

The guardsmen gratefully took coffee from the girls. Abwan tore into a bread roll, shrugging off armour as three bespectacled librarians fumbled with the straps of his dripping armour and dragged it free. He spoke through avid mouthfuls of food.

"We-we rode the east road, sire." The old soldier settled his sword as a girl helped him shrug off his wet robe. "Farmers close to the city saw a group of riders on the road, but the guards at the first road station on the way saw nothing all night. We searched the route off road, and found a haystack torn to pieces in a farmer's field. The farmer, his wife and three children had been slain – dead a few weeks by the look of them. The house had been lived in – food still warm on the table and a fire in the hearth. We found the abductor's horses abandoned in the farm yard."

Raschid nodded, following the story. He gave a long, slow scowl.

"A haystack?"

"Yes, my lord. Torn totally apart, as if something large had been concealed beneath it. Hay was scattered far and wide. There were many muddy tracks in the fields, but the rain turned the surrounding meadows into a quagmire. In the dark and the rain…"

The Shah nodded softly, motioning with his hand to softly quell Abwan's distress. The old soldier was tired near to exhaustion, as worried as his Shah. Raschid tried to settle all the facts inside his mind.

"You're sure the horses belonged to the abductors?"

"We cannot be certain, my lord, but it seems logical. Tired horses – military horses – and the right number."

"I see." It seemed logical. Raschid tried to picture the local area in his mind. He seemed to remember it as being a land of green fields bordering the Amu Daja river. "You are searching the region?"

Abwan pulled on a warm robe that Saa'lu wrapped around him.

"Local commanders are fanning their men out into the fields, my Shah. Messenger squid have been sent flying to all possible bridge garrisons, ferry points, crossroads and all our border posts." It would be uproar – perfect uproar. God only knew whether it would help or hinder an escape.

… But there were no bodies. No one had thrown the corpses of Raschid's wives into the road. They held the women still – and that brought hope that Sandhri and Yariim were still alive.

People entered. Zhu, a slim, buxom and beautiful fox dressed in exotic jewelry. Lady Fatima, Colonel Marsuk, Raas Yomah and Kors Jakoob. Finally old Hassan the Sorcerer came stumping in, leaning on his staff. He irritably chased away a flying squid that tried nesting on his turban, and he sat down upon a tall wooden chair dragged over by a guard.

Leaning on his scabbarded sword, Raschid sat and wearily brought his old friends the facts at his command.

"Sandhri and Yariim are gone. Itbit is gone. Palace guards have been murdered." The Shah leaned heavily on his sword. "Immediately after fleeing the Whispering Hall, Itbit rode out of the city gate upon a blue eyed horse. She rode to the East, and has disappeared." Raschid felt infinitely tired, but had no heart to rest. "While searching the stables for Itbit, Sandhri and Yariim encountered the Emir Had'idh and several of Had'idh's men. The grooms tell us that Had'idh claimed to have found Itbit, that Itbit was injured and needed immediate help. Sandhri and Yariim rode through the palace gate with Had'idh, left the city via the great gate, where they suddenly began to fight with Had'idh's men. One of the abductors was killed by a punch dagger strike beneath his left arm – which will be Sandhri. Another was shot by the bridge house garrison. Yariim's horse was seen to fall. Both women were seized by Had'idh's men, who rode East. They never reached the first road house on the eastern road. Abwan here tells us that there are signs they left their horses at a farm, and removed something from hiding beneath a haystack."

The Shah sighed.

"As for the palace…Prince Tulu Begh, the emissary from the Tsu-Khan's court, has gone. He murdered one guard, and severely injured another. A marksman posted to watch him from cover was stabbed from behind and slain. Tulu Begh could not have reached the marksman: he had help inside this court."

The tall jackal rubbed his eyes, trying to remain regal – remain focused and erect.

"So there we have it. We are presuming the abduction was masterminded by Tulu Begh, with the assistance of Emir Had'idh and a team of traitors. We… do not believe Itbit was a party to the affair, but the abductors may well have seized the opportunity to capture her as well." Raschid found his head drooping towards the floor again, and he forced up his gaze. "We are searching the roads, fords, bridges – guarding the borders. Searching the city, ships, ports…" He sighed. "And now – what can you all advise me to do?"

Zhu looked unhappily down at a small child's toy she held in her hand: it was a knitted woolen ibis she had been making for Sandhri's child.

"We… we lost men?" The fox's voice was soft and sad. "How many guards were killed?"

Abwan rubbed at his eyes.

"Two men, my lady. The third was run through the stomach."

"Oh God!" Zhu pressed a hand against her throat. "Will he live?"

All eyes turned to old Hassan the sorcerer. The old man was supping noisily at a tiny coffee cup. He looked up when he finally noticed all eyes upon him.

"Eh?"

"The injured man." Raschid spoke loudly in the old man's ears. "Will he live?"

"Eh? What?" The old sorcerer irritably thumped down his walking stick and ground it into the tiles. "The injured boy? A hard piece of work! He'll be off his feet for weeks!"

"But he will live?"

"Live?" Old Hassan seemed outraged that the question should be asked. "Course he'll live! Who do you think we are? Franks?" The sorcerer's huge eyebrows flagged in scorn. "Will he live indeed! Of course he'll live!" Hassan was in a foul mood – or fouler than usual at least. He had been up all night, and he was unwilling to seem worried about his old companion Queen Sandhri and his student, the little green mouse. He thumped his stick down once more, and then blurted out to interrupt all conversation in the hall.

"… But what the hell were you all thinking?" He was so incensed that he rose from his seat. "A *blue-eyed* horse? A blue eyed horse, and no one comes to tell me? Did you touch it with relics? Did you test it with spells? No! You just let that poor simple girl leap on its back and go riding about as though nothing were wrong! I can't be everywhere at once, you know! I don't mess about at the stables with horses." The old man paced in frustration and rage. "Did it sweat? No! Did it eat? No! And did anyone come and speak to the college of sorcerers about any of this? No, no no!" Hassan turned. About his wrist, there was a braid of golden hair – the kind of silly gift Itbit would give to her favourite friends. "She is my student! I have a responsibility to take care of the child."

Raschid nodded, eyes closed and pain raging in his soul. He waved a hand to quieten the sorcerer down.

"Have you been able to find any clues with magic, Hassan?"

"None." The old man snorted. " This Tsu-Khan is good. He shields his men and his lands. We have men scrying crystal balls and pots of oil – good men! My best! - And yet we see nothing." Hassan sat painfully back in place. He lowered his head, then took a breath. He gave a calmer sigh.

"My Shah – I believe the horse was possessed. It is a foul magic, an alien magic, but it can be done. That animal will run without rest or pause." The sorcerer leaned thoughtfully upon his staff. "Demons. Possession. Dead souls. Ha!" He gave a snort. "This Khan is no mere sword-waver! This goes far beyond a few magic baubles picked up on the steppes!"

Raas Yomah – head tilted to one side and a straw jutting from his mouth, idly prepared tea.

"He is a servant to the dark one, this Tsu-Khan. Yes?"

"I just said that!" The sorcerer took a bread roll and dunked it in his tiny coffee cup. "This is not some mere soldier! No mere king! They call him the 'Lord of Ghosts'! We hear of walking dead, demons, ghosts – now the horses. Something untoward is happening here!" The old man slurped his bread. "That sort of power doesn't come from bedtime prayer and going to mosque!"

Raas Yomah nodded in slow, silky satisfaction, tilting his head to the other side.

"Yes, yes… A false Mahdi. An Antichrist." He nodded. "It is good."

"Good?" Hassan spluttered. "What the hell is good about it? A demon caller has my student! My Best damned student! The only girl who ever managed to finish all eight volumes of Solomon's Great Key!" The old man was worried. "And they have the bat. The black one – the loud one. She married what's-his-name, the good one. The simple fellow with the long nose…"

"Raschid." The Shah looked fondly at Hassan. "You are tired, Hassan."

"I'm not senile. I just don't like to worry. Sorcery is about making life better." The old man arose carefully. "I must return to those idiots in the tower. They'll have ghee in the scrying pot and sesame oil in the cook pots. I'd best put it all right before they burn the place down." He looked at Raschid, and tapped him on the shoulder with his staff. "Sleep! You're in charge now. You can't go looking for them yourself. So sleep. I get all my best ideas when I sleep." He waddled off towards the corridor. "… And so does that black furred girl .The skinny one! Makes up her best stories after a good night's sleep."

In the silence after Hassan had left, Fatima came forward gracefully, placed a bundle upon the tiles and bowed.

"My Lord Shah? We have searched the apartments of the Emir Had'idh, and have found his entourage has gone. In the apartments of the Emissary Tulu Begh, we have found nothing but this mirror, and this note." The rabbit spread out a piece of paper, which had been written on with a brush and ink in the Eastern style.

The note merely read – *Compliments to his Eminent Majesty, Raschid the Great. Please keep ready to hand.'*

Raschid made to reach out for the mirror, but Kors Jakoob placed his sheathed sword across the mirror's face.

"Do not touch the evil one's mirror, Lord. Send it to your sorcerers to investigate. Yes… yes…" The black fox kept his head tilted to one side, his eyes narrowed. "Think twice before touching anything left by Tulu-Begh."

There was a moment of heavy silence. All present pondered the cups they held in their hands. Raschid swayed, blinked, and sat more stiffly upright.

Zhu sighed and bowed her head, her voice soft and musical.

"So… the Tsu-Khan has Sandhri, Itbit and Yariim…" her hands clenched, and her knuckles stood out taut through her fur. "Are they… still alive?"

"They are alive." Abwan was adamant. "They went to great trouble to capture, rather than to kill."

"But why? What are they trying to achieve?"

Raas Yomah's rich, dry voice rolled across the tiles. "One does not go to the trouble of capturing a man's family unless one has plans." The nomad chieftain had made tea. "We can expect to hear from this Tsu-Khan soon."

Zhu was ashen.

"And what will we do?"

"Yes." Calm and self possessed, Raas Yomah drank his tea. "What will we do."

Raschid heard Raas Yomah. He felt as though he were at the bottom of a pit into which sights and sounds fell with nightmarish lethargy. But yes – this was an attack upon Osra – an attack upon himself. The Tsu-Khan wanted to neutralize the threat of the Osranii army.

Yariim and Sandhri believed in him. He had to carry on the fight. Raschid slowly lifted up his face and addressed his friends.

"The search arrangements are thorough. We will hope, and we will pray. Do not allow your searches to interfere with the deployment of the army." Raschid arose, settling his sword into his sash. "Prepare my staff to move north: I will be joining the army exactly as planned.

"I thank you for all of your efforts."

Kors Jakoob and Raas Yomah both bowed silkily, having expected the order. Fatima and Zhu looked uncomfortable; the soldiers were accepting. Raas Yomah arose and accompanied Raschid as the Shah wandered quietly from the hall.

It was still overcast – still raining. Robes swirling, the tall Jackal walked beside the slim, small desert mouse. Above them, low clouds skidded across skies streaked red with dawn.

The nomad lord halted beside Raschid as they stared at the palace stables. The palace of Sath was no longer the opulent, decadent place it had been beneath the earlier shahs. These were working stables, filled with war horses and work-a-day beasts. Raschid walked slowly over and looked at Marwan's ruined stall.

Raas Yomah planted his fists on his hips, his robes swirling, and looked at the damage with mild interest.

"The young sage has gone. He has decided to rescue your wife, I think." The desert mouse raised one ebony brow. "He has the spirit of a storm, that one. He will not fail you."

"He has gone to see whether a sage can do what swords and armies cannot." Raschid looked quietly at the ruined stall. "I cannot help him. Marwan must look after him now."

A cold wind blew through the courtyard. Raas Yomah's personal guard of twelve men had already brought their riding camels to the fore. The mice sat on their beasts with their robes flapping in the wind, their faces masked by their *keffiya*.

One man silently brought Raas Yomah his camel. The mouse looked steadfastly down at the ground.

"The army is moving. I must go to bring the desert peoples to arms."

"You must go." Raschid felt the world pressing in against him like a wall of needles. Everything seemed unreal. "The campaign plan stands."

The mouse stared at the ground, and then turned and tightly embraced the Shah.

"I would stay with you, if it were for the best, my Brother."

"I know."

Raas Yomah's camel knelt. It was a black beast with a silky look of grace about its face. The nomad chieftain paused before mounting, and looked north, towards the lands of the Khan.

"He has not surprised me, this Meng. I knew he was a hero. He is a hero because he is mad – and God loves the mad." The nomad swung into the saddle of his kneeling camel. "He will find them, my brother. They are not alone."

Raschid looked to the north. His long nose lifted to the wind.

"He will not be following their tracks. He will be deducing where they will be taken." A cold wind stirred Raschid's robes. "They will be taken to the Khan."

Raas Yomah settled his long Osranii rifle across his back. The weapon had been a gift from the Queen. The Desert Nomad raised his hand to the Shah.

"We shall do the work of Allah. We shall cast down this Khan. We shall be guardians of the Light."

Raschid raised one hand. "Go with the Light, my Brother."

"Go with the Light."

They clasped hands, and then Raschid released his friend to his work. Raas Yomah touched his camel, and the beast paced swiftly out across the palace grounds. His warriors closed behind him, and they swept out onto the road. Raschid watched them go, his mind shattered and his heart heavy, and then turned to do the duties that had to be done.

There were papers to sign and officer's commissions to confirm. Yariim had organized so much, and her staff were trying to soldier on without her. Sandhri's own staff worked on hidden and unseen. Her spymasters worked doggedly onwards, appearing briefly to hand discrete folders to Fatima, who brought them to the Shah.

Staff brought in matters for the Shah's seal. Raschid confirmed ten new lieutenants who had been raised from the ranks; commissioned three young noblemen who had requested that they be allowed to abandon the officer's academy and enlist as privates in the cavalry. He removed one incompetent captain, then posted two dishonest quartermasters to the nethermost regions of Aku Mashad. He organised the last great convoy to the north – a thousand wagons loaded with corn, ready to supply the army's horses on campaign. He arranged for Council members to carry on promotions and supply while he was gone. The council would meet in weekly session while he was gone…

…And that was that.

Something round and soft warmed Raschid's feet. He looked down, and there he saw the girl Saa'lu asleep at last, curled at the foot of his desk. She still held Raschid's sheaf of spare paper, pens and ink. The Shah stood and motioned quietly to Saud, who lifted the girl quietly in his hands and carried her to bed.

A Shah came with a lot of baggage. His guards were packing his gear for the move to the north: armour, horses, spare armour, spare bows – and mules loaded with papers and printed forms. The Royal Chamberlain had taken it upon himself to come, and was busily organizing Raschid's household on campaign. The man's moustache bristled so aggressively that no one dared to argue with him

Sandhri - Yariim – Itbit!

The thought was with him every instant, like an ice cold knife stabbing at his heart. Raschid clamped his arms about himself, feeling himself fall slowly forwards. A huge hand came from behind to steady him on his feet.

"Sleep, my Lord."

"No, Saud. Not yet." A Shah could not weep. A Shah could not show weakness. The people of Osra needed him to be their rock.

Saud, of course, would never sleep until Raschid no longer needed him. The huge tiger stood as a shield, hiding Raschid from view as the Shah drew in a breath and mastered his mind.

They stood beside the garden of the sorcerers. Wasps flew in and out on constant patrol, painfully aware that something was amiss. Raschid waved a weary hand as yellow insects accompanied him towards the tower.

"They will need help in the winter. Remind Fatima to make sure hot water gets piped through the line that runs past their hive."

"Yes, my lord." Saud ambled along at Raschid's side. "They have a new princess now. We wanted to make her a little hive near the kitchen chimney."

"Who wanted to?"

"Just someone." Saud looked guilt-bitten; only Sandhri would have suggested the kitchen as a home for a horde of strange, funny bugs. "I forget."

Raschid mounted the steps of the Sorcerer's tower. He had no talent for magic, but he was pleased to see it pursued so thoughtfully and thoroughly. Old Hassan saw him enter, dismissed three arguing apprentices, and stumped over to Raschid's side.

The old man waved to a bench.

"Mirror. They just delivered it." He snorted. "It's magical, but it's old work. Your Tulu Begh did not make this."

They moved to a window beside Hassan's work bench. The old man took up the mirror, shooting a sidewise glance at Raschid.

"More worries?"

"More worries." Raschid swayed with fatigue. "Hassan. Could it be true? Could this Tsu-Khan somehow use the dead as a weapon?"

The old sorcerer lifted up Tulu Begh's mirror and inspected it with a practiced eye.

"No man of God would. Eh? No, no man of God. But *him?*" The old man squinted across the mirror's surface. "Could be done. Ha – must be being done! They wouldn't claim it if he didn't do it!" Hassan rapped the mirror three times with his knuckles, and it glowed with a strange eerie blue light. "Hmph. Scry mirror. Links to another mirror with the same inscriptions. Old work. No one knows how to make 'em any more – mind you' we're trying…"

"Hassan – you say someone like the Tsu-Khan can use the dead?" Raschid felt strangely disjointed from his body – he floated in a haze. "Why someone like the Tsu-Khan?"

"*She* knows. The black one – the storyteller. But she'd never tell…" Hassan let the mirror rest on a table and covered it with a blue cloth smothered in ink stains. "But as for practical advice? I don't know, boy. Lots of nasty possibilities. So keep our sorcerers up tight with your frontline troops, and make sure your musketeers can all load with silver."

"Silver." Yes… Raschid remembered the demon K'aath and her minions all too well. The royal guard always carried silver bullets and silver-inlaid blades. "I will see to it."

Walking familiar paths, Raschid found himself moving down the palace colonnades. Abwan and Saud were beside him, as were two of the Royal council. They somehow seemed to walk in front of him, making him change direction to avoid stepping on their feet. The changes somehow led him to a quiet hall, then past a cool, quiet chamber – and finally into a great, quiet room fragrant with the scents of growing things and rain. It was the royal bedroom, and a great striped ball of fluff lay curled up in the cushions at the door. Raschid looked down dizzily, having trouble focusing on the coltish collection of muscles, curves and tail.

"Saa'lu?"

"The girl was distressed, Lord. She wanted to be near you, in case you needed her." Pandat, president of the Royal council led the Shah gently over towards his bed. "Perhaps you might sit here with her for a while? It might help the girl to sleep."

Dazed, Raschid surged half up off his own bed.

"Too much to do…"

"Yes yes, My Shah – but you can do them here for a while." Pandat signed to someone, and the shutters were drawn, cloaking the room in darkness. "Rest your eyes for a while, my lord – just for a while."

Raschid sat on his bed, and felt himself sway.

"General Abwan…"

"We shall prepare all your travel arrangements, My Shah." The Councilors, and guards withdrew softly. "We shall have you with the army soon."

"Good. Yes…" Fatima was somehow present, helping him remove his robe, his pistols, yatagan and sword. "Yes…"

He lay on his own bed, and the pillows smelled of Sandhri and Yariim. The scent of them was all around him – her could almost hear Sandhri's voice telling quiet stories in the bedroom's peace. Raschid felt himself sinking, then suddenly managed to raise up his head.

"P-Pandat! Melt the palace silver into bullets. All of it!" He sank back down. "Osra's palace has no… no need for frippery."

"Yes, my Shah." Fatima held a finger to her lips and motioned the concerned, anxious entourage to back away. "Ssssh. Rest your eyes, now. All will be done."

She laid Sandhri's old fez underneath Raschid's arm, bowed profoundly low and quietly left the room. She closed the doors, stepping over the sleeping lemur girl at the threshold. Six guards took station in the secret corridor that guarded the Shah's room. Fatima took Saud by the arm, inspected him for a moment, and then pushed him off towards his own bed.

In the ante-chamber outside, Pandat and his senior council, Colonel Abwan and Marsuk all awaited anxiously. Fatima wiped her face and heaved a sigh of relief.

"He will sleep."

"Thank God." The Councilors bowed in relief. "He insisted on doing every little thing himself."

"Activity. He wanted the activity." Fatima dragged fingers through her hair, pulling at her long rabbit ears. Her shoulders were bowed with fatigue. "Hopefully he will sleep for a full day."

Marsuk looked up from toying with his sword – a thin sword made for a girl's small hand.

"Any word?"

"None." Abwan looked as bad as the Shah – worn, torn and muddy. "We're still searching."

There were things to organize. General Ataman needed his Shah with the army, and the elite guard divisions had to be readied for the move. The little core of Raschid's staff moved out into the Whispering Hall, there to deal with the chaos of the day.

A courier arrived at the palace gates – a young officer on an exhausted black horse. The man was taken to the court, where he knelt and proffered a scroll to Colonel Abwan. In lieu of any better arrangement, Abwan took the message and read it quietly. He signed that the courier be given rest, food and drink and walked away. Abwan signed for Marsuk, the garrison colonel and officers of the guard, and the soldiers all gathered quietly in the palace garden.

Abwan pushed the scroll through his belt.

"It's from General Ataman. The Khan is on the move. Scouts have seen enemy troops marching north of the Kakuzak pass."

A garrison officer frowned. "Marching to attack us?"

"No. Withdrawing to the north."

As one, the men all turned to look up at the Shah's shuttered windows. Colonel Marsuk shook his head.

"Ataman needs him."

Abwan gave a grunt. "Then I hope he sleeps." The old dog settled his sword through his sash. "Tomorrow, he will want to march.

"North, to Kakuzan."

***

Cold winds whipped the surface of theAmu Daja into little claws of foam. From time to time, the clouds streaked the far horizon with rain. The lighting was magnificent – moody, dark and shot through with hidden drama. If Meng had thought to bring painting brushes and decent ink, he would have tried to capture it on paper.

Instead, the thin sage knelt in the papyrus reeds beside the river, gazing across the wide, wind-swept waters. Here and there, a reed boat nosed through the shallows as fishermen checked fish traps or cast their nets downwind. Cattle lowed as they settled in the fields, their white hides gleaming in the murky light.

A torn fence and muddy tracks had led Meng this far. Peasants said that they had heard bells ringing in the night – bells, gongs or scrap iron. The trail of confusion had led from a ghastly farm in the middle of the wilderness – a place with a torn haystack and rotting bodies in the fields. It had followed a creek bed, leaving huge tracks that looked like disks gouged into the mud. It had passed without trace along back roads and solid ground, leaving a trail of peasant stories about noises in the night. And now finally it led here…

Whatever it was, Meng was falling far, far behind. Marwan the camel was an admirable companion, tireless and cunning, but he had his limits. Still seasick from the ride, Meng clung onto the camel for stability, swaying as he looked out into the rain.

Whatever it was, it had carried Queen Sandhri, Queen Yariim and all of their assailants. It had been inside a haystack hidden at a farm near Sath – and it moved faster than a galloping camel or a horse. And now it seemed that it had crossed the river. Perhaps by boat? The entire escape route had been well planned.

The downpour would start again soon, and all tracks would be lost. Once over the river, Meng would lose the ability to follow his quarry. He sat cross legged in the reeds, his little tail fluffing out in thought as he placed his chin upon his hand and pondered.

He could not follow – so he must therefore intercept. Captives of so high a rank would be taken to the highest possible authority – the Tsu-Khan himself. And the Tsu-Khan would be with his army far to the north.

There was nothing for it. Meng would have to leave Osra, pass through the wild mountains of Kakuzan and speedily infiltrate the Khan's horde. He would pose as a labourer or engineer and see if he could discover the whereabouts of the missing Queens.

Itbit…

Her name tortured him. Her image hung in his mind. Worried, anxious, driven and dutiful, Meng fretted about her, ferverently hoping that all was well – that Itbit had returned home.

Surely by now she had returned. She *must* be safe – she had to be safe. And when he returned, he would be courageous enough to tell her of the love he felt for her inside his heart.

But first – the Queens! He would do his duty to the Shah, and his honour as a friend. There were boats here that could ferry him across the river, and people who could take a message back to the Shah.

"Graaaaaaaaaawk!"

Marwan made his displeasure known; the camel thought it was high time they were both off on their way. Meng rose to his feet, took the camel by its leading rope, and walked along the riverbank towards the fishermen.

"Very well, you cantankerous beast. We shall continue." The two mismatched creatures plodded off side by side. Meng heaved a sigh. "If it is not an imposition, this humble one will also wash your hide tonight. Please forgive me if I point out your errors, but your odor is unnecessarily strong…"

"Graaaaaawk!"

"Indeed."

The camel had made his objections strenuously known. With a resigned sigh, Meng led the camel off into the rain and wind, pondering on the fearsome task that was now theirs to complete.

Chapter Twelve:

The hut's floor rocked in a strange, diagonal motion – back, forth, back, forth – up, down, up, down. The whole world dipped and slid sometimes as the rhythm jerked and changed. The hemispherical roof overhead echoed to the rhythmic clash and hammer of distant cymbal blows. The floor was deep in uki droppings, and ancient strata of dirt.

Light filtered in through a single door. Emir Had'idh sat on the threshold, facing outward, cursing and snarling in rage. He hit out with a stick at the metal hut that surrounded them, keeping up a constant tirade.

"Left! Avoid the mire, you pointless hovel! Go left! Left!"

The scene outside the door was in constant motion. The hut was borne upon six legs, and the legs carried the hut at phenomenal speed across open, rolling countryside. Made of tarnished brass, the hut clanged and clattered across streams and roads, through woods and grasslands, wincing unhappily every time Had'idh struck it with his whip.

"Useless scrap heap! Faster! Faster! Move your feet!"

Had'idh's curses went on and on. The hut scampered to make more speed. Sitting far back against the rear wall, Sandhri was bucked half off the floor as the hut took a jump over a broken old stone wall.

Drained and disheveled, the bat sat upright on a pile of horse blankets. Blood had crusted in her hair, and one eye was swollen. A foul headache tore at her – a legacy of Had'idh's blow to her skull. Seasick and half suffocated, Sandhri put a hand to the curved wall behind her and tried to keep herself as steady as she could.

Yariim lay on the floor, her head pillowed in Sandhri's lap. The mouse's left thigh was sheathed in dried, black blood, and Sandhri's robes had been torn to make length after length of bandage to wrap up Yariim's arrow wound.

Yariim was running a fever. She panted, her pink tongue always dry, and her body felt burning hot to touch. Sandhri tended her as best she could in a filthy, rocking hut with neither air nor light, but her friend was growing sick. The wound had to be tended properly, and tended soon.

Sandhri glanced up towards the door. Two guards sat facing towards her with blades resting across their thighs, never taking their eyes from their royal guests. Two more tried to rest on pallets spread across the heaving floor. The hut stood at least twenty feet above the ground, and there was no way for a pregnant woman or an injured girl to leap down.

Yariim's eyes flickered open. Her gaze was horribly wild and bright. When she spoke, her voice was barely a whisper in the breeze.

"...Where?"

"North." Sandhri had only a single gourd of drinking water, half empty and lukewarm. She held Yariim's head up and helped her drink, ignoring the dry cracking of her own throat. "Here, drink a little. Little sips – just little…"

The mouse drank weakly, spilling water down her muzzle and into her soft blue fur. Sandhri held up her head, releasing her slowly to pillow Yariim's head back in her lap. Inside Sandhri, her child knew something was terribly wrong. The baby kicked like a bucking bronco. Sandhri held the little creature tight and shushed it, bidding her boy to be still.

Yariim blinked – blinked again – and suddenly her eyes cleared.

"Sandhri – how far have we come?"

"I do not know." Sandhri bent low over Yariim, wiping her brow – talking in a whisper and hiding their faces beneath the curtain of their hair. I t'ink it hass been two days. This hut-thing runs faster t'an a swallow flies!" The bat risked a glance out of the door past Emir Had'idh. "I v'ass unconscious for a long time. But I t'ink v'e are north off the Amu Daja. V'e're climbing high. T'iss might be Kakuzan."

A guard leaned closer, hefting his blade.

"Quiet!"

"Fuck you!" Sandhri was in no mood to be meek. The guards were clearly under orders not to harm wounded or pregnant hostages. "I'm telling a story here! Giff an artist space to v'ork!"

"A story?" The guard seemed to find the concept absurd. "What damned story?"

"It iss the story off the t'ree wild pheasants." Sandhri tried to cushion Yariim as the whole floor tilted and heaved. They were definitely climbing upward through hills or rocks of some kind – and it was getting colder by the minute. Pregnant as hell, Sandhri was generating enough heat for three. She took off the torn remnants of her outer robes and tucked them out about Yariim as a blanket.

> "Now! T'ree pheasants lived in the woods, and each one strutted in splendour through warm summer afternoons. But v'un day, a hunter came and caught them in a trap. He took each bird and cackled as he stuffed t'em into a great big basket, gloating on the profits he v'as about to make.
>
> "Trapped inside the basket, the pheasants were terrified. T'ey knew that tomorrow t'ey v'ould die, and there seemed no v'ay to escape their doom. The first pheasant merely sat in the middle of the floor, his v'ings folded and his face alv'ays serene. The ot'er pheasants fluttered madly about their cage, trying to somehow prize open the bars.
>
> "The bars held tight. V'eeping and v'ailing, the second and third pheasants slumped against the bars and stared into the dark.

> *"In the morning, the hunter laughed and hoisted the basket high. He walked down the road towards the market place – tov'ards the slaughter yards. As he passed beneath a plum tree, the basket struck against a branch, and a fat plum fell down between the bars. The first pheasant looked at the juicy plum in absolute delight.*
> *"A plum! How lucky we are!"*
> *"Lucky?" The other birds were aghast. "Why is a plum lucky?"*
> *"Because it looks delicious!" The first bird offered the plum to the others. "Would either of you care for some?"*
> *"The other two birds wailed.*
> *"How can you eat, v'en v'e are on our way to die?"*
> *"The first bird sucked at his plum with great delight.*
> *"Many t'ings could happen. I could choke on the plum stone and die. The hunter could be struck by lightning and die – or the country could become Buddhist and all meat eating v'ill stop. But at the very least, this iss a delicious plum!"*
> *"He ate quite contentedly, keeping the plum in his mouth as the cage v'as carried in to the slaughter yard. Dead birds hung headless from the branches of every tree, and the chopping axe could be heard v'orking v'ith a hideous regularity. The cage v'as set down beside the chopping block, and the hunter cackled deep inside his soul.*
> *"The hunter opened the cage door to snatch a pheasant for the slaughter. The moment he did so, the first bird spat the plum stone right into the man's eye. The hunter fell back, blinded, and the t'ree birds raced out to freedom, laughing as the v'ind flowed cold and sharp beneath their v'ings."*

One of Sandhri's guards laughed at the tale. Sandhri smiled a sly smile to Yariim, her eyes flicking sidewise to the guards. This was a game she had played before to perfection. She held Yariim up and helped her drink the last of the water from the gourd. Her voice murmured quietly in Yariim's ear.

"T'ere can always be a plum stone, my love. But only if v'e look for one."

The mouse felt burning hot to the touch.

"And if there is no plum?"

"Then I know my honour and my duty, my love." The bat's grey eyes were hard and proud. "I am Queen of Osra – and purple makes the best burial shroud."

With that, Sandhri began pounding on the wall with her fist. She bawled raucously out towards Had'idh.

"Had'idh! Had'idh, you pox-licking goat molester! I haff to pee!"

The Emir turned a look of utter contempt over his shoulder.

"Use the pot!"

"Pot's full. I can use your helmet!" Sandhri dragged the helmet across the floor. "Ooooh! Silk lined, too. Iss lookink like an expensive trip for you!"

Had'idh gave a glance across his shoulder, cursed, and gazed about the world outside. He used his riding whip to direct the hut over to a tangled jumble of boulders, and the metal hut finally began to slow down.

The vehicle stopped, and the silence was deafening. Outside the hut, a cold wind blew. There were green hill slopes, granite boulders and occasional patches of dirty snow. With a creak and groan, the hut suddenly settled on its haunches, and with a horrid thump its belly met the ground.

Stiff, sore and unsteady on his feet, Had'idh tried to rise. The leopard's scarred face was drawn with seasickness, and he leaned against the hut, hanging his head and trying desperately not to be ill.

Sandhri had no such problems. She carefully slid Yariim's head from her lap, and with a grunt she heaved her pregnant self up onto her feet. She pointed commandingly at the two guards.

"You two – pick her up and get her outside into the light. *Carefully.*"

Emir Had'idh jerked up his head.

"Leave her!"

"She has to pee too!" Sandhri stood over Yariim, her tall ears standing proud. "And I haff to heal her leg. If she gets gangrene and dies, you lose half your prize."

Teeth gritted against sea sickness, Had'idh caved in and jerked his chin towards Yariim. The guards picked her up, moving her out into a frosty morning. They were not gentle, but Yariim clenched her jaw and never made a sound.

They stood in a narrow valley gouged across the saddle of a mountain – terrain rough enough to balk sturdy horses and determined men. Breath turned to fog, and moisture into ice. There were patches of old snow clinging in the lee of granite boulders. A stream ran clear and bright along the middle of the valley, its banks rimmed with ice. Tall reeds bent towards the water, bowed over by the weight of crowns of snow.

There was little wind, and no noise except the drip drip drip of water. It seemed an eerie, cold, forgotten place.

Looming over the travelers was a great, tarnished shape – a mighty metal hut that squatted like a monster with its belly to the ground. A huge hemisphere made of ancient brass, the hut had six great, stilt-like legs all ending in metal chicken's feet. A door opened at its front, standing open like an astonished mouth, and two great lenses were topped with a molded metal brow. The hut seemed sad and cowed – unloved and tarnished with the neglect of ages. Sandhri stared at it in wonder, shaking her head as she thought of all the marvelous things there were still for her to see.

A guard threaded a thin line about Sandhri's ankle. The bat looked at the man from across an eight-month-pregnant belly.

"V'at – you t'ink I'm going to sprint so you can't catch me?" With a rude snort, the bat weaved her hand towards the rocks. "Take Yariim over near the stream – and bring blankets! Bring all off t'em!"

Yariim was carried to the icy banks of the stream in the lee of a stand of great black rocks. There was a view down stream and into the fog-shrouded valley below. Sandhri sat beside Yariim, refilling the water gourd, carefully sniffing at the breeze.

Yariim weakly lifted up her head.

"K-Kakuzan. It's Kakuzan."

"Oh?" Sandhri never asked how Yariim knew, but the mouse lifted a hand and pointed to a scrubby tree that loomed over the stream.

"Yalmuk plant. They – they cut it and sell it. You use it to keep moths out of clothing."

"T'en ve're at least five hundred miles from home." Sandhri put a rolled blanket underneath Yariim's head, and then carefully began to remove the mouse's pants. "Damn – t'at hut moves like lightning!"

Trying to keep her face stiff against the pain of her thigh, Yariim rolled her head to look at the huge shape of the walking hut.

"Where did it come from? How did the Tsu-Khan make that?"

"He didn't make it. It's old. It's from elsev'ere." Sandhri worked doggedly on her friends wound. With Yariim's legs bare, the bat could finally see the bandages. They were crusted solid black with blood. Sandhri sat back on her haunches, one hand pressed into the small of her smarting back, and hollered at Had'idh.

"Hey fools! V'e need a fire here!"

The Emir whipped a foul tempered glance towards his prisoners.

"No fire!"

"Fine." Sandhri snapped her fingers. "Then Queen Yariim is dead! I cannot clean the v'ound."

A guard spoke to the Emir – the same guard who had smiled at Sandhri's story. The bat saw the guard sway his Emir, and men began gathering brushwood for a fire. Sandhri stayed patiently beside Yariim.

"A fire, right here. And boil v'ater – lots of it. And I v'ant my dagger back – the thin one that v'ass in the back of my sash. Hurry!"

Men came bringing a cooking pot and chunks of wood. A fire sullenly came to life, the smoke curling idly this way and that in the strange, still fog. Sandhri had a man fill the pot with water and put it on to boil. She saw one of her own pistols in his belt, and held out an imperious black hand.

"Giff me the ram rod. You'll get it back!" She received the tool as her due, then stopped a man from cutting down the living bush nearby. "Not t'at! Iss yalmuk plant! Smells like burning loincloths!" Sandhri chivvied the guards. "Go on, go on! A big fire! The rocks v'ill hide the fire from the valley. Now hurry on!"

Sandhri used warm water to soak the blood-crusted bandages. They peeled stickily away from Yariim's thigh, inch by painful, careful inch. It hurt Yariim like hell. She stiffened, gripping her fists tight, and tried to keep her mind off the pain.

Sandhri's face was intent and deadly serious. Yariim hissed in a breath.

"I… I never knew that you knew medicine?"

"I neffer did. But I am a hill v'oman – and a god damned genius." The bat cursed and used more water, trying to crack dried blood that was fused to Yariim's fur. "Sorry. Bastards! T'iss should have been treated two days ago."

The blue mouse looked up at Sandhri's bloody hair. The left side of her face was swollen.

"You're hurt."

"I'll live, if I can beat the headache." Sandhri hissed as she worked on Yariim's fur – then stiffened and put a hand against her belly. Yariim put a hand on Sandhri's womb, her pink eyes bright with alarm.

"What?"

"Not'ing. Just feels like muscles are torn." The bat took a deep breath, then returned to work. "Bastards left me unconscious for a day. My head bled and stuck to the floor. I tore the scab off trying to get up."

"But our baby is alright?"

"He's alright." Sandhri stroked her belly. "He's still breach, but he's alright."

It took hard, agonizing work to free the bandages from Yariim's fur. They stopped talking as the pain grew worse. Finally the last bandage peeled away in a great, blood-scabbed sheet. Fresh blood welled up from Yariim's bared thigh.

The arrow had gone in parallel to the grain of the muscle. Sandhri reached behind herself with bloody hands and tied her hair up into a knot. She washed her hands, then poured water into the wound, feeling Yariim hiss and stiffen in white-hot pain.

The wound was angry. Red and puffy, but not yet turning to puss. Sandhri probed carefully with the ramrod and the knife, and finally pulled out an infinitesimally tiny scrap of fibre from the wound. Grey-lipped and shaking, Yariim panted in release as Sandhri finally abandoned the wound.

"What – what is it?"

"It v'ass cloth. Cotton." Sandhri inspected the bloody fibers. They were scarcely longer than a little fingernail. "Cloth from your pants v'ass in the wound. The arrow carried it t'rough." The bat gave a sigh. "See – now t'at's v'y I only v'ear silk! Silk doesn't do t'at!"

Yariim swallowed hard while Sandhri washed out the wound. "S-silk. You wear silk b-because you think you might get shot?"

"Nope. Chust makes my arse look good!" Sandhri washed and carefully cleaned the wound. She looked up to see the guards eating bread taken out of a cotton bag.

"Hey! Do you idiots haff supplies?" A guard looked resentfully up. Sandhri held out a hand. "Show me."

There was a cone of sugar, coffee, stale flat bread, and strips of jerked water buffalo that would have made creditable battle armour. Sandhri sniffed and rooted through the sack, then suddenly found a prize.

"Honey. Excellent!"

She poured honey over the wound, then carefully tore new bandages from her shrinking robes. She bound the wound neatly, then sat back, wiping at her brow.

"T'ere. It v'ill heal now. You'll dance again"

"Honey?" Yariim's whole left side felt wooden, stiff and clawed with pain. "Is that a hill remedy? Or did Hassan teach you that?"

"Nope. The v'asps! T'ey steal honey and treat all the children's scrapes and v'ounds." The bat looked about herself. "I could do v'ith about a hundred on t'ose little guys here right now."

Yariim's pants were ruined. Sandhri tucked a blanket about her friend as a skirt. She clandestinely looked about the bed of the stream, examining the beautifully coloured river rocks. Pale and pained, Yariim flicked a glance between the bat and the guards.

"You'll never be able to kill them all with a rock."

"I don't v'ant a weapon. I need rocks to be splitting in two ah! Here!" Sandhri found big flat pebbles, and carefully brought them over beside Yariim. She found a piece of reed grass and dipped it in Yariim's spilled blood, carefully writing little letters onto one of the stones.

She finished her job, and put the stone aside. The bat handed Yariim a fresh pen made out of grass, and then scratched at her lacerated scalp until it freely bled. Yariim tried to hide the motion, looking at the wound in shock.

"What are you doing?"

"V'e are facing the Tsu-Khan. He will try to use magic to be very persuasive." Sandhri dipped the pen in her blood. "Quick – write on the stone!"

Yariim took the pen. The bat let down her hair to hide the activity from the guards.

"Now – Yariim. Do you remember the first time v'e all made love? Do you remember v'at you called me? Write it down."

It was Sandhri's 'bed name' – a name her lovers called her only in the throes of passion and of love. Yariim wrote the words carefully and lovingly, and then Sandhri snatched away the stone.

She split both rocks with a hammer stone, breaking them in two. She wrapped strands of their own hair about the largest half of each stone, and buried them in amongst the rocks. The smaller half of Yariim's stone she pressed into her friend's hand.

"T'ere! Hide it!" The bat looked about to check whether the magic had been seen. "It lasts for a few days. If someone tries to cast a spell on you, it flows into the hidden half of the rock and out into the ground. Your secret name iss like a shield." Sandhri tucked her own stone fragment into her waist band. "Keep it hidden!"

Yariim lolled her head on its pillow and looked at her lover in amazement.

"Is that Hassan's magic?"

"Iss hill magic!" Sandhri's belief carried fervent power. "Shhh! Had'idh comes!"

The Emir stalked forward over the uneven rocks, scarring the frosty grass. His breath puffed in clouds of vapour as he came.

"Well? What's her condition?"

"The v'ound iss clean – but she needs rest! In a bed!" Sandhri helped herself to stale bread from the bag, tore the bread in two and gave Yariim the bigger half. "You keep her in t'at walking hut and you might kill her!"

Had'idh hissed. The fog was too good an asset to waste; it hid the hut from prying eyes, but still let him see the path ahead. The Emir used his whip to signal to his men.

"We move on. We'll rest in two hours once we leave this miserable little pass." He signed to his men. "Pick the blue one up! Get her into the hut."

Men came to pick Yariim back up and carry her to the hut. Sandhri paused to tread down the earth on the buried chunks of stone. A guard took her by the leash and followed her to the hut, where Had'idh was kicking irritably at the giant metal monster.

Had'idh's booted foot rang against the molded brass.

"Up! Come on – we're leaving!"

The hut made a creaking noise and still squatted on the ground. It held out one foot and wiggled it before Had'idh, the hut's claws gleaming huge enough to eviscerate a whale. Metal creaked and groaned, the hut flexing its lower lip to make sad little sounds. The noises only made Had'idh more angry.

"No! We're moving *now!* You worthless heap of junk! You pile of scrap iron!"

He raised his whip to strike the hut. With a cold hiss, Sandhri jerked the whip out of his hand.

"Leave the poor t'ing alone!"

The Emir whipped back his fist, ready to club Sandhri to the ground. The bat stood her ground.

"How long v'ould it take you to die, if the Tsu-Khan finds out you hit me, and I miscarried and dropped dead?"

Had'idh held himself back and contented himself with shoving Sandhri hard.

"You test my limits too much, woman."

"Women haff a pretty good idea off *your* limits, Had'idh." Sandhri gestured to the metal hut. "If you opened your eyes instead off your mouth, you might be smarter."

Awkward from her belly, Sandhri made her way over to the hut. She patted the brass hull with one hand and made soothing noises, and then climbed up to look at his feet.

"Morons! T'iss poor hut hass a stone caught in his foot!" Sandhri clambered up onto the hut's great splay-clawed foot, and prized at a stone that had become jammed inside the machine's toe mechanism. She began to work the stone free, patting the hut kindly on the shin all of the while. "T'ere t'ere. It only hurt for a minute, then out it comes – you'll see." The stone popped out and clattered to the ground. Sandhri smoothed the hut's ankle with clever black hands. "Shhh shhh. All better now. Just work the footsies for a bit, yes? Move it in a circle like this."

The huge hut tilted to look down at its cured foot, then looked up at Sandhri. The bat smiled, and Had'idh strode forward to give the bat a shove.

"Get inside."

"Then lift me." Sandhri gave an arrogant, contemptuous look at her captors. "I'm a pregnant woman."

Had'idh seethed, then jerked his chin at two of his men. The soldiers lifted Sandhri roughly by the arms and hoisted her up into the hut's open door. The hut tilted to give her access, trying to settle to its belly to minimize Sandhri's climb. The men swung aboard, and Emir Had'idh slashed at the hut with his riding whip and gave a savage snarl.

"Enough!" He hit the hut again, and its hull rang like a bell. "That way! North and west! North – and stop wasting time."

A loud *boom* sounded from somewhere in the mist. A low rumble like a barrel rolling over a wooden floor warbled overhead, and then a pile of boulders erupted in a spectacular explosion. Chips of rock and red hot iron clattered from the hut's brass hull. The hut turned, looked behind itself in panic, and then fled at breathtaking speed up the valley and on into the fog.

Sandhri caught a brief glimpse of a distant knot of men – turbaned men with mules and machinery. Long-coated men on horseback spurred after the hut, standing in their stirrups to fire long rifles. The hut rang to the sound of bullet strikes, and Sandhri have a hoot of glee!

"Kakuzaks! And a mountain gun!" It was a border patrol armed with one of Raschid's best toys – a rifled gun that could be carried dismantled on pack mules. "You t'ought Raschid left any pass unguarded?"

Another cannon shot rang out, and the explosive shell hit the valley walls ahead of the hut. Shards of shone rained down onto the hut as it galloped faster and faster over the tangled rocks and scree. A third shot came – and missed wildly. Speed and the fog had hidden the hut. It moved at such speed that the pursuing Kakuzaks would swiftly give up the chase. Expecting no less, Sandhri sat on the floor, one hand on the inside curve of the hull to keep herself steady. The hut gathered itself and leapt spectacularly across a gorge, throwing everyone inside the hull into a heap. Yariim cried out, and Sandhri tried to heft her up off the floor to cushion the ride.

"Fast! Damn – t'is thing can run!" Sandhri saw snow and boulders flashing past. "V'ere almost across the pass."

The hut overleapt a second gorge with scarcely a ripple in its stride. Precipices that made this route impassable to mere men were taken by the hut at breakneck speed. Her bottom numb from the ride, Sandhri gasped as the sensation of torn muscle came to rip at her belly once again.

Yariim was grey-lipped and swallowing, trying to fight her own pain. She looked at Sandhri in alarm.

"Are you alright?"

"I'm alright. Chust shaken." The bat winced, holding her belly in her hands. "I hope v'e get t'ere soon."

The hut ran downhill, out into an open valley covered in little stones. It was a wild ride, but a strangely smooth one. Holding tight to Sandhri's hand, Yariim rolled her head and looked outwards through the door.

"Sandhri – you said you knew where this hut might have come from? That you knew that it was old?"

The bat kept her face turned away as she tended to Yariim.

"It's old."

Yariim looked about the hut in wonder. "Who on Aku-Mashad made it?"

"It's from a tale. I t'ink a great many t'ings here are from old, old tales." Sandhri wet a cloth and laid it across her friend's brow. "Shhhh now. Time to try and sleep."

The hut ran on and on, as fast as the wind. Its claws flicked up the stones behind it as it ran. With mists thinning into a sun-lit day, it sped out into the great steppe lands of the north.

It ran north and west – towards the armies of the Khan…

***

Sour and rebellious, Itbit should have felt on top of the world. By day, she rode wild and free across countryside filled with icy winter. By night, she was a lover. She had broken free from the palace at last, and had become a woman in her own right rather than just Itbit, the palace mascot. She had a Prince as a lover, and a new world to explore…

… In theory, life simply couldn't have been better.

She rode beside her Prince, Tulu Begh. In the light of a winters afternoon, he looked lean and wild and handsome. The blue-eyed horse beneath him sped like an arrow shot from a bow, its muscles gleaming bright as polished metal as it galloped through the hills. Riding so fast that the wind whipped her long blonde hair out in a brilliant stream, Itbit looked at him and felt her heart make a strange, double-bladed pang.

Pride.

Shame.

Where were all her friends?

Sandhri would be crying. Raschid would be stunned. Yariim would be soldiering on and trying to keep the family's spirits bright. And Meng…

Meng…!

Itbit thought of poor gentle Meng, and was sickened by herself. It was a road she refused to let her mind travel. With a harsh cry, she spurred her horse to greater speed, passing Tulu Begh and whisking fast across a mountain stream.

She rode like a girl possessed, urging the horse to mount hill slopes at breakneck speed. Great sheets of spray flew up as she raced through a valley flooded by winter rains. Once, two men in long khaftan coats rose up from ambush and leveled muskets at her. Tulu Begh uncorked a water flask and unleashed a ghost which flew shrieking at the gunmen's eyes. Two musket shots went wide – the ghost flew screaming and weeping off into the breeze, and Tulu Begh laughed as he galloped swifter than the winds across an open mountainside.

Evening fell. They galloped madly past a jet black lake. On the far side of the water, blocking the roadway, campfires gleamed where thousands of men and horses bedded down in tents of felt. These were the Kakuzaks, and they seemed not to see the two riders on their demon horses. The blue-eyed mounts seemed to flicker half in and half out of dreams, speeding like wisps of mist upon a story breeze.

With the campfires many miles behind, the horses finally slowed. They had come down out of the heavily guarded passes, worming along a track scarcely visibly amongst the scree. The great steppes spread before them – a black expanse that looked flat and empty as a grave. An icy wind blew across the oceans of grass, chilling Itbit right down to the bone. Pleased with a day of breakneck travel, Tulu Begh swept off his cap and turned to

Itbit with bright, flashing eyes.

"So much for the passes! A demon horse moving at speed can only be seen by the pure at heart." The nomad prince opened up his arms in a gesture of extravagant triumph. "It would seem purity is a scant quality back there in the hills!"

Itbit's horse stood stock still. After an entire day of running, it neither sweated nor shook. It simply stood like a stone, its blue eyes cold and hostile. Itbit released her reins slowly, wanting to shrink away from all contact with the horse.

Full of high spirits, Tulu Begh leapt down from his own mount with a sprightly jump. He reached up and lifted Itbit from the saddle, holding her on high and relishing her like a delicious prize.

"Ha! You are cold, dear squeaker!" He gave the mouse a squeeze, still effortlessly holding her up off the ground. "Well then- we shall have to warm you up and make you limber. Come see what I have prepared!"

With a triumphant flick of his wrist, Tulu Begh jerked at a shape in the darkness. An old tarpaulin had been spread across a bundle left in the grass, the position marked by a scraggly little tree. Tulu Begh had prepared for his return to the steppes. He opened the parcel to reveal a tent and blankets, firewood and wine. Pleased at his own cleverness, he shook out the tent and pegged it into place.

Itbit stood with her arms hugged about herself. The icy wind blowing from the mountain lakes made her hair stream into the darkness. Hollow eyed, she stared back at the mountains, wanting to see beyond them into Osra – into home.

A little campfire flickered into life, its flames tossed ragged by the winds. Tulu Begh whistled as he produced a frying pan, spinning it in his fingers like a conjurer toying with a silver plate. He set onions frying beside choice slivers of root vegetables, then unwrapped two spicy sausages from his secret treasure trove. He put the sausages to the pan and mulled his wine, while Itbit stood disconsolately in the dark.

The scent of sausage made Itbit wince. Tulu Begh saw to their dinner, and flicked one sly glance at the girl.

"There was a wise man of the steppes – my grandfather, in point of fact. He believed that an *adult* should live a life of no regrets." Tulu Begh pricked the sausages with all the skill of a surgeon at play. "Regret is a weakness brought on by doubting your ability to decide things for yourself."

Itbit's slim back stiffened with pride. Her bottom taut and her hair gleaming, she balled her hands into fists and stared into the dark.

"Itbit has no regrets. Itbit can decide things for herself!" She looked back at Tulu Begh, her pink eyes full of bitterness and rebellion. "No one is going to tell Itbit what she must and must not do."

Tulu Begh looked at her – his narrow face handsome and exotic in the firelight, his eyes challenging and full of promised fire. Itbit strode to him, propelled by pride. She took him in her arms and kissed him, showing this nomad prince that she was no one's little girl. He repaid her with another lesson, and she learned the lesson well.

Lying naked in their shared bed with her lover holding her possessively from behind, Itbit lay for long, long hours, staring off towards the embers of the fire. Flames turned to ashes – and Itbit's visions of a glorious future turned dry and cold. Left with nothing but her pride, she lay listening to the wind.

Her clothing lay beneath her head as a pillow – a pillow with one hard corner that slowly dug into Itbit's face. Trying to keep Tulu Begh asleep, the green mouse moved softly, easing her clothing out beneath her head. She felt in the darkness, and discovered the source of the annoyance – a little book wrapped in her sash. A book no bigger than the palm of her hand.

Meng's birthday gift – forgotten and unread. Itbit had left the palace without even wishing him goodbye.

Meng! The though of him was like a blade twisting through her heart. What would he say about her now? A girl naked and disheveled on an icy steppe – soiled inside and out. Itbit eased out of the blankets and sat silently in the chill, the northern lights outlining her nude figure against the nighttime sky.

The horses both stood watching her through their soulless blue eyes. Neither animal had moved since they had been abandoned. Neither one showed Itbit anything but cold, unwinking disinterest.

Would her horse take her back to Osra if she tried to ride it? And… after all that she had done, how could she ever go home?

Head bowed, Itbit re-wrapped her clothing into a pillow and slid back into bed. A cold wind blew across the steppes, and home was many hundreds of miles away.

Behind Itbit, unseen in the darkness, Tulu Begh's handsome face twisted into a low, sly smile…

***

The sound of marching was rhythmic and unending – boots tramping in unison. Officers calling and horse harness jangling. It had started just after midnight, and would continue for hours: Osranii troops marched long before dawn in order to beat the midday heat. Even in winter, march discipline remained the same. Raschid had seen the first troops off upon their way at three in the morning. He would follow with the royal household after dawn. Until then, there was time for morning prayers, and a long, silent pre-dawn darkness lit by candlefire.

"Sire? Sire!"

Sitting cross-legged at a camp table, reading the Koran, Raschid looked up as the voice called him a second time. Abwan – resplendent in full mail, silvered breast plates and blue brocade, knelt just inside the door.

"Sire– there are some boats pulling up the river. Frankish boats."

Without a word, Raschid stood. Clad in plates and mail, still wearing his scholar's robes, he looked hollow eyed and serious. There was no joy in him – merely unflagging duty. The tall Jackal stooped to exit the low door of his tent, and then exited out into a cold and windswept dawn.

The royal guard divisions were on the march – the finest heavy cavalry in the world, the supremely efficient guard infantry and artillery. With them came the Sultan's bodyguard cavalry from Meepsoor – spectacularly armoured men on henna-dyed armoured horses, armed with steel quoits, punch daggers, lances, bows and gauntlet swords. They added a note of fantastic splendour to the royal blue of Osra's guards.

The guards were marching – long columns of immaculate infantry in blue coats and red turbaned helmets. They carried Osra's secret weapon – the rifled breech loading musket. Infantry marched beside the roads, and the guard artillery rode up the central lane, their cannon gleaming in the dark. Raschid watched courage, pride and technology march off to war, his brown eyes dark and expressionless in the gloom.

Raschid's usual guardsmen knelt about the tent on watch. With them now were ten strange figures – tall, slim leopards dressed in padded cotton armour against the cold. The

Ha' kuto Hanin kissed their hands to Raschid, and their Prince came forward with a bow.

Raschid inclined his head.

"Prince H'utan'tan."

"My Lord Raschid-Shah." The Ha' kuto Hanin Prince bowed low. His men were armed with muskets, spears and shields of Zebra hide. "Raschid-Shah, Frank boat come. Not so many, not so big. Yes."

The slim leopard pointed to the river with his spear. Raschid turned his back to the road and its columns of marching men and looked out towards a river that shone a dark gunmetal grey.

The assembly camp was outside of Sath, down between the ancient pyramids. Coming up into the delta of the Amu Daja were four strange solid, blocky ships. The vessels were utterly barbaric – black hulled and painted with bands of strange heraldic colours. The masts were square rigged, and were clearly crewed by efficient men. Sails flashed in on the yards and opened on the bowsprits as the vessels tacked against the wind. They were low in the water – much like an Osranii ship – but seemed made for slower sailing and far heavier seas.

The ships were ignoring the port of Sath and making for the river beach nearby. Raschid saw a rowing boat down on the shore, where a Frank of some kind was gesticulating wildly and talking to some of the royal bodyguards. Saud seemed to be in charge of the welcoming committee, and the huge tiger seemed bemused to find himself facing a creature as huge, as fearsome and as hairy as himself. The Frank was a black bear hung with mail armour and bearing a titanic two handed sword. He turned and waved to figures on the prows of the incoming ships, clearly beckoning them ashore.

A page came running to Raschid's side, fresh from the beach.

"My Shah – they say they are allies! They say they have come to the summons of our ambassador!" The page's voice squeaked, and he kept his face hidden from the Shah. "They have brought their King!"

Raschid turned from watching the ships grounding themselves deliberately on the sand banks and inspected the young page.

"Saa'lu – you were not to come with the army."

Male dress did little to hide the lemur girl's great stripy tail. She looked up guiltily.

"I go to serve you, Sire! And the General! General Ataman requested my presence." The girl shrank, bowing down. "I do not mean to displease you."

"I am not displeased. But find yourself a sword and keep it with you. There is a spare one in my baggage." The ships had all grounded themselves, and lowered gang planks. They seemed well practiced at swiftly disgorging fighting men ashore. A vast, heavy man made his way down the first gangplank, followed by a standard bearer and a man holding a great chequered bag pierced through with tubes and pipes. Their men from the rowboat met them, pointing up the slopes towards Raschid. The Shah waved back his watchful bodyguards and quietly strode towards the visitors, his white robes swirling in the river wind.

More and more newcomers reached the shores – a chaotic jumble of men, all of them huge, all armed with vast, straight swords, mail and javelins. Here and there a musket or a brace of pistols gleamed. The big men closed protectively around their chief – a huge bear so old that his fur had turned completely grey. The old man lifted his muzzle, hunting for a clear sight of Raschid, then strode forwards with a tread so heavy he almost made the river quake. Beside him came his standard bearer and musician – both of them apparently his grandsons or kin.

Saud came and knelt beside Raschid. The Shah rested a reassuring hand upon the tiger's shoulder, then bowed quietly to his guests. The ancient, massive bear looked Raschid quietly in the face, giving him a long and searching look.

The Frankish musician nodded softly, and leaned to murmur into his master's ear.

<<And he shall be unadorned, for he needs no adornment. He will wear neither silks nor gold....>>

The old man nodded. He swung his titanic sword down off his shoulder and jammed it point down in the soil, planting his fist upon his hip. He bellowed in Frankish – his accent harsh and almost incomprehensible.

"I am The McCallum! The Lord of the Isles!"

In a quieter voice, he spoke to Raschid – his eyes gently watching the Shah.

"We have come. We seek Prester John!"

Raschid folded his hands into his sleeves, unconsciously adopting Meng's quiet dignity. He spoke in Frankish to the old, grey lord.

<<I am Shah Raschid, the ruler of Osra.>> He performed a quiet *Salaam*. <<Forgive me, guests – but I do not know your 'Prester John'.>>

"No doubt." The McCallum flexed shoulders broad enough to lift a tree. "It is an old, old tale – every bard knows it." The old man jerked his head to indicate the musician behind him. "The tales say that there will one day be a ruler. A king of the east who will shelter Christian and Musselman alike. A king who wears no silks. A laird who wears no golden crown."

The young black bear holding the strange musical instrument looked directly at Raschid.

"The wise women came. They said there was a king here who never had a pen out of his hand. That there was a king who had slain a demon with one shot from his bow." The bard looked at the Osranii army on the march beside the river. "They said that Prester John had need of swords."

Raschid looked quietly back towards his army. The river wind ruffled his fur.

"I slew a demon with my bow." He lifted his chin to look towards the shattered ruins that had once been the evil sphinx of Sath. "There, on the headlands. She was the demon K'aath."

The bard and the standard bearer exchanged one quick look, then knelt upon the sand. The huge, ancient 'McCallum' looked intently at Raschid as though he were a man seeing a long awaited son. He stepped forward and embraced Raschid, his muscles feeling hard as teak. He patted Raschid on his armoured back, then took him underneath his arm.

"I am old, Shah Raschid of Osra. But I have stirred myself for this. Our men brought word to us of your ambassadors to those lily livered soft-cocks on the continent. Then our madling women brought us their dreams of you."

They walked slowly on the sand. The four ships were disgorging more and more men, all of whom were armed to the teeth. The old man pointed a mailed fist at his men.

"Nine hundred men, raised on whiskey, beef and a lemon a week. All kin. *Islemen!*" He spoke the word as though it explained all by itself. "When the devil needs a kicking, boy, then an Isleman will administer."

Raschid looked at the barbaric warriors in growing admiration. He turned to look fondly at the mad old man.

"Lord McCallum – how far have you come?"

"From the far ends of the world, my boy. From the far ends of the world."

The old man breathed hard and slow. He stood with Raschid and watched the Osranii royal guard file past. The guard division numbered six thousand men, and they traveled in grim, purposeful silence.

The McCallum gave a quiet, thoughtful nod. His voice was a whisper that carried only to Raschid's ear.

"Is it bad?"

"It is bad." Raschid watched his army march. "We believe we are outnumbered five to one – and none of the Franks will help us."

Raschid looked at the old man and let his wonder and confusion creep into his voice. "Why did you come? *Why?*"

"*Because,* my boy." The old man looked out across the river, staring at nothing but the breeze. "Because the old woman spoke. She told of a coming battle, and said that it might be the *last* battle. The last one that truly counts. The last time true good meets real evil." His voice was quiet, his words drifting with the breeze. "She said that Prester John would lead the last crusade – the Guardians of Light. She said that he would win, and save all – or lose, and the world would fall into darkness."

He looked at Raschid and shook his head.

"That's no battle any man should face without Islemen at his side."

He held out his hand to Raschid. The Shah hesitated, then took the man's huge hand and gripped it hard. The bear thumped him on the shoulder and led the way back to his men.

"Nine hundred Islemen! Any one of them is worth ten soft-cock continentals! So that's the same as bringing you nine thousand." He looked to the road above. "We brought whiskey, lemons, beef and biscuit, but might need to presume upon you lads for supplies."

"You shall have them. You shall have them." Nine hundred men – all of them had come thousands of miles to the fight. Raschid felt a vague stir of flame inside his heart. "Nine thousand. That lowers the odds to four to one."

"Aye lad. That's the way! You point my lads at the killing, and we'll get the damned job done!"

The old man turned to signal his men up onto the road. He swiveled back and looked thoughtfully at Raschid.

"They came, you know. The Order."

Raschid blinked.

"The Order?"

"Aye. The Brotherhood of Light." The huge bear looked thoughtful. "I asked them whether they thought that I should go."

"The Brotherhood…" Raschid remembered plain-gowned men at a banquet long ago. "Yes… what did they say?"

"They said that if any man believed in all it is to be a knight - If any man believed a better world is possible, then let them come."

The old man looked out to where dawn streamed full across the Amu Daja. Ibises flew overhead in great sighing squadrons, line after line of them heading off into the sun. He spoke to himself, watching the flight of the graceful birds.

"It will all be changed, lad. A better world, or a broken one." The McCallum jerked his sword out of the sand. "We're here now – so you can get it started. Lets go bust some cods."

Chapter Thirteen

They were little places, all locked down to endure the bitter northern winter. The first villages were merely clusters of turf-rooved huts that stood beside a church. Snow had cloaked everything with white, but the houses could be seen by the smoke that rose from chimney holes in their ceilings. Here and there men chopped wood, or chipped ice from the stream to fill buckets for the evening stew. Women carried fodder to the winter livestock, while children played snow castles amongst the tall, dark evergreens.

It was the children who died first; they were furthest from the village heart, and easiest to silence. Arrows hissed and bit into flesh with a sound like a cleaver chopping wood. Little bodies were pinned to trees, or left sprawling in the snow forts to stain the ice a brilliant red.

The Tsu-Khan's scouts were old hands at their favourite game. The first places found were always little villages. But to prevent them from becoming running sores of ambush and rebellion behind the army lines, they were always wiped out to a man. The riders burst in from the trees, arrows nocked and murdering in eerie silence. Villagers looked up in shock, spinning as the arrows pierced them. The riders fanned out to hound the fugitives, their swords and long, hooked spears finally coming into play. They did not stop to rape, but killed the pretty girls where they cowered shrieking in their huts. They did not stay to loot, but left slaughtered beasts to lie in the snow as food for the oncoming horde. It took only five minutes to destroy a village – and a handful of horsemen could destroy an entire community. With bloody hoof prints spreading through the snow, the silent raiders kicked their horses onwards, pushing west towards the great ice rivers – to the lands of the Franks.

Behind them, they left bodies torn wide apart. The wounds steamed slowly in the deadly winter chill, and all the world was silent.

Village after village fell – and then the trade towns and little cities with their log stockades and their wooden churches. By the time the first survivors had ridden in panic to the west, the Tsu-Khan had already come.

A quarter of a million riders. Sixty thousand infantry conscripted from the Yellow Empire. It was a blight that smeared Aku Mashad from horizon to horizon, lighting up the winter nights with its countless cooking fires.

***

The King of the Pulski was a grey, scarred wolf, long blooded in bitter battles with land barons to the west and nomad raiders to the east. But he had kin married to the princelings of the cities of the plains. When word came of the nomad horde, he bade the bagpipes sound. The king's red banner was unfurled, and his commoners paraded with their short muskets and with axes on their backs. The nobility gathered in their hundreds, leading proud companies of armoured horsemen, the hussars of the north. The King's army numbered almost sixteen thousand strong. With henna-painted horses draped in the skins of tora birds, they marched East to halt the onrushing nomad horde.

Mounted nomads were an old, familiar foe. The Pulski king had armoured wagons in his army that would serve as a fort. From its shelter, the infantry could fire at their foes. From its heart, he could launch his hussars in a devastating charge once the enemy had blundered into exhaustion. It was the tried and tested way of war – successful for hundreds of years, and the Pulski army sang confidently as they marched.

This far to the north, the great river Kuba was completely frozen. The army marched east across the vast expanse of white, jagged ice and on into the empty plains, looking towards the rising smoke that marked their enemies. The King stood upon a hillside with his son the Prince, both men holding warhammers ringed with gold to symbolize their many victories. They saw their own skirmishers fanning out to probe the enemy, and turned to order the army into its battle lines.

The king sent for his heralds, his dukes and his barons, and made a line across the plains with open arms.

"Deploy the wagon fort."

The wagons rumbled forwards slowly, each one drawn by plodding oxen draped with quilted blankets to protect them from the cold. The wagons were slab sided and tall, their sides pierced with loop holes. Infantrymen piled into the wagons and blew the match chords of their muskets into a brighter glow. Spare matches, ball and powder were passed forward from the supply train as the hussars flooded in to fill the center of the hollow fortress walls.

The first cavalry skirmishers began to appear, fleeing backwards from the distant army of the Khan. The skirmishers sped madly past the wagon fort without slowing their pace, their horses rolling mad white eyes and the soldiers reeling in their saddles. Men and horses sheathed in blood, with arrows jutting from their flesh came next. Some collapsed onto the open plains, while others wove in panic back behind the wagon fort.

The day grew quiet. Deepening clouds promised snow fall, and a breeze plucked at the banners, coats and feathers of the waiting men. The grand army of the kingdom, fully sixteen thousand men, awaited the nomad horde and stared towards the East.

They came on in silence. At first, there was only a darker line upon the horizon – a shape half hidden in the winter gloom. Slowly the line became a moving, living thing – a dark mass that flooded forwards all across the snow.

The line ran from horizon to horizon – a dark wave that seemed to drown an entire world. A quarter of a million men came forward in one vast, unbroken line, converging silently upon the wagon fort.

Inside the fortress, the Pulski king rose slowly to his stirrups. He pushed up the visor of his lobster-tailed helmet and stared across the steppes.

"My God. My God…"

From the invaders' lines sounded deep, vast drums. The first cavalry units detached themselves from the horde's front lines and came racing forwards, fanning out to form a skirmish line. More enemy swept inwards from the flanks, moving to encircle the waiting wagon fort. The King watched the onrushing enemy, never once taking his eyes from his foe.

"My son? Take the reserve hussars. Hold the rear of the fort."

"Yes Father." The Prince removed his helmet. He was a wolf with one chewed ear – tall and ragged furred. He looked to the enemy – the vast, oceans of enemy – then gripped his father's arm. He spurred away, his vulture feathers ruffling loudly in the strange silence of the battlefield. With him went Barons, hussars and aides.

The King watched the first enemy skirmishers flood forwards. He lifted up his warhammer and shouted to his men.

"Fire low! Fire fast! Let no man leave the fortress until the royal command comes!" He waved his hammer to guide the thousands of armoured hussars into cover. "Let them waste their arrows! Eventually, they have to charge and meet good Christian steel!"

- And then the arrows came.

The enemy skirmishers approached at a slow canter – and then began their time tested attack. From each main body, small groups raced forwards at break neck speeds, their ponies speeding fast over the snow. The men atop the horses – snow tigers, minks and lynxes, dholes, bears and wolves – suddenly swerved sideways unleashing dense showers of arrow shafts. They rode hard and fast, crouched low behind the bodies of their mounts, firing arrow after arrow in a maddened blur before returning to their units far behind. Yet more groups came racing forwards, and arrow shafts came swarming through the air.

Arrows slammed into the wagons. Arrows bit into the snow. Behind the wagon walls, stray shots hit oxen, or struck the sheltering hussars. The infantry inside the wagons immediately opened fire, and suddenly the battle was a place of smoke and noise.

The short arquerbuses of the infantry hammered bullets into a thickening cloud of smoke. Even short muskets were dangerous, and here and there a nomad was hurled bloodily to the ground. Horses screamed and men roared. Here and there a musketeer was struck through a loop hole, reeling back into the wagons with blood jetting from his hide. The wounded were passed backwards, corpses were thrown into the snow, and the arrows fell dense and fast all across the wagon line. More nomads closed from the sides and from the rear, and random arrows flickered madly through flame-shot clouds of powder smoke.

The King sat on his horse, and the animal side-stepped nervously as an arrow scored across the blanket covering its flanks. Steadying the beast, the King stood in his stirrups, the roar of musket fire deafening, the blaze of gunfire blinding him. The arrows came through the fog in smaller and smaller numbers, until it seemed as though the enemy had gone.

"Cease fire! Haiduk's cease fire!" Officers took up the cry at the king's command. *"Load muskets – cease fire!"*

The deafening crackle of gunfire dropped away, leaving behind it the sobs and screams of wounded, dying men. The dense wall of powder smoke before the wagons jerked and twisted in the winter breeze, tearing into scraps and slowly drifting on its way. The clearing fog showed a snowfield dotted here and there with bodies – and the vast line of invaders still stationary a thousand yards away.

At the heart of the enemy line, infantry had come forwards. They were uncovering a line of mighty cannon – huge bombards each larger than a house. The line of cannon pointed at the flimsy wagon wall, and the gun crews were slowly loading up the guns with mighty stones.

"Jesus, Michael and St George!" The King turned his horse. "Hussars, to me! To me, and charge the guns!"

The big, armoured men swung their horses towards the East. Infantry scampered to unlock the spiked chains that ran between the wagons, giving the heavy cavalry a route out into open ground. The cavalry spurred forwards fast, and officers chased them onwards without stopping to form the men boot-to-boot in battle line.

"The guns! Charge the guns!"

They charged. The hussars of Pulski were men who feared nothing but the wrath of God. Armoured in metal plate, armed with sabres, lances, pistols, swords and hammers, they gave a wild, bloodthirsty scream and roared forward like an avalanche. Tall strips of wood trailing sheets of vulture feathers were fixed to the hussars' backs, and the feathers roared in the breeze as the horsemen charged. In a vast, unruly mass they came forwards, moving with a violence nothing on Aku-Mashad could possibly withstand. Their king rode at their head, with his barons and his guards. With lances high, the steel hussars screamed madly out for blood.

Horse archers swept out from the Tsu-Khan's battle lines. The Archers raced to meet the onrushing hussars, swarming outwards to enfold the scattered heavy cavalry. A dense line of the Khan's horsemen galloped forwards from the guns, and countless arrows once again came swarming through the sky.

The hussars charged madly onwards, horses falling and arrows striking sparks from their plate armour. The archers before them halted and turned. They fled back the way that they had come, the riders turning in their saddles and opening fire with their heavy bows. Vast clouds of arrows darkened the air, warbling like dense flocks of birds as they came spinning out of the sun. Arrows struck into Hussar horses, sending the beasts rearing and screaming high.

The charge faltered, struck from all sides. Horse archers risked close, fast passes, bringing their bows close enough to penetrate armour plate. Here and there hussars charged towards their tormentors, and the nomad ponies skipped aside. Other nomads charged in with spears and sabers, cutting down the outnumbered hussars before the men could return to safety.

Horses spun and staggered, slamming into one another in confusion. Wounded men were hurled from their saddles. Maddened horses ran wild. The King swore as an arrow penetrated through his shoulder plates. Another stabbed into his thigh, pinning his leg to the saddle. Behind him, a fresh shout raised to the sky.

"Beware! Archers on the flanks!"

The arrows suddenly came in vast, dark clouds. The Khan's heavy cavalry had walked their horses forward, and now these men shot huge volleys into the beleaguered hussars. Outnumbered and split into smaller groups, the hussars still fought to reach the enemy guns, but now their horses balked and refused to come forward against the arrow storm.

Arrows struck helms like steel rain, striking breastplates and spinning wildly aside. The King saw enemy heavy cavalry forming for the charge, taking their long lances from their backs and sheathing their bows. They outnumbered his own men by five to one. Bleeding and wavering in the saddle, the King threw aside his shattered lance and called for six of his best men.

"Cut through to the wagon fort! Tell them to fire the wagons and break free!" There was one hour of daylight left until night might hide the fugitives. "Go south, not west! South, south! Tell my son to take the army and ride for Osra!" The king tore off his golden seal of office and thrust it into a herald's hands. "Ride! *Go!*"

The men protested, then did their duty. Shrieking wildly, vulture feathers flapping, the six hussars rode back through their own men, erupted out into the encircling nomads and slammed into a swarm of men. Long Pulski lances hurtled nomads clean out of their saddles – pistol fire blasted a path for the messengers. One hussar fell, pierced by arrows, but the rest clawed their way through with warhammer and axe. Surprised, the thin screen of horse archers let them through.

A deafening roar of cannon fire began. The guns at the far ends of the line were not masked by the horse archers and hussars. The first round skipped across the snow, grazing the earth, and slammed into a wagon, hurtling the thing backwards in a shower of razor-sharp oaken shards. Men and oxen screamed as blood sluiced across the snow. Hunched with his men, the Pulski King drew his warhammer from his belt and held it high into the sky.

His son needed a full hour's grace to escape into the darkness. The king stood high, drawing arrows like a magnet, and waved his hammer in a circle to his men.

"For God, the King, and Christ eternal!" He swept the hammer towards the Tsu-Khan's heavy cavalry. *"Charge! Charge!"*

The hussars turned, gave a wild scream and charged to glory, littering the fields with broken bodies of their own men. They slammed piecemeal into the Tsu-Khan's horsemen with a hammer-and-anvil crash that almost split the skies.

The dark of winter nighttime was not even lit by stars. Fat flakes of snow came swirling from above, landing with a soft noise across the peak of the Tsu-Khan's mighty tent. The floor of the tent was bloody snow, kicked hastily aside to bare the earth. A wooden floor had been thrown down to cover up the blood-spattered soil.

The Khan was forever surrounded by his Black guard – ten thousand men in black robes and pitch-painted armour, mounted on steeds as black as night. No man entered the guard without first taking ten heads in battle. No man came to the guard unless he took the Tsu-Khan as his living god. The Black Guards stood still and silent in the snow, parting only to let the Tsu-Khan's officers approach the sacred tent.

Inside the Tsu-Khan's tent, there was nothing but the darkness, and a smell of blood. The tent door opened. Guards stood aside as General Gurad entered the tent, threw his sword belt over his shoulder and bowed. His hands were bloody, and his wicked face split wide into a feral smile.

"Holy Person! The army of the Pulski kingdom is scattered to the winds. Our scouts have opened up a road to their capital, Gulay Gudd!"

"Excellent." The Tsu-Khan sat reading quietly from a volume bound in dark, tanned skin. He put the great book quietly aside. "And their men?"

"There is no resistance. The fugitives must have split up and fled!" The general waved his hand to the west. "Not one rear guard remained to block the route to the west.'

"Then they did not go west." The Tsu-khan stood. As he moved, a half-seen flicker of ghosts swirled all around him. "If not west, then where?"

"South." A guard commander grunted, his muzzle bandaged from the fight. "To the north is nothing but the ice sea. They must have turned to the south."

"Towards Kakuzan." The Tsu-Khan looked to the south quietly, and then held out his arms. Men brought him an over robe, and brought him his daggers and his sword.

"Gurad? Our guests are secure?"

"Secure, you Holiness."

"Good." The Khan resumed his seat, bringing the black book close. "Then bring them here, Gurad – and we shall begin to twist the screws."

The general bowed and gave a slow, wicked smile.

"It shall be as you command, Holy Person."

The huge general bowed again, then turned on his heel and marched off into a darkness as black as an empty hell.

Long weeks had passed. A hollow time where Raschid drilled his army, readying it to march. The rains had given way to snowfall, and the army worked to clear paths about its great felt tents. Day by day, the men inured themselves to the cold.

At night, the camp lay hushed and quiet. The sounds of music and laughter from the big tents was muffled by the heavy felt.

In Raschid's tent, there was never laughter. Saa'lu played music when she could, but she was never sure if she was heard. The Shah worked – the Shah drilled beside his troops – and then he slept.

Until one night, the magic mirror gleamed with an eerie blue light.

The glow flooded out to fill Raschid's tent, washing back and forth like a luminescent sea. Raschid's guards saw it instantly, and sent a messenger running forth to interrupt the nightly staff meeting in the army's camp.

The royal guard had reached the southern passes of Kakuzan, joining the great walled camp of the Osranii army. Supplies were still being brought up, but the army was finally ready. The men camped in the chill hills south of the passes, watching northwards where the Kakuzak riders blocked the Khan's roads into Osra.

The tent flap flew open, and a guard ducked in through the door. He was followed by three men carrying lanterns and the tired, haggard Shah. The guard led the way over to Raschid's camp table, where the magic mirror lay bathed in its own strange light.

"Here, my Lord. It began only a few minutes ago."

Saud kept a cocked musket pointed at the mirror, as though expecting a figure to come leaping up out of the glass. Instead there was a whistling noise – tuneless and happy, as though a man were idly biding time. General Ataman shouldered into the tent behind his Shah. Abwan followed, sliding off his helmet to bare his grizzled, lop-eared head. Raschid held up a hand to motion the men to silence, then picked up the mirror and held it in his hand.

The whistling stopped, and a glad, familiar voice pealed out in merry welcome.

"My dear Shah Raschid! How wonderful to see you once again!" Tulu Begh's face radiated smiles. He sat in a tent of his own, all hung with cloth of gold. "You seem thinner. I do hope I find you well?"

Dire, dark and frozen faced, Raschid looked at the man that had stolen his wives, his adopted daughter and his unborn son. The jackal slowly removed his plain steel helm.

"What do you want, Tulu Begh? It is too late at night for passing courtesies."

"Want? Why, merely to assure you that all is well!" The handsome, dashing mouse leaned back in his chair, showing yet more of the magnificent tent behind him. "I have three guests here. Well – almost four, really. Your first wife is really extremely close to term – but is progressing splendidly! They are all three of them in the pink of health!"

Other noises drifted from the magic mirror. From somewhere behind Tulu Begh, a commotion could be heard. There was the sound of a vicious kick, a male grunt, and a chittering voice rich with obscenities.

"...Puking son of a syphilitic goat! May you wed the v'oman of your dreams only to find she hass a penis!" Sandhri was in fullest flood. *"May a tapev'orm raise a circus family deep inside your arse!"*

Tulu Begh looked back over one shoulder and seemed glad.

"Ah – that will be your First Queen. How splendid!" He relinquished his seat. "A colourful woman, but hard to endure for more than a few minutes in the hour. Here we are!"

The mirror swiveled, and there was Sandhri – her long hair hanging, and a look of defiant hate in her eyes. She looked at the mirror, saw Raschid's face, and tore herself right out of her captive's arms.

"Raschid!"

"Sandhri!" Raschid had meant to stay calm, but at the sight of Sandhri his heart gave a leap. Fear, joy, relief and terror flooded through his soul. "Sandhri, are you alright?"

"I'm fine – except for these shit eating pony buggerers!" Sandhri spat at someone out of view. "The baby iss fine. Yariim v'as shot in the thigh. She's getting better, but she can't v'alk! T'ese idiots didn't even haff bandages!" The bat wiped her hair back from her eyes. "Had'idh brought us here in a v'alking metal hut! We're v'ith their army up somev'ere in the snow." Sandhri tried to keep the mirror out of someone else's hands. "Raschid! T'ey've already attacked west! T'ey're killing everybody here! T'ere v'ass a battle, and t'ey killed at least t'venty t'ousand men!"

The mirror was jerked free from Sandhri's hands. Tulu Begh's voice carried over the sound of Sandhri's cursing.

"Enough, enough! Now here is the other one – injured but unconquered." He swiveled the mirror to show Yariim in dirty clothing, her thigh wrapped in bandages and her eyes red rimmed and sunken. The mouse was held by two grinning men in the livery of Emir Had'idh. She lifted her head proudly and looked to her husband.

"Husband, I am healing. Are you well?"

"I am well." Raschid kept his face neutral, just as Yariim would want him to. "I am with Ataman."

"Good." Yariim had understood the message: Raschid was with the army in Kakuzan. "We hope we shall see you soon."

Raschid drew in a breath and called out loud into the mirror.

"Tulu Begh! Where's Itbit?"

Sandhri's voice struggled to be heard.

"Raschid! V'e haven't seen her! T'ey're keeping her separate...!"

"Itbit is very, very well, my Shah." Tulu Begh returned to the mirror, looking extremely pleased. "She has changed somewhat from the girl you knew. More commanding, more accomplished. More... complete." The handsome mouse lounged mockingly in his seat. "Itbit is my lover."

Raschid felt a cold hatred blossom in his heart.

"You lie!"

"No no, Lord Shah. I am a Prince, and have a harem at my command. Why should I claim such a thing if it were not true?" The prince waved a hand. "She is not here. She prefers not to speak with you. She is choosing through the loot of ages, selecting clothing for her wedding day." The mouse tilted his head, enjoying twisting the hook inside the wound. "Really, Lord Shah – how do you think we struck so well? Did it never occur to you that we had help from the inside?"

Raschid looked at the little man in absolute, icy contempt. When he spoke, it was with calculation and with total calm.

"Tulu Begh, I promise your death upon my own blade – unless my wives get to you first."

The mouse prince merrily rested his face upon one hand.

"Promises, dear Shah, are luxuries easy to make and hard to keep. Here, we deal with the *real politic*." He looked up past the mirror and gave a smile. "Ah – reality has come calling. I bid you good night, sweet Shah, and I leave you in better hands."

The viewpoint of the mirror changed as it was taken by new hands and placed upon a stand.

Darkness moved across the face of the mirror. Black robes shifted, and then a cold, slim white face appeared. His face was calm almost to the point of absolute disinterest. His blue eyes were so blank that they could have been fashioned out of ice. The man wore armour fashioned out of blood-encrusted finger bones. Strange shapes seemed to flicker behind the man, just out of view.

The newcomer folded his arms quietly, and regarded Raschid through the mirror.

"I am the Tsu-Khan."

"And I am Shah Raschid." Raschid looked coldly at the other face in the mirror: the Tsu-Khan seemed calm, quiet – almost devoid of emotion. A strange being to find as a warlord, mass murderer and tyrant. Raschid folded his fingers and regarded the other man. "You have kidnapped my wives and my adopted daughter. We consider this to be an instant act of war."

"A pity." The Tsu-Khan was sitting upon a cushioned floor, the cushions stark black and picked out with silver. "It is to prevent war that we have taken them."

"Then you are sadly mistaken."

"And yet your armies were already massing on our borders. Do not feign innocence, Shah Raschid. We divine your purpose, and we cannot allow it to take place." The Tsu-Khan's voice was quiet and hollow, like something once heard in a dream. The Khan leaned forward, his eyes bleak and intent.

"We have heard that the Shah of Osra is a gentle man. That he is a scholar and a lover, a poet and a ruler wise in all the ways of peace. Go back to your peace. This is not your war. This is between the armies of the Khanate, and the Franks."

Raschid's long nosed, jackal's face remained cold and calm.

"We do not believe that you should be given free reign over the Franks.""

The Khan languidly raised one brow.

"You are not a Frank, Shah of Osra – nor should your own men die for them." He raised one slim hand – the white fingers bore a single ring incised with cabbalistic symbols. "We believe that you imperfectly understand our position. We have taken your women, that you may be brought to a more perfect understanding."

The Tsu-Khan leaned closer to the mirror. The man's mismatched eyes were not dead – they were merely pits drained of all compassion.

"The time of the Great Vision has come. Aku Mashad will serve its destiny at last. The under races will be gathered into one great power; alive and dead, they will serve the Lord of Ghosts. Those who oppose me shall not partake of my glory, but shall instead serve me through their agony and screams."

The pale fox gazed upon the Shah.

"Shah of Osra: You will disband your armies and leave our forces to do their work in peace – and we shall enrich you for it. Osra shall share in the campaign spoils, and Osra shall be as our treasured child through all eternity. We shall be as brothers in arms, and you shall have the peace you so earnestly desire."

Raschid's brown eyes were unmoved.

"And if we do not?"

"Then your wives shall serve as a lesson in obedience." The Khan folded his hands inside his jet black robes. "I will set my men to work upon your wives, and they are skilled enough to ensure that neither of them will die. Not that they will not crave for death... but that final mercy shall be denied them." The Khan's face showed its first true emotion – a faint hint of sick anticipation. "We will show it all to you through the mirrors, Shah Raschid. And we shall not cease their torment until you fall upon your face and beg for me to send them the release of death."

From somewhere near the Khan, there came the sounds of a scuffle. Armour crashed, and a male voice retched in pain. Yariim called out to her husband in a powerful voice.

"Raschid! The Khan's army is on the River Kuba, at Gulay Gudd!" Someone tried to muffle Yariim, yelling as she used her chisel teeth to bite into his hand. Sandhri snarled, and suddenly the Khan's mirror tumbled to the floor. Ripping free from her guards, Sandhri looked down into the mirror.

"Raschid - Break the mirror! Break the mirror!" Someone grabbed the bat and dragged her away. *"Kill the bastards!"*

Raschid slammed his mirror flat against the table, then jammed a heavy robe across the top. The sounds from the mirror ceased, and the tent was plunged into an awful, haunted silence.

The long, painful silence stretched. Lit by the flickering lantern, Raschid sat at the table with his face held in his hands. Saud and Saa'lu looked at the floor. Colonel Abwan and General Ataman kept at the tent door, sheathed swords in their hands and awaiting orders.

Taking a long, slow breath, Raschid slowly straightened. He turned his face towards the far, dark recesses of the tent.

"General Ataman – are you there?"

"Here, my Shah!" The huge man was bristling with red hot fury against the Khan. "What are your orders?"

"General Ataman, the army will march north into the steppes at dawn." Raschid hung his head, then drew in a long, slow breath. "Bring your staff up to date, and issue marching orders. We are marching to the river Kuba – to Gulay Gudd."

The big general pushed his sword through his sash.

"To Gulay Gudd, Lord?"

"My wives were willing to give their lives to pass us that information, General. I see no reason to doubt their judgment." Moving slowly, the Shah stood. He groped a hand to hold tightly to the handle of his old, worn yatagan. "I want a departure before first light."

"It shall be done, Lord." The general bowed sharply, instantly rose, and left. The girl Saa'lu looked up after him, and he shook his head briefly at her, jerking his scarred muzzle at the Shah. Saa'lu nodded and stayed in place, meekly hoping to remain unnoticed.

Appalled, Abwan looked at Raschid.

"My Shah? What of Sandhri? What of Yariim?"

"They know what they have done." The tall, powerful jackal kept his face to the darkness. "They have sacrificed themselves for us."

Hollow eyed, old Abwan clenched his hands.

"Will he – he torture them, my Lord?"

The Shah quietly shook his head.

"Sandhri the storyteller will never allow it." His voice quavered slightly in the dark. "She told me once that it was in the power of any being to end their life merely by biting through their own tongue…"

Raschid hung his head. Useless, futile hands gripped his weapons. Abwan looked at him.

"When he sees that it is useless, he may leave them alone, my Lord."

"Yes Abwan. Yes…"

The old soldier rose to his feet and turned to go. He hesitated inside the door.

"I do not believe what was said about our Itbit, Lord."

"It was an attempt to hurt us, Abwan, nothing more." The Shah drew the cowl of his robe over his head, and reached for the nearest book – an Old Testament. "Thank you Abwan."

Abwan drew Saa'lu out of the tent and out into the night. Behind them, Raschid clamped his hand about his stomach and tried not to be sick. He dared not cry. He could not cave-in to the agony and fear. Instead, he rocked slowly back and forth with the bible spread before him in the dark.

Outside the tent, Abwan and General Ataman conferred. Officers ran up from the darkness, listened to the General and then bowed deep. Lanterns flowered into life inside the staff tent, and orderlies brought paper, pens and ink. Colonels and Brigade commanders were woken from their beds, and activity stirred all through the camp.

Watching from their tents nearby, a young pair of soldiers stared at the commotion with wide eyes. They looked about as a tall, slim, swashbuckling officer materialized behind them in the dark. Both soldiers immediately slapped their rifles in salute.

The Officer joined his soldiers in gazing at the command compound. The vast shape of General Ataman stood alone in the dark. The big man gave a sudden roar and smashed his sword into a sapling. The tree sheared clean through, crashing to the ground. Bellowing orders to his officers, Ataman strode off towards the staff tent, kicking anything that stumbled in his path.

The youngest boy – a fennec fox with ears bigger than his hands, looked up at his officer in fright.

"Major – what's wrong?"

Spike – Commander of his own company – gave a smile.

"That, my boy, was an omen." The tall, suave black rat twirled his whiskers with one hand, then called out to his men. "Get two more hours sleep, boys! Then it's full packs, full ammunition, and draw spare flints from the stores!" Spike held his scimitar between both hands and flexed the beautiful silver blade. "We're marching north before dawn."

The young soldiers went back on guard, their eyes straying constantly to the command tents. With a glance to the darkened tent of the Shah, Spike shook his head and went about the business of preparing his men for war.

Chapter Fourteen:

At the northern edge of the Kakuzan mountains, the snow made a ragged carpet across vast swathes of dead, dry grass. From the hill slopes, the north country looked like a restless ocean – all swells and hummocks, stretching off into a grey horizon. The clouds were bringing yet more snow, and the great cold promised at last to come. Even the greatest rivers would freeze solid, and men exposed to the elements at night could freeze right through.

Out on the steppes, there was movement. The first Osranii scouts had surged forwards in the darkness before dawn, their huge, clawed Tora bird mounts running swift and silently across the valley stones. The first small picket posts of steppe men had been overwhelmed with lance and sword, leaving bodies splayed across the snow. The mounted men rode on, their birds' nostrils jetting steam into the frozen air. They fanned out before regiment after regiment of light cavalry on the march: Osranii Bazouks and Kakuzaks. The light cavalry sped out to start their job – the long, sometimes rewarding task of tearing the eyes out of the enemy.

The light cavalry were the army's screen, destroying enemy scouts and spies, blocking their reconnaissance parties, and denying the enemy the slightest knowledge of where the army marched and what it did. Far beyond the fast shoals of Osranii and Kakuzaks, Raschid's bird riders paced swiftly through the snow, standing in their stirrups to scan for dead ground, ambush and enemies.

A tight-knit team of ten men on bright blue birds sped in silence across the snow. The men were from the southern hills of Osra – soldiers used to all weather, hot and cold. They wore turbans with face masks to protect their muzzles from the cold, and some wore goggles of dark glass. Long rifles were in their hands, and slim lances were slung across their backs. Their birds stretched out and ran with heads low and flightless wings spread wide, eating up the miles with their tireless stride.

A darker shape crested a hillside a thousand yards away – a single rider on a shaggy horse. The rider saw the Osranii, stood to scan the land nearby, then waved a bow to signal other men just behind. A dense pack of steppe riders swarmed up out of dead ground – twenty men, perhaps twenty four. They saw the bird riders pacing across the snow towards them, and spurred their horses into the attack.

The bird riders moved with practiced efficiency. They swerved onto a little mound of higher ground, where the birds immediately settled to the snow. The riders vaulted clear and ran into the snow, kneeling and swinging down their long rifles, pulling back the flints.

"Let t'em come! Fire at four hund'ert!" The leader of the hill men knelt on the snow, sitting on one foot beneath him. "For the Queen!"

The steppe riders came on at a fast canter, fanning out and nocking arrows to their bows. They were far out into the open ground before the first Hillman let his gun muzzle settle – adjusted slightly for the wind, and then opened fire.

Rifles crashed, thumping back into shoulders and spitting burning wadding out into the snow. The thinning smoke hung in the air as hill men jerked the levers that opened their rifle breeches, fed in new cartridges and tugged the breeches shut. Powder horns primed the firing pans, flints clicked back, and the rifles were up and ready once again. Out in the open ground, nomad horses reeled. One body sprawled in the snow, and another man fought a maddened, bucking horse. The steppe riders had already spurred into a gallop – and were suddenly sawing sideways in alarm as a row of miraculously reloaded rifles faced them at two hundred yards.

The rifles fired again, bullets thumping out into the smoke. At two hundred yards, hill men did not miss. Steppe riders were whipped backwards from their saddles, bows cart wheeling through the air. Horses screamed and fell. The entire center of the steppe men's line churned bloodily in the snow. Leaderless, the steppe riders sawed at their reins. Some pulled back, but others saw the small group of hill men in the snow, gripped their bows and gave a bloodcurdling scream. A dozen riders raged towards the hill men, and finally the first arrows flew.

Rifles stuttered, slashing bullets through the smoke. Steppe riders tried to swerve into their age old skirmish lines, but wounded horses bucked and screamed. Men fell to the ground. Others turned in the spot, nocking arrows and firing at the small figures who worked their rifles with such hellish speed. Bullets hit home with a sound like axes chopping meat – invisible and terrifying. As the nomads faltered, the hill men suddenly gave a piercing scream and leapt into the saddles of their birds.

Five hill men stayed in place – five vaulted onto their birds and made a screaming charge down hill. The riflemen fired over their heads as the bird riders swept into dead ground. Flayed by bullets, shot down at ranges impossible to understand, the nomads turned and sped away. They turned in their saddles to fire behind them, only to find pistols staring at them in the face. Two more men died as they were pistolled in the back, and three survivors fled madly off into the steppes.

The remaining bird riders on the hill reloaded, mounted, and tugged their lances from the snow. Wounded nomads staggered across the ground. The hill men rode them down with brutal efficiency, spearing the wounded and taking the fugitives as they ran. Their leader blew a bull's horn trumpet and recalled his men, and the bird riders leapt down to swiftly loot the bodies for their valuables.

The leader swept back his face mask. His face was short nosed, black furred and with vast, tall ears – a black bat of the hills. Breath misting about him, the man turned his bird to look back towards the mountain passes miles behind.

The first regiments of regular light cavalry were coming forward across the plains, complete with their batteries of galloper guns. The bird riders did not wait to watch the horsemen. Leaving the regular troops to their job, the hill men wiped their bloodied blades clean on the feathers of their own birds, sheathed their knives and leapt back into the saddle. The birds gave piercing screams of feral glee, then raced off into the dead, blank snow, looking for more prey.

In the hill passes far behind, great caterpillars could be seen winding down onto the planes. Regular infantry in red hats and white turbans made bright rivers that moved inexorably down the passes and out into the north. They formed into marching columns at the bottom of the hills, heavy cavalry guarding the flanks, and then the entire massive army moved out into the snow.

Sixty thousand men.

Moving with a dogged, determined speed, the army of Osra shoved the enemy cavalry screen aside and marched to the north.

To Gulay Gudd, and the waiting army of the Khan.

"Graaaaaaaaaaw!"

Marwan let his annoyance be known to anyone who cared to come in range. The huge animal was in an ugly mood from the cold. Great boots made out of felt and rags, plus blanket after blanket of sheepskin had done nothing to inure him to the snow. For five long weeks he had traveled north with Meng, and in all that time, his temper had never gotten sweeter. Marwan the camel bared teeth the size of chisels at anything organic that came near, ready to take a chunk out of anything too stupid to flee.

Marching at Marwan's side, Meng hunched in the padded cotton coat of a Yellow empire soldier. His head was swathed in a huge fur hat, topped with a metal helmet shaped like a cooking wok. The dragon symbol of an Imperial officer was painted to the coat's front and back – painted by Meng's own fair hand, with enough authentic pictographs surrounding the artwork to make the rank seem legitimate.

The road he followed was a mere river of mud – a vast band of filthy slush hundreds of yards wide trampled by thousands of marching men. Here and there, bodies lay in the snow – always headless, and always in Yellow Empire uniform. The steppe lords dealt savagely with stragglers, and seemed to kill without thought or hesitation. Freezing cold, his arms clamped about his thin body, Meng marched along beside his camel – the only dromedary camel in the entire steppe army – and tried to keep unnoticed at the rear of a vast column of men.

They were Yellow Empire soldiers – all northerners, judging by their accents. In sheer numbers, there were more Imperials here than there were men in the entire Osranii army. At least sixty thousand men marched with the nomads – men so terrorized by the steppe lords that they were almost mad. Meng had couched beside campfires listening to men speaking of ghosts, of torn souls and walking dead - of the price the Tsu-Khan would tear out of a living body that failed to obey his word. The officers were in terror of their lives, brutalizing their own men to keep them moving, keep them fighting – to keep the steppe khan from taking their heads. The Imperial troops were kept in line by fear. They were automata, too blank with horror to fear anything but the Khan.

The Imperial soldiers trudged along beside vast brass bombards cast to look like roaring dragons. The weapons were so huge that they were laid upon vast carts each drawn by teams of sixty oxen. The beasts heaved and pulled at their harness, dragging the carts skidding through the slush. When the guns sank into the mud, infantry threw themselves against the wheels and pushed with frenzied energy, watched by the ever-present cavalry of the Khan.

Meng towed Marwan aside, away from an oncoming gun and its vast array of oxen. As he did so, the camel nudged against him, shifting him aside. One of the Khan's commanders came thundering up the filthy roadway, slashing tardy infantrymen aside with his whip.

The whip accidentally caught Marwan on the rump. It was almost the last mistake the commander ever made. With a wild scream of hate, the camel bit at the armoured man. He tore a tasset of the man's armour free, hurtled it aside, and came back to try and take the man's leg off at the hip. The camel was foiled by the officer's horse, which reared up in fright and spilled its rider down into the slush. Other steppe horsemen laughed, and the officer tore out his blade and rounded on Marwan.

Terrified conscripts backed away in droves. Alone of all the soldiers present, Meng stood his ground. He kept his hands in his sleeves and bowed profoundly to the officer.

"Lord master! Pray do not!" One step closer, and Marwan would take the officer's throat out with his teeth: Meng had already watched, appalled, as the camel had broken a soldier like a matchstick. "He is a chosen animal of the Holy Tsu-Khan!"

Steppe cavalry and conscripts all stared, appalled. Marwan drove them back further with another shocking display of feral blood lust. The muddy officer backed away, his eyes watching the camel in revulsion and fear.

"It is possessed?"

"Truly, Master! And I must escort it to the Khan." Meng bowed again. "A thousand apologies to you on behalf of the Khan."

He had invoked the Khan, and the soldiers nearby all instantly began to go back to their business. The mud spattered officer rose, slapping at his wet clothing, warily backing away. He retrieved his horse, gave a killing glare to Meng, and spurred off down the line of conscripts, flogging at the men who hauled the guns.

Sagging with relief, Meng drew his hands out of his sleeves. He had a pistol hidden there – Sandhri's weapon picked up from the field of her abduction. The young panda felt sick, and pushed Marwan far off the road where he could do no harm.

"Graaaaaaaaawf!"

"I know, I know." Exhausted and dispirited, the scholar watched mile after mile of the Khan's men march bye. They were a blight upon the world, leaving nothing but corpses in their wake. Bodies impaled high upon poles loomed above the road as the Khan's men passed – peasants, old women, farm animals and pets… "Come – we shall find you warmth and shelter in a little while."

There was a distant sound of gunfire on the air. Heavy cannon, firing in erratic stutters. It had nothing in kin with the sharp, fast *crack* of Osranii guns. Meng trudged forward into the acoustic shadow of the hills, and the noise diminished for an hour or two as he plodded wearily along at Marwan's side.

A great city was under siege somewhere up ahead. Khanate troops rode pell mell past the Imperial conscripts, while wagons dragged more and more huge cannon towards the west. A camp had been made, and felt tents had blossomed dun-coloured all across the snow. A quarter of a million men raised a filth, a stench and an ocean of mud that mingled miserably with the freezing cold. Chilled to the bone and staggering with fatigue, Meng wound his way through the edge of the encampment, heading for a vantage point. The

Khan's officers kept a ruthless, bloody camp discipline, but Meng had taken a golden tablet from the coat of the man Marwan had killed upon the road. It was a pass that had led them past many dangers. He showed the insignia to powerfully armoured guards that stood at the bottom of a muddy hill, then mounted up to the hill crest to see what might be seen.

It was a nauseating, squalid vista that oppressed Meng like a vision of the world's final doom. Foul, mud-slathered slopes littered with corpses spread down from the hills towards a frozen brown river. The river surface was crinkled and splashed with filth – blood, mud and wreckage covered the world as far as the eyes could see. All across the river banks, the Tsu-Khan's soldiers swarmed like ants, building, working and piling slush.

At the far side of the frozen river, there stood a city of brilliantly painted wood. Slab sided buildings and a vast wooden church were protected by a tall wall of crosshatched red bricks. Round towers sported onion domes – each one covered in tiles of uncounted different hues, lending an absurdly welcome pomp and splendour to the world.

It was Gulay Gudd – the Pulski capital.

At the banks of the river, the Khan had placed his mighty siege guns. Served by Imperial crews, cast in the Yellow Empire and dragged across countless hundreds of miles, the cannon were each larger than a house. The dragon muzzles gaped almost wide enough for a man to stand in, and the vast stone balls that they fired were being hauled on sleds drawn by terrified, conscripted slaves. Thousands more slaves were tethered to lines of stakes driven into the river ice, forming them into a living shield to screen the invaders from defending fire.

In his studies in the dear, peaceful land of Osra, Meng had seen many sights that had made small sense at first. For instance, the scholar had noticed that Sath lacked the massive curtain walls he had seen around every city he had ever known. Instead, Sath was surrounded by brand new earthworks – geometric, mathematically precise slopes and surfaces designed to glance cannon balls harmlessly away from the wall.

It was a science that no other nation had apparently acquired.

Medieval walls were no match for the guns of the Tsu-Khan. A hit from one of the Khan's huge bombards smashed the curtain walls and scattered rubble to the winds. The red brick walls were being pulverized, and the route into the wooden city was slowly being clawed apart.

Here and there, weapons fired from the defending walls – bombards that lobbed yet more hefty stones. Unwilling to blast apart the tethered civilians that screened the Khan's great guns, the city's bombardiers instead fired at the river ice, trying to make a moat of freezing water between the city and Khan.

It would not work. From where he stood, Meng could see miles down river, behind the screening hills. The Khan was sending his Imperial conscript troops a mile down river, there to cross the ice unharmed. They would assault the city through its broken wall sometime before the end of day.

There would be carnage on the ice, and Meng was helpless to prevent it. Marwan hung his head at Meng's side, oppressed and quietened. The camel nudged at Meng, and the scholar found himself quietly ruffling at Marwan's frozen ears.

"Come, honoured friend. We shall find a fire, and eat what we can."

Meng had merged seamlessly with the army of his enemies. Hidden in plain view, he looked about himself, and let his sharp mind pick at the problem of thwarting the Tsu-Khan.

The Khanate army was divided into divisions of ten thousand men – the *'tumans'* of the horde. At the center of the Khan's army lay the Khan's bodyguard – black armoured and reeking of old blood. A full tuman guarded him night and day. The Khan had a tent made of jet black felt chased with silver brocades, and about it stood the tents of his generals and his officers. The Khan had no harem, nor did he have wives. Meng pondered the view from his hillside, and noticed that one tent amongst the many had garments hanging out to dry above a fire. The garments were women's underwear made of silk in the Osranii fashion, and they flapped bravely in the wind like regimental battle flags.

If only one tent in the Khan's enclosure housed women, then this was where the captives must be kept! But how – how to pass the ever-present guards. How was Meng to steal the Khan's captives out from underneath his nose.

Princess Itbit, Queen Sandhri and Queen Yariim: he had found them at last. Unable to formulate a plan, frozen and discouraged, Meng made his way to a great awning of canvas that had been stretched above a fire. Marwan shouldered conscript troops aside, growling and complaining until he could rest himself beside the heat. With a last snarl of protest against the cold, the camel stretched himself out to maximize his surface area exposed to the fire's heat. Steam rose off his hefty felt boots, and the camel gave a bubbling sigh.

Meng was served tea by a bowing, terror-haunted conscript soldier. The man's uniform showed that he once had been an Imperial Guard. Meng found rice, some sort of fried bird on a stick, and sat himself down wearily on a stool brought to him by soldiers.

Emboldened, Meng hitched his slim 'scholar's sword' out of the way and signed to a passing conscript. He spoke in the rich Imperial dialect of the Court.

<<Soldier – food for the camel! And bring him buttered rice!>>

The soldier looked ashen, and prostrated himself upon the snow.

<<Honoured officer! There is no fodder. We have only straw taken from the rooves of barbarian houses.>>

<<Then let it be straw.>> Meng scowled; Marwan would not be happy. Food for the animals seemed to be growing short. <<If there is barbarian beer, bring it in a bucket that he may drink!>>

<<Honoured Officer, at once!>> The soldier bowed thrice, and backed away, not daring to turn his back upon an officer. <<At once!>>

Straightening his back, Meng tried to play his role with more confidence. A sage took the tools he was handed and found a solution. A sage did not curse the fortunes and blame them for the vagaries of man. He would rescue the three missing women, and he would bring them back and place them in the hands of the Shah – the one man on Aku-Mashad that Meng admired above all. Freed from the awful thought that Itbit might be Raschid's bride, Meng felt his heart soar! Cold, exhausted and numbed by weeks of danger, he forgot his trials in a sudden surge of love.

Marwan was brought old dry straw and a great bucket of malted beer. The camel ate in growling ill humour, turning himself about half way through the process to thaw out his other half before the fire. In all the camel's wildest imagination, he had never conceived of a place as miserable, cold and pointless as the icy north. The camel ate and ate, spreading a cloud of fear about himself that kept conscript soldiers at bay. Meng sipped tea, ate his food, and tried to stave off frostbite from his fingers and his toes. He stayed in place for a long, wary hour, never letting himself rest. He kept his mind turning, and his ears listening to the ragged tempo of the guns.

Riders came into the camp, all holding aloft golden seals. Khanate officers conferred, and men looked to the south. Slow rumours spread through the camp, and the imperial conscripts buzzed with talk. Secretly packing cooked rice into a pouch for later, Meng looked up and caught one man as he raced by.

<<Mendicant of a soldier, what news?>>

The man seemed agog at being confronted by an officer. He dropped to all fours in the slush.

<<Honoured one, rumour tells us that an enemy approaches far to the south.>> The soldier was a ragged raccoon-dog, who kept his face to the ground, not daring to meet Meng's eyes. <<It is said to be the Great Shah of the southern barbarians – a fool who knows not the immortal glory of the God-Khan.>>

Osra! Meng stood and looked to the south. There, far across the snow, an army was on the move. The kingdoms of the south had come to confront the Khan.

The siege cannon had ceased fire. With a sudden jerk of his head, Meng looked to the hill crest. He saw soldiers streaming forward up the hill, their voices raised in triumph as great battle drums began to boom. Seizing as much food as he could carry, Meng tugged Marwan up onto his feet. They abandoned the fires and joined the multitude that crowded cheering on the hill.

The wooden city on the riverbanks had fallen. Its walls lay ruined and its guns were silent. The river welled up through a scant few cracks in the ice. On the far bank, conscript pikemen and crossbowmen slithered clumsily towards the breeches in the walls, piling across the rubble to pour into the streets.

There were no sounds of fighting – no cannon fire. The conscripts surged into the city in a clumsy tide, fanning out to climb onto unresisting city walls.

Khanate officers called to their men, and steppe soldiers began to carefully cross the river. The defenders had fled the city in the night, leaving only a few artillerymen to give the illusion of a defense. Here and there, a fire started by the retreating defenders bloomed into life, but the blanket of snow stopped flames from spreading far. The Tsu-Khan's men flooded into the empty city's houses in their tens of thousands, and the siege was over.

The city of Gulay Gudd had fallen.

The fleeing population could not possibly escape. The khan's cavalry would tear into them like wolves amongst lambs as they fled west towards the river Vistuul. Depressed by the prospect of yet more carnage, Meng hung his head and turned to watch the ocean of soldiers sweep down towards the river banks.

A splash of colour deep in the mass caught Meng's eye. Amongst the countless felt hats, felt coats and looted finery, he saw a sudden gleam of pure emerald green.

Crossing against the tide of men was a figure in a yellow satin coat. Meng's heart jerked as he recognized Prince Tulu Begh. Beside the man was a small figure swathed in a magnificent coat of gold and blue brocade, with an embroidered felt hat low over their head. The figure turned, looking miserably towards the river banks, and Meng's whole world stopped as he recognized Itbit's face.

Itbit!

She hesitated, and Tulu Begh turned and spoke to her. Head hanging, Itbit walked on, heading into a cluster of tents outside the royal compound. Meng swarmed up onto Marwan's back, straining after her, staring until his eyes watered in the cold. The camel joined him, gazing with intelligent attention across the enemy camp.

They saw Itbit enter a magnificent, gold-chased tent. Meng gripped Marwan's pelt in excited fingers, and the camel stamped impatiently against the ground.

Itbit was here! She was outside the royal compound! Had the Khan tried to guard against a rescue by splitting up his captives? Or was Itbit being questioned by Tulu Begh?

No matter. He could rescue Itbit. She had been close enough to the others that she could then help him extract Sandhri and Yariim. Itbit would know the guard rosters and the passwords; she was trained by Sandhri the storyteller, and would already be halfway to her own escape! Meng hissed in triumph. This was going to work! In the confusion of looting Gulay Gudd, there would be an opportunity to rescue one and all!

The army was pulling up its tents and moving across the river. With his heart soaring and new hope burning in his blood, Meng mounted Marwan and followed the crowd.

He would save Itbit, and bring everyone back home to the Shah! Marwan lumbered into a canter, and the would-be rescuers wound their way towards the river banks, beside themselves with glee.

Itbit trudged through the snow and slush with her head down and her chin buried in the down collar of her coat. A magnificent winter hat all chased with gold and gems sat upon her head, protecting her great, delicate pink ears from the cold. Her breath steamed in front of her as she walked, looking as though her soul was slowly bleeding white.

For five weeks, she had been a guest of Tulu Begh and his Tsu-Khan. She had seen the Khan only twice, from a distance, and she had immediately shrunk back in terror. There was a *pressure* – as if a hundred thousand souls were pleading in fright. Although no one else seemed to see it, the Khan was filled by a great black shadow. The shadow always moved an instant before the Khan, as though the shadow were the master and the Khan the puppet. Tulu Begh had spoken briefly with his Khan – had gone into a long conference inside the great black tent, and had come forth pleased, full of himself, and richly rewarded.

Itbit had been forced to celebrate, with all due pretense of eagerness. But her little heart was empty, ashamed and utterly alone.

No one spoke to her – she was kept in magnificent isolation. The army was so fervent in its 'holy' mission that it was utterly monastic; Itbit was the only woman in the entire army camp. The soldiers of the Khan were a fearsome, savage spectacle – outcasts from a dozen different lands, who had found a life mission in total subjugation to their Khan. None of them spoke to Itbit – for which she was thankful. None of them had brought wives, harem slaves or mistresses. There were no servants, grooms or clerks. Every person in the Khan's horde was a fighting soldier. Every man was devoted utterly to the service of his Khan.

And so Itbit sat in a gilded cage, unable to fly out of the open door. She could not go riding without being accompanied by Tulu Begh, who loved to be seen with her at his side. Itbit was a sex object; a magnificent prize Tulu Begh used for display. Like the robes on his back or the sword at his side, she was a symbol of his conquests.

She had learned how to utterly please a vain, demanding man. It was not a skill she could ever have imagined herself learning. But it gave her peace. If she responded as he wanted – posed as he intended her to – then he was satisfied and left her to herself. Sickened with herself, growing thin and hollow, Itbit crouched for hours in the darkness of her tent, or sat numbly in the saddle as the army surged forward across the snow like an all-destroying wave.

Today was yet another day of savagery, ugliness and slaughter. Gulay Gudd – a strange little city made of wood – had fallen. Itbit could not bear it. The murderous army was swarming forwards yet again to loot and kill. Claiming sickness, she had Tulu Begh lead her to her tent.

Inside the tent, there was cloth of gold. There were lamps and inlaid stoves, robes made of finest Torah down or purest silk. But it was all without meaning. Osra's great palace had once had all this opulence and more, and Raschid had given much of it away.

Home was a place of quiet colonnades and laughing voices, where the riches had no meaning except as a gift to share. It was Raschid's warm presence as she sat with him while he taught her how to read. Sandhri shinning with her down a rope, a box of stolen cookies in their hands. It was Yariim dancing quietly beneath a yellow summer moon… It was Meng – dear, strange, silly Meng, painting a picture of her as they sat beneath an old green willow tree. Itbit sat in the middle of absolute splendour, and her ears were filled with the sound of desolation. She hung her head and stared down at her slim pink hands, numbed by all that she had lost.

There was no magic here- only shame.

Itbit was trapped. Having willingly become a part of all this murder, greed and butchery, how could she ever go back? How could she ever look her friends in their wise, quiet eyes again. Sickened at herself, dazed by an endless sense of loss, Itbit could only trudge in the footsteps of Tulu Begh and try to shut out the sound of the army's latest slaughter fest.

She stayed lost in the darkness for a long, long time…

Tulu Begh finally entered the tent, flinging wide the door. Behind him were his men – a squadron of armoured cutthroats recruited from a dozen different lands. The Prince opened wide his arms and gave Itbit a sardonic, possessive smile.

"My dear girl, my dear girl! What on Aku-Mashad are you still doing closeted up in here?" Full of exuberance, Tulu Begh held his sword sheathed in his hand. "We have taken the capital of the frozen north! Come see the loot of Gulay Gudd!"

The men began to disassemble the prince's elaborate tent. Clearly Tulu Begh intended to sleep beneath a solid roof tonight. Crawling with revulsion at the prospect, Itbit rubbed her arms.

"Itbit wants nothing from Gulay Gudd."

Perfectly happy with the day, Tulu Begh let his men roll up the golden carpet beneath his feet.

"But you are the woman of a Prince! A commander of ten thousand!" The handsome mouse took a bow. "Tulu Begh has a share of the spoils, and to you shall fall the choicest tidbits of them all!"

The tent was fast disappearing. Tulu Begh's men lifted it up as a single unit and placed it upon a broad cart harnessed behind a dozen plodding yaks. Left standing on a ring of cleared soil, Itbit shielded her eyes from the winter sun. The days seemed absurdly long here; Meng had once tried to tell Itbit something about midnight suns and endless nights, but the memory eluded her.

The entire camp was being disbanded. The army had moved on into the captured city, and the tail-end units were left to follow. Conscript artillerymen from the Yellow Empire were levering their massive guns back onto their travel carts, while the baggage train with its vast masses of meat ponies and spare cavalry mounts fanned out to be cautiously led across the frozen river. Wrapped in two coats and still chilled to the bone, Itbit delicately made her way across the polluted snow. She stood at the banks of the river, looking out across the rippled plain of ice. Tulu Begh's men brought horses, and Itbit found herself looking once again into the blank, blue eyes of her demon mount.

Itbit hung her head.

"Itbit will walk."

"A noblewoman *rides*, my dear. She always rides!" Tulu Begh mounted his own demonic steed, and the creature watched Itbit with a stark, terrifying gaze. "The ice will bear us, never fear."

There was no choice but to do as they expected. Itbit swung easily up onto her horse –

a superb rider, totally at home in the saddle. Surrounded by all fifty of Tulu Begh's men, Itbit let herself ride side by side with the Prince across the river ice.

Fifty men. Itbit looked around at the soldiers in their looted armour, looted silks and horses, and gave a sudden, vague frown.

"Why is Tulu Begh a commander of ten thousand? Tulu Begh does not have a tuman of his own."

Tulu Begh smoothed his whiskers in great self satisfaction.

"It is an honourary title, dear one. It is honourary because I have certain skills – certain brilliances that the Khan recognizes!"

The mouse girl rode on at Tulu Begh's side, her head bowed and her spirit more frozen than the wastelands around her. The shattered wall of bright red brick had once been smothered with little inscriptions, pictures and prayers; someone had taken enormous love, pride and trouble over that city wall. Itbit guided her horse through the mounds of rubble, heading for the dark, corpse-littered city streets. She wrenched her head away from the bodies on the ground, and looked up towards the piles of rubble beside the broken city wall.

A dromedary camel stood there, framed against the sky. Upon the camel sat a slim, tall figure with a strange, dear way of holding his folded hands. The figure caught Itbit's eye, and Itbit gave a start. A moment later, the camel rider pushed back the rag veil that masked his face from the cold. Meng's panda face looked at Itbit with joy and hope alive inside his eyes.

Itbit felt her whole spirit wrench. Fear, joy, pain, self-loathing. Meng clandestinely bowed to her, signed to her to act as though she had not seen, and covered up his face again. The camel gave a great, bubbling roar full of satisfaction: Marwan saw Itbit and swelled his chest with pride at having come so far. Meng took a last hasty look at Itbit and her entourage, and then drove Marwan lumbering off into the streets to hide.

Itbit wept, staring back at where Meng had disappeared. Her heart ached so painfully that she thought that she might die. The green mouse bit her gloved fist, trying not to let her weeping catch the attention of the soldiers all around.

Tulu Begh looked back to see that Itbit had fallen far behind.

"A little further, my dear! We shall have you in as good a palace as these miserable Pulski can provide." He waved an idle hand. "Solid walls again – that should make you happy. And a real bed at last!" He grinned, let the girl catch him up, then spurred his horse into a proud caracole.

"A fresh conquest! Loot to line our pockets, and a woman at my side!" The Prince unsheathed his spotless sword, and it gleamed with an acid light. "I serve a living god, and all the world shall sprawl beneath my feet!"

He spurred onwards, followed by most of his men. The streets were a riot of soldiers shattering the windows of shops and homes, tossing unwanted goods out into the streets. Itbit gave one last, appalled, yearning look behind her, straining to catch sight of Meng – but the sage had gone. Sick and reeling, Itbit clutched her stomach, hung her head, and let the soldiers lead her wherever their master willed.

***

The southern lands of the steppe kingdoms were the bread basket of the north. Nestled next to the great sand desert, the southern steppes were never gripped by ice and snow. The vast grasslands had been mown, and the hay stored in mighty silos. Granaries filled with corn looted from the starving city states were filled to bursting point. Fodder to supply the mighty horde was concentrated at the city of Urut, there to be shipped onwards to the Khan. Cavalry gathered in the city of Urut, ready to escort the convoys onward. Bactrian camels in their thousands lowed and snarled as they were loaded up with heavy bales of food. The convoys trekked outwards day after day, marching off into a wilderness of wind-swept grass.

It was cold, and yet not snowing. Windy and rain-swept, but not drowned in mud. The desert brought warm winds across the grasslands to chase the rain clouds from the sky.

As the first golden fingers of dawn crept out across the horizon, a mighty convoy assembled beneath the city walls. Five thousand camels stood growling in the darkness, surrounded by cursing men and beaten slaves. The cavalry escorts were filing from the open city gates, while the sentries on the battlements stirred themselves in the dawn.

To the south, where the great sand desert lay, there were only hillocks, scrub and darkness. But on this cold morning, the darkness moved, and surged forward like a desert storm.

"Allah! Allah-hu-Akhbar!"

Trill voices gave their battle scream. Black robed masses swarmed out of the dark, thundering towards Urut in a massive tidal wave. Thousands of camels stretched out into the charge – spears and muskets gleamed in the dawn. A wave of gunfire rippled outwards from the darkness, and the convoy erupted into chaos.

Desert nomads charged out of the darkness in their thousands. There were Beni Mus in pure white robes, and Tuhari warriors in black. Fuzzy haired Darb Haasi mingled with easterners who wore long black braids. One instant, the world had been dark and quiet, and in the next, violence exploded from the night.

The camel-mounted warriors smashed into the convoy, scattering the guards. Supplies meant for an entire army were captured and hauled down to the ground. Fleeing pack animals were shot down, and nomad blades rose and fell amongst the enemy, filling the dawn with screams.

A trumpet sounded from the city gates, and Urut's walls bustled with alarm.

More nomads paced out of the darkness, keeping low behind the shadows of the hills. At the rear came Raas Yomah, elegant and unhurried. He chewed a straw and watched the chaos, nodding to Kors Jakoob who stood nearby. The Darb Haasi chieftain and his kin drew out massive swords and sent their camels racing silently off into the dark, heading through the dead black shadows towards the open city gates.

Massive shapes loomed out of the darkness: war elephants completely sheathed in steel armour. Meepsoori infantry in long velvet brigantines and spike topped helmets jogged beside the beasts, their muskets at the ready. One of their own officers met them, pointed to the city gates, and sent the great beasts padding silently off into the dark. Behind them came Meepsoori warriors carrying muskets, bows and swords. They followed the elephants, making the air jingle with the sound of chain mail.

A slim, parti-coloured dog in gilded armour drew his horse in beside Raas Yomah. The Meepsoori officer had brought his men through the endless sands, following the great pipeline of water the Osranii Shah had run into the wastes. Now the men of Meepsoor and the men of the desert struck at the enemy's underbelly, and the surprise seemed complete. The dog leaned on his saddle bow and looked across the ground.

"Raas Yomah – there are many things I do not understand about your men."

"Indeed?" As a concession to the cold, Raas Yomah today wore a sheepskin coat festooned with weapons. He chewed idly upon a long grass straw. "We find ourselves simple enough."

"Yes – but you bring strangers with your army." The foreign officer pointed with his sword. "My friend - Who are those men on foot who follow behind your warriors?"

"Yes, yes.." Raas Yomah pointed idly with his straw. "Those are satirical poets. We are great poets, we men of the sands. In Osra, the Shah and his Queens invite desert poets to sit at their sides."

"They follow your warriors into battle?"

"Indeed!" Sheikh Yomah rested his crossed feet upon the bow of his saddle. "They will write satirical poems about any laggards in battle. It is a great spur to bravery."

"I see." The Meepsoori was amazed. He pointed to a row of camels behind the battle lines. Each camel was hung with tassels, rugs and talismans, and had a shrouded howdah on its back. "And these?"

"Those are brides – the most beautiful in all the lands. They will choose as husbands only those who show the greatest valour. They will make mock of those who feared to enter battle." The Sheikh pointed to another group of camels. "And here are mothers-in-law, come to watch their daughter's husbands in battle. A man would have to be fearless indeed to bring on himself the blows of a mother-in-law's tongue."

The convoy was scattered, and the one-sided melee was over. The city gates suddenly opened, and steppe-cavalry came flooding out. They charged wildly out behind a shower of arrows, flinging themselves towards the desert raiders. A battle swirled out in the darkness, lit by a constant storm of musket flames.

Watching his men draw the defenders from their walls, Raas Yomah looked out into the darkness with a frown.

"Friend from Meepsoor, I do not understand many things about your own men." Raas Yomah pointed his riding whip towards the dimly seen shadows of the elephants. "Your grey beasts each eat as much as twenty camels, and they drink more water than fifty men. Why do you encumber yourselves with such a burden?"

The Meepsoori glowed with pride.

"Elephants are glory and they are honour! Upon an elephant, a warrior truly rides to war!" The Meepsoori drew himself up in the saddle. "The Sultan's oldest bull is in the lead. Now, you shall see how glory fights!"

The enemy cavalry were swamped by camel riders. Huge camels reared and plunged down onto horse's backs, crushing horse riders and spilling horses to the ground. Nomad muskets fired, lifting steppe riders from their saddles. Gun and bow gave way to spear and sword, the desert men screaming like maddened devils as they flung themselves upon their enemies. The steppe riders were torn apart, and the city closed its gates against fleeing streams of survivors.

The Meepsoori officer signaled to his heralds behind him. The heralds blew great blasts upon long brass horns – and the sound was echoed by an apocalyptic noise out in the dark.

From the shadows of the hills, the elephants charged.

The elephants came storming out of the gloom, shoulder-to-shoulder and moving like an avalanche. Horsemen caught in their paths were utterly obliterated, the elephant's sword-tipped tusks jerking up and down in savage blows that tore men apart and hurtled horses into heaps of writhing blood. Musketeers astride the elephants fired up at the city walls, clearing the battlements beside the gates.

The elephants hit the gates, crashing foreheads into the wooden leaves. The gates shuddered. More elephants came to add their weight, pacing backwards to lumber forwards again. Udat boomed like a hollow drum, the gates bowing inwards and cracking slowly apart. Arrows bounced harmlessly from the elephant's armoured hides, and cannon on the walls were at too high an angle to open fire.

A third blow shook the gates. With a crashing splinter of wood, the gates sagged open. Elephants shouldered the wreckage aside and strode on into the city streets beyond. With a manic howl, the Meepsoori and the nomads poured inwards through the breech, taking sword and daggers into Udat.

Raas Yomah idly pulled his straw from his mouth.

"It is conceded, friend, that the grey-ones are indeed a gift of Allah. May you ride them in joy, and may they ever serve you well in battle."

The Sheikh and the Meepsoori rode forwards towards the city gates. His men had been warned that the citizens were slaves of the steppe men, and were not to be harmed – but a mother-in-law's tongue spurred men to greed as well as into battle. Raas Yomah went forth to control the fight, finding himself another fresh green straw.

"Friend of Meepsoor, the bride in blue has cast her gaze upon you. See? She parts her veil to favour you with a smile." Raas Yomah gestured towards a slim, ethereally beautiful figure who had thrown aside the curtains of her camel howdah. Raas Yomah kicked his camel into motion. "Come! We shall storm their palace and show her your bravery!" He waved his straw. "You should consider a desert bride, my friend. As beautiful as dreams – and should you take her to Meepsoor, you will be comfortably far away from all her relatives!"

The hub of the Tsu-Khan's supply chain had fallen. The desert men and the elephants of Meepsoor surged forward into wealth and victory, while to the east, the steppes glowed bright with the dawn.

Chapter Fifteen:

A cold stormfront of fury swept through the palace of Gulay Gudd. In the courtyards and on the walls, the Black Guards turned their heads to stare towards the palace buildings. Silent and devoted, the men rose to their feet, ready to serve their Khan.

Attended by soldiers, the Tsu-Khan marched through the old palace of the Pulski king. He swept into the old east wing, where guards snapped into bows before their living god.

The Khan stood, flexing his fine white hands.

"Where are they?"

An officer rose from the floor and bowed.

"Holy Person, they are in the great room above the stables, where there are few windows to be watched." He turned to point to a staircase. "They are attended by men of the third tuman. They are ex Osranii, and are thus attentive to the women's wiles."

"Take me there."

Soldiers bowed, took up their weapons and sped to do as their Khan commanded. Men swept ahead of the Khan and opened doors, rousing guards who stood attentively along the corridors.

Above the looted palace coach house, there was a long, empty room. As the Khan approached, he found the door unguarded and closed. A woman's voice came from behind the door, gabbling away as though she had not a trouble in the world. The soldiers accompanying the Tsu-Khan fell to their knees outside the door and bowed, while officers pushed open the doors. The Khan swept silently into the room, and stood gazing silently at a strange tableaux.

Although he had ordered no fires, a brazier of coals glowed in the room. Fresh cheese and a jug of ice cold milk stood beside a platter of home made sausages. The men assigned to guard the royal prisoners all sat on the floor eating sausages and bread, while a heavily pregnant prisoner sat with her back to the door, kneading bread dough on a stone. Sitting in the windowsill to get sufficient light, the blue-furred mouse Queen was stitching baby's clothes out of material swiped from the palace curtains. All six guards had eyes only for the black bat beside the fire. Moving heavily, with an occasional heave of effort and a hand in the small of her back, Sandhri was making fresh home-baked bread for her guards while regaling them with tales. The men clapped her – one played on a long necked fiddle, and the bat waved a floury hand as raucously she sang.

> *"Oh the lord of Steppes, he v'anted sex, and so he v'ent a courting!*
> *And he v'ent at night, cause hiss face vass a fright,*
> *and the dark made t'ings more sporting.*
> *He risked a kiss vit' a big-boned miss he found out in the hay.*
> *She didn't scream, and so it seemed she v'anted him to stay*
>
> *So furry, hot and full of beans, his date soon proved to be.*
> *That the mighty steppe lord stayed till dawn to see who she might be.*
> *But in the light of dawn, my friends, his spirits took a slump.*
> *Iss not undecorous to say – he found how the camel got her hump!"*

Sandhri kept her back to the door, but one huge bat-ear moved slightly as she finished her song.

"Mister Khan!" Queen Sandhri waved with merry insolence, not bothering to look around.. "V'e didn't hear you knock."

The guards turned, stared in shock, then prostrated themselves upon the floor. Quietly, cold and dismissive, the Khan looked about the room.

"I did not knock."

"I know! It v'ass a thin social excuse designed to let you save face." The bat used her hands to help her lever herself around. Her pregnant belly looked huge and taut, it's weight making every move an effort. She raised one brow, inspecting the Tsu-Khan carefully, showing no inclination to bow.

"You haff been collecting more ghosts, eh Khan." The bat's ears twitched, as though she heard things just out of reach of other mortals. "Yes, I see you have…"

The Khan looked at her as an executioner might size up a victim's neck. He fixed upon Sandhri slowly, as though slowly seeing her as an obstacle.

"The beast is insolent…" The Khan slowly walked about Sandhri, a sick intensity gleaming in his empty eyes. "Yes… perhaps it is time we taught you some lessons…"

Back straight and eyes full of disdain, Sandhri looked at him. Her face held a predatory satisfaction.

"He's coming for you, isn't he. Probably marching faster t'an you thought." Sandhri's white fangs gleamed. "Does it make you nervous, Khan?"

"The Osranii are on the march. Much good may it do them. We outnumber your sad little army by five to one." The Khan's face was blank with disinterest. "This world of beasts shall be ours at last, and we shall pave it with your corpses…"

From the windowsill, Yariim looked up, her pink eyes sharp. Her glasses glittered blankly in the window light.

"Let me guess… your supply line is cut."

The Tsu-Khan merely looked at her. Yariim saw the direction of his thoughts.

"No, your guards tell us nothing. But cutting your supply lines is exactly what I would have done. Our husband is more spontaneous than I, but we see much the same goals."

Walking into the room, the Khan spread a cold chill of fear. Half-seen things made up of skulls and freezing rags spread into the shadows. His men remained bowed, their heads to the floor.

Magnificently unconcerned, Yariim adjusted her glasses.

"My husband *has* cut your supply lines, oh Khan? Or is this a social visit. If so, please forgive our lack of hospitality." Yariim slid from the windowsill and made a genteel bow. "I shall make you tea. We have been using acorns and blackberry leaves, but the illusion is acceptable."

Seething with annoyance, the Khan looked down at Sandhri and Yariim in disdain.

"We have no supply lines. We are men of the steppes." Black robes swirled as he lifted a hand to point through the windows to the fields beyond. "We travel with hundreds of thousands of meat ponies. The conquered lands will feed us."

Yariim used an old, discarded saucepan to boil water for her tea.

"Aaah yes. But this is not about food, it is about *fodder*." The blue mouse looked at the Khan in mild interest. "You attacked in winter so that the rivers would be passable. But that means you have to find winter feed for your horses. Hay stored in the farms – that's why your men never burn farms. I've even seen them pulling the thatching down from country houses." The mouse picked up a chipped old cup and idly wiped it clean. "Your southern cities grow good green grass in the winter. You needed that grass to be cut, dried and sent here to feed these horses. But now it's gone. You have to find a new source of fodder, or all end up as infantrymen." She arranged three cups on an old tin plate. "Now let me see – grass doesn't grow under all this snow. So that means you need to find more hay stores, or head south…or turn back?" Yariim peered into the pot, but the water was still slowly melting from ice chipped from the windowsill. She sat back and perched her glasses lower on her nose. "I wonder just how many soldiers are besieging your cities back home?"

The huge old room had once been used as a chapel. The window alcove still held a cross and an old, painted icon of a Christian saint. The Tsu-Khan kept well away from the window as he walked, circling the women slowly. He regarded them as a butcher assesses meat laid on a slab.

"Your husband does not yet understand your predicament. I will have the fingers and toes cut from your body one by one, and sent to your husband every day he does not submit and acknowledge me as his Khan."

In answer, Yariim turned. She proudly slid her robes from her slim back. In the right light, the criss-cross pattern of whip marks could still be seen. Sandhri did not look up at her, but kept suddenly cold, calculating, murderous eyes upon the Khan.

"He was a big man, and he v'anted her to scream before she died." The Bat kept her hand near the hot water pot. "She never cried out, and she never begged. Not v'unce." She looked up at the Khan. "And I killed the one who did it to her v'it' my own hands."

The Khan looked at Sandhri with his empty blue eyes. A darker force seemed to flare inside him – a massive thing of pure black hate - then quell itself back down out of view.

"Be warned, woman – we have a mission, and we will not be defied."

"*V'e?* Iss more t'an v'un of you inside those pants?" Sandhri suddenly cast a piercing gaze at the Khan. "Yes… Yes. I think perhaps there may be. I hear you had a 'vision' v'en you v'ere exiled in the ice mountains long, long ago…"

"You are a storyteller, not a visionary." The Khan scathed Sandhri with his empty gaze. "Confine yourself to childrens' tales."

"Sure!" Sandhri stirred the pot of hot water, and saw the first bubbles finally beginning to rise. "Then let uss have a story v'ith our tea." She motioned to the guards. "Sit up! Eat bread! I v'ould make you biscuits, but v'e haff no sugar."

The Bat eased herself back against the box that served her as a back rest. A pull at her belly made her twinge her face. She waved a placatory hand at Yariim, who came forward to make the tea.

"Now – let me see. V'at might make a good tale?" Sandhri pushed the first tea cup towards the Khan, who utterly ignored it. "Ah! How about the tale off the crab lice? Unless v'e get a bath, v'e might all need to know crab lice more closely, yes?"

The Bat breathed in the steam from her tea cup, and slowly straightened her back. Eyes closed, she seemed to draw a story up out of nowhere…

> "V'unce upon a time, t'ere vass a great big, fat man – the Merchant Jad al Didh. He lived in a mighty house, v'it mighty walls. He had a garden that held vun hundred and eleven types of flower, and his stable had a hundred horses, all of different types. He lived sitting on fat cushions, and all was v'ell inside his v'orld.
>
> "Now- right down deep v'ere the sun it neffer shines, a column of crablice came marching, four abreast and a hundred crablice long. They were hard-shelled, glittery crablice, and their pincers were extremely long. When the chief crablouse saw the wealth of territory, he climbed upon one of Jad al Didh's pubic hairs and addressed the ranks of lice below.
>
> 'My fellow lice! Here we haff the promised land at last. This merchant is fat and full of oil and juicy blood. Here we shall live happily ever after!'
>
> "The crab lice set to, poking holes in the merchant and sucking at his blood. Jad al Didh t'ought not'ing of it, since itches are quite common down v'ere the pants line ends.
>
> "The lice had a fine time, and t'eir numbers grew. Some liked nipping at the merchant's bottom, v'ile others liked to live in the steamy places underneath his belly band. Ot'ers felt the crotch v'ass the choicest place of all.
>
> "As time v'ent by, the old chief died. The crablice multiplied and lived in their separate tribes. All v'ent v'ell, until v'un day, a louse rose up on all its little feet and asked a question of the sky.
>
> 'Who is the supreme leader of the crablice?'
>
> "Some tribes did not care. Some now lived so far av'ay from the original homeland that they neffer saw their neighbours anyv'ay. Some thought that each tribe could best care for its own needs in its own v'ay. But v'un of the rectal lice decided that all lousedom v'ould run amok unless they v'ere ruled by an iron fist (v'ell – an iron pincer). He v'ould make all the other lice bring him droplets of the choicest blood from their own parts of the Merchant. He would feast on everything, and grow powerful! All the other lice v'ould bow before him!
>
> "Some lice said that t'iss v'ass fucking stoopid, and that who cared if all lice bowed before him – v'at the hell did it mean? Also – if he v'anted to haff a piece of all the loot, v'y not travel about and visit folks

instead of chopping them into bits? T'iss v'ass clearly blasphemy and sedition! The big crab louse snipped his detractors in two, and led forth legions of crablice from Jad Al Didh's bum to go forth and bring the ot'er lice to heel.

"Mighty battles raged back and forth across the Merchant's crotch. *Terrible deeds v'ere done. Pincers snipped and crablice died in droves and droves. T'ey sucked blood out of the merchant to grow strong, breed millions of babies and make mightier and mightier armies. The Merchant grew thin and sickly, and developed a most unsighlty rash.*

"*Finally, the evil rectal crablouse triumphed! He had been v'illing to drop to depths of hideous cruelty no vun else could match. The merchant lay sick and yellow beneath his scuttling little feet, but the rectal louse lord climbed atop a pile of slaughtered enemies and raised a huge scream of victory.*

'*I am lord louse! All lice on the Merchant must now bow before me!*'

Sandhri relaxed and sipped her tea. Leaning in intently, his face fascinated, one of the Khan's soldiers opened up his hands, beckoning Sandhri to go on.

"What happened then?"

"Not much." Sandhri drained her cup. "The Merchant Jad al Didh had a hot bath, killed off the lice – and finally got a decent night's sleep."

Unamused, the Tsu-Khan turned slowly. He let his soulless, pale blue eyes rest upon the bat. The darkness within him seemed to swirl and *seethe.*

"The world is not a Merchant's crotch."

"It v'ass just a tale! Forgive me, oh Khan, if you saw any parallels." Sandhri gave an entertainer's bow. "You haff too few legs to ever be mistaken for a louse. Even on a v'orld of beasts…"

He narrowed his eyes then, staring intently at the bat. His hand almost moved towards his sword.

"You might find yourself less amusing, woman, had you not a tongue…"

He almost moved forward – almost drew his knife. The darkness in him seemed to swell and spread its wings…

He pulled away. With one cold snap of his fingers, the Tsu-Khan signed to his guards.

"This audience is over. No one sees these women without my direct permission. No one is to speak with them. No one is to fraternize."

The Khan turned without a backward glance and left the room. Behind him, Sandhri watched him with eyes full of sharp, intelligent calculation. She waved farewell to the guards who she had worked hard to befriend. They gave apologetic bows and locked the doors tight behind them.

Alone at last, Sandhri slumped, grey faced with pain. She pressed a hand low on her belly, sucking in breath.

"Damn!"

Yariim was instantly at her side.

"What is it? Did you pull something again?" Shaking with repressed shock from facing the Khan, the blue mouse took Sandhri in her arms. "It's alright! He's gone. They won't be back." She wiped Sandhri's hair back from her face. "Are you alright?"

"It-it feels like I tore somet'ing!" The bat was clearly in pain, she gripped Yariim's hand. "Iss alright. It passes. It's not a contraction."

Yariim looked about the room in despair.

"We have to get you out of here! Our son cannot be given to these people's hands!" The baby would be a weapon placed right into the hands of the Khan. "We have to get you out!"

"I can hardly v'alk – so I cannot run." Sandhri bowed her head, breathing slowly to control the pain. "Hey – v'ass that true, about the grass? For t'eir horses, I mean. Did you and Raschid think that up?"

The mouse pulled a blanket up around Sandhri's back.

"Yes. It was a clear option. We came up with it a few weeks ago when we wargamed possible campaigns. Raschid proposed it as a problem, and I planned out possible responses." Yariim pulled up the back of Sandhri's robes and exposed her back. She rubbed hard at Sandhri's muscles with the heels of her hands. "If Raschid cut their fodder supplies, then he's trying to control their movements. They have to either conquer a city that has huge fodder stores, or head further south to where grass grows amongst the snow." The Mouse skillfully rubbed Sandhri's back. "Raschid just took the initiative away from the Khan."

Leaning forward beneath the massage, Sandhri looked quietly at the floor.

"I can't do t'at. V'at you do v'ith him – make proposals and schemes. I can't bring him that."

"You do other things. You're the passion, I am the calculation, Raschid is the inspiration." Yariim looked to the tiny pile of charcoal they had been permitted for their fire, and risked putting a few more lumps onto the embers. "We need all three."

"To beat this Khan, Raschid needs calculation by hiss side." Sandhri shivered. The room was cold, empty and silent. "V'e need a v'ay out."

"Then we keep looking." Yariim pulled Sandhri's robes back down and folded her in her arms to keep her warm. She kept a hand over their child, and her cheek resting upon Sandhri's head.

"Sandhri?"

"Yes, my love?"

"Are you sure the baby feels alright? Nothing's wrong?"

"Not'ing. You mustn't v'orry." Hurting badly and trying to keep the pain from her voice, Sandhri gripped Yariim's hand. "No – you must not v'orry. T'ere is bigger things to think of. Think about armies. Think about how you v'ould beat the Khan."

Charcoal popped in the miserable little brazier. The thick glass windows misted over as snow once again began to fall. Sitting together in silence, Yariim and Sandhri watched the coals, while the world outside frosted deadly white.

In the street outside, the Tsu-Khan stood in thought. Dark shapes whispered in the shadows all around him. Strange currents made the snowflakes swirl. With his black robes frosted by drifting flakes of snow, the Tsu-Khan looked left towards his aides.

Emir Had'idh stood waiting. The man wore black armour, and his scarred leopard face was colder than the ice around him. The Khan breathed slowly, his eyes finally filling with emotion.

Hatred, disgust. Calculation…

"Emir Had'idh."

"Sacred One." The Emir bowed in the Osranii manner, touching hand to heart. "How may I serve you?"

"You have already served us well, Emir. But the women are intractable."

"They are harridans, holy one." The Emir laid a hand upon his knife. "What must be done?"

The Khan folded his hands and looked out across the corpses still strewn like garbage in the street. He could slay one of the queens and replace her soul, but that would be a deception hard to maintain. Their willing cooperation would be far more desirable.

The Khan looked out through the falling snow.

"If they would persuade their husband from his current course, that would be convenient." The Khan gazed to the south. "We do not want to break our westward momentum. Turning south to eliminate the Osranii army would cost us many weeks of time."

Emir Had'idh gripped his knife.

"Torture one of them, Great Holy Lord. I will open slits into her flesh until she runs with blood. The other one will beg us to make it stop."

"They are stoic. They are also prepared to die…" The Khan breathed in the chill, bitter air. The scent of blood and corpses still lingered. "A different angle of attack may well produce results."

He turned to his waiting men.

"We will collect fodder for the march. Strip the thatched rooves of their straw. Search cellars for fodder. There will be hay in mattresses and beds. Strip the city, and prepare to move on in two days time."

Emir Had'idh bowed and sent men forth with the message. He bowed once more to the Khan.

"And the other matter, Holy One?"

The Khan turned to one of his men – a dead, cold corpse animated by the spirit of a loyal warrior.

"Go. Bring me Prince Tulu Begh."

The animated corpse bowed low. The Khan turned, and looked back to his men, and walked away into the snow.

***

Tulu Begh was gone and the city was silent. Snowfall blanketed all sound except for the wet, slow sound of snow drifting into the city streets. The soldiers had gone off to search cellars and old houses, and Itbit was once again alone. She sat kneeling, facing the door and trembling. She kept the neck of her robes clutched tight with one hand.

A book lay on the floor before her. A book with delicately brush-written pages. She had not dared to open it, feeling as though she would defile the beautiful pages with her touch. Waiting, heart pounding, Itbit sat and listened for the sound that she knew eventually must appear.

The thatched roof shook slightly, and the straw overhead rustled. Slowly and carefully, a long, thin blade speared down through the ceiling, then silently withdrew. It was followed a moment later by a small mirror on a stick. The mirror swiveled carefully – saw Itbit and froze – then hastily withdrew.

A whisper came down to Itbit through the straw.

"Pssst!"

Itbit looked up, her pink eyes sick with longing, sick with guilt. She saw a slit in the deep straw roof being widened by a mittened hand.

"Itbit! Itbit, it is I! Sixteen Volume Tsau-yi Meng!" The hole pulled wide, and Meng's infinitely dear black-and-white face peered into the gloom. *"Itbit, I have found you!"*

Itbit rose unsteadily to her feet. Meng hung upside down like a mantis on the ceiling, looked about the room, then dropped carefully to his feet. He looked at Itbit in absolute, expectant joy.

"I found you! Thank the ancestors, this unworthy one has found you!" Meng kept a nervous eye out for the guards, crouching behind a table and peering through the door. To his great joy, the coast was clear. Beaming, Meng presented himself before Itbit and made a profoundly low and happy bow.

"Princess Itbit. This humble one overflows with joy to see you once again. I have come to bring you safely back away from those who seized you."

Itbit shook. She felt her hands tremble, and her chest squeezed so tight she thought it might crush her heart. With her tongue half frozen in her throat, she kept her hands clenched tight against herself.

"Meng…" She wanted to run to him, but kept far away where she could not contaminate him. "Oh Meng…"

"Marwan is with me, that most excellent beast! He has weathered ice and snow for you!" Meng swept off his helmet, looking suddenly young and full of joy at his own cleverness. "I am disguised as an Imperial levy! And I have uniforms and food stockpiled to let all of us get away!" He bowed again. "I believe our escape can be effectuated, if we but make sure to start at night, and leave no trail."

Itbit looked at him again, her heart falling. She wilted, her ears dropping, and could not meet his eyes.

"Oh Meng… Why did you come?"

The young man surged forward, wanting to say something unforgivably improprietal. His heart raced at the sight of Itbit, so beautiful in her robes – unharmed, alive, and here! He caught himself and stood a mere foot away, looking at her with love so pure and clear in his eyes.

"I came because we do not abandon those we love. I came because it was the correct action for me to do. To move with no thought, to act with right…"

"That is the way of the Tao…" Itbit felt herself weep. She suddenly bit her knuckles and looked away. Utterly puzzled, Meng could only blink at her from behind.

"Lady – what is wrong?" He clenched his hands together, unsure what to do. "I am here, now. Rescue is at hand. We must merely find out where the others are, then plan our rescue bid."

Itbit felt her ears rise. Her fur prickled. She slowly turned around.

"Others?"

"Well… well yes." Meng did not understand. "Queen Sandhri and Queen Yariim."

Itbit felt the knowledge stab straight into her heart like a blade of ice. It was the final degradation. Tulu Begh had arranged the kidnap of Sandhri and Yariim: Itbit was merely one more hostage. He had used her and deceived her for nothing more than his own pleasure.

Sick and ashen, Itbit felt herself stagger. Meng put an arm about her and helped Itbit sink down to the floor. He pulled herbs from his sleeve and touched them to her nose.

"My poor Itbit! You did not know?" Meng was utterly incensed! Propriety fled aside as he borrowed some of Queen Sandhri's choicest phrases. "Offsprings of overly popular she goats! May their genetalia undergo a unique transformation!"

Keeping a close eye out for the returning guards, Meng knelt down to whisper in Itbit's ear. He had somehow ended up holding one of her hands, and it trembled like a leaf in his grasp.

"My lady, know this. On the day that you were kidnapped, Queen Sandhri and Queen

Yariim rode forth to find you. They were ambushed by the men of Emir Had'idh. Clearly he wanted to take them to the Tsu-Khan for use as hostages. I immediately gave chase, but they mounted a strange animal or vehicle that far outpaced my humble efforts. I deduced that the hostages would be taken to the Khan. Thus, I am here." The young Sage kept a close watch over his shoulder towards the door. "What I must do now is locate the Queens, effect a plan to remove them from captivity, and bring all of you home." Meng put his hands together and made a bow. "Please forgive my tardiness. This unworthy one came to help you as swiftly as his poor skills allowed."

Itbit felt as though she were in a trance. She rose to her feet and drifted somehow across the room. She looked out of the door to where the soldiers were loading mattress hay onto a cart.

"Sandhri and Yariim... Yes. They must be with the Khan."

"Do you know where they might be held?" Meng looked eagerly after her. "I was lost – but when I saw you, I knew that all would be well again! Surely you will have spied upon the guards! You will already know where the Khan keeps his treasure, his magic and his prisoners?" The young sage looked about the room again. It had a carpet laid out upon it, and a huge bed – a man's sword, armour and robes. Itbit's clothes... "Now - where are your guards?"

"Gone." Itbit hung her head. "Tulu Begh was called to a meeting. The household guards have gone to look for something."

"Hay! They're looking for straw, grain and hay!" Meng's face had a grin of joy, his whole being utterly alive. "Something has happened! They're trying to build up a stock of horse feed!" The Sage peered out of a window, keeping low. "Someone has disrupted their plans. That means the Shah! The camp rumours say that the Osranii are only a week's march to the south!"

Itbit thought of Raschid – now perhaps only a few hundred miles away. He seemed suddenly immediate – suddenly present. She felt what he would think of her, and Itbit curled down towards the floor.

She sank to her knees, and finally she sobbed. Her thin shoulders shook as she hid her face behind her long blonde hair in shame.

"Meng..."

The young sage came to kneel beside her. He looked slowly about the room in bewilderment. Tulu-Begh's armour, Tulu Begh's clothes... Itbit's clothing strewn across a great double bed. There were no guards upon the door here. Itbit was neither chained, nor even closely watched... Unable to believe what his reason was telling him, Meng looked about the room again, utterly appalled.

His voice fell to a whisper.

"Itbit..."

"Don't look at me. Don't look at Itbit." Itbit's whisper was hoarse, and tears fell down into her hair. "Please – just go away..."

Meng's entire world collapsed. He sagged, falling back to rest against a wall. He stared across the room with blank, hurt eyes.

"You are not here unwillingly."

Itbit sobbed. She hunched her shoulders, put her face into her hands, and wished that she could die.

"Itbit ran away! No one took me!" The girl sobbed, half choking. "No one was supposed to follow. No one was supposed to be in danger..."

Drained, Meng obeyed Itbit's wishes. He looked away from her and stared at the floor.

"All this time, I wanted to tell you that I loved you. All this time, I was in a nightmare, thinking what might be done to you. But you're with him now – willingly. This is where you desired to be…"

Meng quietly gathered himself. He knelt formally, bowed precisely forwards and kept his eyes upon the floor. His voice was scarcely a whisper in the gloom.

"I thank you, my lady, for pointing out my foolish error."

Itbit wept. She clenched her robes tight about herself in misery.

"Meng – don't."

"I have been a fool – but I still know my duty. A sage puts personal feelings away in the face of noble action." Meng stood tall. "The Shah Raschid has done so. He has brought his armies to face the Khan despite his wives being held as hostages. And.. I shall do so as well."

Itbit stared out through the open door.

"They will kill you, Meng. Itbit has seen them slaughter thousands…" Her voice fell to a horrified thought on the breeze. "You will be killed."

"The courage of a Sage is to uphold righteousness above one's life." Meng turned away. "I have learned that there are worse things than dying…"

Meng settled his sword through his sash. He kept his face rigidly turned away from Itbit.

"I ask you formally, Princess Itbit. Do you wish me to help you to escape to Osra?"

The mouse girl hung her head in misery.

"Itbit… Itbit can never go back."

"Then in the name of the friendship that once was between us, I require your help in rescuing the Queens." Meng looked at Itbit, tall and mastering his own expression. "If you ever loved them, then help them now."

"Itbit… Itbit will help you." The girl remained kneeling on the floor. "Itbit will find where they are held."

"Good. Then I will return here, across the roofs tonight. If you cannot meet me, then please leave a written message in the south corner of the eaves."

The young sage turned and climbed atop the table, then scrabbled up through the hole in the thatch work, dislodging a shower of snow. He hesitated, and below him, Itbit spoke once more.

"Meng…" Itbit hid her face beneath her hair. A single teardrop fell glistening to the back of her hand. "Itbit is sorry…"

Meng hunched, the words driving into him like a poisoned blade.

"I will be here at nightfall, when the great serpent constellation is one finger above the horizon." Meng turned away, and gave a bow. "Goodbye, my lady."

Outside on the roof, Meng was high above the sordid world of streets, of soldiers and mere death. His whole soul felt frozen – torn apart, then turned to bloody strips of ice. He felt it sawing and cutting inside him as he moved. Letting his body move of its own volition, his soul no longer capable of fear, he made his way across the roof ridge, down a gutter and across a stable tiled with bark. Other conscripts stood on distant rooves, tearing up the thatch to throw onto carts and wagons. Meng watched them for a moment, and then slipped quietly away.

Marwan the camel waited for him in an alleyway. The camel kept a careful watch, and stepped forwards to put himself beneath Meng as the sage scrabbled down from the roof above. Settling onto the familiar hump, Meng absently caressed the camel's back. He looked over his shoulder towards Itbit's house, feeling the hope and joy fall from him like flesh made out of broken glass.

With all joy gone, all that Meng had left was duty. Hollow, cold, and impermeable. Meng touched Marwan with his heels and urged him away.

Marwan looked back towards the house and gave an inquiring growl. Meng shook his head in sorrow.

"Come. We have other work before us."

They rode on into a city made of black wood and stark white snow, where bodies slowly disappeared beneath the snowflakes, inch by inch.

Tulu Begh was deep in thought as he walked towards his temporary accommodation. The Khan had been definite. Itbit was to be put to use. There were many different ploys that could be tried, and each one had its strengths and weaknesses. Some rather depended upon the girl's inner heart.

It seemed likely that, one way or another, Tulu Begh would lose his latest toy. He sighed. No matter. She had been extremely entertaining while she had lasted – but the world was wide! The Prince walked past the guard set on the street outside his house, spoke to the men briefly, and then walked in from the street, beating the fresh snow from his robes.

"Itbit! Itbit, my sweet, how are you!"

The girl sat by a small fire, quietly drinking. A skin of cheap wine hung by the fireplace, and she had apparently been working her way steadily through it. Itbit drained her cup in silence, turning red-rimmed eyes upon the prince.

Her voice was slurred and strangely stiff.

"Tulu Begh has been gone for a long time." The girl's whiskers caught the sharp glint of the fire. "To see the Khan – yes?"

"I had the honour, indeed I did!" Tulu Begh found his dining table inexplicably dusted with straw and snow. He swept it clean, keeping puzzled eyes upon the girl. "Wine? I have never seen you drink alone before."

"Itbit iss woman enough to leave her friends, to screw a prince... so she is woman enough to drink on her own." The mouse had the rare ability to be beautiful even when tipsy. But her voice was strangely embittered, and her eyes were hidden behind the blank mask of her spectacles. "Drink. There is plenty here for you."

The Prince found a beautiful communion chalice looted from the cathedral of Gulay Gudd and helped himself to wine. He sat himself upon the table, and Itbit removed his boots.

"Never drink alone, my dear! It can lead to surliness." He drank the wine gratefully; a decent red, despite its unknown origins. "But now, my dear! I have news!"

"Yes. News..." Itbit turned to sourly sit at the far end of the table. "Good news?"

"I think so!" The prince reclined against a wall. "Have you ever thought what you might say to the face of those old friends of yours if ever you met again?"

"Itbit would tell them to go to hell." Itbit poured more wine. "Itbit does not think the chance is very likely."

"Well – there you might be wrong, my dear!" Tulu Begh looked at Itbit in surprise. "You would like to give them a piece of your mind?"

"Itbit would welcome it." The girl hunched and shivered, as though the fire did not warm her bones. "She would welcome it..."

She lifted her face to look at Tulu Begh. "What do you need Itbit to do?"

Surprised and delighted, Tulu Begh beamed for joy. This was turning out far, far better than he had feared. His hold upon the girl showed the true touch of a master!

"My dear, we have a little job for you to do." He moved the wine away. "And if you are properly fortified, we shall discuss it, you and I."

He leaned in to take the girl beneath his arm and hatch his plot and plans.
All in all, it looked like being a most rewarding day!

Chapter Sixteen:

Distant artillery flashes lit the horizon, sending a rumble of gunfire rolling back across the hills. Lowered clouds heavy with snow reflected red and orange gun fire, lighting up the gloomy, snow swept emptiness.

Armoured horsemen galloped up onto a rise, slewing their horses to a halt amidst a shower of snow. Twenty guard cavalry in blue brigantines and mail fanned out to piquet the ridge, lances glinting in the gloom. Other men clustered in a knot behind a tall rider dressed in white. Armoured horses pawed the ground, their breaths jetting frost into the air. The white rider drew out a telescope and stood in his stirrups to survey the ground.

The Tsu-Khan had posted cavalry intended to harass the Osranii march. The Khanate's troops operated as efficient swarms of horse archers backed up by heavy cavalry. Every butchered village could conceal a few dozen ambushers; the larger places had been turned into small fortresses designed to slow Raschid's advance. From the icy ridge, Raschid looked down into a long, shallow valley. A small town made of pitch-painted wood with roofs tiled in all the colours of the rainbow stood beside a massive field of ice. The town looked blasted and torn as though it had been ravaged by wild beasts. Great wounds were ripped through the roofs and the streets. The typical signs of the Tsu-Khan's men were there: long rows of impaled corpses lined an icy defile, and naked, frozen bodies stacked like cordwood stood beside the town's barricaded gates.

The ice field was a river that stretched north and south as far as the eye could see. Once the little town had been a ferry point across the mile-wide river, but now it was a strongpoint for the enemy. The inhabitants stared down from their impaling poles, their ghosts given up to the blades of the Khan.

Osranii troops were at war in the valley. Kakuzak lancers gathered impatiently behind a single battery of eight guns, facing a dense swarm of the Khan's horse archers.

The guns were the Militia artillery regiment of Sath – the 'Queen Yariim's Own'. The artillerymen fought with a new-found ferocity. The artillery fired at the enemy's rally point, throwing the horse archers into confusion. With nowhere to rest their horses and reload, the Khan's men were suddenly forming for a charge. They formed a line, officers waved their bows, and the enemy sped forward in a wave that rippled fast and furiously across the open ground.

The Osranii guns ceased fire, and crews opened lockers to bring out new shot. The horse archers rampaged forward in chilling silence, arrows nocked or swords held low. The artillery let them come to two hundred yards – just outside of mounted archery range – and then opened fire.

The guns bucked backwards like mad things, jouncing across the snow. They fired canister – tubes packed with hundreds of musket balls. The balls flicked spurts of ice and dirt up from the snow, slamming into the onrushing archers. Men and horses were snatched back as the air became a storm of random death. A score of men were ripped into bloody ruin, and others reeled, coughing or screaming in their saddles.

The Kakuzaks instantly lunged forward, whipping their horses and giving wild, savage screams. Long lances lowered as they raced madly towards the enemy. The Kakuzaks were an explosion of barbaric colour – coats and scarves of brilliant hues glittered in the gloom. Their wild charge chilled the blood. Lances slammed into horse archers, punching through felt coats, flesh and bone. The Khan's men scattered and fled, survivors firing at the pursuing Kakuzaks. Carbines and pistols fired in reply – laggard horse archers were ridden down. From the high ridge, it all looked like little dolls at war. Blood sprayed over the snow. The Khan's men were torn apart, and a scattered handful of survivors raced back for the town gates. The Kakuzaks kept their distance from the town, pulling back to help the guns and deal with their handful of casualties.

The artillery limbered up behind their teams of horses, the crews mounting their own beasts. Shedding snow from their wheels, the artillery raced forward to threaten the gates of the river town. Raschid watched the entire engagement in silence, apparently unmoved. He slowly closed his telescope and looked towards the endless fields of river ice.

"So that is the Kuba river."

The men closest to the Shah were in a strange array of costumes. The Pulski Prince wore plate armour and a pointed helm, with tall vertical wooden strips streaming vulture feathers mounted on the back of his cuirass. The McCallum was wrapped in barbaric tartans, and sat on a cart horse that seemed scarcely able to take the huge bear's weight. A Kakuzak Headman and Osranii aides stood nearby. The Royal Guard kept watch over their Shah, the tall horsemen ever scanning the steppes for sign of danger.

The Pulski Prince was as grim and as silent as Raschid. The man stirred and pointed at the river with a red-painted lance lined with eagle feathers.

<<Honoured King, the Kuba runs here and all the way north. It is ice from this point on.>>

Raschid scanned the frozen river.

<<And west of here lies the Vistuul?>>

<<Yes, honoured King. It is broader. Much broader. It too is ice – but below this point, the center of the river still runs free.>> The lance pointed west. <<To cross the Vistuul in winter, you must be maybe one hundred miles north.>>

Raschid nodded, his eyes on the town, the river and the hills. The Khan's men lost heavily against the Osranii skirmish lines of light cavalry and artillery, but still, they occasionally slowed the Osraniis' progress. The town had to be taken, and its garrison destroyed.

Raschid opened the little folding desk that hung from his saddle. He spoke tonelessly as he wrote.

"We will eliminate this garrison. Where is General Ataman?"

An aide rode closer.

"With the main body, Sire. At the road junction."

"Tell him to keep marching. The vanguard brigade will assault the town. Tell Ataman to set new advance guards to replace us." Raschid wrote orders and handed them to the aide. "Go."

The aide spurred away. Raschid spared a brief glance for the terrain, reading it as it would look from the town below. He stepped his horse sideways and spoke to the McCallum.

"I have work for your men, my friend."

"Good!" The huge old Bear leaned forward, relishing the prospect. "There's been too much of this cavalry shite going on so far!"

"We shall be free of it soon." Raschid was aware of the Khan's army. It lay far to the north – but it must choose to move soon. "Lord McCallum – take your men up that defile. It is dead ground. Sound a trumpet when you come level with the settlement. The artillery will fire three volleys into the barricade blocking the gates – and then you can attack." Raschid wrote the orders out on a sheet marked with the date, order number and time. "The First Infantry Regiment will support the attack. Bring the light cavalry onto the flank to cut down the fugitives." Raschid handed orders to his couriers, who jerked their heads in bows, wheeled their mounts and sped off to the infantry, cavalry and artillery.

The McCallum grinned, his huge muzzle gleaming with fangs. He slid heavily from his horse and took his massive two handed sword. He signed for his bagpiper and his kin.

<<*McCallum! McCallum!*>> He waved the sword like a twig over his head. <<*Hands off cocks and fall in! Let's show these nancy horsemen how an Isleman fights!*>>

Islemen gathered in the lee of the hill, forming up with surprising speed into an armoured column bristling with titanic swords. Crouched and stealthy, nine hundred of them moved down into the gully of a frozen stream and made their way towards the wooden town. Raschid watched them go, then turned his horse to look back towards the south – towards the army.

General Ataman led the main march divisions. The army marched in a gigantic oblong formation, with long files of riflemen protecting the massed supply wagons at the army's heart. The whole mass moved with speed and precision across terrain well scouted by the cavalry. Paths had been marked, bridged and cleared by the army's mounted corps of engineers.

The Osranii moved fast and fought hard. They were absolute professionals.

Their Shah slept the required amount of hours each night for health. He ate with his men, eating with a different regiment each night and dining with the private soldiers. The rest of the day and night, Shah Raschid worked. He rode to inspect terrain, he untangled supplies, he directed assaults and sieges. No man in the army dared do less than their Shah. And so the army moved with efficiency born of sheer professionalism. The snow was no more shifting and uncertain than desert sands or southern jungles – the cold was no more dangerous than desert heat. Chilled, tired but driven on by pure purpose, the Osranii army came hunting for the Khan.

The army's numbers had swelled. The shattered remnants of the Pulski army had reached them – three thousand cavalrymen, led by their Prince. Tattered hussars, their armour pierced and their vulture wings dragging, had limped out of the snow. They had been fed, their wounds treated and their dead were buried. Embittered, proud and ferocious, the hussars were posted to the guard division, where they thirsted for revenge upon the Khan. They brought with them invaluable local knowledge – and an invaluable well of hate. Raschid watched as the hussars rode four abreast down the roads below, snapping their heads to face their Prince and the Shah. At their head rode a priest swathed in plain brown robes who bore a silver-framed icon of the Mary and the Christ child. Raschid bowed his head to the priest and the icon, and in return, the hussars dipped their eagle-feathered lances in salute.

Raschid watched them filing past the bottom of the hill. Since the invasion had begun, he had seemed like a machine, avoiding all emotions. Old comrades such as Saud and Abwan remained quiet, knowing Raschid's thoughts and unsure just what to say.

He could not think of Sandhri – of Yariim and Itbit, or of his unborn son. That path led only to madness. Raschid jerked his mind away from images of them a thousand times a day. He forced himself into action, trying to plate his soul in layers of steel.

Emir Jazzak, a short, hefty lion with a clipped, pugnacious nose pulled the scarf back from his face and moved his horse closer to the Shah.

"My Lord – the garrison of that little town must know they cannot hold out." The lion gestured towards the wooden town with his steel hafted mace. "Instead of attacking, we could send out heralds to demand surrender."

In reply, Raschid turned his cold face towards the Emir.

"We are here to destroy them – not to reason with them." Raschid shifted in his saddle. His plate and mail armour rattled. "They already know their choices – withdraw or die."

The army was marching north – deeper into the cold and on towards the Khan. Emir Jazzak rubbed his liver-coloured nose, and spoke again.

"My Shah, we are moving too far north. If we circle west, we can head off their assault into the Frankish lands."

"That would leave them all the eastern steppes to withdraw away into." Raschid looked across the snowfields with his eyes narrowed. He never smiled any more, nor did he waste time on frivolities. "We must not attack until we have maneuvered them into a position from which they cannot escape. Our goal is the total extermination of the Khanate army."

With a last look across his army, Raschid coldly turned his horse around.

"Total – *absolute* – extermination."

The assault against the town was almost ready. Down in the gully, nine hundred armoured Islemen crouched against the gully wall, their swords glinting like a forest of steel. A regiment of infantry jogged from the road towards the town valley, their rifles at the slope and officers chivvying the men forwards with their swords. Raschid saw Spike at the head of his men, and lifted his lance in salute. Spike took two paces forward and gave an elaborate, joyous bow, flourishing the silvered scimitar that had been a gift from his Shah. His men fanned out into two long lines, advancing on the town in echelon. A thousand men moved forward, marching with dogged purpose, their rifles coming down into attack position.

A Kakuzak lancer suddenly stood in his stirrups and stared across the valley.

"The snow moved!"

Raschid instantly jammed his lance butt first into the snow and unshipped his telescope. He trained the instrument on the blank hummocks of snow at the flank of the infantry assault.

The snow was pure and white – and a trampled swathe of hoof prints lead to the hummocks and simply disappeared. Raschid instantly put his telescope away.

"Cavalry! They've tented over some dead ground and hidden cavalry!"

The infantry had their flank to the hidden cavalry, and the nearest covering force was a thousand yards away. With a sudden surge of madness, Raschid jammed his spurs into his armoured horse, snatching up his lance as the animal leapt downhill. He rampaged towards the tented ground, his war cry ringing to the skies.

"*Guard!*" The Shah looked back, lance held high. "*Allah! Allahu akhbar!*"

The twenty bodyguards stared as their Shah led a maddened, lone attack across the snow. Suddenly the Prince of Pulski gave a wild scream of joy and sent his horse racing hard after the Shah.

"*Saint George! Saint George!*"

Twenty guard cavalry spurred after Raschid, joined by a gaggle of couriers, aides and attaches. A herald spurred back towards the road, screaming madly to the winged hussars.

The Osranii infantry marched forwards, their eyes on the town ahead of them, moving past the deadly patch of ground. They never saw their enemy surge upwards out of hiding. Two hundred armoured cavalry – shock troops on armoured horses – thrust up from beneath white tent canvas stretched across a gully. The Khan's horsemen had planned their ambush perfectly. Silent and deadly, the officers waved their swords, and the mass of horsemen shot forward across the empty ground.

"*Allah! Allah defend the just!*"

A single horseman dressed in white raced downhill across the snow. One instant, the Khan's men were turning, and a split-second later a lone lance crashed into their ranks. A man was pierced clean through, shrieking in agony as the impact tore him from his saddle. The Shah of Osra rose, huge in his saddle, and threw his lance aside.

"*Ma'a salaamah! Peace be with you!*"

Raschid's sword was in his hand – living steel, the quicksilver in its hilt shifting down the weapon's hollow spine as he swung. The sword made a brilliant arc, slamming into a steppe warrior's neck beneath his helmet skirts. The body jerked, its head spilling free, and brilliant jets of blood shot across the snow. Another enemy fell back as the Shah of Osra shattered the man's jaw with his steel shield.

Steppe warriors spun, their horses stumbling as the lone warrior smashed into their heart. Raschid screamed in fury, ramming his horse into the Khan's ranks. A mace hammered down towards him. Raschid turned his horse and parried the blow inside the other man's wrist. A severed hand fell free, and Raschid bellowed in fury as he back swung, his sword striking sparks from an enemy's steel shield.

"*Saint George!*"

There was a crash like an avalanche as the Prince of the Pulski smashed into the enemy beside Raschid. The red lance ploughed clean through an enemy. Roaring madly, the wolven Prince drew out a war hammer and joined the Shah, smashing at enemies that closed around them like a swarm of bees.

The Royal bodyguards crashed into the melee with a sound like a hammer smashing down onto an anvil. Outnumbered, the elite guard fought like madmen. Horses snarled and reared, while sword and shields rang in the wild rhythm of war. The Khan's troops halted their advance, men turning to spur in towards the mad battle at their heart.

The Khan's men were old and vicious soldiers. They saw Raschid, and pressed their horses forwards. Beside Raschid, the Pulski Prince fired two pistols at the nearest men, then surged his horse forward into the gap made by his fire. Steel plate rang as blows ricocheted from his armour. The hussar prince crashed his warhammer sideways, staving in a skull, all the time roaring madly for Saint George.

Raschid hacked into the melee with shield and scimitar. Men and horses churned all around him. Out of the chaos, a man came charging at him with a leveled lance. Raschid fired a pistol point blank at an enemy, hurling the man aside. He fired his second weapon, then jerked a steel javelin from its case beside his saddle. The weapon balanced in his hand, then hissed as he hurtled it with all his strength. The spear took an enemy cavalryman in the right arm, piercing through to pin the man's arm to his chest. Raschid spurred forwards, scimitar whirling, and hacked the injured man out of his saddle.

Royal guards were cut down. Khanate soldiers screamed and died. Suddenly winged hussars appeared in the melee – black wolves, white bears and sables roaring as they smashed a path towards the Shah. Suddenly the press of enemies about Raschid faded back. With a maddened scream of hate, Raschid kicked his horse forward and threw himself into the enemy.

Blades ripped at Raschid, and he caught the blows, parried, cut – a whirl of his scimitar, and another man's hand was off. He opened a man's face up with a vicious back-swing of his sword, left his scimitar dangling from its wrist strap, and pinned his victim to the ground with a javelin as the man fell. Raschid saw mailed Islemen with huge swords hacking into the enemy – Osranii tufekchi firing. A Khanate soldier staggered on foot away from his dying horse, and Raschid simply rode the man down. His big horse reared and plunged, its sharp hooves smashing down into a screaming man. Raschid roared in release, sobbing for breath as he waved his sword.

"Kill them! Kill them all!"

A bloody mass spread about him in the snow. Whirling his horse around, Raschid found Osranii all about him. He tried to spur away, looking for more enemies, but a huge figure pushed out of the crowd and gently seized the bridle of his horse.

"Enough. Enough, lad. They're all gone."

The voice spoke in Accented Frankish. Sobbing for breath, teeth barred and blood slathering his muzzle, the Jackal Shah of Osra whirled. The huge figure of the McCallum stood holding his horse, the man's armour and sword streaked with blood. The old bear held Raschid's horse as steady as a rock.

"It's over, lad. It's over."

The fight was over. Hussars, musketeers and Islemen had ploughed piecemeal into the melee, hacking down the enemy cavalry. A dozen of Raschid's bloodied guards spurred towards their Shah. A dead aide lay in the snow. Musketeers ran to kneel and fire after the retreating enemy, who threw away their shields and fled pell mell across the snow. Whooping hussars, their vulture wings rippling in the wind, rode through the carnage bearing bloodied blades.

An enemy horseman spilled to the snow, his horse killed by a musket ball. Leaving his men, Raschid took up his last javelin, hefted it, and spurred forward. His downward strike took his screaming enemy in the back. Curbing in his horse, Raschid turned about. He contemptuously ripped his javelin out of his victim's lifeless back.

The Shah reversed the weapon and slid it back into its sheath. His horse stepped high as he rode back to the McCallum and his men.

"Is the town taken?"

"Aye. They were never even in there. The buggers were out here!" The McCallum looked at the Shah's last victim. "We have the town. We can go."

"We'll use it as a depot." Raschid swung his sword back up into his hand. He wiped the weapon on the brocade housing of his horse's armour. With a hard look across the bloody field, the Shah of scholars turned his horse away.

"March on. The army must cover thirty miles by nightfall."

The McCallum watched as Raschid rode away. Thoughtful and unhappy, the old bear slowly shook his head. He waved his sword to his men, sent them off to see if the dead enemy had any liquor, and went stumping off upon his way.

***

The evening came with a grey, sharp chill. Snow fell slowly over Gulay Gudd, blanking all the signs of carnage and destruction. The world became stark and featureless – bound up in the endless, bitter cold.

Sitting on bare floor boards, her backside aching, Sandhri watched as Yariim gathered curtains up and made them into blankets for their bed. A wide crack in the floorboards looked down into the coach house just below. Sandhri felt a great shape moving down in the darkness, and she heard the dismal clank of chains.

"Pssst! Hey – hey, are you alright in t'ere? Iss t'ere anything you need?"

There was no reply – there never was. Whoever was down there, they seemed to be silent. Sandhri had tried to peer down through the crack, but the room below was dark, and she could never manage to lie flat enough to see inside. She contented herself instead with feeding slivers of bread down through the floor, and telling stories down into the crack where the prisoner could hear.

She presumed the poor prisoner liked the stories. The chains rattled in what she hoped were appreciation, but that was all. Frustrated at the silence, Sandhri sat up and gave a sigh, then looked to Yariim.

The blue mouse was sitting in the barred window, repairing their fraying clothes. Suddenly she looked down through the window, and her whole being seemed to lift up in joy. Ears high, the mouse stared down at the outside world, her fur rising up on end.

"Sandhri! Sandhri – it's Itbit! Itbit's down there!"

Eyes wide, Sandhri tried to heave herself up off the floor. She failed to make the trip. Yariim came to help her, using both hands to haul the bat up onto her feet. Waddling to the window, Sandhri joined Yariim in looking down into a wide courtyard shadowed over by the palace towers.

Out in the courtyard, Khanate officers were in conference. With her head down and her tail dragging, Itbit crossed the yard. Even from high above, it was impossible to mistake that dear, beloved little figure with her great big whiskers and her clever feet. Wrapped in a brocade coat and an immense felt hat, Itbit walked between two officers towards the palace gates.

Itbit's escort stopped to talk to the other men. Left unobserved, Itbit immediately began questing. She looked up at the prison windows, then edged out of sight beneath the coach house eaves. After long moments, Itbit quietly emerged, moving with a casual calculation learned at Sandhri's knee.

From up above, Yariim excitedly clutched her own throat.

"She looks alright! She isn't under a close guard."

"She may not haff to be. T'ey might haff told her they'll shoot us if she tried to run av'ay. *Bastards.*" Sandhri's voice stung with bitter hatred for her enemies. She looked down at Itbit, and slumped against the glass in relief. "So t'en – here she is. V'e're all toget'er at last."

They watched intently, hand in hand as Itbit was led through the doors into the old brick palace. Relief at seeing their Itbit alive and well mingled with a sadness; in their hearts, Sandhri and Yariim had half-hoped Itbit might have managed to escape. Once Itbit left their field of view, the two women sat holding one another in silence. Finally Yariim stood and pulled her clothing straight.

"I believe we are about to have visitors again."

They straightened up their empty room as well they could, and lit home-made candles made of curtain-twine and sausage fat. When the sound of marching boots finally came to the door, they were sitting side by side around their little bowl of coals. The room was rich and dark with shadows.

The door was opened by two soldiers – and Itbit quietly stepped in.

She was looking tall – slim and somehow hollow. She walked as a woman walked – purposeful and possessed. But it was their dear Itbit – all whiskers and green fur. The girl halted, clearly in terror, and looked over to Sandhri and Yariim with haunted, hunted eyes.

Sandhri surged upward from the floor. Arms wide, she came to take the mouse into her arms in joy.

"Itbit!"

Yariim hung back – her head tilted. She watched as Sandhri tearfully grabbed Itbit and held her hard against her heart. Itbit stayed stiff and dazed – her eyes staring off across the room and her arms unresponsive.

The green mouse wept silent, hopeless tears. With her face buried ecstatically in Itbit's hair, Sandhri held her little friend in pure joy. She slowly released her grip as Itbit failed to respond. Wonderingly, Sandhri drew Itbit back to arm's reach and looked into Itbit's hollow eyes.

"Oh Itbit. V'at haff they done to you?"

Itbit shook. It was harder than she had ever imagined. Walking forwards, she felt Sandhri's arm over her shoulder. Her friend must be due to give birth almost any day. The bat moved heavily, always ready for the sudden pull of unaccustomed weight. Itbit wept for all the days she had not been there to help – and for all the days to come.

The green mouse hung her head. When she finally spoke, her little voice quavered in her throat.

"They sent Itbit here to… to threaten you."

Sandhri led Itbit over to the tiny charcoal fire. The green mouse went woodenly, as though she never even felt Sandhri's touch. Yariim and Sandhri stared at their friend in anxious confusion, gently guiding her to sit upon the ground.

Itbit sat quietly, fanning out her coat with the same grace an Osranii courtier used to spread silken robes. The mouse kept her gaze upon the floor.

"Itbit wonders - are you well? Have they been mistreating bat and jiggle-mouse?"

"We are well." Yariim watched Itbit intently. "Itbit – what's wrong?"

"Nothing is wrong. Itbit is well." The green mouse reached out to take a piece of charcoal in her hand. She crumbled it to dust, sprinkling the dust upon the floor. "All is as it should be."

With her back to the door, Itbit sat stiff and still. Her hand wrote letters in the charcoal dust: "THEY CAN HEAR"

Yariim gave an idle sweep of her hand, smoothing over the letters as she reached for a pot to make some tea.

"We were worried about you. We knew you had been taken, but no one would tell us where you were."

"Itbit is as you see. Itbit has… grown." The green mouse looked bedraggled and subdued. Her ears hung like the banners of a defeated army. "Itbit has only just today been told that you were here."

Shadows masked the three women from the watchers at their spy holes. Itbit reached out a finger and quietly wrote in the charcoal dust.

"MENG HERE. ESCAPE POSSIBLE. TOMORROW NIGHT."

Sandhri flicked a sharp eye at the letters on the ground. She brushed them away as she sat up on her knees, drew Itbit close and placed the girl's hand upon her belly.

"V'ell – here v'e all are. But hey – here iss the baby! Can you feel him – the little bugger iss still head up and bum down!" The bat used her body to mask Itbit's other hand as the mouse wrote on the floor. "See – t'at's hiss head, right t'ere. Just a few days now before he's born!" She leaned in close to breathe into Itbit's ear.

"How?"

Itbit's hand wrote in the dust as she bent her frozen face down to listen to the baby.

"BREAK THROUGH FLOOR INTO COACH HOUSE. SMUGGLE YOU OUT."

"Here. Tea. It is terrible – we make it ourselves. They only feed us scraps and dross."

Yariim looked at the dust, wiped it clear as she passed the tea, and wrote an emphatic reply.

"NO. SANDHRI CANNOT CLIMB."

Itbit sighed, her head hanging, and gave a shrug. Looking harder and more calculating, Yariim wrote again.

"WE WILL WAIT. BETTER TIME."

The blue mouse looked Itbit in the face, her eyes narrowing.

"Itbit – where have you been?"

Her voice was hard. Sandhri looked up in surprise. To her shock, Itbit lifted her chin and met Yariim gaze for gaze.

"Itbit has been with the Khan's officers." The green mouse took her tea, and her hands no longer shook. She took a tighter grip upon her cup. "The Khan has spoken to Itbit. His officers have spoken to Itbit. The Osranii army is advancing on the Khan, and the Khan will use you to force Raschid to withdraw."

Sandhri sat erect, her grey eyes hard. "He v'ill not v'ithdraw – no matter v'at the Khan may do." The bat lifted her chin. "Not my husband."

Yariim sat back, her thoughtful eyes upon Itbit.

"Itbit, what has happened? What have they done to you?"

"Nothing has been done to Itbit." The green mouse looked away. Irony sounded strange – it was utterly alien to the Itbit they had known. "Itbit does not have long to speakie with you. They want to use you as a tool against Raschid. Itbit is supposed to be.. be used to pressure you to sending messages to him."

"V'e haff held out so far. And t'ey are not so stupid as to t'ink v'e haff not the means to kill ourselves." Sandhri looked at Itbit in sudden concern. "But t'ey haff you as v'ell, now. V'at if they torture you to make us cooperate?"

Itbit drew her robes tightly about herself and looked steadily at the floor.

"Itbit thinks that they will not…"

She was terribly quiet – and strangely changed. Itbit seemed tall, self possessed – and full of a knowledge that crushed down at her soul. Sandhri looked at Itbit, and suddenly she began to understand.

"Oh Itbit…"

Itbit looked away.

"Nothing has been done to Itbit that she did not do to herself." The mouse looked away. "Nothing…"

Itbit rose to go. She looked down at her hands.

"There is a council of war tomorrow night. They will speakie of you then. If they think they cannot use you, then they will kill you."

Yariim looked steadily at the other mouse. "Then they will kill us."

"But not yet." Sandhri heaved herself slowly upwards, pushing off from the walls to reach her feet. "Itbit – tell your friends t'at v'e are considering your v'ords. V'e haff not been good guests. If the Khan can give us perhaps a few humble furnishings – perhaps a curtain across this hall, some cushions for our guests – we v'ill entertain him tomorrow night and listen more closely to hiss needs. Perhaps just before the v'ar council?"

Yariim hung her head and turned away. Sandhri awkwardly walked up to put her arm about Itbit's shoulders, spreading her own long, pure white hair across the little mouse as a cloak. She leaned in quietly to kiss Itbit's wooden cheeks.

Sandhri breathed softly into Itbit's ear.

"Tell your friend, it v'ill be tomorrow night. The guards v'ill be occupied. Be at the coach house." Sandhri drew back a little and caressed Itbit's face, looking into her unwilling eyes. "Go back to the Prince and the Khan, now. Tell t'em you did well."

Sandhri reached forward to take Itbit's face in her hands. She leaned her forehead against Itbit's trembling cheek.

"Itbit – true love never dies. You are my sister of the heart, my companion and my friend. V'y do you imagine anyt'ing could effer diminish you in my eyes?"

The young mouse's voice caught in her throat.

"Sandhri-bat does not know what Itbit has done."

"My darling v'un – true love does not care."

With a longing, wrenching glance towards Sandhri, Itbit stood and knocked upon the chamber door. The Khan's soldiers came and took her away, locking Sandhri and Yariim back in the gloom. Sandhri quietly crossed the chamber, her eyes thoughtfully upon the floor. Yariim made a swift look about the room for spy holes, then came to take her friend over to the little fire.

Yariim hissed quietly in Sandhri's ear.

"What did you tell her?"

"I told her that hearts are silly, fragile t'ings, and that mistakes are made. I let her know t'at true love neffer turns its back."

"But what was that about curtains and cushions?" Yariim looked back at the doors, keeping her voice intent and quiet. "How long can we play the Khan for time?"

"For as long ass v'e need to, my love. And the first t'ing to do iss to show that v'e are reasonable beings." Sandhri leaned heavily on the windowsill, looking at the rafters in the ceiling. "Ah! Curtains, here, v'ere that crack in the floorboard runs. V'e need to make you a dressing room."

Upset, angered and confused, Yariim waved her hands. "For God's sake, why?"

"The Khan cannot see a Queen of Osra naked!" Sandhri stood. There was work to do. "Tomorrow night, my darling, you dance."

"Dance?"

"Your very sexiest, most v'onderful dance." Sandhri looked carefully at the floor, and whispered quietly into Yariim's ear.

"Tomorrow night, my darling, the floor boards behind the curtain must become a pathway down below, and into the coach house." The bat wrapped her threadbare robes about herself. "To v'ork!" The bat waddled awkwardly over to the doors and hammered with her fist. "Oi! You t'ere! The Khan v'ill be coming tomorrow night! V'e need cloth and thread! Sheets and hammers and nails!"

Yariim went to the window to watch Itbit crossing the darkened courtyard below. Sandhri looked quietly at Yariim – her lover, her partner, her friend. She sat there, simply loving her.

"Tomorrow night, t'en."

Sandhri turned away. Out in the snow below, Itbit took one last, long look up at the window above the coach house, turned up the collar of her coat, and walked quietly away.

Chapter Seventeen:

Over the next day, the huge, empty chamber above the palace coach house was gradually transformed. Yariim stood on a chair atop a table and hammered nails through huge flaxen sheets, curtaining off the rear few feet of the room. Sandhri awkwardly sat on the table, steadying the chair. The old sheets were as stiff as boards – but they would do.

They had grudgingly been given a few cushions, a rug and old copper lamps. With the curtains now screening off the rear half of the room, Yariim yawned, took up a pile of scrap material, and went behind the curtains to sew herself a costume for the night. Sandhri waddled slowly about the main room, fussing with the lamps and fluffing out the cushions. She sang a raucous song at the top of her loud voice.

"Oooooh Old King Cole, v'as a merry old soul, and a merry old soul v'ass he!
He called for hiss v'ife in the middle of the night, and he called for his jugglers t'ree!
Now every juggler had some fine balls... and some very fine balls had heeeeee.
- 'Balls in the air, in the air' said the Jugglers, very fine men are v'e!
T'ere's none so fair as can compare to the men of Anyalie!

Oooooh Old King Cole, v'as a merry old soul, and a merry old soul v'ass he!
He called for hiss v'ife in the middle of the night, and he called for his fiddlers t'ree!
Now every juggler had a fine fiddle... and a very fine fiddle had heeeeee.
- 'Fiddle like hell, like hell' said the fiddlers.
'Balls in the air, in the air' said the Jugglers, very fine men are v'eeee!
T'ere's none so fair as can compare to the men of Anyalie...!"

Covered by the singing, Yariim crouched behind the curtains and took a claw hammer from the bundle of cloth rags. She looked about for a place to work – tested the give on floorboards with her heel, and finally found a board that worked beneath her weight. Treading on the board, she finally got a grip upon the iron nail. The dancer's muscles stood out as she heaved with all her might, slowly drawing the nail free.

> "...Oh,' shove it in the hole in the back', said the faggoters!
> 'I've got v'un thiss big' said the fisherman.
> 'Fiddle like hell, like hell' said the fiddlers
> 'Balls in the air in the air' said the Jugglers, very fine men are v'eeeeee!
> T'ere's none so fair as can compare to the men of Anyalie!"

One nail was out! Yariim worked on a second, and then carefully levered up the end of the board. She peered down into the pitch dark of the room below, trying to see if the room was occupied. Nothing moved, and there was no noise. Yariim waited until Sandhri's next chorus, and then wrenched the board carefully upwards, working free the nails at the other end.

A board was free! Yariim crouched and looked down into the coach house. She saw the vague shape of stables and stalls – a few scraps of light filtered in through chinks in the walls, but that was all. The place was darker than a cave, and utterly quiet. Heartened, the blue mouse went to work with a will, levering the neighbouring floor boards upwards with her hammer.

She made a hole in the floor that was hopefully big enough for a pregnant woman to pass through. Treading the boards carefully down into place, Yariim covered them over with her bedding. She hoped it was not too obvious.

Old King Cole had apparently been a busy man. Sandhri had worked her way through the entire royal household, up to and including stable boys and the puppeteers, and then started on a song even less clean than the last. Yariim finally emerged after scrubbing herself quickly off with rags and water. She took up her sewing, found the spare thread she had apparently been looking for, and smiled to Sandhri.

Sandhri relaxed against the wall, her arms about her belly. The food today was the same as always – flour for making bread, dried meat, a sausage and some sort of sauerkraut. Sandhri was nauseated by the sight of the stuff. She pushed it away, drank from their little pot of melted snow, and sat herself upon the windowsill to watch the enemy.

The massed collection of fodder had gone on all day. Most of the hay and straw was being dragged in wagons off to somewhere in the army camp. But the army was not yet prepared to move. Streams of scouts and couriers came in through the palace gates, as well as officers, soldiers and clerks. The Khan was gathering in his intelligence before lunging the army off on its next orgy of conquest.

Tomorrow or the next day, the army would move on. Sandhri kept her face resting against the glass. She reached out to hold Yariim's hand, squeezing it softly, never showing her beloved friend her face.

"Remember, my love. The Khan's army iss two hundred and fifty t'ousand steppe cavalry. T'ey haff sixty t'ousand Yellow Empire conscript infantry. Mostly pike and crossbowmen." Sandhri kept her face leaning on the window. "Did you understand v'at t'ose officers v'ere talking about, v'en they said the Khan's army fought like a mighty yak?"

"I think so." Yariim squeezed Sandhri's hand, looking at her beautiful, pregnant friend outlined by the window light. Sandhri would deliver her child in days at most. Yariim feared for her. "They spread horse archers out to the flanks to envelop the enemy. Heavy cavalry at the center. I think their guard tuman stays back in reserve with the Khan."

"Good." Sandhri kept a quiet watch on the great outdoors. "And t'eir cannon. You said t'eir cannon v'ere heavy?"

"Siege guns almost a hundred tons in weight. It takes sixty oxen just to move them. Not something they can deploy quickly." Yariim flicked a glance at the doors, then leaned quietly in to Sandhri's hair. She whispered softly, caressing Sandhri's back. *"It's ready! I think we can squeeze you through – but it's dark down there. It might be a long drop."*

Sandhri nodded absently, her quiet grey eyes on the world outside. She stiffened – rose upwards, and then grabbed Yariim by the arm.

"T'ere. Look t'ere. The man dressed in the blue robes."

As evening came closer, more officers gathered for the evening war council with the Khan. Walking through the open gates came a tall, stiff-faced red panda dressed in loose blue robes. Dressed as an officer of the Yellow Empire, he seemed unusually contemptuous of the Khan's troops, who actually bowed to him. Yariim frowned in puzzlement.

"Khanate troops bowing to Imperials?"

"No – look!" Sandhri pointed with one slim finger. "He's not dressed for the cold! No padding, and yet he doesn't even shiver!"

The man in question moved in silence, looking neither left nor right. With a cold, compressed expression on his face, the man walked beneath the window. He did not twitch his ears. He did not curl his long furry tail. His breath did not steam like all those men around him. Shivered by the sense of utter *wrongness* about the man, Yariim drew back from the window.

Sandhri kept watching out the window.

"T'ere are several like t'at. Not many, but a few. Alv'ays ranking officers of cities, conscripts... I t'ink I v'unce saw a Frankish ambassador go in, and come out as v'un of t'ese." The bat looked away, towards Yariim.

"I don't t'ink t'ose creatures are alive."

"No." Yariim felt her spine crawl. "No – you're right. He had no body heat. His breath didn't cloud."

Sandhri gave Yariim an intense, pointed gaze.

"Remember. Anyv'un around Raschid could be replaced by such a creature – but only iff the Khan has access to them. It iss the Khan's doing. Our so-called 'lord of ghosts'..."

"The Khan?" Yariim looked hastily out at the failing light. Soon they would be receiving visitors. "Sandhri, what is he?"

"I do not exactly know." Sandhri levered herself down onto the floor, in the shadows. She reached for Yariim. "Come. Sit, and let me tell you one last tale."

"Last?" Yariim gave a start. "Last?"

"Shhh – iss chust an expression." Sandhri held both of her friend's hands, holding her beloved Yariim in place. "Now quiet – listen now to things unwritten."

She sat behind Yariim, holding the other woman in her arms. She leaned Yariim's head back against her, where she could speak softly into the mouse's soft pink ear.

"V'e do not speak of it, except to ot'er story tellers - our kin. And to pass it on before v'e die. But you are a dancer, and t'at iss a type of storyteller, too."

The bat laid her cheek against Yariim's golden hair.

"I haff told many tales of the birth of Aku Mashad. Of God, and off animals fleeing Eden. Off a place called Earth, v'ere live a race of strange beings like ourselves." The bat squeezed Yariim. "But t'ose are my stories – my very own. A storyteller shapes tales as a lesson – and in making the lesson, t'ey hope to shape a little part off the world. But this iss not a story. This iss history – and in hiding it, the storytellers haff also helped to shape a v'orld. V'e thought it for the best.

"The tale tells us that four great sorcerers lived upon the Earth. Each v'un dwelled at the far corners of the v'orld. T'ey v'ere mighty, and t'ey pulled the strings that controlled religions, nations, queens and kings. So they had lived for many centuries, and so t'ey hoped to live for many more.

"But the magic v'as going out of Earth. Magic is not a permanent t'ing. Magic iss made by souls. Creative magic comes from hope and purity – from love and joy and happiness. Destructive magic comes from terror. But on Earth, technology v'ass spreading. As people understood their v'orld, they feared it less. V'ile no more white magic v'ass made, the black magicians feared that t'eir supply of evil magic v'ould soon dry up. To fight technology, the black magicians v'ould need far, far more power…

"T'ey found their source. The four great evil sorcerers of Earth found the v'orld of Aku Mashad."

The Bat held Yariim quietly, and softly kissed her hair.

"V'e t'ink perhaps our own races already lived here. But to the sorcerers, they v'ere a whole new source of power. So the sorcerers made a great compact. T'ey divided Aku Mashad between them, and they made kingdoms born of terror.

"T'ey abandoned Earth, and t'ey enslaved us…"

The bat's fingers gripped Yariim's fur. Yariim felt the baby stir inside her friend, moving against its cramped, confining womb.

Sandhri kept her voice a merest whisper.

"V'e are told vun came to the Amu Daja Valley, to the center of Aku Mashad. V'un v'ent to the lands that became the Yellow Empire. Vun made his home in a land far av'ay over the seas, and v'un made hiss home in a land v'ere mountains of ice reach to the skies. In each place, they made a vast city of men from Earth. The animal races slaved and died in t'eir hundreds of t'ousands to provide the aliens v'ith luxuries. From the misery and the horror off our people, the sorcerers gathered the power t'at they v'ished to use to v'un day enslave the Earth.

"And so our peoples suffered slavery for a hundred bitter years…

"But all v'as not lost. For the sorcerers used servants from the animal races as t'eir go betweens. These creatures v'ould carry messages and run errands for the mighty ones. But they met v'ith v'un anot'er, and spoke off their hatred for the sorcerers. They v'atched the sorcerers, and t'ey made a plan.

"The Sorcerers v'ere ancient – their bodies long, long dead and v'ithered. If they lost an arm, a leg or even a head, it neffer seemed to kill them. The lost members grew back. But a body servant to v'un sorcerer saw one thing strange about her master's v'ithered husk. Light gleamed from v'ithin his rib cage – for he had a heart of glowing stone."

Sandhri rested her head back against the wall, feeling tired, feeling drained – passing on the tale gave a sense of closure.

"We won, my darling. The messengers arranged a time between themselves, and they all struck. They smashed the sorcerer's stones. All except v'un - that of the sorcerer of ice. The animal races rose up and destroyed the alien cities, killing all the humans they found within. Aku-Mashad v'as purged and made clean at last, and the animal peoples at last had their promised land ordained by God.

"The alien cities v'ere abandoned – nothing taken but a few tools, a few books – holy gospels from religions the sorcerers had long abandoned. The Sorcerer of ice v'as trapped as his city shattered, and v'as buried underground, smashed and forgotten. Time erased the cities, and t'ousands of years erased even the memory of the times v'e had endured.

"But the messengers remembered.

"Some folk remained as go betweens – people who v'andered the world, and remembered that wonder comes from magic, and that true magic comes from joy. Storytellers – real story tellers – look back to those few folk, and keep their memory alive."

Sandhri drew her long white hair about Yariim like a silken cloak, and quietly kissed her ear.

"So now I haff told you. Now you know."

Yariim scarcely dared to move.

"How long ago was this?"

"Millennia, my love. Long ages in v'ich to forget." The Bat stroked Yariim's hair. "To have kept the tale alive v'ould haff made us a people founded in bitterness. So the tale iss neffer, effer told in public. Only true storytellers know it, and pass it only to their trusted kin.

"V'e are the peoples of Aku-Mashad, and v'e know how to embrace wonder…"

Sandhri drew in a deep, slow breath, and reluctantly released Yariim. The contact faded slowly –the feel of Yariim's warmth, the gentle scent of her soft fur.

"I love you, Yariim – my sister, my lover, my partner, my friend…"

Yariim turned to look at Sandhri, her skin crawling. Something was horribly wrong…

"I love you, too." She leaned closer. "Sandhri – what's wrong? Is it the baby?"

"Not'ing iss wrong. All iss as it should be."

Sandhri looked at the door, watching lamp light show her the shadows of the guard's booted feet.

"Now – t'iss Tsu-Khan v'ass once exiled into a wilderness of ice. He came back v'ith powers unlike anyt'ing v'e haff ever seen." Sandhri turned to Yariim. "So *remember* – alv'ays remember. A wizard iss killed not by cutting off the head, but by tearing out the heart of stone. *The heart of stone.*"

Sandhri hung her head, and her hands flexed slowly.

"Osra is science – but it iss also magic. And it v'ill become more and more magical – and people will have a place they can look to, and always say *'yes – t'ere iss hope for the v'orld. Yes – t'ere is a v'ay of peace'.*"

She heaved, trying to get up. Yariim hastened to help, supporting Sandhri's back. The bat nodded in thanks, and slowly made it to her feet. She looked at the rags on the table, and waved her hand.

"Come. Dark iss falling, and t'ey v'ill be here soon. We had best make your finery." The bat fluffed out old silk scarves and pieces of rag. "Itbit v'ould do it far better than you or I. I v'ish she could be here."

Disturbed, Yariim sat and watched her friend. She took up a needle and thread, tried to shake off a strange, half formed intuition, and then tuned her mind to the job at hand.

Nighttime had brought yet more chill, yet more snow. Slow-spinning snow flakes drifted from the sky, landing softly on every surface they could find. Visibility dropped – tracks disappeared…

…All in all, it was a fine night for an escape.

The streets of Gulay Gudd were silent, dark and empty. The inner ring of houses about the palace were occupied by the Black Guard, who sat in their dark groups sharing coarse, hard laughter. Soldiers walked the streets on duty, gathering supplies or heading for their bivouacs. On the palace hill, the officers and couriers, messengers and scouts walked silently and doggedly through the snow, driven by duty and a longing to keep warm.

The palace was surrounded by a dark brick wall. The wall was pierced by a gate. Tall towers loomed overhead, and lights showed here and there upon the battlements. The glint of steel in the night gave the darkened walls an air of deadly menace. Approaching quietly down one narrow, pitch-black street, Meng and Itbit halted just out of sight of the guards.

Itbit looked slim and slight, buried inside a huge fleece coat. Meng stood quietly in the darkness, dressed in his stained Imperial armour. The young sage led two horses by the reins – war horses draped in armour and hung with long felt rugs. He pulled the animals to a halt, and peered quietly around the corner towards the palace gates.

There were two guards, who stood checking the authority tablets of all who entered. Meng felt for his own golden tablet, drawing quietly back into the dark.

"They make no detailed examinations?"

"There is no need. All here serve the Khan, body, mind and soul." Itbit's voice was hollow, and tinged with nervousness. "Meng must lookie as though he has every reason to be here, and he will pass. But if he lookie nervous, Meng will be caught."

The guards stood sheltered in the gateway, protected from the snow. Lights shone through the darkness from the palace walls. Meng kept his face turned away from Itbit, feeling her presence beside him like a blow to the soul.

"This one humbly thanks you for your aid. There is no need to remain. You have done your duty."

"Itbit is not here for duty." The mouse looked away. "Itbit cannot enter the palace – they know Itbit should not be there. She will waitie here, in the darkness, and watch for you."

There was no more to be said. Meng turned and bowed to Itbit, unable to look her in the face, and then took hold of the horses and led them quietly away.

He walked towards the great, dark gates, feeling as though he were observing himself from afar. Itbit had left Meng's soul numb – like flesh stunned by a hammer blow. She had killed his heart as surely as though she had split it with a stone. Meng clung to his duty, tried to keep the demeanor of a sage – and felt like simply falling, weeping, down into the snow.

Instead of collapsing, Meng walked, his face impassive behind the mask of black fur about his eyes. He approached the gate without fear, bowed slowly to the two waiting guards, and proffered the gold tablet he had stolen long ago.

The guards looked at the tablet.

They were Black Guards. Powerful, bow-legged men who had spent their lives in the saddle. Each of them had slaughtered enemy civilians in their hundreds. They looked at Meng through suspicious, squinting eyes.

"This is a pass for a leader of one thousand." The guard looked at Meng. He was a brindled dog with ugly, yellowed teeth. "Why does a leader of Imperial scum need to enter the palace?"

"These are horses from the great stud at Yin-Li-Kwan." Meng coolly indicated the two very ordinary horses at his side. "I have been instructed to bring them for use of Prince Tulu Begh."

The second guard – a tall cat with muscles like steel cables, gave a thrash of his tail. "Tulu Begh." The guard looked the horses over in contempt. "He's skewered some poor bastard in a duel again, and won another prize."

The dog gave a foul bark of laughter.

"He's always skewering something!"

The men laughed. Meng merely bowed, frozen faced, and took back his golden tablet. He moved on, leaving the guards to their mirth.

The palace courtyard was filled with snowflakes that drifted in confusion, blown this way and that by the winds between the palace walls. Officers stood talking at the center of the yard. More soldiers stood tending horses over by the stable wall. The palace itself was a great, block-shaped lump of a building crowned with onion-domed towers. A bulky coach house jutted off to one side, the doors closed and shadowed by a red brick colonnade. Meng took his two horses beneath the eaves and into the shadows by the door. He tied their reins to a post, and then knelt down to check their rugs, their saddles and their hooves.

The horses' armour skirts hung down to hide their bellies. Meng had affixed ropes about the horses' middles, slinging more ropes between them to make a narrow hammock underneath each horse. Hidden by the horse blankets and the armour, they would let a rider cling beneath the horses utterly unseen. Meng checked the knots carefully, keeping an eye upon the courtyard and the officers.

A figure in yellow robes walked across the courtyard with a carefree laugh that cut Meng to the bone. Prince Tulu Begh walked with his fellow lords, laughing and gossiping. Meng withdrew between his two horses and watched the man go – trying not to recognize the great, dark hatred in his heart.

"You there! What are you doing?"

A khanate soldier – a spotted cat as thick as a barrel and wearing a red felt coat – stood with one hand on his bow in its quiver. He looked at Meng in suspicion and contempt. "No one is to approach the coach house! Horses go over there! The far wall! Over there!"

The man expected Imperial soldiers to know only a few words of his speech. Meng simplified his accent, and gave a reverent bow.

"Honoured soldier, this one has been instructed to shelter this most valuable of imported beasts beneath the eaves. It is a desert animal, and has expressed a great dislike for snow."

"Fuck." The cat walked towards the horses. He was a true steppe rider – not one of the Khan's countless foreign converts. The man had the rolling gait that told of a life spent totally in the saddle. "What use is a horse that can't take the chill. Get them out of here now, or we'll have you flayed alive."

"At once, great soldier." Meng bowed. The officers standing in the courtyard had gone, and the grooms had walked away from their horses. "I thank you for your instruction."

The soldier spat into the snow and turned to go.

Meng drew his long slim blade in one great, fluid flow. He lunged forward, punching the needle-sharp sword through felt coat, flesh and muscle. He ran the khanate soldier clean through from behind, punching his scholar's sword out through the man's chest.

Run through the heart, the soldier jerked. He tried to scream, but only coughed. He fell thrashing and jerking to the ground, words half croaking from his throat. Meng knelt swiftly, looking left and right, but the courtyard was blank and bare.

"I ask your forgiveness. This humble one will undergo contrition for this deed."

The soldier died. Feeling hollow, Meng looked at the vast mass of red, steaming blood melting through the snow around the corpse. He pushed the dead man underneath the eaves and dragged snow over the corpse. Yet more snow was strewn over the already freezing pool of blood. Meng stood back, his heart pounding, wiping his hands again and again on his coat. He could still feel the impact of the sword piercing through a living body, and it played through his senses again and yet again. He felt the moment would plague him for all eternity.

Someone laughed over at the far side of the courtyard. A soldier came out to piss against a brick column near the other horses. From the shadows of the stables, other soldiers cheered. Meng looked around quietly, and then backed towards the coach house door.

The rickety doors were held in place by a single bolt, and the bolt was locked in place. But the coach house doors opened outwards – and this meant that the hinges were on the outside of the doorframe. Long bronze pintels passed down through the hinges. Meng unfroze the metal with a flask of hot water from his belt, then used a knife blade to ease the long metal pin out of the lowest hinge.

No one saw – no one heard. Meng reached up and quietly dealt with the upper hinge. The horses beside him stamped and snorted – but all was quiet, save for the sound of female voices from somewhere up above.

Female. The Khan's army had no camp followers, no female slaves or wives. The voices must be the captive Queens. Meng looked up at the floor above, satisfied that he had done well.

He took a pry bar from a pack of tools upon one horse, and wrenched the door carefully open, pushing against the piled snow. He needed it open wide enough for a pregnant woman to pass. Meng froze as the great doors gave a screech of tortured wood. He looked about the courtyard, then suddenly heard footsteps coming through the snow from behind. The young sage flung himself face down in the snow beside his horses, the pry bar held tight in his hand.

Men laughed – Khanate officers were laughing in the snow. Emir Had'idh was amongst them, striding into the palace. The men passed by the horses at the coachouse – walked past Meng without looking into the shadows. They met guards at the main palace doors, and with much laughter passed inside.

Meng waited no longer. He slithered on his belly through the crack he had made in the coach house door. He crept silently into a great, cold, empty world that echoed in the gloom.

Wooden floorboards formed a roof overhead, and candlelight filtered down through cracks to stripe the empty space below. The floor was beaten earth frozen hard as steel in the cold; a few wisps of straw, and the upright posts of stable stalls made stark shapes in the gloom. Meng moved quietly inwards, and he heard the sound of Queen Sandhri's voice through the boards overhead. It was like a draft of pure joy to the soul!

Something stirred in the darkness, and Meng whipped his head about and shrank in fear.

A huge shape loomed in the chamber – a great hemisphere the size of hay stack. A black hole at its front gaped like a mouth, and flared metal brows drooped on either side of that strange face. The great figure had six huge, folded legs equipped with chicken feet big enough to throttle a war horse. Each leg was shackled to brick pillars with a heavy length of iron chain.

Meng stared, frozen in shock. The huge hemisphere moved slightly in its chains, making metal scrape on metal. Meng's heart hammered in his throat, as he rose quietly, put his hands into his sleeves and gave a bow.

"Please forgive this humble person for disturbing you."

The great shape stirred as Sandhri's voice came from overhead. The Queen's voice lilted in her usual much-beloved tones. The great bronze hut lifted itself up, apparently listening to Sandhri's voice, and the hut seemed suddenly to be less sad.

The voices rose – more feet walked the boards overhead, and Meng settled down to wait.

"My Lord Had'idh! My Lord Tulu Begh. How very t'oughtful off you to join us!" Pregnant as she was, Sandhri did not kneel and bow. Instead she put a hand over her belly and bowed her head, her long hair sweeping theatrically down about her like a cloak. "Please do grace our humble home."

The hall above the coach house was still horribly dark and cold. A huge curtain made from sheets screened off the far end of the hall, hiding the more squalid aspects of captivity from view. The little charcoal brazier was heaped with coals that tried unsuccessfully to keep away the bitter cold. But a rug had been found and dragged into the room, allowing old cushions to be placed for Sandhri and Yariim's guests. Yariim knelt beside the door and greeted the armed and armoured soldiers as they entered, her blonde hair gleaming above her worn and ragged clothes.

Yariim's hatred was implacable, but she hid it behind a stiff demeanor of gentility. Sandhri, on the other hand was full of irrepressable life. Heavy with pregnancy, she moved with difficulty, but the life and lilt were in her hands and in her eyes.

Tulu Begh, Emir Had'idh and four grim, hard-bitten commanders came in through the door. Sandhri leaned upon a stick and bid them enter with a wave.

"A hill v'oman washes the feet of her guests! But giffen the temperature, you might find it unkind!" Sandhri bent over with a grunt and fetched the tea kettle. "So I v'ill offer you somet'ing hot instead."

One soldier walked forwards to yank open the curtain and look briefly over the bedding on the floor. The toilet bucket in the corner convinced him to retreat. Sandhri made a show of presenting the man with tea.

"Our hordes of assassins haff the evening off." Somehow, the scoundrel of a bat had managed to bake scones. "Please make yourself comfortable."

Yariim poured the acorn tea. Soldiers watched her with mingled cold appraisal and watchful lust: The second Queen of Osra looked impossibly beautiful, even in rags. Yariim's every movement was schooled to sensuality and grace. She served her guests and withdrew back to sit at Sandhri's side.

Tulu Begh watched both Queens with a satisfied, predatory grin.

"Well, your Majesties. You seem comfortable enough!"

Yariim looked at Tulu Begh. Her pink eyes were level, and her thoughts about him were her own.

"I have endured worse."

Sandhri supped her tea with satisfaction.

"And I v'ass a street beggar, Tulu Begh. Here at least, v'e haff scones!" Sandhri threw one to the Prince. "Here!"

Emir Had'idh watched the Queens through eyes filled with an undying hate.

"Why have you asked us here?"

Yariim gave the man a glare. Sandhri gave a hoot of mirth and passed the man a scone.

"V'e did not ask you here, Had'idh. V'e think you are a clinker off the arsehole of the devil. But v'e did ask the Khan – and he t'inks that haffing you here iss a grand little joke. But anyv'ay – haff some tea and a scone." The bat slid her glance over to Yariim and arched her brows. "Yariim – perhaps you v'ill pour?"

Yariim was nervous. Tonight, as the Khan's war council met mere yards away, Yariim and Sandhri somehow would escape. She could not quite see how it would be done, but Itbit and Sandhri had a plan. She concentrated on acting the hostess, and kept her fear of failure from her eyes.

Boots marched up to the sealed door. There was a shift of light in the wall – the hidden guards that peered through spy holes moved aside.

The door was thrust open by armed men who stank of blood. The men stood with blades bared – scalps hanging from their belts.

Behind them, stood the Khan.

The Tsu-Khan's thin, pale face stood clearly out amidst his jet black robes. The man's fox muzzle gleamed bone white – his blue eyes looked at ally, victim or prisoner with the same lack of emotion. The lords and officers in the hall all put their foreheads to the floorboards in worship, and the Khan's presence seemed to flow into them like a dark, black stream of ecstasy.

The Tsu-Khan brought with him a sinister black energy. To his men, it was the breath of life, the surge of hope, and a dark, undying dream. Sandhri felt it too – and to her it was a living, watching, slithering *awareness*. A predatory, seething *thing* that watched her out of pale, dead eyes...

The Khan walked into the room, and the candles guttered.

Sandhri kept to her seat, and gave a solemn bow.

"Lord Khan! Such an honour. V'e are so glad t'at our message v'ass passed on to you." The bat indicated a seat by the coals. "You are most gracious, to attend our little home av'ay from home."

The Khan looked about the room with his blank, dead gaze. One of the men behind him was dressed in the outlandish armour of a Yellow Empire officer. Another wore the robes of a Pulski priest. Both men had skins covered with frost, and neither man's breath smoked as they stood. Yariim looked up from her place kneeling by the door, and then bowed to the Tsu-Khan.

"Great Tsu-Khan. It is a pleasure to see you again. Please be seated. Please allow us to show you such hospitality as we can muster."

Sandhri fussed with tea, fetching scones. The Khan's frost-covered priest and guard made no move to accept the gifts and eat. With a look of cold impatience, the Khan waved the food aside.

"We have no time for trivialities."

"Pray, indulge our taste for hospitality." The blue mouse bowed again. "Please be seated. Allow us to entertain you."

The Khan looked left and right to his attendants. They sat in an arch behind him. The Khan settled carefully onto a cushion with a black-bladed sword placed carefully at his side.

"Time is pressing." The Khan's voice was as blank and uncoloured as his fur. "If you have words for me, then say them now."

"Indeed." Yariim managed to look demure and quite contrite. "But allow us to receive you properly as our guest." Yariim put a hand upon her heart. "We have been remiss. I shall dance for you, as a guest should for her host."

The Khan turned a disinterested, icy gaze upon the mouse.

"I need no dance."

"But you must!" Sandhri brooked no opposition. "You haff not truly lived until you haff seen Yariim of Osra dance!" The bat fought her way up to her feet. "Come come! V'e can show you v'e are reasonable, educated ladies. Iss a good basis for business, yes?" The bat stood and put a finger to her sharp little teeth in thought. "Now... a sacred dance, or somet'ing a little spicier?

An officer answered darkly for his Khan.

"A sacred dance."

"Off course." Sandhri looked at Yariim with cool grey eyes. "Yariim?"

"The ode to Buraq should be eminently suitable." Yariim bowed to the Khan. Less skilled at outright deception than Sandhri, she kept her eyes on the floor. "Will that suffice, oh Khan?"

The Tsu-Khan kept the women under the gaze of his pale, unfriendly eyes. "I care nothing – provided it is not too long." The Khan swept a gaze across his men. "The council of war convenes in but half an hour."

"And v'e are grateful for your time." Sandhri inclined her head. "V'e shall not take up too much of your evening, great Khan. And the Ode to Buraq requires Yariim to ritually cleanse herself after the dance is finished – so you v'ill only haff my poor, pregnant self as company."

Yariim stiffened, then shot a hidden glance towards Sandhri. No dance in the world required any such damned fool thing – but the bat was already pouring tea for one and all.

"My Khan- we regret that v'e haff perhaps behaved badly as your guests. V'e wish to open the door to… more complete communication betv'een ourselves and your August majesty – and effen our husband Raschid! I am sure you will understand."

"Proceed, then." The Khan let tea cool unnoticed at his side. "But let it be brief."

Sandhri inclined her head, then made her way over to Yariim. Yariim slipped from her ragged outer robes, assisted by her friend. She leaned in to whisper anxiously into the bat's tall ear.

"Sandhri! What are you doing?"

"Meng iss in the courtyard. V'en the dance ends, go down to him." Sandhri put her arms about Yariim. She put her face into the mouse's hair and held her tight, breathing in her scent.

"I love you."

Moving purposefully, Sandhri let her best friend go. She perched herself in the windowsill, where she had an old brass cooking pot and a ring of discarded sleigh bells ready. The bat awkwardly sat in the windowsill, then upturned the pot and skillfully began using it as a drum.

To simple percussion, Yariim began to dance.

She *flowed*. With her old robes abandoned, the mouse gleamed blue as a summer sky, dressed in wisps of brilliant cloth. She floated slowly, reverently – in perfect control. With effortless strength, Yariim sank to the ground in a graceful split – only to rise up as she danced without putting a hand to the floor. The drum thumped, bells rang, and slowly the soldiers became trapped in Yariim's spell.

Yariim was living – graceful and quiet. An image of perfection, of art and reason – all that made Osra shine as the jewel of the world. Yariim poured all of her soul into her art, and Sandhri loved her for it.

She moved past the watching audience in a swirl of rags, blue fur and golden hair. Tulu Begh watched Yariim in shameless admiration.

"Remarkable." The Prince admired the perfect curves of Yariim's backside as she danced. "Voluptuous. Intelligent. Supple as a dream. No wonder the Shah of Osra is so smitten."

General Gurad – dark, black and massive in his snow-spattered armour, looked unsmilingly at Yariim.

"Osra is a blight upon the face of the world."

"They slew your family, dear General. But that was because your family supported the

Shah's brother in his abortive coup – is it not?" Tulu Begh kept his eyes upon Yariim. "A tad short sighted of them. For myself, I find it best to keep away from politics."

The General put his hand to his sword.

"You would do well not to anger me, Tulu Begh!"

"I have risen beyond your sphere, General Gurad." Tulu Begh was deceptively at ease. His hand was placed idly where it could reach his slim, plain hilted sword. "The Khan has seen fit to reward success. My star has risen higher than your own. Where are the mighty victories you promised him? Where are the great lands laid at his feet?"

"You are a canker!" The General watched Tulu Begh. "Never forget that your position relies solely upon *me.*"

"The Khan begs to differ." The Prince breathed Yariim's scent as she went bye. "It seems the Khan has need of men of subtlety and… flexibility."

Swirling, Yariim danced before her captors – proud, intelligent and utterly controlled. Sandhri's eyes never left her – those grey eyes full of love. Yariim looked at her and felt her hackles rising. Somewhere, something strange was pulling Yariim's heart. The blue mouse swept into the last graceful flutter of her dance, falling like slow autumn leaves upon the wind. She ended flat to the floor, spread in a carpet of colour amongst the flat old boards.

Tulu Begh was enthusiastic in his applause. The other soldiers followed suit, begrudgingly recognising the force of the performance. The Khan and his two undead companions sat in silence, uninterested and unmoved.

Sandhri stood and bowed slowly, then held a hand to take Yariim from the floor. She squeezed Yariim's hand in her own, and faced the watching officers.

"V'e thank you, Great Khan – great lords. T'ank you for your indulgence." The bat smiled only with her face, and not her eyes, which she kept hidden as she bowed.. "Ass you know, Yariim must leave us now."

Sandhri took her friend by the hands and kissed her softly. Taking Yariim against her heart, Sandhri breathed quietly and sadly into Yariim's ear.

"Goodbye, my love. God speed."

Suddenly Yariim *knew*. She knew that Sandhri had never intended to go. Yariim tried to cling to Sandhri, but the bat firmly turned away. She kept her face from Yariim, and turned back to the Khan.

"Yariim v'ill cleanse herself, Gentlemen. But I v'ill be your hostess. If you – Tulu Begh! Yes – If you could reach me that cushion for my poor bum..."

Yariim stood, horrified, and looked to the floor, bowing low. She backed to the curtains, and risked sending Sandhri one last, awful glance. Sandhri met her eyes and nodded once, telling her to go. Yariim bowed to the room and faded back through the curtains.

Numbed, Yariim moved as though driven by some disconnected, guiding hand. She took her robes in hand, quietly levered up the floorboards and slid through into the darkness below.

In the main room, Sandhri straightened her back as though a burden had left her. False emotions masked over her grey eyes as she looked up towards the Tsu-Khan.

"More tea, oh Khan?"

The Tsu-Khan drew in along, slow breath and stared at Sandhri.

"In mere minutes, the council of war gathers at my command. Queen of Osra – why do you waste my time?"

Sandhri gave a sigh, her shoulders wilting. Ears flattening in sour defeat, she looked humbly to the ground.

"If you give me the means – paper, pens, v'un off those magic mirrors – I v'ill write to my husband Shah Raschid." Cowed, Sandhri clenched her hands. "I v'ill ask him to negotiate an end off hostilities v'ith you – if you v'ill promise to release myself, Yariim and Itbit to him unharmed."

There was no swift, immediate reaction. The Khan regarded his prisoner in thought.

"Your husband has already led his troops out to attack."

"You haff angered him, My Lord. His attack on you iss in vengeance more t'an anything else." Sandhri looked away. "Vengeance."

Tulu-Begh raised his brows.

"Vengeance, oh Queen? Is that like a scholar-king?"

The bat lifted grey eyes to look at Tulu Begh.

"He iss the Shah of Osra, of the House Dinaq, of a line extending back for a t'ousand years of royalty." The bat breathed slowly. "Neffer underestimate the force and futility of anger, and of pride."

Emir Had'idh looked at Sandhri in loathing and suspicion.

"A remarkable turn about in attitude."

"A v'oman is a weak instrument, lord Emir. V'at can v'e do in the face of so much power?" Sandhri looked at the floor her body bent in defeat. "I ask v'un t'ing. Do not hurt my Itbit."

Soldiers sat taller as the light dawned. They looked at Tulu Begh in sly respect. The Prince had worked a miracle yet again. With an air of secrecy, the men looked back at the bat and smiled in victory.

The Khan was unmoved. He finally decided to taste his tea.

"Tomorrow morning, you shall present me with a letter written to your husband the Shah. It will beg him to halt his armies and to retire to his own borders, in order that you be returned to him unharmed." The Khan's pale, empty eyes fixed softly upon the bat.
His voice was soft and smooth.

"Let us understand each other, my lady. Your life or death are nothing to us. For our pleasure, we would tear your living child from your womb and impale it slowly on a spike. We would drag your shrieking body down the halls so that your agonies might pleasure us as you die. We would flay you alive before our court. We would have a saddle cloth made from your skins, and feed your bloody carcasses to the Torah birds..." The Khan failed to make Sandhri meet his eye. "All these things shall come to pass, unless you bow before our will."

Queen Sandhri made certain that the Khan never met her gaze.

"V'e are aware off the alternatives." The bat's voice had a hard edge, and she softened it carefully. "I haff come to accept many t'ings in this last day. No matter how beautiful, some t'ings cannot be. And no matter how dreadful, some choices must be made, because t'ey are *clean...*" Sandhri gave a bow. "You are late for your meeting. V'e are sorry to haff kept you."

The soldiers rose to leave. Sandhri clambered to her feet, crossed to the curtains and peered behind. She nodded to the occupant within. "Yariim – our guests are leaving..." Sandhri listened to an unheard end of the conversation, and bowed. She dropped the curtain and crossed to the door.

"Yariim bids you good night. V'e trust the evening has been of profit."

The Khan left without a word, his black robes swirling and his slight figure surrounded by a unseen cloud of evil. His men left one by one. Tulu Begh came last of all, and made a great show of kissing Sandhri's hand.

"My dear Queen – this has been a pleasure!" Tulu Begh bent over Sandhri's hand. She looked on him as she would gaze upon a scorpion dipped in vomit. Prince Tulu straightened with a smile. "And to you also, Queen Yariim! An exquisite privilege to be with you once again."

Sandhri cocked one huge ear as though listening, and gave a sour smile while looking at Tulu Begh in clear distaste.

"Yariim v'ishes you well."

"I'm sure." Tulu Begh gave a satisfied smile. He bowed towards the curtains, and departed.

The doors closed with a hollow *boom*. Lights flickered as the hidden watchers took up their places outside the door. Left alone in the cold, Sandhri walked slowly back towards the curtains, her face hidden by her pure white hair.

The baby stirred inside her, pushing against its confinement. He moved anxiously, knowing that something was wrong. Sandhri squeezed her eyes shut against the tears as she stroked her son through her belly, shushing him quietly back to sleep.

She moved behind the curtain into the emptiness behind. Moving quietly, Sandhri tamped the loose floorboards back into place, holding a one-way conversation with Yariim all the while. She banked up the blankets in their ragged bed to look as though Yariim were asleep, then rose and drew the curtains aside.

"T'ey're gone now, my love. Iss alright. It had to be done – you haff to understand. T'iss v'ass the only v'ay."

Sandhri sat with her back to the spies near the door, so that none could see the tears coursing softly down her cheeks. Sandhri took up one of the nails Yariim had removed from the floorboards – a nail that Sandhri had carefully flattened and honed to a knife-edge against the bricks. She slid the little blade into hiding inside the stitching of her sleeve, and leaned back against the wall.

She had made her choices.

"Now – let us haff a story together. Something bright. Something v'onderful." Sandhri wept, but her voice was bright. She had given her gifts – and she knew that it was right.

"Long ago and far av'ay, there vass a little story teller in a market place." Sandhri caressed her son beneath one hand, and stroked the cold pile of blankets with another, and focused her eyes far, far away.

"A storyteller, and a handsome, gentle Prince…"

In the darkened coach house, Yariim dropped silently to the floor. She felt a familiar presence call out in the darkness. Weeping, Yariim fumbled towards the sound and found a warm, slim hand reaching out to take her own.

"My Queen."

Meng. Dear, wonderful Meng. Yariim hugged him tightly, her shoulders shaking with her tears. Meng crouched down to whisper into Yariim's ear.

"Forgive this one's tardiness in locating you. I have a way to smuggle you outside." Meng crouched and looked up towards the floorboards overhead. "Is Queen Sandhri following?"

Yariim hung her head.

"Queen Sandhri will not be following." The mouse tried to master herself, rising unsteadily to her feet, tears running freely down into her fur. "We must go."

Meng froze, appalled. "Majesty – where is she?"

"She is covering our escape." Yariim kept her back turned to the escape hole high above. "It is her gift to us. We must go."

Meng stared at Yariim in the gloom. Overhead, Sandhri's voice could be heard speaking to the soldiers and the officers of the Khan. Meng looked up towards the sound in sadness and awe. He then placed his hands inside his sleeves, faced the sound of Sandhri's voice, and gave a long and reverent bow.

Chains stirred as the giant metal hut moved against its bonds. Great guy ropes ran back and forth across the hut, holding it down in place. Yariim saw the hut and touched it quietly, feeling it try to arch into her touch.

"Poor thing."

Meng made his way to the coach house door, peering out into the dark. He looked back at the hut. "Lady – what is it?"

"It is a magical thing." Yariim stared at it, feeling its age, its loneliness. "A thing from fairytales…" The mouse touched the hut with the back of her furred hand; the metal was cold enough to stick to unprotected skin. "One day, we shall free you. I promise you."

With that, they left. Yariim squeezed through the coach house door, and Meng slid the lower hinge pintel back into place.

The courtyard was dark with night and swirling with snowflakes. Light filtered down through the arrow slits and windows overhead. Meng looked towards the nearest group of soldiers at the stables, but all seemed quiet.

He helped Yariim slide beneath a horse. The mouse fed herself into the narrow hammock, and Meng pulled the ropes tight. Clamped face-up against the hot belly of the horse, Yariim clung tight to the ropes, and felt the great horse sway slowly into motion. The hooves stamped through the snow, the tail swished… curtains of cloth and armour hid the world from Yariim's view. The mouse felt herself being led across the courtyard, then down a slope towards the palace gate.

Exposed to night and snow, Meng kept his pace even and refrained from looking behind himself. He led the two horses towards the gates, plodding quietly through the snow.

At the gates, the two guards had a fire to keep them warm. It threw huge light into the street, and cast great shadows up onto the palace walls. The men finished eating dried meat as Meng approached, and reached for their spears.

Meng gave the men a bow.

"My Prince declares the horses to be acceptable. He instructs me to take them to his quarters."

The knotted black cat leaned on his spear and spat.

"Tulu Begh is a fool. These prissy toys are only built for speed."

The second guard gave a laugh, looking sourly at his fellow. "You haven't even seen them run!"

"No need to – look at the barrel!" The cat slapped the nearest mount upon the chest behind its shoulder. "Too short."

"They look good enough." The other man gave a caw of laughter. "Firm in the arse – just like a good woman."

"No. No stamina!" The Cat grabbed the edge of the horse's blanket and wrenched it up. "Look at the belly on it!"

The horse stamped in impatience. The horse's belly was exposed – stripped of straps and hammocks. Meng had kept the horse without a passenger closest to the guards. He looked politely at the horse's belly, and bowed.

"Honoured soldier, it may be so. This humble one is no one to judge. But a free horse is not to be dismissed lightly."

The two guards laughed. One swatted the nearest horse on the backside, starting it forward. Meng led the beasts on into the alley, keeping his pace quiet until he turned a corner into a darkened lane.

Meng sagged, fear rushing through and out of him in a gush. He spoke quietly to the wind.

"My Queen – we are in the city streets."

Itbit was waiting for him. She came forward timidly – anxious, frightened, but trying not to meet Meng's eyes. Hands clamped together and body tight, she edged closer to the horses.

"Meng…"

"All is well." The Sage felt a wrench at his heart. He kept his back firmly turned upon the palace. "Swiftly – we must go."

They walked through streets filled with ghostly noise. Impaled corpses frozen into bloody, silently screaming chunks of ice gleamed high above the streets. The houses were home to soldiers who ate, laughed and shattered furniture. Men spilled into the streets here and there, walking through the snow. Meng kept a tight hold on the horses and led them at a steady pace down the streets towards the river gate.

Itbit kept her head down, her eyes upon the snow. Her furless pink tail had been sheathed in a long sock of padded cloth, and it swished sadly behind her as she walked. A strain of silence webbed between herself, Meng, and the unseen passengers.

The river gate stood open, but the gateway was home to a guard of at least a hundred soldiers. Houses by the gate thronged with men. The soldiers of the Khanate did not drink alcohol, nor did they waste their time with women when on campaign. The men talked and joked – played instruments or oiled their weapons. A cockfight held the attention of a large, blood thirsty crowd. Itbit kept her head down, and Meng tried to look neither left nor right.

Guards arose and demanded to see a pass. Meng pulled out his much-used golden tablet. The guards looked in contempt at his foreign uniform, then jerked their heads to tell him to be on his way.

The Yellow Empire conscripts were housed in tents outside the city. Meng led the way out, far away from the city and its noise, and off towards the great, dark expanse of the Kuba river. Here, flat snow was broken up with jagged blocks of dirty ice. The horses were moved quietly to the lee of a great, jagged block of ice, and quietly halted in the dark.

Meng climbed the ice block and looked about himself. Campfires made a vast ring about the city, spreading out along the river banks and up into the hills. A quarter of a million men were encamped out in the snow, and their fires spread out like the stars in the sky. But here, on the frozen river, all was dark. Men feared to tread the ice, no matter how thick it might be, and no men walked here in the dark. Satisfied, Meng slid down and began to wrench the armour from the nearest horse. Itbit ran to help, tugging at the frozen straps and hauling at the heavy rugs, hurtling them aside.

Yariim swung down from her cradle beneath the horse, dragging loose hair out of her eyes. She made a swift look out into the darkness, wiping frozen tears from her fur. Itbit half ran forward – hesitated – then was swept up into Yariim's arms. The two mice clung to one another, holding tightly, faces buried on each other's hair.

"Itbit! Oh, Itbit!" Yariim held the girl as tight as she could. "Forgive me."

Itbit clung onto Yariim as though her soul depended upon it. Meng finished stripping the horses of their armour, then covered them back in their felt rugs.

"My lady. We are ready."

A great, looming presence rose up out of the dark. Growling fit to terrify the dead, Marwan the Camel surged up from beneath a snow-covered sheet. He shook himself free of snow and padded forward in his big rag boots, stretching out his neck to head butt Yariim in welcome. The blue mouse clung to Marwan's head in gladness.

Itbit slowly pushed away from Yariim, looking about the piles of rugs and armour in growing uneasiness. Her voice was hushed almost to a whisper.

"Meng – where is Sandhri?"

Yariim answered. She kept her face buried against the thick felt blankets that covered Marwan's neck.

"Sandhri stayed behind, Itbit."

The green mouse sagged, sitting on the ice in shock.

"Why?"

"Because she is too pregnant to run, to climb or ride. Because she needed messages taken to Raschid." Yariim's voice broke with tears. "She knew she would never get away…"

Looking away, Meng hunched his shoulders, then reached to take up a bundle from the snow. He dusted the bundle off, then slung it up onto Marwan's back as the camel knelt upon the ice.

"Here are blankets and a tent. A bottle of alcoholic beverage, which will not freeze. Tinderbox and a pot in which to set a fire. Use only twigs in the day – they make no smoke. At night use only coals, and bank snow to hide the glow." He dragged out a clattering pile of clothes. "Here is a steppe man's clothing. Felt hat, sheepskin coat and boots. Keep your face masked with the woolen scarf."

The Sage knelt and pointed off into the darkness. "Travel down the river. The center of the river is rough ice caused by the banks freezing inwards to the middle. Use it as your guide. Travel at night, and hide in the day. The Osranii army is reputedly due south of us, perhaps two hundred miles." Meng pulled Marwan's saddle straps tight. "A camel has greater endurance than a horse. Marwan should outdistance the pursuit. His tread is soft upon the ice." Meng knelt to offer Yariim a knee up onto the camel. "Give my duty to the Shah. Tell him the Khan's army has fodder enough to last it for a few days – no more."

A sudden voice barked out across the snow.

"You there! Halt!"

A khanate soldier in a felt coat stood on the ice nearby, his horse held by the reins behind him. The man saw the two women with Meng and took a step closer, reaching for his sword.

"Imperial scum! What do you do here with these women?"

Something flashed in the dark. The soldier suddenly arched, one hand groping at his throat. A thin-bladed knife stood buried to the hilt in the man's windpipe. As he fell, Itbit threw a second knife that caught the man right in the eye. He jerked and fell thrashing to the snow, blood spilling out black and slick in the darkness.

Yariim turned and stared at Itbit. The green mouse ran to her victim and kicked the sword out of his spasming hand, looking back as she took possession of the blade.

"Itbit thinks is danger here. Yariim mouse should go!"

Yariim stared at the soldier's corpse.

"You killed him!"

"Sandhri taught Itbit to throw." Itbit jerked her knives free and wiped them in the snow. "Yariim must go. Itbit and Meng will take care of Sandhri now."

"Itbit!" Yariim came forward, reaching out a hand. "Itbit, they will come for you when they find I'm gone! You have to come with me!"

"Itbit will find Sandhri and bring her to Raschid." The slim green mouse stood, framed by bloody snow, her eyes sharp and proud. "Got to Raschid and the army. Helping them because they need you now. Sandhri knew that you can do things she cannot do." Itbit took a coat and hat Meng had clearly intended for Sandhri's escape, and wrapped herself inside them. "Bring our army. Kill the Khan."

Yariim looked to Meng, who held out a hand to beckon her onto Marwan. She hesitated. "I should stay."

"Forgive me for pointing out your error, but Lady, you must go." Meng bowed to Yariim. "Queen Sandhri wanted you with our army for a reason. Your duty leads you to your husband's side."

"Itbit and Meng will save Sandhri." Itbit ran over the snow to take Yariim's hands. They kissed. "Please – going fast, going safe. But *go."*

Queen Yariim gripped Itbit, then came to Meng. To the sage's shock, she kissed him full on the mouth, holding him in her arms and then resting her forehead against his cheek. A moment later, Yariim swung easily up onto Marwan's back, and the huge camel surged up onto his feet.

Yariim looked quietly down to Meng.

"Meng – take care of Itbit." Yariim pulled at Marwan's reins and turned him towards the great, black sky to the north. "Thank you."

Marwan knew his task. The great bull camel paced swiftly off into the darkness, moving with the silent lope that had always served him so well. Within seconds, he was gone. Snow fell, covering the camel's tracks, and the river lay still and quiet in the darkness.

Itbit came nervously over to Meng, and copied his style of bowing.

"Does a sage forgive error?"

"A sage forgives error. A sage knows that an error is a lesson." Meng bowed slowly to Itbit. "I have behaved… badly."

"Itbit thinks you have been magnificent." The green mouse looked up at him, yearning and sad. "Sandhri taught Itbit many things. The last lesson that she taught Itbit was that love never turns itself away."

"Yes." Meng looked to the city. "Then let us not turn away."

They walked past the dead soldier, leading three horses back towards the city. Snow fell, covering their tracks, the blood, the body- drifting down to mask the world beneath a haze of ice.

"Itbit – this humble sage would be pleased to hear your suggestions. How do we now slip into the palace and save the Queen?"

The green mouse nodded her head in thought.

"To slither through gaps, we needie a worm."

Meng nodded. "Do you indeed know a worm?"

"Oh yes. Itbit knows a worm." The green mouse walked on into the snow. "Come come! Itbit thinks it is a good job that combinies businesses with pleasure."

They quietly held hands. Side by side, with quiet steps, they walked across the fields of ice.

Chapter Eighteen:

The Osranii army marched. Sixty thousand men.

For weeks, the main army had marched in a gigantic oblong, the baggage carts with their huge loads of fodder, food and ammunition at the center. This close to an army of steppe cavalry, the army prepared itself to open fire in any direction, ready to respond to an attack wherever it might come.

The vanguards of light cavalry, artillery and skirmishers were outthrust into the countryside. The rumble of artillery and the crackle of small arms sounded at intervals all through the day. But there had not yet been serious resistance. The Osranii were dogged by scouts and piquets, ambushers and guerillas – the Khan had not yet decided to face the Osranii with his men.

Raschid rode his horse up to a hill top to unship his telescope and look at the road ahead. Saud and Abwan stayed with him – both awkwardly mounted on spare horses. Saud rode a cart horse, and the beast still looked as though it were about to have a hernia. But Abwan was no longer willing to let his Shah out of sight. They stood their wheezing horses, standing in their stirrups to watch for danger while the Shah looked carefully at the surrounding countryside.

There were Osranii light infantry pushing forward into a thicket of woods perhaps a mile away. Raschid could see the dead bodies of Khanate skirmishers the men left behind them in the snow. Skill and technology were proving a deadly counter to the horse archers of the steppes. Raschid had now seen enough to know the measure of his men. He watched the light infantry move in rushes, flushing enemy horse archers out of the woods. Rifle smoke drifted in the distant breeze as the Osranii skirmishers advanced.

An infantryman shared the hill with Raschid. The man wore the long white felt coat of the Osranii, with the obligatory ten silver bullets lining his breast pockets. His fleece cap had been circled with a green turban. The man nodded to the Shah, but kept his rifle cradled in his arms and scanned the marching army carefully as it passed.

His rifle was long, clean and efficient. A long brass telescope ran along the barrel. Raschid's sharp shooters were equipped with rifles of his own design, and the Shah rode over to join the infantryman.

The soldier gave another nod.

"My Lord."

"Soldier." Raschid looked at the man's rifle. "Are there any improvements you would like to see in the design?"

"It suits me well, Lord Shah. We just have to adjust the sights after a few shots."

"Ah." The Shah looked at the rifle and frowned. "The reason?"

"The cold, sir. The rifle barrel expands and contracts depending on the hot or cold."

Raschid shook his head. There was little that could be done about the cold. His men were well equipped and dressed, but still there had been frostbite. The only good news was that the troops were healthy. The sorcerers were keeping disease away from the men, and the icy chill had served to freeze a goodly supply of limes and lemons for the men.

Beside him, the infantryman suddenly rose up from a crouch.

"Mine!"

A figure had lain in the snow, waiting for the Osranii army to pass. The figure was a steppe horseman, who now pulled his horse up out of a snow bank and swung onto his mount. Up on the hill, five hundred yards away, the Osranii skirmisher took aim. The man let his rifle muzzle settle – lift – and then he fired. Smoke jetted, and the bullet hummed off down field.

The spy's horse reared, kicked and slewed sideways as the bullet slammed into its haunches. The rider fell, and Osranii horse archers spurred out of the marching column to intercept him. Up on the hill, the sniper shook his head unhappily and adjusted his sights.

"Drifting to the right. It's enough to make a temper pique." The rifleman reloaded and locked down the breech. He looked apologetically up at Shah Raschid. "Sorry, my Lord."

Raschid gave a snort. 'A cantering horse at five hundred?" He reached for a flask of palm brandy. "That was good shooting, Corporal…?"

"Yammak, my Lord."

"Good shooting, Yammak." Raschid tossed the man his brandy flask and gave a *salaam*. "Well done."

The Shah had a hundred body guard cavalry a few paces behind him. Raschid heard yet more hooves, and turned to see a slim girl with an absurdly long tail riding up from the army. A troop of Kakuzak lancers followed devotedly behind her. Saa'lu reigned in and bowed before her Shah.

"My Lord, General Ataman says that the Prince of Pulski and The Isle King have joined him for lunch. The main body is about to halt and eat."

"Ah." Raschid looked to the north. Enemy resistance had not been stiffening. Did that mean the Tsu-Khan was retiring north? "And what else did General Ataman say?"

The girl blushed from amongst her fleecy robes.

"He-he says I should make you move your royal arse off this hill, and make you come down to eat a proper meal – Sire."

Raschid had no interest in eating, except when he must. He shrugged, having eyes only for the terrain. Saa'lu crept her horse a little closer, and unwrapped a bundle before the Shah.

"My Lord? We caught a fish yesterday, in the ice. I have made fish dumplings. I cooked them myself -the way Lady Fatima taught me." She proffered the food. "She said that you liked them…"

The jackal Shah slowly turned his head. He pulled his scarf away from his face, his brown eyes looking quietly at the girl. He reached out and covered over the hot food, then gently patted the girl upon the hand.

"That is too kind a gesture to waste. Come – we shall eat together, with the General and the Princes." Raschid turned his horse. "Thank you, Saa'lu."

He began to ride back, then shot a sudden glance back at the girl.

"Has that idiot General proposed to you?"

The girl blushed.

"No, Sire."

"I am not sure what to make of a General who misses opportunities." Raschid hammered his spurs hard into his horse. "Come – we'll eat!"

They turned and rode back to the army. Raschid spared a glance for the land to the north.

Where was the Khan? Where were his armies?

What would Sandhri and Yariim have advised him to do?

He wrenched his heart away from the constant pain of loss. Followed by a hundred bodyguards in royal blue, Raschid returned to his men.

Hooves pounded on the ice. From her haven between two ice blocks, Yariim peered out beneath a fold of cloth and watched her enemies ride past.

They were light cavalry – one of them bloodied. They rode towards Yariim's refuge from the south, passing her by to race towards the north – towards Gulay Gudd. Yariim took it as a sign that the Osranii were drawing closer. She crept low across the snow and rose to watch her enemies depart, and then returned to Marwan's side.

There had been no sign of pursuit. Yariim had hidden herself at dawn, letting Marwan rest after a long, long gallop that had run for hours in the dark. God only knew how far they had come. Snow still fell fitfully, and the clouds were low. There would be a half moon tonight – more than enough to let Yariim see her way.

Marwan needed another half an hour of rest – and then Yariim would push on. The snowfall seemed heavier, and so she would risk traveling in the day. Anything to put more miles between herself and the Khan.

She had to reach Raschid.

Yariim bore a note. Sandhri had hidden it inside Yariim's hair ribbon, and it had fallen free as Yariim undid her hair. Yariim had stared at it for an endless age, softly caressing the ill-formed letters on the little strip of rag.

> *"My darling.*
> *In your heart, you know that I could never have come with you. But go to him. He needs you. And in this way, I save a part of us.*
> *Tell our husband that I shall send them to him. All of them. We will have victory. Our dreams will live.*
> *- Do not grieve. Our son and I will always be waiting for the both of you, at the old stone wall, beside the beach of dreams.*
> *I love you.*
> *Sandhri.*

PS: *I will try to hide your disappearance for at least one day. The Khan should have known better than to drink my tea."*

Yariim carefully shielded the note from falling snow. If she breathed in slowly, she could still smell Sandhri's spicy scent clinging to the rag. She cradled it softly, then folded it quietly away and slipped it in against her heart.

The world seemed silent – all except for the soft sound of falling snow. It seemed unreal to be free again after so many long weeks in captivity. Yariim felt exposed – as though a hundred thousand eyes were watching her every move. Forcing herself to be rational, she stood up carefully and climbed atop a chunk of river ice to scan for enemies.

The horizon was a blur. Snowfall masked everything but the very edges of the riverbank. There was an impression of dark, looming trees – forests of evergreens that were as silent as a grave. Yariim shivered, finding the whole landscape alien and horrible. She longed for the quiet rivers, the palm trees and the warm skies of home.

"Marwan – do you smell anything?"

The Camel looked up: He had been dining on a package bale of beans, malt and hay that Meng had packed for him. The camel stretched – vented a vast fart that echoed like a gunshot, and clambered to his feet. His long nose swiveled to search the wind, and yellow teeth champed in thought.

Satisfied, Marwan stepped over to the ice block. Yariim wrestled her tent back into its pack, slinging it over Marwan's back. Pain jabbed through her injured thigh, the arrow wound smarting after yesterday's exertion. With a genteel curse, Yariim climbed carefully up onto Marwan's back. The camel waited until she was settled, and then took off at a shocking speed towards the south.

He ran hard and fast, head stretched forwards, his breath huffing. He ran with dedication, eating up the miles. Marwan knew speed was of the essence, and spared himself nothing.

Clinging onto the camel's back, Yariim blessed him. She went without sleep, without rest, and sped on through the snow, wondering if she would ever run herself dry of tears.

The night had not been kind to Tulu Begh. By morning, he was still abominably ill – hollow eyed, quaking and gaunt. He had spent an entire night on the latrine, and the ailment showed no signs of easing up by morning. Shuffling along in old robes, he felt as though a bomb had gone off deep in his insides. He was too ill to face breakfast – too ill to tolerate company. He had sent his men away, and prayed that the sky would fall and somehow end his misery.

The cramps struck yet again – and the Prince was forced to run.

Prince Tulu Begh had been forced to turn a window that fed out into an alleyway into his latrine. With a pot full of hot coals in front of him, his front end was toasty warm – but his backside hung out into the freezing air, and he had begun to fear frostbite. He had to sit thus for hour after hour, sick, dazed and agonised, making his quarters echo to his moans.

His guards had made themselves suitably scarce, offering the Prince a measure of privacy. Holding on for grim death, Tulu Begh called hoarsely out into the other rooms of the house.

"Paga-shan! Bring me medicine!"

A door opened. Standing tall and suave in a padded coat and snow-dusted hat, Itbit leaned idly back against the door frame. She toyed absently with a riding whip and looked with hooded eyes at Tulu Begh.

"Itbit thinks you have had an entertaining night."

Tulu Begh looked up in alarm, and then relaxed as he saw Itbit. Sick and shaking, he gave the girl a watery smile.

"I-Itbit!" The Prince squeezed his eyes shut. "I.. I am indisposed, my dear."

The green mouse ignored him. She warmed her spectacles with her breath and wiped them clean.

"The palace is all closied up. No one getties out or in! The army is moving, and mister Khan does not want to be disturbed."

"Yes – we're moving west." Tulu Begh gasped as the pain wracked him again. "We-we have found a… a Frankish city at the Vistuul river. And a… a Frankish army is on the move. If we take out their army, then their city and supplies…"

That was as far as he managed to go. There was an unpleasant interval, much punctuated by Tulu Begh's wails and moans. Itbit leaned one elbow against the door, her head propped on her hand, idly eating cheese and waiting for a break.

"What you need is nice teasies. Tea made from something sweet." Itbit finished her cheese. "Flush out your system. Is poison inside."

"Oh – Oh Itbit!" Tulu Begh looked relieved. "You can cure me?"

"Of course." Itbit shrugged. "Sandhri taught Itbit many things. Sandhri made tea to make all of you sick – so Itbit will make you well again."

Tulu Begh looked at Itbit, suddenly chilled.

"Queen…Sandhri?"

"She used ivy plucked from the palace walls. Itbit is too nice a girl to think about what else she might have put in." The mouse drew a pistol from her robes – part of Tulu Begh's spoils. "She wanted all of you to be shittie-sick, just for a few hours."

The Prince froze. He flicked his eyes to his sword belt, which lay with his trousers on the floor. Itbit leveled her pistol at him, and suddenly the girl did not seem quite so funny any more.

Itbit's slim face looked at Tulu Begh in cold, hard hatred.

"It is not nice, Tulu Begh, to bed a girl you intend to betray." Itbit pulled back the pistol's lock, and the pawl clicked loudly in the air. "You were going to let the Khan kill Itbit inch by inch if she had not gone to see Sandhri and Yariim so willingly. You would have killed Itbit, just to pressure her friends into sending letters to Raschid." The Prince gave a stammer, and Itbit twitched the pistol to cut him short.

"Did it give you feelings of muchly power, Tulu Begh?" Itbit leveled the pistol at his head. Her glasses glittered, blanking her pink eyes behind a mask of light. "How do you feel now?"

A noise outside the window gave the answer. Itbit gave the Prince a look of absolute contempt. She stepped aside from the door, and Meng entered with his long sword drawn. He cast an eye at the Prince, then quietly closed the door.

"The guards have gone to the main camp to gather the Prince's horses." Meng turned from Itbit to the Prince. He flipped his sword beneath his arm, put his sleeves together and gave the Prince a bow. "Prince Tulu Begh. This humble one offers commiserations for your current embarrasment. A sage must realize that pride goes before a fall." He bowed again. "Please to forgive the intrusion. This unworthy one must ask you not to cry out or cause trouble, otherwise he will be forced to act to your detriment."

Meng looked to Itbit. "We are alone."

"Good." Itbit kept Tulu Begh covered. "Meng, please to findie many, many jugs of water. Melt clean snow. There is honey and some lemons in the cupboard in the kitchen. Do please put a little in the water." Tulu Begh edged in his seat. Itbit motioned him to keep still as a stone. "Sit down! We give you muchly water, and you will drink – then sit and let nature take its course."

Tulu Begh shook. He tried to gather up his dignity.

"Itbit! Now Itbit, my dear…"

"Quiet." Itbit rested one hand on the hilt of her stolen nomad sword. She leaned back against the wall, her eyes carefully watching Tulu Begh.

"Meng – do you havie the bomb?"

"Bomb!" Tulu Begh looked shocked. "Oh now, let us be reasonable…!"

"Hush!" The green mouse polished a fleck of snow from her pistol barrel. "And now – Itbit wants to hear a story."

"A-a story?"

"Yes." The mouse tilted her head in interest. "Tell Itbit special things, Princie Begh. Tell her about a metal hut with legs. Tell her *everything*."

The Prince's heart hammered in his throat. "And… and what then?"

The green mouse gave an evil smile.

"And then Itbit thinks all good friends should go off visiting." Itbit looked back and moved aside as Meng entered the room. "Ah! Here be medicine! Now drink and shit profusely. Itbit is a little pressed for time…"

They all walked the streets together like one happy family – close together and swathed in felt and fleece. Tulu Begh walked to the fore, his hands inside his sleeves. Itbit walked at his side, her arm through his and the pistol up her sleeve and pushing into the Prince's ribs. Meng came behind, and a string held in his hand linked to something underneath Tulu Begh's coat. The Prince stumbled, and Meng gave a frown.

"Please to exercise caution!. If the string pulls hard, then the bomb's fuse will be lit. It would sadden me immensely to lack any remains to present to your family."

The Prince panted, his eyes flicking about himself in panic. He truly seemed afraid.

"You won't get away with this! I am a Prince of the blood!"

"Shut up!" Itbit jammed the pistol hard into the Prince's ribs. "Itbit say – we have gotten away with it. Itbit thinks Tulu Begh should keep mouth shut or he go *bang* like big wet meaty firecracker!"

They approached the palace. The red brick walls loomed high and dark. Mounted soldiers swarmed through the streets, and the noise of hooves, of harness and of shouting men was deafening. There seemed to be a search being made – soldiers were bursting into houses and looking inside haystacks. Shoving Tulu Begh into a hidden doorway, Itbit barred her chisel fangs in hate.

"If one strand of Sandhri's fur has even been touched, Itbit will kill you slow!"

"It isn't my doing – I swear!" The Prince looked around for help. "… but if the Holy Khan…"

Meng kept an eye upon the palace.

"Where is the key, Tulu Begh?" The Sage watched a troop of soldiers ride by. "Lead us properly, and you shall be saved. When we have accomplished our task, we will set you free."

Itbit gave a snarl.

"*No!*"

"We do not need him then, nor can he do more harm." The panda looked to Tulu Begh. "But remember the bomb, Tulu Begh. Your hands are tied. You could not free your hands in time to save yourself."

Tulu Begh scowled, panting hard. The handsome mouse looked at the snow, then jerked free from Itbit's grasp and stood on his own feet.

"The key is kept in the quarters of the Steward of the Royal Stables. That is all I know."

"Then take us there."

Tulu Begh led the way through the throng of soldiers towards the palace gate. Black Guards stood at the gates, fully armoured and with swords and bows. Men left the palace, but none entered. The army was moving out to attack and destroy the west.

Tulu Begh presented himself before the guards, tightly flanked by his companions. He kept his face sourly neutral, feeling the gun jammed hard into his ribs.

"I am Prince Tulu Begh. I must enter the palace."

A guard glared.

"None may enter."

"I must see the Khan."

"The Khan will pass here within the hour. " The guard motioned to other supplicants waiting outside the gate. "Remain here."

Itbit murmured softly in Begh's ear.

"Tell him you have news from the Osranii Shah himself." She ground in her pistol barrel. "Tell him!"

"It is a message!" Tulu Begh hissed, then jerked his chin to signal the guard to get out of his way. "A message from the Osranii Shah himself!"

The guards murmured. One motioned to Tulu Begh, and then led the way inside. They passed through the gate and out into the courtyard, where hundreds of the Khan's black-clad bodyguard were saddling their horses. The guard pointed at a wall.

"Wait here!"

The guard departed for the main palace, threading his way through busy soldiers. The black guards poured heated water into a horse trough to allow their beasts to drink. Others gathered nets of fodder to bundle up behind their saddles.

They were in! Meng and Itbit met each other's eyes - frightened and appalled – half daring to hope they might succeed. Itbit looked about herself, wondering what the hell they should do next.

Soldiers swarmed past, each man with a hundred jobs to do. Meng looked left and right, then singled out a passing man.

"Forgive me soldier – but where is the Steward of the Royal stables?" The sage bowed. "Prince Tulu Begh must see him."

Annoyed and busy, the soldier pointed into the stables. Meng bowed, and Tulu Begh was tugged into the fetid darkness of the stable stalls.

Foul-tempered horses crowded the eaves of the stables – at least thirty of the beasts stood, pawing and made restless by the activity.

A side room had been turned into luxurious quarters all hung with stolen carpets, silks and sheets. Men passed one another carrying saddles, saddle blankets or huge sheets of rawhide horse armour. Hanging on one wall of the room was a heavy iron key. Itbit saw it and nudged Meng, who took his chance and marched across. He took the key swiftly from the wall, looking neither left nor right, and shoved it into the breast of his robe.

Itbit looked quickly out into the courtyard. Over at the far side, at the coach house doors, men were kicking free the snow. One man hit something solid, knelt, and wiped snow off the corpse Meng had left there last night. The soldier grunted, then turned to bellow for an officer.

Itbit jerked back into hiding.

"Shit!"

Tulu Begh suddenly kicked the girl with all his might. Itbit tumbled sideways. Tulu Begh ran free, and the string still held in Itbit's hand tugged, then jerked loose. Screeching in fear of the bomb, Tulu Begh ran pell mell to the horse tough and leapt into the water, half drowning himself and screeching out in fear.

"Assassins! Assassins!"

"Damn!" Itbit untangled her pistol. The Prince wallowed in the horse tough, babbling in fright as he tried to douse the bomb tied to his back. Since the 'bomb' was merely a parchment tube filled with ashes, the man was fairly safe. Soldiers ran to him as the courtyard dissolved into confusion.

Racing to Itbit, Meng gripped the key.

"Is this the right key?"

"Itbit doesn't know!" Itbit looked out at all the soldiers. "What now?"

"We move!"

Meng drew his sword and cut at the ropes holding the rows of horses in their place. He cut at the horses' rumps with his blade, sending the animals bucking and screaming out into the courtyard. Meng took Itbit by the hand and ducked, running behind the stampeding horses as the animals bowled over soldiers and ran wild.

They ran for the coach house doors. The soldier kneeling at the corpse saw them and rose up, drawing his sword. Itbit leveled her pistol and fired, and the bullet snapped the man's head back, turning his muzzle into a mask of blood. Itbit skidded down in the snow, reloading from a flask and bullet bag while Meng tried to tug the hinge pintel free.

Soldiers were bashed aside by horses, or ran after the creatures, hurtling lassos. But amidst the chaos, men helped Tulu Begh from his bath. The Prince pointed through the stampede towards Itbit and Meng, and the soldiers whirled to see the pair at work upon the coach house door. Meng dragged the pintel free and hauled on the edge of the door, opening a crack for Itbit to crawl through.

"My Lady! Go!"

A soldier leveled a bow and fired an arrow at Itbit, but a horse ran in the way, rearing and screaming at the arrow jutted through its haunch. Itbit scrabbled through into the darkness. Meng crouched down, then forced the crack wider and shoved himself inside. Itbit held the door open, and as Meng slithered through, she kicked the door shut right in a nomad's snarling face.

The vast coach house was partly lit. Floorboards above had been torn open, and daylight streamed down. Meng threw Itbit the iron key. The mouse caught the key and threw Meng her gun.

The hut loomed in the gloom, half rising in its chains. Itbit raced towards it, suddenly fearing that the key might not be the right one for the hut's huge manacles. The little mouse flung herself on the hut's chains, while behind her the coach house doors boomed to the impact of the men outside.

She looked up through the wide, torn-open ceiling, then shot up a pillar to look into the upper room.

"Sandhri be gone!"

"She cannot be far!" Meng saw the doors prize outwards at the broken hinge. He carefully fired the pistol through the gap, killing his man. "We can find her!"

Itbit fumbled with the keys. The hut was simply incredible – a huge, sad thing of brass and bronze which seemed to stare at her in hope. The girl placed herself between its claws and grabbed the rusty locks.

"I am Itbit! Sandhri sent me! Sandhri and Yariim." The girl scraped the key inside the lock, twisting with all her might. The metal scarcely budged. "Where is Sandhri? Do you know?"

The hut nodded.

Behind Itbit, the coach house doors shook to a massive blow. Wood began to splinter. Meng took his sword and lunged it through a crack. A lance stabbed through the gap, and Meng kicked the weapon aside.

There was a battering ram outside the doors. From the rooms above, shouts began to sound. Itbit looked about herself in panic, then threw her whole strength into the lock, straining mightily at the keys.

"Where is she?"

For the first time in long years, the Tsu-Khan was furious. With anger blazing ice-cold all about him, he crashed open doors with his fist a moment before his bodyguards could open them wide. Soldiers in the palace corridors stood to attention, not daring to watch the Holy One pass.

The Tsu-Khan smashed forward into the western corridor. Guards peered through spy holes into the upper coach house. The Khan swept past the guards and thrust open the doors to hear a story in full flow.

Sitting by her bedside, her hand upon a figure underneath the blankets, Queen Sandhri looked up at the Khan with a raised brow. Sweeping forwards, the Khan ripped back the bed covers to reveal a pile of rags and old sheets wadded up to look like a sleeping woman. Queen Yariim was clearly no longer in the room. The Tsu-Khan flexed his hands, and spoke without looking at his guards.

"Find her."

Men bowed and ran off into the palace. Others kicked the bedding away, found the loose floorboards and tore them aside, peering down into the empty coach house down below.

Two men dragged Sandhri to her feet and held her dangling above the ground. The bat looked straight at the Khan, defiant and magnificent, giving him the level stare of a dedicated enemy.

"I know v'at you are. I know how to kill you." Sandhri gave a look of undying hate. "And now Raschid knows as v'ell…"

Without even changing the expression on his face, The Khan struck Sandhri across the jaw. He hit her again and again, left and right fist, working slowly and precisely. The bat never gave any sound other than a grunt.

The sound of fists on flesh sounded like gunshots in the room. The Tsu-Khan looked at his victim with pale, dead eyes.

"My Generals have spent an entire night, an entire morning in the latrines!" The Khan struck Sandhri yet again. "One man is a misfortune. Half a dozen men is poisoning. And where else might all of my Generals have fallen ill?"

Seeing stars, Sandhri hung in her captor's arms. Her face was one great explosion of pain. She lifted her head, feeling blood drooling from her lip, looking at the Tsu-Khan in hatred through one half-closed eye.

"Storytellers neffer forget." The woman spat blood at the Khan. "You v'ill neffer, *neffer* have Aku-Mashad."

Ignoring her words, the Tsu-Khan lifted Sandhri's head by the hair. His voice remained calm and quiet.

"Where is Queen Yariim. What plans were made for her escape?"

In reply, Sandhri gave a bloody, feral smile.

"T'iss time, v'e were ready for you…"

The Khan breathed out slowly. Dark presences swirled about him, tracing patterns of light and shadow across the Khan's skull. He let Sandhri's head drop, and moved to the door.

"Bring her to the battlements."

Sandhri felt her baby shifting – kicking in rage as though wanting to slaughter the Khan. He sensed Sandhri's pain. She let herself be dragged down corridors and up an interminable circular flight of stairs. Blood dripped from her mouth, and her lips were aflame with pain. She forced her head to clear, trying to make her legs move to her command.

A door was hurtled open, and snow-thickened air swirled into Sandhri's face. She felt herself being dragged out into open air, where her blood spattered onto clean white snow.

They were high above the city, five levels up above the palace courtyard. The Tsu-Khan stood at the edge of the walls, his black robes swirling in the wind.

"Bring me a knife."

A guard brought the Khan a long, hook-bladed knife. He held it bare in his hand, and then turned to look out across the dead city of Gulay Gudd, and out towards the horizons of the world.

"It shall be mine…"

The Tsu-Khan breathed slowly. Dead souls swirled about him, swerving away from iron weapons and iron nails. They grew more tangible – skeletal and savage, and their passage kicked up eddies in the snow.

The Khan looked out across a waiting world.

"It shall be mine. All mine! This time there shall be none to share my power! This time, all shall bow before me and tremble – or they will die. Their dead souls shall serve me, and their lifeless, rotting husks shall be my slaves!" The Khan turned to stare at Sandhri with his empty eyes. "And this time, it shall last for all eternity…"

Sandhri looked at the Khan in loathing.

"Raschid *knows.*"

"Then Raschid shall die, along with all those who serve him, and all those who know him." The Khan hefted his knife. "We shall extend our hand, and all of Aku-Mashad, all of Earth, shall be ours. Glory unyielding, world without end…"

Faint shouts were coming from the courtyard far below – horses screamed and men roared. The noise had finally become intrusive. With eyes only for Sandhri, the Tsu-Khan spoke to a guard.

"What is that?"

The guard bowed. "I know not, Holy Person."

"Discover."

The man left. Sandhri hung between the arms of two armoured guards. Far below her in the courtyard, wood splintered and horses screamed.

The guards were horsemen. Their heads turned towards the sounds of horses. Sandhri put her left hand into her right sleeve, drew her sharpened steel nail and drove it length ways between the knuckles of one guard's hand. The man screamed, and Sandhri twisted away. She changed hands and hammered the blade into the inside elbow of the second guard, tearing herself free. With a bloody weapon in her hand, Sandhri gave a feral laugh and staggered back, planting herself against the battlements. Her long white hair streamed over the walls like the banner of a saint.

A weapons chest stood against the wall. Sandhri climbed atop the chest, then onto the very edge of the battlements, moving her bulk with fluid ease. She stood with her back to the yawning gulf behind her, and lifted her bloody face to snarl at the Khan.

The palace shuddered. There was a sound of crashing masonry and splintering wood, mingled with a sound like ringing bells. The Tsu-Khan merely watched Sandhri as she climbed, the spirits all around him staining the air like smoke.

One guard held his bloody arm – the other had blood streaming from his sword hand. Both men swore foully, reaching awkwardly for weapons. The Tsu-Khan waved them away. He held his dagger and looked levelly at Sandhri.

"Your life is mine."

"My life v'as neffer yours to give or take." Proud and magnificent, Sandhri reversed the blade in her hand, facing the point towards herself. "I am Sandhri the Storyteller – and my revenge shall damn thee."

The whole palace shook, and the sound of ringing metal grew deafeningly loud. Sandhri suddenly looked down behind herself, then turned a gaze of feral glee upon the Khan. Her whole face lit up, and she gave a howl of triumph!

The Khan surged forward, robes swirling in the wind.

"Kill her!"

With a crash, a huge bronze claw reached over the wall, gripping the battlements and shattering red bricks. A great shape heaved over the edge of the walls like a titanic spider. The bronze hut lashed out with one foot, sending guards sprawling back across the roof. Itbit clung to the lip of the hut inside the door, waving a hand out towards Sandhri.

"Sandhri! Jump!"

With a savage laugh, Sandhri moved. She turned to the Khan, her face vicious, and whipped her hand forward. Her blade hissed through the air, and the Tsu-Khan put up his arms as a shield. The sharpened nail went right through his palm, and the Tsu-Khan gave a snarl of pain.

The Hut crashed its threshold down onto the battlements. Meng leaned from the hut and caught at Sandhri's clothes. The bat was dragged to safety, and the huge hut clawed its way back down the palace walls. The metal hut rammed its claws through windows, using them like the rungs in a ladder as it made its way back down to the courtyard.

Inside the hut, Sandhri crashed against the back wall, cushioned by Meng. The sage had the breath smashed out of him. The hut rocked, then reached the ground, righting itself and sending its passengers tumbling across the floor. Itbit clung in the door, holding on for all that she was worth.

"Smash the gates! Itbit says – that way!"

The hut crashed forwards,. Horses reared and screamed, fleeing madly from its path. A storm of arrows sped out from the courtyard, pattering like rain against the brass hull. Arrow shafts flickered in through the open door, striking sparks from the metal and clattering to the floor. Itbit lay flat – the hut rocked madly, and suddenly the hut reared up onto its back feet.

Huge claws reached out to the locked palace gates and crashed hard against them. The wood splintered, and the hut stepped back, tearing the wreckage clear. Overjoyed to be free at last, the hut surged forward. Soldiers in the streets opened fire with bows, and the hut ignored them. It looked left and right down the open streets, happy as a puppy. Itbit clung onto the edge of the door, ducking as arrows flickered past.

"Left! Go left!"

"Right!" Sandhri held her belly, feeling something wrench inside her. "Hut – go right!" The bat felt sick. "T'eir army iss leaving by the main gate. But v'e can climb right over the city v'all."

The hut settled into a canter, outstripping even the fleetest horse. Sandhri blundered forward, her hand reaching out to grasp Itbit. She drew the mouse girl to herself and held her hard against her heart.

"Hello Itbit."

"Hello." Itbit drew back, and her hand gently held Sandhri's face, careful of her swollen eye. "You silly bat. You should have known Itbit would come."

"You came." Sandhri carefully held Itbit. She wept quiet tears. Itbit looked up at her, then clung against her, clenching her fingers inside Sandhri's fur. Sandhri stroked the girl's golden hair and held her tight.

"True love neffer turns its back."

Meng climbed forward along the bucking floor, reaching the hut's open door. The arrow fire had gone – the hut had outdistanced the pursuit. Soldiers scattered from the streets, and the hut stamped a cart full of loot into ruins. Meng took command, politely asking the hut to steer towards the city wall. Sandhri watched him, and reached out to stroke his face quietly with the back of her hand.

"Meng." Sandhri looked at him through her battered face with love. "Our truest knight."

Another cramp ripped through her. Sandhri hissed and held tight to Itbit, hissing in pain. Looking back from the hut's door, Meng stared at her in alarm.

"My Queen! Your injuries are severe?"

"No. No." Sandhri put back her head, gulping for air. "Fast! Go fast as you can, Meng. As fast as you can…!"

Sandhri panted hard, reeling in pain. Head down, Meng gave the hut a pat, and the creature sped into a gallop. The world rang to the clash of metal feet as the hut carved its way over the walls of Gulay Gudd and out into the snow.

On the palace battlements, the Tsu-Khan hissed. He slowly drew the iron nail out of his own hand, letting it drop onto the ground. With the iron out of his flesh, the wound hissed with steam and instantly healed, leaving no mark behind it – not even a scar.

Broken bricks lay scattered all across the snow. Black-armoured bodyguards charged up out of the door into the palace, fanning out over the roof. The Tsu-Khan waved them away, walking quietly to the battlements and flexing his healed hand.

The city down below was spread out before the Khan like a child's toy. Toy soldiers, huts and houses – bridges and trees. The main street stretched out into the distance, and there, hundreds of yards away, the metal hut clambered over the city walls. The hut moved like a daddy longlegs, alien and awkward. But it ate up distance as it moved. Seconds after crossing the walls, the Khan saw the hut mounting the surrounding hills.

A guard commander flung himself down before the Khan.

"Sacred Person! Shall we pursue?"

The Khan quietly waved one hand. He quietly shook his head, his eyes upon the hut as it dwindled far away. He drew in a long, slow breath, and opened up his hands.

"Come…"

Darkness spilled across the rooftop, like blood liquor flooding from the mouth of a corpse. With it came chittering things – dark shapes half unseen. They crept like spiders, then chattered like centipedes – with skeletal hands and eyes of ice, they hissed and quested through the darkness, seeking prey.

The Khan lowered his gaze, looking at the skeletal monstrosities that stood awaiting his sacred word.

"Here is her blood." The Khan tore the sleeve of his robe and threw it to the rooftop. The sleeve was spattered with Sandhri's blood.

"Find. Kill. *Destroy…*"

With a half heard scream of lust, the shadows gathered, then lunged out across the rooftop and out into the open air. The currents caught them, and the evil shapes disappeared from view. The Khan's guards coldly watched them go, then bowed to put their faces to the ground as the Khan turned upon them with his untroubled eyes.

"We are changing our deployment. Have the Generals come to me at once. All troops are to embark upon the march."

The Tsu-Khan looked slowly to the south – towards Raschid. Towards the army of Osra.

"We march south. We march to destroy the Osranii Shah."

Chapter Nineteen:

Raschid's army employed the finest engineers in all of Aku-Mashad. His army had a pontoon bridge, all disassembled and carried on a train of carts. It had cranes, portable forges and surveyors. Minor gullys were crossed on portable briges, and the army marched more swiftly that any non-Osranii would have believed possible.

They swung across the deep gullys that rimmed the Kuba River, crossed the mighty ice river, and moved west. Raschid stood his horse beside the river crossing, watching his men slog across the ice. Snow had fallen, and the wretched stuff made marching laborious. Raschid watched and met each unit as it crossed the ice, raising his hand and acknowledging the cheers of his men.

He looked tall and powerful in his white robes and plain armour. Leaning forward, he gave his absolute attention to each unit as it came, nodding to the countless faces he recognized. The men looked well – cold but not suffering. The thick winter clothing had served them well. They looked in good spirits. Thus far the cavalry had taken much of the glory, and the infantry were eager to fight. Raschid pointed the units onwards to the west with his sword, pointing to the night's encampment that had been fortified by walls of ice and snow.

"Just a while longer, lads. One mile more. We sent the cooks on ahead, so there's hot food." The Shah saw a fresh regiment of infantry approach – all in broken step, so as not to risk cracking the river ice. They carried a banner showing the severed head of the demon K'aath. Their Colonel led his horse at their head, and Raschid raised a hand in welcome.

"Sergeant Marsuk!"

"My Prince." The Colonel looked dead tired, but the one eyed mouse looked up and gave Raschid a smile. He swung atop his horse as he reached solid ground. The horse itself had been a gift from Raschid. "We're heading west, my Lord?"

"West." Raschid had the beginnings of a plan – a way to tempt the Khan to battle. He looked down, saw Marsuk's elite light infantry company crossing the ice, and gave a rare smile.

"Spike – your men look like rogues."

The dapper rat saluted with a flourish of his scimitar a grin.

"They're all bastards, Sir! Even a couple of noble's boys amongst 'em!" Spike shook his head in mock disappointment. "You can't trust the nobility. Thieves to a man!"

The troops marched on, and Raschid lifted a hand in blessing as they lifted up their guns and cheered him. He looked for wounded men, and found only six frostbite victims being dragged on sleds. He sent for the sorcerers, and turned to look westward, towards the evening's camp.

A huge man in plate and mail armour thundered towards Raschid on a horse the size of an elephant. General Ataman, his standard bearer and his aides slithered gleefully to a halt beside their Shah, and threw severed heads at his feet. Ataman was bloodied, his sword crusted in crimson ice. He threw open his arms and gave a great, wild roar of joy.

"Sire! We found some of the buggers! Light cavalry – about three thousand of them!" The General's armour was spattered with blood. "And now there's about two thousand seven hundred!"

He gave a great, booming laugh, then passed a black helmet to the Shah. The helm was of Steppe Nomad make, painted glossy black. Raschid took the helmet in his hands and looked to the north.

"Three thousand?"

"Three fucking regiments of the mama-buggers!" General Ataman threw open his arms, immensely pleased. "We fled backwards, and they followed into an artillery ambush! That will stop the buggers from farting in Mosque!"

The General drew closer to Raschid. More calm and conspiratorial, he gestured to the north and west with his sword.

"They came down river – scouts out front. A big recon patrol. I led out the bird riders and the southern horse. Stopped them hard."

Raschid nodded.

"Black armour. They all had black armour and black horses?" Raschid looked up, and the General gave a great, pleased grin of his fangs. Raschid put the helmet aside. "Black Guards. They report directly to the Khan."

"So he's gotten serious about us! Maybe he's coming at last!" Ataman was in a high state of excitement. "Do we pursue?"

"No." Raschid signed for an aide to bring him a map. "We want them to tell the Khan the location of our main body. Now we're here, we want him to come to us."

"Excellent, Lord." Ataman flexed his sword, anticipating a fight. "A victory today – a fight tomorrow. But for now, we camp!" The General looked around. "Where's that stripy-tailed bugger of a girl?"

"Saa'lu?" Raschid pointed back to his staff. "I ordered her to camp – so she's wearing a spare suit of armour and is trying to hide amongst the guards." The Shah raised a brow and looked at Ataman. "Or did you give her the armour?"

"She is an independent woman. But all woman!" Ataman rode off towards Raschid's guards, calling back across his shoulder as he rode. "*All woman!*"

At least someone was happy. Raschid let them go, and watched over the last of his men. His thoughts pierced through the snowfall to the north, bent towards the Tsu-Khan and his men.

The Khan had sent his personal scouts to find Raschid. Perhaps that meant the man was coming at long last. Raschid felt a cold, hard flood of anticipation, and tried to still the hatred in his heart.

A sage did not hate. A sage acted for the right.

Raschid would kill the Khan – and then he would be free to weep at last.

***

They found her on the evening of the second day, just as night began to fall.

Marwan had been moving at a fast, steady lope – ten miles an hour, seemingly for time without end. He paused to catch his breath three times a day, looking more and more exhausted as the journey went on. Yariim tried to bid him lay his head in her lap and sleep, but the camel clambered to his feet each time after a scant half hour of rest and insisted on moving on.

They ran down the frozen river, hour after hour. On the banks were burnt, dead villages or the ruins of towns, each one topped by its inevitable crown of impaled corpses. The Khan had nailed the skins of flayed victims to the trees where his troops had passed. Yariim made herself look, fixing the horror into her memory.

The Khan would pay. He would be stopped. The world would be made clean.

To kill a sorcerer, break the heart of stone…

She should have traveled only at night – but the journey would have been made at a crawl. So it was in the last dregs of daylight, that Yariim looked to her right, across the ridge of ice at the middle of the river, and saw the black horde slowly bearing down.

They were black armoured men on jet black horses, and their banners were as dark as night. Yariim had seen such men day after day in her captivity. There were hundreds and hundreds of them, riding north away from her. Although two thousand yards separated them from the river, they had seen the strange figure of Marwan pacing doggedly down the ice. A swarm of riders split off from the darker mass and rode to investigate, while the great body of riders spurred off into the north.

The smaller group of riders numbered a hundred or more. They moved at an ambling gait, angling themselves to intersect Yariim's course. The Mouse reined-in Marwan and stood, hearing the camel wheeze, feeling his huge ribs labouring. She looked back behind her to see the enemy coming towards her. The nearest riverbank was a place of dense brushwood and tall trees. Marwan would not be able to move swiftly in the tangled briars, and a hundred enemies would soon search Yariim out. To the West, the sun had dipped below the horizon, and the ice sent huge, dark shadows reaching out over the snow. In an hour, nightfall would have come, and Yariim might be able to dodge into the trees and hide.

"Marwan, my old friend – it seems you must run." She patted the camel on the neck. "Can you run for an hour? Maybe two?"

The camel looked back to the north, at the oncoming horses, and gave a low, vicious growl. He lumbered about to face south, down the river, and broke into his great splay-footed run.

The enemy horsemen kicked their mounts into a canter, and the chase was on.

The Khan's horsemen fanned out into two wide lines, one behind the other, curling out over the ice. With his head down and his neck stretched low, Marwan ran, his foot falls echoing loudly on the ice. Yariim spoke to him, leaned her weight forward to help him, and let the camel run. Behind her, the Khan's troops advanced in total, chilling silence.

The horses gained. They ran faster than Marwan, and their riders drove them hard. The first line of horsemen were a thousand yards behind Yariim – mere shapes on the ice. Soon they were five hundred yards away, then four hundred. Yariim heard a hiss in the air, and saw a dozen shapes flicker past her in the gloom.

Arrows hissed, losing power and dropping almost vertically into the snow beside Yariim. One actually hit her, falling to strike her felt coat under no more power than its own weight. The arrow fell away, and Yariim looked back to see the Khan's horsemen gaining slowly, inch by inch and yard by yard.

Marwan looked behind himself, and his yellow eye suddenly seemed cunning. The camel gave a roar and stretched out in a sudden burst of speed, his back swaying in a smooth "S" as he flew across the snow. Yariim looked back and saw what the camel had in mind.

The enemy horses were flagging.

The Khan's horsemen must have already ridden far that day, and they had underestimated Marwan's speed. They had pushed their speed too fast, too soon, and now Marwan went into his fastest run. The Khan's soldiers fell slowly behind. Arrows arced upwards across the five hundred yards separating the riders from Yariim, but no archer could hit a target at such a range. The light dimmed, and only the last few deep tobacco-coloured clouds lit the skies as Marwan raced down the river of ice.

Yariim gave a savage laugh and patted Marwan's neck. The camel followed a turn in the river, and the Khan's men fell far behind.

All bar one.

One horse reared. One man stared towards Yariim, and his horse gathered itself and shot off in pursuit. The animal came on fast. Yariim lost sight of the other men and ran out into the dark.

She turned the river bend, and her pursuers dropped out of sight. Yariim saw a gap in the central ice, and urged Marwan through onto the west side of the river.

The camel could run on thin ice, using his rag-booted feet. He left no tracks. Yariim saw flat ice gleaming, and set Marwan racing across it towards the nearby banks. Dense thickets of little trees would hide her from the enemy.

Marwan galloped between snow banks, crossing the open river. The ice here creaked beneath Marwan's weight – some surge of the river seemed to have made the ice sheet wafer thin. Yariim looked down in shock as a sound like a pistol shot came from underneath. Great cracks split left and right beneath Marwan's feet.

The camel left the dangerous ice behind, climbed the river bank, then raced between the trees. Branches whipped at Yariim's face, and she fended them off with her hands. She ran Marwan up into a stand of evergreens, then leapt down from his back. Her thigh gave a warning stab of pain, but the Mouse ignored it and pulled Marwan down, making the camel kneel in the shadows of the woods.

Marwan breathed hard, wheezing – almost spent. Her heart hammering, Yariim tried to hide the steam jetting from his nostrils with her robes as she watched out across the night-bright river, staring out into the dark.

Hooves sounded. A horse was galloping on the ice, coming insanely hard and fast. The animal hit the patch of weakened ice, and its hooves broke through with a noise like shattering glass. The rider gave a shout, and then there was a harsh sound of churning water as an animal thrashed helplessly in the ice water.

Yariim rose carefully, expecting to see a tragedy out on the ice. Instead she saw a horse half immersed in the water. The beast half swam, half lunged forward, splintering the shelf ice with its forequarters. It's rider stayed unconcernedly in the saddle. Ignoring temperatures that should have killed it deader than a doornail, the horse lifted its head, looked towards Yariim, and simply swam on.

The horse had pale blue eyes.

Even from a hundred yards away, Yariim could feel the creature's stare. The horse gave a scream of absolute hatred for all life, and clawed its way out of the water and up onto the shore.

Yariim clumsily drew the sword Meng had provided with her disguise. The blade felt as though it weighed a hundred tons. She swung herself swiftly up onto Marwan's back, and urged the camel back onto his feet.

"Come on, Marwan! Look for snow!"

Soft snow – the camel might be faster in the soft snow. But Yariim had seen the demon-horses of the Khan before. They never tired, never slept and never seemed to rest. Yariim turned Marwan due south, heading madly off into the trees.

The army was to the south. What had Meng said – two hundred miles? She had been riding for two days and a night. How far had Marwan traveled? Yariim urged the camel onwards, hearing the sound of brushwood splintering somewhere just behind her. She rode up a steep slope – almost had a low branch tear off her head – and then crested a rise between the trees. On the slopes below her, she saw fires twinkling – hundreds and hundreds of fires! It was the army! Yariim was saved! She saw a strange figure rising from the bushes nearby – a musketeer with a matchlock that glowed in the dark. The man raised up a shout in what sounded like Frankish, then turned to bellow a warning back towards the fires.

Yariim rose in her saddle, full of joy – and then an arrow came scything fast out of the dark.

She ducked. Hooves hammered as the Khan's man rode at her, a new arrow nocked like lightning in his bow. He fired, and Yariim bent backwards, flattening herself. The arrow sliced fibers from the belly of her coat, jerking her whiskers with its wind. The rider made to gallop past, but Marwan turned and slammed his neck straight into the face of the demon horse.

The horse spilled sideways, screaming in hate. Hooves flailing, the beast landed in the snow. Marwan fell on it in a foaming rage, rearing and stamping down. The horse's bones cracked beneath Marwan's weight, and the camel bit his teeth into his enemy's face.

The black horse jerked, and flung itself back onto its feet.

The demon horse bled, but its wounds glowed with a pale blue fire and disappeared. The rider shook himself, stunned. Armoured in black, the man turned a muzzle full of wicked teeth towards Yariim. He snatched out his scimitar, bared his fangs, and the demon horse charged.

Marwan ran straight at his enemy, crashing chest to chest with the demon horse. The horse gave a guttural noise and snapped its teeth, tearing at the thick rugs about Marwan's neck. The camel shoved, using his more massive weight to try and crush the horse down, hoping to pulp the rider. He reared and flailed his neck, trying to grapple with the horse. The black guard hacked his sword at Marwan's neck, and Yariim managed to put her own weapon partly in the way. Steel rang on steel, and the enemy blade thumped into Marwan's blankets without sufficient force to cut the inch-thick felt. The soldier gave a roar and cut at Yariim, who ducked fluidly backwards away from the hissing blade.

Camel and demon horse crashed and fought like dragons, hurtling into each other with absolute savagery. Marwan streamed blood from a gash ripped in his cheek. The demon horse reared and struck with his hooves, thumping into the camel's shoulder with force enough to shatter bone. The camel turned with the blow and swung his huge neck like a club, staggering his enemy aside. Yariim cut down with her sword, but the enemy soldier easily parried the blow aside.

<<*Saint George! Saint George!*>>

The night thundered to the crash of hooves. Suddenly a huge figure burst out of the darkness. It was like an alien being – a creature totally sheathed in armour plates until it looked like a clockwork nightmare. It rode a horse clad in yet more armour, with a steel spike upon its brow. The huge figure carried a lance thicker than Yariim's arm. It rode straight at the demon rider and gave a bellow that echoed in the night.

<<*Saint George!*>>

The khanate soldier whirled and threw up his shield. Driven by an avalanche of horseflesh, muscle, bone and steel, the newcomer's lance blasted a hole right through the enemy's shield, armour and his chest, smashing bloodily out his back.

The demon horse reared, throwing off its rider's corpse. Marwan lunged for its face, teeth snapping, and the demon horse turned and fled. It ran with unbelievable speed, heading to the north. Muskets fired in the darkness, but the demon horse ignored it all. Within seconds the horse had disappeared. Yariim slid to the ground. Marwan was bleeding, his blankets torn. He staggered, flanks heaving and exhausted. The mouse threw her arms around him and hugged him tight, feeling the camel's heart pounding like a drum.

"Marwan! Marwan, are you alright?"

Halting before her, the newcomer stopped and looked down from on high. It was a man – merely a man, but in armour so monstrously heavy, so rigid and complete that it was impossible even to guess his species. The suit needed a monstrous horse to bear the weight – and the rider's beast was a vast thing bigger than a cart horse. The rider gazed down at Yariim, faceless behind a visor of gleaming steel. He swung down from his horse. To Yariim's shock, he knelt to her with head bowed and a hand upon his heart.

<<My Lady! This Knight thanks God that he could be of assistance.>>

The man spoke Frankish! He stood, and levered open his visor. The thin, dapper face of a red fox peered out at Yariim. The fox smoothed his whiskers with an elegant hand.

<<The House of Malvern is at your service, Madam.>>

Frankish! Yariim switched smoothly into the language, touching her hands to her heart, her lips and brow.

<<Peace be with you, Rider. I am Yariim ibn-Dinaq, Second Queen of Osra. I have escaped the Tsu-Khan, and seek my Husband, Shah Raschid.>>

<<Majesty...!>> The Knight bowed, his armour so perfect that it expanded and contracted as he moved. <<I am Randolph Malvern, Duke of Chetter. I am honoured to be of service.>>

Foot soldiers came running from the camp – piquets armed with matchlock arquerbuses or enormously long bows. The men wore morion helmets and dense coats against the cold. Sir Randolph let one man lead his horse, and proffered an arm to Queen Yariim.

<<Majesty...>>

Marwan walked behind Yariim, hovering protectively over her and looking bloody, foul and dire. The foreign soldiers stared at the great beast and kept well clear. Yariim used her own scarf to bind Marwan's wound and led the limping creature tenderly downhill.

<<Good Knight, my mount is hurt. He is a hero. Have you a ... a treater of horses?>> Yariim looked towards the camp fires. They were very few in number – the Khan's army literally lit up entire plains. This was too small to be the army of Osra. Perhaps a camp of scouts?

They reached a rise, and looked down at tall tents hung with banners. Horses stood in rows beneath canvas awnings. Foreign soldiers in a dozen different costumes sat at fires making meals, playing pipes and laughing. The piquet lines were archers with enormous long yew bows – tall foxes, ferrets, martens, dour badgers and watchful wolves. Down by the horses, servants were polishing and storing suits of armour for the knights. There were no cannon, no rifles – and no Osranii men in sight. It looked as though soldiers from a dozen different nations had all come here into the snow. No two men seemed to be costumed alike – but all of them wore a badge shaped like a golden sun.

Over it all, there hung a banner – a pure white field on which there shone a sun of gold. Runners had preceded Yariim. Beneath the banner, men awaited her – tall men, all wearing plain white robes over their gleaming silver armour. There were three men wearing the crowns of Kings – more men with lesser golden circlets, or chains of office. More and more white robed knights came from the tents, there to quietly wait for Yariim.

Queen Yariim stood, awed and humbled, as the sea of knights knelt to her in the snow. At their head were two huge men – a badger and a grey-maned, scarred old lion. She recognized them in shock as the strange Franks that had visited Osra long, long ago.

The Lion knelt and kissed the hem of Yariim's torn, stained robe.

"Queen of Osra – the Lady Blue…"

"You…!" Yariim turned to gaze about herself. More and more knights had appeared. Five hundred – a thousand. Armour plate gleamed like liquid silver in the firelight. <<Why are you here?>>

The Lion lifted up his heavy, grizzled chin.

<<Majesty, we are the Order of the Sacred Light – a knightly brotherhood that crosses all mere boundaries of nations and of Kings.>> The man arose. <<Nations refused to heed Osra's call, but Chivalry did not. Here is the flower of all that is good in our lands. The most virtuous, the most valorous – the most faithful knights in Christendom.>>

Their army was small – so small. It contained Princes, Dukes and Kings – all leveled to the same rank with their white robes. Yariim looked at them in amazement.

<<Why are you here, Sir Knight? Why does Christendom's flower wait in the snow?>>

The Lion looked up at their banner, high above.

<<We come because nations are not the people. We come because faiths are not God. We come because a true Knight will always know a true King.>>

The old Lion turned to his men.

<<Might must be used only for right. Power must be used only against injustice. Valour is a shield against evil.>> He finished, facing towards Yariim. He proffered her the hilt of his sword.

<<We have come to serve a true King. Because this is the One Great Battle – and he must not stand alone…>>

Yariim quietly laid her hand upon the sword's hilt. All around her, armoured knights drew their blades and held them to the sky. They shouted for Yariim, for God and glory, while all around them, golden banners streamed.

The Franks had come – and Osra was not alone.

"Contact front!"

A light infantry scout saw the flash of metal glinting in the dawn. Before full light, the Osranii army was already on the march. Row after row of rifle barrels gleamed in the pre dawn light. Snow compacted down into filthy slush as regiment after regiment marched in the same path. But the scouts and flankers were out and alert. The moment the cry went up, riflemen doubled forward from the marching columns, and cavalry pushed out to protect them from enemy horse.

A line of light infantry had mounted a hillock overlooking a vast, broad valley. There were looted, destroyed villages and roadways lined with bodies. But there, at the far side of the valley, metal gleamed. First a single point of light, and then row after row. The valley held the night's shadow, hiding any details. Osranii soldiers unwrapped oiled cloth covers from their rifle locks, and checked their frizzen pans for damp powder.

Sharp shooters raced forwards with their telescopic sights, kneeling behind banks of snow. Corporal Yammak uncapped his sight and looked through the telescope. Behind him, cavalry officers skidded their mounts to a halt, and unshipped telescopes of their own.

A force was moving at the far side of the valley, perhaps ten miles away. The still dawn held not a hint of snowfall, and seemed almost magically clear. The darkness at the far end of the valley held an impression of mass – marching figures, banners and horses. They were cutting south, across the valley floor.

Sparks and flashes flickered in the darkness. Small arms were firing. The oncoming troops were shooting at something here and there. Yammak squinted through his sight, fixing on a few figures that rode onto a hill crest and fired pistols at something hiding in distant trees.

"Whoever they are, they have muskets." The Corporal watched carefully. "Aye – slow ones, but still muskets."

Captain 'Spike' knelt in the snow beside Yammak, peering off into the gloom.

"What is it?"

"More Pulski? Looks like a marching column. Might be shooing-off some Khanate scouts." The Corporal lifted his head and frowned. "Must be Pulski. They can't be Khanate men."

The Shah himself arrived. Faint across the valley came the distant sound of small arms. Now that the darkness had faded, a long column of armoured cavalry could be seen crossing the valley, heading south. Infantry marched behind them – possibly archers, dense columns of pikemen and a few musketeers. Heavy cavalry lumbered, trying to chase off a cloud of horse archers who had come to dog their rear. The Shah watched in puzzlement, then signed for an aide.

"Who's the nearest light cavalry?"

"The Hill men, my lord."

"Good." Raschid raised his telescope again. "Have some Pulski officers join them. Those people down there have no light cavalry. Ride down and give assistance."

A smaller group of riders broke off from the head of the armoured column. There were armoured men on glittering, steel-clad horses, all robed in white. They carried banners as pure at the snow around them. In their midst, a great ungainly shape waded through the snow, shoving the little horses aside. It was a swaying shape, lank and unlovely. From across the valley came a faint and hideous growl.

The beast's rider threw off a cloak and hood. Even from such a distance, blue fur gleamed in the light. The Shah stared, then gave one wild cry and stabbed his heels into his mount. His horse took off downhill like a bullet. He rode madly down into the valley, while his long-suffering staff could only stare.

Saud rode up on a horse that looked no bigger than a donkey. The huge tiger set his mount ambling happily after the Shah. Coming close behind, Abwan stood his horse, rose in his stirrups to stare, then gave a yip of joy and rode pell mell after the Shah. Bodyguards and staff joined in pursuit, and suddenly half the army seemed to be flooding down the hillside towards the oncoming men. A cheer rose up that set the skies alight with joy.

Queen Yariim! The Blue Queen had returned!

Down on the valley floor, two tiny riders met. Yariim and Raschid scrabbled off their mounts and into one another's arms. They held each other, while the Brotherhood of Light and Osra's army, Winged Hussars and Islemen met amidst a storm of cheers.

Chapter Twenty:

Marwan the camel felt due for a reward, and was perfectly happy to be pampered. He lay like the lord of all creation in the middle of the Shah's own tent, a fire thawing out his bones and a rug beneath his rump. He had drunk beer from a bucket, eaten apples and dates, and let grooms brush him inch by inch. Smug and contented, he lay with his neck stretched out and eyes closed, growling strange, hostile noises in his sleep.

Marwan's feet had been worn bloody beneath his old rag boots. It had taken two sorcerers to heal him. Bloodied but unbowed, the camel slept a hero's sleep, his head pillowed on Raschid's own robes.

Raschid and Yariim sat naked together beneath a single blanket, foreheads resting quietly against each other. They had sat there quietly together for an hour, mostly in silence, naked and warm. Tears had long bled away, and now there was merely the feel of one another, close and alive – the slow sound of one anothers' breathing. Raschid breathed in the scent of his beloved's fur, and gave his thanks to God.

Finally, he drew his face away, looking at Yariim. He slowly caressed her cheek with the back of his hand, looking quietly into her face.

The blue mouse held his hand against herself. Her voice was a whisper in the softness of the tent.

"You have grown thinner, husband."

"The way has been long. Endless walking. Endless nightmare." Raschid quietly stroked Yariim's hair. "I did what I had to do, to guard what we have made."

"We knew."

They sat together and looked at Marwan as the camel slept. His torn face was healing, but was missing patches of fur. It did nothing to improve the camel's looks. Raschid stroked his old friend Marwan along the neck, cherishing him as the noblest animal in all creation.

"Marwan and Raas Yomah. Meng. Abwan and Marsuk. Ataman and Saa'lu. Sandhri and Yariim…" The Shah's long Jackal face looked elegant, wise and sad. "I fear I am a man of little talent… but I have been fortunate in my friends."

They hung their heads, thinking of Sandhri. Raschid's hand flexed into a fist. Miserable, Yariim drew the blanket more tightly about herself.

"She knew what she was doing."

"I know." Raschid impotently closed his eyes. "I know."

"I tell myself that I should have stayed with her." Yariim stared at the ground. "But she sent me to you. She wanted me to be with you." The mouse hung her head, then drew in a deep, slow breath, putting the fear and grief away inside her. Impotent fear and regrets did not serve Sandhri.

Yariim's voice fell to a whisper.

"Husband – I have seen the Tsu-Khan's work. I know his methods. And I have seen his magic." The mouse sat cross legged, gazing at the bowl of coals that warmed Marwan's flank. "He can place the souls of his servitors inside the bodies of the dead and make the corpses walk and speak again. He gathers and torments the souls of his army's victims. He is not merely here to conquer bodies and lands. He comes to enslave our souls for all eternity."

Raschid sat quietly and listened. "My God…"

"He is *ancient*, Raschid. He has lain patiently for thousands of years, waiting for his chance. And now, we are all that can oppose him.

"Sandhri *knew*. And she wanted to make sure that I passed the knowledge on to you, my husband." The mouse held Raschid's hand, looking intently up into her husband's eyes. "We already knew this was an evil that must be stopped, Raschid. But it is more. This is the Great War – the One Great Battle. If we fail, then all of Aku-Mashad is gone. The very souls of all living creatures will be condemned to insanity and pain."

Quietly listening, Raschid looked into his wife's pink eyes.

"Sandhri told you this?"

"Sandhri told me this as we watched his works." Yariim leaned in more closely. "And she told me to tell you - To slay a sorcerer, you must break their heart of stone."

"A heart of stone…"

Raschid rose slowly. He stood, naked, his head bowed in thought. He strode to the map table, and stood gazing down at his charts.

"He has taken the Yellow Empire, Yariim. The Yellow Emperor is his vassal. So now, we are the only ones who oppose him."

Yariim looked up at her husband in quiet trust.

"We can destroy him?"

"We have the means. We have the skill." Definite and purposeful, Raschid held out a hand and beckoned her to his side. "Come – let me show you what I intend."

They stood together, leaning naked over an old trestle table. Raschid had maps of the frozen north – the great rivers Kuba and Vistuul running vertically across the maps, acting as moats protecting the west from the east. Coins had been laid out to represent the Khan's men – concentrated at Gulay Gudd, but with scouts and raiding forces facing the Osranii troops. The Osranii army was a pile of spare rifle flints encamped a thirty miles west of the Kuba river.

Raschid's long finger traced a course from the Osranii army to the west.

"Here, we have the last great river that protects the west from the Khan. The Vistuul. Wider than the Kuba. And to the south of here, it is not entirely frozen – the Pulski tell me that the middle of the river still runs free. Thick ice shelves on either bank." The Shah's map even marked the strengths of currents and the river's depth. "This is why the Tsu-Khan has forged so far to the north."

Raschid planted a fist on his hip, looking at the maps.

"Our aim must be the absolute destruction of the Tsu-Khan's army. Somehow we have to pull his entire force in against us, and bring them to battle."

Yariim sat on the table, looking up at him.

"And so you have a plan."

The Shah nodded.

"Problem: The Tsu-Khan's army is made up of mobile forces – cavalry and horse archers. If we defeat him in open battle, he will merely pull back, and hit us from another direction. Solution: therefore, we must fight only where he cannot escape. And it must be his *entire* army – led by the Khan. We must make him want to crush us quickly in the hope he can salvage his westward momentum before the ice thaws."

Yariim looked softly at the maps.

"Sandhri says that she is sending him to you – with all of his men."

"Then it can be done." The jackal breathed slowly, feeling events moving slowly into his grasp. "We must let him stall us – must let him think he has outmaneuvered us, and then he will be ours."

Raschid showed Yariim on the map. He showed her his plan in absolute detail, with reports from his Pulski scouts, his surveyors and his engineers. When he was done, the Shah sat back, staring at the map. Yariim was silent, her mind racing hard and sharp.

"You have told no one about this?" The mouse settled her glasses on her nose. "If we fail, there is no escape."

"If we fail, then escape would be pointless." The Shah shook his head. "One way or another, the battle will be final."

Yariim looked carefully at the maps, then took off her glasses and folded them away.

"It is brilliant."

Unburdened, Raschid closed his eyes and nodded. He rubbed at the crease between his brows.

"How long until the Khan arrives?"

"They can advance eighty miles in a day." Yariim looked north. "If they left a day after my escape, then they might be here within twenty four hours."

"Then we must force march tonight for the Vistuul river." Raschid reached for his clothes. "It is time to move."

They stood and dressed – Raschid in his scholar's robes, and Yariim in clothes fetched from her own dear palace and carried here in hope. Raschid kissed her quietly, and then went to the door.

He hesitated, and then looked at the floor.

"Meng and Itbit… Have they a chance?"

Yariim closed her eyes.

"Sandhri taught them well."

Raschid nodded. He opened up the tent and called quietly for his guards.

The grave-faced Crown Prince of the Pulski entered the Shah's tent. With him came the McCallum, huge and forever full of life. General Ataman brought in the Royal staff – infantry, artillery and cavalry officers dusting the snow from their boots. Behind them came the leaders of the Franks – the Brothers of the Order of Light. Their ranks included Bishops, Princes, Dukes and Kings. To all, Raschid offered the small comforts of his tent.

"Salaam, my brothers Peace be with you. Peace and light." Raschid bowed gently, and then met his visitors with his warm, brown gaze. "I am Raschid, Shah of Osra. Pray grace my humble tent with your presence."

The tent was made much smaller by the snoozing camel at its midst – but there was heat, mulled wine and Yariim bowing to her guests. The Blue mouse moved elegantly, taking her new guests by the hand.

"My Husband – I present the Most Chivalrous Brotherhood of the Order of Light." Yariim's etiquette remained forever perfect. She indicated the huge, grizzled old lion with one hand. "I present the Grand Constable of the Sacred Order, Sir Huliam D'Artois. Sir Huliam – I present Raschid al Dinaq, the Shah of Osra, guardian of all faiths – the Scholar King."

Fully armoured, and like Raschid, robed in white, the old lion gave a profound bow.

"My Lord – may God be with you."

"And with you, Grand Constable." Raschid looked at the newcomers in tired, gentle hope. "Your coming is a blessing unlooked for."

"Pray forgive our tardiness." The lion turned, and extended an armoured hand to introduce the brothers beside him.

"My Shah -This is Crown Prince Albrecht Von Keller of Huss, Knight Commander of the Order. Prince Pedro Abriganza of Nejarre, Knight Commander of the Order. Duke Giacomo Spezzate of the Trade Republic of Trebenizzi, Knight Commander of the Order - and Bishop Hugo Du Salle, Knight Champion of the Order."

Hound and Otter, Rat and Badger – the four knights knelt to the Shah. Yariim brought forward another man – a dapper fox with his whiskers twirled into a natty moustache.

"…And this is Randolph, Duke of Chetter – a knight of the Sacred Isle, and my particular saviour."

Raschid warmly embraced the surprised fox.

"I am in your debt, Sir Knight. Let you but speak a need, and it shall be fulfilled." The Shah took the Pulski Prince and the McCallum on his arms and led the men to the map tables. "Come, then. We will tell you what we know. My wife will speak to you of the Khan – and I will show you what Osra intends."

Raschid's old band of brothers was there. One-eyed Marsuk the mouse, his uniform sparkling with frost. Saud, huge and understanding nothing but the need to help his friends – Abwan, commander of the royal guard. Raschid leaned across the map, and brought his commanders close.

"Now – this is what I intend…"

Behind them, Marwan gave an enormous yawn. He opened one eye – saw the men in conference, and knew it would soon be time to wake. Wise enough not to lose a moment, the huge camel closed his eyes and drank up every last second of rest.

***

"Contact, my Khan!"

A black-armoured scout knelt in the snow with an arrow jutting from the rear shoulder of his rawhide armour. Blood dripped down the man's arm to spatter bright red droplets beside him. He never moved, waiting with eyes downcast beside his heaving, steaming horse.

The air thundered to the sound of hundreds of thousands of marching cavalry. It was a storm of noise – surging, endless and deafening. The Tsu-Khan's army marched beneath a ghostly, shimmering storm cloud of looping, shrieking souls. The regiments were headed by tall, unbreathing men who rode horses that had stark blue eyes. Skeletal, half seen things clung and gibbered about the army's standards, flying low above the numbed, grey-faced conscript infantry.

Column after column, line after line – the Khanate army seemed to cover an entire world. It marched onwards in a single direction, never pausing, never resting, driven by the ice cold will of the never-sleeping Khan.

The black regiments of the guard rode their horses forwards, parting to flow about the Khan as he sat upon his dread white horse. The Khan sat quietly in the saddle, his black robes stirring in the breeze, surrounded by his generals and his staff.

Ten bloody men from his scout cavalry knelt before him and dripped blood into the snow. The Khan looked at them softly, tilting his head to inspect the men like a raven peering at corpse.

"Contact?"

"Yes, Holy One." The scout had to almost shout to be heard above the all-pervading noise. "Our trailing troops encountered the Osranii attempting to proceed north up the Stalonji valley. We engaged their scouts, and now their army seems to have turned away and is heading west, towards the Vistuul river."

Generals looked at one another. The Khan merely turned his pale blue eyes towards the scout.

"Why was this not reported by magic mirror?"

The scout bowed lower.

"Forgive me, Sacred Person. Our command group were slain by enemy cannon fire. Our company split. Half of them attempted to recover the mirror, while half of us cut through the enemy cavalry to report to your Holiness in person."

The Khan nodded slowly, his thoughts apparently meandering elsewhere. General Gurad – vast, bristling and with his muzzle bearing yellow fangs, leaned forwards.

"The Vistuul? You're certain they are heading for the Vistuul?"

"Yes General." The wounded scout bowed again. "Their marching columns turned to the west. They are moving very rapidly, crossing gullys with portable bridges."

The Khan's narrow, fine-furred face turned back to the scout. He inclined his head slightly towards the man.

"You have done well. Report for healing, and then guide a new scouting unit to tail the Osranii troops." The Khan looked away. "That is all."

The scout had to be helped to his feet and led away. Blood loss made the man stagger, yawning and near collapse. With the army still moving past them like a vast, slow tide, the generals brooded on the news.

General Tsai-Chung leaned onto the pommel of his saddle.

"This is a matter for concern. Why are we consistently losing so many men? These are light cavalry of the Sacred Guard! They should not be taking such casualties from mere Osranii hirelings."

The Khan raised one slender finger.

"Their full effort is being sent against mere scouting detachments of our own. When we meet them one-to-one, they will not stand before us. When we meet them five-to-one…" The Khan lifted a hand, indicating the titanic army all around him. "They shall be as ashes blown before the wind."

The Khan lifted his muzzle to look towards the south. His tail did not weave, nor did his ears twitch in thought.

"Tulu Begh – you know these people. What do they intend?"

At the rear of the silent army staff, Tulu Begh sat upon a fine golden horse. The usually-elegant mouse looked drawn, hollow eyed and ill, tinged with a seething, boiling sense of anger. He rode forward and bowed briefly to the Khan.

"Holy Khan, the Osranii Shah is a scholar and a thinker – not a warrior. He will attempt to outsmart us." The Mouse shuddered, still sick from Sandhri's concoction two nights before. "If he wants to go north, he will not fight your screen. He will try to find a way around."

General Gurad gave a vicious, pleased growl between his fangs.

"He has finally realized our might. He fears us at last."

Tulu Begh sourly shook his head.

"Never forget that his aim is to cut us off from conquest of the West. He may simply be hoping to block our western progress."

The Khan sat quietly and pondered.

"How would this best be done by a small force facing a larger?"

"By defending an opposing river bank." General Tsai-Chung nodded slowly. "The Vistuul has steep embankments. Properly handled, an army could make our forces fight at a tactical disadvantage."

"Yes. A scholars way of making war." The Tsu-Khan finally bared teeth – the first sign that he was eager for the slaughter of his enemies. "He would be a cautious man, this scholar."

Tsai-Chung's long black-and-white striped tail lashed. The snow tiger signed for an aide, who brought out a hand painted silken map and spread it out upon a board.

"Sacred Person, he may be trying to outrace us to the Vistuul. He is already considerably west of our position." Tsai-Chung's mailed finger pointed to the positions of both armies on the map. "We are still far north of their army."

Gurad gave a growl.

"The scouts first found him heading to the North! He only turned west when our scouts fought their cavalry screen!" The big man swept out one hand. "Why would he march north if he intends to cut off our progress to the west?"

In reply. Tulu Begh rocked back in his saddle, infinitely pleased. He closed his eyes and saw everything blooming beautifully before him.

Tulu Begh gave a wondrous smile.

"Because they come from a land of sand and palms!"

The Generals turned to look at Tulu Begh. Suddenly full of sly, confident life, Tulu Begh smoothed back his long fine whiskers.

"They are not familiar with rivers that freeze! Do you see? They thought to merely march across the Vistuul river – but now they have finally met some Frankish guides. They are too far to the south! The Vistuul is still unfrozen at its middle this far to the south. They are trying to head north to a frozen crossing point!" The mouse was immensely pleased. "Our Scholar has not been quite clever enough!"

It made perfect sense. One glimpse at the Osranii change of march route made it obvious. The Osranii were trying to head north, slipping west of the Khanate army to beat them to the river.

The Osranii were almost at the Vistuul – but there was no way across. There were no bridges, boats or fords. This was the great open plains of the Vistuul: Cavalry country. The

Generals looked at the map, and Gurad leaned forward with a smile.

"Here. We have them!"

He pointed to a loop in the river just behind the Osranii army.

"The Vistuul river makes a deep bend here, do you see? It becomes like a vast bag with a narrow mouth where the river almost doubles back to touch itself." Hills acted as a 'plug' at the mouth of the great sack. The river bent in a loop, and within the loop was flat, open terrain. "If we can force the Osranii army into that sack, they will have the river on three sides of themselves, and only us to their front! We can crush them against the river and drown them like lice!"

General Tsai-Chung looked at the cul-de-sac and pondered.

"A moderate force could bottle them there and virtually hold them under siege."

"We lack fodder!" General Gurad slammed his fist against his saddle horn. "The horses are losing condition! We must destroy the Osranii, capture their corn supplies, and capture new feed in the west!"

The Tsu-Khan's voice drifted into the conversation.

"We will attack the Osranii. They must be annihilated. Swiftly."

The Generals turned. Behind them, the Khan sat on his horse with his eyes quietly closed.

"She has reached him. The blue Queen has reached him. She will have passed forbidden knowledge to the Osranii." The Tsu-Khan looked at the skies. "They must all now die. It is the command of the Khan, your God."

The Khan turned to Gurad.

"Can it be done?"

"Easily, lord!" General Gurad's savage muzzle twisted in a smile. This huge leopard's tail lashed in predatory joy. "We must split the army into two wings. One will force march towards the river. The other will force march directly south, then west. We will approach the Osranii from above and to the side – the river prevents him from going west. We will force them back into the river bend – into the trap!"

"Inside this 'sack', the river will protect their flanks." Tsai-Chung was unhappy. "We will be unable to envelop them."

"Which is why they will choose to make a stand there." Gurad smiled evilly. "Inside the river bend, it is flat terrain! *Cavalry* terrain! A charging horseman can cross the range of a musket before it can reload. One charge, and we shall smash them back into the river."

The Khan came to look at the maps. He sat and breathed in the breezes stirred by wheeling spirits, his fur rippling as the dead souls passed. Finally, the Tsu-Khan nodded to his men.

"We shall slaughter the Osranii and their allies within the bend of the Vistuul. We shall give their bodies to our blades, their blood to the snows, and their souls shall be playthings for our joy. Not one of them must be allowed their life. We shall flay the skins from the living Shah and his Queen, and I shall use them to cover up my throne." The Khan breathed in the vision, seeming to swell and draw strength from another world. "General Tsai-Chung, you will take the army's left wing and proceed south, driving the Osranii into the river bend. The main body will force march west immediately."

Tsai-Chung's long black-and-white tail lashed.

"Sacred Person - to move swiftly enough, we will have to abandon all cannon and all baggage. We can carry nothing but a few light rockets."

"We shall return to collect the baggage once the enemy are dead." The Khan nudged his horse and rode on. "We ride."

Gurad looked to Tsai-Chung in bloodthirsty glee.

"Two days! One day to catch them – one day to destroy them! Two days from now, the Queen of Osra will be screaming as I tear out her living womb!" The big general stood in his stirrups and bellowed for his officers. *"Commanders to me! Fresh mounts, and abandon all baggage! Fresh mounts! Fresh mounts!"*

The army cast aside its hundreds of thousands of remounts – its tents and supplies, its cannon and its siege tools. The main body of one hundred and fifty thousand horsemen rode west at a canter, making the frozen soil shudder to the impact of their hooves. Like a tidal wave they swept off towards the distant Vistuul.

Baggage, tents and tethered horses made a vast blanket across the snow, guarded by the few walking wounded left behind. General Tsai-Chung sat in his saddle, watching the main army canter westwards. He shook his head, looked back to see his own men ready to march, and motioned for his standard bearer to signal the advance.

"At the trot – advance!"

One hundred thousand cavalry moved south. Sixty thousand conscript infantry clung to the cavalry's stirrups, jogging at the horses' sides. Yet more cavalry advanced behind the troops, coldly ready to slaughter any infantrymen who dropped out of the march. Abandoning its cannon and supplies, the troops moved out across the hills, leaving behind them a scarred wasteland of garbage, slush and snow.

***

"Stop! Stop the hut!"

Sandhri's voice cut through the clang and clatter of the hut's galloping brass feet. Ever helpful, the hut screeched to a stop, tilting its hull madly and collapsing Itbit and Meng together in a heap. Braced against a wall, Sandhri managed to stay in place by jamming her feet against the floor.

The hut subsided. Itbit hung half out of the door. Sandhri's breath hissed between her teeth, and her voice strained out past barred fangs.

"I'm sorry, Children, but t'iss iss as far as v'e go."

"Oh no!" Itbit clung in the doorway, suddenly looking ashen. "No!"

"What?" Meng looked at Sandhri, and suddenly his eyes bugged out with shock. "No!"

"Ooooh yes!" Sandhri had her head back, and her breathing was… well, laboured! She shuddered her hands into fists as a spasm gripped her hard. "Damn! Alright people, Mama needs herself a safe place vit' no passing armies. And some stones! Find me some stones!"

The hut had galloped through a long night and a difficult day, its pace slowed by the need to keep Sandhri comfortable. They had run far west towards the Vistuul river, hoping to lose the pursuit. Next they had gone south east to angle back towards the place the Osranii army had been rumoured to be. The hut had clambered through dark fir forests, across hills and past dead, burned towns. It had sped down roads lined with frozen corpses impaled upon poles. Khanate cavalry had appeared from time to time, and the hut had moved into a run and swiftly lost the pursuit. Then for long hours they had lain hidden in a copse of trees as vast, dark regiments of Khanate soldiers had thundered past them, riding hell-bent to the south.

On a hill overlooking the Kuba river, they had found a vast patch of trampled slush well scattered with horse droppings and old campfires. It seemed that the Osranii army had moved on. Old tracks in the snow showed that the army had gone west. Gullys and deep creeks had all been bridged by Osranii engineers. For an hour, the hut had been following the army's trail. Then the path had been joined by a vast trail left by Khanate cavalry. From the hilltops, the Tsu-Khan's army could be seen – a dark line advancing due west in pursuit of Raschid's force.

On a hilltop, beneath a pair of trees, the hut craned onto its tippie-toes. Meng and Itbit stood in the hut's door and watched the distant evil smear that was the Tsu-Khan's army. The army stood between them and Raschid. Itbit bit her lip, and took Sandhri beneath her arm.

"Itbit thinks - maybe Raschid is not far? Maybe friends in big brass hut should try to run straight through the Khan's army?"

Sandhri shook her head, her long hair limp with sweat.

"No. They haff lariats and ropes. Thiss time they v'ill know to trip the hut over. And…." Sandhri held her belly, looking in pain. "No – I can't travel any further. The contractions are too close."

Meng looked back into the hut, then perched on the jutting front step of the hut to look to the north. A line of hills were nearby, and might offer better shelter if night should come. The panda turned back anxiously toward the Queen.

"My lady – how swiftly will the baby come? Need we plan for the night?"

"Yes you need to plan for the night!" Sandhri's temper snapped. She was in pain. "T'iss iss going to take a few hours, and v'e're not goink nov'ere!"

Meng sat on the doorstep and directed the hut to the north. The big, gentle, clumsy thing started moving. Chastened and nervous, Meng looked back to Sandhri in the hut.

"Does it take long to… to have a baby?"

"Don't t'ey teach you this at scholar school?" Sandhri looked at the frightened scholar and gripped his hand. "Hours. Sorry. I'm sorry." Sandhri closed her eyes tight and clenched her teeth. "I haff been having these things for hours. The waters broke before nightfall, back v'en I went to pee."

Itbit tore at her own hair.

"Sandhri-bat has been having these for hours and hours?" Itbit was frightened and appalled. "Why silly bat not tell!"

"V'at good v'ould it haff done? It v'as better to try and find… find Raschid." Sandhri lifted half off the floor as a contraction came. Itbit fumbled for her hand. Sandhri gripped tight, and Itbit almost had her hand crushed to pulp. She never made a squeak. When Sandhri finally collapsed, panting, the bat looked drawn and sweating.

"D-damn! How close are they apart?"

Itbit shrugged helplessly. Extracting her hand, she looked towards Meng. The scholar shrugged in panic.

"Five minutes? Ten?"

Sandhri's temper cut back at him. "T'ere's a hell off a difference between five and ten!" Panting, the bat tried to see out of the front door. "Are you finding a place to stop, or am I goink to haff to kill you?"

Looking hurt, Meng concentrated on guiding the hut on its travels. Crestfallen, Sandhri touched his back.

"Sorry. Sorry." The bat fought hard for breath, sick with pain. "Damn. I'm sorry."

"It's alright, my Lady. I do understand." Crossing into the hills, Meng spied a steep gully littered with boulders. "Here! This might be good."

The hut tried to move carefully. Huge delicate chicken feet trod carefully on snow and scree as the hut nosed its way along a long thin gully that ran between two steep hills. The gully was dotted with granite boulders, half of which had split in the frost. The gully was a place of stones and eerie silence, shadowed by a tangled rim of dead scrub, old wood and leafless trees.

The hut ducked beneath a low hanging tree, pad-pad-padding quietly up the gully. At the end of the passage, a granite shelf made an overhang, and beneath the overhang there was a rough wall made from dry piled stone.

The hut clambered into cover beneath the overhang. Meng patted the hut thankfully, and the huge creation settled down onto the ground as gently as it could. Meng drew his slim sword and stepped out onto the snow, looking carefully around.

Still holding Sandhri, Itbit lifted up her face, long whiskers a-quiver.

"Itbit feelsies something. There is a spirit here."

Meng led with his sword, his eyes wide.

"How do you know?"

"Itbit knows what an Itbit knows." The mouse's fur stood on end. She looked towards the cave. "In there. It's quiet, and…and a little sad."

The wall had been left untended for long centuries. Tufts of dead grass jutted from between the stones, and some of the rocks had slithered free. Ghost or no ghost, the cave had promise. Meng sheathed his sword and carefully pulled aside stones one after another, making a path beneath the low-slung ceiling. Behind him, Sandhri let herself be helped up to her feet. Hobbling, she set foot on the snow and looked about herself. The hut made a mournful, creaking noise and nosed gently against her. The bat leaned her face against the cold brass hull and embraced him with her arms.

"It's alright, nice hut. Thank you for taking us so far, so safely." She patted the metal hull quietly. "Can you be a guard for us now? Chust for a few hours, eh?"

The hut nuzzled adoringly against Sandhri, and then clambered awkwardly about to face back down the gully. Sandhri leaned on Itbit, who followed Meng up beneath the granite overhang.

A distant, giggling scream seemed to hover on the wind. Sandhri and Itbit both looked back towards an empty sky. Sandhri nodded softly.

"Itbit – v'at's good?"

The mouse stared intently off down the valley.

"We needie a barrier. Itbit will make some writing. Bury iron beneath the threshold - perhaps your sharpened nail. And then make a line of virgin's pee..."

"Good." Sandhri signed to Meng. "Meng?"

Flabbergasted, the young sage drew up straight, embarrassed beyond belief.

"My Lady – what makes you think…!"

"V'oman's intuition. Just pee."

Meng was stiff with shame, and tried to cover himself with a cough. "Well – just to humour you."

"Right. V'at effer. Thank you, Meng." The bat hobbled under the overhang, leaning on Itbit's arm. "This iss good. Yes – this v'ill do."

The dry stone wall had sealed off a low, cold chamber. Rocks made steps that led awkwardly up into the dark. Itbit pulled a tinderbox from her nomad belt and struck a spark, blowing it carefully to life against a tiny stub of candle. Sheltering the candle flame behind her hand, the green mouse led the way up the rocks, pausing to let Sandhri lean upon her shoulders for support.

The steps led up into a great, high ceilinged chamber. Two great slabs of sheer granite leaned together overhead to make a natural roof, and the floor spread broad and relatively even down beneath. Sleeping peacefully in one corner was a hefty, warm blooded, fur-bearing skink at least three feet long – apparently hibernating the winter months away. Apparently it had entered through the hole in the stones. The animal never even stirred from its slumbers as Itbit and Sandhri wandered past.

Meng joined them, looking mortified. He peered in interest at the skink, intrigued by its markings, and then quietly rose to point at pictures painted on the granite walls.

The pictures were crude – drawn with charcoal and ochre. They showed lovingly rendered images of skin tents and people hunting, fishing and catching wild birds. The people in the pictures were of all manner of species – fox, wolf, bear and rabbit, squirrels and short-tailed mice. They rode horses across timeless, ever growing grass, and taught children to ride ponies and play beneath the sun.

At the side of the cave, there was a shelf, and upon the shelf, a bundle lay. A skeleton lay on its side, curled like a sleeping foetus. Skins wrapped the bones, and long strings of amber beads held the shroud closed tight. A folded, faded blanket woven in a thousand stripes of colour served as a pillow. The skull had the long snout of a fox or slender dog. Beside the body, pots and clay urns had been arranged, with clay dolls dressed in skins and fabric seated all around.

Sandhri came carefully closer.

"I think she v'ass a v'oman. A mother. See – her family made dolls off themselves to be beside her." The bat looked up into the shadows. "She's still here."

Coming quietly forward, Meng knelt, put his hands into his sleeves, and bowed towards the bones.

"Honourable bones! This humble one begs your indulgence for this intrusion. We ask your sympathy for a woman in great need." Meng bowed three times deeply to the skeleton. "With the gravest, most sincere respect, we promise to behave as guests."

There was an unseen stir up above. Itbit craned her face to watch, sensing something moving high above.

"Itbit thinks that she is happy to let us stay." The mouse had flippantly and eagerly studied books of sorcery. Little good it did her now. "If we makie fires at the back of the cave, the smoke won't hurt those nice pictures."

Meng went forth to collect brushwood and old logs, while Itbit swept the back of the cave clean. Sandhri wanted to walk, and so she hobbled back and forth, feeling her womb contract and strain in hard, vicious spasms. Her pelvis ached – her back ached, and she felt weak at the knees. The feelings down between her legs were definitely unpleasant. Her breath steamed in the icy air as she forced herself to walk through the pain.

Itbit found two pieces of leather thonging from her belt. She had a knife – a rag torn from her dress. There were no more tools. She collected snow and put it inside her water bottle, hoping it might thaw.

- There seemed so little she could do. Anxious and with a crawling sense of fear, the young mouse looked back at her friend.

Sandhri already seemed tired.

"Thank you, Itbit."

"Is it right?" Itbit wrung her hands, keeping her distance from her oldest friend. "Is it enough?"

"It iss perfect." The bat held out a hand to draw Itbit near. "Now come here, my angel. Come…come."

A shelf of rock at the back of the cave formed a natural seat. Sandhri took Itbit tight beneath her arm, and they walked together to sit in the gloom. The single candle just barely managed to light the edges of the walls.

Sandhri gently swept away Itbit's hat. She caressed the mouse's face, and they leaned together, cheek to brow. Sandhri softly kissed Itbit's golden hair.

"Itbit, I am sorry."

The mouse moved, bowing her head softly. Sandhri held her tightly.

"You v'ere neffer a child to me. But you v'ere a friend. A soul mate. The sister in mischief I had alv'ays dreamed of." The bat rested her face on Itbit's fur. "You know v'at happened to my family. So you v'ere little sister, playmate - my friend. I could giff you all of the fun and cleverness, v'ith none of the pain."

"I'm sorry t'ere vas pain. If I could take it for you, t'en I v'ould."

The mouse began to cry.

"Itbit failed you."

"Never. Never did you fail me. Look how you grew up! Look how you are v'ith me now." The bat kissed her softly, then turned the tearful green face up towards her own. "V'e were your world, Itbit. And I know you v'anted to be a lover as v'ell as a friend. But you haff to understand – v'e loved you as our best friend. For us, it v'as not a thing that had dawned upon us." The bat lifted Itbit's chin and wiped the mouse's eyes. She kissed away the tears.

"I t'ink it v'as for the best, in the end. I t'ink something very precious v'as v'aiting for you to find it. You see, in the middle of hardship, I found my own great, true love. And I believe you are about to find v'un all of your own…"

The bat hissed as another contraction came. This time it was huge! The bat arched and scrabbled for Itbit's hand, clinging tight until the pain had ebbed slowly away.

Mouse and bat clung close. Sandhri had her eyes screwed shut, and was panting as the pain sprung tears into her eyes.

"Itbit – I talk too much. But now I haff to talk again, just a little."

The mouse kept an arm about Sandhri, holding her friend's hand and trying to help.

"Itbit is here for Sandhri."

"I love you, Itbit." Sandhri's head reeled. She drew in a breath and mastered herself.

"Itbit. There are no sorcerers here. I am very small, and the baby is very big." Itbit's eyes widened in horror. Sandhri held her tight and made the mouse listen. "Itbit! If the worst happens, you must be mother to my son! If you can do it, get him to Yariim and Raschid. If not – Raas Yomah." A new contraction came, and Sandhri fought it back. The bat's wild soul sparked clean and clear in her grey eyes. "Raise my son! Tell him I will alv'ays be v'ith him! Alv'ays!"

Itbit ran a little hand over Sandhri, her heart racing. Suddenly she felt cold.

"It will be alright. Itbit will make it alright! Sandhri must not think it! Sandhri will be alright." The mouse wept helpless tears. "It will be fine! Is just a birthing! Sandhri never fails. Sandhri will be alright!"

"Yes. Yes.." Sandhri hissed, letting her head slump back against the cave wall. She opened her eyes and managed to give Itbit a watery smile. "It v'ill be alright. It v'ill be alright. I know v'at I am doing."

They held hands for a while, leaning back against the wall while Meng carried in armload after armload of firewood. He set a blaze going, feeding it carefully, and even piled stones to shield the sleeping skink's eyes from the light. The chill came off the room slowly, and the warm light of the fire seemed to make fears fade away. Sandhri leaned forward, pillowing her head on the wall as Itbit rubbed her lower back.

Somewhere out in the distant world, a rumble echoed in the air. It was not thunder. It was short, sharp, and staccato: a ripple of cannon fire.

Breathing slowly and carefully, trying to control her reaction to her body, Sandhri lifted up her head and looked towards the west.

"Showtime."

Chapter Twenty One:

Raschid led the army past the cold, free flowing river, and up into a narrow range of hills. The hills served as a plug in the neck of a long, deep bend of the Vistuul. From the heights, the river could be seen flowing down from the north, flowing miles to the south, then doubling back and bending in towards itself. Granite hills served to swerve the river away once more, sending it east and away into the steppes

The result was a peninsula of flat land extending two miles north to south, bordered on three sides by the river, and to the north by granite hills. The river that belted the cul-de-sac was almost a thousand yards wide, and the central hundred yards flowed icy cold and free. The river banks were bordered by steep banks eroded by centuries of water and ice. A single village stood at the base of the peninsula – unplundered and totally intact. The tall church steeple could be seen clearly from the hills.

Pulski horsemen led the way into the plain below, speeding onward to warn local villagers of the danger. Behind them raced Raschid's engineers, riding fast wagons filled with lumber saws, crowbars, ropes and steel pegs. The Shah stood on the hill tops surrounded by his bodyguards, watching the army flood over the hills and into the lands below. He turned to speak with Yariim, when suddenly the rearguard of the army erupted into cannon fire.

The Tsu-Khan had finally come.

Two vast forces had closed upon Raschid's force. From the vantage point of the hills, Raschid could see them approaching like tidal waves darkening the horizon. To the North there was a vast ocean of cavalry, extending miles back into the snow. They covered the surface of the world like a locust plague. To the east, smaller and yet still uncountable, came the second force, swarming over the snow. Both enemy armies had shot forth huge advanced guards of cavalry, and these forces sped in from north and east, trying to cut off

Raschid's rear guard. The Shah stood in his stirrups, watched the approaching forces, and saw how his rearguard's artillery forced the Khan's cavalry to swerve aside from the guns.

Raschid flipped open his portable desk and wrote swiftly and clearly on printed order sheets.

"First regiment of Guard cavalry – with me! Second regiment – remain here in reserve." The tall jackal turned to Yariim, who sat on her own horse, looking at him calmly. "Yariim – Keep the main body moving. Split off the light horse to cover our retreat."

She kissed him, and then let him go. Raschid swept his lance forward, signaling the premiere regiment of his guard cavalry.

"The Guard – advance!"

They were magnificent – blue armoured men upon blue armoured horses, armed with lance and bow, pistol, javelins, mace and scimitar. Boot-to-boot the guard cavalry of Osra moved forward in ranks that wavered slightly with the undulations of the ground. At their head, the royal banner flew beside a figure dressed in white robes who rode an armoured camel.

Raschid rode Marwan. The camel would tolerate no other beast to carry his master. The huge beast now wore a magnificent armour made of plates and chain, with tassels swaying brilliantly in the breeze. Effortlessly bearing the weight, Marwan broke into a trot, his savage growl booming out across the sound of cannon fire.

Dressed in full armour, with white silk robes trimmed in pure white down, Queen Yariim turned her horse away from the sight of her husband advancing into battle. She was armed with a slim, curved sword and a painted dancing fan. She waved the fan towards her guardians, bringing them to her side.

Saud and Abwan were infantrymen – soldiers of the Foot Guards. They stood beside their horses, and came over to Yariim, unhappy about letting Raschid ride from their grasp. Colonel Abwan cast a worried glance after Raschid, and gave a bow.

"My Lady?"

"I am taking the main body onwards to the river. The Foot Guards will take rearguard position with the Queen Yariim's artillery. March south, fast as you can." Yariim tried to keep her back turned calmly to the battle, but she felt the pressure of thousands of enemies behind her. She fought the urge to duck as a cannon roared. "Where is General Ataman?"

"With the advance guard at the river, My Lady."

"Saa'lu? Ride and tell him we are coming within the hour." Yariim looked to Saud. The vast tiger leaned on his two handed sword, his rifle slung over his back. He stared unhappily off towards the north. Yariim leaned down from her horse and stroked the huge man's whiskers.

"Saud – it's alright. He said you should look after me now."

They rode south, down from the saddle of the hills. Far behind them, a distant roar of voices and screaming horses echoed through the sky. With the sun fast disappearing and the world turning a soft indigo blue, Yariim rode to catch up with the fast-marching columns of Osranii infantry.

Cavalry and artillery guarded the rear of the marching columns. Yariim's standard bearer waved the cavalry commanders closer. Yariim saw tall-eared bats on fleet tora birds speed over in response, and she tried to keep her heart sealed away from its ache of grief and fear for Sandhri.

The bird riders from Osra's hill country led their speedy mounts to Yariim's side. Their commander placed his hand over his heart.

"My Queen?" Even his voice sounded like Sandhri's. "V'at iss your desire?"

"Brigadier – the light cavalry is to concentrate here, below the hills. Deploy to cover the rearguard's withdrawal." Yariim looked at the sun, finding it low on the horizon, just grazing the snow. Long shadows streamed eastwards from the lines of marching men. "Make sure your animals are rested. We have a long march ahead of us before nightfall."

With a piercing whistle, the bat summoned his tribesmen. Torah birds plumed in yellow, orange, blue and red spread out into lines of attack, facing back towards the granite hills.

The battle rose to a pitch of sound somewhere on the far side of the hills. Yariim shuddered and hunched her shoulders beneath the oppressive weight of sound.

The old hound, Abwan, stroked whiskers back from his snout.

"My Lady – I could send men to go back and watch for him."

Yariim shook her head.

"He will return. Raschid has his duty." The mouse deliberately straightened her back. "… As have I."

She kicked her horse into motion. There was an army to march, a battle to deploy, and a miracle to arrange by dawn. Her armour jingling, Yariim sped off and left her husband to cover her back while she led the men to war.

The north face of the hills echoed to the sound of swarming warriors. Horse harness, armour, arrows in quivers – hoof falls and boots. The small force of Frankish longbowmen had shaken themselves out into line, and had planted arrows in the ground at their own feet. Behind them, sergeants from the Brotherhood of Light dressed the line and waved new companies forward with their swords. Raschid stood high on Marwan's saddle, and looked across the heads of the waiting bowmen and down into the open steppes beyond.

The enemy army had come.

Dark masses of cavalry trotted towards the hills in a menacing mass. Line after line of them, a hundred yards apart. They were coming right at the center of the bottleneck, up the one obvious road – heavy cavalry in armour, on horses slathered with rawhide, mail and plate. Raschid unshipped his telescope and steadied Marwan, then looked carefully at the line.

The range was a thousand yards. It looked like an advance force – the bulk of the enemy army was still back at the horizon. His mind crisp and steady, Raschid divided the front line of the nearest unit into half, then half again, then counted heads. He fought down the panicked impulse to believe the enemy had vast numbers, and did the math.

"I make the leading line one thousand. A thousand in the following lines – four lines in total." He swung his telescope carefully, looking past the front line. "The second line have better armour. They plan to pass through and attack."

Four thousand horsemen were assaulting a hilly position held by a thousand infantry. Raschid felt no need to panic. He waved his bow over his head and signaled to the massed cavalry of his guard who stood their horses behind them.

"Dismounted action! Bows and firearms!" He pointed a hand to each end of the Frankish line. "Half the regiment on each end of the line! I want the household squadron mounted and ready as a reserve!"

The thousand men of the First Guards thundered into action. Big men on big horses rode to the ends of the Frankish line and swung down from their saddles, their full armour jangling. With bows in hand and pistols through their belts, the men ran forward, nocking arrows with practiced speed. Five hundred armoured Osranii fanned out on each side of the Frankish line, the steel and compound bows of Osra sinking into firing position.

Behind the Frankish infantry, a dapper figure in gleaming silver plate walked along quite happily. From the towering height of Marwan's back, Raschid made a Salaam.

<<Sir Randolph. Good evening.>>

<<Sire. Your arrival is most welcome!>> The Fox knight wore full plate armour, and had a sword across his shoulder that could have decapitated an elephant. <<Have you seen our lads shoot yet?>>

<<No, Sir Randolph.>>

<<Ahh. Well, you're in for a pleasure then!>> The knight seemed utterly unconcerned about facing odds of four-to-one. <<Not so scientific as your own lads – but by God, they pack a punch.>>

From a vantage point, the two commanders stood and watched the enemy come on. The range had closed to eight hundred yards, and the rocky hillside was throwing the enemy cavalry into confusion. Raschid searched with his telescope, hunting for the enemy commander.

He saw two men behind the fourth line. Big men in expensive armour, each followed by a skull-topped standard hung with scalps hacked from living victims. Keeping his eyes on his enemy, Raschid lent his glass to the Frankish Knight.

<<There – with the five-tailed standard. Gurad." The Jackal Shah felt strange – detached, almost as though time was slowing down all around him. <<He was the General of the Northern army under my Father. Fought to make his own kingdom in the north when I was crowned. We beat him in a campaign, and he fled to the Steppe Cities with all his nobles.>>

Beside Gurad, a familiar figure loomed – a cheetah, spotted and scarred, dressed in the full regalia of a Khanate Nobleman.

<<The second man is Had'idh. One of my Brother's old Emirs. We took back the lands he had stolen from the hill people and relocated him closer to the capital.>> Raschid took back his telescope. <<He kidnapped my wives.>>

He watched them come. The range closed to seven hundred, and the Osranii guards lifted their bows. They had fitted arrow channels to their weapons, and began firing short, light darts. The small arrows fell in shoals into the advancing enemy – vast clouds of them hissing and rattling up into the sky. The sound of darts striking armour gave a continuous, musical ring.

The Frankish archers were bemused by the Osranii's range. Randolph looked up in astonishment, but Raschid seemed unimpressed. He kept his eyes on the enemy front line.

<<Just darts, Sir Randolph. They won't penetrate armour, but they can sting an unarmoured horse. But it starts sewing confusion, which is what we want.>> Raschid kept a close eye out for flanking enemy cavalry, but there was none. <<They're coming right for us. They want to carry the position fast.>>

Sir Randolph leaned on his titanic sword and watched the enemy come.

<<Should we send for your riflemen?>>

The Jackal shook his head, his eyes upon the fight. Arrows flew upwards in clouds, jostling as they arced, hung, then plunged down into the dense-packed lines of enemy.

<<Your musketeers are in the rocks – and they'll be slow shooting, sir Randolph. We want them to think of muskets as being slow. Most of them haven't met Osranii rifles.>> Raschid watched the vast lines of enemy close, the men hunching forwards as darts hit and span away from armour. Here and there a dart lodged in an armour joint, slashed a horse's leg or made an animal dance nervously aside, but the enemy line held a brutal, rigid discipline. <<We need to hold them back and let our army reach the river – but we don't want to frighten the enemy away. We need to make them think we have been forced out of this position.>>

He clapped his telescope shut.

<<Bows. We'll do it with bows. They're good against mounted men.>>

Randolph reached up to grip Raschid's proffered hand.

<<I wish you joy of the fight, Sire.>>

<<Take good care of yourself, Randolph. I am still in your debt.>>

Four hundred yards – and suddenly the real fight began.

The enemy cavalry in loose order, the horses weaving to pass through rocks and shrubs. The slopes were steep, and their lines wavered. A thousand horses laboured forwards, their armour ringing with the strike of darts. The riders hunched beneath lifted shields, ducking as the darts hissed down onto them from the skies.

The advance came to just out of true archery range. The riders closed ranks, ducking as darts hit their armour, but otherwise quite silent. General Gurad had his standard lifted, and a heavy drum began to roar.

The cavalry were unleashed.

They gave a sudden, demonic scream. Four thousand armoured horses crashed forwards, their riders howling in a maddened lust for blood. The riders nocked arrows to their own bows, and rode pell mell up the slopes in four massive, armoured waves.

A Frankish officer with a long staff paced behind his men.

<<Yeomen! Nock!>>

<<Draw>>

<<Loose together!>>

The Frankish archers were squat, hefty men – huge shouldered from long, hard hours of practice. Raised to shoot almost before they could walk, the men nocked arrows and bent back their tall bows. When they fired, the very air thrummed to the shock of the departing arrows. Without looking to see if their first arrows struck home, the archers were already reloading, moving shockingly fast.

The first arrow volley struck.

There was a hammer and anvil sound – metal striking metal, punching leather, or thumping into flesh. Horses screamed and men swore. Charging at the archers, the enemy line jerked in shock, then surged forward, the riders kicking horses forwards. Chargers reared and screamed. Horses fell kicking in agony. But Eastern armour had been designed to soften arrow blows. Studded with shafts lodged in their armour plates, men and horses charged onwards, speeding up the slopes in maddened rage.

The horsemen came to two hundred yards, and opened fire.

Steppe horsemen liked to close to point-blank range, but the Khan's leading men were trained in the Osranii style. They fired in shoals, concentrating on set points of the enemy line. Arrows flew, passing each other in the sky. The first arrows thumped into the ground amongst the Franks. Some smacked into bowmen, folding shrieking men onto the ground. But the Franks kept shooting, working like machines – shot after shot, the bows level as the enemy came into point blank range.

The Osranii guards ran their open flanks forward, enfolding the enemy like wings. The arrow channels were still in their bows – and now the Osranii loaded with solid steel darts.

"Fire!"

The heavy darts sped forward with blinding speed. The steel shot punched into armour, tearing through horseflesh and piercing men. Attacked from the flanks, the enemy bunched inwards. The front rank stalled, moving forwards at a walk, horses shying and men cursing..

The wild scream of the charge had changed into the shouts and curses of hard-pressed men.

The sounds of arrows made a constant rush. Raschid stood on Marwan, and the camel stamped sideways as an arrow flickered from his steel shod flanks. Raschid watched the fight, the clouds of arrows making dense shadows in the sky.

Light was failing. Already night stained the river banks, the river gleaming silver. There would be a half moon tonight, and it already rose behind the Khan's men. The enemy ranks became a dark mass, almost lost against the shadowed ground behind them. And still the arrows flew and soldiers died.

The Frankish archers were holding. The enemy front line collapsed. A second rank gave a scream and forced their horses through and over the ramparts of injured and dead. Arrows met them, smashing into steel and leather. The firefight intensified as the enemy drove fresh troops into the attack.

A Frankish Sergeant limped back from the left flank, an arrow jutting from his thigh.

"Beware the flanks! Beware the flanks!"

Raschid rose to look. The rear ranks of the enemy horse had fanned out and were racing to envelop the archers. He signaled with his sword.

"Osranii guard – refuse the flanks!"

Cavalry trumpets sounded. and the Osranii guards looked back. They had taken almost no casualties, being heavily armoured and set on the battle's flanks. The Osranii swung their lines backwards like gates hinged upon the Franks, angling backwards to protect the line from the swarms of horse archers that sped outwards and around the fight.

The left flank of the allied line knelt and fired at the onrushing enemy. From rocks nearby, Frankish musketeers opened fire with their arquerbuses. The short, smoothbore muskets coughed smoke, and bullets began to fly. Snatched back from the rocks, the clambering Khanate cavalrymen were knocked back from the left flank. Armour that kept arrows at bay was no more use against lead bullets than papier mâché. The fire was slow, inaccurate – but the musket flashes stabbed bright and frightening in the dark, and enemy horsemen shied back from the violence of the sound.

The right flank was not so lucky. The hill made a flat saddle here, devoid of rocks and shrub. Sensing a clear road to victory, the enemy cavalry drove fast towards the open flank. Five hundred of them rampaged past the Osranii bows and made for the rear. With a nod to Sir Randolph, Raschid took his lance from an aide and sent Marwan gliding to the head of the mounted reserve.

"The Household Squadron will advance!" Raschid pointed his long lance forward. *"Advance!"*

There were only a hundred and twenty men in the squadron, but they were Osra's best – the companions to a King. Boot-to-boot, they formed a massive wave of blue brocade and polished steel. With the white-robed Shah on his armoured camel at their front, the squadron drove forward in a packed hammer blow of steel. Raschid rode through the darkness, never looking back – sensing the men behind him. He saw the enemy horsemen swinging onto the open hill top, then gave a violent roar and let Marwan plunge into the charge.

Marwan ran, stretching out into a gallop that came on like an armoured avalanche. Metal armour, mail and plate thundered as he ran. Raschid bellowed, picked his target and smashed an enemy's head back with his lance. Marwan crashed chest-to-flank with a steppe horse, and sent the smaller animal tumbling aside.

The household cavalry hit the enemy in the flank, smashing the formation apart. Raschid hurtled his bloody lance into the melee and drew his mace. Huge and raging, he rode in his stirrups and smashed the steel head down. Two massive blows sent an enemy horsemen sliding from the saddle. Marwan turned, clubbing enemy horses with his armoured neck and rearing to plunge down, crushing a rider beneath his chest.

Osranii guards rode past, lance pennons streaming. They sped in pursuit of enemy riders who broke and fled into the dark. Seeing nothing but dead and wounded enemy around him, Raschid turned Marwan and brought the camel lumbering over to his heralds.

"Sound the recall. No pursuit! No pursuit!"

A trumpet blew the recall for the Osranii cavalry. Raschid wanted no mad pursuit off into the dark. Night had fallen, and the hills were a maze of black shadows and hidden pitfalls. He saw that his men were returning, piked a fallen enemy with a borrowed lance, and rode hurriedly back towards the center of the line.

The noise had gone. There were only screams – shrieks from dying horses, and occasional musket shots. Marwan picked his way forwards, and Sir Randolph emerged from the gloom.

The enemy had gone.

A dense tidal line of dead horses showed where the line had reached to thirty yards from the Frankish bows. But the terrain had been too rocky and uneven for the horses to gallop, and the slopes had blunted the charge. It had been a beginner's mistake, to send cavalry uphill in the rough. The mistake of a man with something to prove in a hurry.

Raschid looked out across the carpet of dead and felt nothing. These were the men who had stolen Sandhri and his unborn son. These were the men who amused themselves by flaying victims alive. A rider rose from the pile of dead, staggering and dazed. Raschid drew a pistol and shot the man dead.

Sir Randolph waded forwards through countless arrows that jutted through the grass.

<<They've gone, my Lord.>>

The enemy had stood in the arrow storm, trying to force their horses forward through the rocks. It had been too slow a route. The Frankish arrows were heavy, and fired by fearfully skilled men.

The carnage was largely hidden in the gloom. Raschid felt his body sitting stiff and strange – like a thing experienced at a distance. He made himself look to Sir Randolph in gentle concern.

<<What are our casualties, Sir Randolph?>>

<<Twelve dead. I think we lost two of your lads. We have – ooh – twenty five, maybe twenty six wounded.>>

They had killed perhaps a thousand of the enemy. Raschid looked back down the slopes towards the enemy army. It was still coming forward – but slowly. Only slowly. Its speed had gone.

<<They will reach the bottom of the hills and camp. They will send infantry here to clear the hills.>> It had been a good thing the enemy cavalry had not thought to dismount: Bows were no match for determined infantry. <<By the time they discover we are gone, the main body will already be encamped.>>

It was done. The enemy were stalled, and the main army could deploy. There was time for the great plan to be begun. Raschid turned his camel away from the enemy.

<<Thank you, Sir Randolph.>> Louder, he called in Frankish to the archers who gathered all around him. <<*Thank you. Thank you all! Never have I seen men shoot so well.*>>

They cheered him then. Archers came forward, Frankish and Osranii. Marwan stood proud and vigilant and growled, while the gentle Shah moved amongst the troops and touched outstretched bow staves and reaching hands.

"Well done. Well done."

He felt strange – like a player in a role. Leading his men quietly down the rear hills towards the river bend, Raschid prepared himself for the real work to come.

The river gleamed – a vast, silver roadway that bent about the army and off into the night. In the dark of night, with clouds hanging over the starts, the half moon still made the open river gleam. The clear water at the center of the river shone black and slick as jet, while the ice gleamed cold and deadly in the gloom.

The army lit its fires. All inside the great "U" bend of the river, regiments were bedding down. The campfires glittered, shooting red light across the frozen ice.

Behind the steep river banks, the army seethed with activity as men prepared themselves for the coming day. The hiss of steel on oilstones rippled through the dark as men put edges on their swords, their scimitars and yatagans. Men obsessively oiled their rifles, cleaning the barrels and checking the flints. Sharp shooters milled their own powder and carefully hand loaded cartridges, polishing the bullets smooth so that each one would fly true.

Lights showed far out in the river ice. Walking arm in arm with Yariim, Raschid made his way through the foot-deep snow. He walked carefully, finding his footing, helping Yariim as the mouse picked up her tail from the slush.

They stood together, arms about one another. Each of them was armoured in mail and draped in sheepskin coats against the cold – but warmth still came through the clothing. They could feel each other' heart beat. Could breathe each other's scent. They stared out across the river towards the pitch dark lands beyond.

At the center of the river bend there was a small village. The sound of hammers and saws sometimes drifted from the houses, and teams of men chanted as they dragged heavy loads to the river banks. Yariim turned to slowly trace the path downstream, the river gleaming like cold black glass. Her breath clouded into frost as she stared into the night.

Bagpipes sounded from the Islemen's distant camp. Big men in woolen kilts were dancing, apparently unconcerned with the coming battle. They were drinking with Raschid's Foot Guards, and laughter in a dozen accents could be heard. Raschid stared at the line of fires and watched tiny figures dance.

"They're good men." Raschid looked towards the men who danced over crossed swords beside their camp fires. He felt distanced and estranged. "Keep them by you."

"I will keep them by me. They are our reserve." Yariim held tight to Raschid's arm. "Ataman and I know what to do."

The hills that bottled in the river bend twinkled with the lights of enemy watch fires. Side by side, Yariim and Raschid stood and watched the evidence of the distant enemy. Mouse and Jackal stood quietly in thought, their breath clouding softly as they breathed.

Raschid's tail moved slowly and disjointedly with his thoughts. In the darkness and the quiet, with Yariim by his side, he softly, sadly looked into the night.

"Where is she?"

"I feel….something." Yariim looked out into the night, her pink eyes gleaming, her whiskers silver in the moonlight. "I feel her."

"I wish I could." Raschid closed his eyes, yearning for some sense of communion with Sandhri. But Sandhri was life, and here there were only men preparing to deal death. "I try – but I can't seem to hear her."

"She is there, Husband."

"She is there. I have faith." Raschid breathed the cold, still air. "She will return to us.

I have faith in her. I have faith in Itbit, and I have faith in Meng."

"Faith…"

Yariim closed her eyes and nodded quietly. "I think the essence of all of this is *faith*. A belief that something better can be made. A belief that the future holds golden promise, if we can only hold onto a love of joy."

Horses galloped as an artillery team sped towards the river. The weapon and its crew were a lonely shape racing through the dark.

Yariim gave a sigh.

"What would Sandhri say to us right now?"

Raschid gave a watery smile, a rare light coming to his eyes.

"She would tell a story – the essence of which would be to "stop v'inging and kill the buggers'."

The Shah looked at his army.

"And so we shall."

With a firmer stride, the two crossed a rise. A steep, long slope rose from the plains to the river, then cut alarmingly down to plunge towards the river itself. Long millennia of erosion had worn the river Vistuul deep into the soil. Here, out of sight of the watchers on the hills, the army's true strength lay.

The men were busy.

Campfires burned, and here the Franks, the Pulski and Osranii infantry were at work. Slabs of river ice were being hauled up onto the banks to make long gleaming walls. Other men packed snow in front of the walls, ramming the substance hard into place. The result were walls thick enough to ruin arrow fire – and a stumbling block for enemy horse and infantry. The soldiers were delighted by the wicked cunning of the idea. Some men even threw snowballs as they worked.

The true magic was already almost complete. Osranii engineers had worked like demons through the day, disassembling houses from the village and laying entire walls flat upon the river ice. Vast ice slabs had been sawn from the river and used to make a floating bridge across to the other shore. Water had been poured to freeze as cement. The army had a bridge that led out into the dark.

Kakuzak cavalry were already crossing, walking their horses carefully. The ice creaked, but held. A gun team had already made it across. As long as the chief engineer was willing to stand at the middle of the bridge and drink to each passing unit's health, the men were happy that the bridge would never fall.

The engineers were tired – but the night's work was scarcely begun. The bridging wagons with their tin pontoons were the next in line to cross. Their crews were experts. With a crack of whips, the dray teams were started on their way, and the pontoon bridging companies cautiously drove out across the bridge of ice.

The army's officers had gathered in the great, echoing wooden hall of the village church. Entering the church, Raschid bowed to the light of the eternal presence that burned upon the altar, then turned to face his men. The room was cold, and mens' breaths steamed. But the men were well fed, warmly clothed, and their weapons were perfection itself.

There were tufekchi colonels from Osra, and Winged Hussars in plate armour. Knights from a dozen strange lands and Kakuzak chiefs. The McCallum had chosen himself pride of place at the table's foot, pouring whiskey for the officers with a lavish hand.

Saud the tiger met Raschid at the door. The Shah clasped the man's hand, seeing that the huge tiger was unhappy. Shadowed by the man, Raschid took Yariim to the table's head and placed his helmet quietly on the boards.

"Gentlemen."

"My Shah!" Huge, clad in armour thicker than a safe door and with whiskey in his hand, General Ataman bowed. "Your unit commanders."

"Excellent. Thank you all." Raschid took a whiskey from the McCallum's own hand, but did not drink. Instead, he saw to the careful unrolling of the map. "I expect that the enemy will begin an assault upon this position before dawn tomorrow. Here is what I intend."

They were all professionals – and even the foreigners were now steeped in the thorough, scientific methods of the Osranii. The officers leaned in to look at the map, brows creasing in thought.

Raschid smoothed the printed paper flat.

"Our infantry will fortify this position and prepare for a holding action. The army's entire shock cavalry complement will cross the river. That is the Brotherhood Knights, the Winged Hussars, the Guards and the Heavies. We are taking one regiment of Kakuzak scouts, and half of the galloper batteries." The Shah drew a route upon the map with one mailed finger. "We will cross to the far side of the river and proceed three miles downstream, hooking behind the enemy army. Screened by the woods *here*, we will construct a pontoon bridge and re-cross the river." The finger tapped on the map. "We will remain concealed until we are certain that the enemy army is entirely engaged. The enemy must be completely drawn into the river cul-de-sac. We then become the hammer to the defending force's anvil, attacking the Tsu-Khan from behind." He pushed the map aside. "Our objective is the total destruction of the Khanate army, and the death of the Tsu-Khan."

The heavy cavalry officers studied the map. Osra's infantry colonels looked grim, anticipating the fight to come. Raschid spoke to them.

"We will need you to hold this position against any odds for as long as it may take. When you feel the time is ripe for us to cross, you will signal us with rockets. Three green rockets fired vertically in succession. The signal will be repeated by a signal team the cavalry will leave half way back along our route of march." Raschid looked at his commanders. "The defending force is under the command of General Ataman. The right wing will be commanded by the Grand Constable. The left wing is under the command of Queen Yariim. The shock force will be under my personal command.

"Are there any questions?"

Old Abwan – commander of the First Foot Guards and looking resplendent in his blue brocaded armour, lifted his grey muzzle to the Shah.

"Have you a time limit, sire? If the signal fails, will you attack in any case?"

Raschid placed crosses on the map.

"We will still leave hidden piquets on the far bank. Signal the piquets, and they will ride to tell us that it is time to attack." Raschid tapped the map. "If all else fails – then we are downstream. Send a boat."

"Yes Sire."

"Are there any other questions?"

Full of a seething, predatory joy, General Ataman looked up at his Shah.

"By this Saint George and by the tits of Buraq, we are going to slaughter the bastards!"

Raschid took up his helmet.

"Be aware that the enemy has sorcerous powers. Remember – silver weapons have been given to you. Remember, love of comrades is a shield against the dark. No matter what sorcery they try, they are servants of slavery. They lack the strength of love."

Looming huge and shaggy in the firelight, the McCallum poured whiskey and thumped down his jug. He held up his battered old tin mug, and the officers, Shah and Yariim joined him. The big man gave a growl.

"Lads! My Lady. A toast before we go!" The old man hefted his cup. "Here's to love and honour, faith and reason. Here's to those who guard the Light!"

"Faith and reason." The officers responded, drank, and thumped the mugs down on the table. Yariim drank, feeling the stuff burn like lightning down her gullet. Deeper down, she felt her stomach give a swoop of nausea.

Raschid looked at her in quiet concern.

"Is anything wrong?"

"Nothing. I will tell you another time."

Yariim took up her own helmet. The officers moved outside into the snow. Here, the long, long lines of cavalry were waiting. Winged hussars, their vulture plumes catching the firelight. Knights on armoured chargers, and Osranii heavy cavalry fantastically housed in mail and silk brocade. Meepsoori warriors in brilliant brigantines.

Saud looked unhappy. He stood beside Marwan, and the armoured camel looked about himself suspiciously and growled. A warhorse in full armour stood nearby, and the camel glared at the beast in suspicious dislike.

Raschid patted the camel, and turned quietly to Yariim.

"I can leave you only the things I have always trusted most." The tall Jackal passed the protesting camel's reins to his wife. "Marwan will look after you. Saud will protect you." Saud was unhappy to be letting Raschid from his care – but the huge tiger was no cavalryman. "And love. Always my love."

They kissed softly – embraced – and then Yariim let him go. Raschid held Marwan and whispered into the camel's ear.

"Look after her."

He went to his war horse and took the reins from a soldier. Waiting beside the other officers was a slim, dapper black rat with an extravagantly curved scimitar. Raschid clapped the man upon the shoulder.

"Spike – we are splitting off the light companies to form a reserve brigade. You're a Colonel." Raschid found an old one-eyed mouse at his side. "Marsuk – Ataman wants your regiment to hold the center. We're making you up to Brigadier." The Shah sought out the old hound who had served him as friend, bodyguard and soldier for so many years.

"Abwan – the Foot Guard regiments are yours. I'm putting the entire reserve under you. That's the Guard foot, the Guard Light – the Islemen and the converged light companies." The Shah pulled forth a golden chain and proffered it to the old hound. "You're a General."

The old hound stared. With a tear in his eye, he bowed.

"My Shah."

"And when this is over, find a wife. I want your children as companions to my son."

Raschid mounted, swinging easily up into the saddle. Ignoring the mournful protest from Mawan the camel, he lifted up his head and took a deep breath into his lungs.

"The air feels clear."

Riflemen raced past the headquarters staff, carrying boxes of ammunition. Turning to Ataman, Raschid grasped the General's hand.

"General Ataman – I leave the army in your care."

"Take care, Lord!" The huge man grinned with great crocodilian teeth. "And not to be hurrying on our account! Don't spoil our fun!"

Raschid took his lance and shield, settling himself. Without looking around, he spoke to a shadowy armoured figure hiding in the ranks of the guard.

"Saa'lu?"

"Y-yes, lord?"

"No."

Crestfallen at being discovered, the lemur girl crept her horse shamefacedly into the light.

"But…"

"Yariim will need an aide. Stay by her."

The girl looked up.

"Not by Ataman, Lord?"

"He has not proposed to you yet. His brain may have gone soft." Raschid walked his horse slightly forward towards Yariim and looked down at his wife.

"I love you."

"I love you, husband." Yariim held Raschid's hand and pressed it against her sapphire cheek.

"Defend the dream."

The Shah of Osra rode.

They followed him – the Grim, savage hussars of Pulski – the knights in shining white. Osra's blue-armoured guards, and the heavy cavalry in jingling plate and mail. They rode behind an armoured man draped in plain white robes who spurred his horse on into the darkness and the ice.

Yariim stood to watch them all go. She did not weep, for it was her duty to be strong. She did not fear, for fear clouded the mind. She watched her husband and all those noble horsemen slowly disappear, and then quietly turned back towards the army's fires.

"Saa'lu?"

"Yes, Majesty."

We have work to do." Yariim turned to go. "We shall be having visitors before dawn."

Chapter Twenty Two:

"Something is coming."

Meng arose, staring out through the cave mouth. The dark, stony gully had turned sheer black with night. He sensed something lifting and whispering through the air. He retreated a step to whisper hoarsely back towards the others. "My ladies! Something is coming through the air!"

Sandhri was walking, bowed over and leaning heavily upon Itbit, breathing hard. She lifted up her sharp face and seemed to sniff the breeze.

"Itbit?"

The green mouse looked up at Sandhri in alarm.

"Will Sandhri-bat be alright?"

"I can manage." Sandhri had been walking back and forth for hours. "See! See if the spirit fence holds!"

"But what will Itbit do if the fence be broke?"

"You v'ill haf to fix it." Sandhri leaned hard on the wall, her thin back bowed. "You v'ere Hassan's favourite student. So do v'at you can."

Flitting past the shrouded mummy in its niche, Itbit ran softly to Meng's side. She held onto his arm, craning to peer out into the dark. The hut was with them – huge and gleaming beneath the overhang of rock. The hut craned to stare at something hidden in the night.

There, out in the deep gully, Itbit saw dim figures move. Ghostly, skull faced things of rags and tatters, claws and blood were swirling through the scree. They sensed Itbit's gaze and gave a savage snarl, lunging straight towards the cave.

Itbit squeaked and jerked back. The spirits hit an invisible line and curved away, hissing and screaming in hate. The urine and the buried iron seemed to be keeping the enemy at bay. The spirits curved back and slammed against the barrier once more, coming back and back again, screaming out for blood.

Shaken, Meng stared at the creatures in fright.

"The barrier has held them." He seemed surprised. "I had thought it was mere superstition. An old wife's tale."

"Sandhri knowsies every old wife's tale in the universe. That's why she will live to be an old wife." Itbit backed away slowly from the spirits, her pink eyes watching to see if the fence would hold. "Itbit does not know if the fence will hold for long."

Evil spirits snarled and tore against the barrier. Suddenly something shot out of the mouth of the cave. A haze of ribbons, bells and bones, the spirit of the cave arced up to dance furiously in front of the savage ghosts. The barrier glowed. Each attack was blocked by the bristling cave spirit, until finally the evil ghosts screeched and crept away.

From deeper in the cave there came a sharp hiss of breath. Sandhri's voice echoed in the dark.

"Itbit! Meng!" Sandhri sounded in distress. *"Itbit – quick!"*

The two friends came at a dead run. They passed the mummy, overleapt the fire, and found Sandhri leaning on the wall, panting with a strange, high 'yip' in her voice. It was an entirely new sound. Fumbling, Sandhri wound her hair up into a knot, pulled it tight, and looked to her friends.

"C-come on. It's time!"

Itbit paled.

"No!"

"It isn't… isn't all just fun and play, my darling. But this also iss beautiful. I haff taught you much – and now I haff to teach this to you as well." Sandhri caught herself, squeezing her eyes shut and making her little yips of pain once more. She had managed to untie her tunic. Meng stiffened, and made a smart about-turn.

"My Lady! I shall stoke the fires and keep watch for the enemy!"

"Ooooh no. Come here!" Sandhri was brooking no evasion. "Meng – haff you effer seen naked woman before?"

The Panda blathered in embarrassment. "My Lady – I…. Well only once! But I tried not to look!"

"V'ell I need you to look now." Sandhri tried to remove her tunic, but failed. She put her back to Meng. "Help me! The clothes are making me choke!" Sandhri felt another hard contraction and caught Itbit for support. "Come on – get them off!"

He helped her, fumbling his hands against the tunic hem and lifting it out and around Sandhri's pregnant belly. He clumsily undressed her, and she leaned against him, resting her face against his chest. Naked, she clung to him, moaning and clenching tight as her body rippled from inside.

She held on tight to Meng, and he put his arms around her – appalled that any woman should be made to suffer so. He stroked Sandhri's hair and babbled something in her ear, letting her fingers clamp into his flesh without complaint. Sandhri stiffened, yipped for long, hard seconds – and then finally let go. Panting, she weakly held onto him. Meng quickly brushed her hair back from her face.

Sandhri kissed him. The feel of her breasts against Meng's front was shockingly soft and warm.

"Hokay. G-good man. Good man…"

The contractions were coming close and hard. Sandhri felt her way over to the far end of the cave. A ghostly, unseen presence seemed to glimmer overhead. Sandhri touched it with her hand and stroked it absently.

"Iss OK. Iss OK. He's moving. I feel him." Keeping a tight hold on Meng, Sandhri backed into the rear of the cave. "Alright. Here v'ill do. Meng – I'm going to squat. I need you to hold me from behind and support me – yes? You can sit on the shelf." The pain was coming back again. Sandhri threw back her head and swallowed hard. "I-Itbit? Itbit – get naked. T'ere's no spare clothes, and v'e can't ruin the only ones v'e have."

The green mouse stood just out of reach, biting her fist in appalled dismay. Helpless, she panted in fright.

"But Itbit is little! What can Itbit do?"

Sandhri fumbled for Itbit's hand.

"Itbit – I need you! He's coming out backv'ards. It will be safe, but I need you. You'll have to help to guide the baby out. His chin might get caught – so you v'ill haff to put your hand inside me and feel to see if it's OK." Itbit moaned, and Sandhri brought her close and buried her face into Itbit's ear. "Itbit. My-my son and I, v'e need you now."

The green mouse swallowed, looking into Sandhri's eyes.

"Itbit will not leave you."

Sandhri gripped Itbit and kissed her hard. She reached back to grope for Meng.

"Meng – You're going to hear an awful lot of swearing now!"

"I... I understand, my Lady." The panda sat the naked queen half on his lap and held her warm and tight. "Like this?"

"Good man. Good man." Sandhri took a grip upon his hand. "Shit – here v'e go!"

**

Raschid whipped his head about. A sharp sound had seemed to hover in the night – a Toraki bird hunting prey? He swiftly took off his helmet, aware that something somewhere was wrong. Tall jackal ears lifted, and he strained towards the sound, but it was gone...

He stood on a moon-shot hillside. Below him, Winged Hussars were passing in column of fours, moving as quietly as horse shoes and plate armour allowed. There was no talking and no sudden sound. The galloper guns behind them moved with a rumble, but the buckets and equipment had all been well wrapped in rags.

Raschid's force had cut the chord of the river's arc, moving behind the hilly banks and a mile behind the great bottleneck over the river. Now they were heading for the crossing point. A small, dark forest of fir trees hid the sight of enemy camp fires. Regiment by regiment, the force was gathering and being sent into concealment in the gullys by the riverside.

Horse hooves thumped into the snow as a rider galloped past the hill. Raschid lifted his hand, and the rider changed course and rode quickly up towards him.

It was one of Raschid's aides – a slim, slight young fox – Hanna's younger brother. The young man looked atrociously young as he saluted his Shah.

"My Shah?"

"How long?"

"The lead wagon broke an axle, my Shah." The boy had ridden so fast and hard that he was almost sick. Raschid signaled to his bodyguards to bring the lad a drink. "They are fixing it as fast as they can!"

"How long?"

"The artillery limbers use the same axle, Lord. Ten minutes at most."

Raschid tried to be patient. Fears and annoyances served no one. Accidents had to be expected. The pontoon wagons would come as swiftly as they could. Meanwhile the troops could be profitably hidden, fed and rested.

Raschid tried to estimate the time. Assembling the army's pontoon bridge might take three hours. It took far longer to disassemble and store the huge pontoons on their wagons, to retrieve the anchors that held the pontoons steady – to tie down the loads and get underway. Which was why the army had used a bridge of ice to first cross the Vistuul.

The night seemed clear, although clouds half masked the moon. Standing on a hill to watch over his men, Raschid looked to his magicians.

"Sorcerer?"

Four of old Hassan's best acolytes were standing with heads bowed in concentration. One man looked briefly up at the Shah.

"Shields are holding. They have spirits on the wind, but we are not yet seen." Old Hassan had chosen his men well. "They are concentrating on the main army."

An eerie light lit up the darkness. Men turned to see a streak of brilliant flame appear above the trees, dwindling out of sight. It was followed by another and another. Bright red flashes lit the undersides of the low clouds.

"Rockets."

Raschid spoke for the wondering leaders of the Brotherhood who had come to join the Shah. They had clearly never seen such a weapon before. <<Enemy Rockets. Not ours.>>

The fire escalated into a full artillery bombardment, lighting the horizon with streak after streak of rocket tails. The red glow came from far behind the cavalry – back at the distant river where the infantry held against the storm.

The Tsu-Khan was making his first attack.

Raschid turned his back upon the light.

"Clear ground for the bridge footing. Make sure everybody eats a meal. Keep everybody quiet, and no fires."

The boom and crash of far explosions seemed strangely unreal. His wife was there somewhere – his friends and followers. Raschid tried to put it from his mind.

"Eat. Rest." He walked his horse down from the hill. "That is the best thing we can do."

<<Jesu!>>

Islemen ducked as rockets ripped fiery trails through the air above and slammed into the snow. Wave after wave of light came screaming down from above, the rockets smashing into the ground around the Osranii lines. One rocket hit the church steeple and flew wildly off across the river. Others hit the ground and bounced into the air, exploding uselessly high. Still others hit the river, the empty snow, or merely flew wildly off at weird angles through the sky. But enough of them hit the wooden village to light up the night with fires. Explosion after explosion deafened the troops, and the rocket trails screamed like demons as they tore across the dark.

Osranii soldiers ran to their entrenchments. They had not been foolish enough to man the village itself, for it was a target big enough to draw heavy fire. But still the rockets took a toll. Ducking beneath a shower of earth, Yariim ran low, seeing runners from the village blown apart before her eyes. She found a team of gunners sitting underneath their guns. The men were watching the rockets and heaping scorn upon their accuracy, spitting in contempt. The sight of the men was calming. With Saud looming protectively over her and Saa'lu tripping along behind her, Yariim ducked beneath a cannon and yelled through the noise.

"You there! Where's Brigadier Marsuk?"

A sergeant rose and pointed through the fire flashes to a line drawn in the snow. Yariim thanked the man and ran on, coming to the end of a huge line of Osranii infantry. The men lay in the snow, their rifle locks protected by their coats. The rockets were hissing well over their heads.

A single figure walked along, outlined by the blazing village just behind. Brigadier Marsuk had two whole regiments deployed into line, and he showed not the slightest bit of concern about artillery fire.

"Lie down. Check your flints. Make sure you're loaded." The one eyed mouse walked steadily, gruff and unconcerned. He found one young soldier who had a wobbling flint in his rifle lock. "Loose as a good woman, boy! Screw it tight!" He walked on. "Lie down, check your flints, make sure you're loaded…"

Buckling on her helmet, Yariim managed to slow to a genteel walk. She used all her skill to keep her voice calm and unconcerned.

"Brigadier!"

"General." The Mouse gave Yariim a salute. "Here's where they'll hit."

Yariim looked back at the burning village. The blazing fires illuminated the pitch-black battlefield. The purpose of the bombardment had been to create light as much as chaos. She flicked a glance out into the open plains and nodded.

"They'll be coming."

"Aye. And they'll soon be going." The old mouse scratched beneath his eye patch. "With your permission, my Lady?"

"Carry on."

Out in the darkness of the plains, something glimmered. There was a distant sound that came through the blast and scream of rockets – a thumping, pulsing tidal wave that grew ever nearer. Marsuk planted his fists on his hips and signaled the nearest colour party to stand.

"The first and second infantry regiments will form two ranks. Close order. *Form – ranks!"*

Two thousand infantrymen scrambled to their feet. They were all manner of species – mice and rat, rabbits and foxes, ferrets, bears, aardvarks and weasels. Turban-wrapped fezzes were on their heads, and the breast pockets of their long coats gleamed with silver bullets. The men formed side by side in close order with their long rifles at their sides. They lined the ramparts of ice and snow, while behind them other men opened boxes of spare cartridges.

"Fix… bayonets!"

Each man had a long yatagan hanging from his belt beside his scimitar. The men drew the long, snaking yatagan blades and slotted them beneath their rifle barrels. Raschid's passion for innovations would finally be put to a destructive test. The men slammed to attention, facing out into the dark. A vast ripple of motion could be seen in the darkness – a tide flooding across the plains, revealed by rocket trails and powder flash.

Brigadier Marsuk always carried a rifle. He shouldered his way into the front ranks of his men.

Movement.

The enemy was there – a broad line of armoured bowmen on horseback. Arrows hissed out of the darkness, hitting the battlements, hitting snow and ice. Somewhere in the dark, an arrow thumped into flesh.

The enemy horsemen came on at a manic gallop. At two hundred yards, they were black shapes lit by the distant flames. They broke into a scream, and came on like an avalanche. The entire night shuddered to the thunder of their hooves.

Marsuk adjusted the leaf sights of his rifle.

"At one hundred yards..." The men fixed their back sights to the required range. *"Present! Individual rapid fire...."*

With a wild howl, the enemy flung themselves into the gallop. Their horses lunged forward shoulder to shoulder in an all-destroying wave. Marsuk took careful aim.

"Fire!"

The effect was apocalyptic. Two thousand muskets fired in a single devastating blast. Muzzle flames lit the night, and the air seemed to punch outwards in shock. In the darkness, horses reared and screamed. Riders sawed sideways, tripping other men. Bows and lances cart wheeled. Still, clouds of arrows came from the enemy. The air thrummed with arrows, and the Khan's men came on.

The Osranii reloaded with practiced efficiency. The men bobbed down, levered open smoking breeches and shoved paper cartridges home. The breech levers were yanked closed. Powder horns primed the firing pans. Flints cocked back, and the men stood to fire – some faster, some slower, but all of them reloading in four or five seconds at most. The next volley came in one huge blow, flailing at the stalling line of horsemen. Powder smoke coughed out to thicken up the night.

"Pour it in, boys! Kill the bastards!"

Saud loomed between Yariim and danger, sheltering her with a steel shield. Arrows flickered from the darkness, and one struck a spark from the shield. Making her way forward, battered by the deafening noise of rifle fire, Yariim shouldered through the ranks towards Marsuk.

"Marsuk!" He heard her. He had stains up the side of his face from powder flash, and seemed immensely happy. *"Marsuk – I have the first brigade on your right, and the frontier brigade at your left. The Guard are back behind the village. I'll leave a rider who can find me if you need support!"* A fresh rush of enemy came leaping their horses over the dying, flailing horror of the first line. Arrows ploughed into the Osranii defenses – hitting the ice wall. Here and there a man fell back, screaming or dead with an arrow buried in his flesh. *"You'll hold?"*

"Against cavalry?" Marsuk shoved a fresh cartridge into his weapon. *"We'll hold."*

Yariim left. The Khan was attacking the center. She left her dispositions as they were expecting the Khan to attack the far ends of the battle line once he thought Osranii reserves had been drawn into the fight. Ducking under a fresh storm of rocket fire, she went back behind the infantry lines.

Saud knelt between Yariim and the arrow fire, his shield held high. In the powder smoke and flames, the vast tiger looked feral and dangerous. He held a rifle in his hands that seemed no heavier than a twig.

Saa'lu ran forward and found Marwan, dragging the irritable camel over to Yariim. Saud kept between her and danger as she climbed into the saddle.

"Saud – I think we are out of arrow range."

"Raschid said that Saud should take care of you." The tiger was in a stubborn mood. "Saud will take care of you."

"Thank you, Saud."

The enemy attack was developing swiftly. Ataman sent aides to observe, but kept himself back behind his center, coordinating the overall defense. Yariim summoned one of her small band of staff, wrote out one of Raschid's printed report sheets and sent it off to the

General. She hauled Marwan around, took a telescope from its saddle sheath, and stood to watch the assault.

Marsuk's men fired like the furies. The front of their position was a rippling sheet of flame. The enemy horsemen pulled back, gathered, and then stormed fanatically forward again and again, taking unbelievable casualties.

They preceded their attacks with dense-packed shoals of arrow fire. Yariim saw her own men being snatched back. The enemy were trying to blast a hole that they could tear wider with their blades. Once in amongst the infantry, it would be all over in a blood-soaked minute.

A night attack had been a good idea. Although they did not know it, the Khan's men were denying the rifles their huge advantage in range. Here, bow and rifle were almost even. Yariim looked to her left flank, still expecting a second attack, and then rode back to her second line.

"Guns."

An artillery battery stood limbered up and ready. They men wore the dark uniforms of militia, and all bore Yariim's sky blue scarf about their waists. Their colonel rode eagerly to Yariim's side.

"My Lady!"

"Pass through the first brigade. Flank that attack, and open fire with canister." Yariim snapped shut her telescope. "I can give you one squadron of hill riders to cover your flank."

"Yes lady!" The artilleryman swelled with pride and called back to his battery. *"Queen Yariim's Own artillery will advance at the gallop. Move!"*

The guns charged forwards, accompanied by yelling bird riders. Yariim willed them into position, moving closer behind Marsuk's line as the fighting intensified. Arrows whirred and flickered past. Saa'lu joined Saud in sheltering Yariim, and the blue mouse had to let Marwan the camel push them both aside so she could see the action to her front.

Marsuk's regiments had been shorn of their light companies. He had a single company in reserve for each unit, and a third regiment in reserve behind the battle line. Yariim saw the darkness in front of Marsuk's left hand regiment boil with shapes. A dense wave of cavalry burst into the feeble light at a screaming gallop. The enemy fired bows with fluid speed. Osranii infantry were snatched back, and a gap was punched in the line. The enemy horsemen spurred for the gap, screaming wildly in victory.

Marsuk's reserve company charged forward, halting and firing a volley by platoon ranks. Hammer blows of lead smashed into the cavalry who had poured through the line. Again and again the clockwork volleys blasted at the horsemen – but more and more cavalry spurred for the rallying cries of their men. At the edges of the breach, infantry with bayonets fought to keep screeching horsemen at bay. The sound of steel on steel mingled with the relentless sound of dying horses and rifle fire.

"Aide!" Yariim looked about her, and saw Saa'lu. "Saa'lu! Here's an order sheet. Have the reserve regiment pass through the front line and blast those cavalry away."

"Yes, Majesty."

Saa'lu had a white steppe pony looted from a skirmish in the snow. Long and lean, wearing armour and with an unaccustomed sword flapping at her side, the girl rode pell mell into the dark. As the fight at the front line grew more frenzied, Saud reached up and passed his shield to Yariim.

"Yariim must hold this over her body." The big tiger cocked his musket. "Duck."

A trio of screaming cavalry hacked through the gap in Marsuk's line. They spurred forwards, bloody swords in hand, and rode straight at Yariim. Saud knelt and fired his rifle, blasting one man from the saddle. Then with a terrifying berserk roar, he charged.

The huge two handed sword swept up off Saud's back. He slewed into the snow in front of a charging horse, cutting the beasts front legs from under it. The rider catapulted to the ground, screaming in rage. Saud hacked down and split the man completely in two.

The third man rode for Yariim. She let Marwan turn into the enemy horse and crash into it chest to chest. She hid beneath her shield as the enemy's sabre flailed at her. Yariim lashed out and somehow hit his horse across the muzzle, and the animal staggered aside.

Marwan smashed into the wounded horse and shoved. The horse rolled under Marwan's armoured bulk, crushed aside. The rider went crashing to the ground. He scrambled to his feet, and then whirled as he heard a roar behind him. Saud's blade smashed down through helmet, skull and rib cage, killing him with a single savage blow.

Infantry trumpets blew. Drums marked the beat. With colours flying, the reserve regiment marched forward in two ranks, the lines of readied rifles tipped with steel. The colonel sketched Yariim a salute with his sword, then brought his men at a steady march, keeping his lines dressed tight.

"Bayonets! Bayonets, you bastards! No one stops to shoot until we're in amongst 'em!" The colonel – a scholarly aardvark with a pair of spectacles perched upon his nose led his men from horseback. "Charge! Charge!"

The line went forward with the ecstatic, ululating scream of Osranii battle cries. The bayonet line slammed into the milling cavalry, driving horses back. Rifles fired, and in the dense musket smoke Yariim saw a horseman physically lifted from his saddle. The gap in Marsuk's line was sealed – the milling horsemen driven back. The new regiment passed onwards beyond the ice ramparts, firing madly into the dark.

From the darkness to their flank, a sudden chain of explosions roared. Gun flash lit the shapes of Osranii cannon bucking backwards, the crews already running forward to sponge out and reload. Though only muzzle loaders, the cannon fired barrel loads of musket balls into the flanks of the enemy attack. The sound of small shot ringing from lances, sword and steel helms mingled with the butcher's sound of metal punching into flesh.

The advancing infantry regiment formed ranks and leveled muskets at the dark.

"Volley by ranks! Front rank... fire!"

"Rear rank... fire!"

"Front rank.. fire!"

The regiment stepped forward over screaming, dying horses. Bayonets flashed and swords scythed down as men dispatched wounded enemies. The rifle volleys punched smoke into the darkness, while on the flanks the cannons bucked and roared.

"Cease fire! Cease fire!"

The rifle fire died out. Osranii banners jutted above the smoke, and men moved forward through enemy dead. There were no more cavalry in the dark. Only screaming horses beating their lives out in the dark. The Osranii infantry drew back behind their ramparts, and the guns and bird riders returned. Yariim greeted each unit as it came. Her couriers returned one by one, and she sent them out again.

"Issue ammunition. Bring the ambulance teams forward." Marsuk seemed alive and well – but there were many Osranii bodies in the snow. A hundred? Two? The regiments would give her a body count soon enough.

Saa'lu was waiting. Yariim passed the girl a note.

"Compliments to General Ataman. Local attack in the village sector held. All regiments intact." The mouse suddenly felt tired and drained. "Well done, Saa'lu."

The lemur gave a shy smile, much smudged by powder stains. Yariim watched her ride away, then let Saud take Marwan's reins and lead her back away into the dark.

A thin line of grey lit the eastern horizon. It was not yet dawn, and already the dying had begun.

"Alright – *push!*"

It was a mistake. Meng was trying to be helpful, and instead, Sandhri gave him an earful.

"I know how to push! You t'ink I don't know v'en to push? I push v'en I want to focking push!" Sandhri suddenly arched her neck and heaved. Her flailing hand caught Meng's fingers, gripped like steel and almost pulped his bones. She gasped hard – grunting, clinging tight to Meng, her small body unbelievably taut and strong in his grasp.

Panting, she swam back out of the contraction in a string of swear words that considerably expanded Meng's Osranii vocabulary. Itbit's as well, for that matter. Sandhri shook her head, clearing the mist from her eyes.

"Push, push! Don't you tell me to push! Who's havink the baby here? You v'ant pushink, you do it yourself and let a lady v'ork!" The tirade cut short as another contraction came. Sandhri gave a snarl of sheer effort, but never once cried out in pain. "T'ere! He's coming out. Itbit? Do you see?"

Kneeling naked between her best friend's legs, her hair knotted back and panting with the moment, Itbit timidly tried easing in a hand.

"Itbit can't see anything!"

"Get your nose in there and look! I can feel the little bugger!" Sandhri heaved again. "Damn it! Shit...!"

She dissolved into yet more swear words that crossed at least four different languages.

The brass hut came crowding in to the opening of the cave, wanting to offer moral support. It made a mournful, anxious sound, striving to come closer, making the rock wall creak. Yipping as she hung in Meng's arms and fought for breath, Sandhri managed to fix the hut in her eyes.

"Not long! Not long now!" Wiping her own face, Sandhri looked down at Itbit. "Itbit?"

The green mouse heard spirits screaming outside the cave and looked towards the cave mouth.

"Those ghosts might still be out there."

"Who gives a shit!" Sandhri grabbed a handful of loose skin on Meng's hide, and gave a convulsive squeeze that almost jerked off his pelt. "Crap! Just put your focking hand in t'ere! Stop pissing about!"

Itbit obeyed.

"What if Sandhri tears?"

"I v'on't tear. I'm flexible ass an eel, and I whacked off while you buggers were outside before!" Sandhri bore down hard, teeth barred, pushing with a dedicated skill. "Jesus! God bugger it! There! You feel that? T'ere!"

"Itbit feels him!" Itbit seemed utterly shocked. "His bottom's there! Itbit sees him!" She squealed for joy. "We're having a baby!"

Sandhri threw her head back. She held on tight, shuddering for breath.

"I'm holding back! I...I can't do it long!" The skinny bat held back the urge to push. "You'll need to ch-check his chin! Help his chin t'rough!"

Meng looked down in a daze and tried to be helpful again.

"Lady! Y-you should concentrate on something else." Itbit had a look of total concentration on her face as she wormed her hand up inside her friend. Meng swallowed, about to be sick. "M-maybe you should tell a story?"

"I'm giffing birth, you idiot! I haffn't got time to bang out verses in iambic pentameter!" Sandhri would have said more, but a huge contraction came. "Shit! Itbit?"

"Itbit has him! She has him!" Itbit sounded utterly ecstatic. She worked firmly and carefully, covering herself in goo. "Here! Sandhri! He's here!"

Out he came – bum first and tiny, out into the world.

He slithered out easily, and Sandhri panted in triumph. Itbit eased the baby out into her arms, and wept ecstatically as she held him.

Sandhri looked almost savage – her hair plastered to her face and a feral joy swimming through the pain. Itbit delivered the baby straight up onto Sandhri's naked belly, and the bat took her son into her arms.

He was red hot and tiny – a little blind thing with fur plastered white and sticky. Huge ears were folded down flat against his head. Quite definitely a boy, the little creature hunted his face across his mother's breast, and Sandhri sobbed and held her son in joy.

Still holding Sandhri in his arms, Meng softly stroked her hair back from her face.

"May heaven shine and bless you. This humble one offers his congratulations on the birth of your new son…"

They eased Sandhri down onto the floor, wrapping her and the baby roughly around with robes. Itbit hurriedly tied the chord with her own hair ribbons. Still in a daze of adoring triumph, Sandhri bit through the umbilical chord with her own fangs. Panting, battered and bleeding, Sandhri looked up with tears in her eyes at her two friends.

"He's beautiful!"

Tiny little fingers clasped the air as the baby moved. Sandhri caressed him, unable to see too much of him. She lay propped in a rough bed against the cave's wall, looking as though she had fought an entire army. The fight faded from memory as Sandhri held her son.

"He's *beautiful*. Just beautiful…" Sandhri's head swam. She reeled, exhausted and panting, and drank water Meng held to her mouth. "Beautiful…"

They rested together, all dazed by the event. Meng fetched water, sponged Sandhri's face, then hurriedly banked up the fire.

Itbit was still at work with rags and water. Meng looked down, and leaned forward in alarm.

"She's giving birth again!" The sage almost died in fright. "It's twins!"

"It isn't twins." Itbit looked up at the man in scorn. "Afterbirth."

"Af…" That did it. Sage or not, Meng finally felt sick. "Oh…"

Outside the cave, the spirits still screamed. Sandhri was half dazed, lovingly cradling the infant against her heart. She caressed ther baby, groped weakly for Meng, and fumbled for his hand.

"Meng?"

"I'm here, my Queen." Meng held her hand against his heart, wiping her face tenderly in respect and awe. "You did it, my Lady."

"Thank you, Meng…" The bat closed her eyes. "My v'onderful friend Meng." Sandhri's breathing was ragged and tired. She was tired as hell, and far too excited to sleep. She took a better grip upon Meng's hand. "Meng – the spirits… out there."

Sucking in a hard breath, Sandhri opened up her eyes. Her voice suddenly grew clear.

"Meng – write our secret love names on stones – v'un for each of us, the hut and the baby. T'en split the stones. Hide v'un half off each carefully. Each of us hass to keep the other half off t'eir own name." Sandhri's head fell back. "Iss… iss hill magic!"

"Stones." Meng looked about. The cave certainly had a good supply of those. "Love names, My Lady?"

"True names. The baby's name. My name. For me, put… put *'Buru'shan'*. Black angel. My…my mot'er…" Sandhri sighed – just wanting to lie back and hold her son. Her beautiful son…! "And the baby's name. Just…just write his real name down."

She lay there, nestling the tiny baby against her heart. The panda rose and quietly moved back into the empty cavern. Itbit came to him. They held each other, looking at the sleeping mother and child.

"What do I write?"

"Private names. The first name you were ever given – or a name given to you in love." Itbit looked up at Meng, disheveled and utterly beautiful – warmed with triumph. "A name the spirits out there do not know."

The Sage looked at Itbit, and then quietly stroked her face.

"But where will I find a name of love?"

"From someone who loves you…."

She quietly stroked his face, and Meng touched her gently in return. Itbit kissed him, and he held her. They murmured names into each other's ears – held tight, then pulled away. Itbit grasped Meng's hand in her own, looking at him in love – tired and worn, elated and shy. Meng pulled away, and ran to find the stones.

He wrote in the practiced, flourishing hand of a sage – each brush stroke pure perfection. Soot and water were his ink, and a chewed twig was his brush. He stumbled forward to the hut, making a stone for it as well. With a great blow of a bigger stone, he split the name stones into two.

He hid them in the rubble of the fallen wall, burying them deep.

For the baby's name, he used the name he had heard Sandhri use before – the only name that came to mind.

…And when all was said and done, "Prince Sinbad" seemed indeed a name fit for a King…

Chapter Twenty Three:

The great standard of the Tsu-Khan had been raised upon the plains. Standing their horses in a dark, sullen mass, the commanders of the army looked to the red smudge of fire to the south. The distant village still burned, and musket shots still flickered here and there in the dark. Three tumans had been sent in for the night attack – thirty thousand men in all. A mere ten percent of the army, but they had been badly mauled, and the losses hurt the generals' pride.

The retreating units were bloodied beyond belief. A single Tuman had led the attack, and not one man in four had returned. The rest were dead out in the darkness – and the survivors were reeling in shock, with wounds and fatigue. The immense roar and flash of musket fire had hurtled men into shock. It was as though the gates of hell had opened, and the apocalypse had come. The Osranii had fought with demoniacal precision. Men and horses had died beneath the rifle flashes, or had been blasted apart by the mincing machine of the guns. The survivors had been withdrawn to focus their minds upon the Tsu-Khan's glory and re-learn the sacred mission of their lives.

The other two tumans had been separated from the first in the dark. One had arrived late, only to be entangled in the first tuman's retreat. Another had attacked a far end of the line, where it had been beaten back by bows and by infantry armed with pikes. Sitting on their armoured horses, their mood black and foul, the Tsu-Khan's generals watched the survivors return, and stabbed dour thoughts towards the Osranii battle lines.

General Gurad seethed with hate.

"We have lost ten thousand effectives. Half of those will merely be lost in the dark." His demon horse sensed his impatience and stamped its hooves. "Five thousand dead is no matter. We have felt out the disposition of his battle lines."

A tall, slim chieftain of Steppe Nomads looked at General Gurad. The man was a steppe wolf – long, thin and dusty grey.

"I do not understand why your wing made a night attack."

"It almost succeeded!" Gurad whirled on the other man. "It was a chance to split them apart before the dawn assault!"

"Almost…" General Tsai-Chi had come from the foot of the hills, where his own tumans and the Yellow Empire infantry had camped. "A near success is still a failure." He looked to Gurad as the bigger man went for his sword. "Do not attempt it. The Tsu-Khan would have no mercy on your dead soul."

Banners made from womens' scalps stirred in an unseen breeze. Vague, skeletal shapes looped and twisted in the dark. The demon horses stirred and stamped, tossing their dark manes. Eerie corpse-lights burned and flickered at the tips of steel blades.

The Tsu-Khan had come.

He came in a perceptible chill of power – a cold, surging force that gripped the officers and made each man straighten in his saddle. The soldiers turned their horses and bowed, total dedication gripping their very souls.

Riding his small, pale horse, the Khan moved forward shadowed by his battle banners. The two great standards of the army were topped with living skulls that hissed and champed their jaws. Each skull had been taken from a screaming, living king, and their ghosts still jerked and danced in agony above.

The Khan's black robes stirred softly in the pre-dawn breeze.

It was still dark. A grey haze of dawn stole inward from the east, lighting the icy river a translucent silver. The lands beyond were nothing but black hills and silent forests.

The Tsu-Khan lifted his long muzzle and slowly breathed the winds that blew chill and icy from the plains.

"We have made a night attack."

Gurad bowed, his bluster gone.

"Sacred Person – I thought it wise to probe for weakness in the enemy lines. Three tumans attacked at night. Two of the units sustained casualties."

"Two damaged tumans..." The Tsu-Khan's voice showed neither regret, anger or compassion. He looked towards the burning village in the river bend below.

"Did we discover weaknesses?"

Gurad bowed lower. "The Osranii Shah was ready for us, Sacred One. Our force was blunted." The General bowed his shoulders. "But we have fatigued them. Their night has been spent in action, and our own main army is well rested."

The Khan's main army waited on the far side of the hills, outside of the cul-de-sac. A mere hundred thousand men had come to the south side of the hills, and they stood before the Khan like a dark, dire ocean. Horsemen spread from the east bank of the river to the west, packed deep enough to totally obscure the snow. Dark as it was, their banners made tall silhouettes against the creeping light of dawn.

The Khan spread his hands open, his eyes upon his enemy. He spoke as a man totally preoccupied with deeper thoughts.

"Recommendations?"

General Tsai-Chi made a short nod of his head.

"Holy One! We must attack at dawn. Allow me to lead an assault against one end of their line. A cavalry body could be kept back in reserve. If they attempt to swing in from the center to aid their flanks, then, the second body can attack."

Gurad derided the idea.

"Limited attacks are not our way! The army of the Tsu-Khan hits like a storm! Total impact – total destruction of the enemy. We must engage at all points of their line at once and smash them utterly apart!"

The steppe chieftain's quiet voice drifted from the gloom.

"Gurad has already shown the folly of piecemeal attacks." He ignored the dire glare from Gurad. "We have the numbers to attack their entire line at once. This means that different sectors cannot send reserves to their neighbours." The man looked to the distant Osranii lines, now lit by a crisp, clear dawn. "A total assault will achieve a breakthrough somewhere in their line. Once a single gap appears, it is over. Our cavalry will simply claw them apart."

Tsai-Chi was unimpressed.

"We are still unsure of their capabilities. No one has yet faced the Osranii main body in battle. By an oblique approach, building pressure in a well supported...."

Gurad chopped down his hand.

"You are planning a battle that might last for days! We have three hundred thousand men! An all-out assault could give us victory before noon!" He pointed angrily at the troops below. "We still need fodder for the horses! Every day of delay weakens us against the Franks!"

The Tsu-Khan quietly held up his hand. All talk immediately ceased. His generals turned to listen in intent, intelligent devotion to their lord's commands.

The Khan leaned forward in his saddle and quietly inspected the enemy battle line. The sun rose above the nearby forests, and the first slivers of light slanted low across the battlefield. The ground before the village was scorched black and littered with dead animals and men.

The Khan rose.

"We shall use speed of horse." He signed to his couriers and aides. "Bring the entire army over the hills. We will attack across their entire front – six tumans wide. Six more tumans immediately behind the main assault to act as reserves." The Khan threw back his robes. He was armoured in blood encrusted finger bones, with a black sword at his side. "Let us see how this Scholar fights the Lord of the Dead."

He slowly turned his head to stare at General Gurad.

"Gurad. You will personally lead the assault."

The General gave a mad, savage grin of his fangs. He shot a look of triumph at Tsai-Chi, and spurred away to gather his officers. In the hills far behind, the great war drums sounded, summoning the entire army over the hills and onward to the slaughter of Osra.

Dawn lit up the snowfields a brilliant white. Gazing at the enemy, the Tsu-Khan spoke into the wind.

"Tulu Begh."

The slim, dapper mouse spurred forwards. Much recovered, dressed in immaculate armour and with a quiver full of arrows hanging beside his slim, plain sword, he made his obeisance to the Khan.

"Holy Person!"

"Tell me, Tulu Begh. Where would he be, this Shah of Osra?"

"With his household troops at the center of his army, Sacred One." Tulu Begh pointed to the vicinity of the burned village miles away across the plains. "Osranii Royal Guard regiments dress in royal blue. He will be with his Guards." The Prince spoke in hate. "He is the soul of Osra. Slay him, and their cause collapses."

"We shall slay him, and reap in his soul to be our play thing..." The Khan searched for sign of blue uniforms miles away across the plains, but saw nothing.

Tulu-Begh had other means. He unshipped the brass telescope he had brought from Osra long ago, and trained it across the plains. He steadied the telescope on the shoulder of a bodyguard, and peered through the lens.

The enemy lines two miles away were suddenly sharp and clear.

A great fan of dead bodies radiated outwards from the burned village. Here and there, huge rockets stood jutting from the snow, some of them still smoking evilly. The Enemy infantry lined the high crest of the river banks. Other troops must have been hidden in the dead ground behind...

On the left, there were Frankish banners. In the center, Pulski and Osranii. On the right... a forest of Osranii regimental flags. There were Osranii infantry in red fezzes and white turbans....Light infantry in greys and greens...

Blue. Royal blue stood out in the lens. It was a mere impression – a line of colour painted in the snow, but it was there.

Tulu Begh held his breath. No bigger than ants, individual figures moved along the enemy battle lines. Horsemen and cavalry... and there, on the right, a tall swaying animal that towered above the passing couriers.

"There!"

Tulu Begh pointed, his hunting instincts utterly alive. "There, Holy One! A White robed man upon a dromedary camel." Tulu Begh was triumphant. "The Shah!"

"Excellent." Teeth barred in a cold, feral snarl, the Tsu-Khan suddenly seethed with blood lust. He called out to General Gurad. "Gurad! The Shah is at the right of the burned village. Make that your heaviest point of attack!" The Tsu-Khan stared intently towards his distant enemy, willing death and destruction upon the Shah. "We shall draw him into battle, and we shall hurt him. When we have hurt him, we shall destroy him. With him dies his knowledge, and his hope.

"And then, this world shall be ours at last..."

The army came.

Tens of thousands of warriors moved across the hills behind the Khan. They moved in silence, filled with deadly purpose. Horses stamping, armour gleaming. Bows in hand and banners dipping in obeisance to their Khan, their cause, their living god. The Khan spread open his arms as if taking in their love, breathing deep and closing up his eyes.

"You are not an army of mere conquest! You are an instrument of will! You were created to fulfill the destiny of entire worlds. To break the bonds of mere mortality and create an undying empire!" The Khan turned to the south, towards the Osranii, and his eyes blazed with a pale blue fire.

"Go, my children. Kill!"

"Kill!"

"Kill!"

The army moved forwards. Behind them, the Tsu-Khan flung open ecstatic arms and embraced a living dream.

The river creaked and groaned as it flowed. The ice lifted to the surge of water through the river's center, and the hollow, mournful noises echoed in the dawn. The army stood silently, facing to its front. Banners flapped in the breeze, the sound strangely loud. Here and there a horse stamped; riding birds cawed raucously to greet the incoming dawn. But the sounds of ordinary life were gone.

Fifty thousand troops faced into the north. There were Osranii riflemen in ordered ranks – mice and rabbits, foxes, rats and hounds. Behind them there were the Osranii light cavalry – bird riders, horse archers and Kakuzaks, all kneeling low beside their mounts. Frankish pikemen were behind the front lines in reserve – the perfect instrument for hurling back cavalry. Longbowmen were waiting behind the riflemen, ready to add weight to their fire. Cannon batteries waited, gleaming in the sun. The men all looked north, towards the enemy.

At the rear, the Generals waited together on their mounts. Couriers, aides and bodyguards stood at hand. Hot bread had been baked, and the Osranii had broken open their last supplies of coffee. Men dragged carts forward to each regiment, throwing hot bread to the troops and pouring hot coffee into tin mugs. The scents of breakfast seemed intensely homely, and the sudden upsurge of good humour amongst the men was a balm. The men ate, the men drank and joked. The ranks broke as men brought food to friends and comrades. Yariim looked down the long, long lines of men – a thin line curving off around the river, finally curving in to anchor its flanks against the river banks. The numbers seemed awesome – thousands and thousands of men, all brought together in one place for this one fight. They seemed confident, laughing and professional. Yariim felt her pounding heart settling its pace.

The dead enemy from the night before had been hauled up against the ice ramparts. They had already frozen into a ghastly extra layer of protection. Yariim tried to remain focused on the job, and ran the numbers through her head.

Easily six thousand enemy had been killed. Her own losses had been five hundred men – small in proportion, but those men had all been sorely needed. The night attack had come close – but it had shown Yariim and the men that the enemy could be beaten. Firepower was the telling factor: firepower and tenacity.

General Ataman –a huge hairy man – sat on a huge hairy horse that seemed to be made entirely out of scar tissue and mane. He was scanning the horizon with a much-battered brass telescope. Beside him, the Grand Constable, Sir Huliam, tirelessly scanned the plains. He conferred with Ataman, and then rode to follow the wagonloads of hot bread being taken to his men.

Over by Yariim, Sir Randolph sat nattily upon a horse completely sheathed in silk and steel. The animal had a raffish air about it – as though it knew a dirty secret or two it half intended to share. The fox knight waved a hand beneath his snout as the ration parties trundled past.

"My lady – what is that stench?"

"Coffee." Yariim's attention was on her men. Troops were boiling water behind their lines and using the hot water to clean their musket barrels. She had to remember to bring up some firewood. "It is a drink we often have in order to relax."

"Ah. Relax." To Sir Randolph, the coffee apparently smelled quite, quite vile. "Yes – ah. A novelty from the east."

"Should you like some?" Yariim had been waiting her turn to be served with bread and coffee, but rank had its privileges. "You may find it to your liking."

"I shall remain content with wine, my lady." The knight gave a bow. "But I thank you for the offer."

Marwan growled, noisily chewing his cud. The camel had been fed by men from the Royal Guard, who stood in reserve beside the burned village. A party of guardsmen came past the three generals, carrying a cauldron filled with hot sausages. The men passed sausages to their commanders, and were soon joined by a group of huge barbarians all armed with titanic two-handed swords.

Their leader was grey as steel, and seemed to actually enjoy the cold. Yariim waved to him with her fan.

"My Lord McCallum!" Yariim was surprisingly fond of the huge old barbarian. "A second breakfast?"

"When I get bored, I eat, Lady!" The old man pounded on his huge belly. "If they take much longer, I'll have to go find some proper exercise!"

Preoccupied, Yariim looked out towards the ramparts of the dead.

"You are eager to begin, McCallum?"

"I am old, my Lady! I have good sons." He shook his head. "It's not right for a McCallum to die in bed."

Yariim lifted one elegant brow.

"Surely that would depend on what you were doing at the time?"

The Royal Guardsmen heard her, and they laughed. The laughter and good will spread. The old McCallum laughed and hefted his sword over his back.

"Not enough, my lady! Not enough. But seeing you makes a new man out of me!" He departed back to his men. "It's never too late to have a few more sons!"

From General Ataman, there came a sudden grunt of anticipation. The big man kept his telescope glued to his eye.

"Ha! That took you buggers longer than you expected, eh? Hard to move quickly when you have so many men!" The General stood in his stirrups. From the rise before the village, he could see clean over his entire line of troops.

The open ground to the north turned black with moving men.

The haze of light above the snow shimmered as countless thousands of the enemy moved forwards. They came first as a haze, and then as a black line that stretched for miles across the plains. Horses made a churning wave of oncoming motion. The riders were a dark mass tipped with gleaming steel. The rumble of hooves was primal; elemental and savage. It felt as though a force of nature had risen up to wage a war.

The enemy were coming in great strength. Used to seeing their standards, Yariim unshipped her own telescope and studied the slowly closing mass of enemy.

"Six tumans across – that's sixty thousand men." The blue mouse studied the oncoming line. "They'll have at least as many men right behind the front." The mouse carefully focused her lens on the center of the line. "Red tailed standards. They're Gurad's men. The Center banner belongs to Emir Had'idh."

"Had'idh!" Ataman was exultant! He anticipated the fight as a man longed for bed with a new-wed bride. "Stupid arseholes are coming at us mounted! They're going to use speed to cut down their closing time!"

He almost laughed as she slammed shut his telescope. "An easy one for the first attack of the day!" The big man stood in his stirrups and bellowed in a voice that boomed across the snow like cannon fire. *"All regiments – finish your coffee and Stand To! Ambulances to the rear!"*

Ataman turned to Yariim and Sir Randolph.

"My Lady. Sir Randolph. To your commands." The big hairy General saluted his subordinates with his massive sword. "God bless."

They saluted him, then turned their mounts. Sir Randolph paused to give Yariim a dapper salute, apparently immensely pleased that the Osranii had a female General. He rode off at astonishing speed, his horse still sniggering at its own private jokes.

The reserve division was forming into attack columns behind the village. The officers of the foot guards and the light infantry came running over to Yariim. The men clasped hands with their Queen, wishing her well – offering bread, coffee or sausages. Yariim took a little of each, riding amongst the men and touching well loved faces.

"Abwan! Spike!"

The old hound and the handsome rat awaited her. Armour jangling, Marwan strode over to the men and growled. Well used to him, they took the camel by the head and fed him sugar.

"My Lady." Dressed in his blue armour, old Abwan came up and kissed Yariim's hand. "Keep back out of the fight. And listen to Saud. He knows what he's doing."

"I do!" Saud sat on a ridiculously small horse, looking mildly offended. "I always do, but no one listens!"

"I will listen, Saud." Yariim kissed the huge tiger on the cheek – then Abwan, then Spike. "God willing, you will have a quiet day."

"God willing." Old Abwan held Yariim's hand. "We'll see Queen Sandhri today! She'll never miss a story's ending, never you fear." Abwan looked out across the snow. "Remember what she says, My Lady. Trust in the bounty of Allah…" The man passed Yariim a pistol. "…and keep a pistol hidden at your back."

Yariim accepted the pistol, then stuffed it into the back of her sash. With a salute, she turned Marwan towards the left flank of the army – her own command.

"Come, Marwan!" The Queen kicked the camel into a gallop across the snow. *"Yah!"*

Saa'lu came racing after Yariim, weighed down in a helmet one size too big for her. The lemur was followed by a trail of heralds, couriers and troopers – and Saud, whose horse was not quite up to the tiger's massive weight. They covered the long thousand yards to the left flank of the army, and Yariim met her Division commanders and led them forward to the men.

Generals of division went to their commands. Brigadiers sat on their horses between their regiments of infantry. The regiments finished eating their breakfast in full sight of the enemy, draining every last drop of coffee they could find. The men rose, put their cups and canteens away, and formed into rigid, close order lines. A fight against massed cavalry was no time for skirmish tactics. Ataman intended to face the Khan in two deep lines of riflemen, packed shoulder to shoulder and spitting out a dozen aimed shots per minute.

The regimental banners were unfurled, and bright silks streamed out into the sun. Osra's army was resplendent in its red caps and turbans – its uniforms of white and black, of green and blue. It made a bold, glorious sight against the dark oncoming mass of enemy. Yariim felt her heart catching in her throat as her men sent a prayer to Allah soaring up into the morning sun.

> *"Allah! God of battles!*
> *To the right, give now your strength.*
> *To the unrighteous, send now your wrath!*
> *Blessed be Allah, who gives each man the right to be his own salvation!"*

The enemy were approaching. They had closed to a thousand yards. Yariim could see individuals amongst the masses; silver armour here and there - a white faced horse. The enemy came in two lines: the first of skirmishers, loose packed and chafing, ready to speed into the gallop. Behind them, the bulk of the cavalry were locked tight together, ready to charge home with lance and sword.

From the Frankish lines, there came singing – alien, strange and beautiful. It made

Yariim's hackles rise. She turned to see the Frankish pikemen and archers with their helmets off, singing their hymns. A Frankish priest turned to Yariim and made the sign of the cross protectively over her. She touched her heart in acknowledgement, and gave the man a bow.

The brigades were formed with two regiments in the front line, and two in reserve. Yariim rode Marwan up behind her front rank troops. A bespectacled aardvark Colonel saluted her with his sword.

"Maximum effective range, colonel."

"Maximum effective it is, Ma'am." The man polished his glasses. He kept his eyes on the enemy and called out to his men. *"Prepare for rapid fire – front!"* The colonel's voice echoed across the snow. *"Sight for six hundred yards!"*

Saud shouldered his little horse forward to Yariim.

"Queen Yariim must not be in the front lines. The enemy will fire arrows at her."

He was right. Yariim's place was back behind the lines, directing the men. She slowly turned her camel away, edging back, but wanting a front line seat for the start of the battle.

The colonel sloped his scimitar across one shoulder.

"Stand... ready!"

The enemy horsemen came on steadily. Eight hundred yards, and now finally they broke into speed. With a wild cry, the leading lines of skirmishers whipped their horses into a canter. The skirmish line sped forward, bows at the ready, the horses weaving back and forth across the plains.

Yariim had seen her troops hammering pegs into the ground in front of them- range markers placed at one hundred yard intervals. The enemy line – a wave that seemed to stretch millions of miles wide – rampaged forwards, engulfing the first of the pegs. Snow flew up from their hooves, the earth shuddered and the enemy's screams rang wild and deafening in the air.

All along the allied lines, colonels raised their swords.

"Present!"

The long, dense lines of infantry seemed to take a half turn to the right as men brought their rifles to their shoulders. Twenty five thousand rifles – the pride of Osranii science – were lifted, glinting evilly in the light.

Out on the plains, horse archers screamed like banshees, and broke into a gallop. They wove madly from side to side, throwing up gouts of snow.

"Individual rapid fire...." Beside Yariim, the Colonel paused.... waited... saw the enemy pass the second range marker, and suddenly swept down his sword.

"Fire!"

The rifles fired, and the world dissolved in rage.

Chapter Twenty Four:

In the soft, grey dawn, the ancient cave slowly filled with light. In the fireplace, logs glowed with velvet coals. Warmth stole outwards past the rocks, and filled the air with peace.

In the quiet and the gentle warmth, Itbit and Meng made love.

It was loving, and it was beautiful. Slow and wondering – then passionate. When it finally was over, Itbit lacked the strength even to laugh or cry. Instead, there was only a feeling of absolute and total peace.

They clung together, Itbit lying softly atop her love, her long blonde hair streaming down about them like a silken sheet. She fell asleep with him still inside her, and for the first time in long, long months, Itbit drifted in pure, quiet joy.

When they awoke, they made love again – exploring, worshipping. Afterwards, they lay looking at each other, hands gently tracing the lines of each other's faces. Clothes and blankets were piled across themselves, keeping out the cold.

Meng stroked the soft fur of Itbit's cheek with the back of one hand.

"This one humbly proffers his apologies for acting in the manner of a fool."

Itbit simply looked at him in love. "Itbit thanks you for pointing out her errors."

They lay together, Itbit pillowing her head upon Meng's chest and listening to the slow, quiet beating of his heart.

Dawn stole golden fingers into the cave, caressing the pictures painted on the walls.

"You were wonderful yesterday. You looked after Lady Sandhri well." Meng caressed Itbit's hair. "I was so proud of you then."

"You wrote all those poems for Itbit." The green mouse lay quiet, no longer able to feel sadness or regret. "Such beautiful thoughts you wrote."

She moved, looking up at him and gripping his hand. He brushed the golden hair back from her face, and Itbit gave a rueful smile.

"A sage learns?"

"A sage learns." They put all behind them, and spoke of it no more. Meng smiled as he pulled Itbit into his arms. She rolled on top of him, adoring him, and they kissed. Itbit reveled in it, feeling things she had not thought possible. Lifting up her face, she nipped Meng and straddled him, letting him caress her naked fur.

"Itbit never thought Enlightenment was supposed to feel so good!"

The panda adored her with his hands.

"Enlightenment has a magnificent rear..."

Leaving them in peace, Sandhri tip-toed past the lovers' alcove. Shaky on her feet, but full of life, the bat carried her treasure out into the morning light. Her little son felt warm and tiny in her hands – his little face had his father's nose, his mother's ears, and gorgeous jet black fur. Sinbad made little mewling noises as he sought the warmest place in Sandhri's arms. Aching, tired and battered, the triumphant mother took her son out into the world.

The gully streamed with golden light as sunshine came through the fingers of the winter trees. The Cave's spirit hovered protectively overhead, but there was no sign of the Tsu-Khan's evil ghosts; dawn's light seemed to have chased them clean away. Gleaming bright, the huge brass hut crowded happily forward. Sandhri took her son to him, and happily showed the hut her little boy.

"Hey mister Hut! See v'at we made!" She caressed her son, looking down at him in total adoration. "He's perfect. Iss utterly perfect."

She sat in the rocks as bright sunshine warmed the snow. Sandhri stroked the cold brass hull of the hut, propping up the baby so that the hut could see. The cave spirit, all ribbons and half-seen rags, swirled down to hover above the child. Sandhri showed him off to both of her friends, reaching out to touch the spirit with her hands.

"V'e haff called him Sinbad. But his middle names shall be *'idn hutta, idn shaaru'* – Child of the Hut, Child of Spirit – because v'e owe the two off you so much."

The hut seemed to beam. Overhead, the cave spirit jerked back in wonder, then came closer to look at the baby, then at Sandhri. It seemed to change colours somehow, radiating a sudden, quiet joy.

The bat looked up at the ghost in wonder and affection, the dawn light streaming through her long white hair.

"Hey spirit – do you v'ant to stay t'ere in your cave?" Sandhri touched the spirit with gentle fingers, feeling it as soft as a ghostly moth. "If you v'ant, you can come v'ith us. T'ere v'ill be a palace v'ith a garden. In the garden, t'ere are frogs and flowers, ponds and children, and stories told beneath the quiet trees." The bat stroked the ghost carefully. "If you no longer v'ant to rest, then perhaps you might be happy t'ere?"

They all sat quietly together for a while. Sunshine streamed through tree twigs that sparkled with countless gems of frost. Sandhri reveled in the warmth amongst the snow, keeping the baby swaddled in against her breast. The little creature nuzzled her, his little face hunting, and then finally he suckled from her. He made little noises – quiet, happy sounds. Sandhri softly sang a song that somehow rose out of her memory.

She remembered her own mother, in the good times. A white painted house with a tree in the dusty yard... Chickens and a duck pecking busily through the grass. Her mother holding a neighbour's baby, singing the same song. She looked to Sandhri with a quiet, loving smile. Long white hair swirled in the breeze.

"Look, Mama. I did it." With tears sparking quietly in her eyes, Sandhri looked up at the sun. "V'e haff a child..."

Her mother's smile lingered long after the other images had gone. White snow glimmered in the sun. Gully walls shone bright where a painted house had stood. Tearful and peaceful, Sandhri wept a little, strangely glad, and sat in peace and quiet with her son.

Itbit crept softly out into the light – looking dazed and shy with the beauty of new discovery. Sandhri looked at her in love, and Itbit crept beneath her arm. Sandhri kissed her gently, and they sat together side by side.

Sandhri carefully passed the baby to Itbit. The green mouse marveled at the soft, warm feel of the tiny little body in her hands.

Meng came quietly from the cave, looking tired and wonderfully happy. He looked to the women and smiled, bobbing down to collect clean snow to melt over the fire. Sandhri kept a warm arm about Itbit, and watched Meng in approval.

"Itbit… V'at you v'ant in life, iss not someone to sleep v'ith, but someone you long to wake up next to." She held Itbit, and the mouse snuggled into her, happy and content. "To come awake and feel that person sleeping naked beside you. You hold them, look at them, and feel thankful that this gift v'as giffen to you. *That* is a treasure given to you by God."

She stroked Itbit's face, and the mouse looked up at her – embarrassed, and yet so happy. Sandhri looked into her eyes, and gave a smile.

"I'm glad it came out right."

A distant noise shook the dawn: a pulse, like a deep breath being sucked into the world's lungs. Long moment's later, a strange, elusive sound shimmered in the distance. It sounded like twigs crackling in a distant fire. Echoes lifted and shredded on the fitful morning breeze.

Meng scarcely caught the sound, but straightened in puzzlement. Itbit heard more – but Sandhri's tall ears locked onto the noise. She looked to the southwest, her eyes grey and intelligent.

"T'ey' ve started."

Itbit passed the baby back and stood, her big pink ears lifting, her long whiskers questing. She heard it properly now – sound of rifle fire many, many miles away. Something about the breeze made the noises ebb and flow, but here and there, there came a subtle pulse of cannon fire.

Sandhri gripped the rim of the hut's door and tried to stand. It took her two tries.

"Itbit? Can you get me a stick to lean on? I might need it later. Meng? V'e need the bedding brought into the hut." Sandhri looked to the spirit that fluttered anxiously above. The creature seemed all ribbons bright with bells. It suddenly swirled inside the hut and made itself at home.

"Meng – v'e haff a new traveling companion." The bat painfully made her way into the hut. "Can you please brick up the cave before v'e go?"

Itbit and Meng held one another and looked in trepidation at the bat.

"My Queen!" Meng blinked. "Surely we are in no danger here?"

"V'e're going to the battle." Sandhri had difficulty standing up; her backside was aflame, and her belly still felt like it had been kicked by a drunken mule. "Neffer miss a story's end, my darlings. Iss rude!" The bat made herself a nest of rags and blankets, and carefully sat down with her baby in her arms. "Hey – haff v'e got any food?"

The sounds of battle drifted into hearing again. The rifle fire was now one unceasing, endless blur of sound. Itbit ran for the clothes and blankets. Meng carefully bricked up the cave wall. With a last bow to the cave, he backed out and ran to the big brass hut, leaping nimbly inside.

The hut rose up onto its tall, sturdy legs, stretching out the kinks like a delicate great cat. Turning to the sound of rifle fire, it marched steadily off towards the horizon, its great feet ringing like a dozen temple bells.

Rifle fire was a constant storm of noise, the weapons blasting flame and smoke out into the air. A roiling cloud of smoke hung before the infantry, choking off the morning sun. Thousands of men stood in line, working their rifles with dogged efficiency. The men moved fast, loading, priming and firing, the rifles kicking back hard to blast yet more smoke into the dawn.

Inside the smoke cloud, a living hell was being carved out of flesh and bone.

The cloud churned as a living wave of hate sought to fling itself onto the Osranii line. There was a ringing sound as rifle bullets hit drawn swords and metal armour. A hefty meat-axe sound came back as bullets punched through living men. Horses reared and screamed, flailing at the sky. Riders were snatched backwards, blood misting in the air. They came forward, surging madly over the ramparts of dead. The dense black mass of enemy seemed never ending. It came in waves and surges a thousand men wide. Horses flung themselves madly at the Osranii lines, galloping through the storm of lead. Rifle fire snatched the riders back in ones and twos, spilling horses screaming in the snow. Arrows showered from the horsemen, hitting the ice ramparts, slamming into snow or ripping into men, but the relentless rifle fire flayed the enemy alive. The charging horses sawed aside, fear maddened and foaming. In their thousands they churned about in chaos, their riders trying to force the beasts on into the attack. The attacks disintegrated into nightmare, the solid masses of horsemen withering away into blood and screaming ruin.

And still they came.

The Khan's men screamed war cries, surging forward in the smoke. Arrows drifted in strange, slow clouds overhead. Yariim's artillery thundered, firing canister out into the smoke. Like titanic shot guns, the huge weapons blasted the tin cans of musket balls out over the snow, the metal striking into the enemy with a sound like pebbles smacking into a brick wall. The screams of horses, the yelling men, all churned into one hellish chaos that seemed to swallow up the world.

All along the allied line, the guns were at their work. The ice ramparts were flecked with black from powder residue and burning wisps of paper cartridges. Here and there a horseman made it right up to the muzzles of the rifles, only to be shot out of the saddle. One huge rider flailed briefly at the infantry with his sword, but a sergeant felled the horse with a stroke of his rifle butt, and infantry bayonets made short work of the fallen man.

The scene was repeated a hundred times over all through the allied line. Regiment after regiment, line after line, all standing in their places. The muzzles of the rifles were smoking hot, and men fell back to fit new flints or clear their priming pans.

Fifty yards behind each regiment in the front line, a second unit stood at the ready.

The heaviest enemy assault came straight at Yariim. The enemy had fixed on her command as their point of break through. Yariim watched the proportion of men falling back from her front line to clear their guns, and then signaled to her standard bearer.

"Signal passage of lines. Replace the front line regiments."

Division commanders saw the flag. Orders went to brigadiers. Up and down the rear line, orders echoes through the cannon fire.

"Line passage – march!"

The rear regiments marched forward in breathtaking precision. The front units edged into rows as they fired, each man taking one last shot and running back through the approaching regiment. The old front lines reformed their ranks and retired fifty yards. The new regiments fired a massive volley that smashed through the air like a thunder blow. Yariim stood in her stirrups to make sure the movement was complete. The enemy cavalry had not been able to exploit the pause in fire.

"Excellent. Have water, spare flints and cleaning tools sent to the men."

Saa'lu saluted and rode off. An arrow had cut her cheek, and the blood flowed unnoticed. Yariim turned back to watch her artillery at work.

A sergeant with a bloody bandage about one hand walked along behind the rear regiment of men.

"Don't cool your guns with snow! Don't cool your guns with snow! Piss in them if you can't get hot water!" The sergeant saluted Yariim in passing. *"Don't cool your guns with snow...!"*

If one had wanted a leader for a band of desert raiders, Sandhri would have been a wonderful choice. Devilish, wild and full of energy, she would have done an excellent job. But for tenacious, relentless infantry work, Yariim was a perfect commander. She stood her camel right behind the front lines, her eyes constantly on the battle. She kept the men in place, the ammunition moving, and never quailed as the enemy came on.

There were casualties in the Osranii lines. The ice ramparts were a godsend, but enemy arrows found their marks in ones and twos. Ambulances raced forwards – small, well-sprung carts pulled by fast ponies. They sped back to the medical tents and the sorcerers, carrying burdens of pain.

Still the enemy came on in one great screaming mass. Yariim's fist tightened around the handle of her fan. Beside her, Saud patiently held a shield to cover her from arrow fire. Her own regiment of artillery was to her front, working their sponges and rammers like demons, the ammunition parties running forward with budge-barrels of powder through a storm of arrow fire.

Further back behind the lines, Frankish infantry stood. Archers flanked a block of pikemen, and the men all stared in shock at the Osranii troops. The storm of fire poured out by the riflemen was simply numbing. The infantry ignored casualties and fought like demons, each man sticking in his place.

A sudden shower of arrows drifted up, hung arcing in the sun above the smoke, and plunged downwards. The arrow shower came thick and fast, scything into one concentrated point of the Osranii line. Saud gave a warning shout and pointed the attack out to Yariim. She took her telescope and tried to see what was happening through the smoke.

Dim shapes moved forwards – shapes on foot. The enemy were attacking on foot, leaping from their horses and taking cover behind the dead. A dense, impromptu swarm of bowmen was being marshaled, and the archers were showering arrows onto the Osranii line. Yariim saw a figure swipe off its helmet and clap a hand against one bleeding cheek: an orange, spotted hide gleamed in the sun.

"Had'idh!"

Emir Had'idh waved his sword, calling in more cavalry to dismount and add weight to his firing line. Out shot by the rifles, the archers were flung back, dying in swarms – but they were still managing to hammer one segment of the Osranii line. A dense shadow far back in the smoke told of a cavalry charge forming to take advantage of the crack in the Osranii line. Yariim slammed her telescope shut.

The retired lines of Osranii riflemen were frenziedly refitting flints or cleaning out their rifle barrels. Many of the men shook with shock. Yariim took one look at them, then rode the length of the line, reaching out to touch the hands held up to greet her. She rode

Marwan back towards the Franks, and found a knight in half armour awaiting her command.

<<Sir knight – please follow me.>> Marwan stepped into place beside the Franks. <<We're sending in a pike assault.>>

A courier arrived in a slew of hooves, breathless from his ride.

"My Lady! General Abwan wishes to know if you need support?"

"Tell the General we are not yet in dire need." Yariim was concentrating on the best route to the threatened point of her line. Marwan's long stride gave the courier's horse trouble in keeping up. "Thank him."

The Frankish pikemen were impressive. Armoured in plate corslets and steel helmets, they carried wicked spears with red-painted hafts eighteen feet long. The men fought in a phalanx sixteen deep, and in battle, they came on like a forest of spear blades. They marched in step, their armour clattering as they headed toward the arrow storm, and Yariim sat tall and elegant in her saddle as she accompanied the men.

Saud wrinkled up his nose.

"Lady mouse should lead from the back."

"From the front, I think." Yariim searched her lines, looking for other units that seemed to be disengaged. She saw artillery with her own colours flying. "Colonel Muradah! Can you spare a battery for a charge?"

"Allah is kind!" The Colonel whirled on his horse towards his ranks of brass muzzle-loaders. *"Yariim's own! Number one battery, limber up! Fetch your horses! Fetch your horses!"* The gunner colonel waved his scimitar. *"Prepare for an artillery charge!"*

Frankish archers fanned out to make a skirmish line. Bird riders mounted up and covered the pike phalanx's flanks. Marwan gave a great, anticipatory growl, and had to be sharply reigned in as he tried to surge eagerly towards the battle lines.

The rifle fire was deafening. The flash and shock of muzzle flames dazed the mind and eye. The pike assault passed through the rear units of riflemen – past litter strewn across the snow, and scores of dead and dying men. Arrows stood up from the ground like a forest of reeds, and stray shots began to fall amongst the pikes. They hit the tall spears and clattered harmlessly down, falling to the ground.

Yariim fought an urge to duck. The Frankish commanders walked with huge two handed swords, or with long rapiers and bucklers beneath the front ranks of pikes. The banners of the Sacred Order flew, each one shining with a smiling, lordly sun.

<<Assault step... march!>>

The front rank regiment of Osranii was near. Arrows hammered into the ice ramparts, spraying chips and ricocheting high into the air. Countless other arrows blurred overhead, humming in a vast, dark rain to fall into open ground. But the weight of fire was bringing death. Riflemen span out of line, clutching arrow wounds. Men were snatched back. One man winced as an arrow shot clean through his turban, staying wedged through his fez like a weird plume.

"Saa'lu?"

Yariim called out, but the girl had not returned from her last mission. The mouse sent other couriers racing forwards. The Osranii officers and sergeants looked back to see the pike regiment marching forward to the front lines. They called out to their men, and orders surged up and down the lines.

Out in the hell-swept cloud, the enemy had thickened into an ocean of men. Thousands of archers packed dense and deep were firing blindly through the smoke. Bullets whipped flat through the chaos, smashing archers aside, but Emir Had'idh screamed out orders, and still his men drew their bows and fired. He saw the Osranii line grow thin at the impact point; men wavered, and then the turbans went back down behind their own ramparts in a surge. Had'idh drew his sabre and screamed in victory, leading his men forward in the charge.

Had'idh's archers ripped out their swords and ran shrieking at the breach in the Osranii line. Cavalry came thundering in their wake. Like a massive hammer blow of flesh and steel, the Tsu-Khan's men hurled themselves towards their victory.

A forest came across the ice ramparts. Spears four man-lengths tall appeared, rank after rank. White banners emblazoned with a golden sun came forward through the smoke. The phalanx flooded down onto the plains, relentlessly advancing into the smoke.

<<*Charge your pikes!*>> Frankish knights on foot waved their blades forwards. The forest of pike points sank down. <<*Charge!*>>

The pikemen screamed like banshees and came forward at the run. Four rows of pike points jutted past the first ranks. The pikes slammed into the onrushing enemy like a battering ram, tossing men clean off their feet. The pikes shuddered with the impact – stabbed and twisted, the blades coming back bright red.

The phalanx surged forward, the ranks wavering as the men stepped over bodies. The Khan's men fought back with swords, hacking hopelessly at the pike points that stormed savagely forwards. Emir Had'idh took a pike thrust to one leg and screamed defiance, trying to slash a way past the pikes and into the men beyond.

Had'idh's dismounted archers broke and ran backwards, trying to reach for their bows, but the pikes were fast behind them. An instant later, the Khan's cavalry rampaged out of the smoke. They came in a scattered mass, sabres drawn and screaming war cries. Horses slammed into the pikes and died, or pulled up in panic, tumbling riders to the ground. The first surge of cavalry balked, only to have the rearward ranks crash into them from behind.

<<*Onward! Kill the bastards!*>> A Frankish knight waved on his men. He cut at a fallen cavalryman who tried to spear one of his men. <<*Forward at the march!*>>

Yariim rode beside the phalanx, feeling like an actor in a play. The men around her knew what they were doing. More and more cavalry came thundering out of the smoke, hitting the hundred-wide phalanx in piecemeal attacks. The pikes went forward. Here and there, arrows swarmed flat out of the smoke. Some hit pikemen's breastplates and ricocheted. Some cut pikemen down. None of it served to stop the relentless forward march.

The enemy surged and churned in a chaotic mass about the phalanx. Osranii bird riders covered the flanks, and Frankish archers fired. The pressure of the attack simply shoved the Khan's men aside. Yariim stood in her saddle, elated and overjoyed.

There was a sudden scream of hate. Bird riders surged and fought a mad melee with Khanate cavalry. A knot of armoured horsemen cut their way through, and charged screaming straight at the flanks of the phalanx. Yariim saw the attack, found a group of archers standing at her back, and waved them forward with her fan.

<<You men – follow me!>>

Marwan sprang forward, released at last. The big camel charged, hurtling his massive weight of armour at the enemy. He crashed into a horse and tossed it aside, then suddenly Yariim found herself sword to sword with the enemy.

They were big men and they knew what they were doing. Yariim yelped and shielded herself as a sabre crashed against her blade. She swung with all her strength, and hit an enemy horse, cutting off its ear. The horse reared, and Marwan instantly had his teeth in the poor beast's throat. He shook the horse like a doll, and the rider fell screaming to the ground.

"Witch!"

Had'idh was amongst the enemy riders. Frankish archers ran into the melee, hurtling themselves at the horses and grappling riders to the ground. Daggers rose and fell in a vicious gutter fight. Had'idh skipped his horse contemptuously past the infantry. He drew his sword, raked back his heels, and charged screaming straight towards Yariim.

Marwan whirled, snarling, ready to kill Had'idh. The Emir sawed his reins sideways, and his horse careened sideways straight into Marwan. The camel snarled, side stepped, and staggered as he trod upon a fallen horse. A blade slammed against Yariim's sword, and she fell from the saddle and crashed into the snow. Her sword went spinning from her hand.

Had'idh turned his horse and charged straight at Yariim. He gave a howl of triumph, raising his voice into a great bloodthirsty scream.

"Death to the Queen!"

Yariim pulled the pistol from behind her sash and fired. The bullet smashed into Had'idh's throat, blasting out through the top of his skull. He rode over her, the steel-shod hooves of his horse clipping Yariim's shoulder. The mouse cried out, then felt herself lifted from the snow by Saud's huge hand.

An Osranii voice bellowed orders through the screams and rifle fire.

"Ram your pieces!... Prime your pieces!...Aim and fire!"

A shuddering thunder of explosions came one after one. Artillery was firing, blasting canister into the gun smoke. Blood and horror misted through the air as the divan's artillery fired from the flanks of the melee.

Master gunners skipped back and jerked their lanyards, and the flintlocks on the cannon snapped down. The huge cannon bucked backwards, firing canisters packed with musket balls point blank into the enemy. Entire files of cavalry were thrown backwards, torn apart into a horror of metal, flesh and bone. The shock of impact slammed the charging horsemen aside, tangling them into a churning mass of horses and frightened men.

"Fire!"

Yariim stood on her own feet, steadied by Saud's huge, gentle hand. Her shoulder burned like fire, and her hand felt numb. She still held the smoking pistol in her fist. She watched her artillery pivot and blast fire into the flank of the Khan's main attack. The pikemen stood their ground as the rifle smoke slowly cleared.

The enemy had gone.

They were racing back across the snow – a mass of horses, riders and stumbling, wounded men. An insane carpet of dead, of blood and offal lay all across the snow. The rifle smoke drifted skywards as all along the Osranii line, the infantry ceased fire.

Cheers sounded – distant at first, and then spreading wildly down the line. Men ran to the ramparts and stood waving their turbans, cheering their survival – jeering the fleeing enemy. Yariim swayed, then saw Marwan pacing gruffly over to her. The camel knelt in the snow, annoyed at having lost his rider. Yariim mounted gingerly, and Marwan swayed her back aloft.

The pike phalanx had come three hundred yards out of the line, literally crushing everything in its path. The line of destruction looked like a road of death across the snow. The Frankish soldiers cheered, and the artillerymen threw their caps into the air. Tired and drained, Yariim watched the last of the enemy run away.

The northern horizon was black with men. The Khan had two hundred thousand men still in reserve. Yariim looked to the vast mass that began slowly approaching, and waved a hand at her men.

"Well done. Pull back. Bring your wounded back."

It was only two hours after dawn. The Khan's first attack had stalled –
- and the second was already on its way…

Out on the plains, the Tsu-Kan watched almost half of his army wither away. Twelve tumans – a hundred and twenty thousand men – rampaged forward toward a ludicrously thin line of infantry. The Osranii lines had erupted into smoke; raw violence of unbelievable scale had smashed into his men. A smoke cloud had hidden everything from view as unit after unit charged into an inferno, never to return.

Gurad's attack had failed. An hour of hard fighting ended when the Osranii musket fire trailed away. Fleeing, shattered cavalry came stumbling from the smoke, riderless horses racing madly ahead and dripping blood across the snow. Shocked survivors staggered and fell. Dying men fell in their tracks. The dead numbered in their thousands – and the Osranii cheered.

The Tsu-Khan gripped his reins and stared towards the drifting cloud of powder smoke. He saw his defeated General leading the survivors. The Khan leaned to murmur quietly in the ears of his closest guards, and the riders sped away.

Summoned by a rider, General Tsai-Chi rode up and bowed before his Khan.

"Holy Person."

"General Tsai-Chi." The Khan seethed with an implacable, cold fury as he stared at the Osranii. "You will make your attack at once."

"Yes, Sacred One!" The eastern General rose in his saddle. He turned to bark orders to bring up the infantry. "It shall be done!"

"Excellent." The Khan gestured, and his guards came forward. They held Gurad's severed head impaled upon a spear. "Gurad has volunteered to lead your men."

The Khan's army had twelve fresh tumans of cavalry, sixty thousand infantry, plus the Khan's ten-thousand strong Black Guard. Leaving the guard behind, Tsai-Chi signaled to the leaders of his men, and took the remaining army of the khanate on across the plains.

The General knotted his armour tight, and rode on into the certainty of victory.

The sounds of battle were shockingly loud, and came without a cease. Rifle fire rose to a mad crescendo, never slackening. The sound went on for what seemed like hour after hour, while the Shah sat upon his horse and looked steadily to the south west.

No signal rockets were fired. No riders came. And so the Osranii hammer blow bided its time.

A pontoon bridge had been thrown across the icy river. Anchors had been towed upstream to anchor the great tin-plated floats. Planks had been laid, and a great felted roadway rolled into place. The bridge thrust straight across the river behind the Tsu-Khan's men, and it shuddered as the cavalry crossed in droves.

Armoured men led their horses by the reins, walking their beasts across the deadly river. Kakuzak riders had fanned out at the other side, hiding in cover to watch for the enemy. Armoured knights were already crossing, to be followed by regiment after regiment of winged hussars. The bridge crossing was two hours behind schedule. Raschid tried to keep a veneer of calm

Frozen engineers shivered, wrapped in horse blankets. They were forbidden a fire, but Raschid did all that he could. Chunks of ice swept down river had knocked an anchor free, and the center of the bridge had been almost swept away. Men had gone into the water to save the bridge. Raschid's sorcerers were busily trying to treat the half-frozen men.

The distant battle shuddered the sky with its violence. Raschid lifted his face to the sky, wondering what the battle was like. He had brought a new age to the battlefield; perhaps he would be remembered more for the slaughter he had wrought than for the good things he had made...

The Prince of the Pulski rode up to join Raschid. He looked anxiously off toward the battle.

"My Lord! Do you think the enemy is fully engaged?"

"No." Raschid's horse stamped a hoof, and the armoured jackal quieted the beast with a pat of his mailed hand. "No- Ataman knows his art."

Quite suddenly the sounds of battle faded away. The silence was shocking. Every man had been listening to the fight, and now faces turned in their thousands towards the silent battlefield. Troopers halted midway across the bridge, searching for the sound of war.

"The Tsu-Khan is being taught a lesson in firepower and dedication." Raschid's voice carried to the staff who waited nearby. The words were echoed out to his men. "Listen."

Faintly on the breeze, there came the sound of cheers. The voices drifted, surged and boomed. It did not seem like the sort of sound that might come from the army of the Khan.

With his eyes looking towards the sound, Raschid spoke quietly to the air.

"Well done, you three. Well done."

Twenty thousand of the finest heavy cavalry in the world were crossing the River Vistuul. Raschid turned to watch his own Royal Guards file onto the bridge, and lifted up his hand.

"Cross the bridge. Form up, and then dismount. Rest your horses! Rest your horses!"

The battlefield remained a silent mystery. Raschid eased off his helmet and let the cold river breeze hiss through his fur. His long-nosed face searched the south, back along the river, and then turned quietly away.

The general staff were the last men to cross the Vistuul. Raschid dismounted and quietly led his horse into the shadows of great, silent woods, and then went to make the rounds of his men.

The troops ate. The horses were fed from bags of corn laboriously transported from Osra, so far away. Even in the snow, the corn still held a faint smell of summer sun and desert palms.

In the distance, the sound of cannon fire suddenly crashed out again. It came faintly – like a far away thunder clap. The intensity never varied, remaining at a constant crackle and boom.

Horses stamped. Men walked about the lines, their armour jangling. Here and there low voices murmured, but otherwise, the cavalry were silent. The men all watched towards the distant battle, trying to read the flow of sounds.

Something flickered in the sky. A moment later, three small streaks climbed up against the sun, bursting into green showers of stars. The signalers on the river bank had repeated the rocket signal sent up by Ataman and Yariim. Raschid watched the green stars shower slowly through the sky, and then reached up to grab the armoured neck of his horse.

"Mount up."

He swung himself up into the saddle, his body springing up despite the huge weight of his metal armour. Raschid draped his robes in place, slid his steel shield onto his arm and took his lance in hand. The Royal Standard was unfurled, and with it were the banners of the Pulski and the Sacred Order. All up and down the lines, the officers called to their men.

Twenty thousand cavalry mounted in a mighty crash and clatter of steel.

"Mount up in columns of march! Mount up in columns of march!" The units were deployed in line as they would be for battle. The horses all then made a turn to the right, and the battle formation instantly became long marching columns. Raschid cantered along the long, long lines, seeing the winged hussars with their dark plumes of vulture feathers – the Knights of the Brotherhood of Light in gleaming, polished steel. Osra's heavy cavalry were there, resplendent in plate and mail, silks and velvets, with pistols, carbines, lances bows and shields. Meepsoori riders, their faces covered up by mail, readied their *chakram* quoits and lances. The Kakuzak riders fanned out to guard the flanks, and Raschid reached the column's head with banners streaming in the wind.

"At the fast trot – march!"

Twenty thousand horses moved. The crash and clatter of iron shod hooves roared like thunder. Lances streamed forwards, banners lofted in the breeze.

With a scholar at their head, the finest cavalry in the world rode towards the sound of the guns.

Chapter Twenty Five:

Rifle fire roared. The breeze had changed, blowing back towards the river, and gun smoke whipped back from the Allied lines. The din was something you became used to. Yariim saw General Ataman arrive with his staff, and by leaning in towards him, she could hear him loud and clear.

The entire battle line along Yariim's front was once again engaged. Her infantry blasted lead into the enemy. Elsewhere, the Osranii were standing quiet: Enemy cavalry to their front were hovering just out of effective range. With a screen of cavalry, the Tsu-Khan was effectively pinning two thirds of the Allied army impotently in place.

The incoming attack against Yariim was being made with infantry. Massed pikemen were still twelve hundred yards distant, being driven forward by vicious officers with blows of whips and swords. A vast screen of skirmishing crossbowmen – easily twenty thousand men in armour – were rampaging forward, screaming like banshees as they tried to close the range. Osranii rifle fire was ripping into their ranks, hurling men backwards and melting their ranks away.

Behind them, forty thousand pikemen and halberdiers marched fast – heading in deep columns straight towards Yariim's line. They were Yellow Empire soldiers, and they came on like men possessed. Ataman reigned in his horse and looked out at the incoming attack, then turned happily to Yariim.

"They don't like you!"

"I'm an artist!" Even in mail, Yariim's figure was arresting. "Even a negative audience reaction is still valid emotion!" Her rifled cannon were firing. Shells and solid shot ploughed into the vast, teeming enemy attack columns. The oncoming infantry simply seemed to soak up the shot. Their packed ranks barely rippled as each shell punched home. "This time they're doing it more cleverly."

"Not cleverly enough!" Ataman saw what Yariim was doing. Her muzzle loading cannon had been withdrawn and massed into a single battery of forty guns, wheel to wheel. She was planning to concentrate her artillery to make a savage hammer blow against the incoming attack.

Ataman approved. He leaned in to bellow into Yariim's ear as artillery bucked and roared.

"I am ordering an advance of my center and the right." The big general pointed out the movements he intended with one scorched hand. "We'll make a rifle rush, get three hundred yards closer and open fire. We'll try to force them to attack or bugger off!" He pointed back towards the village. "That will open up a gap between the center and your troops. I'm giving you the reserve division! The Guards and the Islanders. Have them move forward into the gap, pivot left, and attack your enemy in the flank!" The huge general leaned forward. "Do you see what I mean?"

"I see it. Go!" Yariim had her fan in hand, and was directing a racing artillery battery towards its place. "Thank you for the Guard!"

"I wish you joy of battle!" The General bared his fangs happily with his departing wish. He turned, and rode back to direct his attack.

If the cavalry facing the main allied line could be engaged, then that would bring the whole of the Tsu-Khan's army into battle. The signal could be sent to Raschid. Yariim looked back to the river bank, where Ataman's signalers stood beside the hospital. But a fresh crescendo of insane battle screams sounded out across the plains, and Yariim turned to face the Khan's attack.

They came on at a dead run – a vast column of men two thousand yards across, spears gleaming, banners streaming – whipped into fury by raw fear of their officers and the madness of the fight. Surviving crossbowmen thickened up their ranks as they thundered forwards into the attack, racing towards the thin Osranii line.

The Osranii took a half turn to the right. Their lines were tipped with countless rifle muzzles. An instant later, the crash of rifle volleys came. Osranii artillery blasted out solid shot that whipped through the onrushing spearmen, blasting entire files of men into bloody ruin at a time. Still the attack rampaged forward, fanatical, blood crazed and unstoppable.

Lead swarmed through the air. Spearmen spun and fell, their weapons cartwheeling through the sky. Spears jutted from the ground. Behind the attack came the Tsu-Khan's cavalry, slashing with their sabres at the men who fell behind. Wounded men who failed to claw their way forward were speared where they fell. The blue-eyed demon horses stamped the dying into offal, lifting up their heads and screaming in their lust for blood.

The attack slowed as the front ranks fell. Rear ranks overleapt the dying and the dead, screeching like maddened banshees. They closed to one hundred meters – fifty – ten. At close range, they were blown literally clean off their feet.

The churning mass of madmen faltered – was rammed backwards by the storm of lead. At their center, massed artillery pieces fired canister and simply disintegrated every living thing in their path. But the attack gathered, bleeding and screaming – and then suddenly lunged forward in a last, maddened howl.

There was a crash as the spearmen suddenly smashed against the Osranii line.

Spears outreached Osranii bayonets. Some Osranii fired, but others slung their muskets, screamed and drew their swords. They stepped back from the collapsing ice ramparts, and as the enemy clambered awkwardly over the barrier, the Osranii tore into them with swords.

The fight instantly changed. No more rifle fire and artillery – this was steel on steel, halberds versus bayonet – swords and flesh and screams. Yariim saw her lines step back, then surge forward to meet the charge. With a curse, she turned Marwan back and headed for her reserves.

"Saa'lu! Bring in the Guard!"

Elsewhere on the battlefield, a new storm of rifle fire exploded into life as Ataman attacked. Three green rockets climbed into the sky. Yariim watched them go – saw the triple burst of bright green stars, then turned back to the fight. She waved her Frankish pikemen forward once again, and once again went with them into the melee. The world rang to the screams of fighting men, the blast of rifles and the ring of steel. With Saud beside her, Yariim drew her sword and led the charge.

"Forward the Guards! Forward!"

Old Abwan waved his scimitar at his men. In deep column they stormed forwards with bayonets, screaming as they hurled themselves into the attack. Beside them came the Islanders, the big men moving at a dead run, pistols and two handed swords in hand. A weird, screeching instrument flayed the men forward into the attack, spreading a red madness wherever the sound came. The McCallum and his pipers led the Islander attack, and his men gave a scream like demons as they flung themselves into war.

Collapsed on the snow, Abwan bellowed to his passing men. Old Abwan cursed, holding his leg. A crossbow bolt jutted from his thigh. Two of his corporals broke ranks and ran to him, signaling for more men. Abwan waved them aside with his sword.

"On to them! Fire and steel! Fire and steel!" He fell, losing blood. "Kill the buggers!"

The Guard rampaged forward. On their flanks, Spike brought his light infantry, the crack marksmen fanning out to drop into skirmish line. Their rifle fire was slower than the infantry of the line – surgical and precise. They fired on the Khanate officers behind the enemy infantry, snatching the men out of their saddles one by one.

The Islanders and blue-armoured Guards smashed home into the flank of the enemy attack. Steel driven by the maddened strength of huge men crashed into the enemy. Yellow Empire troops reeled, their lines smashed and compacted by the huge impact on the flanks. The Islander's vast swords literally sheered men in two. The McCallum led his men from the front, roaring like a torah bull, his pipers driving Guards and Islanders forward to roll up the enemy line.

Abwan laughed, weakening. He tried to rise, using his sword as a crutch, but the supple blade bent, and he fell. Hot blood spilled past his hands as he tried to grip tight to his thigh.

"We've got you! Wait – we've got you!"

Hands held him. Abwan blinked, and saw a grizzled old Mouse with an eye patch bending over him. With him was a lemur girl – slim and absurdly young. Her face was scorched with powder, smeared with blood, and she looked like an angel. Moving fast, the girl tore off her coat and tunic, and tore away her own sash.

They used the sash as a tourniquet, tightening it with a length of broken spear. The lemur girl called for stretcher bearers. She fought her way back into her coat, sprang astride a steppe pony, and rode off at a gallop, sword in hand. The girl followed the Guards, directing companies forward, waving her ridiculously narrow sword.

Abwan gasped as two men came and lifted him into a stretcher. Marsuk the mouse, old in war, gripped Abwan by the hand.

"You'll live."

His head swimming, Abwan tried to see the fight.

"Are they breaking?" He tried to rise. "Where's Colonel Tuk? I have to hand over command!"

"Tuk's handling it. The enemy's broken." Marsuk patted the stretcher bearers. "Go!"

The stretcher men ran off towards the hospital tents. Limping forwards, his left leg cut open by an enemy spear, Marsuk found his horse. With a bandage in place and a musket in hand, he rode awkwardly forward towards the battle lines.

Ataman and the Grand Constable had taken their men forward, and the fight raged thick and fast. The Yellow Empire infantry had broken, the survivors fleeing back across the snow, artillery blasting holes into their swarming lines. They left perhaps thirty thousand corpses behind them – a nightmarish carpet of dead.

The Osranii infantry in Yariim's lines were staggering. The melee had cost them dear. Men who had once been two files apart were suddenly finding themselves neighbours. Battalions had sometimes shrunk from a thousand men to six or seven hundred. The ambulance carts raced backwards, and the rifle regiments collapsed in place, too torn and exhausted to pursue the enemy infantry.

Marsuk rejoined his brigade. He looked left and right at exhausted faces – rats and mice, one eared rabbits, foxes gasping with fatigue. He waved them back towards the crumbled ruin of the ice ramparts.

"No one told you to stop working!" The mouse rode stolidly forward. "Fall back – salvage ammunition. Check your weapons." He spied his colour party standing about their flags. "You there! Canteens! There may still be some coffee for the men."

Out further in the field, the light infantry were coming back in high spirits, guns over their shoulders. At their head, Spike waved a bloody sword towards Marsuk.

"Sir! I want to put in a request for compassionate leave? I believe I'm suffering from stress!"

Spike's men laughed. Marsuk slowly shook his head and turned to his own troops.

"That, lads, is what happens when you opt for beauty over brains." He waved his men back. "Back behind the ramparts. Set your piquets and rest!"

Out in the plains, the battle still raged – but here, in a grotesque tangle that seemed to cover half the world, there was nothing but tangled heaps of enemy dead.

Tulu-Begh blanched, his demon horse stamping beneath him as the creature sensed his mood. The torn, bleeding fragments of an army streamed past him, staggering and dying in the snow. Yellow Empire soldiers limped and reeled in shock. They were caught by black-armoured cavalry of the Khan's own guard who spurred forward to brutally force the survivors into line.

More cavalry tumans had been savaged. The Osranii main body had run forward from its fortifications and had brought the cavalry under fire. Stung, the cavalry had disobeyed its officers and had tried to charge home. The result had been decimated units, fields of blood, and a wilderness of dying, shrieking horses kicking their lives out in the snow. Shaken by the fate of the dawn attack, the tumans had sped back and withdrawn, leaving a quarter of their number dead or dying on the ground.

General Tsai-Chi had been shot. His right shoulder was a mask of blood beneath a ragged bandage. He staggered forward from the shocked mass of infantry, surrounded by his officers. They crashed to their knees, making obeisance before the watching Khan.

"Holy One – we have failed." The General sounded sick with shame. "Their bullets are too much! Allow me to expunge my failure with my life."

He held out his knife to the Khan, panting raggedly – exhausted and swaying on his knees. The Khan looked quietly down at the officers with his strange, pale eyes, and then quietly swept back his pitch black robes.

"We watched your attack with interest, Tsai-Chi. You served with diligence." The Khan lifted his eyes to look icily at the Osranii lines. "This scholar's science should have been more carefully studied."

Tulu-Begh stiffened, feeling the rebuke. The Mouse spurred swiftly forwards to the Khan.

"Holy One! They were muskets! Merely muskets! There was no way to know…"

"Enough!"

The Khan stabbed a displeased glance at the mouse, and Tulu-Begh pulled back in fear. The Tsu-Khan spread a palpable chill of utter fear.

A bullet whipped overhead. At the range of almost two thousand yards, someone had actually tried to fire upon the Khan. Black Guards shielded him with their bodies, but the Khan paid the sniper no heed.

"The attack was well made, Tsai-Chi." The Khan looked to his guard officers. "How many dead are on the field?"

"Beloved Person – perhaps thirty thousand conscript infantry. Perhaps ninety thousand cavalry." The soldier seemed as though mere death were nothing worthy of note. "More than one third of our numbers."

Tulu Begh blanched. Should they withdraw? Attacking the allied army when its flanks and rear were protected had been a clear mistake! Tulu-Begh almost felt the words rise in his mouth, but he ducked his head. He extricated himself slowly to the rear of the conference.

The Tsu-Khan sat in his saddle, his slim face turning towards the battlefield – towards the immense carpet of corpses lying splayed across the snow.

The Tsu-Khan smiled.

"General Tsai-Chi. Will you endeavor to attack a second time?"

"Yes, Adored One!"

"Then you shall have victory." The Khan quietly folded back his sleeves. "I will give you a shield against these bullets. A wall that their rifles cannot pierce. Your men need fear their guns no more."

The Tsu-Khan took direct command. He whirled his horse, rode along the face of the exhausted, terrorized Imperial infantry, then looked at the long lines of his battered cavalry. He had thirty thousand conscripts – with perhaps half of them too wounded to fight. He had seventy thousand cavalry who could still ride in an attack. The Khan looked along his lines, and signaled for his Black guards.

"Kill the wounded conscripts."

The Guard tuman lunged forward, the big horses braying in lust as the riders butchered screaming men. The Khan watched the massacre with a look of anticipation upon his face.

"The Guard will remain mounted as a reserve. Dismount the other men. We will now close with the enemy." Bloody corpses were tossed to the snow as the Black Guard stabbed the wounded conscripts with their lances. "And drag this offal with us."

Orders were bellowed all up and down the line. There were sufficient men to match the Osranii line, and the Khan's army had the deeper formation. The surviving conscripts were driven forward to form a human shield for the front lines.

Satisfied, the Khan rode forwards. His men made a long, slow march towards the enemy lines. All around him, the soldiers of his dark dream walked without fear. The banners of flayed scalps and skins streamed in the breeze. The men brought lances, bows and swords forward to slaughter the Osranii. Behind them came the Black Guard, lances ready, their weapons dark with dripping blood.

They came to the first scattered tangles of dead. Osranii artillery had a long reach. But this time, no shells came. The Osranii were conserving their ammunition, and the Tsu-Khan gave a savage smile.

"Excellent."

Tulu Begh rode a horse behind the rest of the general staff. He edged backwards from a corpse that lay strewn madly across the ground. The Khan watched the Prince, and fixed him in his cold blue eyes.

"You are fearful, Tulu Begh?" The Khan swiveled, his pale stare shining with a soulless light. "Then open your eyes and see. Know now why I am the master of the dead…"

The dead made a foul carpet that stretched miles wide. At the edge of the vast field of corpses, the Tsu-Khan's army halted in its place. The men waited as an icy wind stirred past their spears.

Ragged, half seen shapes had come forward with the Khan – skull faced things that swooped and whirred unseen, touching at the living with claws of hate and rage. The Tsu Khan slid from his horse. With his black robes flapping in the fitful breeze, he walked out before his troops and faced the ocean of the dead.

A bullet came whirring from an Osranii sniper. The Khan idly held up one hand, and the lead bullet splashed into molten metal as it struck against an invisible shield of air. Spreading his arms wider, the Khan bowed his head, and darkness seemed to flow out across the snow.

The sun darkened. Clouds appeared, and a chill fell over the battlefield. Hanging above the army, hungry spirits looped and screamed out for living blood.

"Death does not end duty." The Khan lifted up his hands. *"I am the Tsu-Khan. I am the destined ruler of Aku Mashad. I am the Earth Born, come to make all creatures bow before me, living or dead."*

A glowing light opened from the Tsu-Khan's breast. A blazing rift appeared – a gate ripped into the world of the dead. The Khan's voice bellowed – deep, powerful and commanding, and from within the gate there came a chorus of screams.

"All those who defy me, shall know pain! All those who receive pain, shall plead before me! All those who plead before me, shall grovel at my will!" A storm wind blasted from the glowing gate, whipping out across the waiting men.

"Slaves to my power, I command thee! Worms who fell before me, I call thee forth! Thou who have learned the penalty for defying me – obey my will!

"Come forth!"

They blasted out into the living world – screaming ghosts, weeping and lost in madness – tormented by the Khan into gibbering, howling strands of hate. They were the lost souls from conquered cities – slaughtered innocents in their tens of thousands. Entire cities had died beneath the Khan's blades, and now their souls were his demented slaves.

"Enter the dead and arise! Arise and kill! Slaughter those who would defy me!" The Khan laughed, roaring as the power jetted from his soul.

"Arise. Arise! ARISE!"

All across the battlefield, the dead jerked and quivered as hellish life blasted back into their bones. Corpses ripped into splays of entrails and slime by the artillery – bodies slain by bullets, bayonets or blade. The mad souls plunged inside the cold dead flesh of horses and of men. Jerking and flopping madly, they turned to the allied lines. Dragging themselves on shattered limbs, on blood slime or staggering forwards howling in lust, the dead arose and marched upon the enemy.

The Khan laughed. All along the Osranii lines, the rifles opened fire. Bullets smacked into the walking dead unheeded. Impact staggered corpses back, but the corpses marched slowly on. Laughing, the Khan turned to Tsai-Chi. He opened up his arms and waved towards his men.

"Follow! Use the dead as your shields! Slaughter the enemy, my children, and know that there is no death for those who serve the Khan!"

The Khan's soldiers stared, then gave a great, maddened screech of joy. The men ran forwards, crowding in behind the wall of walking dead. Bullet strikes staggered corpses. Here and there, a man fell, but the attack surged forwards behind a wall of death.

Standing before his guards, the Tsu-Khan watched his army storming forward into glory. The Osranii would die, and the last threat to his destiny would finally be gone. With a howl of triumph, the Khan flung open his arms, and ghosts came to dance and scream high in the skies.

Chapter Twenty Six:

Rounding the forest and out into the hills, Raschid's cavalry rode parallel with the great bottleneck, then came to a halt. The ranks closed up, the troops turned to the left in place, and the march columns had instantly become battle lines. Kakuzak horsemen galloped in from the piquet lines, forming a loose screen on the flanks. Raschid rode fast up the lines, the horse's armour jangling, and took his place at the head of the attack.

Twenty thousand men.

The Frankish knights were formed up boot-to-boot, so close that a loaf of bread thrown at their ranks would have been impaled upon a lance. Their huge horses stamped and smoked in the cold. Beside them ranged regiment after regiment of winged hussars in plate and mail, their horses painted red with henna and their vulture plumes rustling in the breeze. In the main formation, the heavy Cavalry of Osra filled the wings. At the center, the blue armoured Royal Guard regiments were in their perfect ranks. Blue brocaded armour gleamed like turquoise in the sun.

The cavalry advanced.

Row after row, immaculately spaced. Big men on huge horses, all clad in armoured steel. Silken banners flew in the wind, and the horses moved forwards in an inexorable wave. Twenty thousand men, two formations deep across a frontage of almost a mile. It was like seeing a living tidal wave of glory surge across the land.

It was the final charge; the last time lance and blade would ever decide a battle. In the distance, the roar of rifle fire spoke of the future. It would be guns and science – or it would be nothing but the darkness of enslavement to the Khan. And so the old ways came to go out in a blaze of glory, and to carve a path in legend forever more.

The lines advanced.

They swept in line abreast up the undefended hills, passing bodies left lying from the previous day's battle. The riders crested the range of hills and paused, dressing ranks and gazing down across the plains below.

The horizon was a churning mass of smoke and flame…

The river curved. Tight against the river were the allied infantry – a place where tiny coloured lines of troops fought to hold the line. The entire front of the defending army was a boiling cloud of smoke. Rifle fire blasted flame into the fog bank, hiding the infantry from view.

Their flags were still flying. It was too far to see the details, but the line had held.

The enemy were moving forward on foot. Their horses were picketed at their rear, left tethered while their riders marched forwards with bow and sword. Vast numbers of troops marched deliberately forward towards the rifle smoke. Before the dense-packed ranks, there was another strange swarm of shapes – a hundred thousand shambling figures moving purposefully towards the allied lines.

A thousand yards behind the enemy attack, a vast, black-armoured cavalry formation stood in reserve. The Tsu-Khan's guards, ten thousand strong, faced the Allied lines. Raschid took in the view, looking at the regiments spread like toy soldiers on a table top, and swept his lance point down.

"Forward."

It was two miles to the river bank. Two miles: twelve minutes at the trot. The infantry would have to hold for twelve minutes more. Raschid's twenty thousand swept forward down the hills. The enemy remained facing the Allied infantry. No scouts had sped to warn them of Raschid's approach.

The lines rode forward, two regiments deep, shining in the morning sun. They kept their pace – fast and steady, never giving in to the urge to scream forward in a scattered rush. The blow had to be delivered in a single mighty crash: boot to boot, lance and blade. Discipline and terror.

Six minutes passed. More than half way there. The rifle fire rose to a mad crescendo. Something was strange – Raschid felt it in the air. The sky suddenly darkened, and black clouds obscured the sun. A dark wind seemed to swirl in around the Khan's sinister black cavalry.

The allied cavalry closed the gap.

Ten minutes had passed. The Black Guard were close – five hundred yards away. Finally someone in the rear ranks of the enemy turned. There was a stir of motion as the enemy cavalry suddenly saw the threat in their rear.

It was too late.

The Allied cavalry halted, the ranks locking tight. Raschid summoned his wing commanders, who cantered to his side. The Shah of Osra bowed in Salaam to the Pulski Prince..

"My Prince – lead the hussars around the right flank of the Black Guards and attack their infantry from the rear. My Lord Commander – take the Knights of the Order and do the same on the other flank." Raschid signaled his men. "The Osranii heavy cavalry will engage the Black Guard."

"Yes, my Lord."

"God go with you."

Raschid rode his horse out before his men. With lance in hand, he stood in his stirrups and bellowed out to all the regiments who had come so far and fought so hard.

They stood their horses in long ranks, their lance points gleaming in the morning sun. Raschid's voice carried to the furthest edges of the battle lines.

"We are not soldiers fighting for mere nation. We do not fight for greed or gain. Our treasure is the future. Our only cause is freedom!"

The Shah turned his horse. His long nose pointed at the enemy, and his armour gleamed beneath the eerie light of the battlefield.

"In the name of Christ – of the Buddha and Allah!" Raschid raised his lance on high. *"Faith and Reason!"*

"FAITH AND REASON!"

Twenty thousand horsemen shook the skies with the cry. In one massive wave, they started forwards in a solid wall of steel. To the front, the infantry battle raged. The Black Guards sawed at their reins, trying to turn and face the oncoming wave of enemy. Raschid stood in his stirrups, waved his men forward, and let the trumpets call.

"Charge!"

"Jesus!"

The brass hut perched atop a hill crest, looking down into a great sack-shaped bend in a half frozen river. From here, the battlefield took a moment to make sense. The inside curve of the river far away was wreathed in smoke. Cannons jetted thick white fumes into the clouds. Osranii infantry were locked in a ferocious battle with a dark mass of shambling enemy that waded forward into the choking powder smoke.

Behind the infantry battle, a vast line of black cavalry was trying to form into line. Rampaging towards it was a great checkerboard of astonishing horsemen. There were units armoured in silver, armoured in red or royal blue. Terrifying horsemen with upright wings fixed behind their armour rode like wild men, leveling lances that were striped like candy canes. The roar of horse hooves almost drowned out the sound of gunfire. At the head of the middle regiments, the flag of Osra gleamed. From inside the door of the brass hut, Sandhri watched in astonishment. She held the baby in one arm. Meng and Itbit stared at the titanic battle. The sheer numbers of men facing the allies was beyond belief.

The allied cavalry threw themselves into the charge. Trumpets sounded distant in the stormy air. Somewhere, thunder boomed. Lightning lit the battlefield an eerie blue. In the flash of light, Sandhri saw a white robed figure, impossibly tiny in the distance, charging well ahead of the Osranii Royal guard.

"It's Raschid!" She tried to struggle to her feet. *"Raschid!"*

The baby mewled, unhappy with the strange new sense of evil pulsing through the air. Meng had a telescope. He searched the battlefield through the lens, trying to understand the events below.

"It must have been a flank march. Remarkable!" Thousands of heavy cavalry had been delivered behind the Khan to deal a mortal blow. "The Shah split his forces in the face of superior numbers. Most remarkable."

"Remarkable? Off course he's bloody remarkable!" Sandhri held her son safe against her breast. "V'at's that at the other battle? V'at's that in front off their infantry?"

Half out of the hut and carefully scanning the hills around them, Itbit rose and gripped the metal hull.

"Meng!"

All across the hills, dead bodies lay feathered with arrows. Suddenly the bodies jerked and arose. Screaming, ghostly shapes swerved across the ground, looped up and sank into the bodies, and the corpses came to life. Frozen and ungainly, their limbs cracked as the cadavers slowly struggled from the ground.

"Jesus!"

Sandhri swore. Walking dead were shambling to their feet in their hundreds. The dead eyes swiveled towards the friends inside the big brass hut. Two of the monsters clawed at one of the hut's long legs. The hut kicked them away, shying back as more and more dead bodies came slowly up out of the snow.

The dead laughed.

They cackled madly – they wept, they crooned, they screamed. Dead jaws howled, creaking with ice. With arrows jutting from eye sockets, some lacking arms, some lacking jaws, the dead came forward with weapons in their hands.

They had bows, and arrows were dragged out of their own death wounds. Itbit squawked and dove inside the hut as arrows slammed into the metal hull. Sandhri ducked back from the door, hunched protectively around her baby. The hut pranced backwards and kicked out with its big feet, stamping on bodies as they came close.

Out on the plains, the infantry battle raged. Holding on for dear life as the hut smashed its way through a shambling horde of enemies, Itbit looked towards the rifle smoke.

"Bodies! They be fighting bodies!" Itbit stared out towards the battle. "Itbit thinks the Tsu-Khan has summoned up the dead!"

"Bugger! T'en they're in trouble!" Sandhri gripped tight to the door. An arrow blurred in through into the hut and clattered from the back wall. "Hokay – v'e fix it up!" The bat looked back at Itbit, where she lay clinging to the floor. "Itbit – v'ere's the Khan?"

"With the Black Guards!" Itbit slid towards the door. Meng caught her, then drew his sword and hacked at a dead hand that came groping across the threshold. "Always with the guards!"

"Then v'e hit the Black Guard!" Sandhri whacked the brass hut with her hand. "Hey hut! Go, hut – go! *Charge!*"

The hut span on its long, lanky legs, threw off a dead swordsman that was clambering up its shin, and then lumbered down the hills. Arrows rattled and rang from the brass walls as the hut ran like the wind. Sandhri tried to shelter her baby from the motion as the hut stretched into a manic gallop, its legs flailing wildly to either side. Hanging on for grim death, Meng struggled forwards to the door.

"My Lady!" Meng hunched in the wind as the brass hut charged across the snow. "This humble one wonders - what are we doing?"

"Anot'er lesson!" Sandhri had eyes only for the battle, willing the hut to greater speed. "Alv'ays remember! If you v'ant a job done right, you haff to do it for yourself!"

Ringling like a mad church bell, the hut rampaged forwards, while all across the battlefield, the dead men rose.

The front lines of Yariim's troops boiled with panic. Some ranks were firing at the oncoming enemy. Others were locked blade to blade with the dead. Corpses jerked and slithered across the snow – some almost whole, and some of them mere scattered scraps of organs, limbs and bones. The nightmarish army had arisen, and slowly walked into the Allied battle lines.

Osranii dead were also staggering to their feet. The rear ranks of units turned and fought hand-to-hand with the dead. Slow, ungainly and mutilated, the dead were all the more horrific for bearing the faces of dead friends. Those that still had jaws screamed and laughed like maniacs, screeching and howling out for blood.

Surrounded by corpses, Yariim's staff fought their way through a knot of dead artillerymen with their swords. Yariim rose in her saddle and hacked downwards with her scimitar – a gift from Old Abwan. She smashed the blade down into a dead man's face, hacking again and again, sobbing as she finally battered the dead head free. The decapitated corpse staggered blindly away, falling on its side and bucking madly in the snow.

Dead horses were amongst the risen. The animals brayed and staggered as though unused to moving on four legs. Those cut in two by artillery crawled forward on their front hooves, dragging entrails behind them in a slime of blood. Yariim gagged, half turning away – and then her guns blasted canister into the nearest ranks of dead men, literally blowing the corpses away.

The butchered fragments still writhed and moved, creeping forwards with a hellish life all of their own. The allied infantry fought like demons, but the rifle fire had ended. Behind the walking dead there came dark columns of the Tsu-Khan's men – seventy thousand armoured men roaring forwards, waving spears and sabres in the air. The enemy broke into a charge, crossing the ground that had been so deadly only minutes before. Scarcely a single one of them fell to rifle fire as they charged at Yariim's men.

Artillery fired, the crews working fast and hard. Shells hammered into the onrushing horde, blasting men into the air. But the shambling dead reached the guns, and crews had to fight the monsters away with rammers, staves and swords. The artillery fire slackened as the living suddenly locked in combat with the dead.

Marwan turned and turned, crashing into dead men and knocking them aside. Yariim loaded a silver bullet and fired at a screeching corpse. With silver in its dead flesh, the body seemed to fall down like a marionette bereft of strings. Saa'lu spurred her horse forward and fired two silver pistol bullets into the nearby dead, and the bodies span away and lay bonelessly in the snow.

Yariim wasted no time with the dead. She rode Marwan behind her battling men.

"Pull back! Pull back!" Yariim's voice cracked. She had never been trained to make her voice carry, and she sounded thin against the crash and roar of battle. *"Everyone, pull back thirty yards!"*

Saud came to the rescue. The huge tiger boomed out an echo of Yariim's commands.

"Back thirty paces! Back thirty paces!" The Tiger swept his sword out to point at the new battle line. *"Face the enemy and fall back thirty paces!"*

Her larynx aching, Yariim held a hand to her throat and waved the Tiger forward.

"Saud – get them to load with silver! Pull back and volley fire"

The tiger understood. He stood atop a broken cart, booming out to the troops. The men came backwards step by step, outdistancing the dead and firing uselessly into the enemy.

"Load with silver! Load silver!" Each man had ten silver bullets lining his breast pockets. Saud waved a bullet above his head. *"Shoot them as they come over the ramparts!"*

Brigadiers and division commanders came racing to Yariim. The back lines were a charnel house of dead slain again and yet again. The officers slewed their horses to a halt and surrounded Yariim.

The blue mouse had her helmet off. Her blue fur and golden hair were a banner marking her location to her officers. As the infantry went backwards step by step, the first of the gibbering mass of dead came clawing their way up over the crumbled lines of the old ice ramparts.

"Shoot them once they cross! Kill them as they mass on this side!" The mouse waved her sword to show the army's new firing line. "Control the fire. Volleys!" The men only had ten shots each, and then it would be hand-to-hand combat against an enemy that felt no pain. "Fire our ten shots – then swords!"

Artillery horses screamed. The dead were in amongst the guns, and artillerymen fought desperately against enemy claws, spears and swords. Yariim saw the Islemen standing to her rear, and she swung Marwan about to face the big barbarians.

'Saud! I can't shout anymore. Call out the volleys for me! Then lead them forward!" Marwan growled, wanting to head back to the fight, but Yariim curbed the angry camel in. "Be careful!"

"My Lady must be careful! Be careful!" Saud shouldered his sword, ready to command the tired, bleeding lines of soldiers. The huge tiger put a hand upon Yariim's shoulder in concern. "Keep friends close! Keep out of fighting."

Yariim rode away. She sped Marwan over to the McCallum, pointed the old gentleman at the artillery, and the big swords went screaming off to save her guns. If the artillery could blow back enough of the walking dead, then the day could still be saved. Explosive shell and canister seemed to do the trick.

"Make ready!"

Saud's voice boomed like a god. The huge tiger stood between two regiments, spreading his arms wide. His huge sword was like a toy in one of his hands. *"Silver shot! Volley fire! Present...!"*

Corpses clawed across the old ramparts, spilling into the snow and fighting back to their feet. More and more bodies crowded in behind. And behind them, the Khan's army came. The enemy gave a sudden roar and broke into a run, their spears and swords gleaming, their legs pounding as the hurtled themselves forward in an all-destroying charge.

"Fire!"

The rifles gave one great roar. Shambling dead were hurtled back, pierced bodies simply dropping in their tracks. Silver worked its miracle, smashing down the dead.

Yariim let the men do their work. Wiping her face, she cast about, and saw a dear, familiar figure limping up to her side. Abwan had a bloody bandage about his leg, but his sword was in his hand and his men were waiting in the rear. Yariim trotted Marwan over as a second volley thundered out into the air.

"Abwan! Abwan – form up the Guards!" Yariim pointed up to the center of the line. "Load silver and relieve the guns!"

The old hound cut at her. Yariim threw up her hands, and Abwan's scimitar spat sparks from the steel braces about her mailed forearms. The old soldier cut again and again, and Yariim blocked with one arm and frantically fought to bring up her own blade.

Abwan giggled, shrieking incoherently. He sliced at Yariim and hit her leg, numbing her armoured knee. His scimitar dragged a bright line across Marwan's armoured flank. The camel whirled on the dead soldier in a fury, slamming his neck into the dead man. Abwan span aside, and Saa'lu rode past, leaning from her saddle and - throwing her full weight behind her blade. Her slim sabre sliced off Abwan's head. The old soldier's body staggered back towards Yariim, slicing with its sword at empty air. It fell sideways into the snow, still writhing and jerking with appalling energy.

Shocked and sick, Yariim could only stare. Above her, the volleys slammed into the dead time after time – measured, slow and deadly. But the enemy infantry had almost reached the wall, and Yariim heard their war cries rise into a victorious, joyful scream.

"Peace be with you...!"

The Royal Guard slammed into the Khan's black-armoured horsemen like a sledge hammer of flesh and steel. Huge horses drove raw power behind the lance points. Ten thousand strong, the Black Guards counter charged, but Raschid's regiments had the speed, had the skill, and had a power born of pride and joy. The opposing lines smashed into one another at fantastic speed, and men were hurled screaming through the air. But Osra's blue armoured men ploughed forward like a mailed fist, shattering the Black Guards and crushing them aside.

The cavalry melee broke ranks into a furious swarm. Osranii officers led tight knots of men clean out of the enemy ranks, reforming into squadrons, then charging back into the enemy. The discipline and ferocity were a savage pleasure to behold. The Osranii Guards fought under absolute control.

Raschid cut his way through the melee, his magic scimitar a blur in his hand. The ironic Osranii war cry rang in the air, and he bellowed it himself as he slammed home with his sword.

The Black Guards were grim and merciless, but today God was with the Just. Osranii scimitars crashed into Nomad sabres, blurring fast and hard. Osranii cavalry fired pistols inside the melee. Steel javelins struck down the enemy; Osranii maces and dagger axes hammered into black armour all across the fight. The big armoured horses snarled and bit, and the Shah of Osra led his men screaming through the fight.

A huge enemy rider came at Raschid. Letting his sword drop to its wrist strap, Raschid drew a pistol and fired at the man's horse. The animal died with a bullet in its brain, and Raschid rode his horse clean over the fallen man. He let his warhorse dance and stamp, hearing the enemy's bones crack, he spurred quickly away and hurtled a javelin at a man who bore a standard topped with screaming, howling skulls.

Beside the fallen standard bearer, a small man sat upon a pale horse. The man was absurdly slim and delicate in this place of death and steel. He wore black silken robes. Raschid sawed his horse to a halt and faced the man with his scimitar in hand.

White robes and black jerked in the breeze. The Tsu-Khan stated at Osra's Shah, and his pale eyes blazed with hate.

From the battlefield came the scream of maddened men. A splintering crash rang in the air. The winged hussars of Pulski had crashed into the rear of the Khan's infantry. On the other flank, the Knights of the Sacred Order thundered home their charge. Lances smashed into the backs of the Khan's men, and exultant riders forged through their enemies, smashing downwards with their swords. The Khan whipped his head around, saw the fight, and then opened up his arms.

There was a pulse of darkness. Suddenly a hemisphere of black oily film sealed Raschid and the Tsu-Khan off from the battlefield.

The silence was sudden, and it was shocking.

Raschid slammed home his spurs and charged.

He hurtled a javelin, and the steel shaft thrummed as it flew. It hit the Khan's blue-eyed horse, and the beast crashed sideways as the spearhead rammed into its shoulder. The Khan drew his own sword and met Raschid blade-to-blade. Sword and scimitar crashed as the two horses fought chest to chest, tearing at each other with their teeth.

Snarling horses circled, lunged and reared. Raschid fought with sword and shield; A big man, he moved fast, his blows smashing down with dreadful strength. The Shah fought in silence – scientific and savage. His blade was coldly met by the black sword of the Tsu-Khan.

The blades rang. Outside the hemisphere, the cavalry battle raged. Men tried to force their way in to help their dueling leaders, but none could pass through the barrier.

The wounded demon horse was not weakening. The Khan dodged Raschid's blade with insolent ease. He speared his own sword hard at the neck of Raschid's horse, plunging his sword in beneath the armour plate between the beast's neck and jaw. The horse reared and screamed, spraying blood, and Raschid kicked free and rolled off onto the ground. His horse fell. The Tsu-Khan spurred towards him, his straight blade head forward like a spear.

Raschid drew his old Yatagan and held it in his shield hand. He blurred sideways, taking the Khan's blade on his own. The yatagan was rammed home deep into the demon horse, the silvered blade slamming deep. Raschid ripped the wound wide, yanking out the blade and whirling, hacking his magic scimitar across the animal's neck. He took the horse's head off with a single blow, sending the Khan tumbling to the ground.

The black-robed figure rose, shaking out his robes. The Khan's slim face now looked annoyed. Throwing back his sleeves, the Tsu-Kan stared at Raschid in icy hate.

"Beast!"

Swaying on his feet, Raschid readied scimitar, yatagan and shield. He swirled his sword, loosening his wrist.

"My wife had many things to say of you, Tsu-Khan." The tall Jackal moved forward with the sharp, diagonal steps of a swordsman. "Yield your men."

The Khan watched Raschid in absolute disdain.

"Fool! Fur-bearing freak! You are all nothing but beasts masquerading as real men!" The Khan held out his own hand and looked at it in loathing. "A mockery! Toys made for a child!"

Raschid moved cautiously forward to attack.

"But not you."

"None of you know the truth! Your storytellers know nothing but a shadow!" The Khan flung out one arm. "You are mine to command, to break or destroy! It is the will of God!" He opened up one hand, and black fire blazed in his palm.

"And man was given all dominion over the birds of the air. Over the trees and lands, the fishes of the waters and the beasts of the field!"

Raschid moved forward, and the Khan moved back, watching Raschid critically as though waiting for an opening. The jackal watched his enemy, needing to keep clear of the thrashing hooves of the Khan's headless horse.

"You are a beast too, Tsu-Khan."

"Do you mean *this?*" The Khan laughed at his own body. "Borrowed. Taken from a fool who delved too deep, too far."

The Khan side stepped; Raschid saw that he was trying to reach the javelin that jutted from his dead horse's neck. Raschid moved to keep the man away. The Khan kept his eyes cautiously upon Raschid's face.

"He came where he should not – into my prison of ice! He hunted for the tools to make him great – and he found more than he could have ever dreamed!" The Khan's eyes had the same weird blue light that shone from the demonic horses of his officers. "I took him, and came forth to claim Aku-Mashad at last."

Raschid maneuvered to attack. The Khan was cautious, pulling back.

"What did they tell you - that blue dancer and that black witch?"

"They told me enough." Raschid angled his shield. "They told me you could die!"

He leapt forward with a roar, his scimitar a blur of steel. The Tsu-Khan flowed sideways, whipping about as he dropped, and sweeping at Raschid's ankles with his heel. Raschid kicked out his shin to meet the blow, his armoured leg crashing against the Khan's. The jackal span, and sparks showered as blade met blade in a deadly dance of steel.

They fought fast and hard. The Tsu-Khan had an unearthly speed, and a weird, fluid fighting style. Raschid had intelligence and strength, meeting blow after blow and driving back the Khan. He landed a savage blow, but the sword cut flashed and healed. The Khan laughed and lunged, and his sword point pieced the shoulder of Raschid's mail.

Raschid staggered back, blood springing from his wound. The Khan leapt high, scything down his sword. Raschid caught the attack on his shield, but the Khan's blade cut through the tempered steel and crashed into Raschid's helmet. The Jackal's cut scalp blazed like fire. Shaking his head, Raschid leapt over a leg sweep, punched his shield out as he attacked, and knocked the Tsu-Khan's blade aside.

Break the heart of stone!

With one massive lunge, he ran the Khan through with his sword.

He ran the evil creature clean through the heart, twisted the blade – and the Khan laughed in his face.

The sorcerer crashed his sword hilt against Raschid's snout. Shaking his head, Raschid staggered, rising up to see the death wound in the Khan's chest close and heal. Blue light shimmered, and the wound had simply gone. The Khan roared and opened up his arms.

"Do you see, beast?" Raschid flicked a glance at the shield walls all around him. "No – none of them will help you. What power is there that can conquer sorcery? What can conquer a magic that can conquer entire worlds!"

The Shah almost laughed as he stood to face the Khan.

"Love."

Raschid threw his shield. The Khan ducked, and Raschid crashed into him like a charging bull. He tackled the Khan in full flight, smashing him off his feet. Roaring in fury, Raschid stabbed his yatagan down again and again into the smaller man.

The old blade punched deep into the Khan's chest – deep into the right side, opposite a normal heart. The Khan's eyes shot open – and finally he screamed.

The yatagan went flying. Raschid bellowed, bunching his strength to rip the Khan's ribcage open bare handed. The Tsu-Khan screamed and hammered a dagger into Raschid's side, gouging at the mail. Raschid tore open a vast wound in the Tsu-Khan's chest, then hurtled aside his Yatagan. He punched an armoured gauntlet into the cold, undead ribcage, and fastened fingers about a heart of stone.

The stone burned like fire.

Screaming in pain, Raschid tore out the heart. It glowed hellish blue, like blazing ice, smoking as it bit through his leather glove. Raschid dropped the heart, and it landed in the snow. With one massive blow of his fist, the Khan broke free of Raschid. He whipped his sword low, and cut Raschid's right leg through the mail. The Jackal toppled, crashing to the snow. The Khan strode past the smoking heart, advancing on the jackal with his sword.

He gave a sickly smile.

"Not - good - enough!"

"Hey fuckwit!"

The air rang to the sound of hellish bells. Crashing through the black shielding came a huge, ungainly vehicle – a brass hut with six great spindly legs. Love burst the magical shield. From a door in the front, a slim figure rose – long white hair gleaming like a waterfall, and white fangs gleaming in the light.

"Did you miss me?"

Sandhri fired a pistol. The silver bullet slammed into the Khan, spinning him aside. Dragging his leg, Raschid lunged and reached the icy heart. He grabbed it tight, felt it burn into his hand, and then threw it through the air towards the hut.

"Sandhri!"

The stone heart skittered in the snow. The Khan rose and saw it land. He stared, then looked up to see a black bat looking down at him with knowing eyes – and a great brass foot poised in the air.

"And t'ey all lived happily effer after…!"

The hut stamped down its foot, and the stone heart shattered into dust.

The Tsu-Khan gave a lost, piercing scream.

The black barrier flew apart. All across the battlefield, the walking dead dropped in their tracks as tortured spirits were set free. The ghosts span wildly up into the air, looping high to climb into the sun. At the heart of his slaughtered guards, the Tsu-Khan stood, arms wide and mouth open in a helpless wail.

Wounds burst open where Raschid's blade had struck. The Khan's flesh decayed to slime, falling from the bones. His body fell into his black robes, stinking as it decomposed. Maggots writhed, and still the hellish scream went on.

Delicate as a bird, the huge brass hut lifted up its foot and worked its toes, scattering fragments of the crushed heart into the breeze. The Khan's scream faded, dying away, until the soul behind it was finally dead and gone.

Rifle fire crashed, and the sound seemed exultant. A cheer was ringing through the air. Armoured horsemen surrounded the Shah, cheering him as the weird brass hut settled to the ground. Passing her pistol back to Meng, Sandhri took a little bundle out of Itbit's arms and eased herself down to the snow. She came hobbling to Raschid, who sat up bleeding in the snow, reaching up his hands to her, love and wonder shining in his eyes.

Bloody and bruised, he held his beloved Sandhri. She came to him, and his fingers wound into her hair. The bat held him tight, and in triumph, she lifted up the baby so that Raschid could see.

"Our son! Raschid – t'iss iss our son!"

The baby's little face seemed impossibly small and wise. One tiny hand groped at the edge of the baby's blankets. With one scorched and bloody gauntlet, Raschid took his son's fingers in his grasp. He leaned forward to smell the baby, caught up in wonder. He looked to Sandhri, and the bat wept with him in joy.

"V'e haff a son!"

Meng and Itbit leapt down from the hut and into Raschid's arms. Men came to bandage the Shah's leg, helping him to his feet. All about the battlefield, there came the sound of joy. Cheers rang in the air as the men of Osra, the Franks and the Hussars surged towards each other in victory.

At the infantry lines, the Osranii and the Franks surged back to the ice ramparts. They kicked through the dead, and found the enemy infantry stalled twenty yards short of the line. The enemy surged, turning to the rear. Behind them, winged hussars and Frankish knights smashed bloody paths into their ranks.

With a roar, the Osranii charged forward with their bayonets. Islemen charged forward swinging swords, and the pike phalanxes marched. Bagpipes mixed their music with the beat of Osranii drums. The standards, ragged and proud, all went forward towards the enemy.

Walking her tired old comrade Marwan beside the lines, Yariim looked at the Khan's infantry. They were surrendering, flayed by cavalry, driven back by rifle fire and bayonets. The enemy were giving up at last. Yariim let Marwan plod slowly to a stop, and she watched her men go forward into victory.

Beside her, Saa'lu wiped powder stains from her face and pointed to the north.

"My Lady – look!"

A tall brass hut crouched like a titanic daddy long legs far off amongst the heavy cavalry. Figures danced and waved. Yariim could see green fur – white robes – and then a slim figure with great clever ears and jet black fur. Bloody, tired and weaving, Yariim looked towards her husband and her wife with tears springing to her eyes.

"Then everything is well…"

Ataman rode up at the head of the Guard Infantry. The men were bloody, tired and exultant. They surrounded vast swarms of prisoners.

"Yariim!" The huge General waved his battered sword at Yariim, pointing her towards her husband and Sandhri. "Go! Go!"

She went. Yariim kicked Marwan into motion. The huge camel looked up, caught sight of Sandhri and Raschid from afar, and gave a joyful growl. Scattering infantry aside, he lumbered through the troops racing towards his waiting friends.

Saa'lu rode over to Ataman. She wiped her face clean on her mail sleeve. She leaned from her saddle and kissed the General, clinging to him in gladness. He held her in his arms, and then the two of them rode on at the head of the Guards, marching on to greet the Shah.

They all came together in a circle. Sir Randolph – his armour dented and rent, Ataman and Saa'lu, The Pulski Prince and the old Lion Master of the Brotherhood. Saud and Marsuk limped in from their regiments. The McCallum, a bandage about his brow, came roaring from the fray, absurdly full of joy.

They surrounded the Shah, his wives and a tiny baby, absurdly glad. Itbit clung to Meng, and Raschid held the green mouse in his arms. Above the allies, their banners flew, and there was suddenly not a dark cloud in the skies.

Scrambling back through the snow, Tulu-Begh struggled to carry saddle bags laden down with gold. His demon horse had suddenly dropped stone dead, leaving him stranded on the ground. Fleeing the fight, the Prince ran for safety, distancing himself from the disaster.

The world was wide, and he still had loot, he still had looks, and he still had a silver tongue! There were horses scattered all across the battlefield. If he could flee into the open plains, the Prince knew a golden future could be found. The steppe cities would be in chaos with the death of the Tsu-Khan. A man could carve himself an empire and rule as a king!

Horses scattered before him as he ran. Tulu Begh cursed and tried to round up a beast, finally catching hold of a horse's mane. He mounted, hefting his saddle bags over his shoulder. The bags held golden tablets looted from dead officers of the Khan – a good stake for a man going on the run.

He sped away across the snow, laughing like a demon. He was handsome, he was brilliant, he had a new future rising from disaster! All the world would bow before the glory of Tulu Begh!

Five hundred yards away, Spike and his sharp shooters rounded up a stunned group of prisoners. They jerked their weapons, motioning the enemy soldiers to plod off towards the river.

One sharpshooter looked up as a figure on horseback streaked away across the hills. Wiping his muzzle, Corporal Yammak uncovered the lens of his telescopic sight, and knelt in the snow.

"*Mine!*"

Walking along with a young ensign – a rather young spotted hamster – Spike turned an eye towards the fleeing enemy.

"One of theirs?"

"Looks like" Yammak carefully primed his pan. "He's in a hurry."

The young ensign looked at the speeding horseman in doubt.

"It must be five hundred yards away! No one can hit that!"

"Indeed?" Spike walked happily on his way. "Yammak?"

Behind Spike, a single shot rang out. Without looking back, Spike walked side by side with the young officer, swishing happily with his sword.

"Faith, my boy! In life, we all need faith. Wonderful what a man, a woman – a hut, a camel or a bat can do, with just a little bit of faith inside them." Spike looked happily off towards the army, where the smoke of camp fires finally began to rise.

"I have a friend you must meet, my boy. And he will tell you that before or after battle, one should always have a drink of tea." Spike felt in his pocket and found a much battered pouch of herbs given to him by Raas Yomah long, long ago. "Come along, and I shall make you some. It's good for the complexion."

The soldiers walked on across the bloody trampled snow, while high above, the sun shone bright and clear.

.

Chapter Twenty Seven:

In springtime, the city of Sath wreathed itself in flowers. The new white battlements were a forest of brilliant blooms; the palm trees blazed with yellow flowers while the fields shimmered with wildflowers in yellow, red and white.

Free men had died to keep the dream alive. They had buried those men on the steppes of a far distant land – but here they raised their monument. It was a monument of walls and stone, of flowers and city streets. Sath lived – and the dream of a better world lived on.

The allied army had gone its separate ways. The Pulski Prince had been crowned King upon the battlefield, to the accolade of Osra and the Brotherhood. Troops had gone on to liberate the Steppe Cities from the yoke of the dead Khan: Osra would have yet more work, sending her teachers, doctors and engineers to help to heal the massive destruction wreaked upon the north. But in time the city states would bloom, if only given patience and help.

More Osranii engineers had stayed to help the Pulski rebuild their land. But their King had come to make a pilgrimage. A service of thanksgiving would be held where the great fight had begun – in Sath, at the heart of Osra. A bumbling, happy hut of brass had carried him faster than the winds, bringing him to an ancient, mellow land of palm trees, flowers and sun.

They all were gathering: the Princes, Dukes and Knights of the sacred brotherhood. The leaders of the desert nomads, the Meepsoori, the Kakuzaks and even the Ha'kuto Hanin. They brought with them a brotherhood forged in the snow and fires.

They brought with them the beginnings of something wonderful and new.

- A broader world.

It was springtime in Sath. The boom of signal guns rolled over the city as Frankish ships came into port, the sailors being met by cheering crowds. Children ran through the streets waving long sticks trailing streamers. Ibis wheeled overhead, their white wings brilliant in the sun. The children laughed as they ran, flocking to the puppet theater where Fallahim welcomed them with a great booming laugh.

Marwan the camel sat dozing in the sun, flanked by two females and apparently well content. Leaning back against his shoulder was Raschid, his turban down across his eyes and a look of total peace upon his face. Yariim lay with her head in his lap, her fingers holding Raschid's hand against her heart.

They lounged in a common courtyard down by the market place. Wasps from the palace gardens were collecting pollen into little baskets overhead. A flying squid hooted in the trees. Water spilled from a great brass frog to bubble into a basin made of bright blue tiles. Somewhere, bread was baking, and lamb sizzled on a grill. The city took a break from festival and had the first snooze of a long, warm, sunny afternoon.

Children had gathered here in the soothing shade – royal wards and neighborhood children, and the offspring of visiting dignitaries. The new King of the Pulski sat with a little boy at his side, showing the child the keys inside a wind-up music box. Sir Randolph, a tad nonplussed, was the darling of three girls from Fatima's dance class. Fatima herself – pink and pregnant, lay back in Saud's arms, holding tight to the huge tiger's fingers and never letting go.

Raas Yomah, exotic and mysterious in his desert robes, had come with Hanna, his wife. Ataman and Saa'lu lay on their bellies in the sand, excitedly designing a courtyard garden for a house. Looming above it all, the brass hut lay like a vast, boneless spider, his legs splayed wide and his beautifully polished metal dappled by the shade. He had a carpet on his floor, and baby toys dangling from inside his roof. Warmed by the sun, the magic creature dozed the pure sleep of the just.

A ghost lay across his threshold like a pet torah bird dozing by its water bowl – chin on the sand and a long, half seen body of ribbons and mist trailing out behind. The spirit of the cave had taken up residence inside the hut, and the two of them seemed perfectly content together. The spirit wagged her streamers slowly like a fish cruising in a summer stream, content to listen to the soothing rise and fall of Sandhri's clever voice.

Sandhri sat beside the huge brass frog, surrounded by children and friends. In her arms, she held her little baby. Sinbad had grey eyes like his mother, and Raschid's long and clever nose. He suckled happily at Sandhri's breast. She stroked her hair back from his face and looked down at him in love.

She had ice cold milk in a pitcher beside her, and a hunch of crusty Frankish bread – made into a sandwich with Frankish bacon, fresh lettuce and chunks of a chicken dinner someone had left unguarded in the palace. Sandhri drank lustily, ate a mouthful that showered crumbs across her belly, and waved Zhu away as her friend the fox tried to hold up her food for her as she nursed the child.

"No no! Iss fine!" Sandhri had returned to being as skinny as a slick black eel – and still had the appetite of a shark. "Hey – you should try t'iss chicken bacon thingy!"

"Must you eat that?" Zhu the fox rolled her eyes. Her own litter of cubs were clustering close about Sandhri, peering at the baby and wanting to touch. "Bacon?"

"Crispy bacon. And the Franks do t'iss fantastic sauce!" Sandhri reveled in the taste. "Hey – Sinbad gets the best off all possible v'orlds! Eastern science *and* bacon sand'viches!"

Hanna – Jewish and content to be so, raised one brow.

"Were you going to tell a story, or what?"

"Soon, soon!" The bat grandly lifted up one finger. "Genius must not be rushed!"

Sandhri held her child against her heart, simply adoring him. "I make the most amazing t'ings."

With her snout wryly wrinkling, Zhu looked to Yariim.

"Did she drive the Tsu-Khan mad?"

"The worst mistake he ever made." Yariim lounged happily. "He hadn't been so annoyed in three thousand years."

"Ha! V'ass tactics! Can you believe that man actually found poor little Sandhri irritating?" The Bat tossed bread to Yariim. "Hey blue tits! How's the bladder?"

"It's fine!" Yariim put a hand to her belly. "Damn! Why did you have to say that?"

Trying to follow the Osranii banter, the new King of the Pulski looked to Yariim. A slim grey wolf, he had an air of energetic, casual innocence that had drawn Fatima's dancing girls as a flower drew bees. Doting on his every word, the girls closed in, fluttering lashes as the Prince spoke to the Queen.

"How far into term are you, My Lady?"

"Ten weeks." The blue mouse could still scarcely believe it. When she lay still, she imagined that she could feel the tiny baby deep inside her. "Ten whole weeks."

"Two nights before the battle!" Sandhri toasted her lovers with a cup of milk. "Quite a homecomink! Ha!"

Raas Yomah stirred a teapot that simmered upon a little metal stove.

"My Queen – we should drink tea."

"Tea? Oh – tea!" Sandhri sat bolt upright, careful to keep the baby cuddled in against her breast. "T'at's the story for today!" She shied a twig at Raschid. "Aha! Oi, you! Jackal? Are you ready?"

"Ready." The Shah of all Osra opened his eyes and hefted a pen. Beside him, a vast sheaf of pages bound in leather covers lay upon the ground. "Always ready."

"Good! Genius can't v'ait for silly jackals and siestas!"

Children gathered closer. The Bat looked down at her baby in infinite love, tenderly caressing him as he nursed. Holding his tiny hand inside her own, she gave a quiet smile.

> "Long ago and far away, in the high places of the Yellow Empire, t'ere v'ass a mountain old as old as time." Sandhri's voice drifted in the shade beneath the trees, matching the drowsy murmur of the fountain. "It stood high above the city, and high above the farms. Great forests of bamboo soared into the sky, and forests of tall trees overhung the mountain waterfalls. Two little villages had been atop the mountain for as long as anyv'un could know, divided by the forest and sharing their mountain home. The villages v'ere called 'Clear Dawn' and 'Golden Dusk', and they lived v'ith one anot'er in perfect harmony."

The brass hut had crept closer to listen to the story, and the cave spirit slid out to lounge behind Sandhri above the fountain.

Carefully measuring tea into an iron teapot, Raas Yomah cocked an eye at the strange apparitions, and then pulled down his veil.

"A thousand pardons, my little Queen – but what has this to do with tea?"

"Shush! Iss set in the Yellow Empire, and the empire makes good tea!" Sandhri waved the man away. "V'y iss it alv'ays Sandhri who must know effery t'ing?"

Lady Fatima looked up.

"Have we heard from the Yellow Empire, my Lord?

Raschid leaned back against Marwan, immensely pleased.

"Yes! Hassan hooked up some of the Khan's magic mirrors! The Khan's agents fell dead in their tracks ten weeks ago. They must have been corpses possessed by the Khan." Raschid caught up with Sandhri's story, his pen giving a great flourish. "Their Marquis Hu-Zhei-Pei in the south managed to talk the invading northerners into peace. We are supporting him as claimant to the crown, pending advice from our good friend Meng." Raschid looked up. "Where *is* Meng?"

"V'ith Itbit!" Sandhri waved her bacon sandwich at her husband. "Hey! Are v'e listening to the story teller here or v'at?"

Much chastened, the gathering shrunk in their seats. Sandhri sat up and glared at them with a piercing eye, finally content to settle back in place.

"Now – v'ere were we? Ah! The mountain!"

One elegant black hand swept up to mould magic in the air.

"The villagers of Dawn and Dusk each lived on the opposite side of the mountain, joined by the mountain shrine hidden deep inside the trees. They fished and farmed, wove clothes and danced. In the summer time, visitors v'ould swap between the villages bringing cakes, music and tea." Sandhri stuck a sharp tongue out at Raas Jakoob. *"V'en they needed things from far av'ay, they v'ould cut firewood and bamboo and cart it down the mountainside. In the city, they could sell t'eir v'ares for a few coins and use the money to bring a few strange little luxuries back home.*

"Now – v'un day, the main street of the city v'as darkening v'ith night. Beside the city gates v'ere two stalls selling bamboo and firewood – one stall from the village 'Dusk', and V'un from 'Dawn'. The villagers v'ere closing down their stalls, v'en a man came stride-stride-striding down the road in a great deal off a hurry. The man – a big fat panda bear v'ith a black lacquered hat as tall as a cake, halted by the stalls. He 'hummed' and 'hawed' – and then strode over to the villagers from Dawn.

'You t'ere! Humble woodcutters! How much for one bundle of wood! V'e are going to entertain, and I need to start a barbeque!'

"The wood sellers from Dawn gave a shrug.

'Four bronze coins, sir! That iss v'at v'e haff alv'ays charged.'

Scowling, the fat panda v'alked across the street to the stall from 'Dusk.'

'Ha, fellows! It iss evening already. Surely you cannot expect to sell your wood for four whole coins?'

"The villagers from Dusk put their heads together. It was a long way back up their mountain, and they had no wish to carry their wood all the way back home. It seemed best to offer the panda a discount. One villager put his hands inside his sleeves – just like Meng – and bowed three times with funny little bobs.

'Honoured sir, we can sell you this bundle of wood for three bronze coins.'

"Sold!" The panda paid his coins and went off happily. The villagers from Dawn looked resentfully at the other stall, then lugged their own remaining wood all the long v'ay home. V'en they arrived, their backs were sore. T'ey v'ent into the village inn and there they drank two whole

> *cups of millet wine.*
>
> "*The village head man – a teeny little mouse fellow with a beard that trailed two whole yards down from his chin – came over to the men. They asked the old man for advice.*
>
> '*Honoured Elder! The villagers from Dusk village made a sale v'en v'e could not! We wished to charge our usual rate for wood, but the other village dropped their price to t'ree bronze coins!*'
>
> "*The Elder walked about the inn in thought, his beard narrowly missing a few puddles. Finally, he came back to speak to the woodcutters. The entire village had gathered to hear v'at the elder had to say.*
>
> '*My sons, v'e must not lose our ability to sell our wares. V'e need money to buy the t'ings we do not make here on the mountain! Silks for the ladies, hinges for our doors – nails and wool and magazines!*'

"Magazines?" The Pulski King blinked. "Magazines?"

"Ah." Sandhri leaned in to whisper into the Pulski King's ear. "Recreational magazines, you understand. It gets cold and lonely in the mountains."

"Oh!" The King blinked. Osranii dancing girls were crowding close to him on either side, and one kept offering to rub his back. "I – er – I see!"

"You, I t'ink, v'ill neffer need them." With a sly glance at the ever-worshipful dancing girls, Sandhri eased her baby from the breast. The little fellow had slipped quietly off to sleep, and he cuddled against her, making little noises as he dreamed.

> "*Anyv'ay! The next morning, the wood cutters of Dawn village v'orked hard. They cut and stacked up all the wood they thought they could handle, and took the bundles on their backs, v'alking to the city. With a sniff, they saw their comrades from Dusk village giffing them a wave. T'ey ignored the ot'er villagers, and put up a great sign written in bold black ink:*
>
> '*Firewood – two and a half coins per bundle.*'
>
> "*Astonished, the villagers from Dusk village came racing over. T'ey stared at the sign in absolute bev'ilderment.*
>
> '*Honoured neighbours, are you mad?*' *T'ey pointed at the sign. 'Surely you mean to charge four coins for your v'ood?*'
>
> "*The men from Dawn village put their noses in the air.*
>
> '*You saw fit to steal a customer from us last night. Clearly underselling the other stalls will bring us more money in the long run.*'
>
> "*Just then, a customer appeared. V'en he saw how low priced the wood v'as at the Dawn villages' stall, he ran to find his friends. Soon people v'ere besieging t'em for wood. The Dawn village sold out its stock, and happily packed up to go home. Poor Dusk village had not made a single sale. They gathered together in their village inn that night v'ith their own headman, and muttered far into the night.*
>
> "*The next day, both villages had stalls open almost at the crack of morn. The Dusk village stall had a sign of its own; 'Wood – two coins per bundle' – and 'Cheapest Bamboo in town!*'
>
> "*The Dawn village saw the sign and hastily rewrote their own. Prices dropped during the day to a single coin – t'en to 'Free Bamboo v'ith*

every wood bundle!' Boys from both villages had to run back up the mountain and ask for more wood and bamboo.

"The price war v'ent on. In order to keep prices low, the villages each had to make wood and bamboo harvesting more efficient. The time that had been spent making cakes, tea and wine for the neighbours v'as now spent in harvesting wood. Everyv'un, young or old, had to help cut twigs and bamboo. They made carts to haul the wood more quickly – penned up the nice v'aterfalls to make fish farms to feed the hungry workers. In the city, the price war reached silly levels until finally every house in the city had all the wood and bamboo they could stand! No v'un bought from the stalls any more, and both Dawn and Dusk village blamed each other for the loss of sales.

"It was the time of the moon festival, v'en gifts from each village were carried into the forest shrine, v'ere both villages v'ould prepare a feast for v'un another. The people of each village had exactly the same thought.

'Sales are gone – but v'e v'ill let the ot'er village think that v'e are too wealthy to care! V'e v'ill make the most magnificent feast t'ose idiots haff effer seen!'

"And so they laboured like heroes! Each made the most stunning gifts imaginable to giff to the other village. Each village cackled as they made complicated dishes for the feast, sure that their rivals v'ould be shamed and overawed. In great pomp and ceremony, the two villages each set off into the forest on the appointed day. They met at the path that led to their sacred shrine, and eyed each other in suspicion.

"Each village had made almost exactly the same dishes. Each village had made gifts similar to one another for their offerings. The women and the cooks, the tailors and the woodcutters, the children and the wives all began to furiously argue v'ith v'un anot'er. They accused and scoffed – derided and yelled in fury! Finally the two old head men almost came to blows! The battle lines v'ere being drawn, v'en suddenly from thin air there came a horrid yell!"

Sandhri leaned forward to the children, waving her free hand like a claw.

"Suddenly, every villager had a little demon gripping their backs. The critters had great big horns and long tails tufted green! Some had striped feet, some had wings – but all of them had great long sharp claws. They gripped the villagers backs and dug in tight, and the villagers could only roll around and scream!

"The people fled the glade, beating at their backs v'ith sticks and rocks. As they left the sacred glade, the little demons faded av'ay. Each village turned upon the other in accusation.

'You haff defiled the shrine v'ith your horrid blasphemies!"

"And v'ith that, the villagers stormed off to their homes."

Sandhri stroked little Sinbad, telling the story for him, caressing his ears softly as she spoke.

> *"Things grew miserable upon the mountain. There v'ere no more visits – no more cakes and tea and music as the sun spread glorious colours all across the lands below. The villagers had the finery they had bought v'ith their cash. They wore their new clothes in pride, no matter how impractical they v'ere for life amongst the fishes and the trees.*
>
> *"After a long, long time, a visitor came to the mountain. It v'as a nun – a nice lady who had v'unce been the prettiest girl in either village. Her name v'as 'Clarity', and she had a big straw hat and a smile upon her face. She had been av'ay for many years, and had become a Taoist priest."*

Sitting adoringly at Sandhri's feet were the children from the palace – all Sandhri's special loves. She let one little girl hold the baby carefully, and drew the others underneath her arms. One boy looked up at Sandhri in puzzlement.

"What's a Taoist?"

"Ah! Like a Buddhist, but able to laugh a whole lot more!" Sandhri waved a hand. "T'ey like to say all things are connected, and all are v'un – yes?"

"Oh!" One skinny hyena girl with glasses and dust over her spots looked up in joy. "Like the Zen Buddhist!"

"Zen Buddhist?" Sir Randolph scowled, then brightened as he made connections somewhere in his head. "Was he that chap we saw the other day? The one working at the puppet show?"

"T'at's him! He came out good after all!" Sandhri was immensely pleased. "He finally put two and two toget'er and figured out t'at I v'ass full of crap!"

Yariim lazily lifted up a finger. "It does take some people a little time…"

"Hush! Who are you to question Sandhri – enlightener off the lost?" Sandhri brightened as Raas Yomah stoked his little stove and brought out a bundle of raw sausages. "Oooh! Food!"

Three priests – one Christian, one Islamic and one Buddhist monk came walking amiably side by side into the square. They had a chessboard and a folding table. The three men set up their game in a shady doorway. Sandhri longingly watched the preparations as Raas Yomah prepared his sausages until Raschid tossed a twig at her.

"Sandhri? The Taoist nun?"

"None?" Sandhri blinked. "Oh – nun!" She brightened and forgot the sausages in an instant, even though they sizzled as they were placed onto the grill. "Yes. Little 'Clarity' – she v'ass clever, and she v'ass beautiful – so obviously she v'ass a bat!"

"Oh obviously."

"A v'ite bat, very thin, v'ith tall pink ears.'

Sandhri sat up in place.

> *"The nun came v'alking as calm ass you please up the mountain path. She visited first v'un village, and then the other, looking at the fine clothes and art objects the people so proudly displayed. She made a simple meal, and began to wander off into the forest all alone. V'en they saw v'at she v'ass doing, the people of Dawn village came running over in dismay.*
>
> *'Dear Priestess! Do not enter the forest – demons will get you v'ith*

their claws!'

"*Clarity faced the villagers and gave a humble bow.*

'*My friends, I have seen that your villages are greatly troubled. I intend to pray for you at the forest shrine.'*

'*V'e cannot allow you to go in there unprotected!' The Dawn villagers gathered in consternation. V'e shall send some men to guard you.'*

'*It is not necessary, but I shall welcome the company.' Clarity bowed v'unce more. 'I believe Dusk village offered to giff me an escort of twenty men.'*

The Dawn villagers bridled.

'*Twenty? V'ell v'e can top that! V'e shall send you thirty – no fifty!' The old head man swelled with pride. 'Our entire village shall escort you! That should show those dusk villages how much more pious than them v'e are!'*

"*Clarity gave a bow, and v'andered happily on her v'ay.*

Sandhri gathered her audience about her. Yariim was sitting, a sly smile on her face as she anticipated future turns. Raschid smiled with her, writing without looking at the page. Zhu wriggled closer, in amongst the children and Raas Jakoob.

Sandhri steepled her finger tips.

"*Now – v'en the people of Dusk village saw v'at was going on, they too came running. Both villages glared at v'un another, each trying to out do the other in piety and diligence. They marched in step behind the priestess – who looked back at them with a sly gleam in her eye.*

"*As they reached the sacred glade, Clarity bowed to the shrine and quietly began to make her prayers. But no sooner had they entered the glade, v'en the villagers all began to scream and wail! On each back there v'ass suddenly a little green demon, digging, nipping, piercing v'ith its claws!*

"*The people writhed about and screamed – ran to leap into ponds or climb up trees, but nothing took the demons from their backs. Serene and calm, Clarity walked through them all, weeding the shrine and making everything nice and neat again.*

"*With extra big spotty-botted demons on their backs, the two head men cried out to Clarity.*

'*Run! Why don't you run?' The demons swiped at their flesh, and both men gave a squeal of pain. 'Can't you see how much pain these demons can cause?'*

"*Clarity never looked around. Instead she happily put flowers in the shrine.*

'*Good sirs – I gave up carrying demons on my own back many years ago. Why do you insist upon carrying yours?'*

Sandhri put her hands together and gave a smile.

"*At that moment, the villagers had an Enlightenment. They suddenly knew what the demons were. Their own jealousy, greed and pride had come to tear at them. Brimming tears, the people of Dawn and Dusk fell to their knees and bowed to Clarity.*

> '*Honourable Priestess – v'e thank you for pointing out our error!*'
> "When they realized their sin and were contrite, the demons lost all power over them. Swiping irritably with their claws, the demons tried to hurt the villagers, but their claws just seemed to pass right through. Irritated, the demons all stomped off into the forest, keen to go and ruin someone else's day."

Sandhri reached out to gently take her sleeping baby from her students. She kissed the little creature on the cheek, then took the other boys and girls underneath her arm.

> *"And so the villagers has a new moon festival – this time without the finery and without the jealousy. Clarity presided over everything, and took to living in a grass hut where she could watch the v'aterfalls. The villages prospered, but they let their finery stay in the cupboards where it belonged."* Sandhri ruffled the childrens' hair. *"After all – it interfered with cakes and tea, and music in the quiet evening times…"*

Sausages sizzled, the tea boiled. Sandhri's audience sat back to bask in the story for a while. Warm, fed and acutely aware that there was work to do, they lounged about for a while, watching ibises drift above the palm trees.

Sandhri took three sausages and nestled in with Raschid and Yariim. She passed them food, and gave a satisfied sigh.

"That v'un was for Meng. And it iss the last story in my book. V'un t'ousand and two stories. Not a bad little job." The bat gave a great yawn, tired and warm. The baby stirred and opened up his eyes, and Raschid leaned down to talk to his little son.

Yariim mused at Sandhri with sly suspicion in her eyes.

"Where is Meng?"

"Aaah – where any lad would want to be." Sandhri leaned back against Marwan, feeling the camel snore. "Off discussing architecture and fiscal policy v'ith a heavily stacked princess…"

Raschid opened up one eye.

"He what?"

"Sandhri knows what a Sandhri knows. " The bat lounged back between her partners with her baby cuddled on her bare, warm stomach. "I t'ink everything v'ill be fine."

She leaned in to whisper quietly to Yariim.

"Psst. V'un hour. Raschid is going to 'tummy time' the baby, and we can go!"

Yariim gave a sly smile and snuggled down. One hour… but in the mean time, there were sausages and sun. The blue mouse kissed Sandhri, and they sat there together lying the baby atop Yariim's belly, introducing him to his sister-to-be. The sun shone, the tea simmered, and all seemed bright and pure…

*****

"…And here! This will be the great hall." Meng opened his arms and showed Itbit the lines pegged into the soil where a vast building had been planned. "All the students will come here to eat. It's all been budgeted for!"

They stood at the heart of a vast flat piece of river land. Vague outlines had been planted in the ground with pegs and string. The army had been home only for two weeks, but plans had been made en route. Excited, Raschid had spent an afternoon hammering in the pegs himself, explaining his vision to the Brotherhood of Light, the Pulski King and Meng.

Removing his hat, the young panda turned around and around, looking at the vision laid out beside the walls of Sath.

"Think of it, Itbit! The university of Aku-Mashad! Not a place for nations, creeds or race, but a place where knowledge makes all peoples one! We will bring Grand Masters from the Yellow Empire – philosophers and legendary artists from the Franks. The Hak'uto Hassin will send herbalists. We will make a place where all may come and learn!" Meng looked about himself in awe. "There is a dream here. We humble ones have the chance to bring it all to life…"

He spread his arms, looking alive and wonderfully excited. Itbit hoped up onto a rock, sitting on her wonderfully rounded bottom and hugging her knees to her chest, her head tilted and her pink eyes brim-full of love.

"Tell Itbit about it."

She already knew. Raschid had told her everything – but the green mouse was in love, and she adored the light in Meng's eyes as he told her of his dream.

"It can be a new age, Itbit. Here, where learning and joy are sacred, we can bring them all here. The children of other nations – their future rulers, their future citizens and scientists and statesmen. Here, we can educate them where all of them are like one giant family. No one need grow up fearing men of another nation; the cultures and the ideas of our neighbours will be familiar, beloved things! New generations will grow who have learned not to fear, not to hate. Generations who have learned that synthesis is strength, and that statesmanship is measured by joy and peace that it provides!" The panda's hands jittered when he was excited, and he jammed them into his sleeves. "Cross fertilization of ideas and faiths. And… and we shall make campuses in places all around the world. Students will travel as part of their learning, seeing other places and taking the people into their hearts!"

He stood, staring at the river Amu Daja – slow and brown and peaceful amidst its fields of flowers.

"… But *here* – where love and learning are sacred. Here will be the start."

Osra was warm and filled with the scents of spring. Dressed once again in her beloved harem pants and halter, Itbit opened up her arms. Meng came to her, holding her, caressing her. He brushed her flowing golden hair back from her face and kissed her so softly, so intently that Itbit felt like she could soar.

They sank into the grass. There, amidst the poppies and the dandelions, the two of them made love. Itbit cried out for the freedom and the beauty of it, sending white birds starting up out of the grass. Meng held her, adoring her, skilled and passionate and gentle. He brought Itbit down just as he had set her flying, setting her adrift in a wonderful universe of peace.

They lay naked in the grass together, where the cicadas sung and whirred. Lying peacefully against her love, her golden hair gleaming in the springtime sun, Itbit whispered Meng's love name into his ear. He answered her with her own secret name – a secret only the two of them would ever share. They looked into each other's eyes, while overhead white clouds shone in a perfect sky.

Itbit lifted her face and propped herself where she could gaze down lovingly at Meng. Her breasts felt wonderfully warm where they lay against Meng's naked chest.

"Itbit went back to school today. Hassan says he will take her as a *real* student. He will train Itbit as a sorcerer." The Green mouse stretched; the perfect muscles of a dancer moved along her back beneath Meng's caressing hands. "Itbit will go and learn. One day, she will be able to throw a real magic spell."

Already under her spell, Meng traced the sweet, sly lines of Itbit's face.

"And you will dance?"

"Always dance. And find stories and wonderful things." The Green Mouse looked smilingly into a strange, warm future. "And be kind to wasps and frogs and horses – and show Meng how to play dice… And always, always *always* be with Meng."

She kissed the side of Meng's mouth, and he kissed her in return. For a long, delicious moment, they were content. Finally, Itbit pulled away. They lay on their sides together, still coupled, as Itbit softly stroked the black markings about Meng's loving eyes.

"And what about Itbit's friend? What will dear Meng do?"

"The Honoured Shah…" Meng blushed to use the familiar name of a King. "Raschid. He… He asked me if I would consider taking tenure here as the first Dean of the university."

"That is wonderful!" Naked and wonderfully disheveled, Itbit kissed Meng's hands. "Itbit is so happy!"

"He is naming the university hall 'Sixteen Volume Hall'. They have asked me to be a Godfather to their children." The young sage blushed. "But dare one as humble as I take such a position?"

"Itbit asks - Why not?"

Meng gave a sigh.

"So many students will be nobility in their own lands. I abhor the sentiment – but perhaps they might not respect a Dean who is of inferior rank?"

Lying on her side, cradled in the warm spring grass, Itbit stroked her man and loved him for his silliness.

"Did you know Itbit really is a Princess now?" The green mouse ran fingers through the warm, soft fur that covered Meng's silly head. "Sandhri and Yariim, Raschid and Sinbad – they really *are* Itbit's family now." She gave a watery little smile. "Itbit has a real family at last…"

Meng kissed her lovingly, and missed the point entirely.

"I am so happy for you, beloved one." He smiled. "One of us at least, is real royalty."

Itbit ruffled Meng's fur, loving him for being an idiot.

"Does Meng love Itbit?"

"I will love you forever and always with all of my heart." Meng simply adored her. "All I want is to be forever by your side."

Itbit looked at him, waiting – letting the idea filter by osmosis into his brain. Finally his eyes went wide. Itbit put a finger to his lips and held him, burrowing softly into his fur.

"In time, my love. All in good time." The girl stroked Meng's fur and felt her heart take wings. "We have all the time in the world."

Out in the grass a few yards away, Sandhri quietly arose. She took Yariim's hand, and they walked quietly alone, leaving the two young lovers in peace.

Sandhri held a great, heavy volume in her hand – one thousand and two stories, all lovingly written down. It was her gift to tomorrow. Her own gift of love.

Yariim looked at the book and smiled.

"So it is finally finished?"

"It iss finished now. It iss finally done." The sun was warm, and Sandhri felt it streaming down into her soul. She put her arm about Yariim's waist, and the two of them meandered off beneath the trees.

Yariim let her long blonde hair intermingle with Sandhri's. She turned to watch the river banks, where Raschid and Saud were showing Sinbad all the dragonflies.

"Are you sad, now that it's over? Now that the book is at an end?"

"No, my darling." Sandhri watched her baby son staring in wonder at the dragonflies. "Because good stories neffer end. V'e can visit them time and time again. And they neffer die – because the good ones reach out like ripples in a pond, touching souls. Who start ripples of their own, that touch more souls…"

Great, slow sail boats cruised up the river. Overhead, a flock of ibis whirred past the city walls. Sandhri stood with Yariim and looked out over it all, and Sandhri gently took her good friend by the hand.

"In the kingdom of Osra, by the banks of the Amu Daja, lay the ancient capital city, Sath; a tarnished jewel in a comfortable crown…"

In the grass behind them, where the lovers would find it in good time, a wedding scarf gleamed clean and pure in the sun.

Sandhri knew what a Sandhri knew – and all was well with the world…